THE PRIVATE EYE

IMAGE COMICS, INC.
Robert Kirkman – Chief Operating Officer
Erik Larsen – Chief Financial Officer
Todd McFarlane – President
Marc Silvestri – Chief Executive Officer
Jim Valentino – Vice-President

Eric Stephenson – Publisher
Corey Murphy – Director of Sales
Jeremy Sullivan – Director of Digital Sales
Kat Salazar – Director of PR & Marketing
Emily Miller – Director of Operations
Branwyn Bigglestone – Senior Accounts Manager
Sarah Mello – Accounts Manager
Drew Gill – Art Director
Jonathan Chan – Production Manager
Meredith Wallace – Print Manager
Randy Okamura – Marketing Production Designer
David Brothers – Branding Manager
Ally Power – Content Manager
Addison Duke – Production Artist
Vincent Kukua – Production Artist
Sasha Head – Production Artist
Tricia Ramos – Production Artist
Emilio Bautista – Digital Sales Associate
Chloe Ramos-Peterson – Administrative Assistant
IMAGECOMICS.COM

CHAPTER ONE

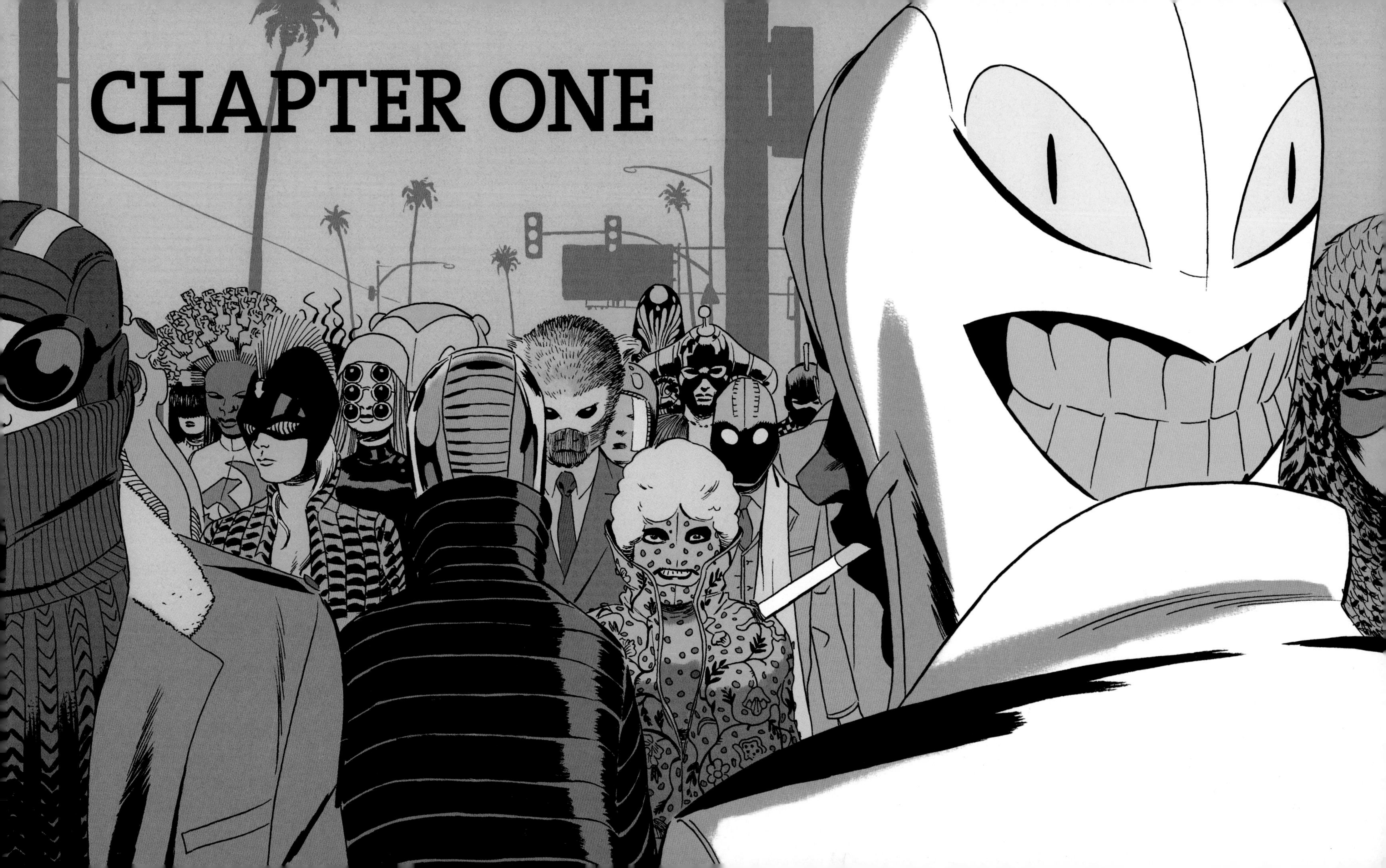

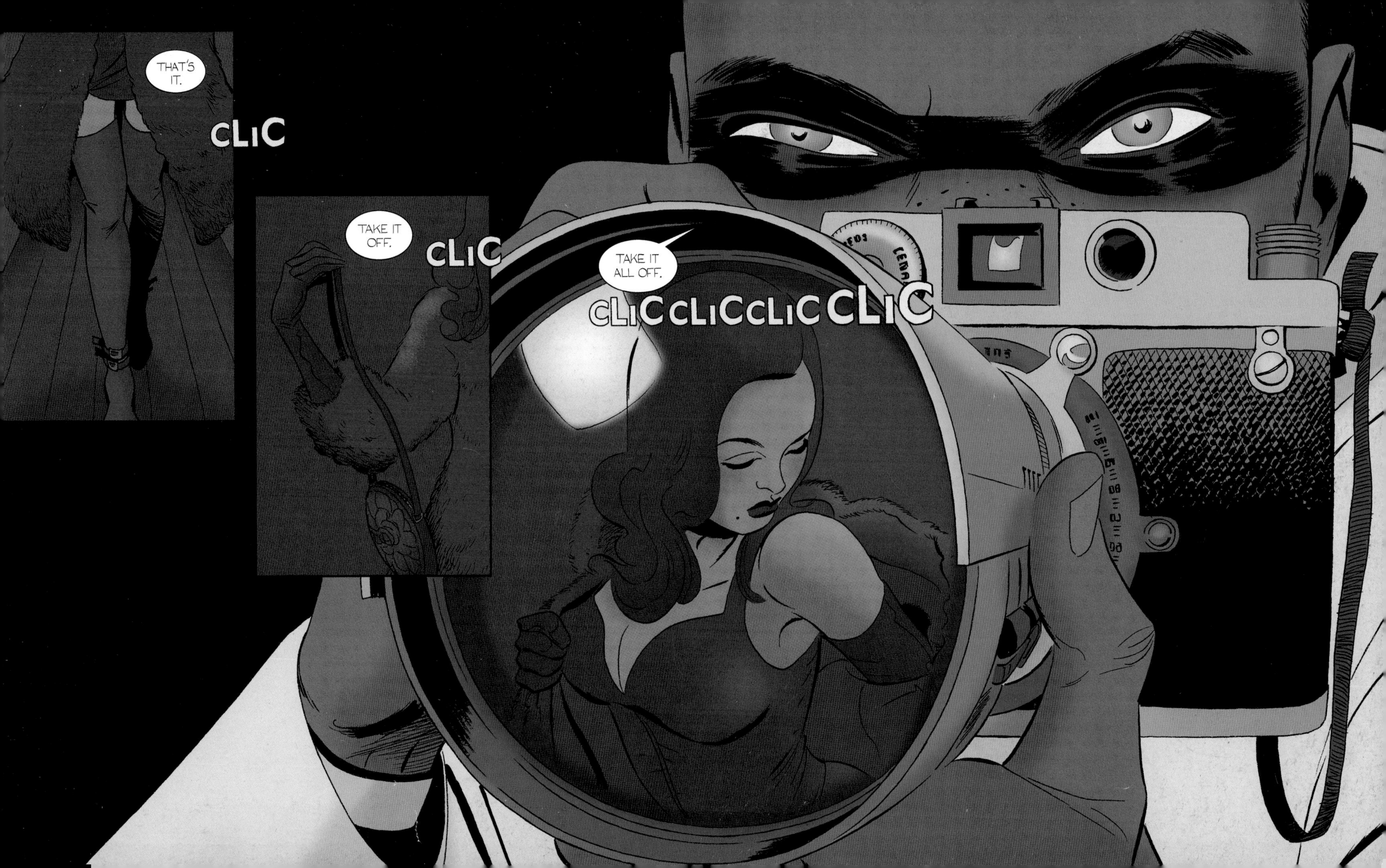
THAT'S IT.
CLIC
TAKE IT OFF.
CLIC
TAKE IT ALL OFF.
CLIC CLIC CLIC CLIC

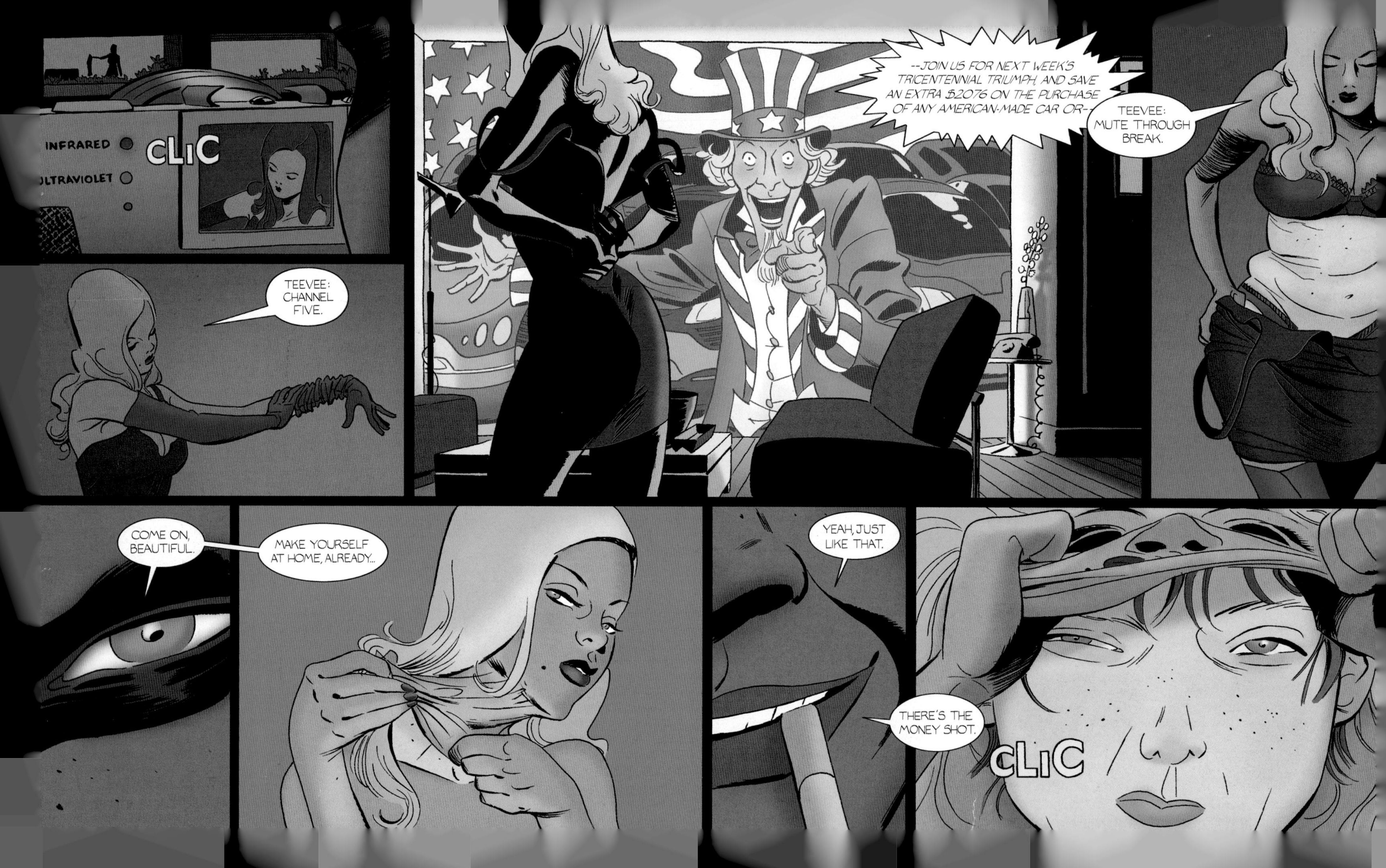
INFRARED
ULTRAVIOLET
CLIC
TEEVEE: CHANNEL FIVE.
--JOIN US FOR NEXT WEEK'S TRICENTENNIAL TRIUMPH, AND SAVE AN EXTRA $2076 ON THE PURCHASE OF ANY AMERICAN-MADE CAR OR--
TEEVEE: MUTE THROUGH BREAK.
COME ON, BEAUTIFUL.
MAKE YOURSELF AT HOME, ALREADY...
YEAH, JUST LIKE THAT.
THERE'S THE MONEY SHOT.
CLIC

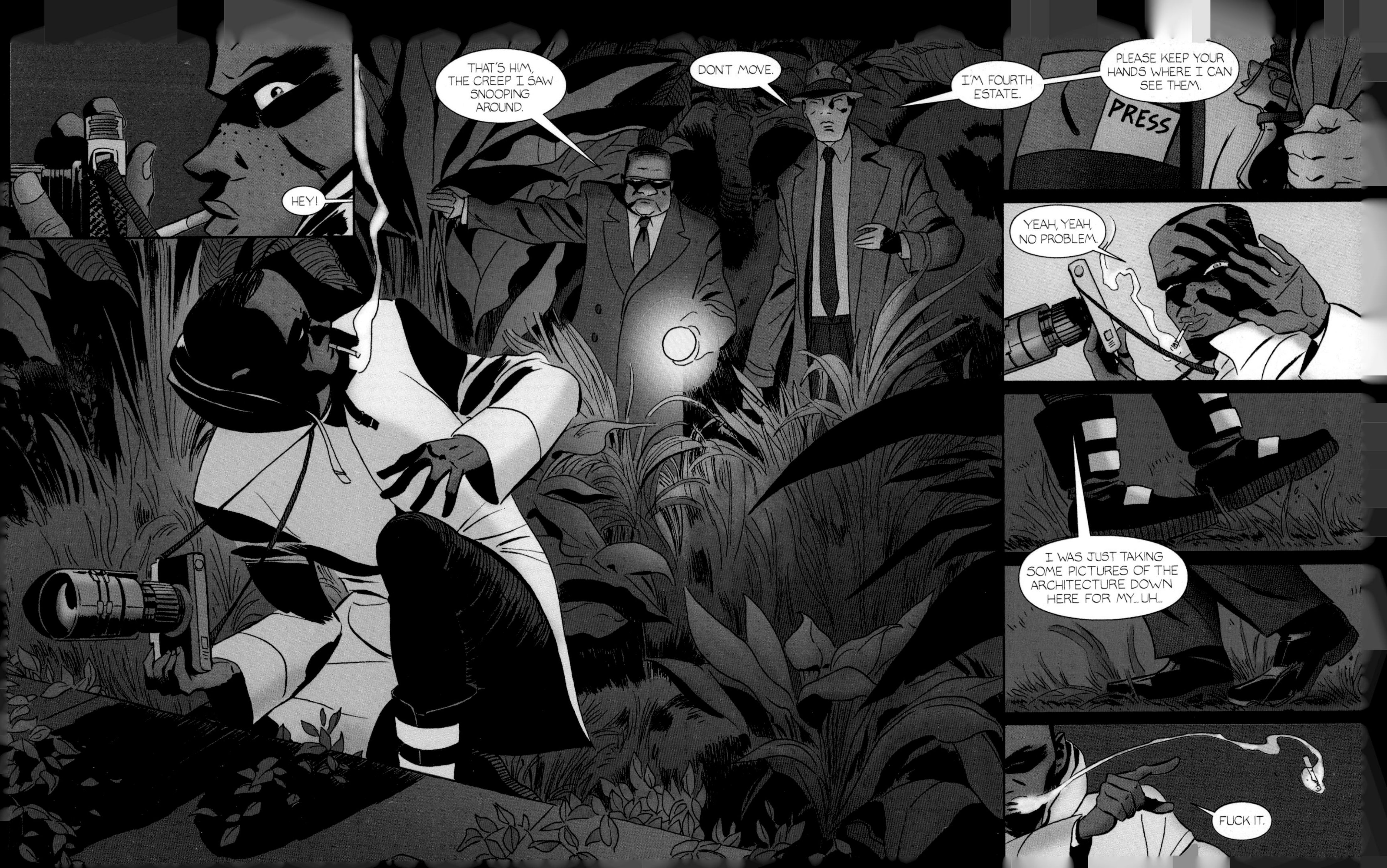
HEY!
THAT'S HIM, THE CREEP I SAW SNOOPING AROUND.
DON'T MOVE.
I'M FOURTH ESTATE.
PLEASE KEEP YOUR HANDS WHERE I CAN SEE THEM.
PRESS
YEAH, YEAH, NO PROBLEM.
I WAS JUST TAKING SOME PICTURES OF THE ARCHITECTURE DOWN HERE FOR MY... UH...
FUCK IT.

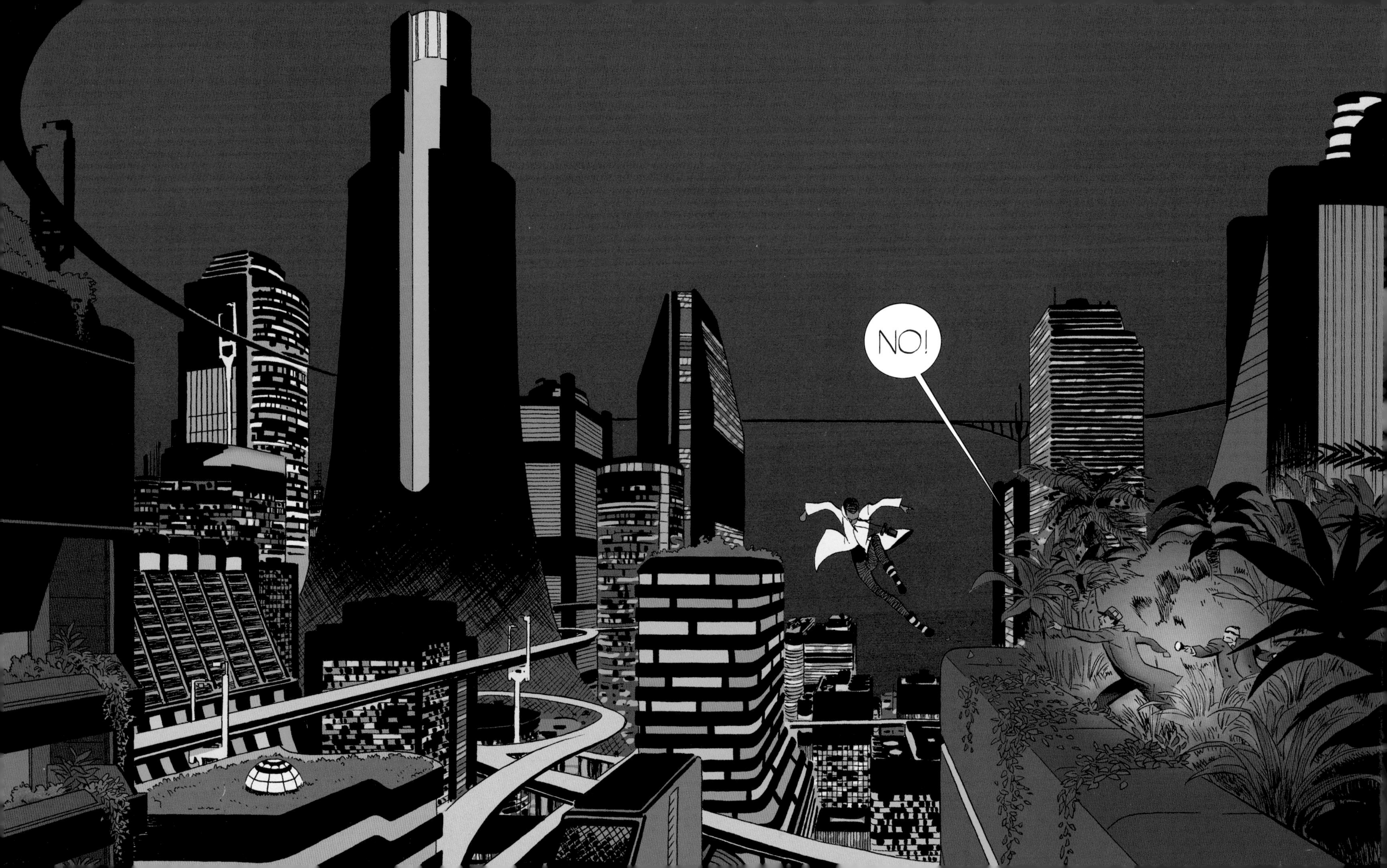
NO!

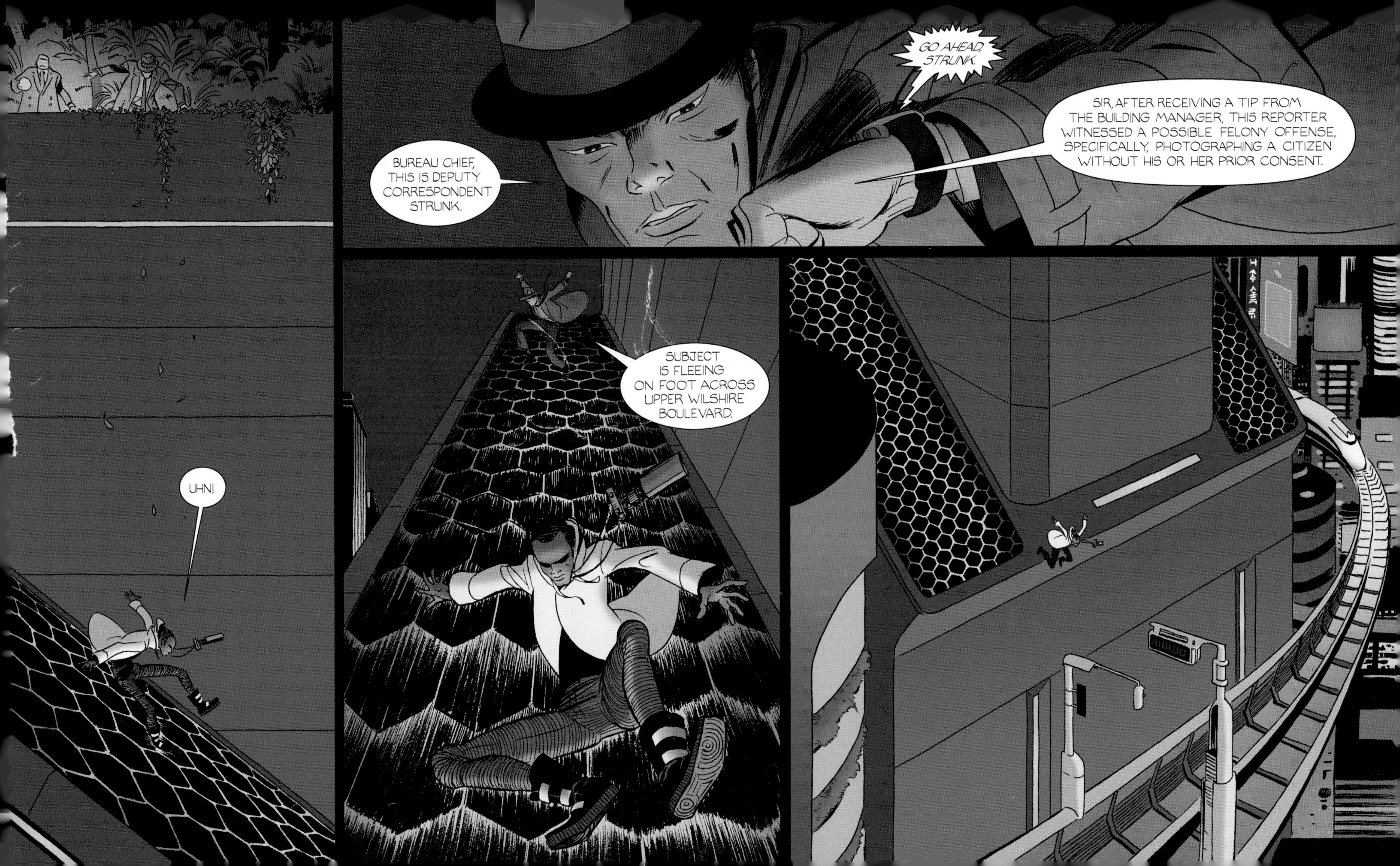
GO AHEAD STRUNK.
BUREAU CHIEF, THIS IS DEPUTY CORRESPONDENT STRUNK.
SIR, AFTER RECEIVING A TIP FROM THE BUILDING MANAGER, THIS REPORTER WITNESSED A POSSIBLE FELONY OFFENSE, SPECIFICALLY, PHOTOGRAPHING A CITIZEN WITHOUT HIS OR HER PRIOR CONSENT.
UHN!
SUBJECT IS FLEEING ON FOOT ACROSS UPPER WILSHIRE BOULEVARD.

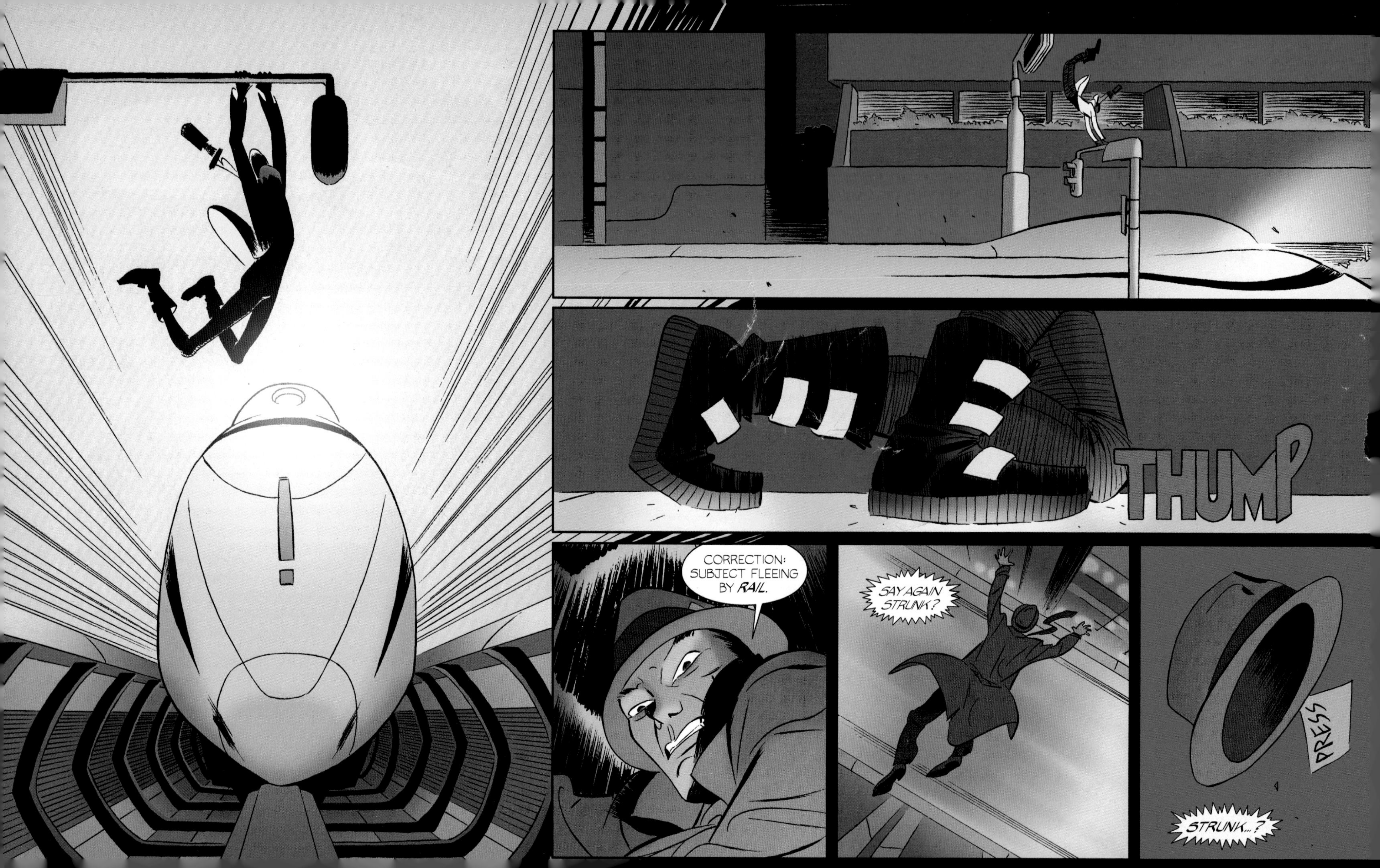
THUMP
CORRECTION: SUBJECT FLEEING BY RAIL.
SAY AGAIN STRUNK?
PRESS
STRUNK...?

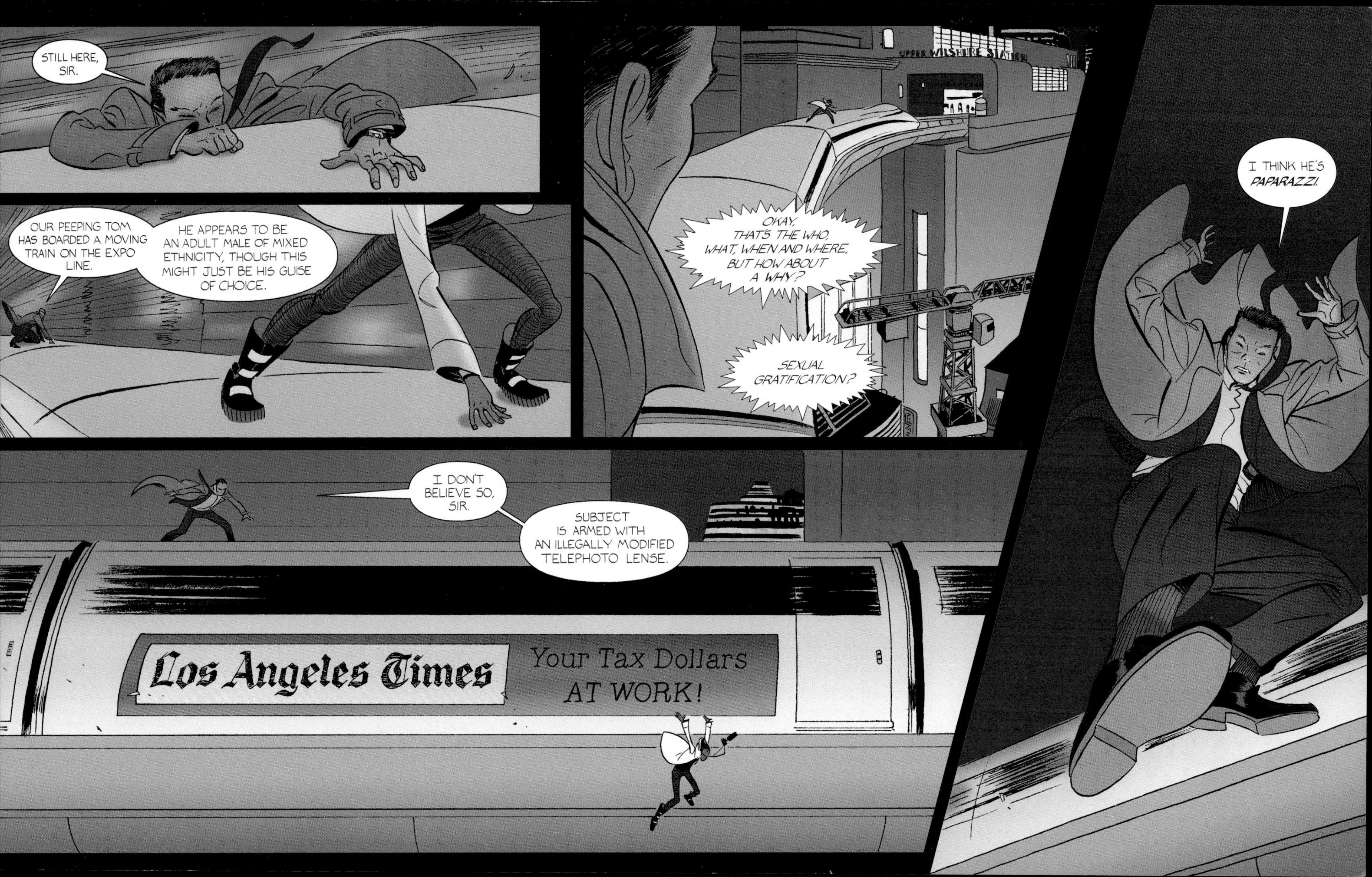
STILL HERE, SIR.
OUR PEEPING TOM HAS BOARDED A MOVING TRAIN ON THE EXPO LINE.
HE APPEARS TO BE AN ADULT MALE OF MIXED ETHNICITY, THOUGH THIS MIGHT JUST BE HIS GUISE OF CHOICE.
UPPER WILSHIRE STATION
OKAY, THAT'S THE WHO, WHAT, WHEN AND WHERE, BUT HOW ABOUT A WHY?
SEXUAL GRATIFICATION?
I THINK HE'S PAPARAZZI.
I DON'T BELIEVE SO, SIR.
SUBJECT IS ARMED WITH AN ILLEGALLY MODIFIED TELEPHOTO LENSE.
Los Angeles Times
Your Tax Dollars AT WORK!

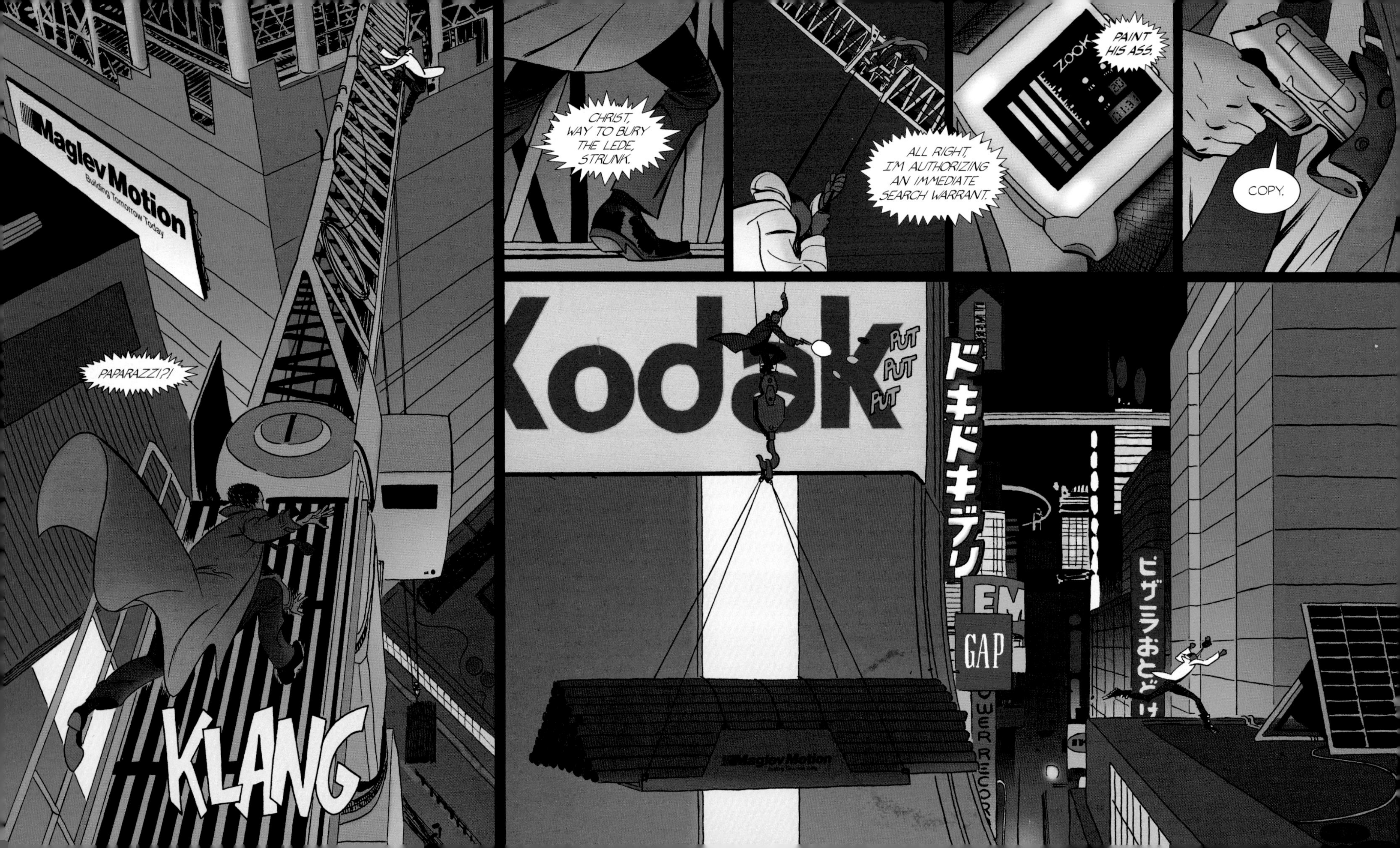

Maglev Motion
Building Tomorrow Today
PAPARAZZI?!
KLANG
CHRIST, WAY TO BURY THE LEDE, STRUNK.
ALL RIGHT, I'M AUTHORIZING AN IMMEDIATE SEARCH WARRANT.
ZOOK
PAINT HIS ASS.
COPY.
Kodak
PUT
PUT
PUT
ドキドキデリ
GAP
ビザラおとどけ
Maglev Motion

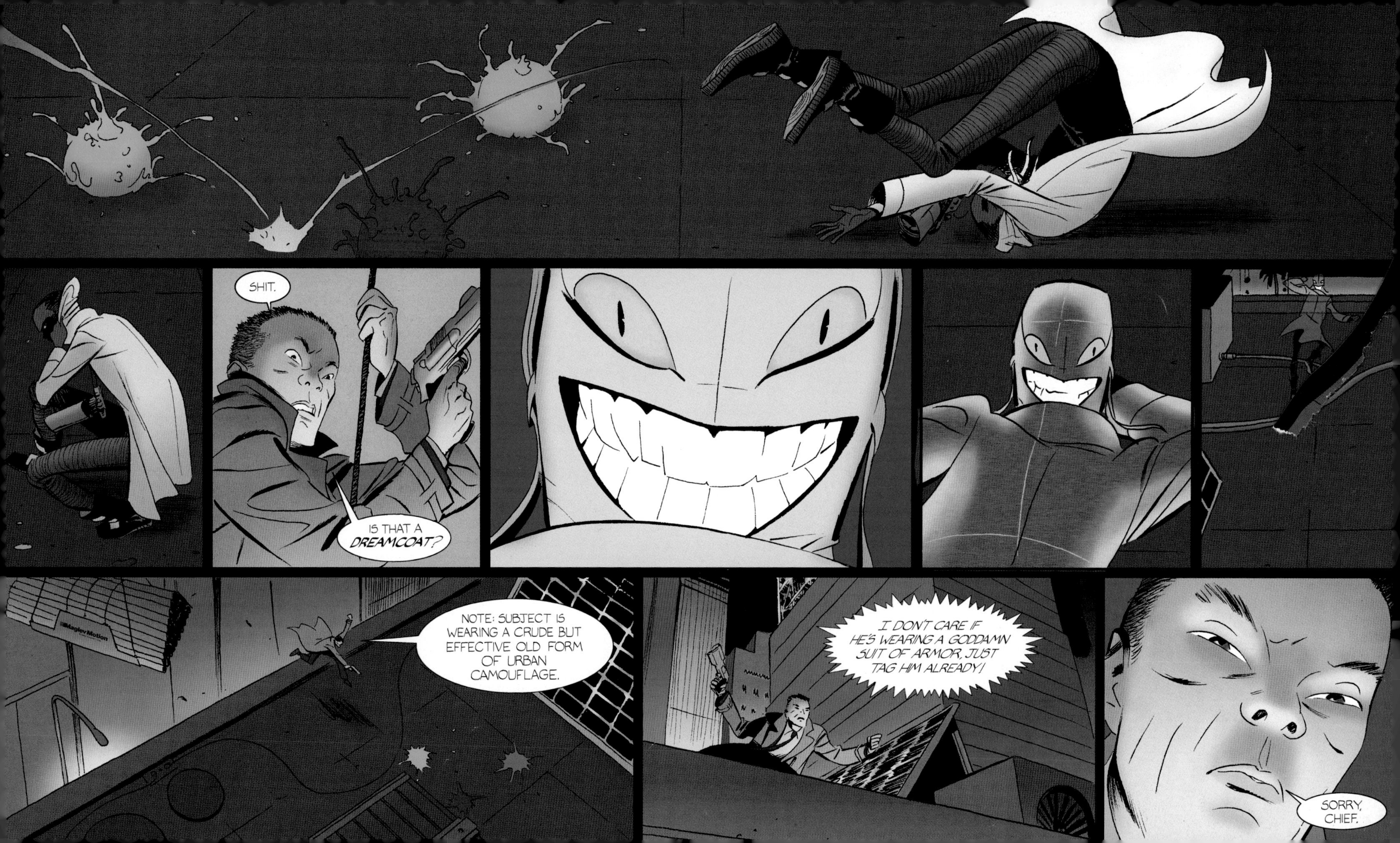
SHIT.
IS THAT A DREAMCOAT?
NOTE: SUBJECT IS WEARING A CRUDE BUT EFFECTIVE OLD FORM OF URBAN CAMOUFLAGE.
I DON'T CARE IF HE'S WEARING A GODDAMN SUIT OF ARMOR, JUST TAG HIM ALREADY!
SORRY, CHIEF.

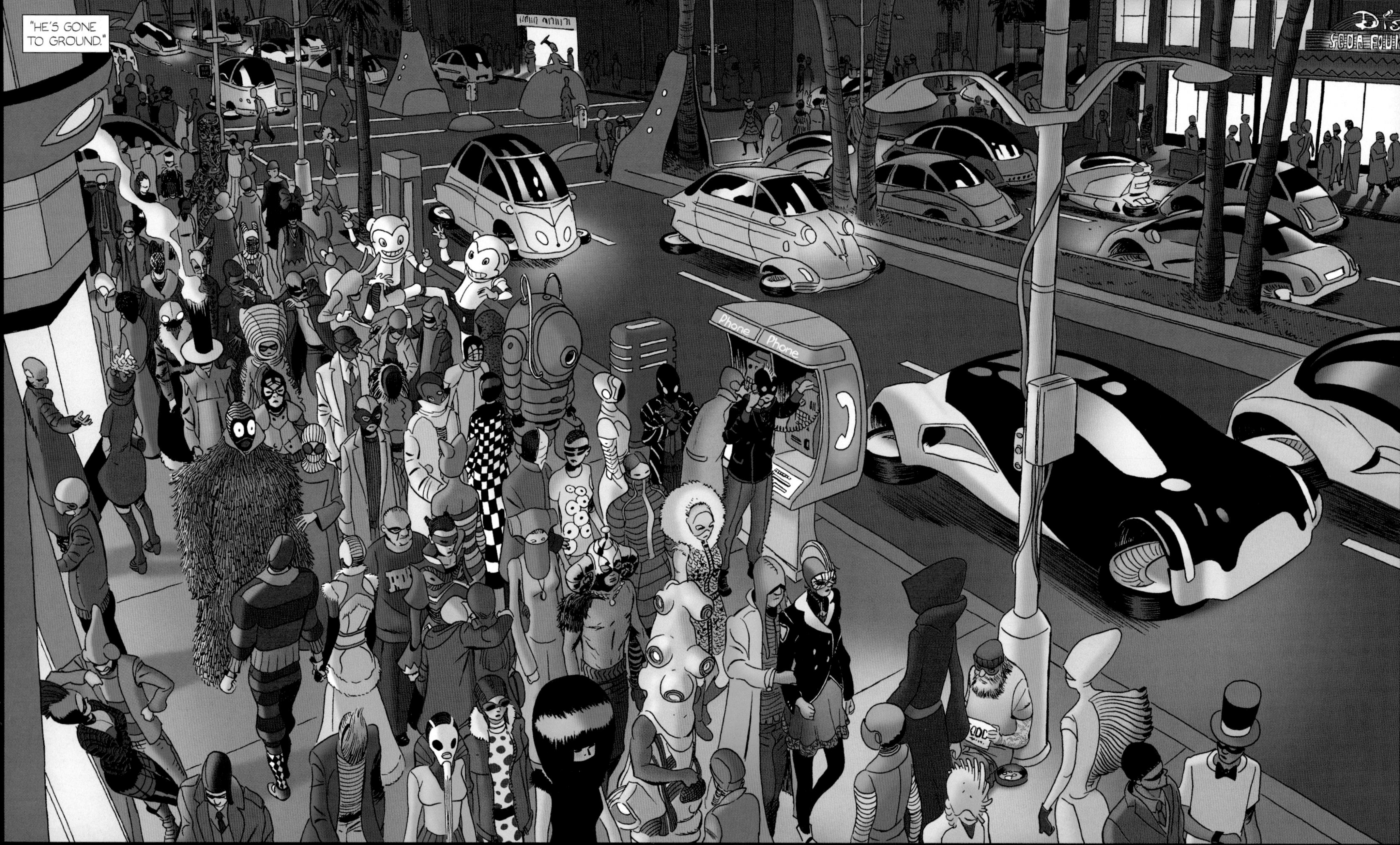
"HE'S GONE TO GROUND."
Phone
Phone

BRIAN K. VAUGHAN　　　MARCOS MARTIN

THE PRIVATE EYE

WITH
MUNTSA VICENTE

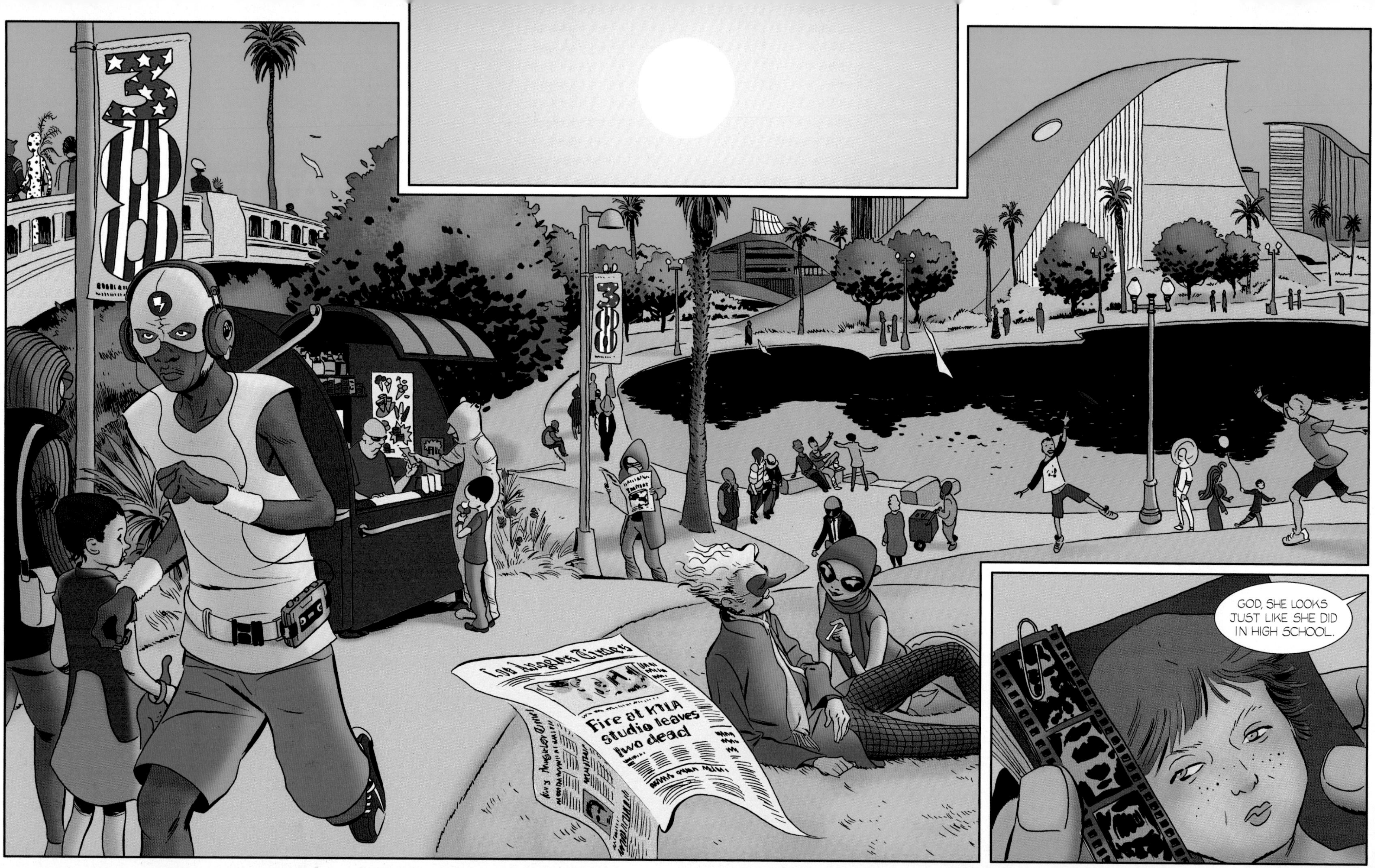
Los Angeles Times
Fire at KTLA studio leaves two dead
GOD, SHE LOOKS JUST LIKE SHE DID IN HIGH SCHOOL.

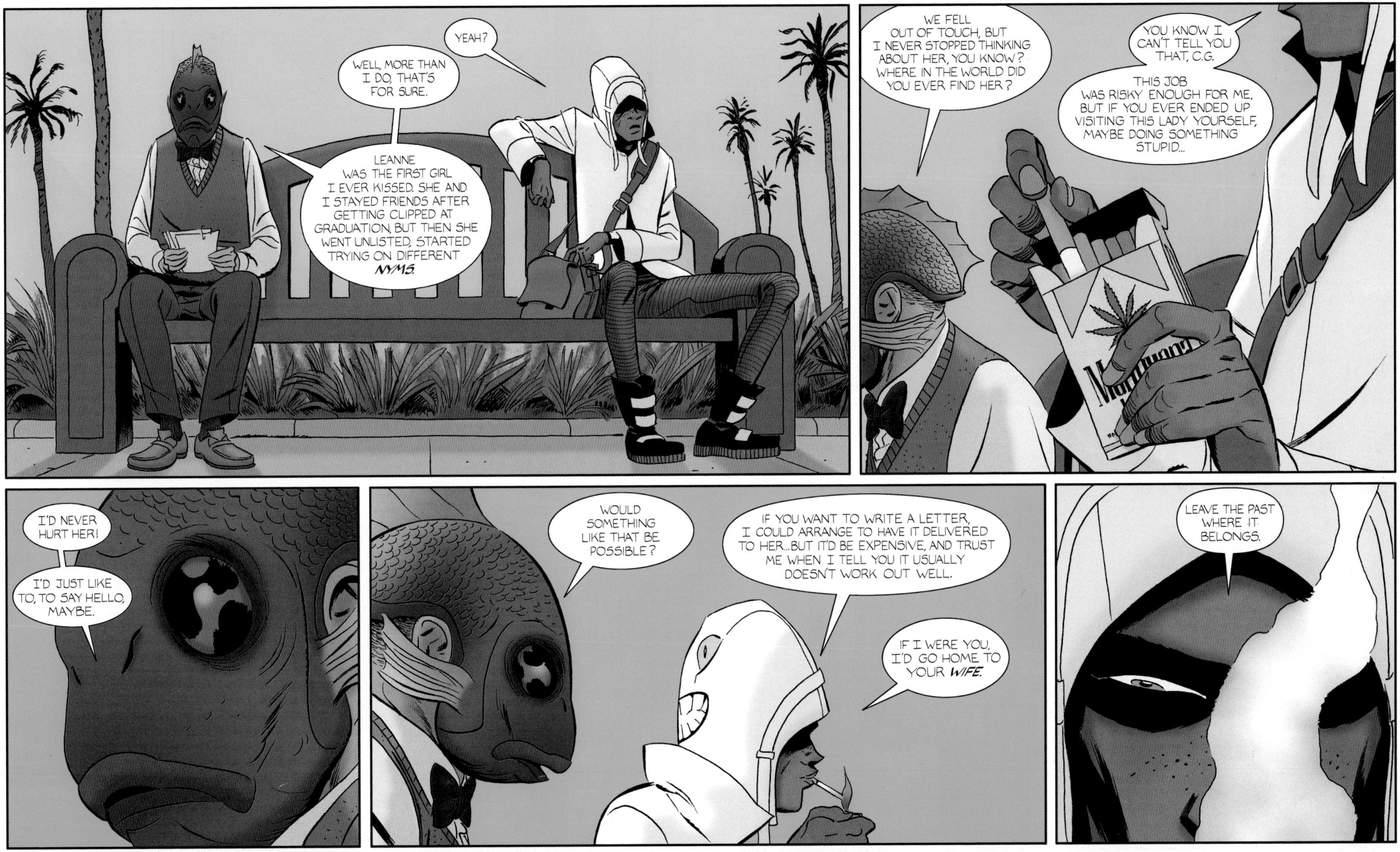
LEANNE WAS THE FIRST GIRL I EVER KISSED. SHE AND I STAYED FRIENDS AFTER GETTING CLIPPED AT GRADUATION, BUT THEN SHE WENT UNLISTED, STARTED TRYING ON DIFFERENT NYMS.
WELL, MORE THAN I DO, THAT'S FOR SURE.
YEAH?
WE FELL OUT OF TOUCH, BUT I NEVER STOPPED THINKING ABOUT HER, YOU KNOW? WHERE IN THE WORLD DID YOU EVER FIND HER?
YOU KNOW I CAN'T TELL YOU THAT, C.G.
THIS JOB WAS RISKY ENOUGH FOR ME, BUT IF YOU EVER ENDED UP VISITING THIS LADY YOURSELF, MAYBE DOING SOMETHING STUPID...
I'D NEVER HURT HER!
I'D JUST LIKE TO, TO SAY HELLO, MAYBE.
WOULD SOMETHING LIKE THAT BE POSSIBLE?
IF YOU WANT TO WRITE A LETTER, I COULD ARRANGE TO HAVE IT DELIVERED TO HER...BUT IT'D BE EXPENSIVE, AND TRUST ME WHEN I TELL YOU IT USUALLY DOESN'T WORK OUT WELL.
IF I WERE YOU, I'D GO HOME TO YOUR WIFE.
LEAVE THE PAST WHERE IT BELONGS.

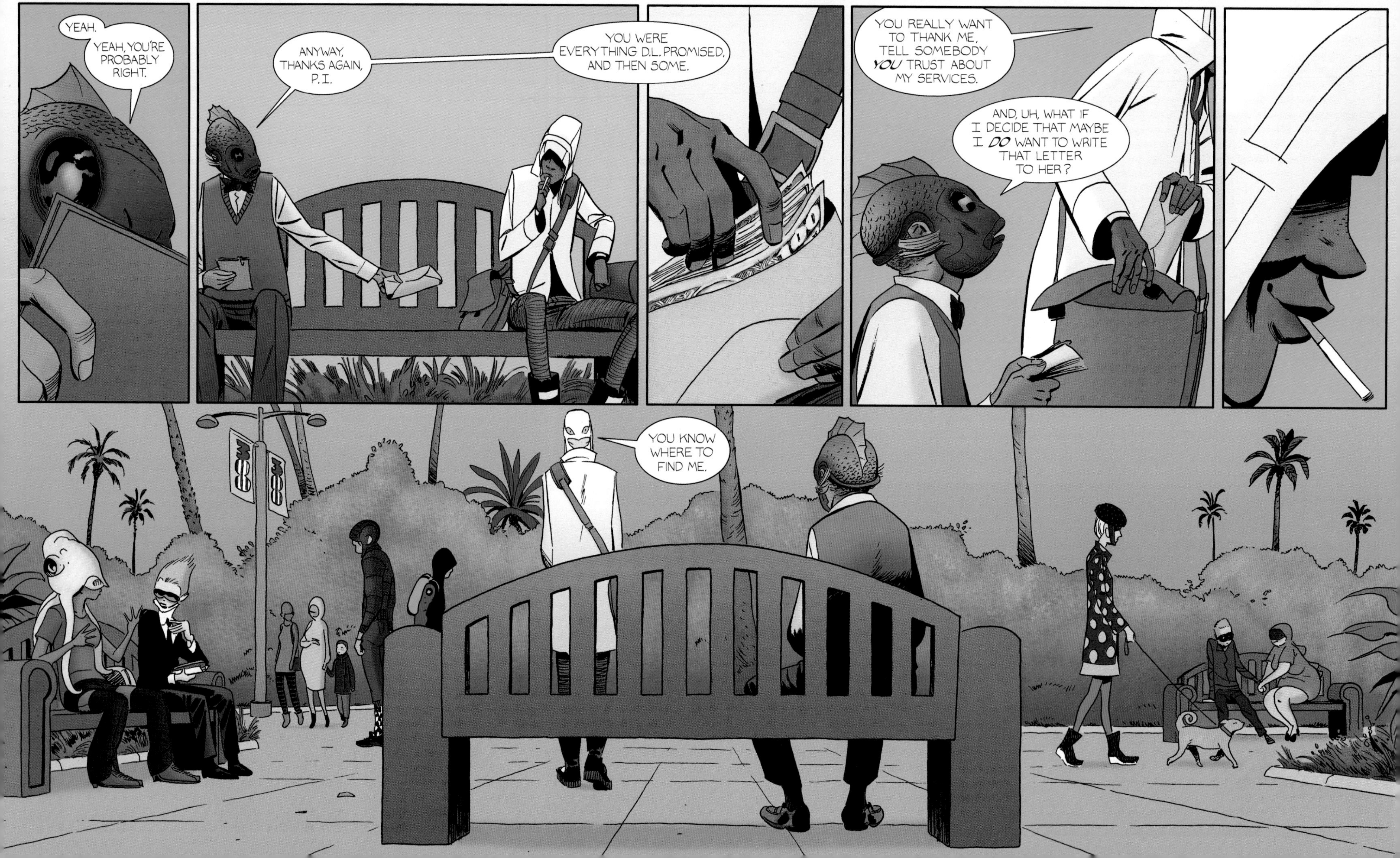
YEAH.
YEAH, YOU'RE PROBABLY RIGHT.
ANYWAY, THANKS AGAIN, P.I.
YOU WERE EVERYTHING D.L. PROMISED, AND THEN SOME.
YOU REALLY WANT TO THANK ME, TELL SOMEBODY *YOU* TRUST ABOUT MY SERVICES.
AND, UH, WHAT IF I DECIDE THAT MAYBE I *DO* WANT TO WRITE THAT LETTER TO HER?
YOU KNOW WHERE TO FIND ME.

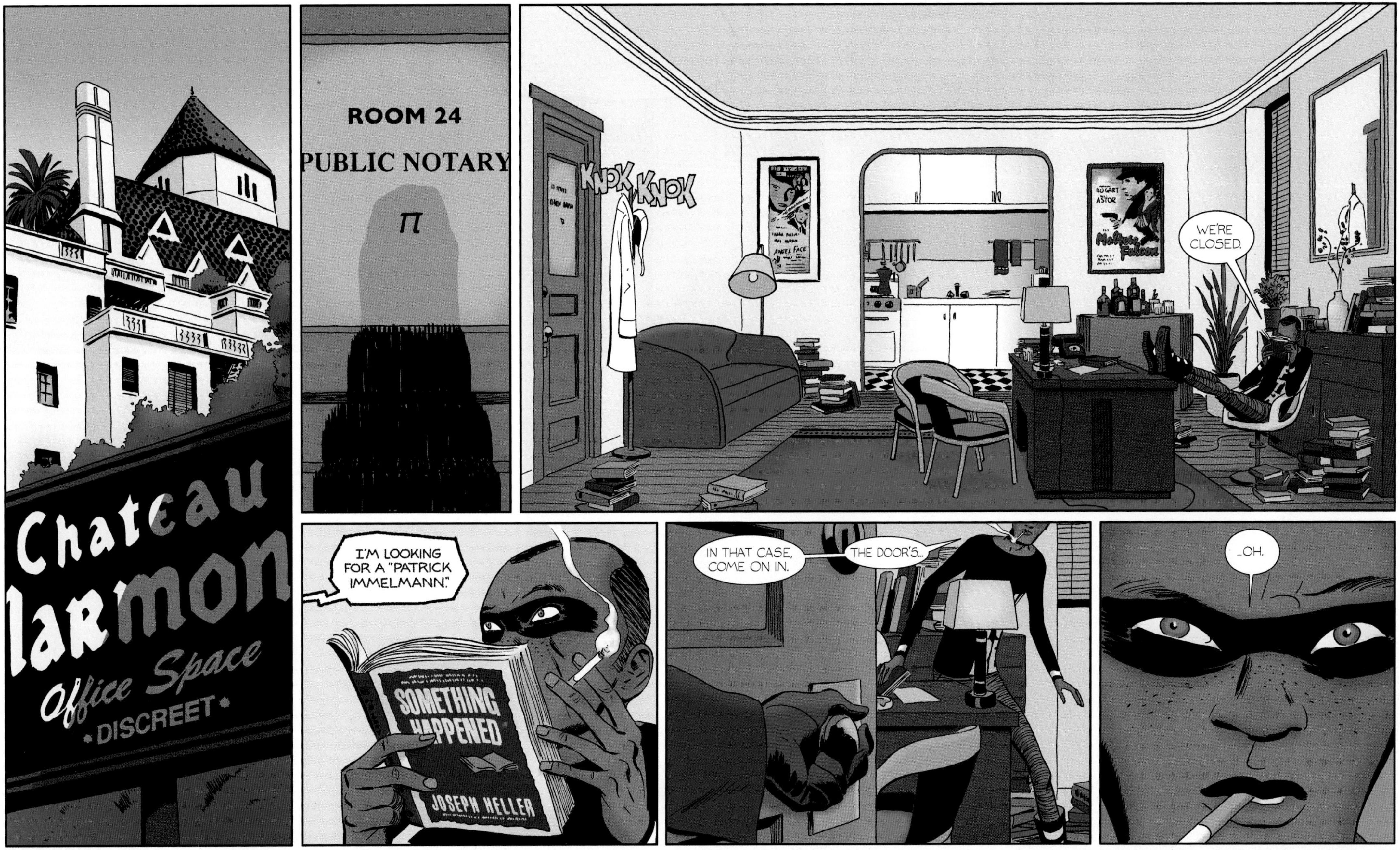
Chateau Marmont
Office Space
DISCREET
ROOM 24
PUBLIC NOTARY
KNOK KNOK
ANGEL FACE
BOGART
ASTOR
Maltese Falcon
WE'RE CLOSED.
I'M LOOKING FOR A "PATRICK IMMELMANN."
SOMETHING HAPPENED
JOSEPH HELLER
IN THAT CASE, COME ON IN.
THE DOOR'S...
...OH.

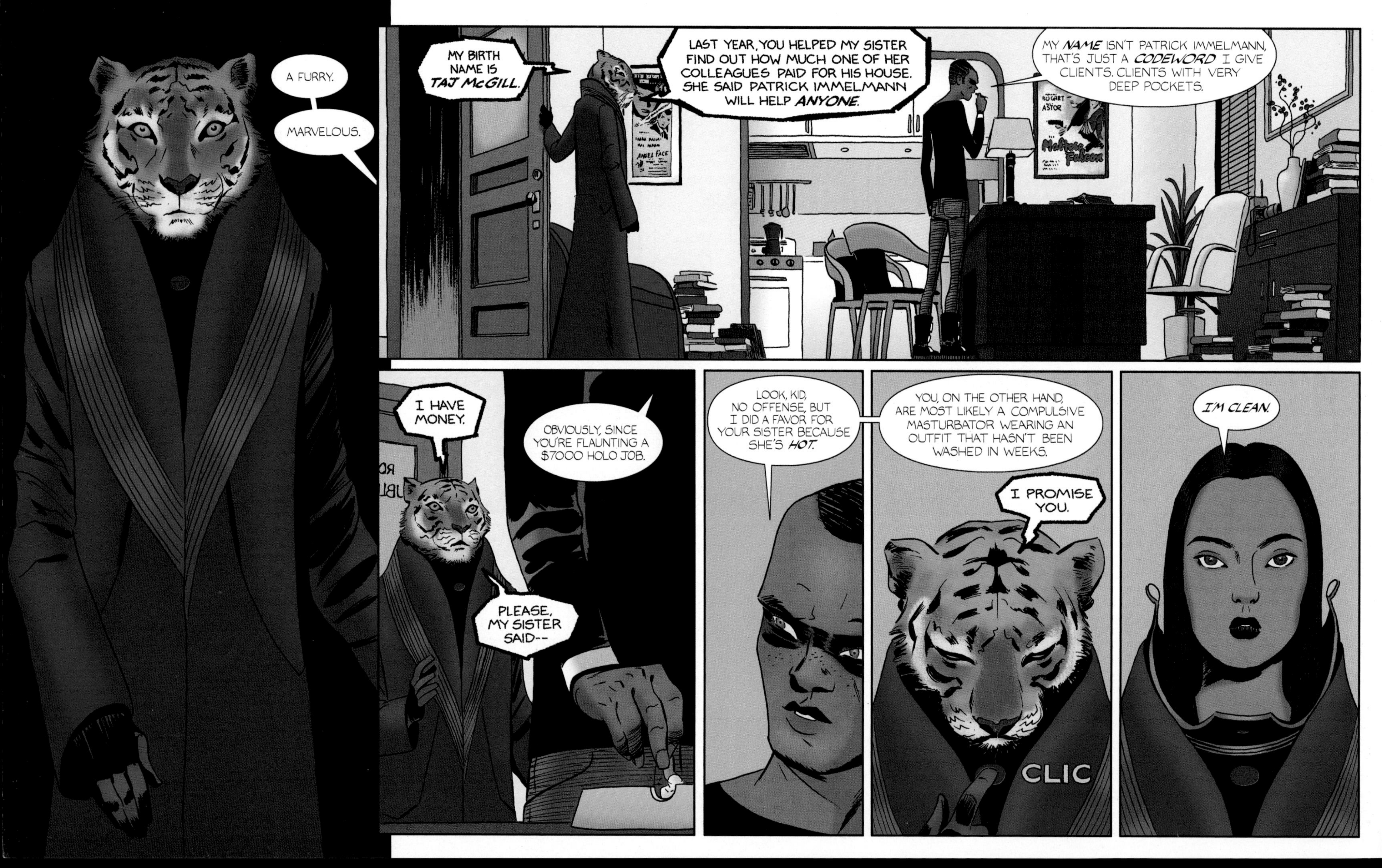
A FURRY.
MARVELOUS.
MY BIRTH NAME IS TAJ McGILL.
LAST YEAR, YOU HELPED MY SISTER FIND OUT HOW MUCH ONE OF HER COLLEAGUES PAID FOR HIS HOUSE. SHE SAID PATRICK IMMELMANN WILL HELP ANYONE.
MY NAME ISN'T PATRICK IMMELMANN, THAT'S JUST A CODEWORD I GIVE CLIENTS. CLIENTS WITH VERY DEEP POCKETS.
I HAVE MONEY.
OBVIOUSLY, SINCE YOU'RE FLAUNTING A $7000 HOLO JOB.
PLEASE, MY SISTER SAID--
LOOK, KID, NO OFFENSE, BUT I DID A FAVOR FOR YOUR SISTER BECAUSE SHE'S HOT.
YOU, ON THE OTHER HAND, ARE MOST LIKELY A COMPULSIVE MASTURBATOR WEARING AN OUTFIT THAT HASN'T BEEN WASHED IN WEEKS.
I PROMISE YOU.
CLIC
I'M CLEAN.

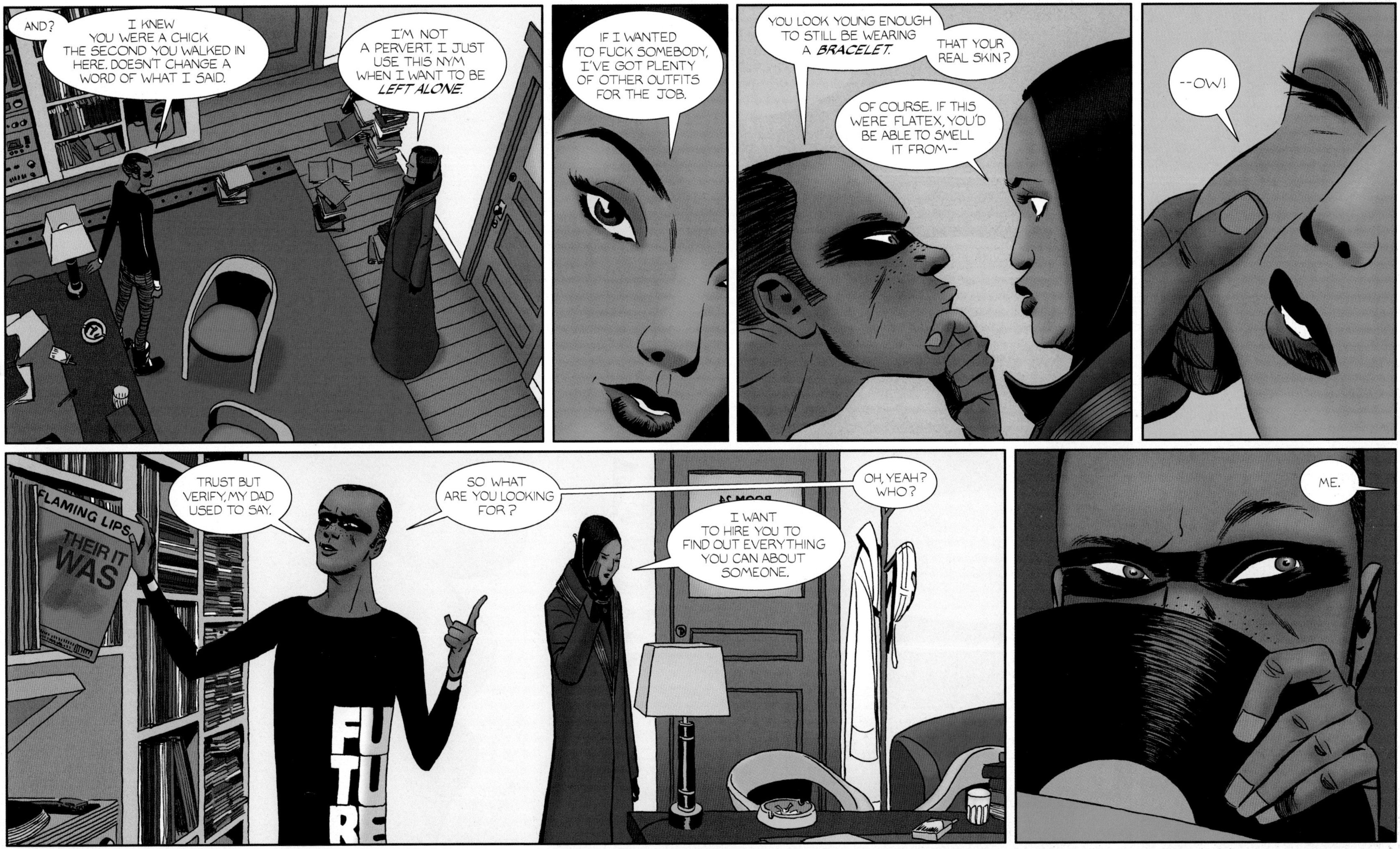
AND?
I KNEW YOU WERE A CHICK THE SECOND YOU WALKED IN HERE. DOESN'T CHANGE A WORD OF WHAT I SAID.
I'M NOT A PERVERT. I JUST USE THIS NYM WHEN I WANT TO BE *LEFT ALONE.*
IF I WANTED TO FUCK SOMEBODY, I'VE GOT PLENTY OF OTHER OUTFITS FOR THE JOB.
YOU LOOK YOUNG ENOUGH TO STILL BE WEARING A *BRACELET.*
THAT YOUR REAL SKIN?
OF COURSE. IF THIS WERE FLATEX, YOU'D BE ABLE TO SMELL IT FROM--
--OW!
TRUST BUT VERIFY, MY DAD USED TO SAY.
SO WHAT ARE YOU LOOKING FOR?
I WANT TO HIRE YOU TO FIND OUT EVERYTHING YOU CAN ABOUT SOMEONE.
OH, YEAH? WHO?
ME.
FLAMING LIPS
THEIR IT WAS
FUTURE

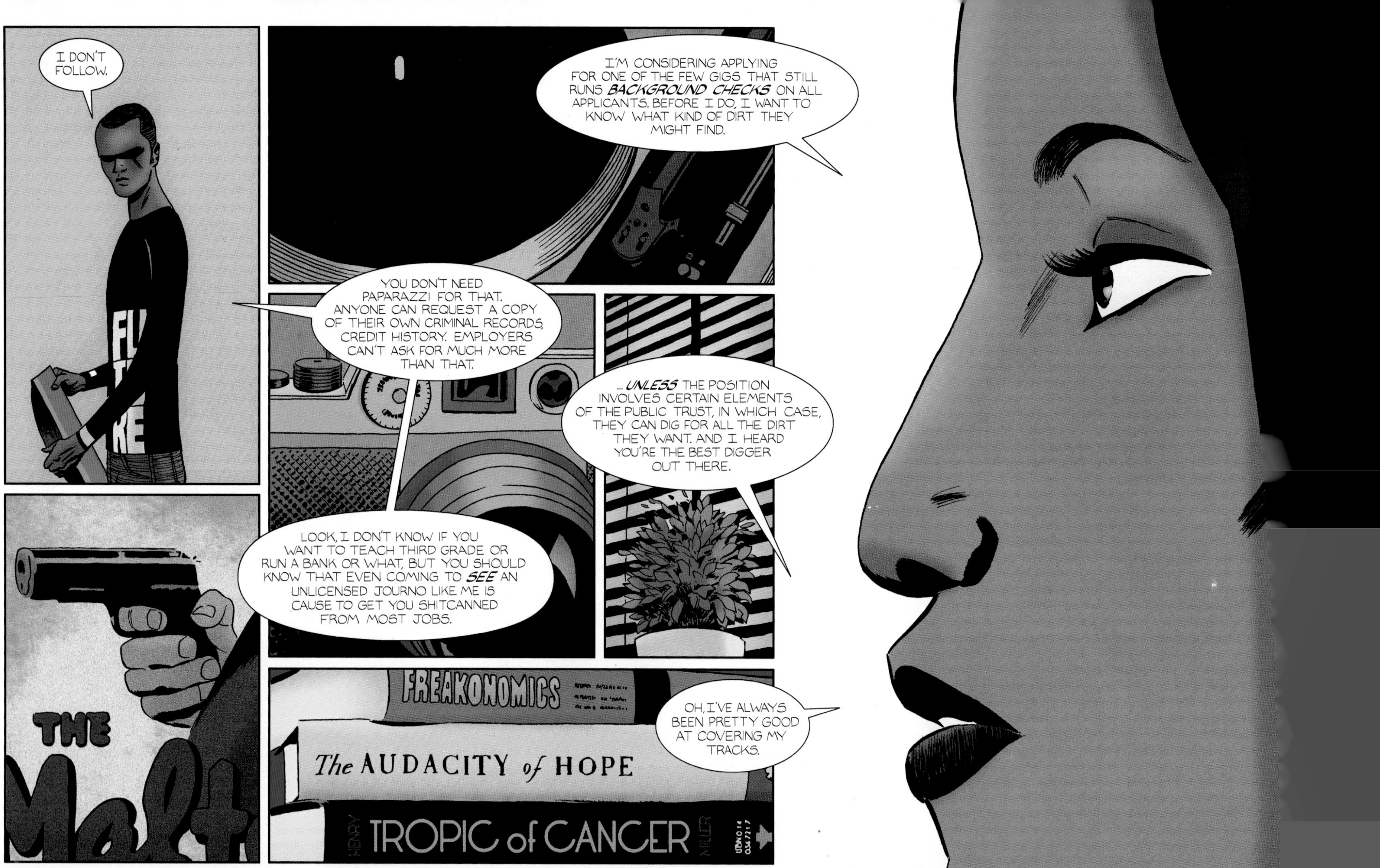
I DON'T FOLLOW.
I'M CONSIDERING APPLYING FOR ONE OF THE FEW GIGS THAT STILL RUNS *BACKGROUND CHECKS* ON ALL APPLICANTS. BEFORE I DO, I WANT TO KNOW WHAT KIND OF DIRT THEY MIGHT FIND.
YOU DON'T NEED PAPARAZZI FOR THAT. ANYONE CAN REQUEST A COPY OF THEIR OWN CRIMINAL RECORDS, CREDIT HISTORY. EMPLOYERS CAN'T ASK FOR MUCH MORE THAN THAT.
LOOK, I DON'T KNOW IF YOU WANT TO TEACH THIRD GRADE OR RUN A BANK OR WHAT, BUT YOU SHOULD KNOW THAT EVEN COMING TO *SEE* AN UNLICENSED JOURNO LIKE ME IS CAUSE TO GET YOU SHITCANNED FROM MOST JOBS.
...*UNLESS* THE POSITION INVOLVES CERTAIN ELEMENTS OF THE PUBLIC TRUST, IN WHICH CASE, THEY CAN DIG FOR ALL THE DIRT THEY WANT. AND I HEARD YOU'RE THE BEST DIGGER OUT THERE.
THE
FREAKONOMICS
The AUDACITY of HOPE
HENRY TROPIC of CANCER MILLER
OH, I'VE ALWAYS BEEN PRETTY GOOD AT COVERING MY TRACKS.

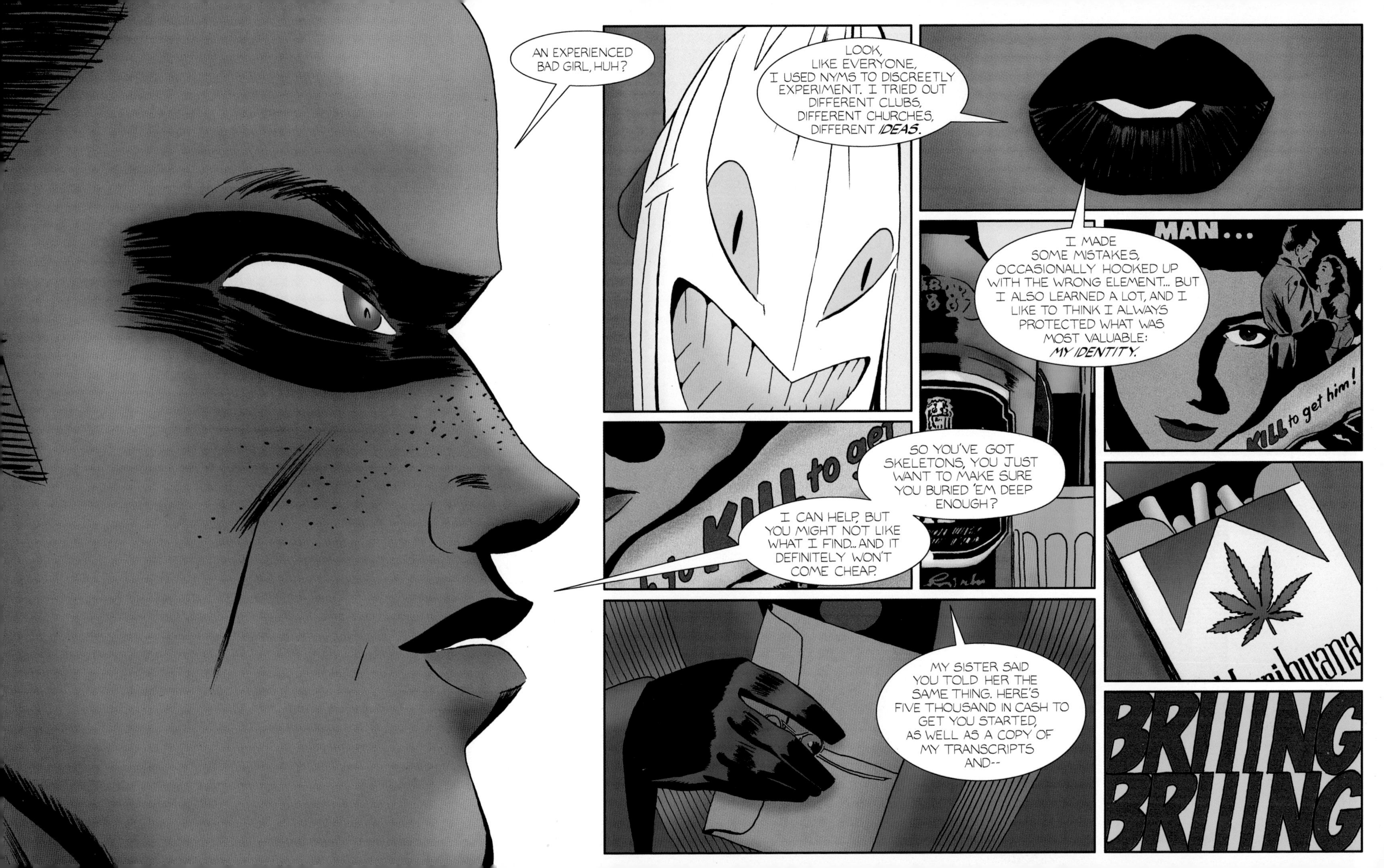
AN EXPERIENCED BAD GIRL, HUH?
LOOK, LIKE EVERYONE, I USED NYMS TO DISCREETLY EXPERIMENT. I TRIED OUT DIFFERENT CLUBS, DIFFERENT CHURCHES, DIFFERENT *IDEAS*.
I MADE SOME MISTAKES, OCCASIONALLY HOOKED UP WITH THE WRONG ELEMENT... BUT I ALSO LEARNED A LOT, AND I LIKE TO THINK I ALWAYS PROTECTED WHAT WAS MOST VALUABLE: *MY IDENTITY.*
MAN...
KILL to get him!
KILL to get
SO YOU'VE GOT SKELETONS, YOU JUST WANT TO MAKE SURE YOU BURIED 'EM DEEP ENOUGH?
I CAN HELP, BUT YOU MIGHT NOT LIKE WHAT I FIND... AND IT DEFINITELY WON'T COME CHEAP.
MY SISTER SAID YOU TOLD HER THE SAME THING. HERE'S FIVE THOUSAND IN CASH TO GET YOU STARTED, AS WELL AS A COPY OF MY TRANSCRIPTS AND--
BRIIING BRIIING

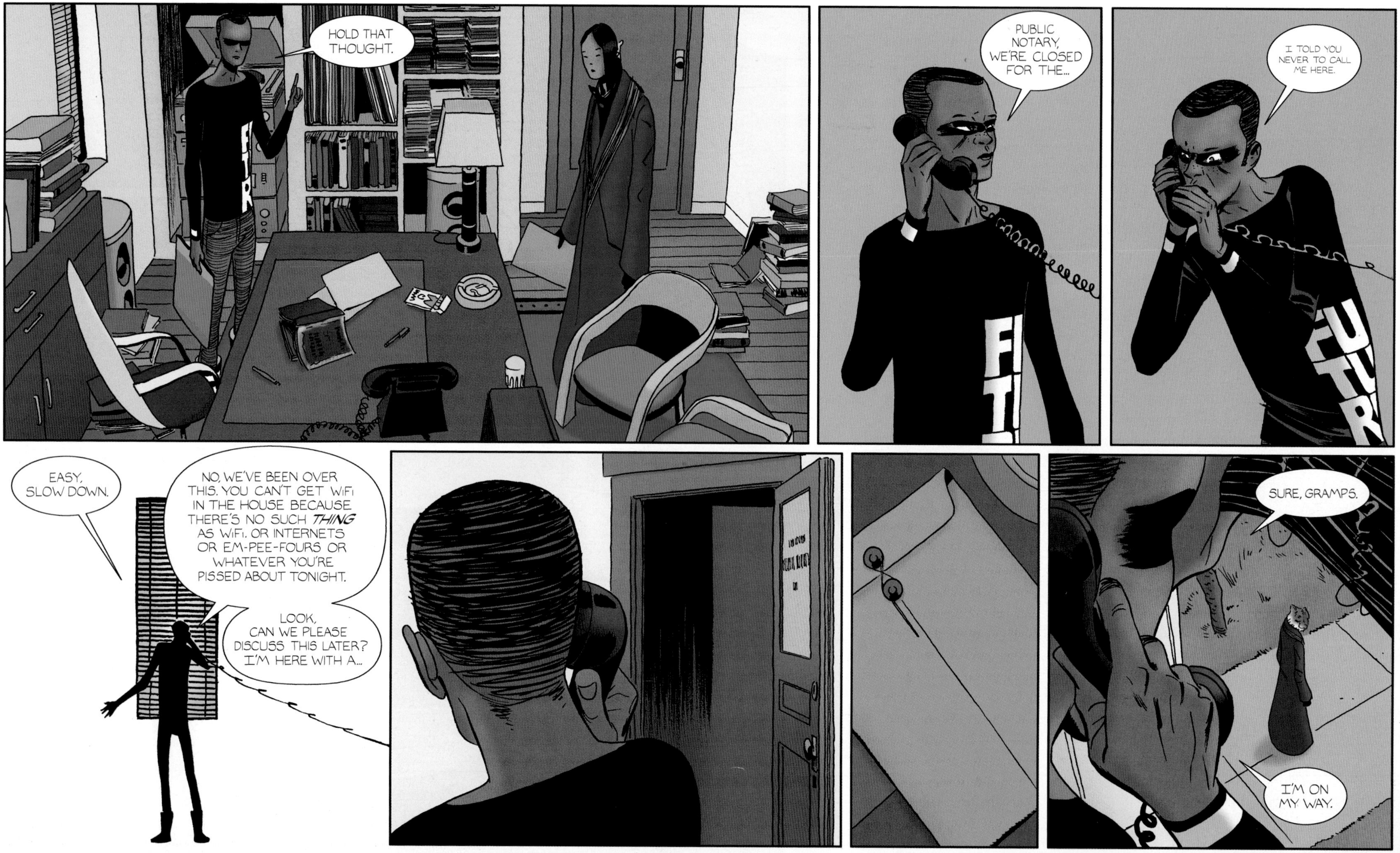
HOLD THAT THOUGHT.
PUBLIC NOTARY, WE'RE CLOSED FOR THE...
I TOLD YOU NEVER TO CALL ME HERE.
EASY, SLOW DOWN.
NO, WE'VE BEEN OVER THIS. YOU CAN'T GET WiFi IN THE HOUSE BECAUSE THERE'S NO SUCH *THING* AS WiFi. OR INTERNETS OR EM-PEE-FOURS OR WHATEVER YOU'RE PISSED ABOUT TONIGHT.
LOOK, CAN WE PLEASE DISCUSS THIS LATER? I'M HERE WITH A...
SURE, GRAMPS.
I'M ON MY WAY.

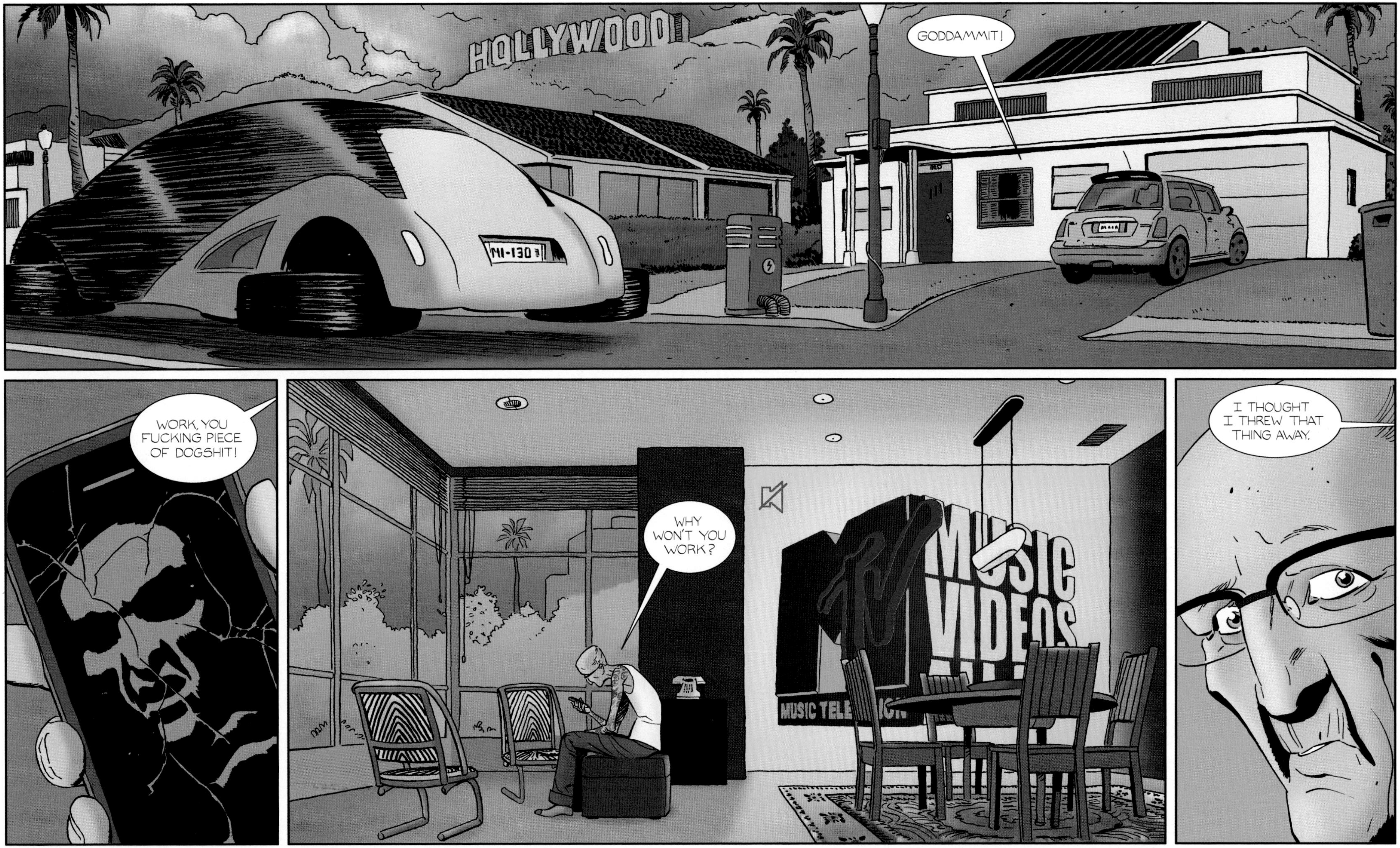
HOLLYWOOD
MI-130
GODDAMMIT!
WORK, YOU FUCKING PIECE OF DOGSHIT!
WHY WON'T YOU WORK?
MUSIC VIDEOS
I THOUGHT I THREW THAT THING AWAY.

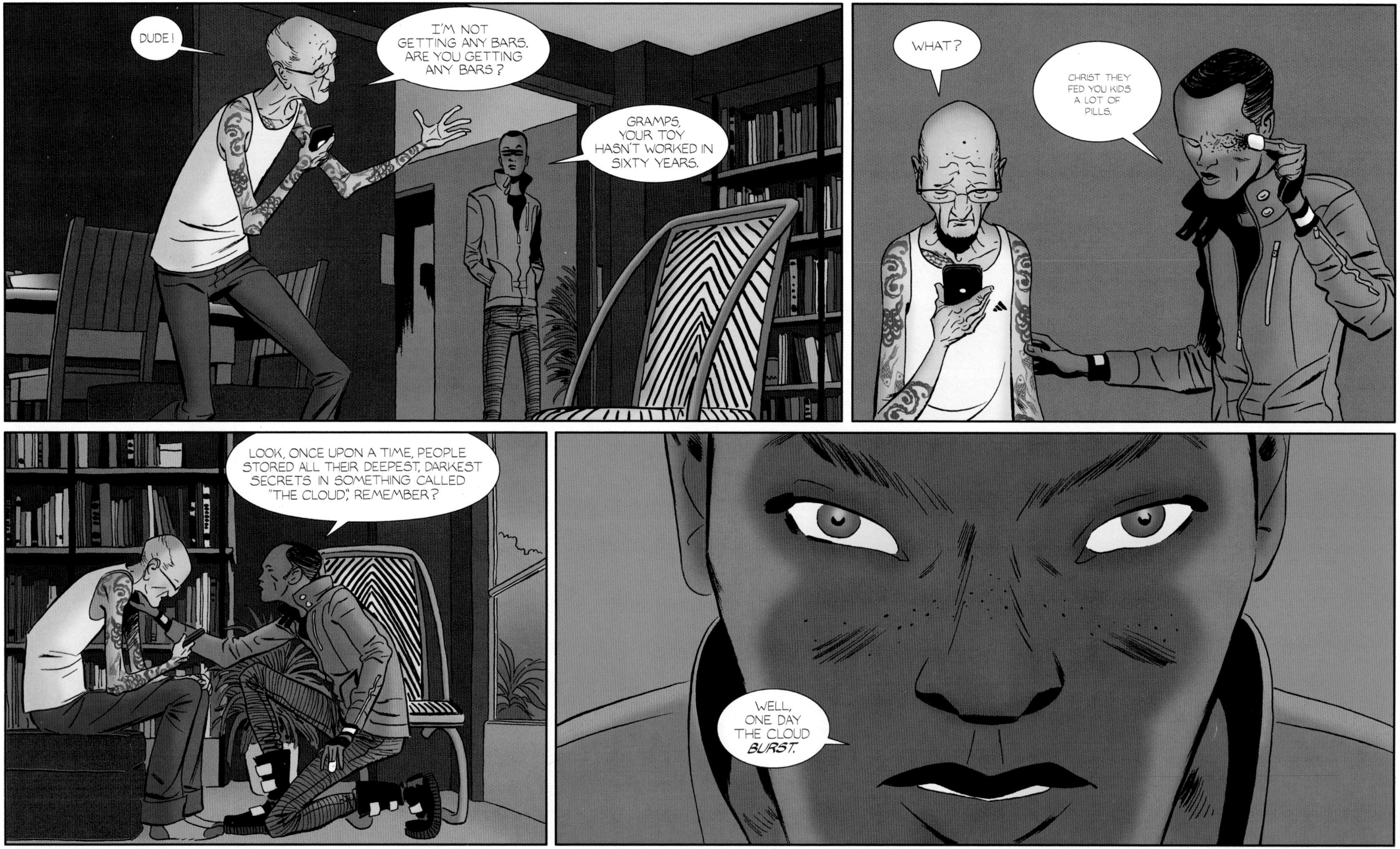
DUDE!
I'M NOT GETTING ANY BARS. ARE YOU GETTING ANY BARS?
GRAMPS, YOUR TOY HASN'T WORKED IN SIXTY YEARS.
WHAT?
CHRIST THEY FED YOU KIDS A LOT OF PILLS.
LOOK, ONCE UPON A TIME, PEOPLE STORED ALL THEIR DEEPEST, DARKEST SECRETS IN SOMETHING CALLED "THE CLOUD," REMEMBER?
WELL, ONE DAY THE CLOUD *BURST.*

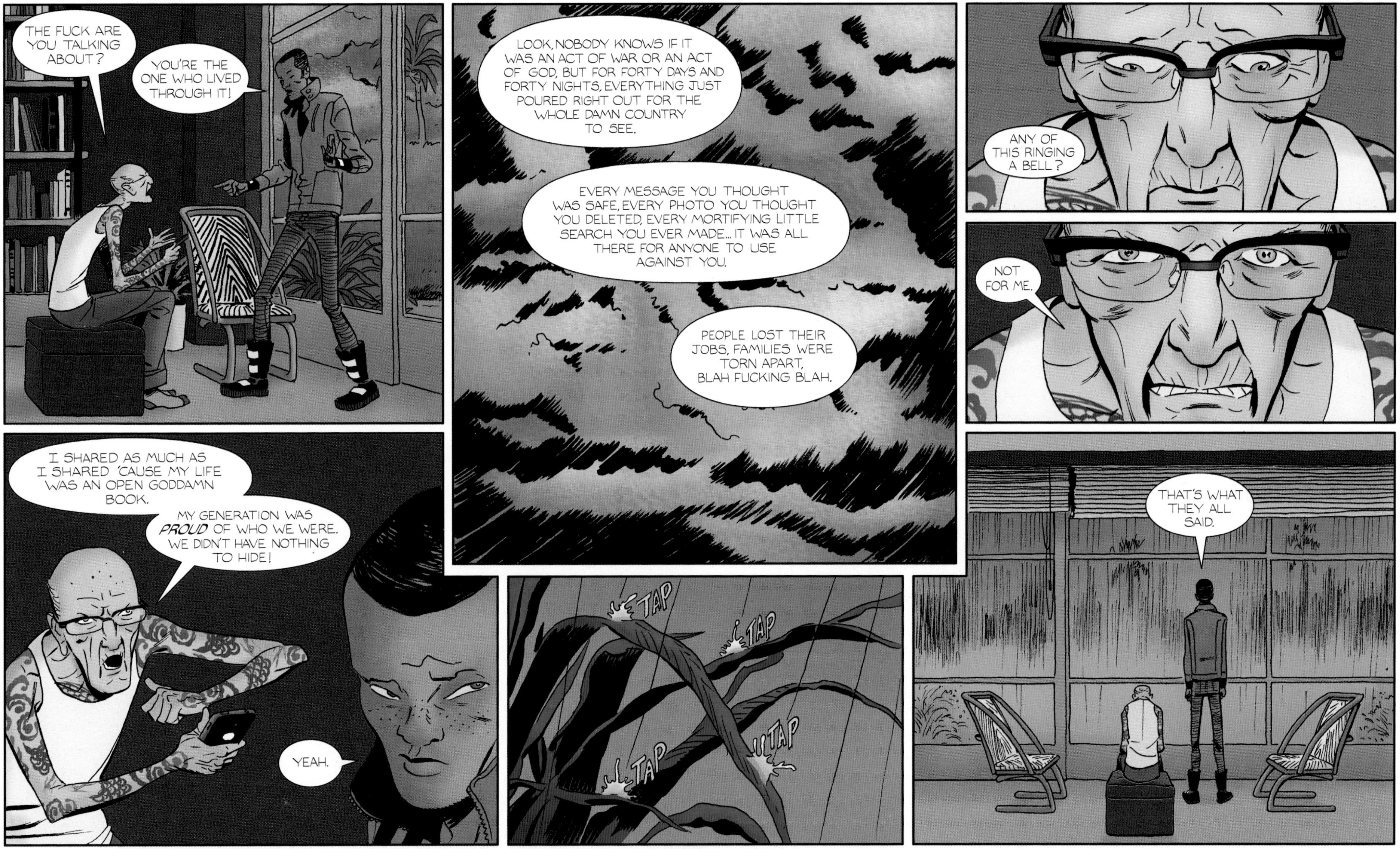
THE FUCK ARE YOU TALKING ABOUT?
YOU'RE THE ONE WHO LIVED THROUGH IT!
LOOK, NOBODY KNOWS IF IT WAS AN ACT OF WAR OR AN ACT OF GOD, BUT FOR FORTY DAYS AND FORTY NIGHTS, EVERYTHING JUST POURED RIGHT OUT FOR THE WHOLE DAMN COUNTRY TO SEE.
EVERY MESSAGE YOU THOUGHT WAS SAFE, EVERY PHOTO YOU THOUGHT YOU DELETED, EVERY MORTIFYING LITTLE SEARCH YOU EVER MADE... IT WAS ALL THERE FOR ANYONE TO USE AGAINST YOU.
PEOPLE LOST THEIR JOBS, FAMILIES WERE TORN APART, BLAH FUCKING BLAH.
ANY OF THIS RINGING A BELL?
NOT FOR ME.
I SHARED AS MUCH AS I SHARED 'CAUSE MY LIFE WAS AN OPEN GODDAMN BOOK.
MY GENERATION WAS *PROUD* OF WHO WE WERE. WE DIDN'T HAVE NOTHING TO HIDE!
YEAH.
TAP
TAP
TAP
TAP
THAT'S WHAT THEY ALL SAID.

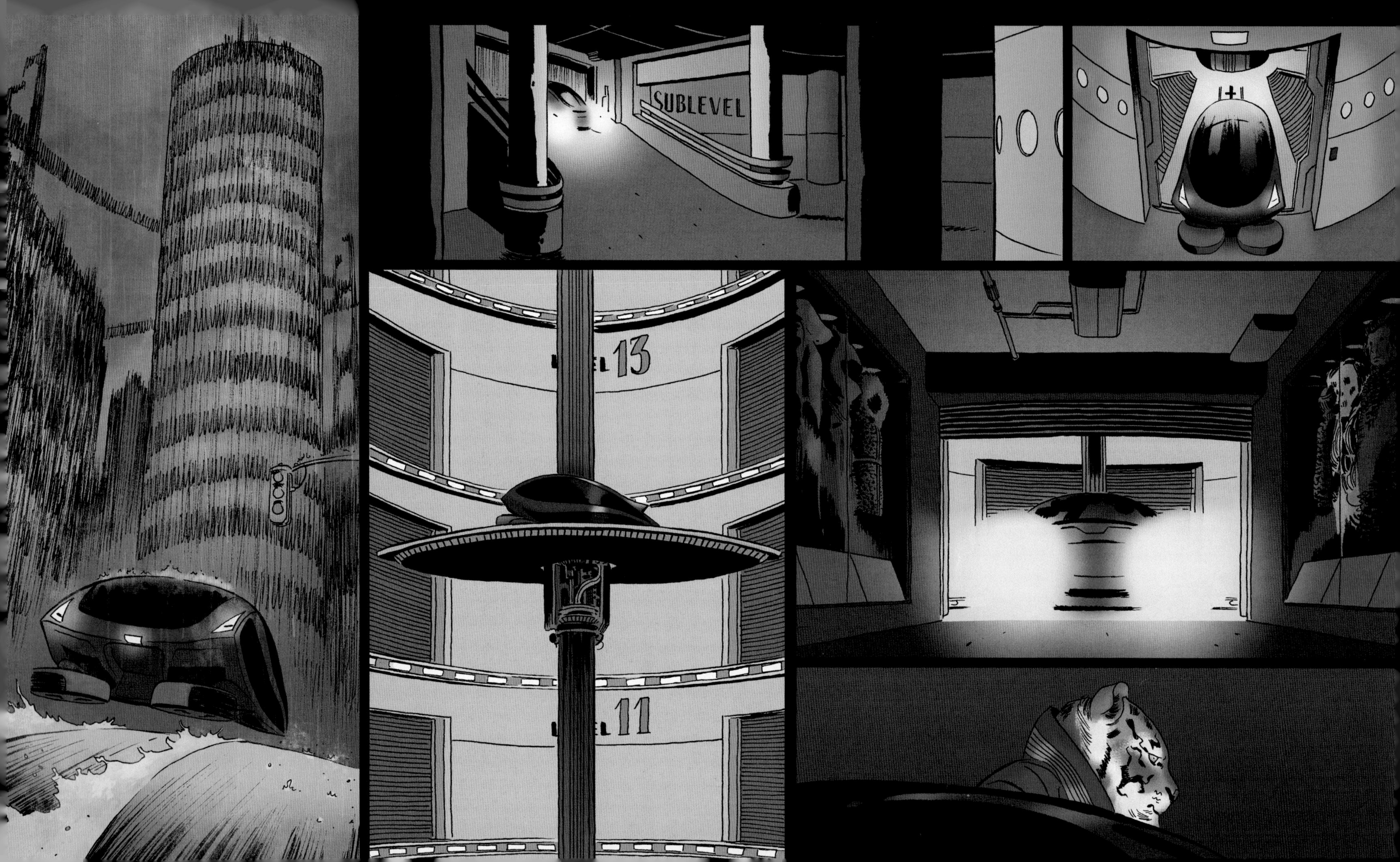
SUBLEVEL
EL 13
EL 11

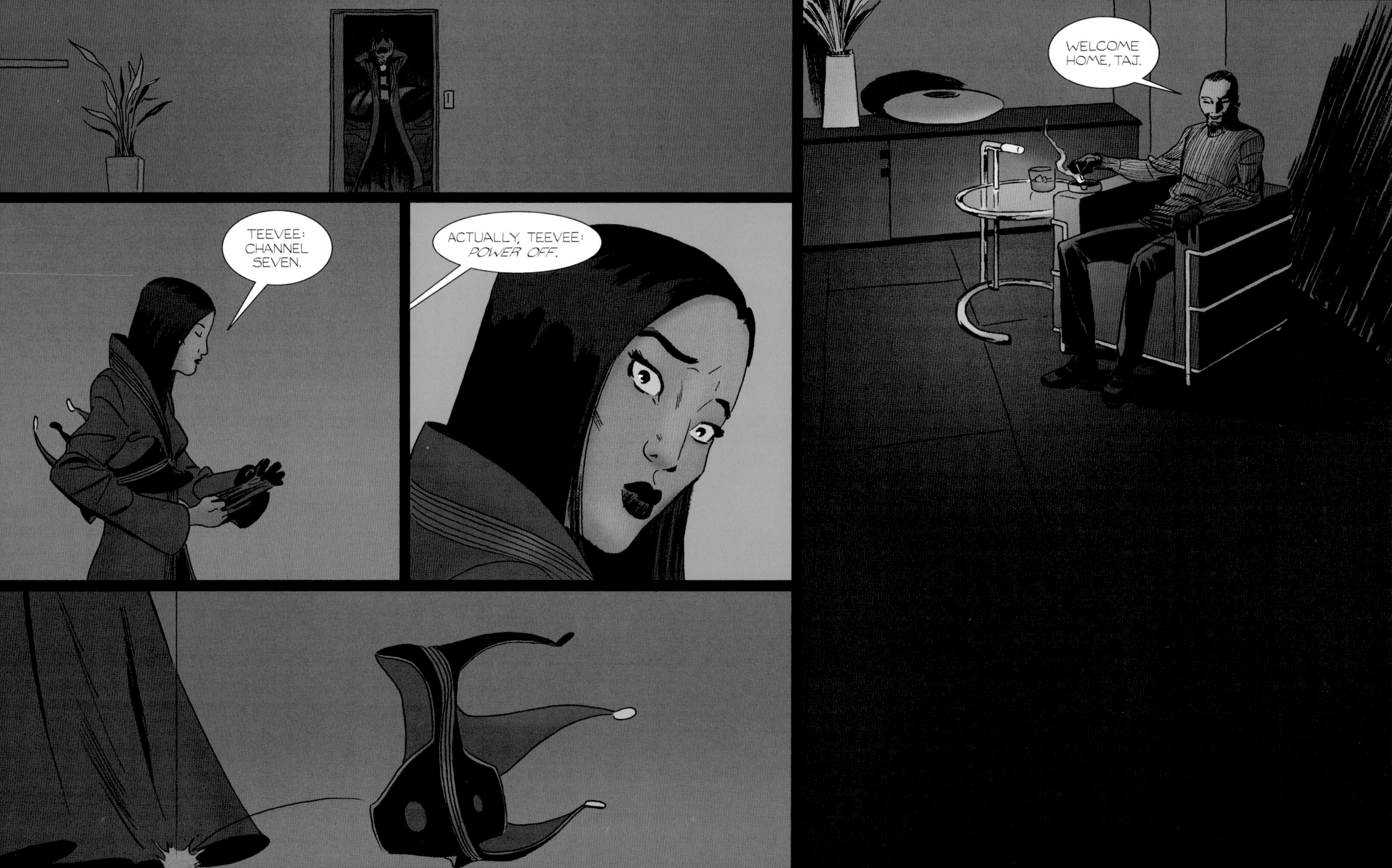
TEEVEE: CHANNEL SEVEN.
ACTUALLY, TEEVEE: *POWER OFF.*
WELCOME HOME, TAJ.

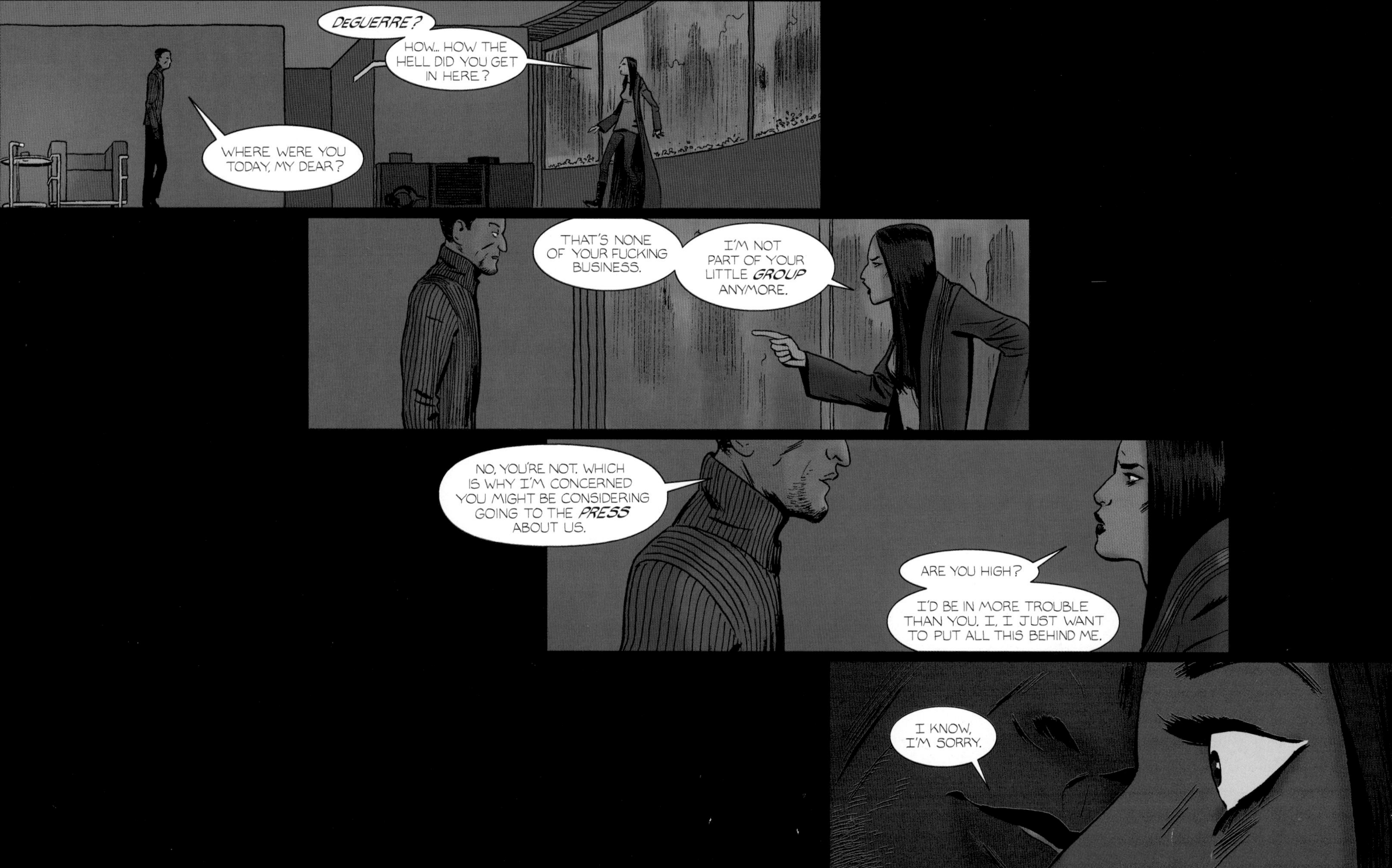
DEGUERRE?
HOW... HOW THE HELL DID YOU GET IN HERE?
WHERE WERE YOU TODAY, MY DEAR?
THAT'S NONE OF YOUR FUCKING BUSINESS.
I'M NOT PART OF YOUR LITTLE GROUP ANYMORE.
NO, YOU'RE NOT. WHICH IS WHY I'M CONCERNED YOU MIGHT BE CONSIDERING GOING TO THE PRESS ABOUT US.
ARE YOU HIGH?
I'D BE IN MORE TROUBLE THAN YOU. I, I JUST WANT TO PUT ALL THIS BEHIND ME.
I KNOW, I'M SORRY.

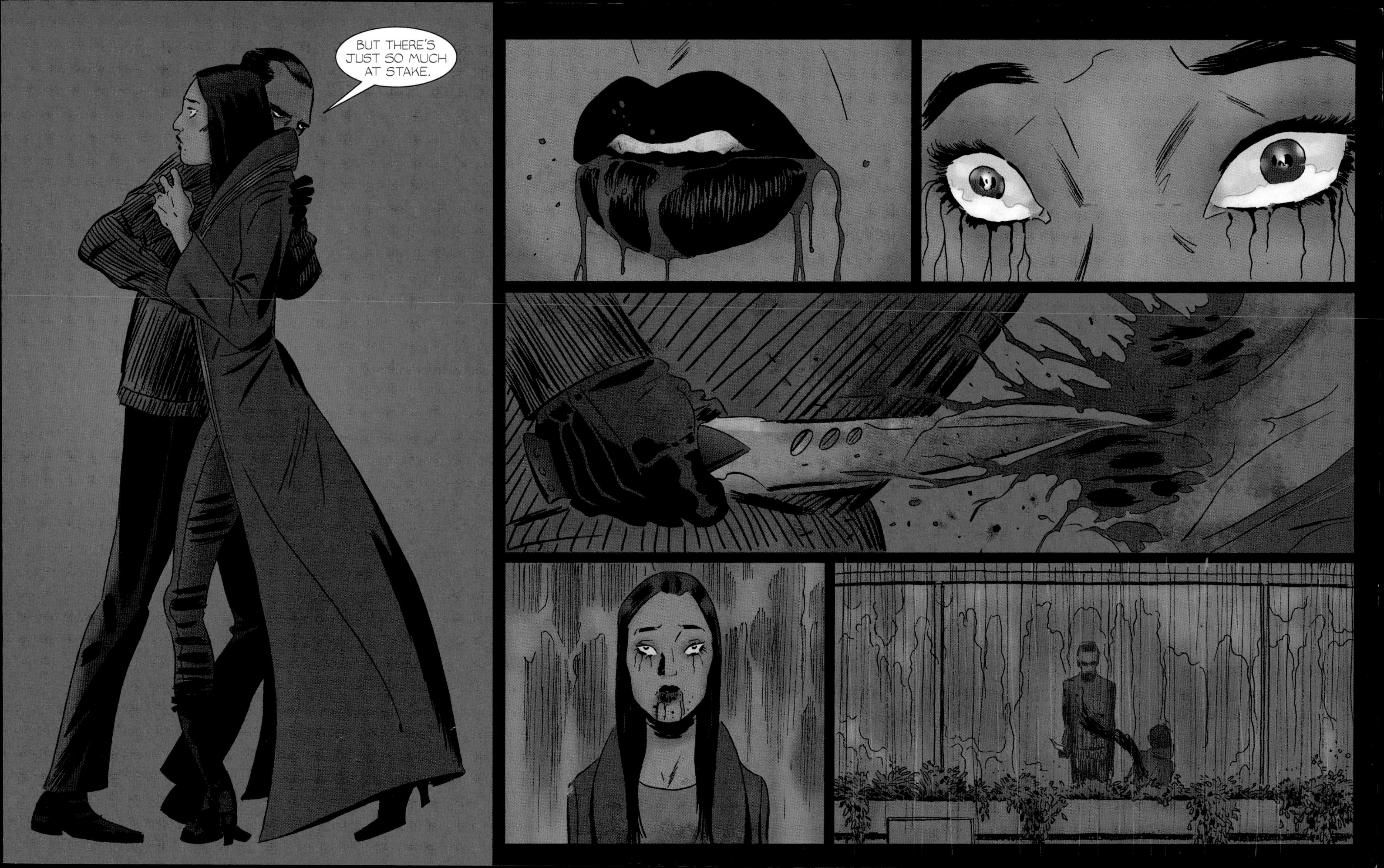
BUT THERE'S JUST SO MUCH AT STAKE.

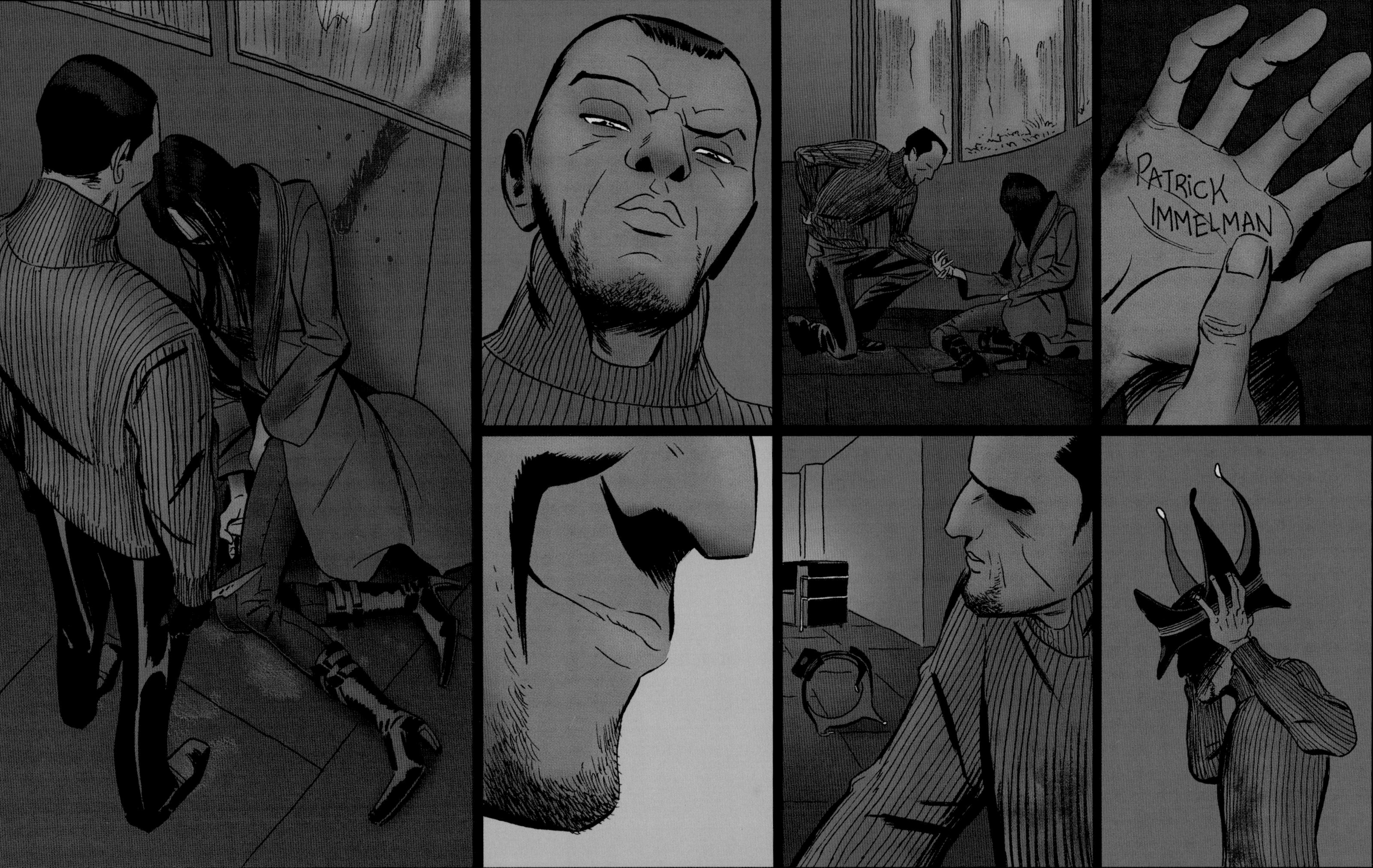
PATRICK
IMMELMAN

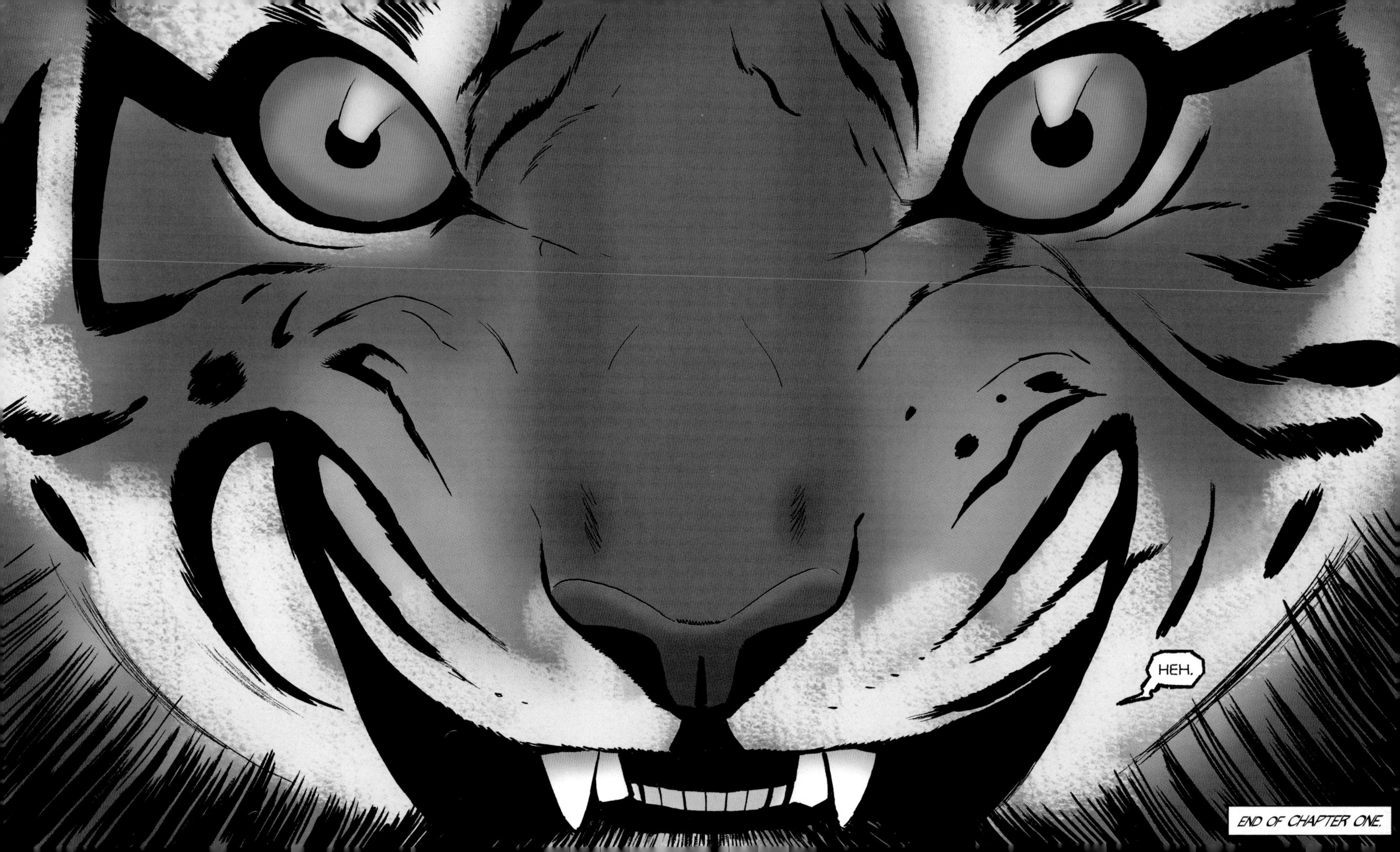
HEH.
END OF CHAPTER ONE.

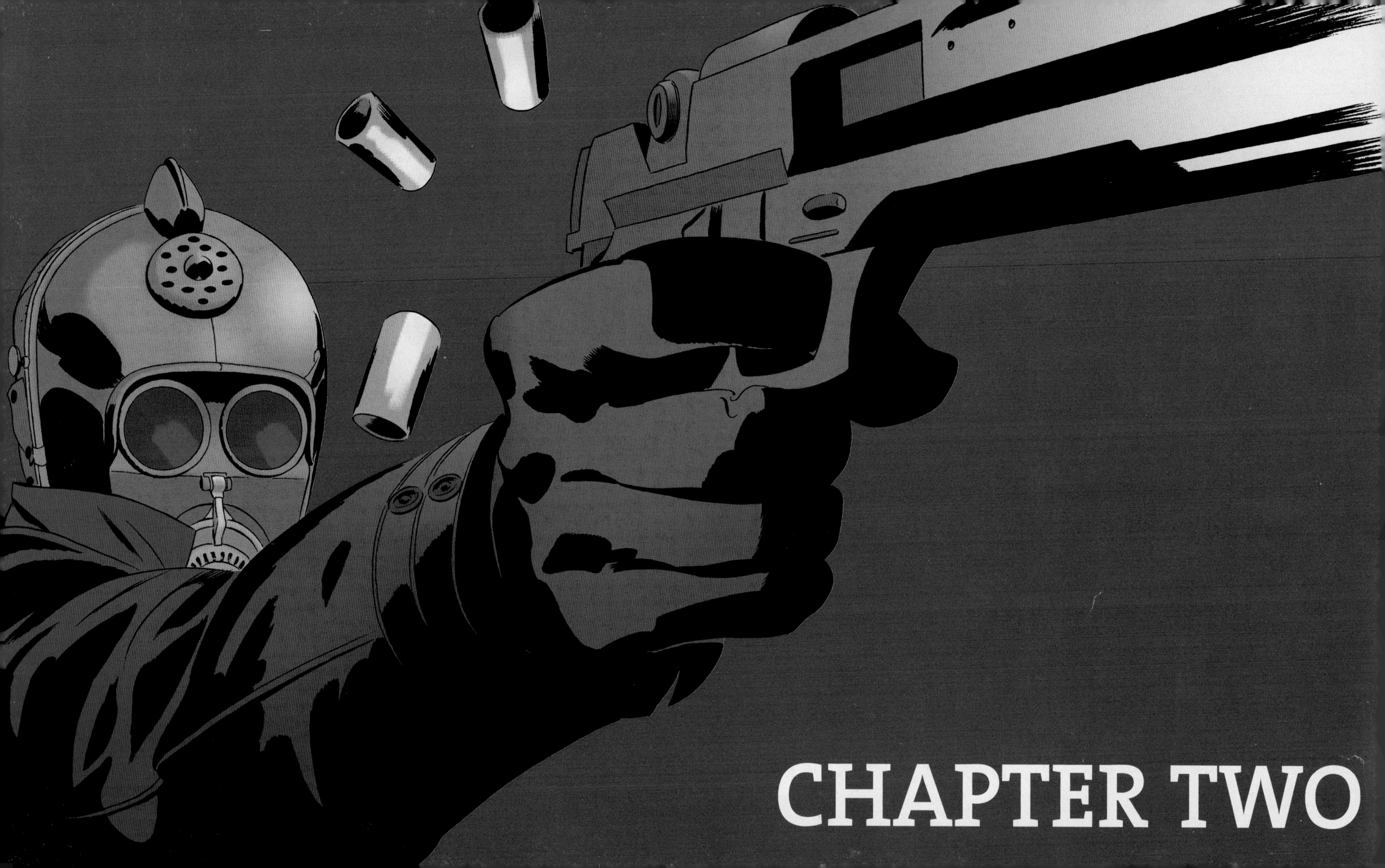

CHAPTER TWO

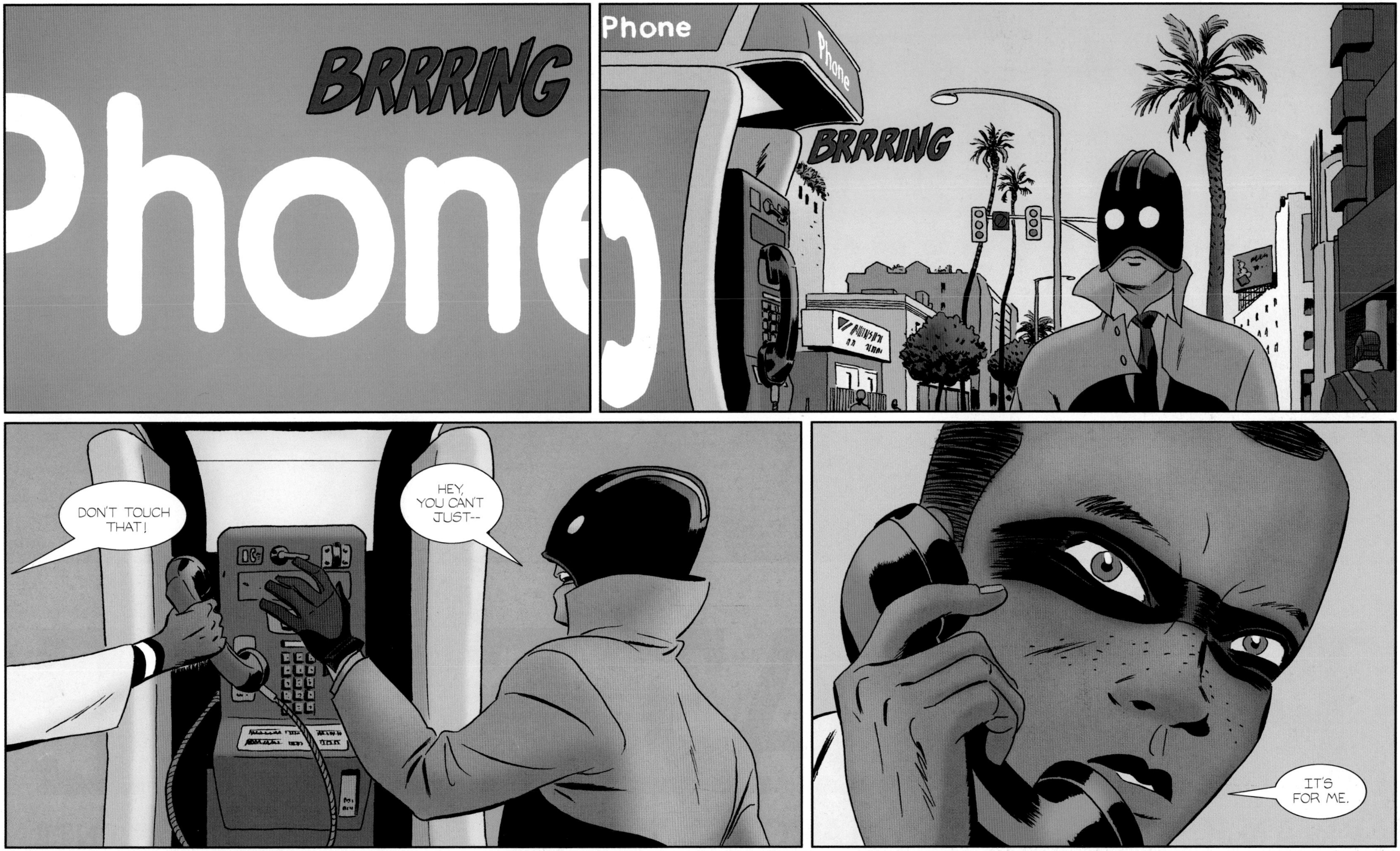
BRRRING
Phone
Phone
Phone
Phone
BRRRING
DON'T TOUCH THAT!
HEY, YOU CAN'T JUST--
IT'S FOR ME.

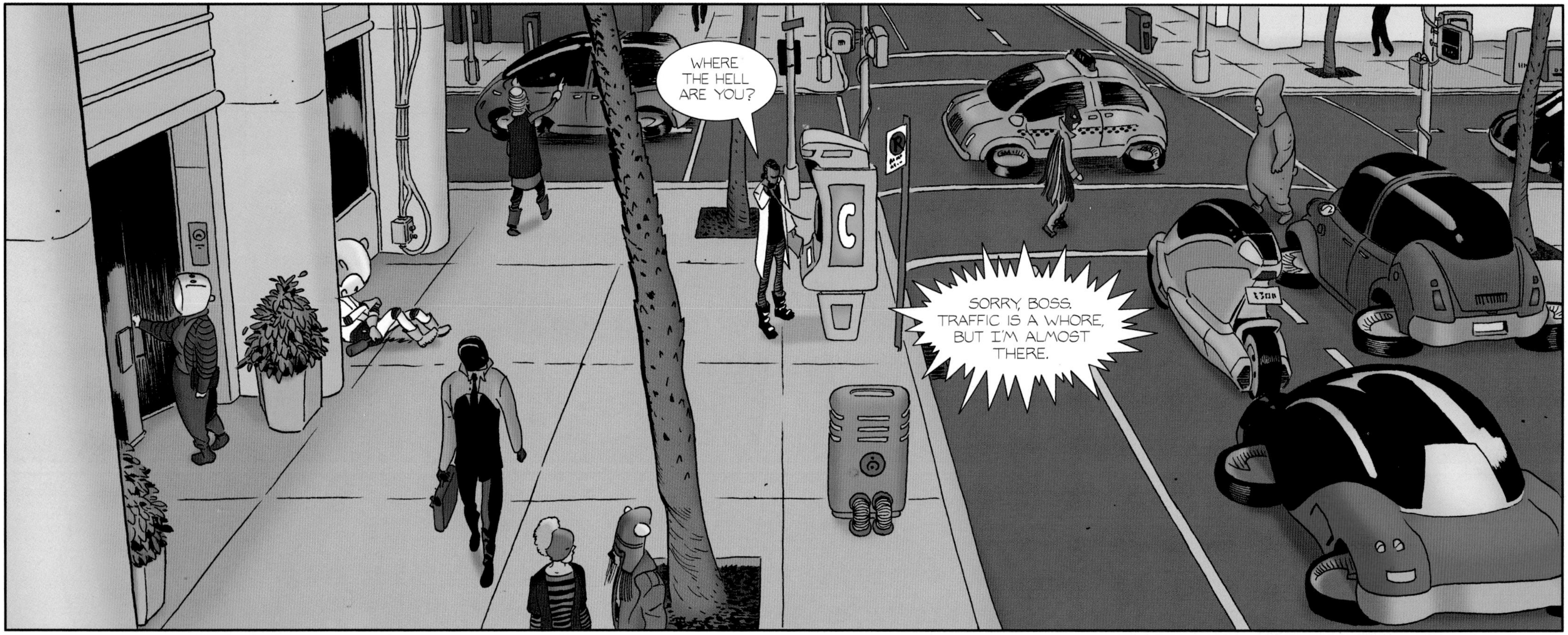
WHERE THE HELL ARE YOU?
SORRY, BOSS. TRAFFIC IS A WHORE, BUT I'M ALMOST THERE.

THE PRIVATE EYE

BRIAN K. VAUGHAN MARCOS MARTIN WITH MUNTSA VICENTE

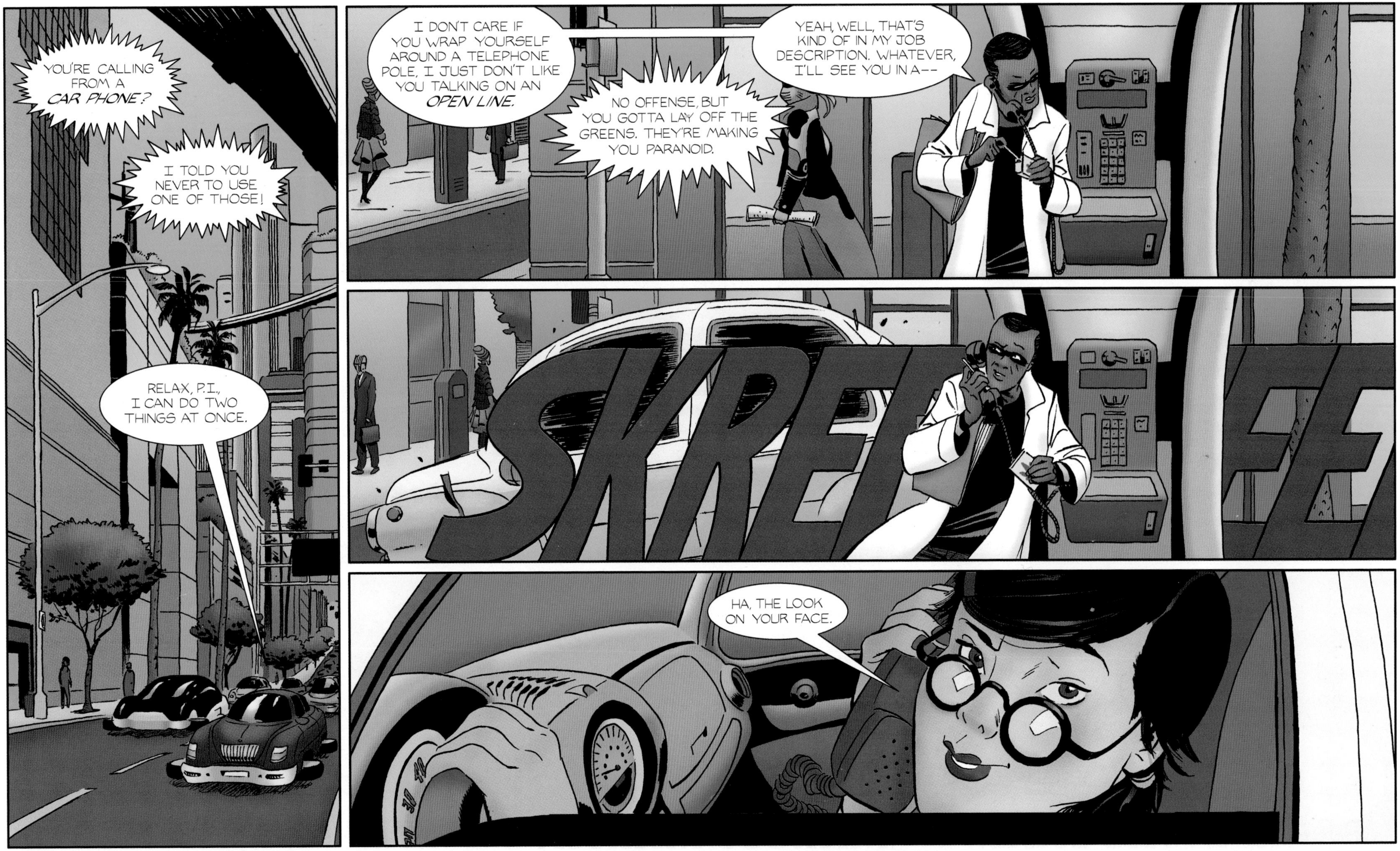
YOU'RE CALLING FROM A *CAR PHONE?*
I TOLD YOU NEVER TO USE ONE OF THOSE!
RELAX, P.I., I CAN DO TWO THINGS AT ONCE.
I DON'T CARE IF YOU WRAP YOURSELF AROUND A TELEPHONE POLE, I JUST DON'T LIKE YOU TALKING ON AN *OPEN LINE.*
NO OFFENSE, BUT YOU GOTTA LAY OFF THE GREENS. THEY'RE MAKING YOU PARANOID.
YEAH, WELL, THAT'S KIND OF IN MY JOB DESCRIPTION. WHATEVER, I'LL SEE YOU IN A--
SKREE
EE
HA, THE LOOK ON YOUR FACE.

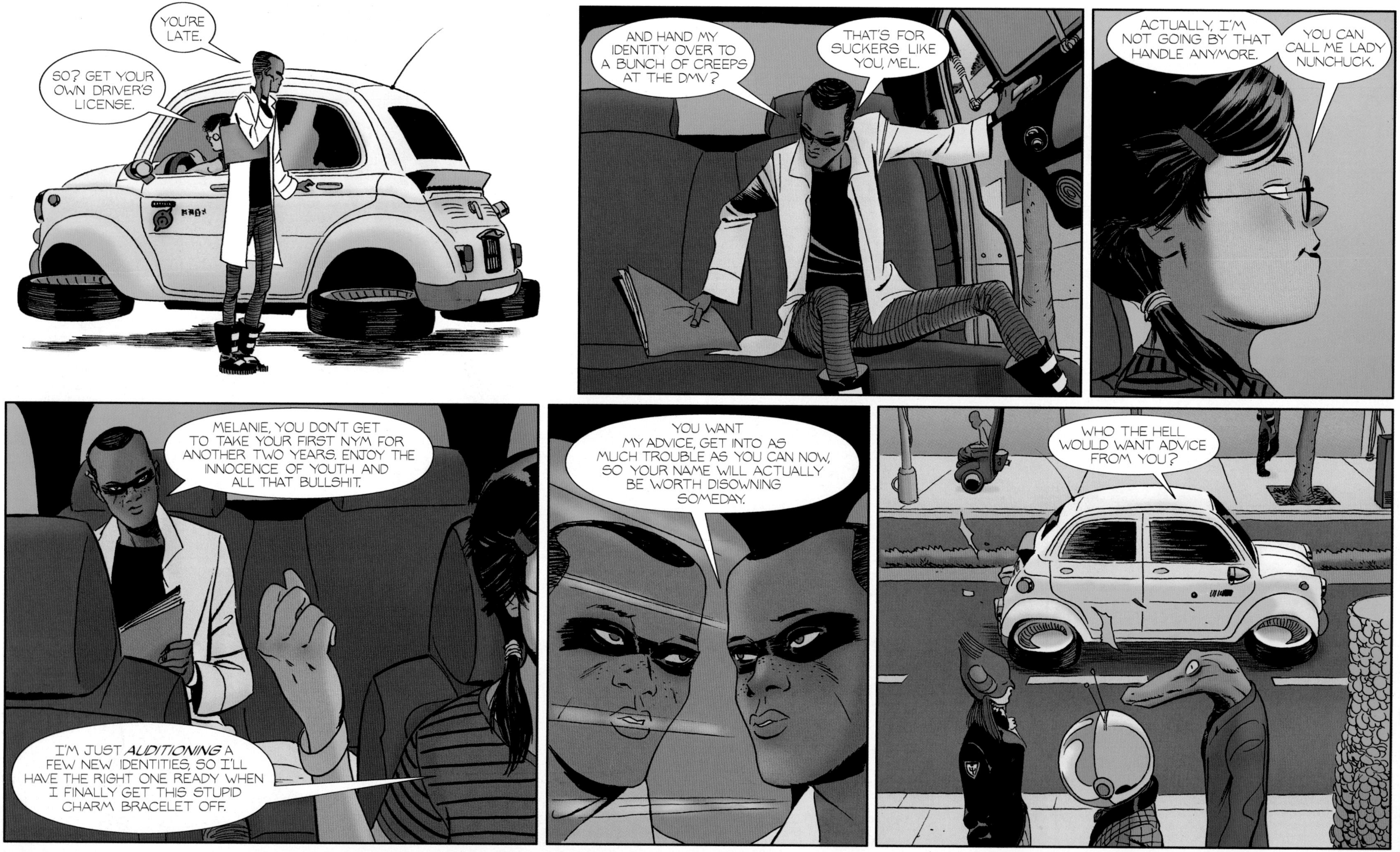
YOU'RE LATE.
SO? GET YOUR OWN DRIVER'S LICENSE.
AND HAND MY IDENTITY OVER TO A BUNCH OF CREEPS AT THE DMV?
THAT'S FOR SUCKERS LIKE YOU, MEL.
ACTUALLY, I'M NOT GOING BY THAT HANDLE ANYMORE.
YOU CAN CALL ME LADY NUNCHUCK.
MELANIE, YOU DON'T GET TO TAKE YOUR FIRST NYM FOR ANOTHER TWO YEARS. ENJOY THE INNOCENCE OF YOUTH AND ALL THAT BULLSHIT.
I'M JUST *AUDITIONING* A FEW NEW IDENTITIES, SO I'LL HAVE THE RIGHT ONE READY WHEN I FINALLY GET THIS STUPID CHARM BRACELET OFF.
YOU WANT MY ADVICE, GET INTO AS MUCH TROUBLE AS YOU CAN NOW, SO YOUR NAME WILL ACTUALLY BE WORTH DISOWNING SOMEDAY.
WHO THE HELL WOULD WANT ADVICE FROM YOU?

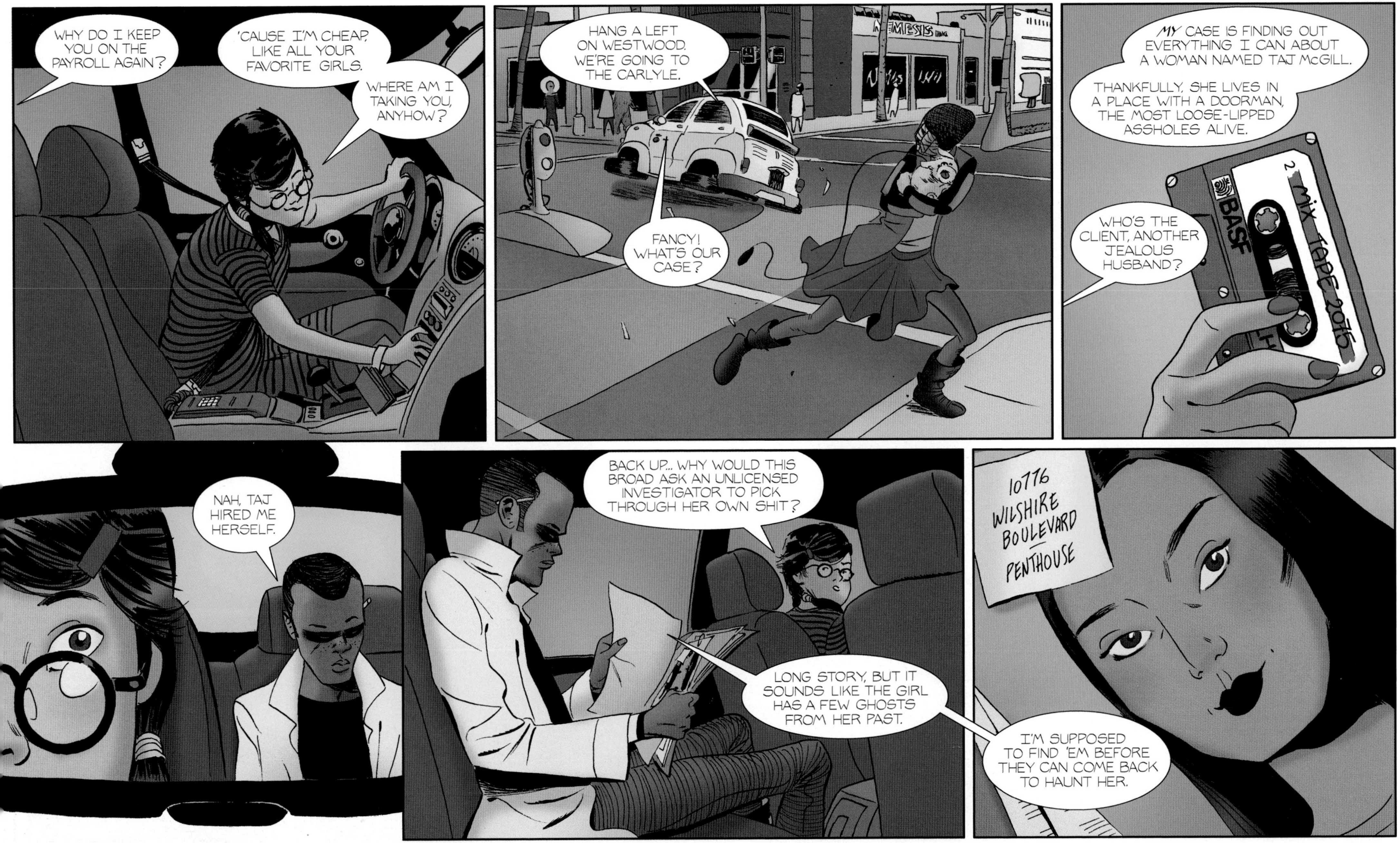
WHY DO I KEEP YOU ON THE PAYROLL AGAIN?
'CAUSE I'M CHEAP, LIKE ALL YOUR FAVORITE GIRLS.
WHERE AM I TAKING YOU, ANYHOW?
HANG A LEFT ON WESTWOOD. WE'RE GOING TO THE CARLYLE.
NEMESIS INC
FANCY! WHAT'S OUR CASE?
MY CASE IS FINDING OUT EVERYTHING I CAN ABOUT A WOMAN NAMED TAJ McGILL.
THANKFULLY, SHE LIVES IN A PLACE WITH A DOORMAN, THE MOST LOOSE-LIPPED ASSHOLES ALIVE.
BASF
MIX TAPE 2015
WHO'S THE CLIENT, ANOTHER JEALOUS HUSBAND?
NAH, TAJ HIRED ME HERSELF.
BACK UP... WHY WOULD THIS BROAD ASK AN UNLICENSED INVESTIGATOR TO PICK THROUGH HER OWN SHIT?
LONG STORY, BUT IT SOUNDS LIKE THE GIRL HAS A FEW GHOSTS FROM HER PAST.
10776 WILSHIRE BOULEVARD — PENTHOUSE
I'M SUPPOSED TO FIND 'EM BEFORE THEY CAN COME BACK TO HAUNT HER.

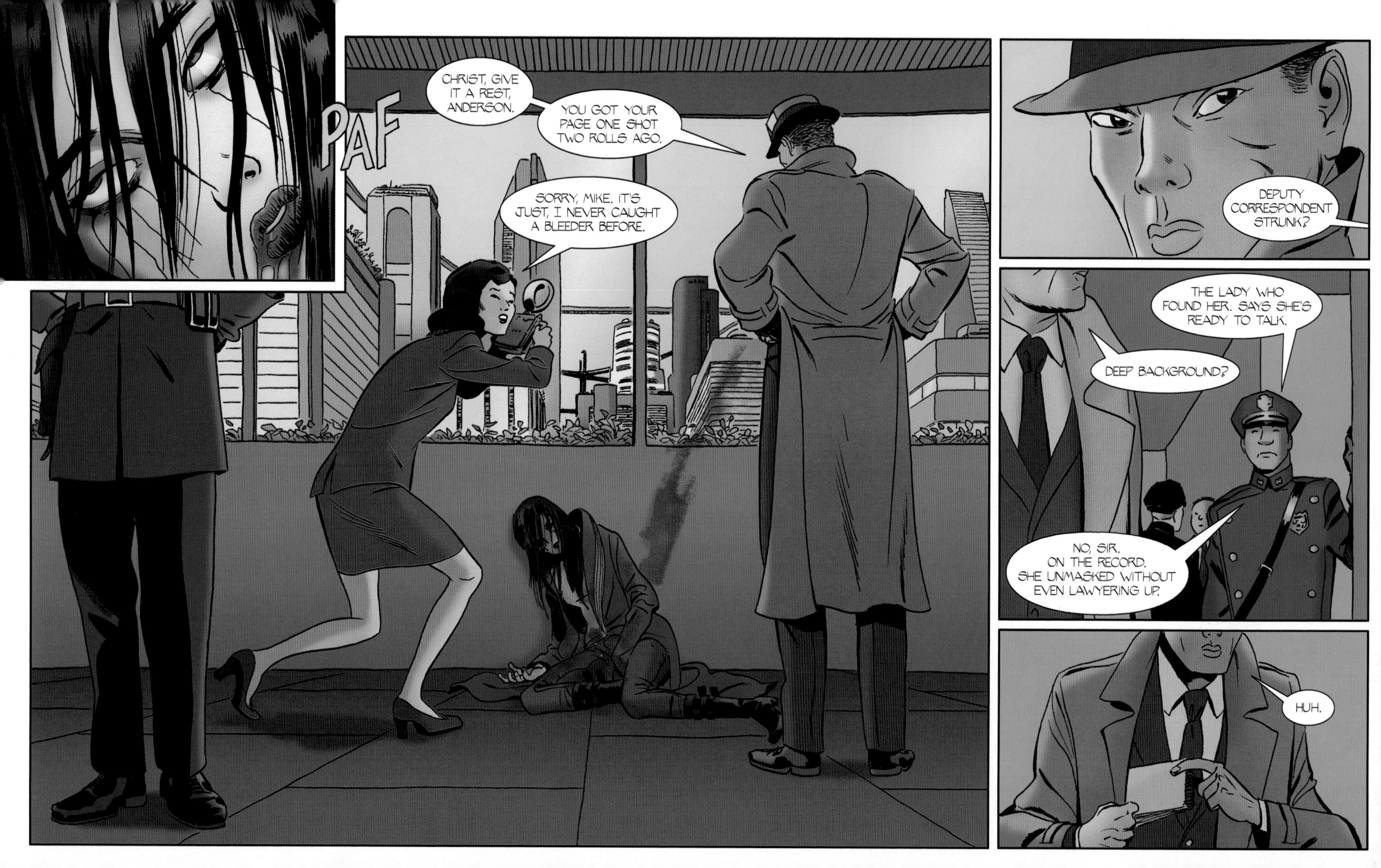
PAF
CHRIST, GIVE IT A REST, ANDERSON.
YOU GOT YOUR PAGE ONE SHOT TWO ROLLS AGO.
SORRY, MIKE. IT'S JUST, I NEVER CAUGHT A BLEEDER BEFORE.
DEPUTY CORRESPONDENT STRUNK?
THE LADY WHO FOUND HER. SAYS SHE'S READY TO TALK.
DEEP BACKGROUND?
NO, SIR. ON THE RECORD. SHE UNMASKED WITHOUT EVEN LAWYERING UP.
HUH.

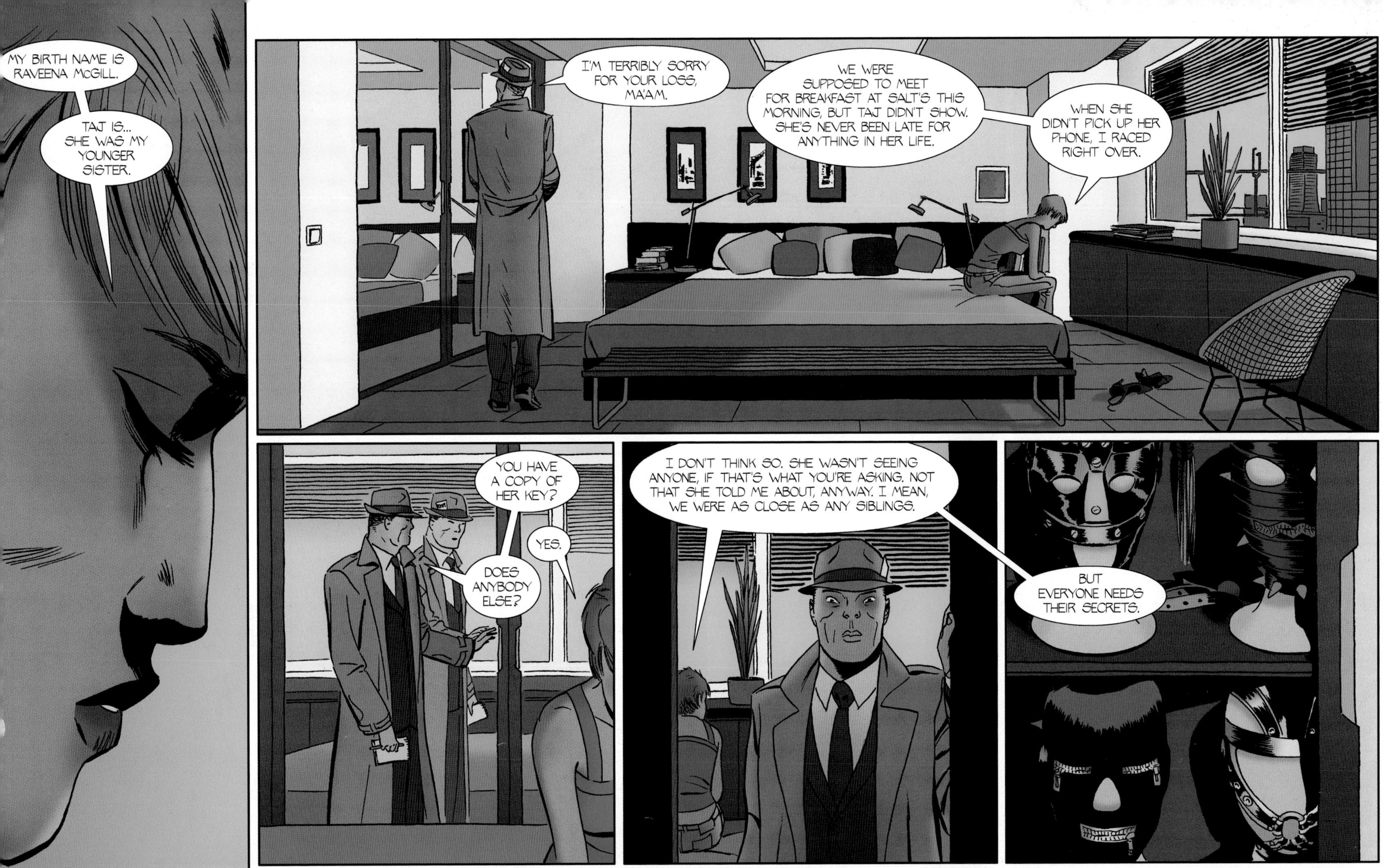
MY BIRTH NAME IS RAVEENA McGILL.
TAJ IS... SHE WAS MY YOUNGER SISTER.
I'M TERRIBLY SORRY FOR YOUR LOSS, MA'AM.
WE WERE SUPPOSED TO MEET FOR BREAKFAST AT SALT'S THIS MORNING, BUT TAJ DIDN'T SHOW. SHE'S NEVER BEEN LATE FOR ANYTHING IN HER LIFE.
WHEN SHE DIDN'T PICK UP HER PHONE, I RACED RIGHT OVER.
YOU HAVE A COPY OF HER KEY?
YES.
DOES ANYBODY ELSE?
I DON'T THINK SO. SHE WASN'T SEEING ANYONE, IF THAT'S WHAT YOU'RE ASKING. NOT THAT SHE TOLD ME ABOUT, ANYWAY. I MEAN, WE WERE AS CLOSE AS ANY SIBLINGS.
BUT EVERYONE NEEDS THEIR SECRETS.

OF COURSE.

DID SHE HAVE ANY ENEMIES YOU WERE AWARE OF? PEOPLE WHO MIGHT WANT TO HURT HER?

I CAN'T IMAGINE.

AS FAR AS I KNOW, SHE SPENT MOST OF HER DAYS INSIDE GOODHUE.

THE LIBRARY? WHAT WAS SHE RESEARCHING?

I WISH I KNEW.

I DON'T EVEN HAVE A CARD.

YEAH, I'M MORE OF A TEEVEE GUY, TOO.

JUST ONE MORE THING. IT LOOKS LIKE YOUR SISTER HAD A NAME WRITTEN IN INK ON HER HAND. "PATRICK IMMELMANN". DOES THAT MEAN ANYTHING TO YOU?

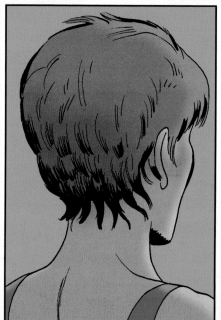

I CAN'T SAY THAT IT DOES.

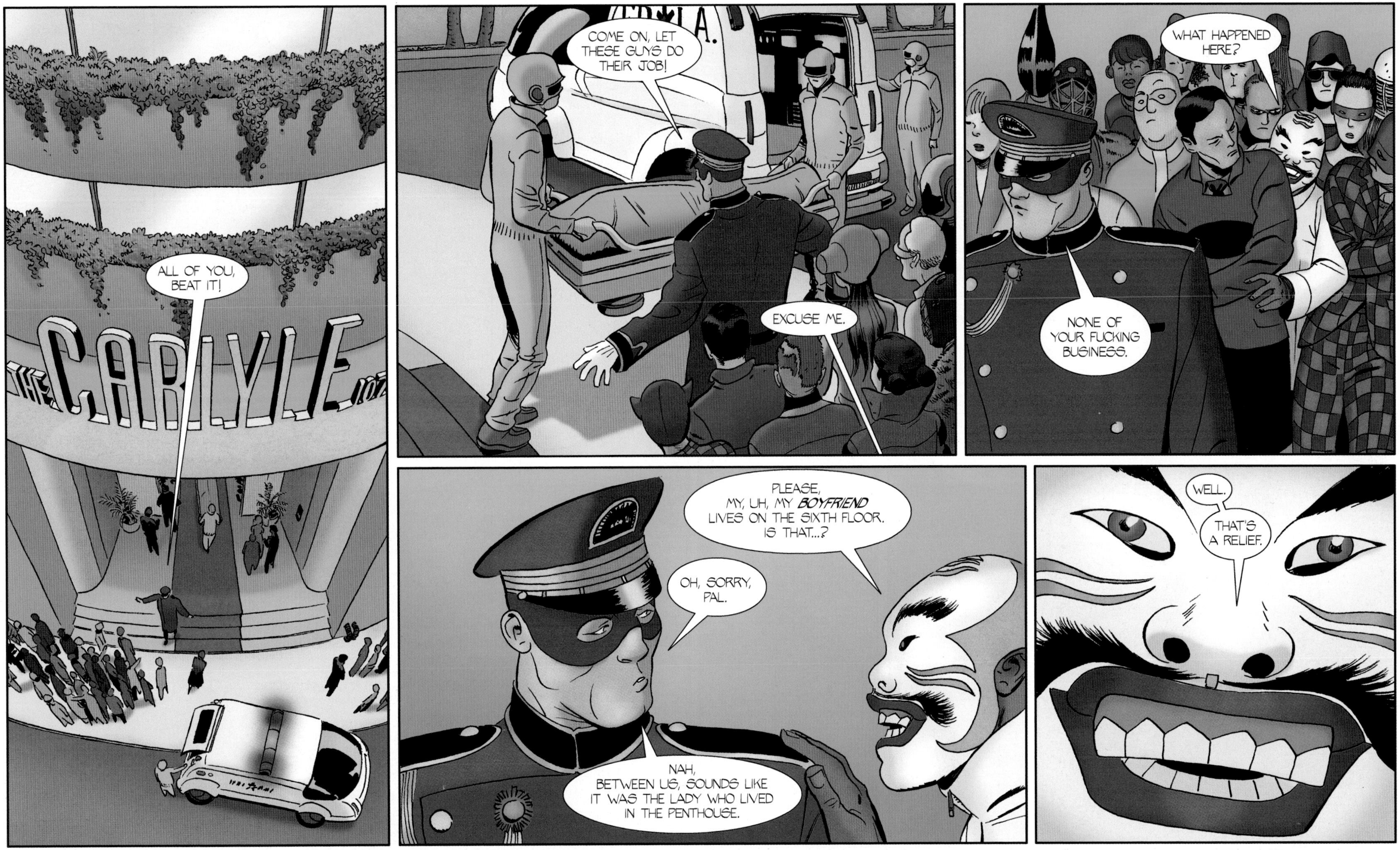
ALL OF YOU, BEAT IT!
COME ON, LET THESE GUYS DO THEIR JOB!
EXCUSE ME.
WHAT HAPPENED HERE?
NONE OF YOUR FUCKING BUSINESS.
PLEASE, MY, UH, MY BOYFRIEND LIVES ON THE SIXTH FLOOR. IS THAT...?
OH, SORRY, PAL.
NAH, BETWEEN US, SOUNDS LIKE IT WAS THE LADY WHO LIVED IN THE PENTHOUSE.
WELL.
THAT'S A RELIEF.

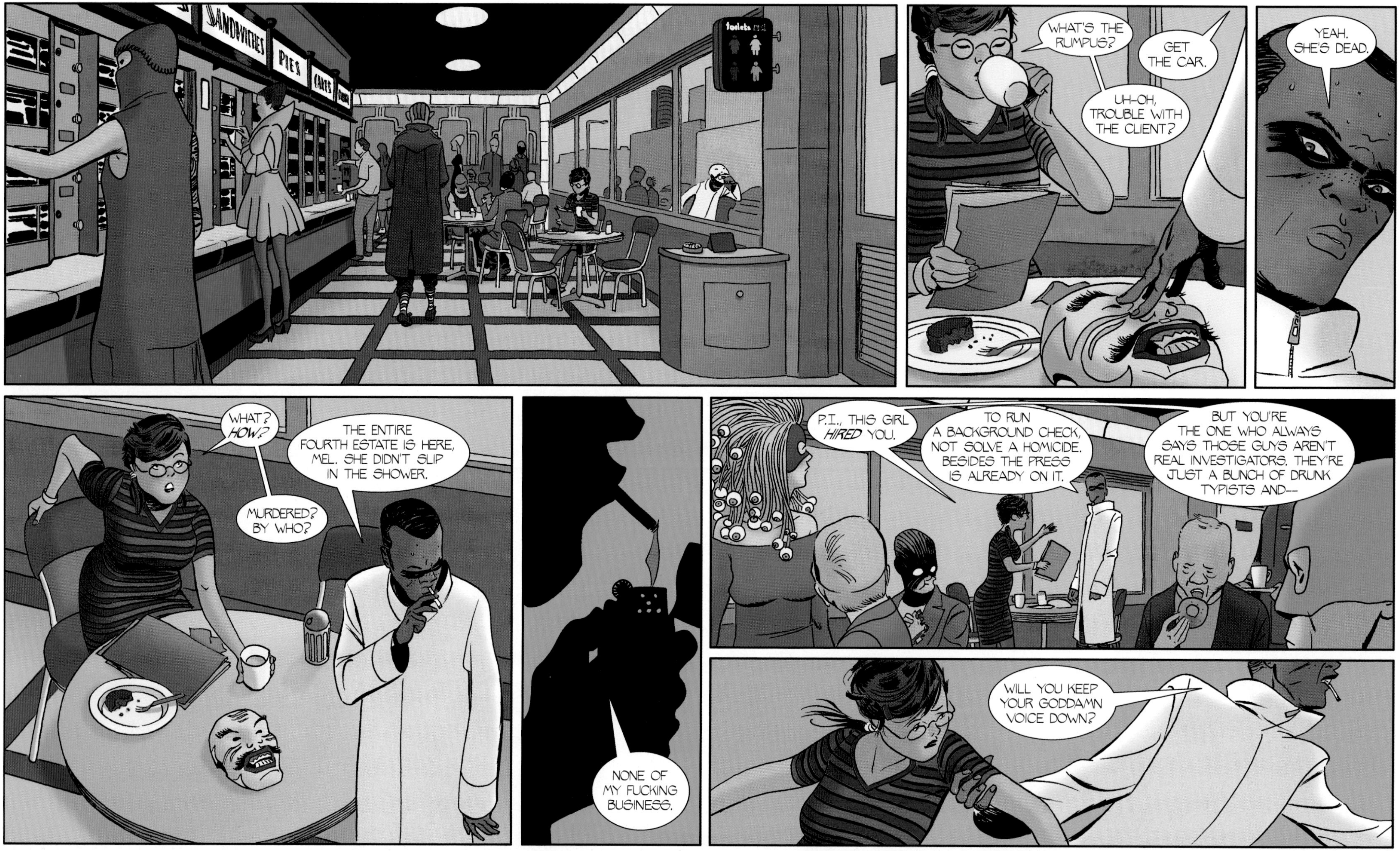
SANDWICHES
PIES
CAKES
toilets
WHAT'S THE RUMPUS?
UH-OH, TROUBLE WITH THE CLIENT?
GET THE CAR.
YEAH. SHE'S DEAD.
WHAT? HOW?
MURDERED? BY WHO?
THE ENTIRE FOURTH ESTATE IS HERE, MEL. SHE DIDN'T SLIP IN THE SHOWER.
NONE OF MY FUCKING BUSINESS.
P.I., THIS GIRL HIRED YOU.
TO RUN A BACKGROUND CHECK, NOT SOLVE A HOMICIDE. BESIDES THE PRESS IS ALREADY ON IT.
BUT YOU'RE THE ONE WHO ALWAYS SAYS THOSE GUYS AREN'T REAL INVESTIGATORS. THEY'RE JUST A BUNCH OF DRUNK TYPISTS AND--
WILL YOU KEEP YOUR GODDAMN VOICE DOWN?

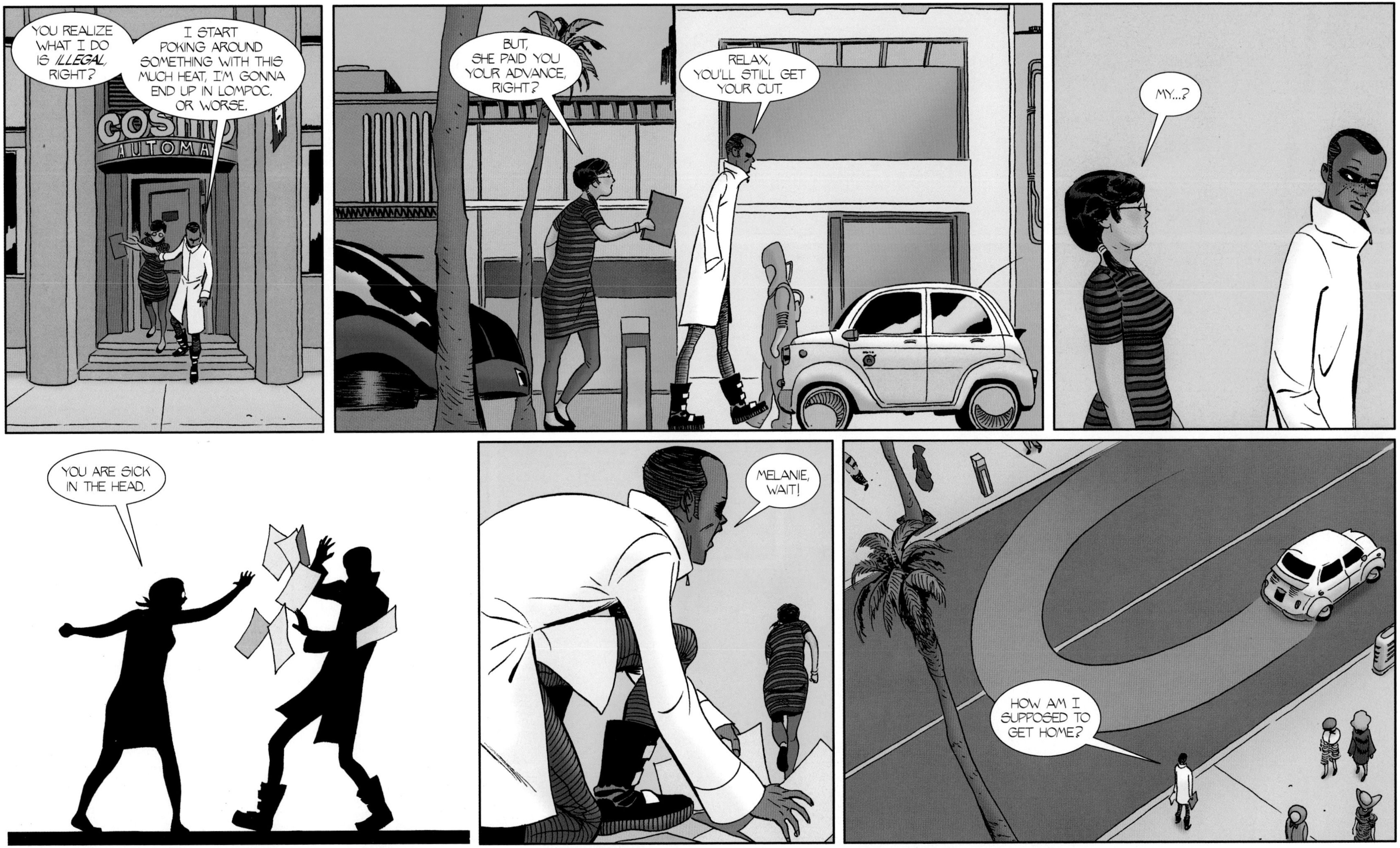
YOU REALIZE WHAT I DO IS *ILLEGAL*, RIGHT?
I START POKING AROUND SOMETHING WITH THIS MUCH HEAT, I'M GONNA END UP IN LOMPOC. OR WORSE.
COSMO AUTOMA
BUT, SHE PAID YOU YOUR ADVANCE, RIGHT?
RELAX, YOU'LL STILL GET YOUR CUT.
MY...?
YOU ARE SICK IN THE HEAD.
MELANIE, WAIT!
HOW AM I SUPPOSED TO GET HOME?

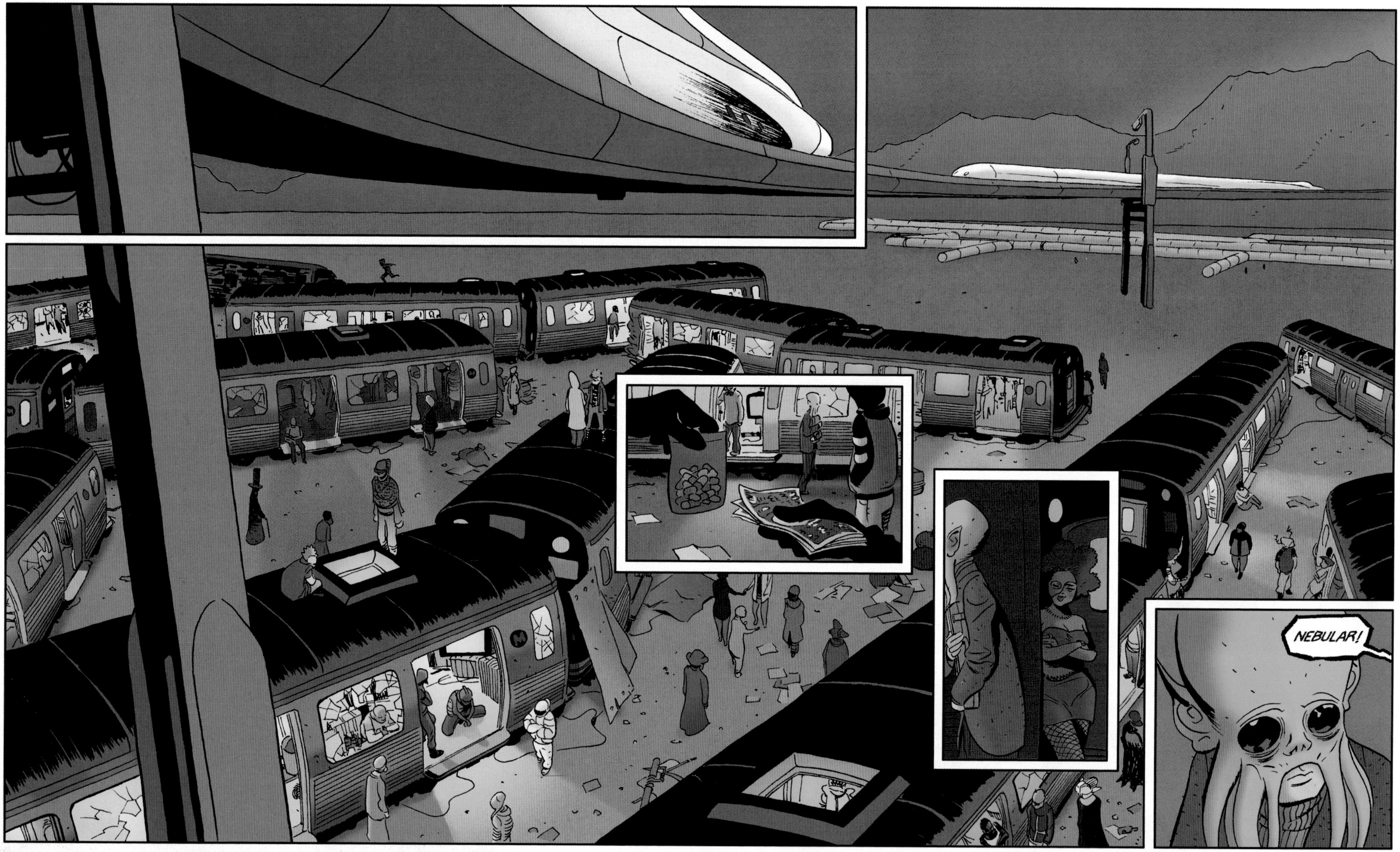
NEBULAR!

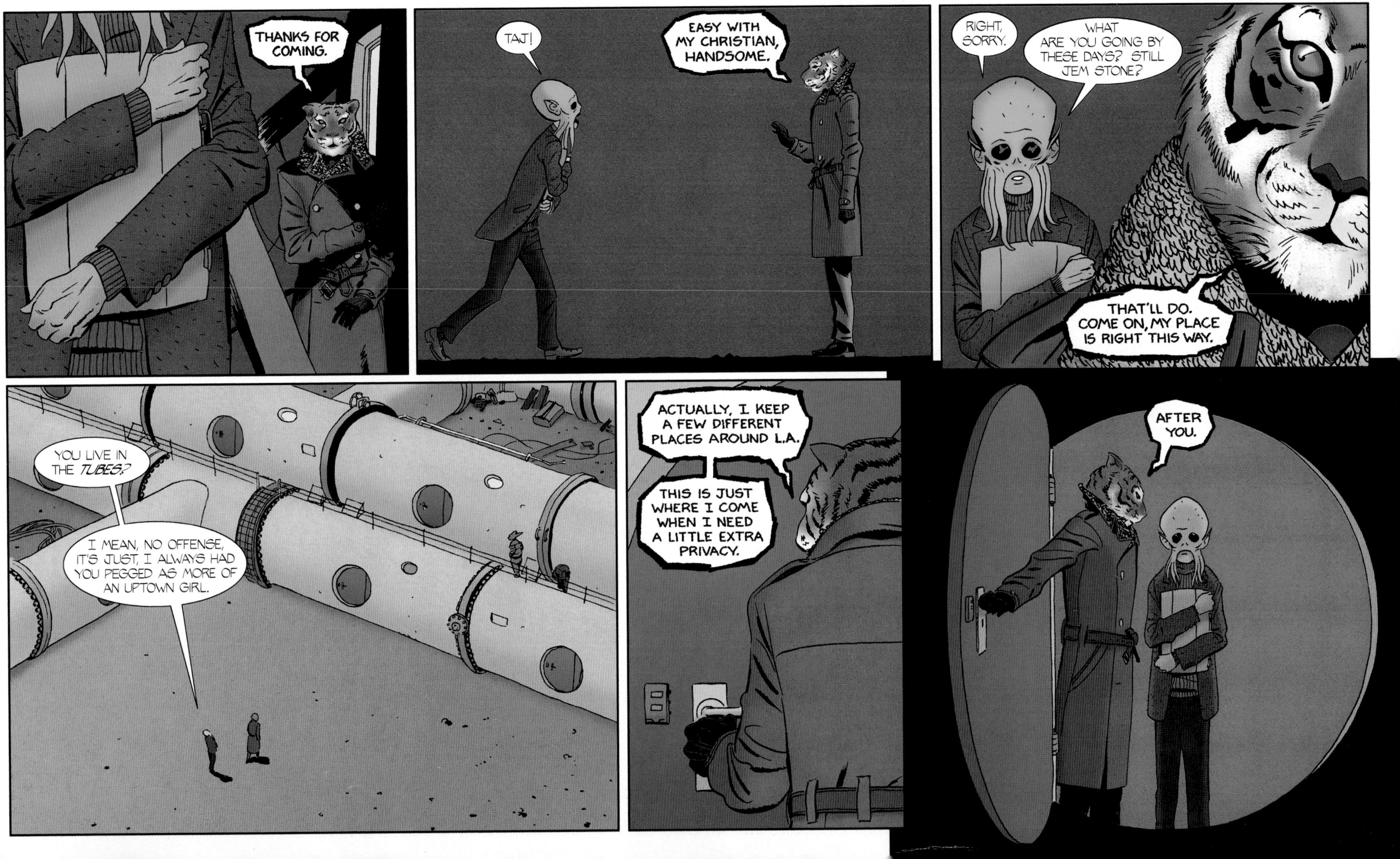
THANKS FOR COMING.
TAJ!
EASY WITH MY CHRISTIAN, HANDSOME.
RIGHT, SORRY.
WHAT ARE YOU GOING BY THESE DAYS? STILL JEM STONE?
THAT'LL DO. COME ON, MY PLACE IS RIGHT THIS WAY.
YOU LIVE IN THE *TUBES?*
I MEAN, NO OFFENSE, IT'S JUST, I ALWAYS HAD YOU PEGGED AS MORE OF AN UPTOWN GIRL.
ACTUALLY, I KEEP A FEW DIFFERENT PLACES AROUND L.A.
THIS IS JUST WHERE I COME WHEN I NEED A LITTLE EXTRA PRIVACY.
AFTER YOU.

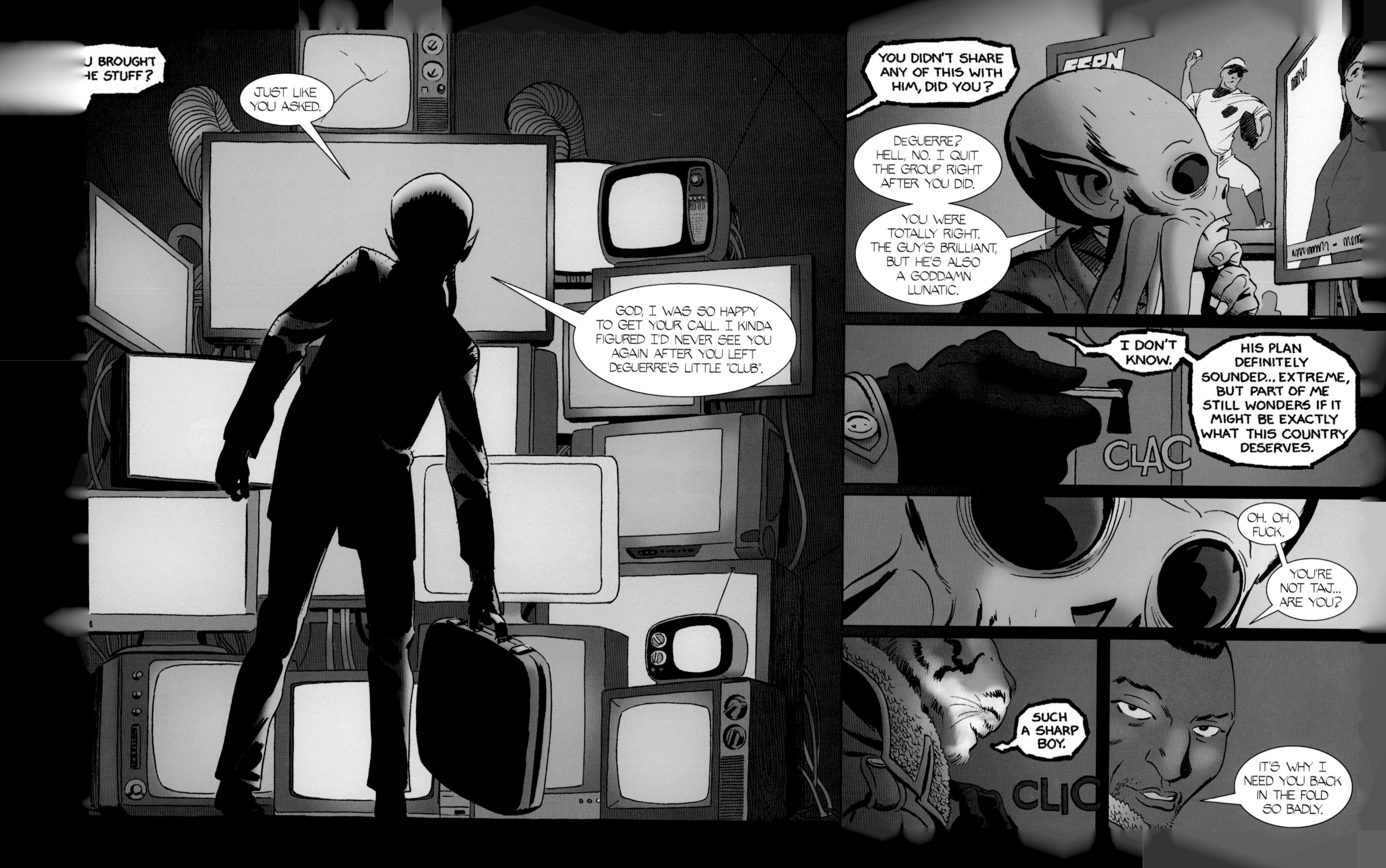
U BROUGHT
HE STUFF?
JUST LIKE YOU ASKED.
GOD, I WAS SO HAPPY TO GET YOUR CALL. I KINDA FIGURED I'D NEVER SEE YOU AGAIN AFTER YOU LEFT DeGUERRE'S LITTLE "CLUB".
YOU DIDN'T SHARE ANY OF THIS WITH HIM, DID YOU?
DeGUERRE? HELL, NO. I QUIT THE GROUP RIGHT AFTER YOU DID.
YOU WERE TOTALLY RIGHT. THE GUY'S BRILLIANT, BUT HE'S ALSO A GODDAMN LUNATIC.
I DON'T KNOW.
HIS PLAN DEFINITELY SOUNDED... EXTREME, BUT PART OF ME STILL WONDERS IF IT MIGHT BE EXACTLY WHAT THIS COUNTRY DESERVES.
CLAC
OH. OH, FUCK.
YOU'RE NOT TAJ... ARE YOU?
SUCH A SHARP BOY.
CLIC
IT'S WHY I NEED YOU BACK IN THE FOLD SO BADLY.

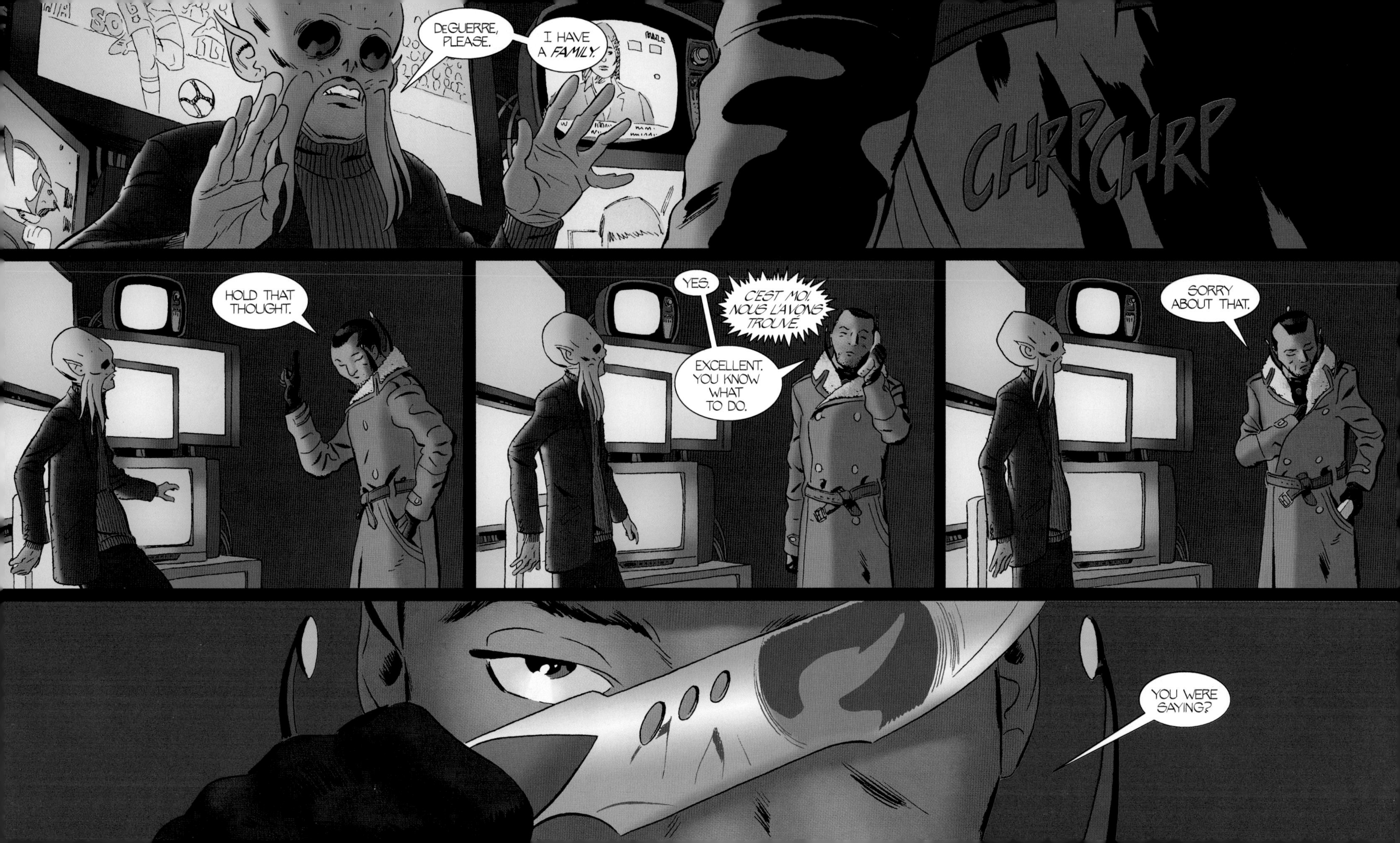
DEGUERRE, PLEASE.
I HAVE A *FAMILY.*
CHRP CHRP
HOLD THAT THOUGHT.
YES.
C'EST MOI. NOUS L'AVONS TROUVÉ.
EXCELLENT. YOU KNOW WHAT TO DO.
SORRY ABOUT THAT.
YOU WERE SAYING?

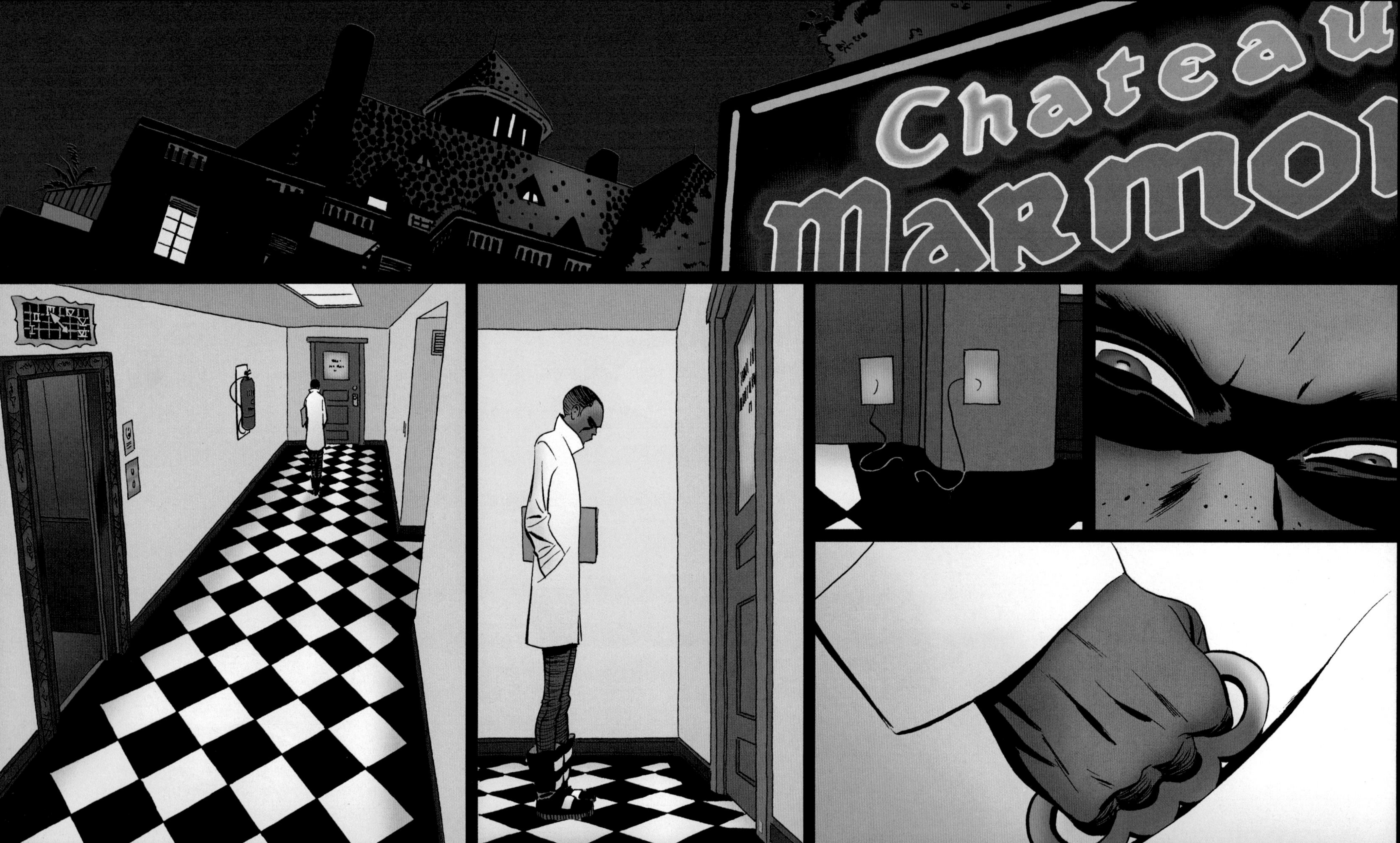
Chateau
MARMO

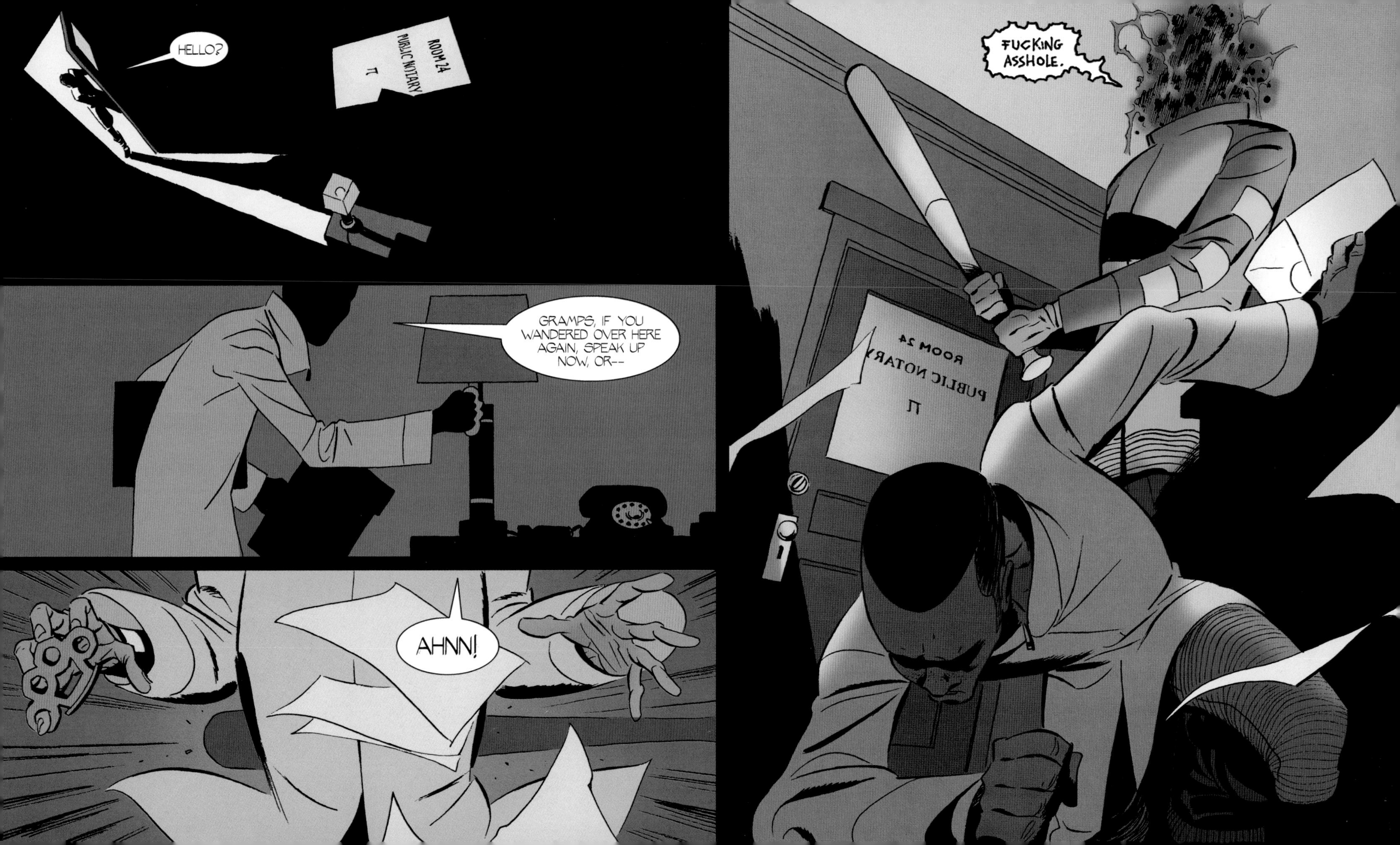
HELLO?
ROOM 24
PUBLIC NOTARY
GRAMPS, IF YOU WANDERED OVER HERE AGAIN, SPEAK UP NOW, OR--
AHNN!
FUCKING ASSHOLE.

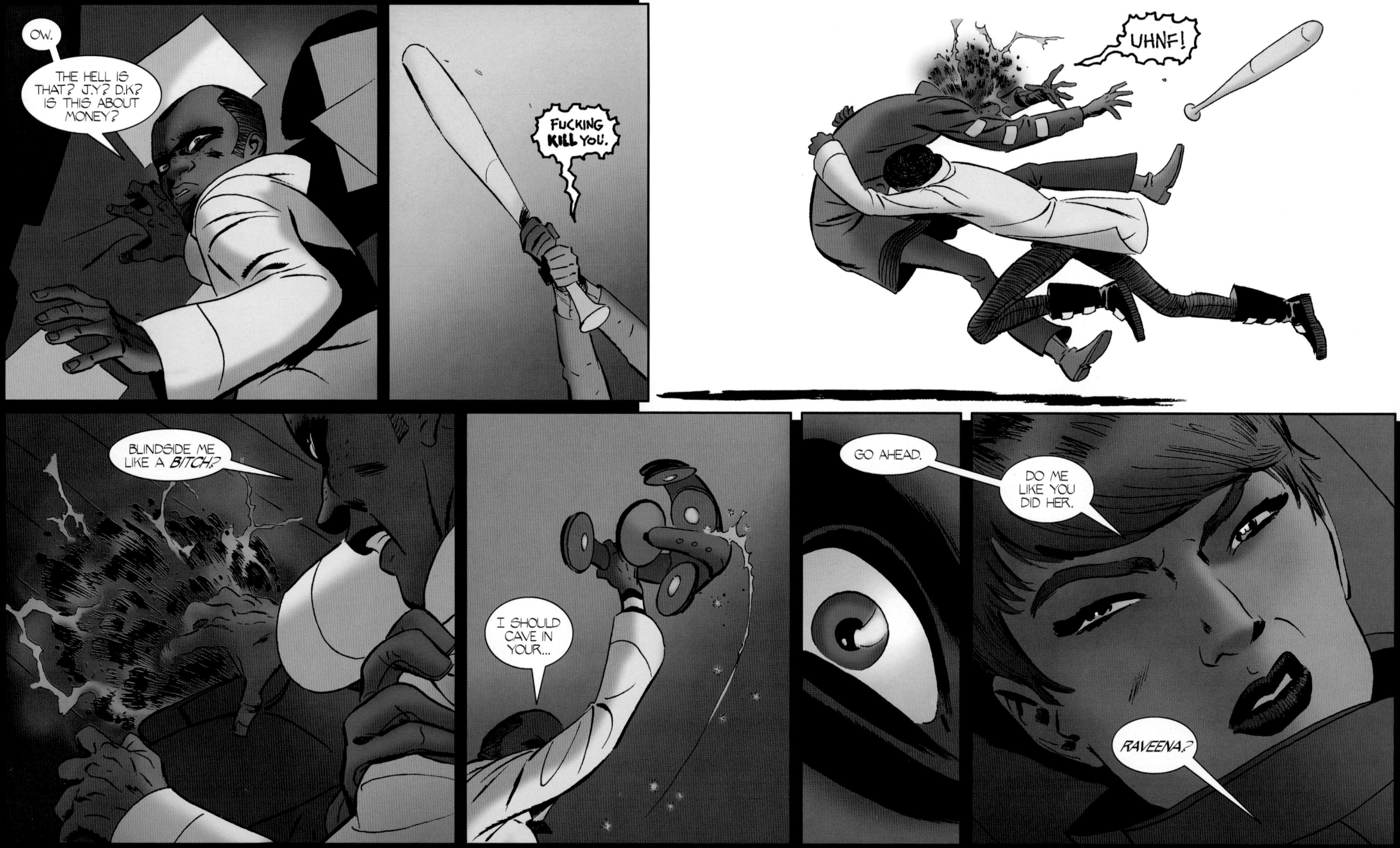
OW.
THE HELL IS THAT? J.Y? D.K? IS THIS ABOUT MONEY?
FUCKING KILL YOU.
UHNF!
BLINDSIDE ME LIKE A *BITCH?*
I SHOULD CAVE IN YOUR...
GO AHEAD.
DO ME LIKE YOU DID HER.
RAVEENA?

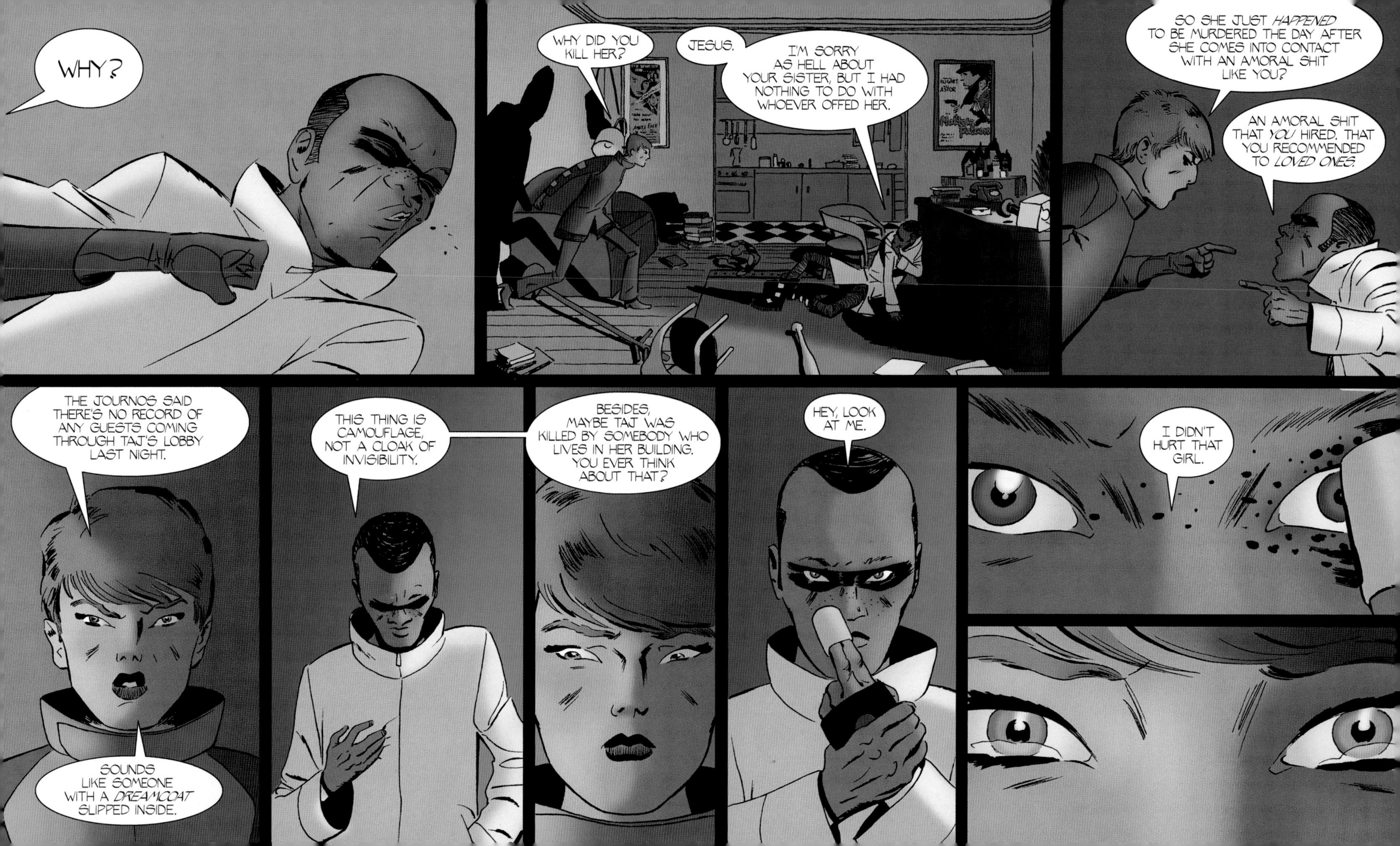
WHY?
WHY DID YOU KILL HER?
JESUS.
I'M SORRY AS HELL ABOUT YOUR SISTER, BUT I HAD NOTHING TO DO WITH WHOEVER OFFED HER.
SO SHE JUST *HAPPENED* TO BE MURDERED THE DAY AFTER SHE COMES INTO CONTACT WITH AN AMORAL SHIT LIKE YOU?
AN AMORAL SHIT THAT *YOU* HIRED. THAT YOU RECOMMENDED TO *LOVED ONES.*
THE JOURNOS SAID THERE'S NO RECORD OF ANY GUESTS COMING THROUGH TAJ'S LOBBY LAST NIGHT.
SOUNDS LIKE SOMEONE WITH A *DREAMCOAT* SLIPPED INSIDE.
THIS THING IS CAMOUFLAGE, NOT A CLOAK OF INVISIBILITY.
BESIDES, MAYBE TAJ WAS KILLED BY SOMEBODY WHO LIVES IN HER BUILDING. YOU EVER THINK ABOUT THAT?
HEY, LOOK AT ME.
I DIDN'T HURT THAT GIRL.

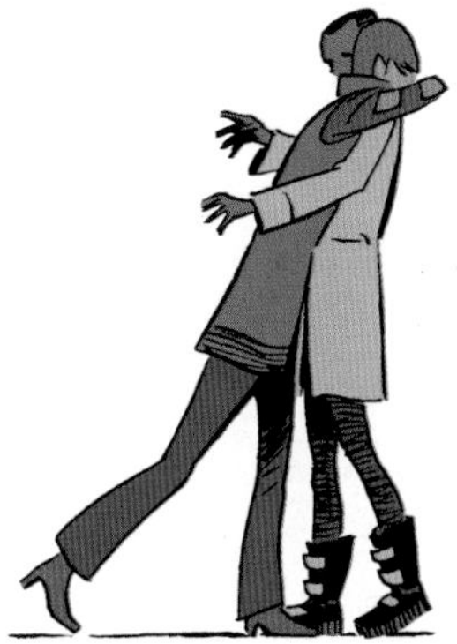

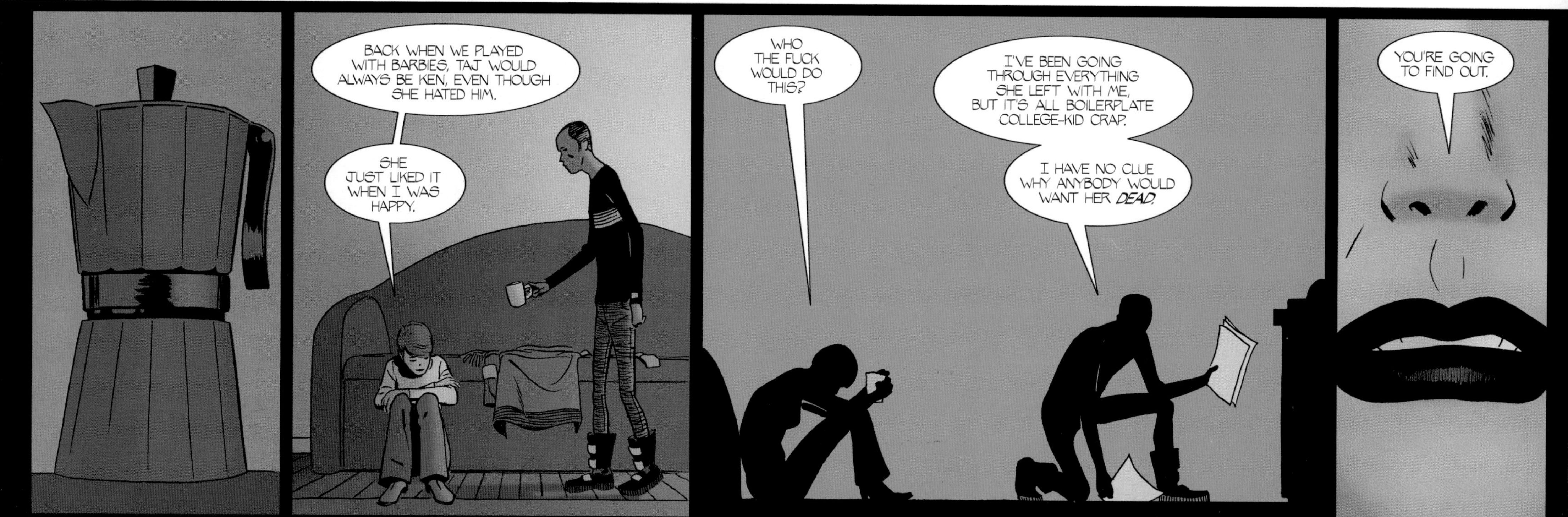
BACK WHEN WE PLAYED WITH BARBIES, TAJ WOULD ALWAYS BE KEN, EVEN THOUGH SHE HATED HIM.
SHE JUST LIKED IT WHEN I WAS HAPPY.
WHO THE FUCK WOULD DO THIS?
I'VE BEEN GOING THROUGH EVERYTHING SHE LEFT WITH ME, BUT IT'S ALL BOILERPLATE COLLEGE-KID CRAP.
I HAVE NO CLUE WHY ANYBODY WOULD WANT HER *DEAD*.
YOU'RE GOING TO FIND OUT.

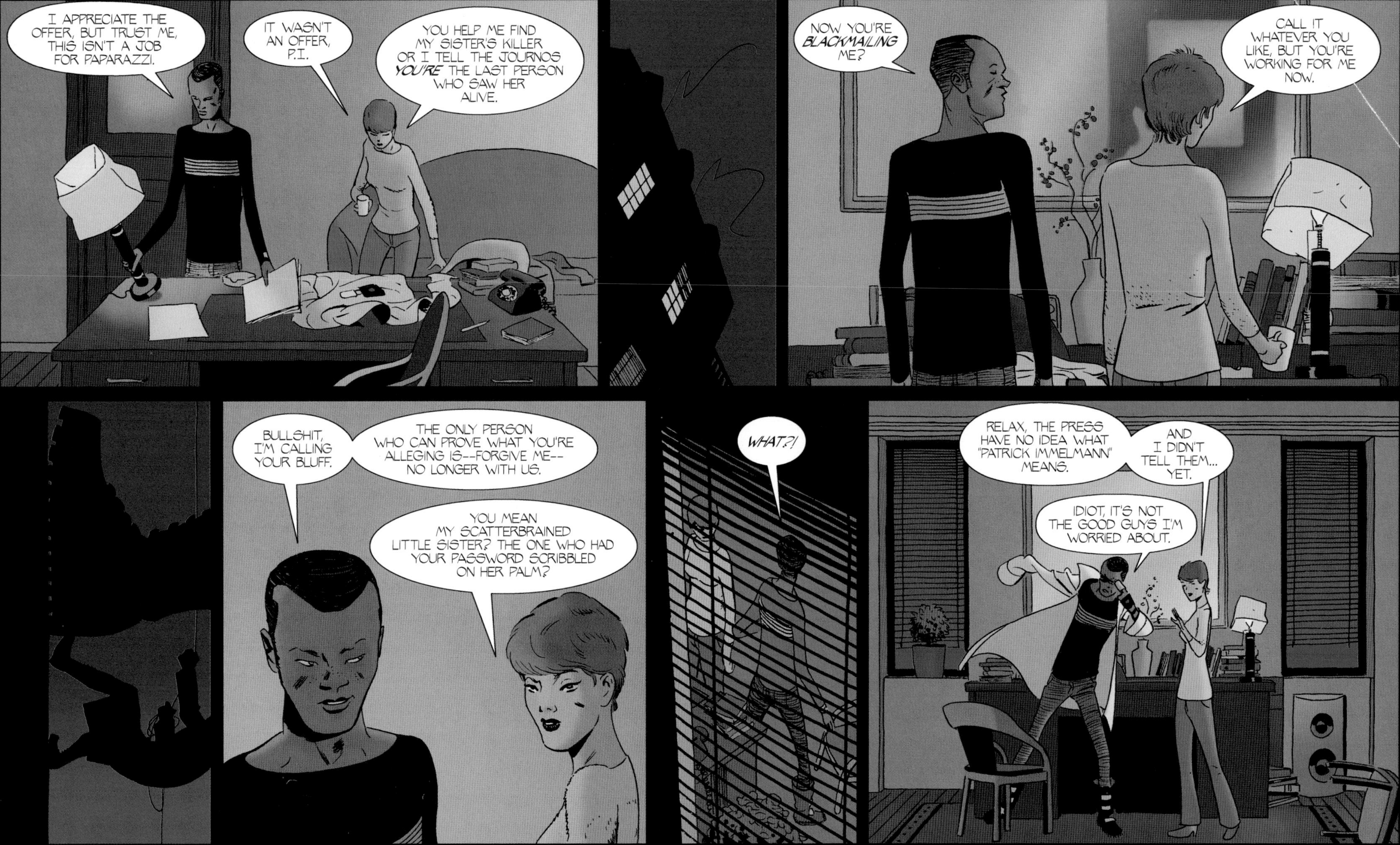
I APPRECIATE THE OFFER, BUT TRUST ME, THIS ISN'T A JOB FOR PAPARAZZI.
IT WASN'T AN OFFER, P.I.
YOU HELP ME FIND MY SISTER'S KILLER OR I TELL THE JOURNOS *YOU'RE* THE LAST PERSON WHO SAW HER ALIVE.
NOW YOU'RE *BLACKMAILING* ME?
CALL IT WHATEVER YOU LIKE, BUT YOU'RE WORKING FOR ME NOW.
BULLSHIT, I'M CALLING YOUR BLUFF.
THE ONLY PERSON WHO CAN PROVE WHAT YOU'RE ALLEGING IS--FORGIVE ME--NO LONGER WITH US.
YOU MEAN MY SCATTERBRAINED LITTLE SISTER? THE ONE WHO HAD YOUR PASSWORD SCRIBBLED ON HER PALM?
WHAT?!
RELAX, THE PRESS HAVE NO IDEA WHAT "PATRICK IMMELMANN" MEANS.
AND I DIDN'T TELL THEM... YET.
IDIOT, IT'S NOT THE GOOD GUYS I'M WORRIED ABOUT.

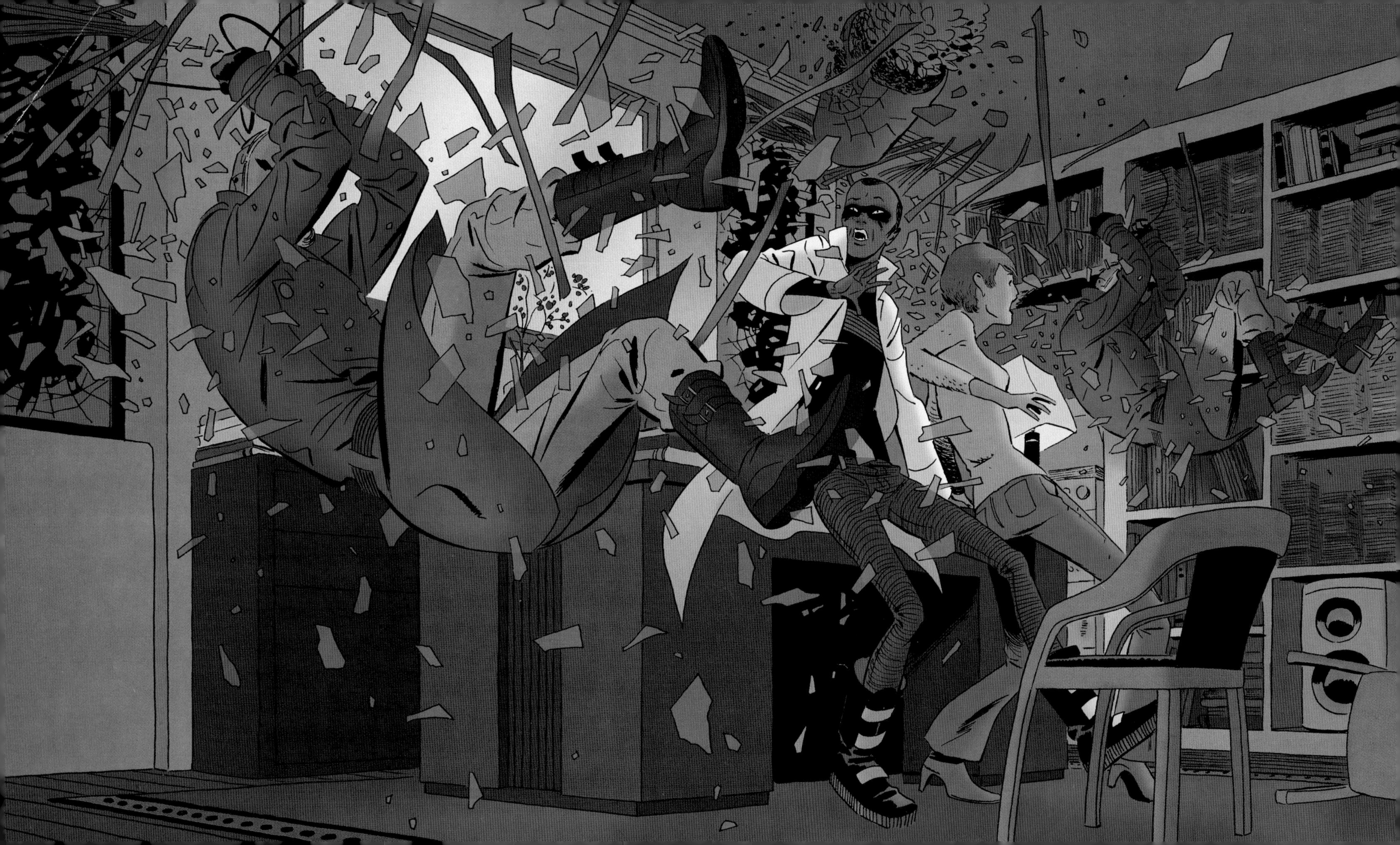

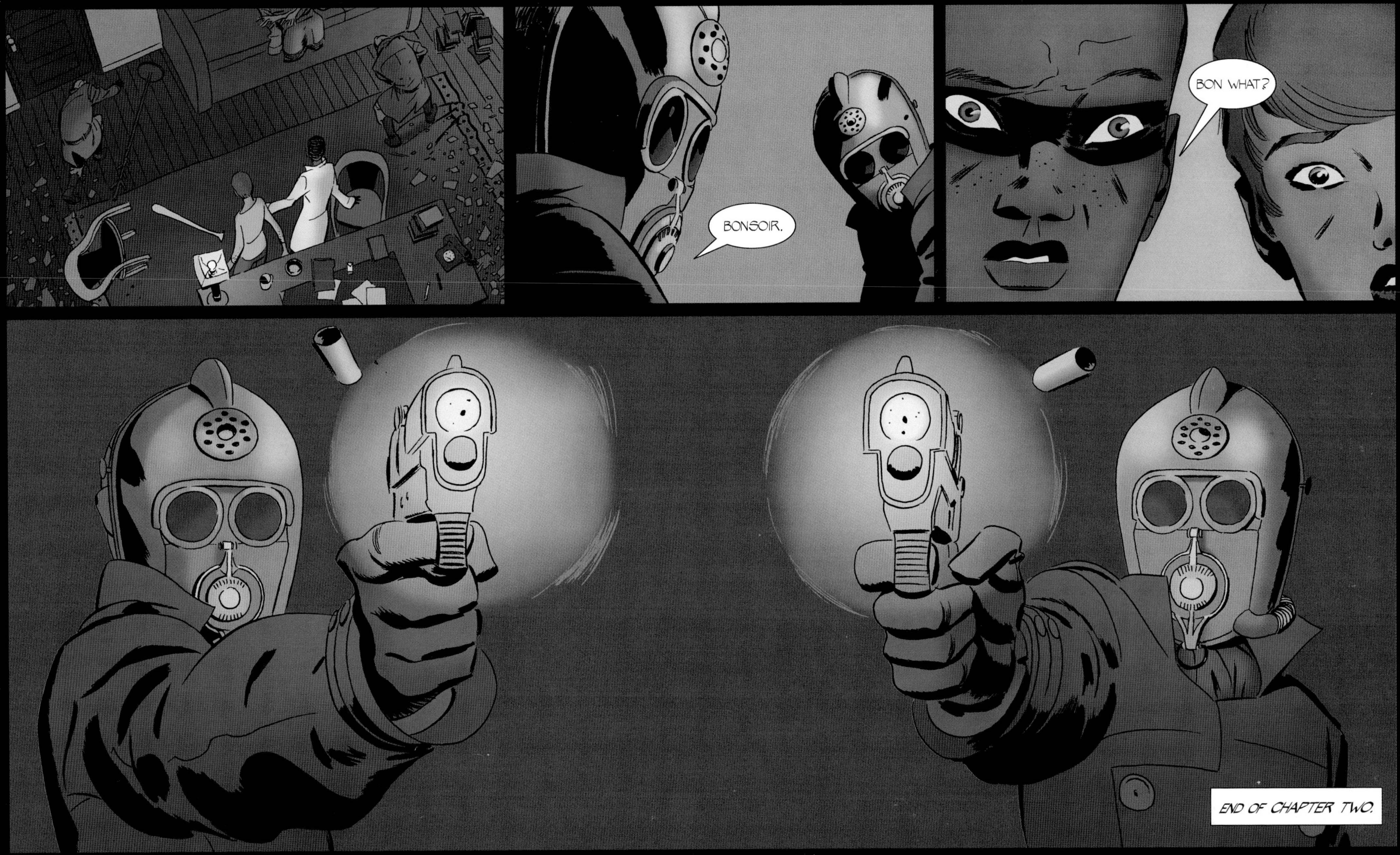
BONSOIR.
BON WHAT?
END OF CHAPTER TWO.

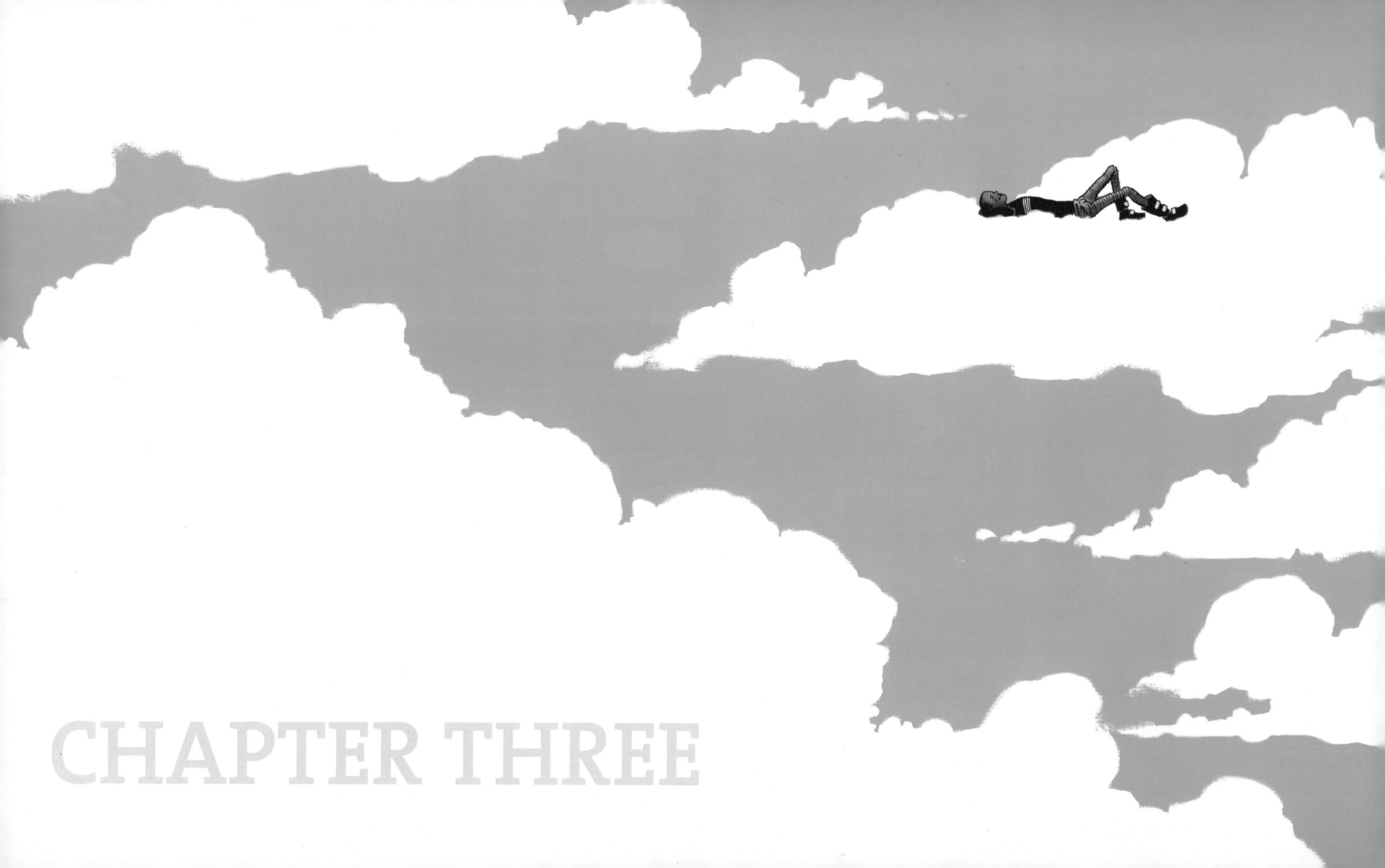
CHAPTER THREE

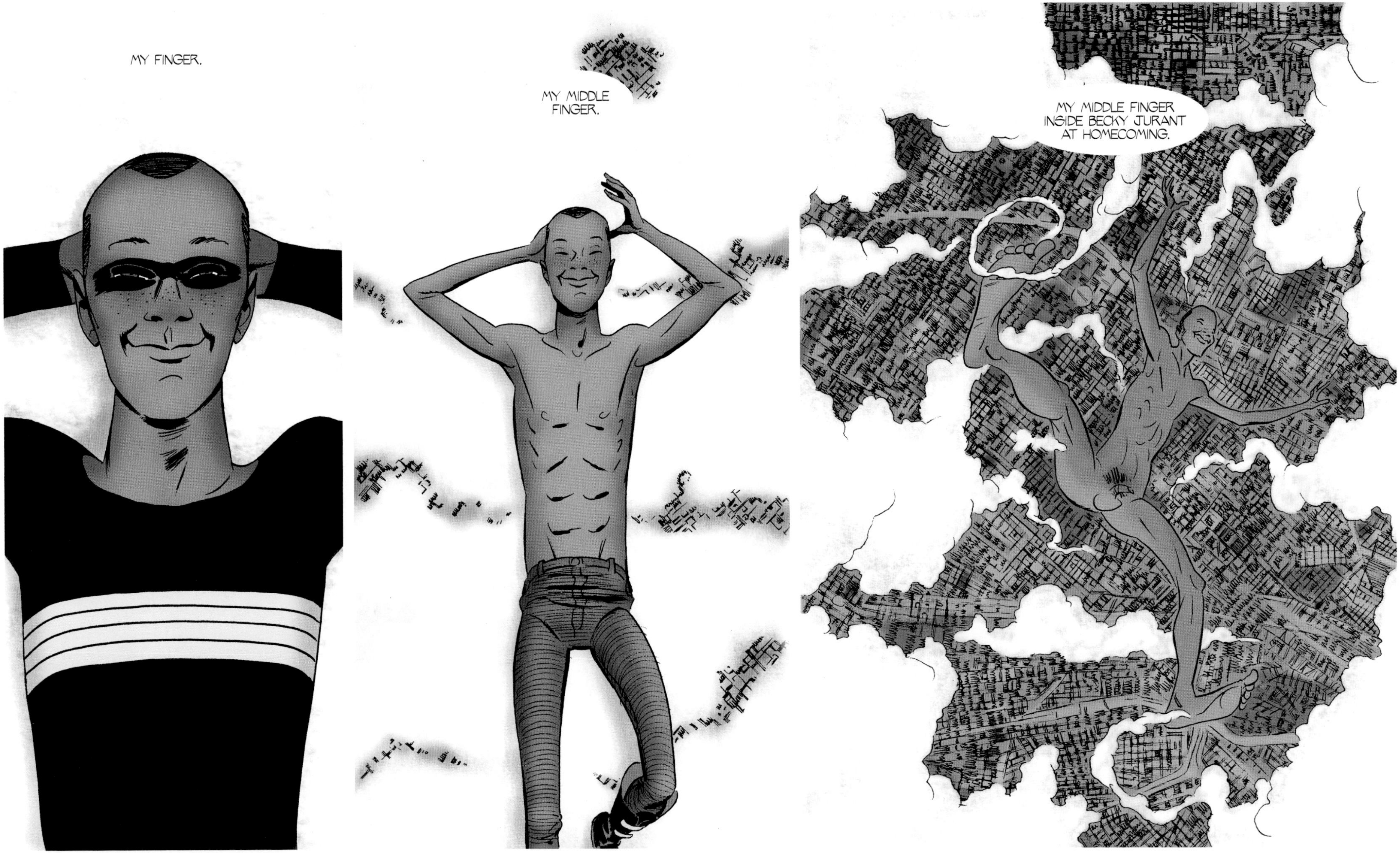
MY FINGER.
MY MIDDLE FINGER.
MY MIDDLE FINGER INSIDE BECKY JURANT AT HOMECOMING.

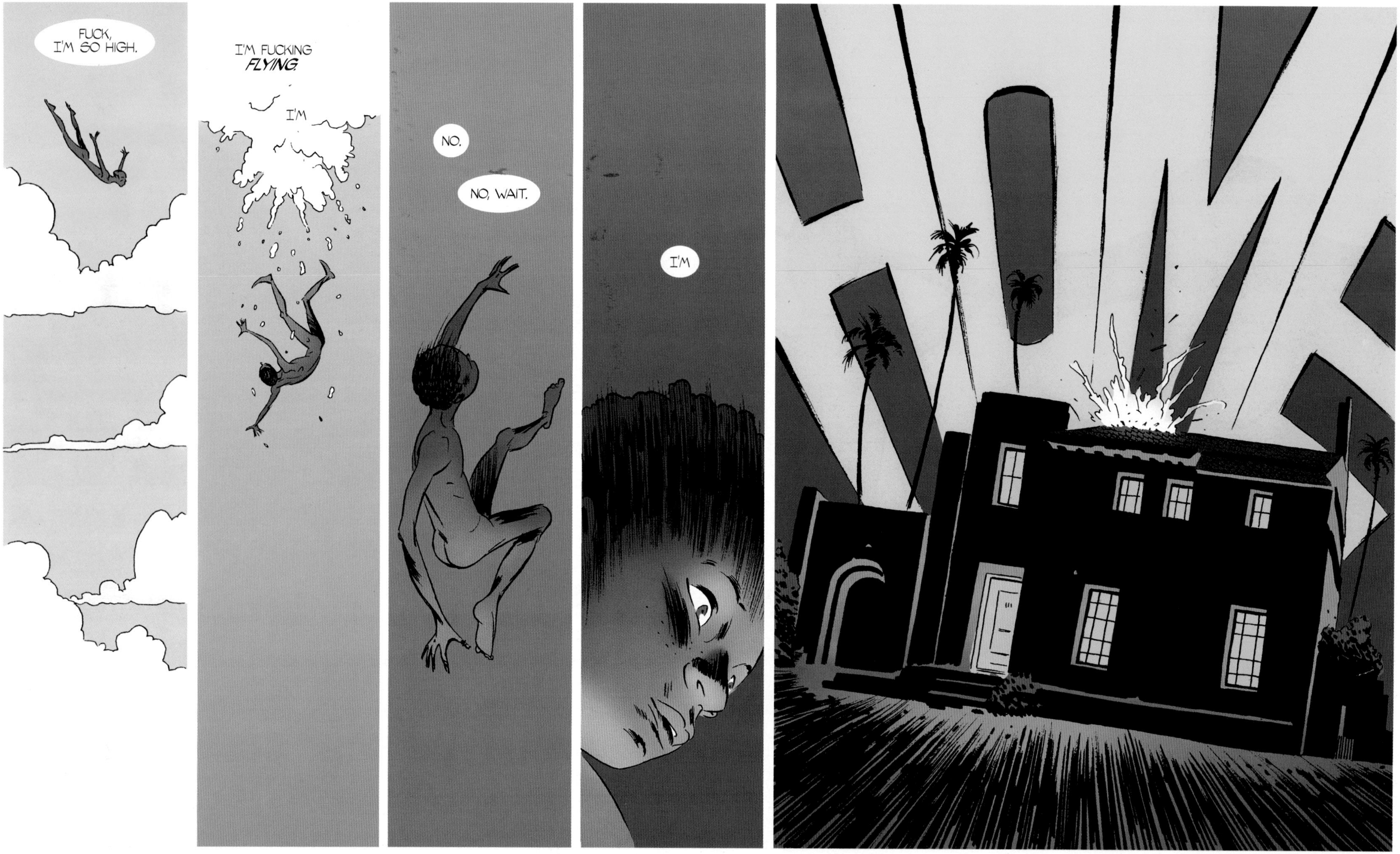
FUCK, I'M SO HIGH.
I'M FUCKING FLYING.
I'M
NO.
NO, WAIT.
I'M

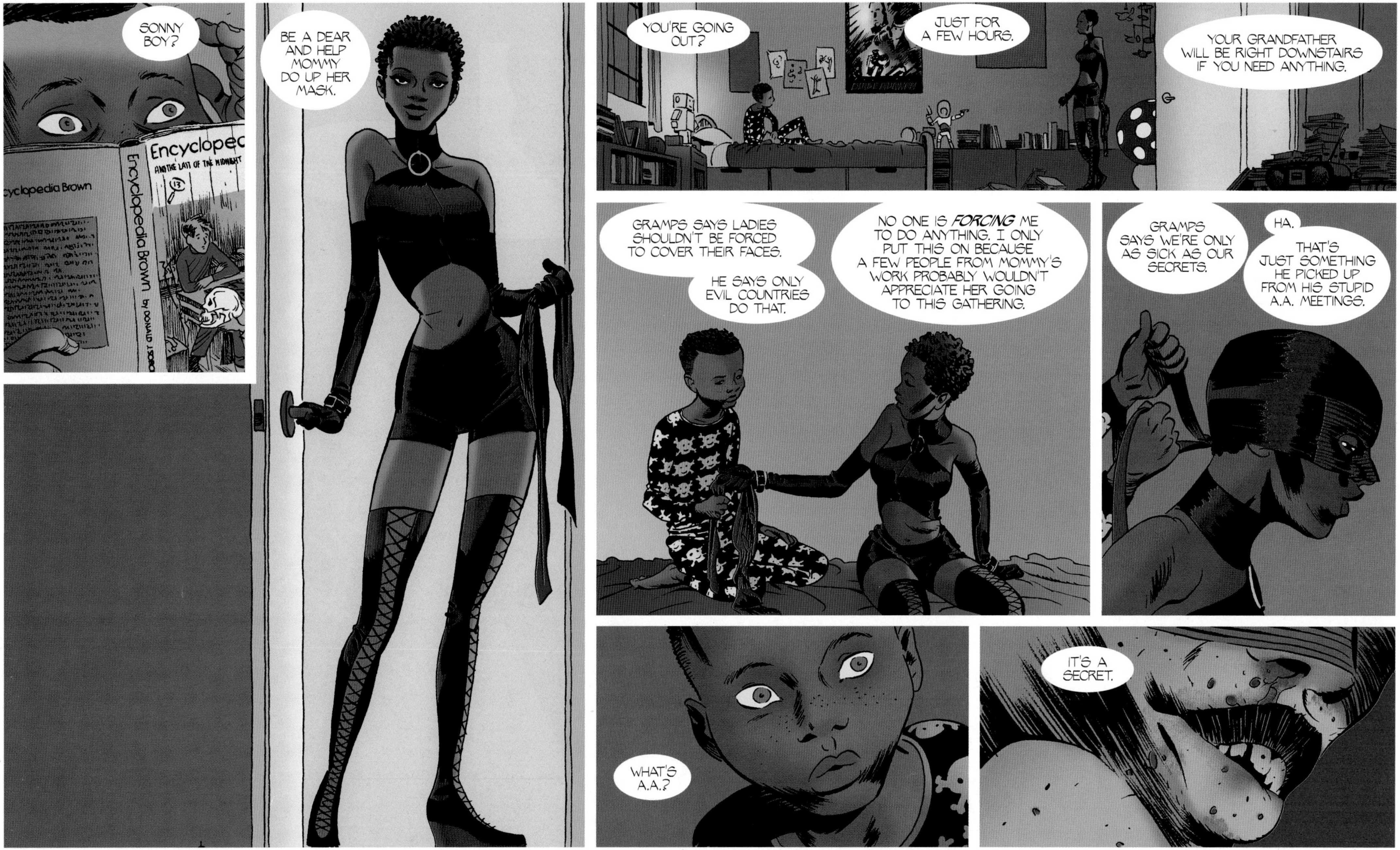

SONNY BOY?
Encyclopedia Brown
BE A DEAR AND HELP MOMMY DO UP HER MASK.
YOU'RE GOING OUT?
JUST FOR A FEW HOURS.
YOUR GRANDFATHER WILL BE RIGHT DOWNSTAIRS IF YOU NEED ANYTHING.
GRAMPS SAYS LADIES SHOULDN'T BE FORCED TO COVER THEIR FACES.
HE SAYS ONLY EVIL COUNTRIES DO THAT.
NO ONE IS *FORCING* ME TO DO ANYTHING. I ONLY PUT THIS ON BECAUSE A FEW PEOPLE FROM MOMMY'S WORK PROBABLY WOULDN'T APPRECIATE HER GOING TO THIS GATHERING.
GRAMPS SAYS WE'RE ONLY AS SICK AS OUR SECRETS.
HA.
THAT'S JUST SOMETHING HE PICKED UP FROM HIS STUPID A.A. MEETINGS.
WHAT'S A.A.?
IT'S A SECRET.

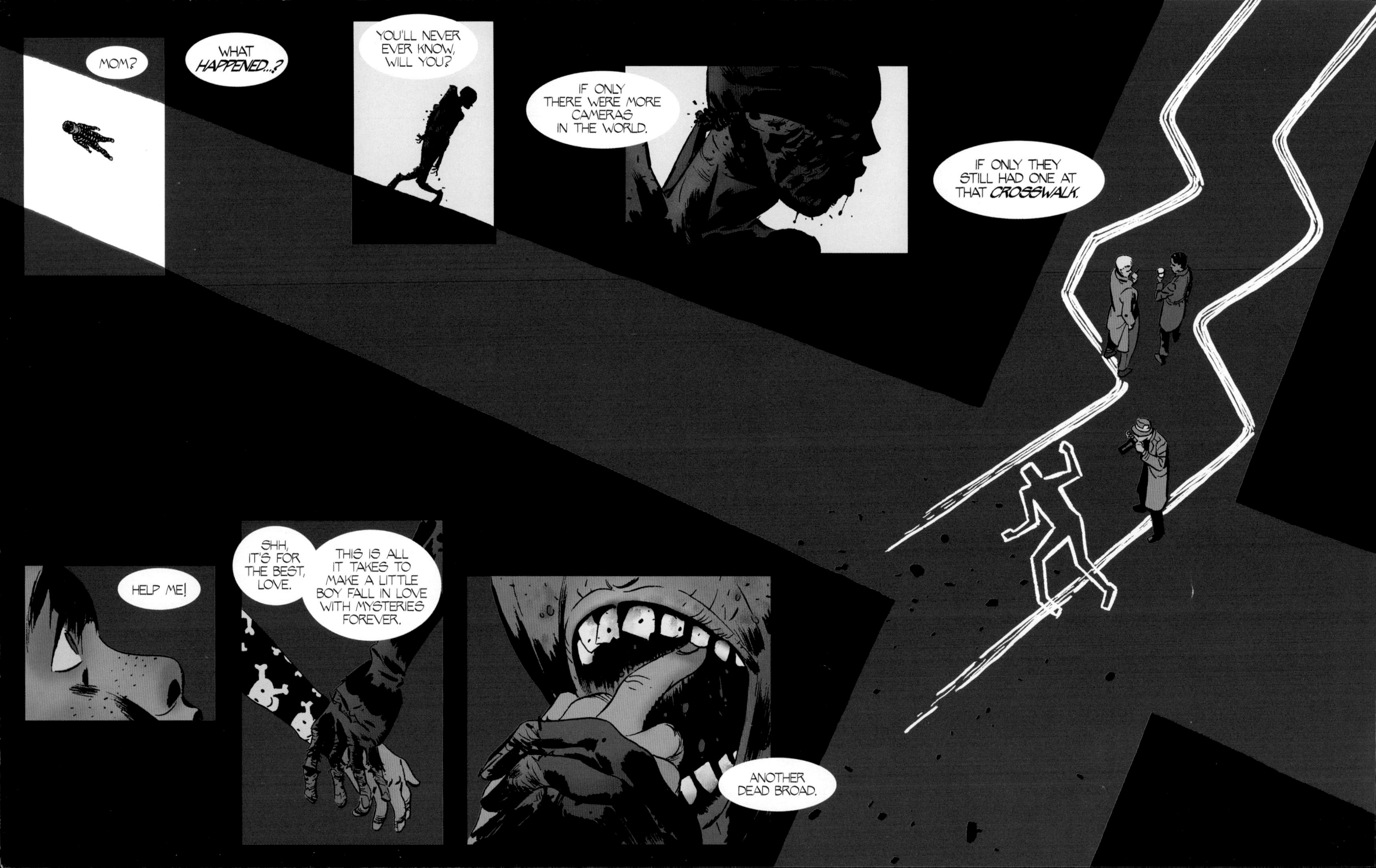
MOM?
WHAT HAPPENED...?
YOU'LL NEVER EVER KNOW, WILL YOU?
IF ONLY THERE WERE MORE CAMERAS IN THE WORLD.
IF ONLY THEY STILL HAD ONE AT THAT CROSSWALK.
HELP ME!
SHH, IT'S FOR THE BEST, LOVE.
THIS IS ALL IT TAKES TO MAKE A LITTLE BOY FALL IN LOVE WITH MYSTERIES FOREVER.
ANOTHER DEAD BROAD.

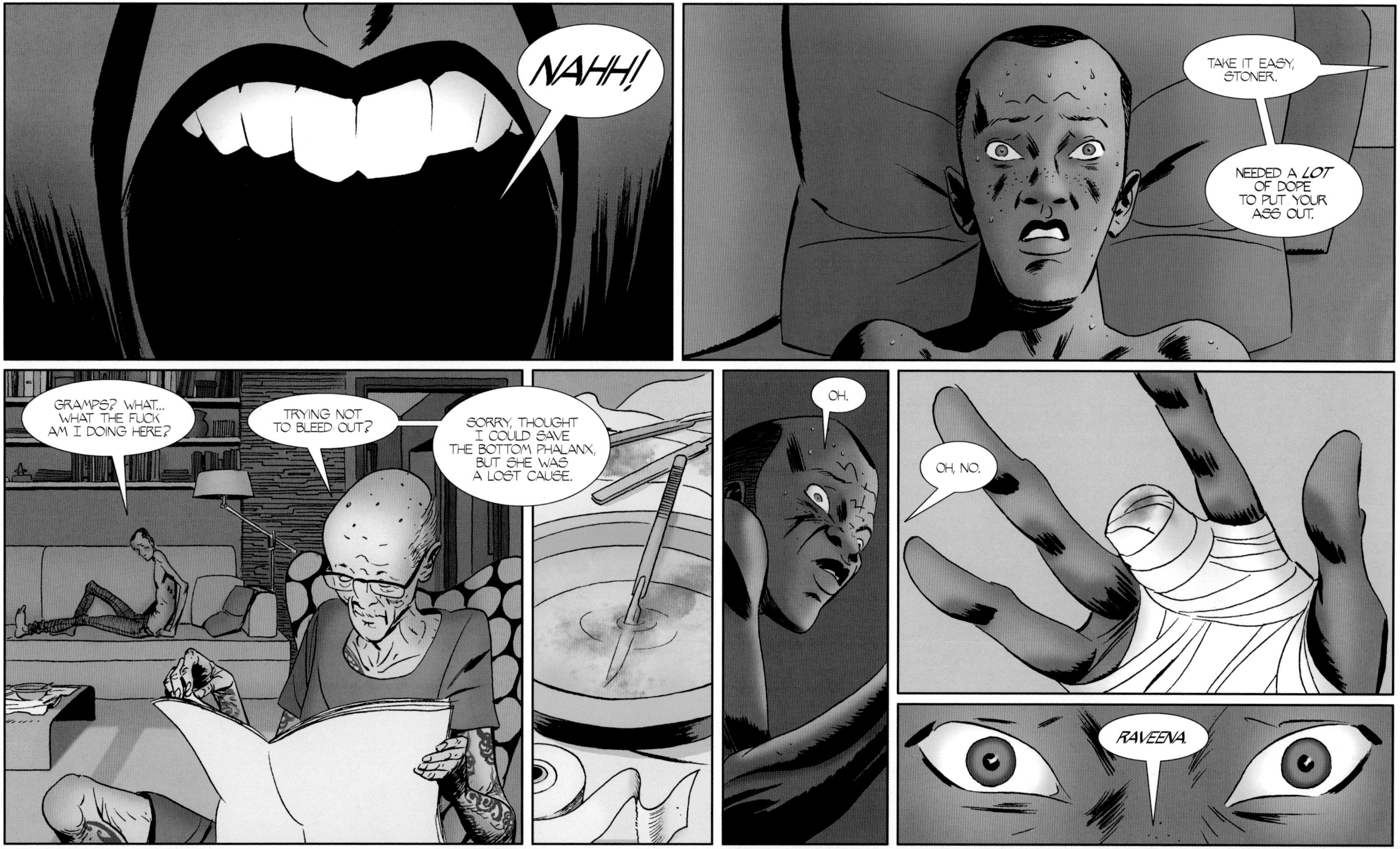
NAHH!
TAKE IT EASY, STONER.
NEEDED A *LOT* OF DOPE TO PUT YOUR ASS OUT.
GRAMPS? WHAT... WHAT THE FUCK AM I DOING HERE?
TRYING NOT TO BLEED OUT?
SORRY, THOUGHT I COULD SAVE THE BOTTOM PHALANX, BUT SHE WAS A LOST CAUSE.
OH.
OH, NO.
RAVEENA.

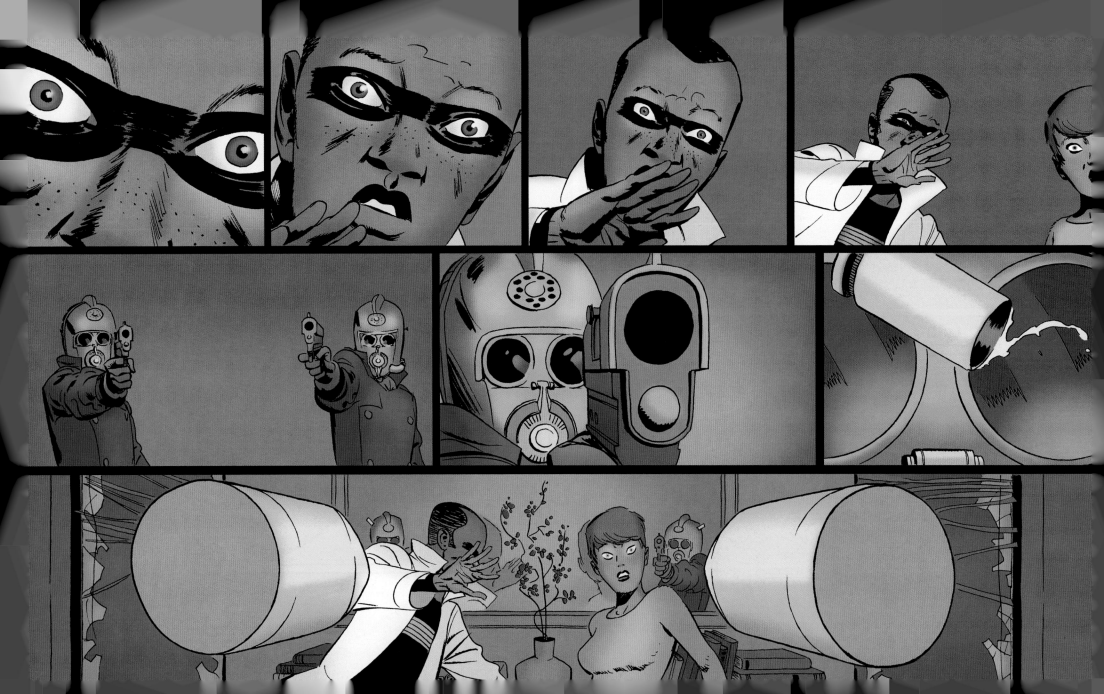

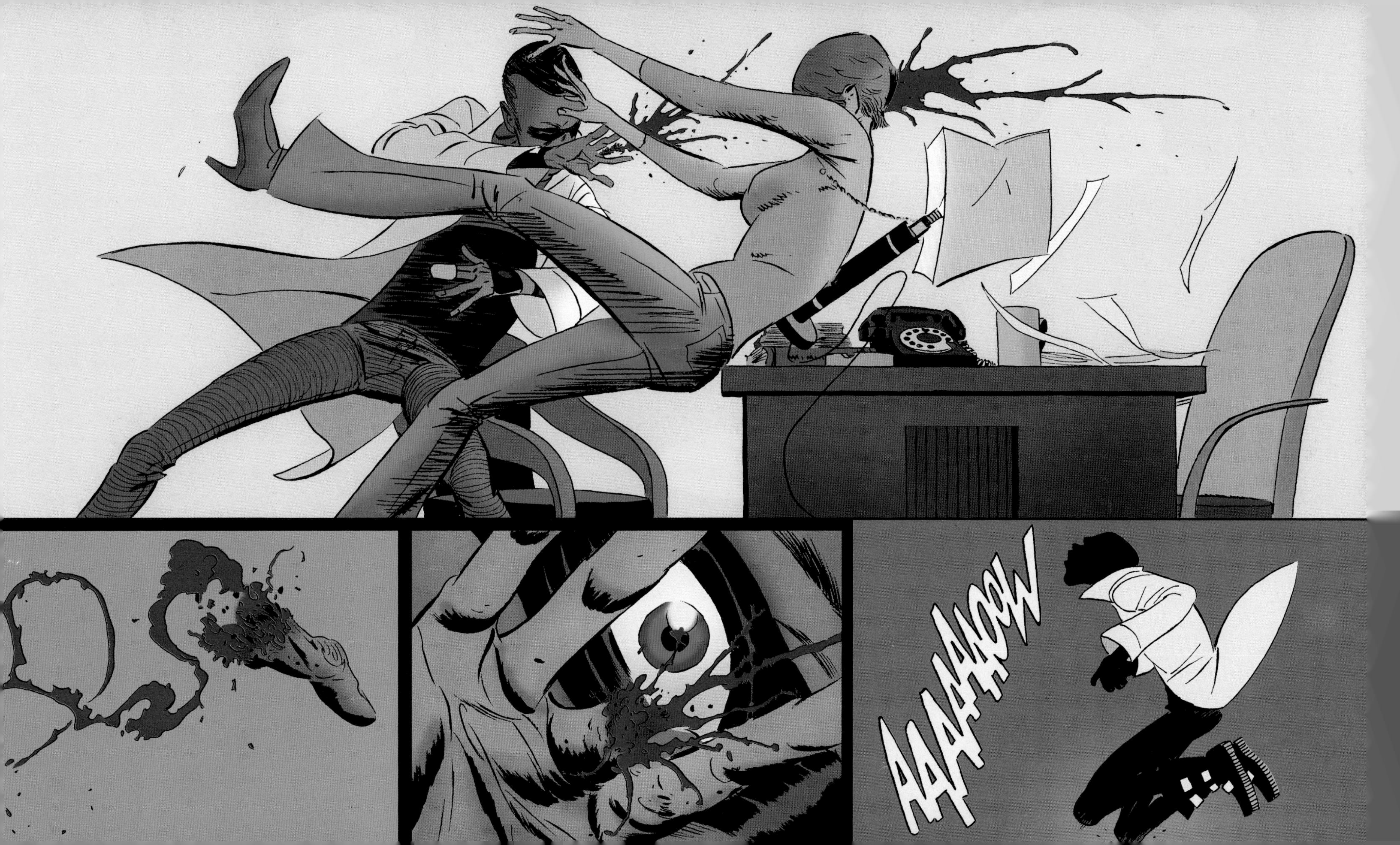
AAAAHOOW

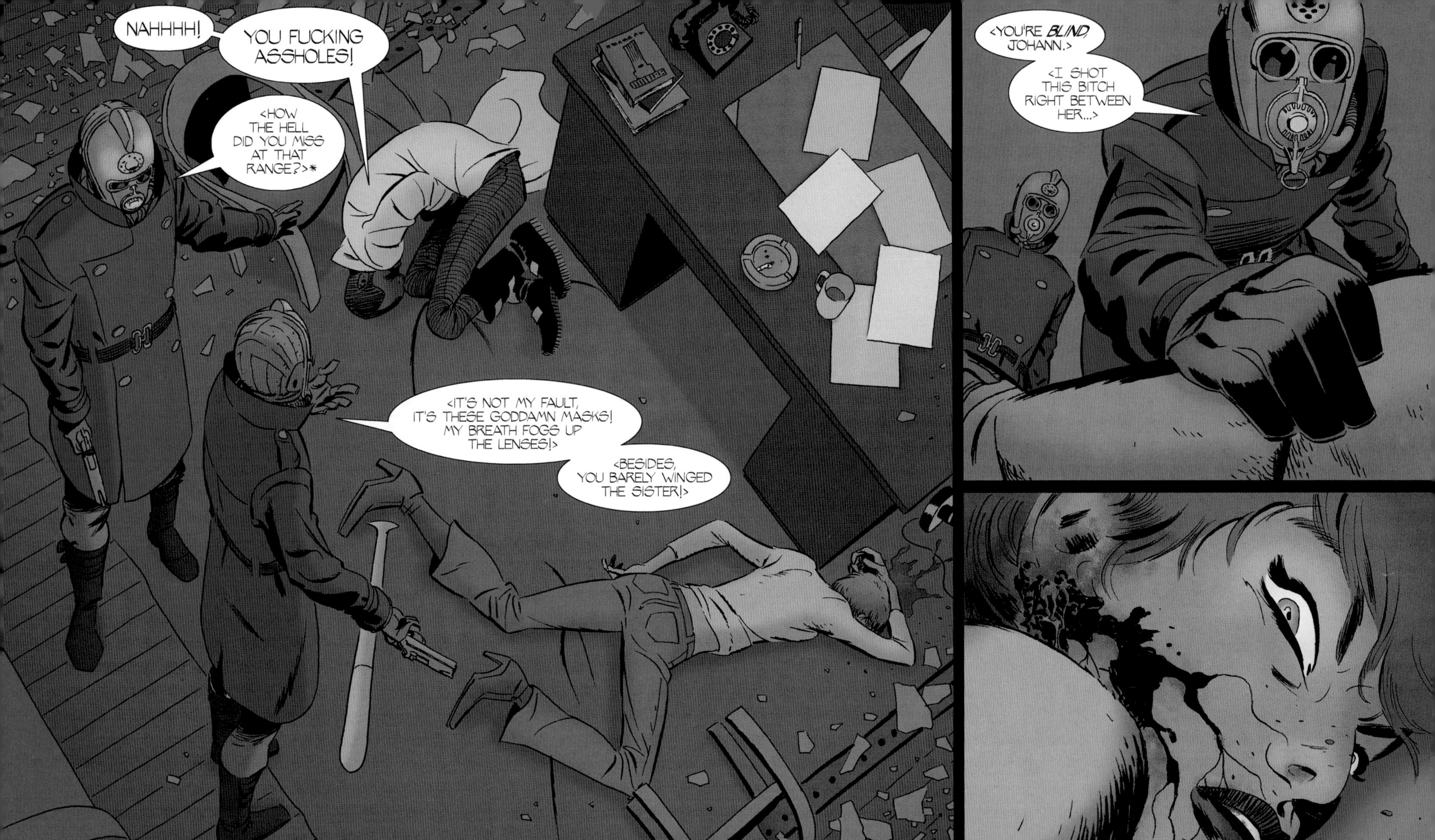
NAHHHH!
YOU FUCKING ASSHOLES!
<HOW THE HELL DID YOU MISS AT THAT RANGE?>*
<IT'S NOT MY FAULT, IT'S THESE GODDAMN MASKS! MY BREATH FOGS UP THE LENSES!>
<BESIDES, YOU BARELY WINGED THE SISTER!>
<YOU'RE *BLIND*, JOHANN.>
<I SHOT THIS BITCH RIGHT BETWEEN HER...>

* Speaking in French.

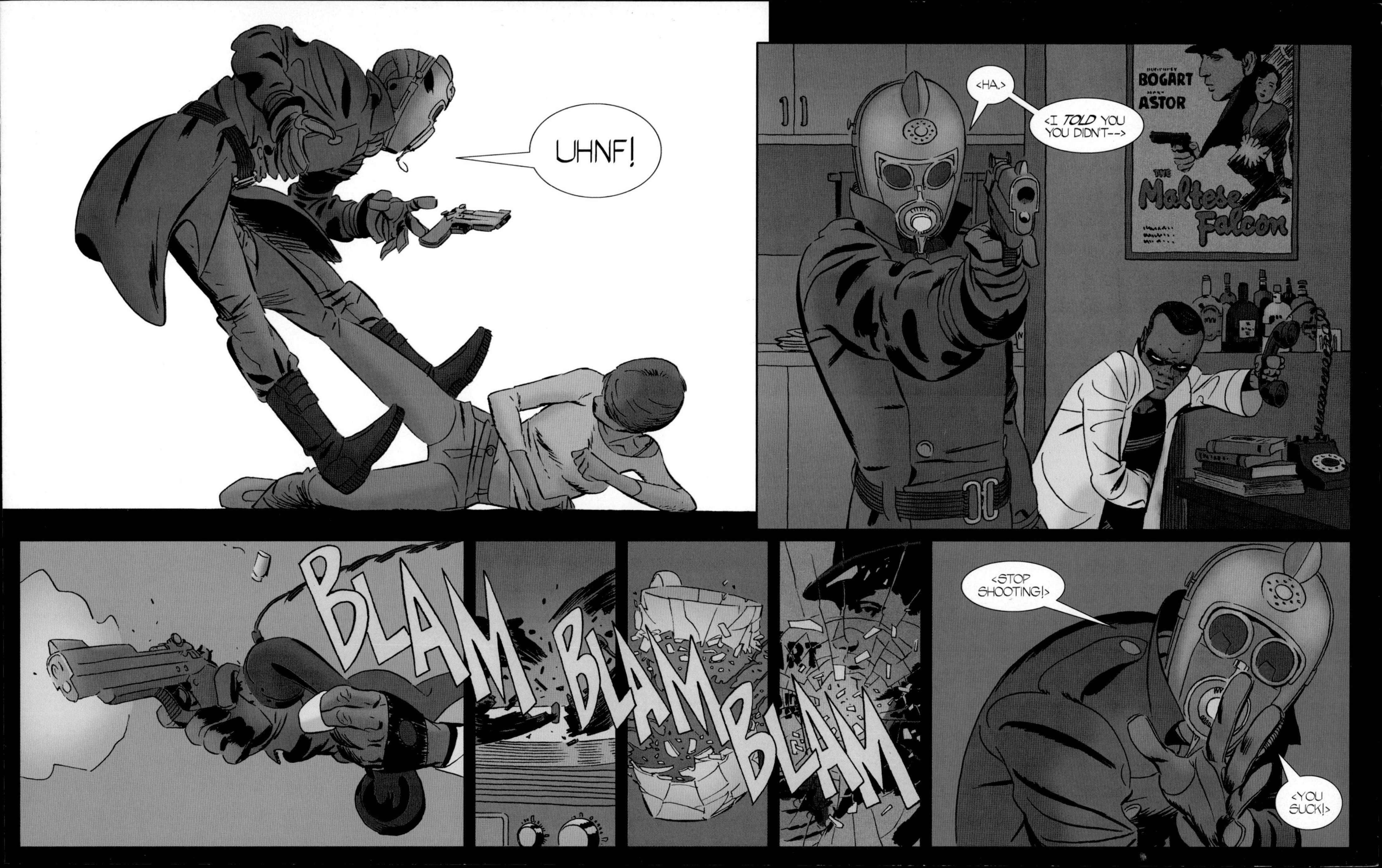
UHNF!
<HA.>
<I TOLD YOU YOU DIDN'T-->
BOGART
ASTOR
The Maltese Falcon
BLAM
BLAM
BLAM
BLAM
<STOP SHOOTING!>
<YOU SUCK!>

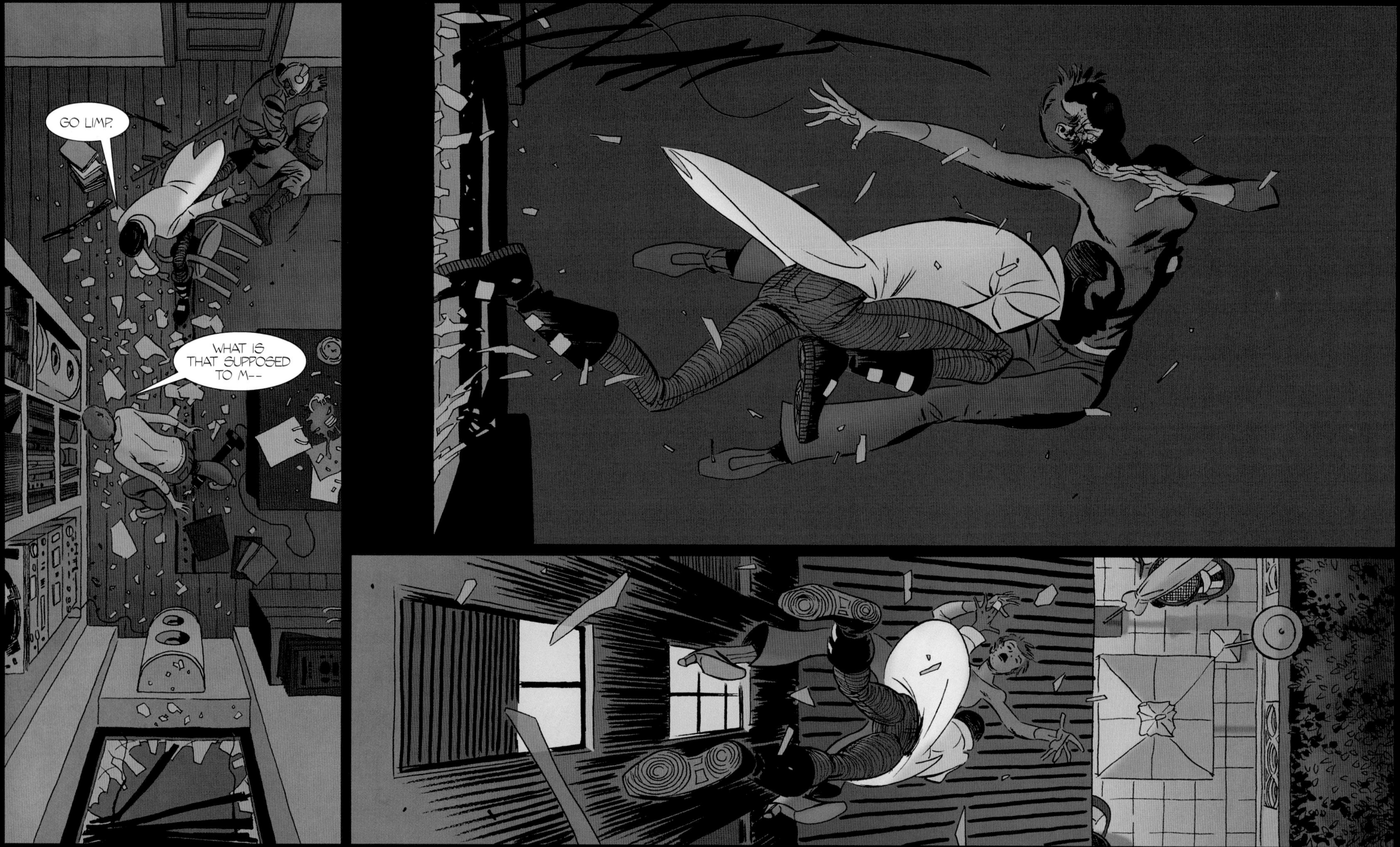
GO LIMP.
WHAT IS THAT SUPPOSED TO M--

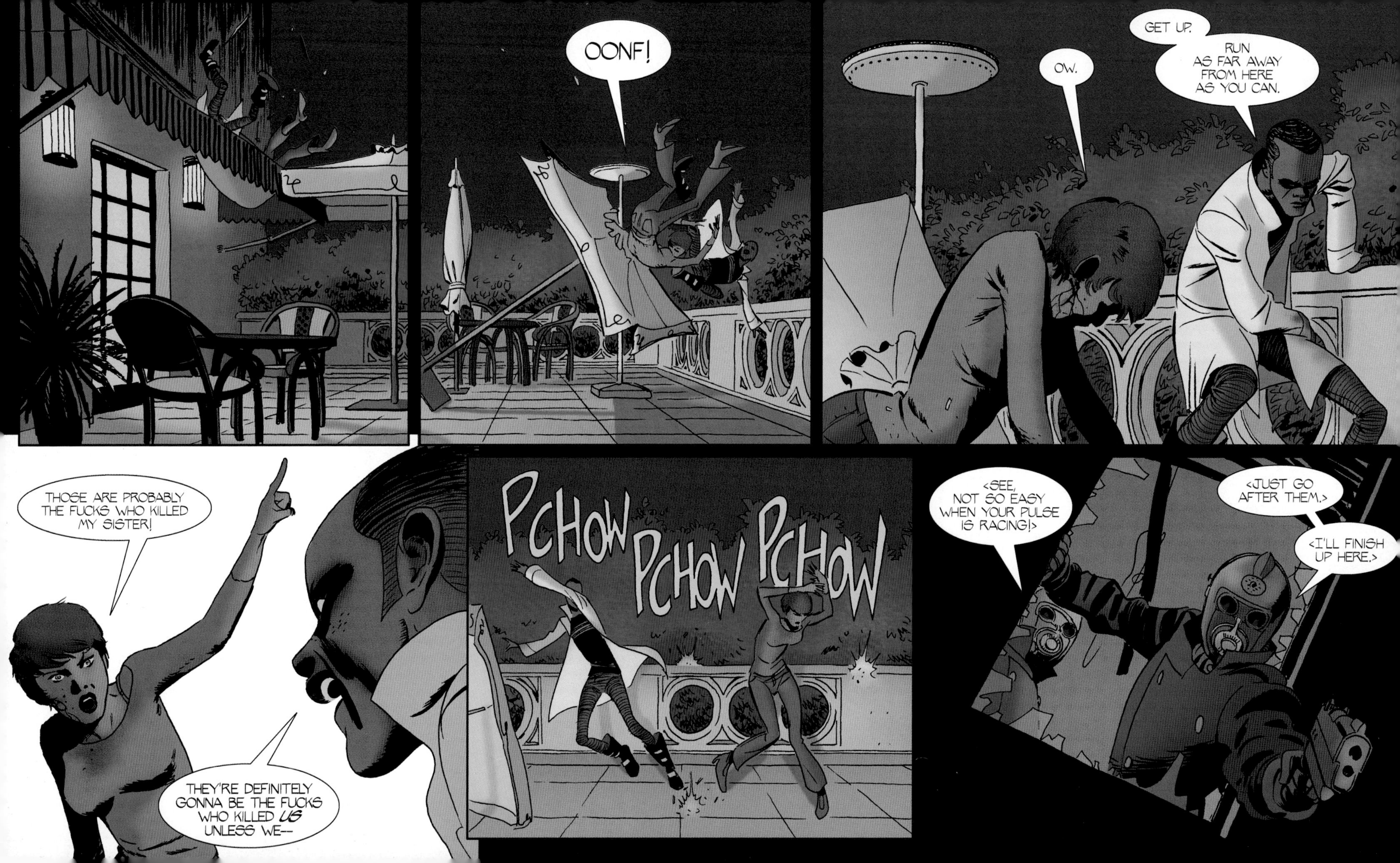
OONF!
OW.
GET UP.
RUN AS FAR AWAY FROM HERE AS YOU CAN.
THOSE ARE PROBABLY THE FUCKS WHO KILLED MY SISTER!
THEY'RE DEFINITELY GONNA BE THE FUCKS WHO KILLED *US* UNLESS WE--
PCHOW PCHOW PCHOW
<SEE, NOT SO EASY WHEN YOUR PULSE IS RACING!>
<JUST GO AFTER THEM.>
<I'LL FINISH UP HERE.>

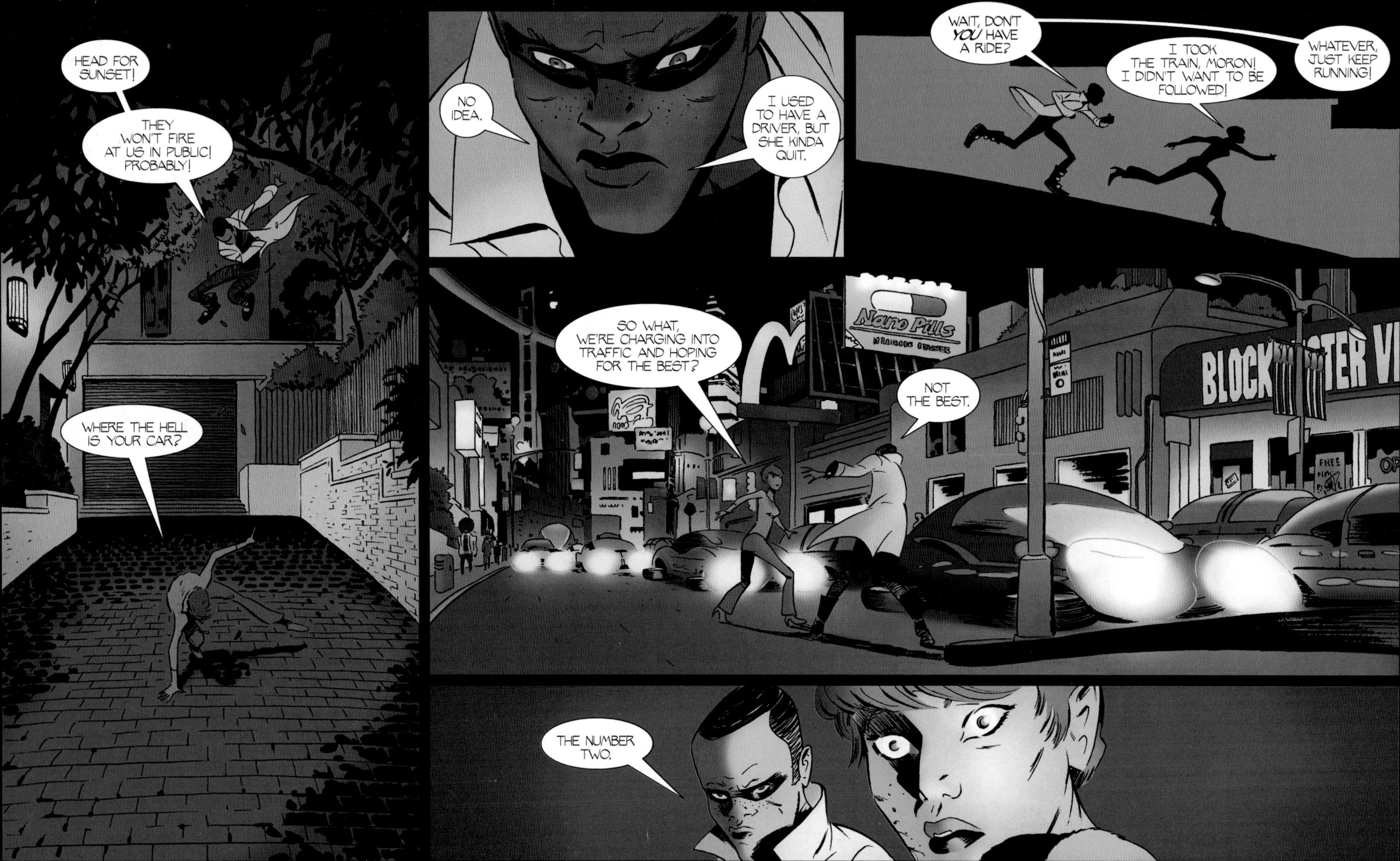
HEAD FOR SUNSET!
THEY WON'T FIRE AT US IN PUBLIC! PROBABLY!
WHERE THE HELL IS YOUR CAR?
NO IDEA.
I USED TO HAVE A DRIVER, BUT SHE KINDA QUIT.
WAIT, DON'T *YOU* HAVE A RIDE?
I TOOK THE TRAIN, MORON! I DIDN'T WANT TO BE FOLLOWED!
WHATEVER, JUST KEEP RUNNING!
SO WHAT, WE'RE CHARGING INTO TRAFFIC AND HOPING FOR THE BEST?
Nano Pills
NOT THE BEST.
THE NUMBER TWO.

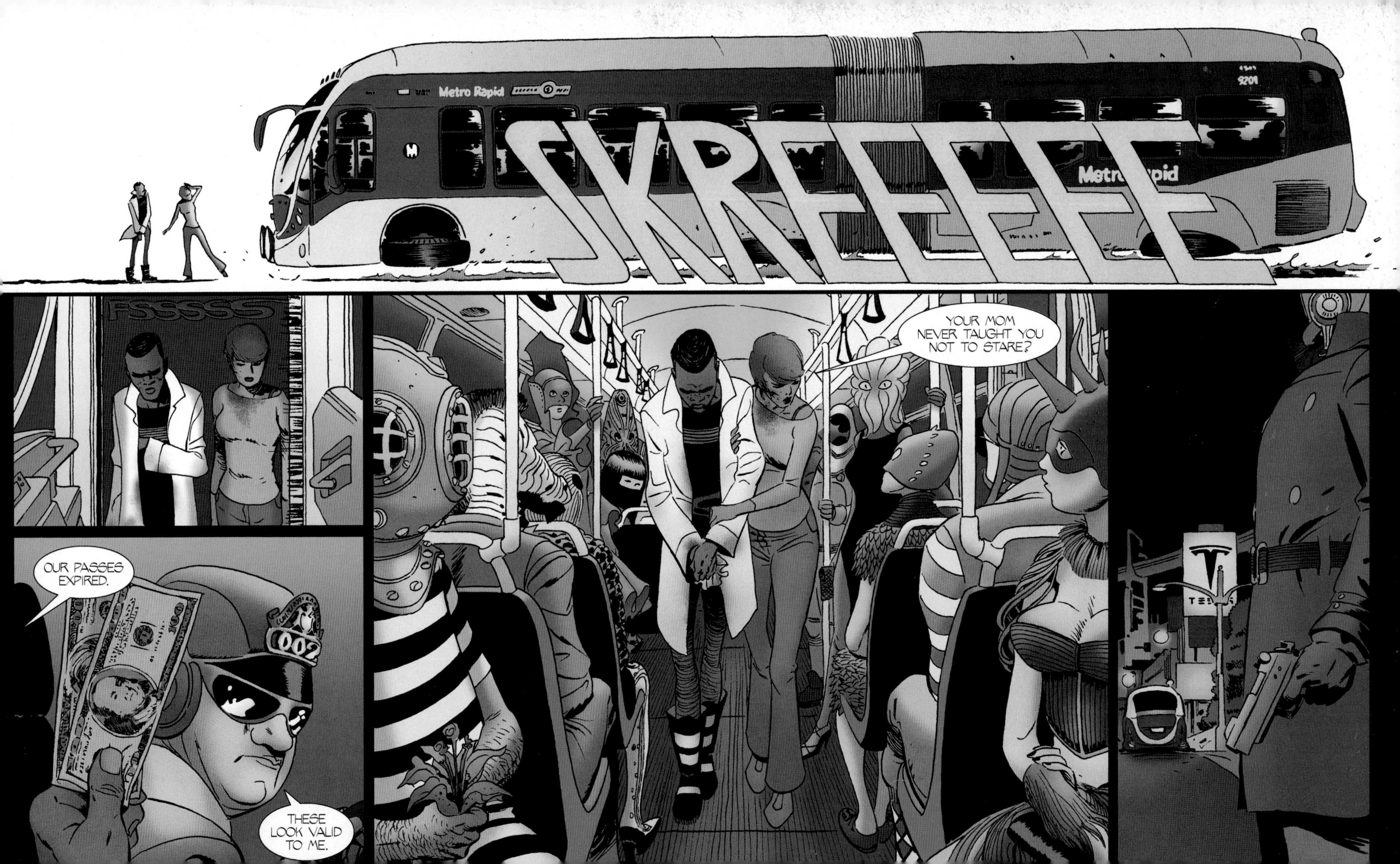
SKREEEEEE
Metro Rapid
9201
FSSSSSST
OUR PASSES EXPIRED.
THESE LOOK VALID TO ME.
YOUR MOM NEVER TAUGHT YOU NOT TO STARE?

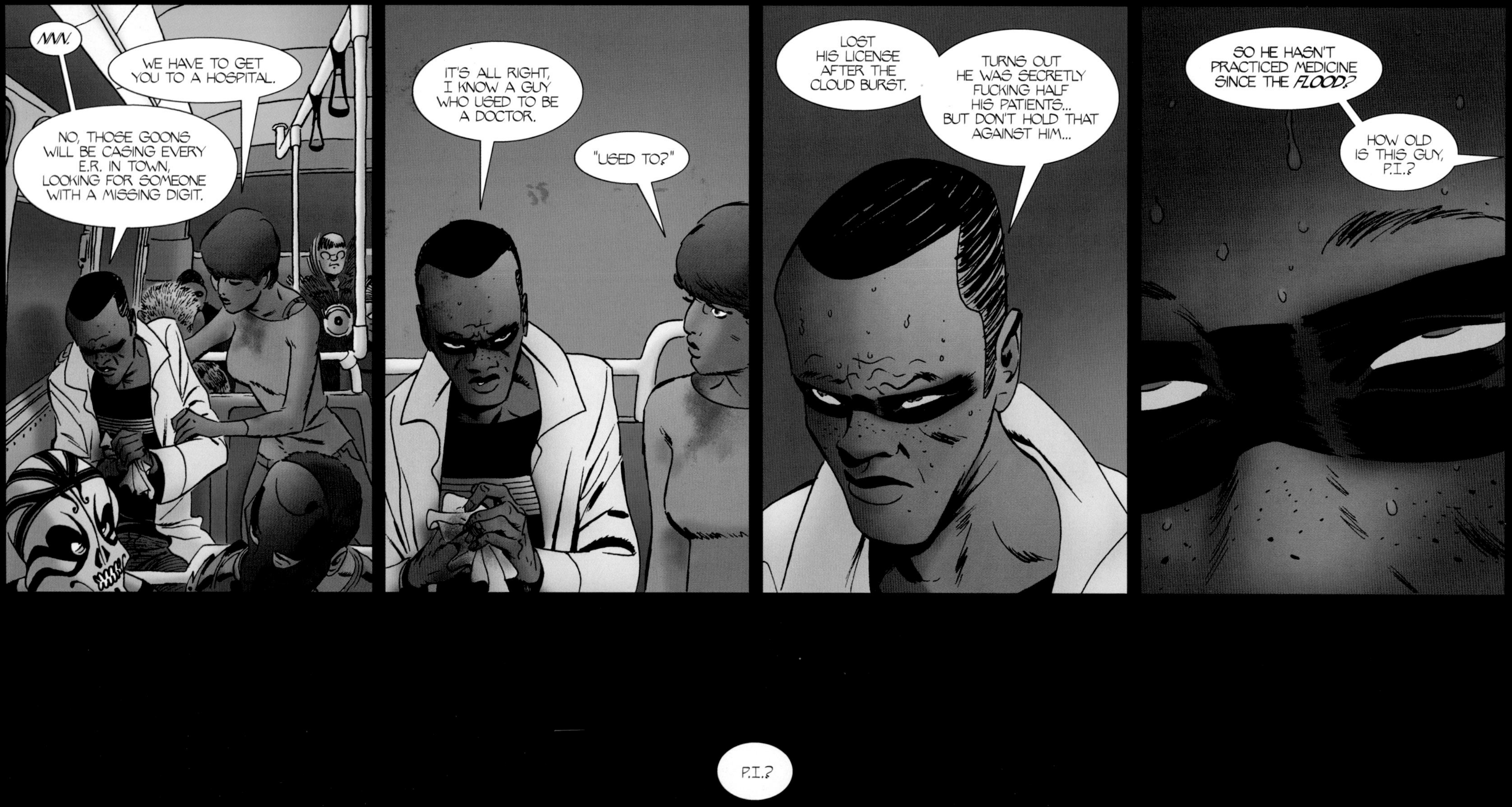

NNN.
WE HAVE TO GET YOU TO A HOSPITAL.
NO, THOSE GOONS WILL BE CASING EVERY E.R. IN TOWN, LOOKING FOR SOMEONE WITH A MISSING DIGIT.
IT'S ALL RIGHT, I KNOW A GUY WHO USED TO BE A DOCTOR.
"USED TO?"
LOST HIS LICENSE AFTER THE CLOUD BURST.
TURNS OUT HE WAS SECRETLY FUCKING HALF HIS PATIENTS... BUT DON'T HOLD THAT AGAINST HIM...
SO HE HASN'T PRACTICED MEDICINE SINCE THE *FLOOD?*
HOW OLD IS THIS GUY, P.I.?
P.I.?

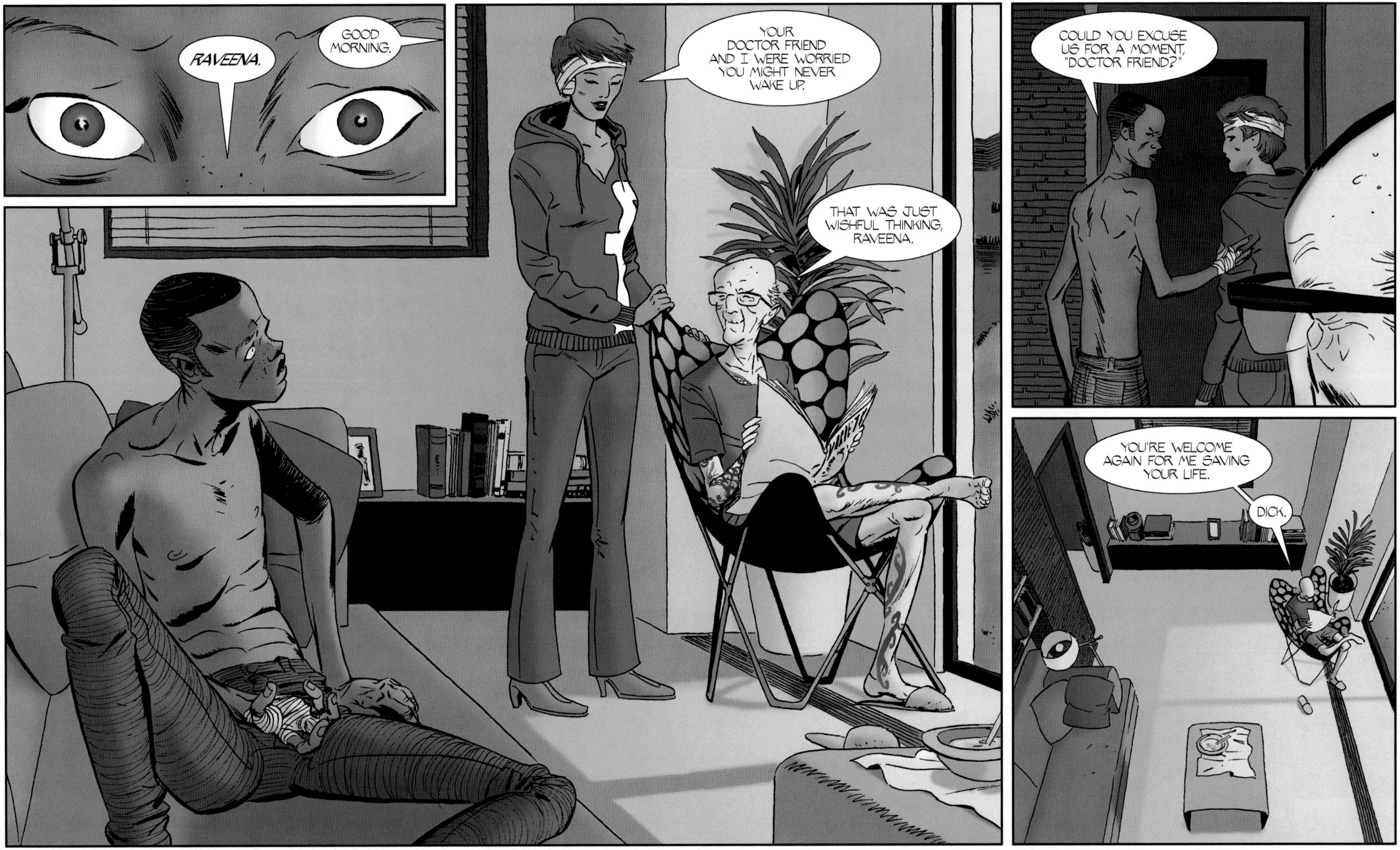
GOOD MORNING.
RAVEENA.
YOUR DOCTOR FRIEND AND I WERE WORRIED YOU MIGHT NEVER WAKE UP.
THAT WAS JUST WISHFUL THINKING, RAVEENA.
COULD YOU EXCUSE US FOR A MOMENT, "DOCTOR FRIEND?"
YOU'RE WELCOME AGAIN FOR ME SAVING YOUR LIFE.
DICK.

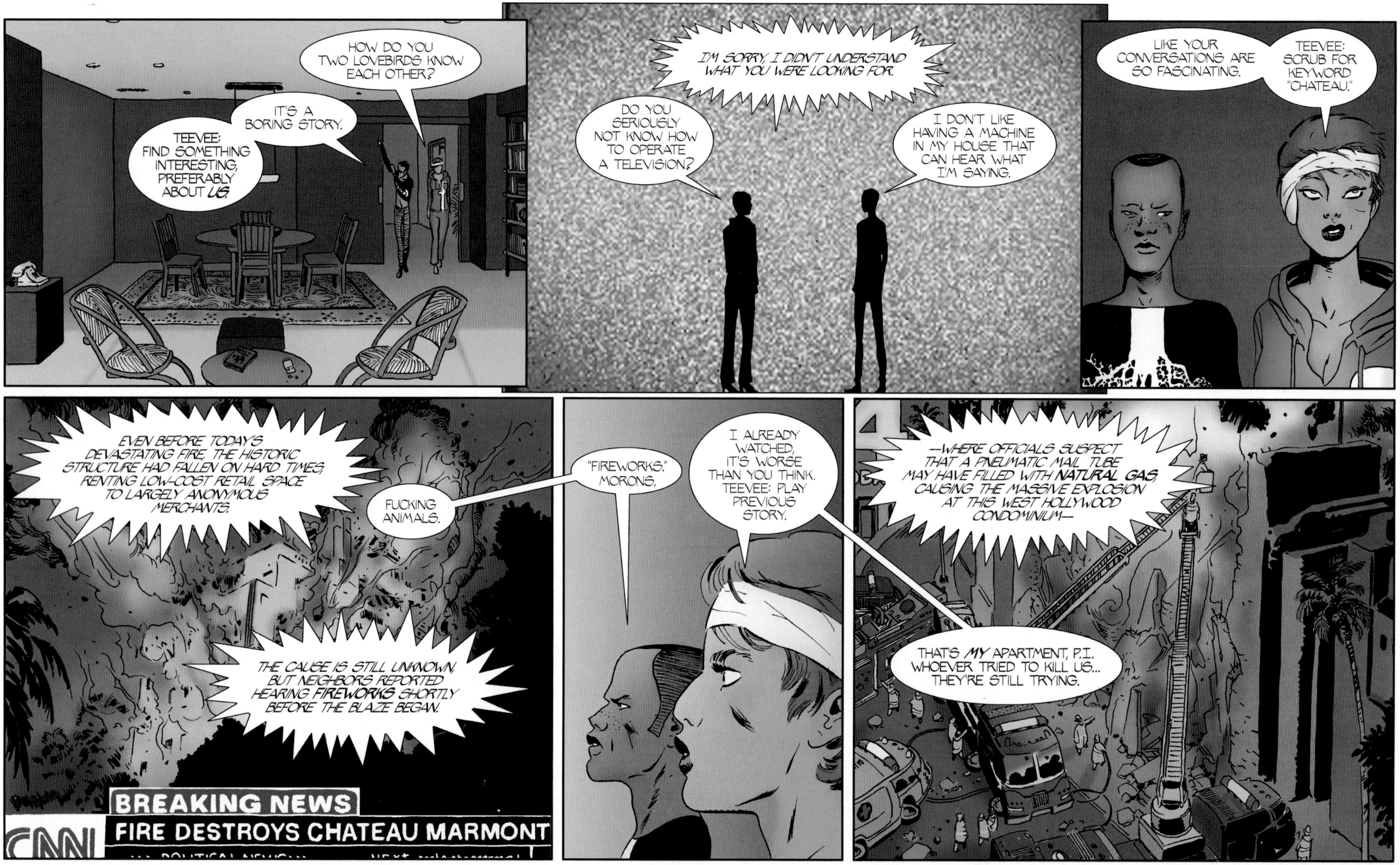
HOW DO YOU TWO LOVEBIRDS KNOW EACH OTHER?
IT'S A BORING STORY.
TEEVEE: FIND SOMETHING INTERESTING, PREFERABLY ABOUT *US*.
I'M SORRY, I DIDN'T UNDERSTAND WHAT YOU WERE LOOKING FOR.
DO YOU SERIOUSLY NOT KNOW HOW TO OPERATE A TELEVISION?
I DON'T LIKE HAVING A MACHINE IN MY HOUSE THAT CAN HEAR WHAT I'M SAYING.
LIKE YOUR CONVERSATIONS ARE SO FASCINATING.
TEEVEE: SCRUB FOR KEYWORD "CHATEAU."
EVEN BEFORE TODAY'S DEVASTATING FIRE, THE HISTORIC STRUCTURE HAD FALLEN ON HARD TIMES, RENTING LOW-COST RETAIL SPACE TO LARGELY ANONYMOUS MERCHANTS.
FUCKING ANIMALS.
THE CAUSE IS STILL UNKNOWN, BUT NEIGHBORS REPORTED HEARING **FIREWORKS** SHORTLY BEFORE THE BLAZE BEGAN.
BREAKING NEWS
CNN
FIRE DESTROYS CHATEAU MARMONT
"FIREWORKS." MORONS.
I ALREADY WATCHED, IT'S WORSE THAN YOU THINK. TEEVEE: PLAY PREVIOUS STORY.
--WHERE OFFICIALS SUSPECT THAT A PNEUMATIC MAIL TUBE MAY HAVE FILLED WITH **NATURAL GAS**, CAUSING THE MASSIVE EXPLOSION AT THIS WEST HOLLYWOOD CONDOMINIUM--
THAT'S *MY* APARTMENT, P.I. WHOEVER TRIED TO KILL US... THEY'RE STILL TRYING.

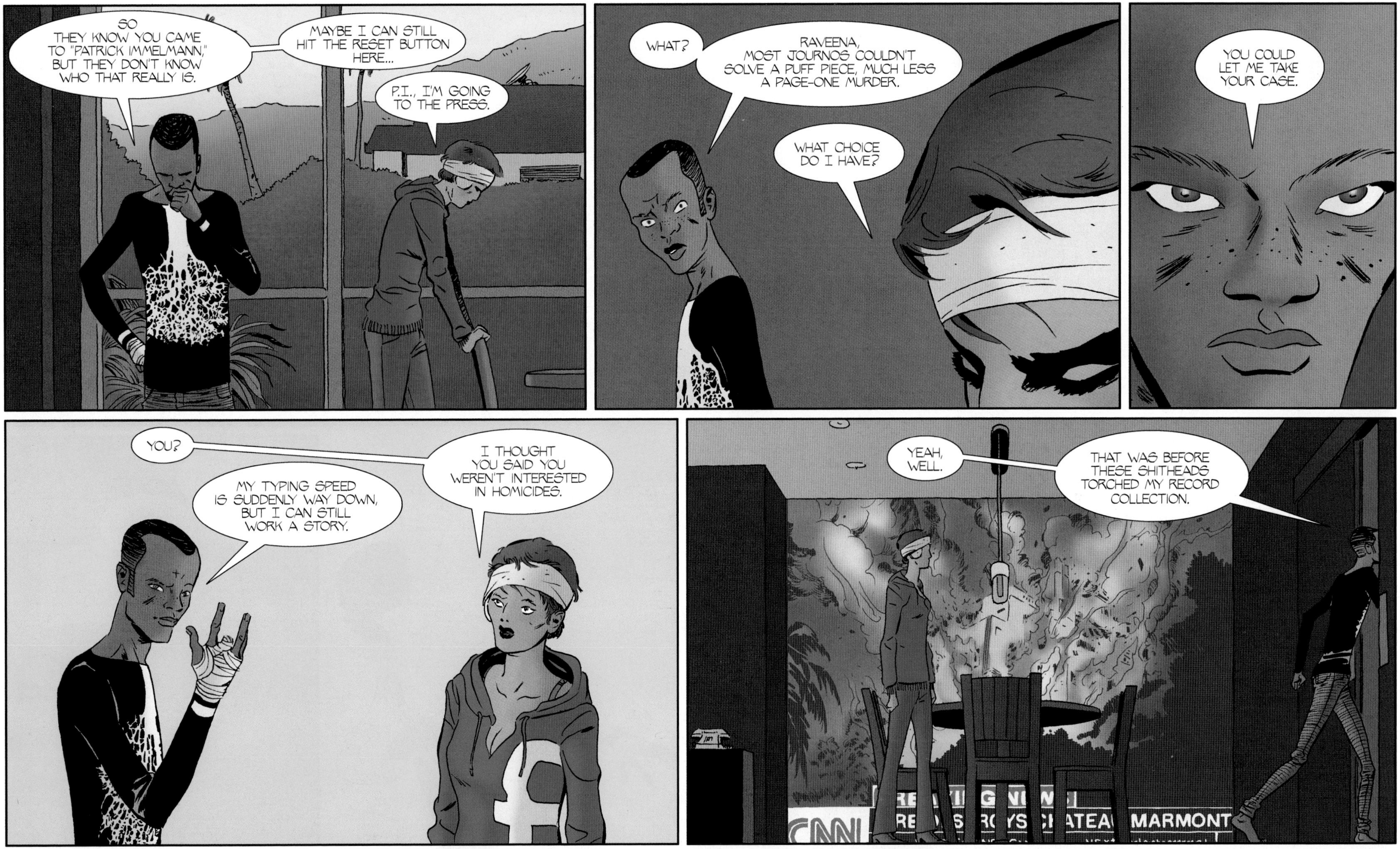
SO THEY KNOW YOU CAME TO "PATRICK IMMELMANN," BUT THEY DON'T KNOW WHO THAT REALLY IS.
MAYBE I CAN STILL HIT THE RESET BUTTON HERE...
P.I., I'M GOING TO THE PRESS.
WHAT?
RAVEENA, MOST JOURNOS COULDN'T SOLVE A PUFF PIECE, MUCH LESS A PAGE-ONE MURDER.
WHAT CHOICE DO I HAVE?
YOU COULD LET ME TAKE YOUR CASE.
YOU?
I THOUGHT YOU SAID YOU WEREN'T INTERESTED IN HOMICIDES.
MY TYPING SPEED IS SUDDENLY WAY DOWN, BUT I CAN STILL WORK A STORY.
YEAH, WELL.
THAT WAS BEFORE THESE SHITHEADS TORCHED MY RECORD COLLECTION.

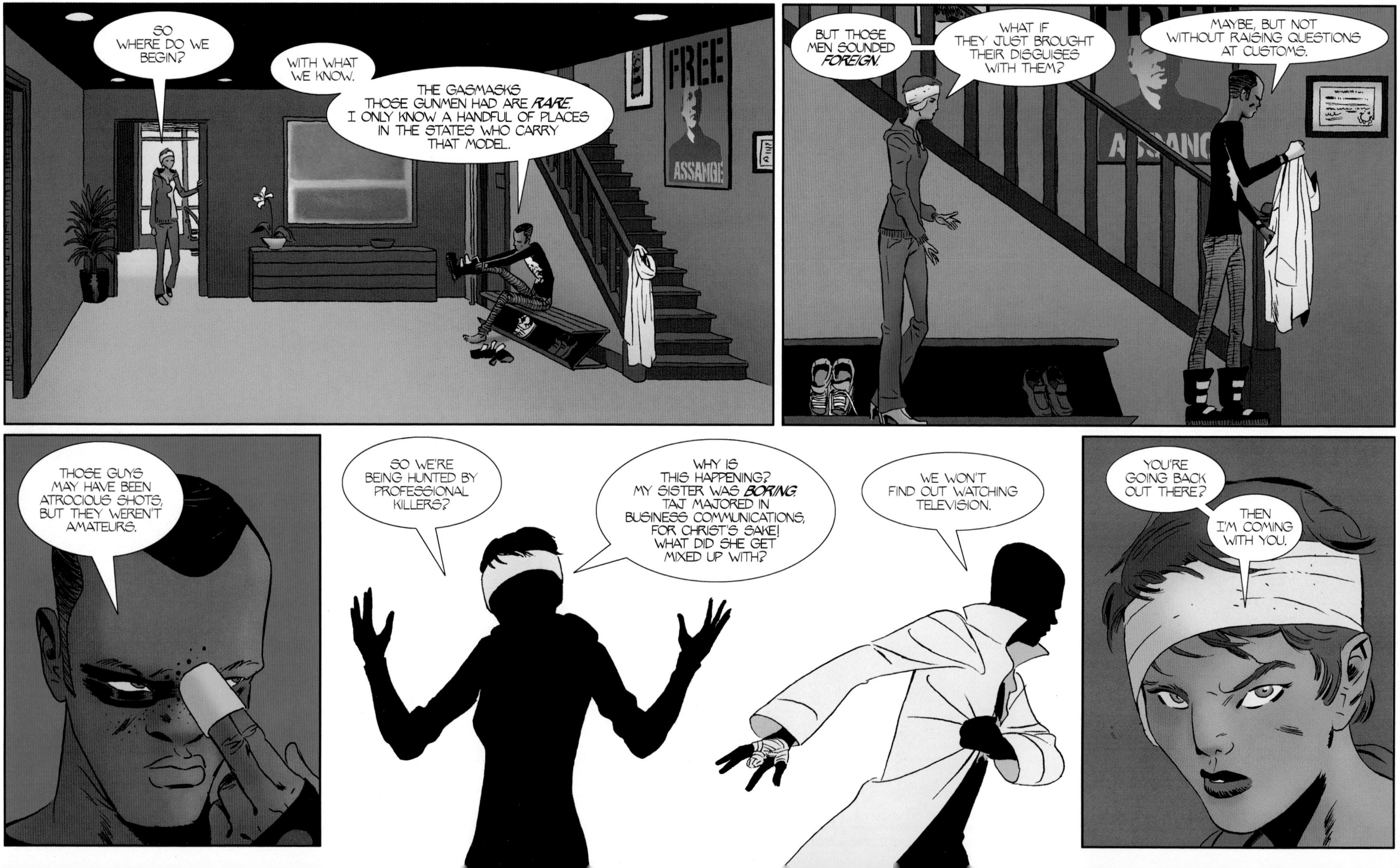

SO WHERE DO WE BEGIN?
WITH WHAT WE KNOW.
THE GASMASKS THOSE GUNMEN HAD ARE *RARE.* I ONLY KNOW A HANDFUL OF PLACES IN THE STATES WHO CARRY THAT MODEL.
FREE
ASSANGE
BUT THOSE MEN SOUNDED *FOREIGN.*
WHAT IF THEY JUST BROUGHT THEIR DISGUISES WITH THEM?
MAYBE, BUT NOT WITHOUT RAISING QUESTIONS AT CUSTOMS.
ASSANGE
THOSE GUYS MAY HAVE BEEN ATROCIOUS SHOTS, BUT THEY WEREN'T AMATEURS.
SO WE'RE BEING HUNTED BY PROFESSIONAL KILLERS?
WHY IS THIS HAPPENING? MY SISTER WAS *BORING.* TAJ MAJORED IN BUSINESS COMMUNICATIONS, FOR CHRIST'S SAKE! WHAT DID SHE GET MIXED UP WITH?
WE WON'T FIND OUT WATCHING TELEVISION.
YOU'RE GOING BACK OUT THERE?
THEN I'M COMING WITH YOU.

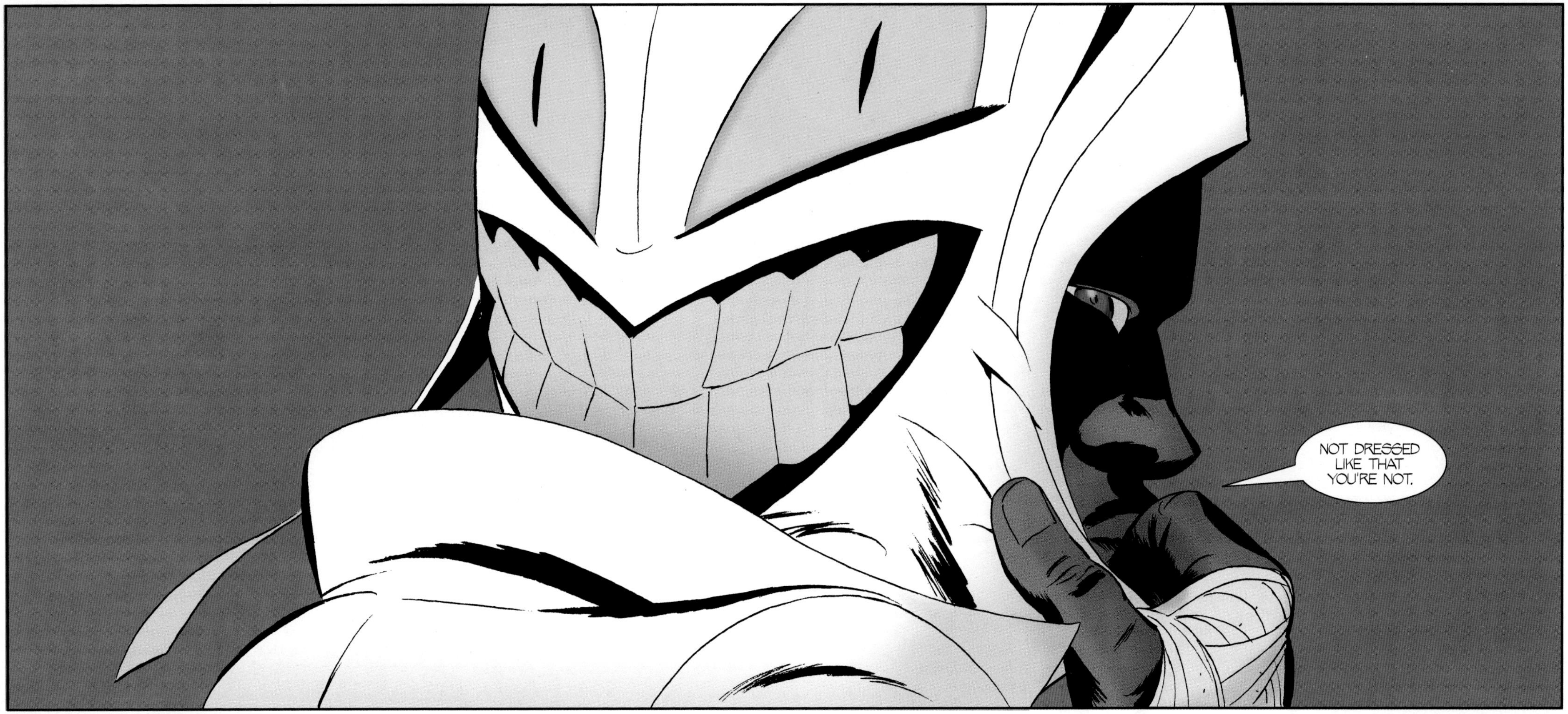
NOT DRESSED LIKE THAT YOU'RE NOT.

THE PRIVATE EYE

BRIAN K. VAUGHAN
MARCOS MARTIN
WITH
MUNTSA VICENTE

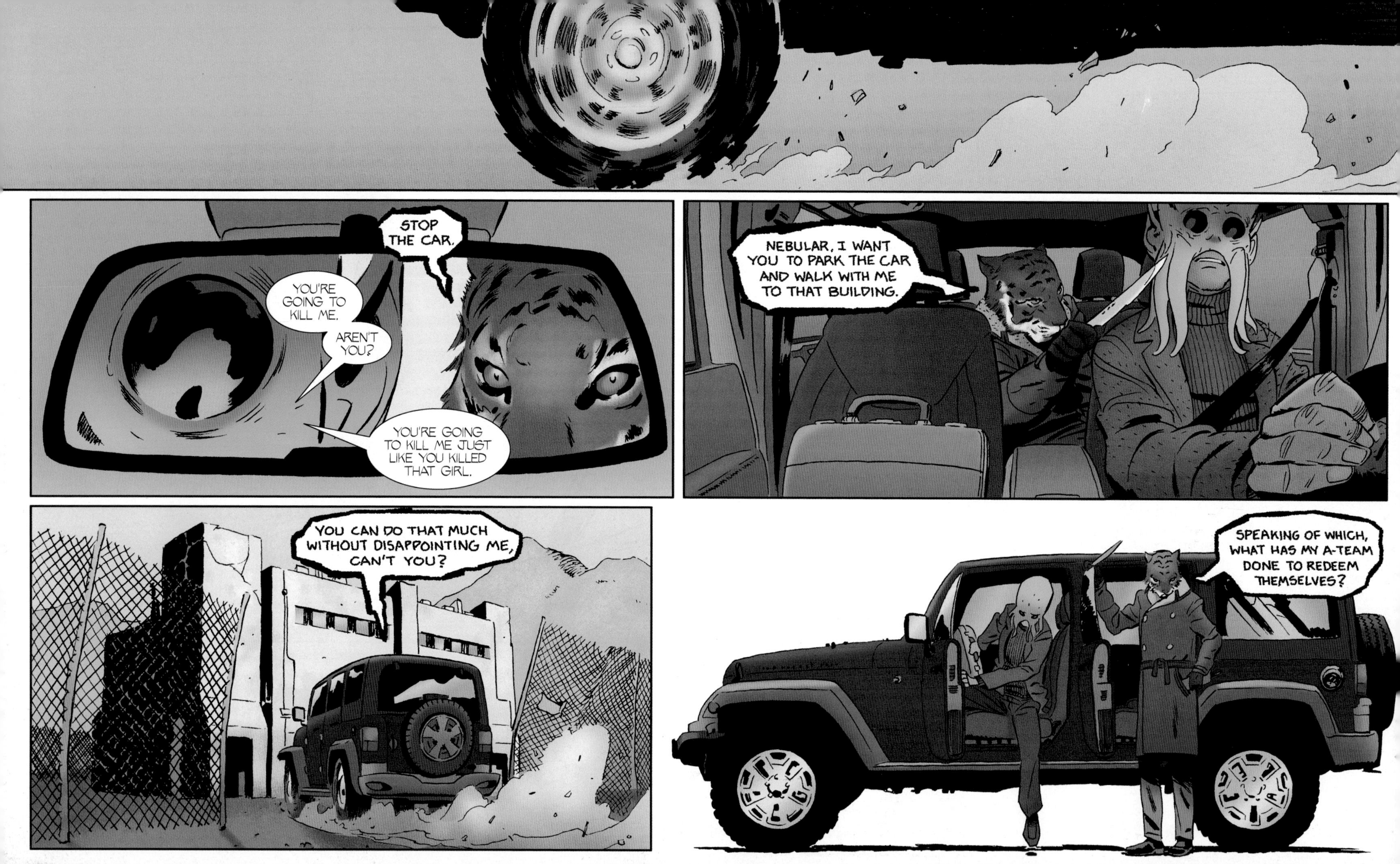
STOP THE CAR.
YOU'RE GOING TO KILL ME.
AREN'T YOU?
YOU'RE GOING TO KILL ME JUST LIKE YOU KILLED THAT GIRL.
NEBULAR, I WANT YOU TO PARK THE CAR AND WALK WITH ME TO THAT BUILDING.
YOU CAN DO THAT MUCH WITHOUT DISAPPOINTING ME, CAN'T YOU?
SPEAKING OF WHICH, WHAT HAS MY A-TEAM DONE TO REDEEM THEMSELVES?

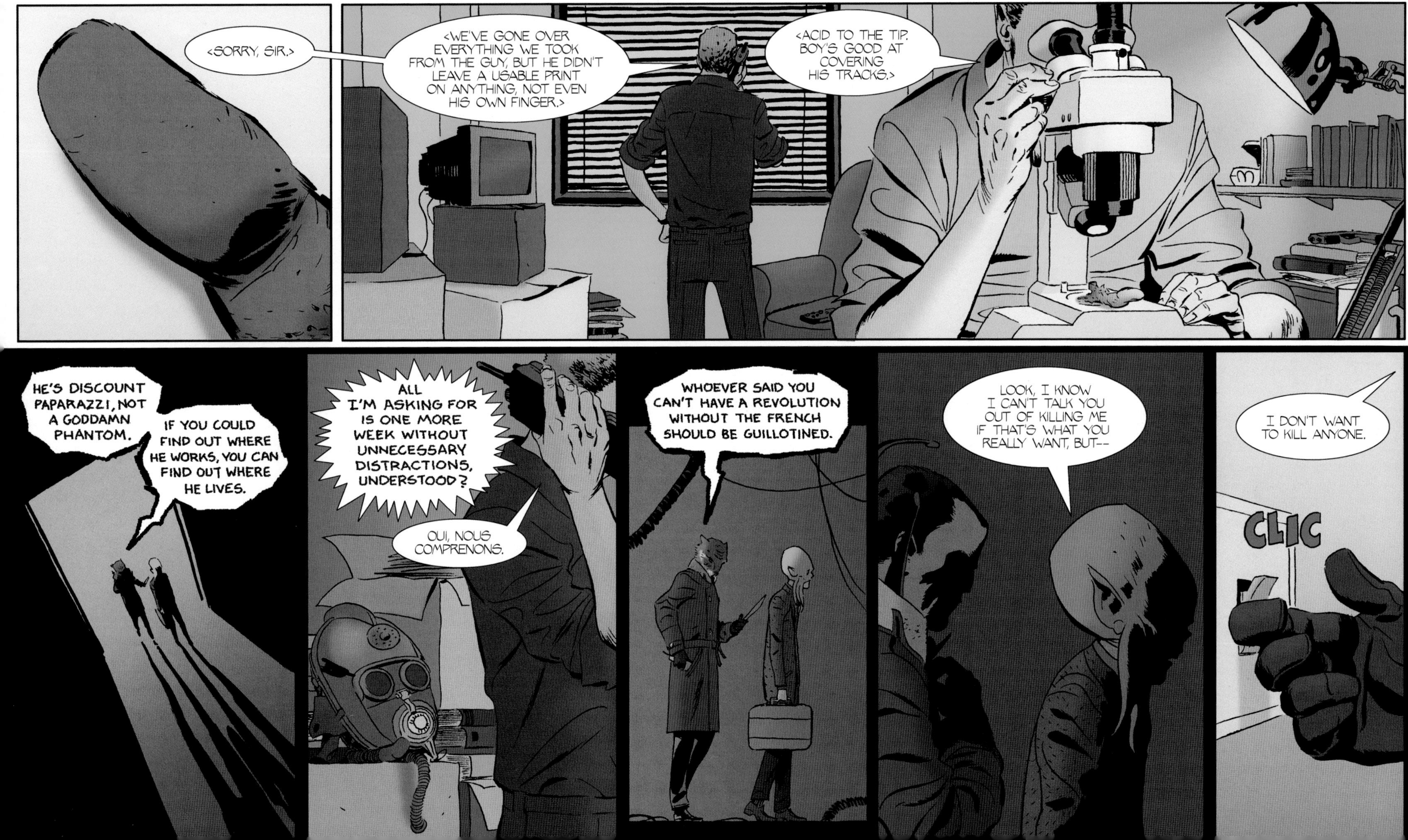
<SORRY, SIR.>
<WE'VE GONE OVER EVERYTHING WE TOOK FROM THE GUY, BUT HE DIDN'T LEAVE A USABLE PRINT ON ANYTHING, NOT EVEN HIS OWN FINGER.>
<ACID TO THE TIP. BOY'S GOOD AT COVERING HIS TRACKS.>
HE'S DISCOUNT PAPARAZZI, NOT A GODDAMN PHANTOM.
IF YOU COULD FIND OUT WHERE HE WORKS, YOU CAN FIND OUT WHERE HE LIVES.
ALL I'M ASKING FOR IS ONE MORE WEEK WITHOUT UNNECESSARY DISTRACTIONS, UNDERSTOOD?
OUI, NOUS COMPRENONS.
WHOEVER SAID YOU CAN'T HAVE A REVOLUTION WITHOUT THE FRENCH SHOULD BE GUILLOTINED.
LOOK, I KNOW I CAN'T TALK YOU OUT OF KILLING ME IF THAT'S WHAT YOU REALLY WANT, BUT--
I DON'T WANT TO KILL ANYONE.
CLIC

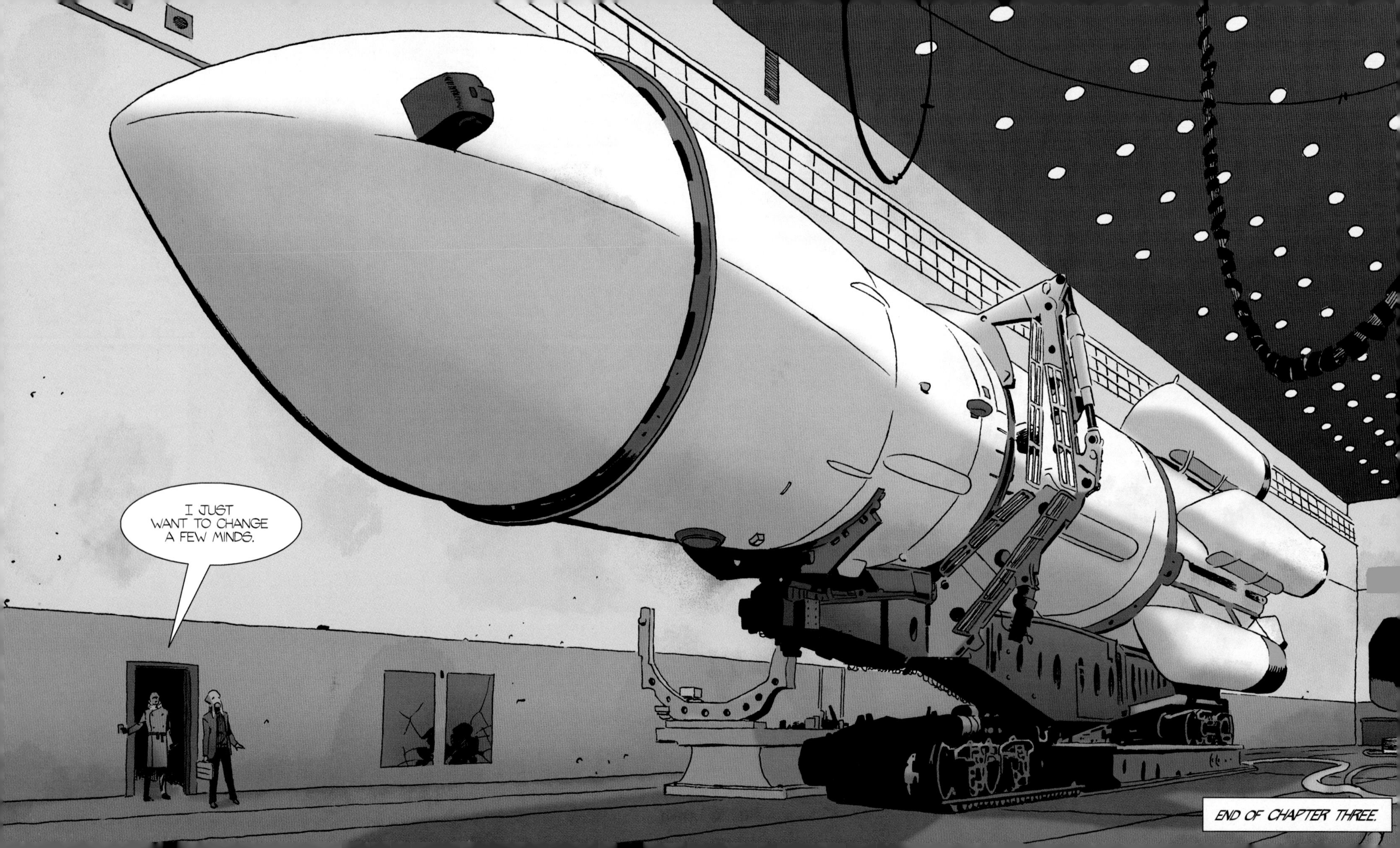
I JUST WANT TO CHANGE A FEW MINDS.
END OF CHAPTER THREE.

CHAPTER FOUR

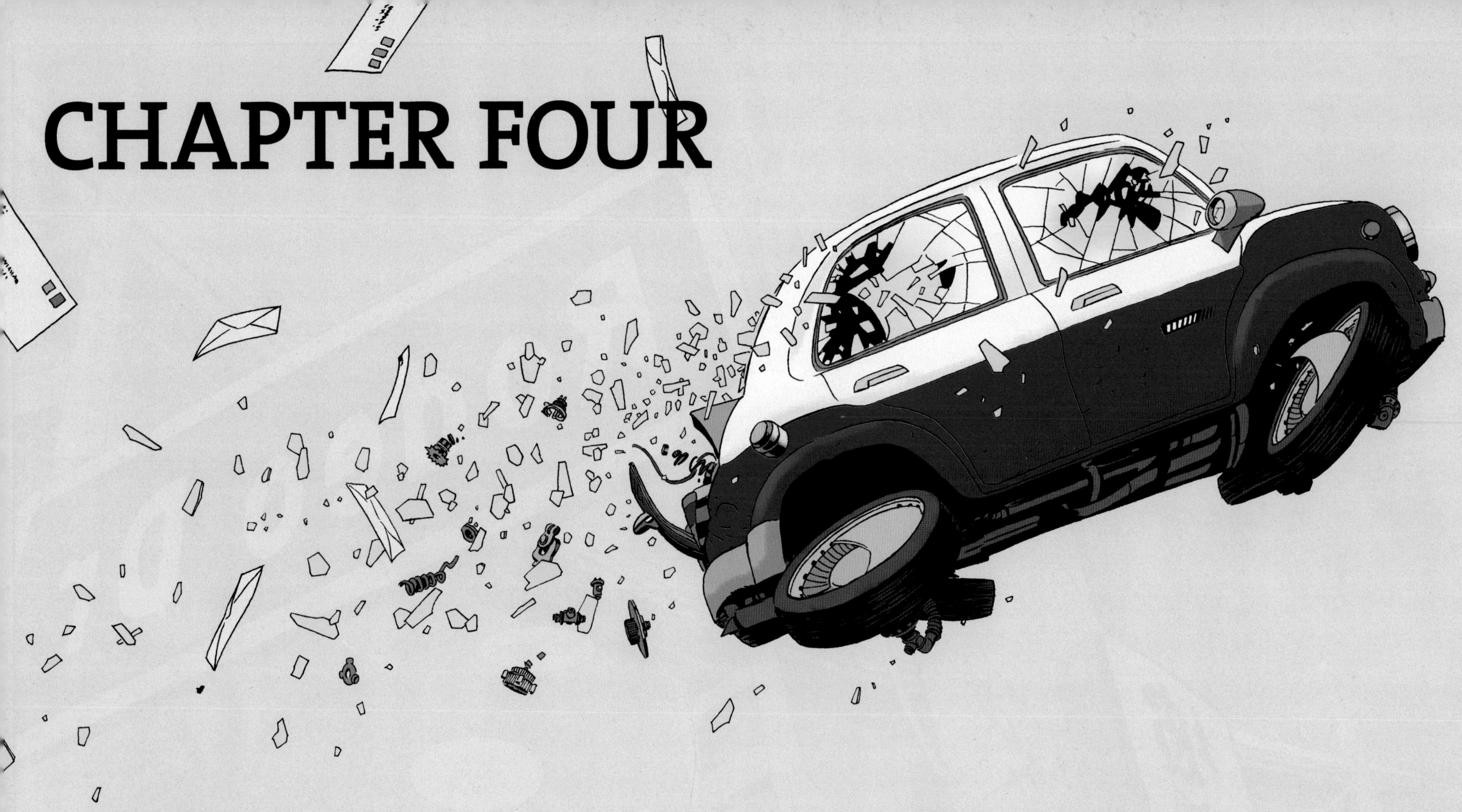

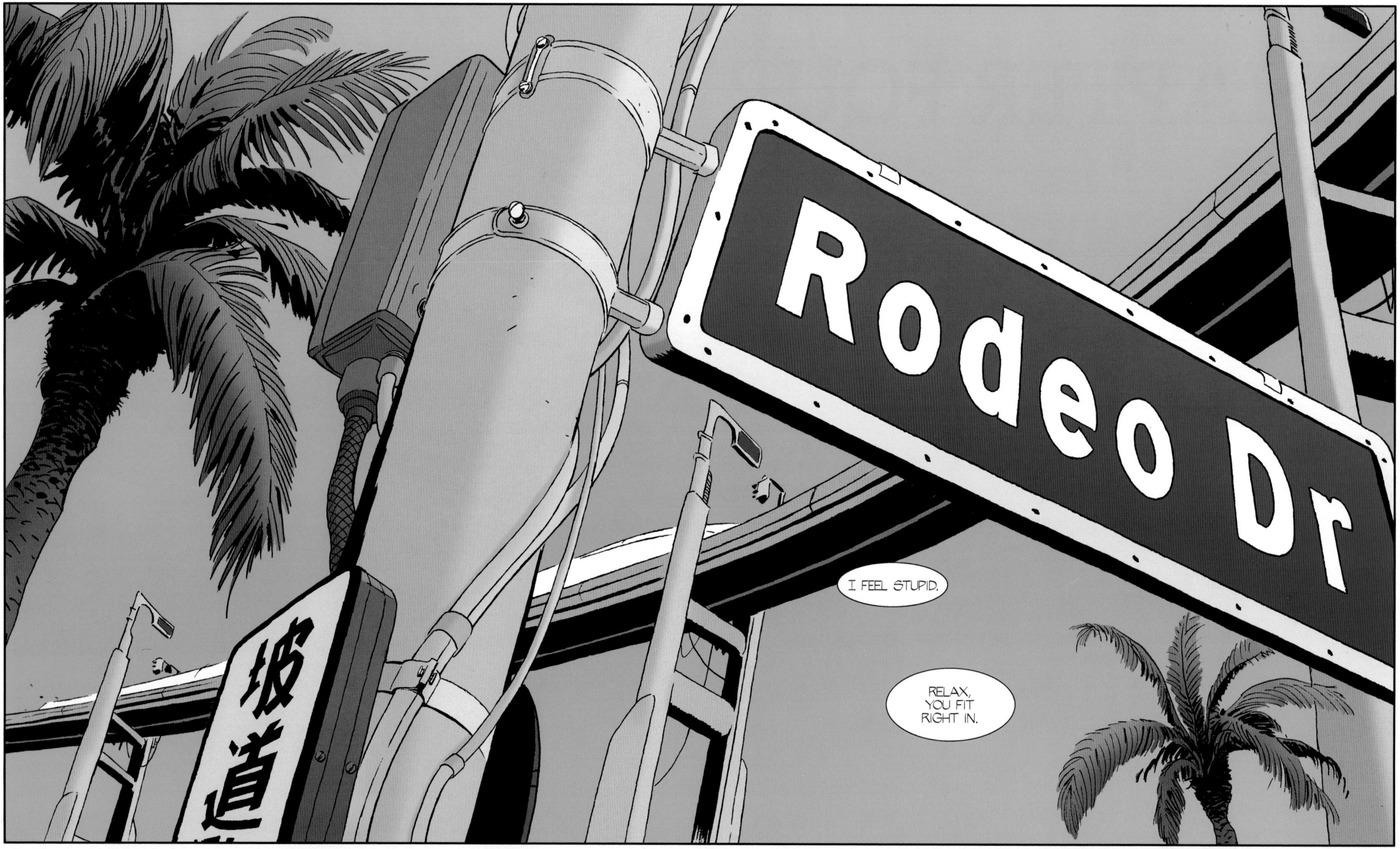
Rodeo Dr
坂道
I FEEL STUPID.
RELAX, YOU FIT RIGHT IN.

I'M SERIOUS, P.I.

I'VE NEVER BEEN COMFORTABLE WITH THIS IRONIC RETRO SHIT.

IT'S NOT RETRO, IT'S VINTAGE.

SMELLS LIKE ARTIFICIAL FRUIT AND OLD BLEACH.

YEAH, THAT WAS A WEIRD CASE.

ANYWAY, IF YOU HATE MY WARDROBE THAT MUCH, YOU CAN BUY YOUR OWN DISGUISE.

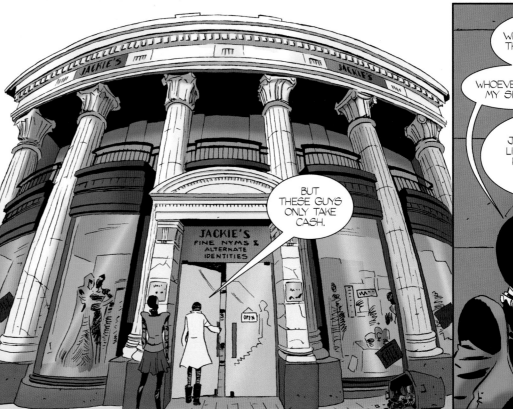

BUT THESE GUYS ONLY TAKE CASH.

JACKIE'S FINE NYMS & ALTERNATE IDENTITIES

IS THAT WHY YOU THINK THEY SHOPPED HERE?

WHOEVER KILLED MY SISTER?

RAVEENA, JUST BROWSE LIKE A NORMAL PERSON AND LET ME DO MY JOB...

OPEN

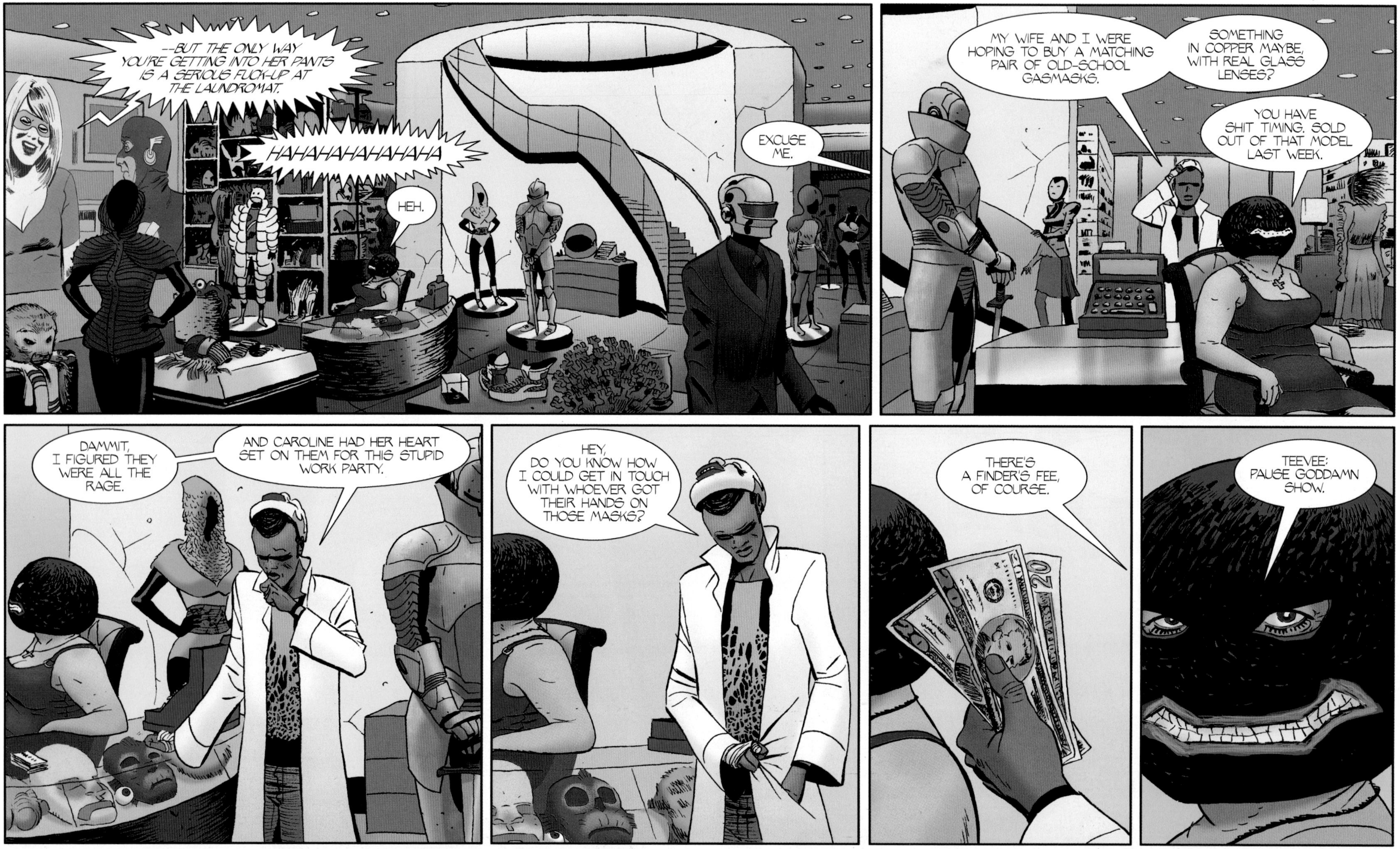
--BUT THE ONLY WAY YOU'RE GETTING INTO HER PANTS IS A SERIOUS FUCK-UP AT THE LAUNDROMAT.
HAHAHAHAHAHAHAHA
HEH.
EXCUSE ME.
MY WIFE AND I WERE HOPING TO BUY A MATCHING PAIR OF OLD-SCHOOL GASMASKS.
SOMETHING IN COPPER MAYBE, WITH REAL GLASS LENSES?
YOU HAVE SHIT TIMING. SOLD OUT OF THAT MODEL LAST WEEK.
DAMMIT, I FIGURED THEY WERE ALL THE RAGE.
AND CAROLINE HAD HER HEART SET ON THEM FOR THIS STUPID WORK PARTY.
HEY, DO YOU KNOW HOW I COULD GET IN TOUCH WITH WHOEVER GOT THEIR HANDS ON THOSE MASKS?
THERE'S A FINDER'S FEE, OF COURSE.
TEEVEE: PAUSE GODDAMN SHOW.

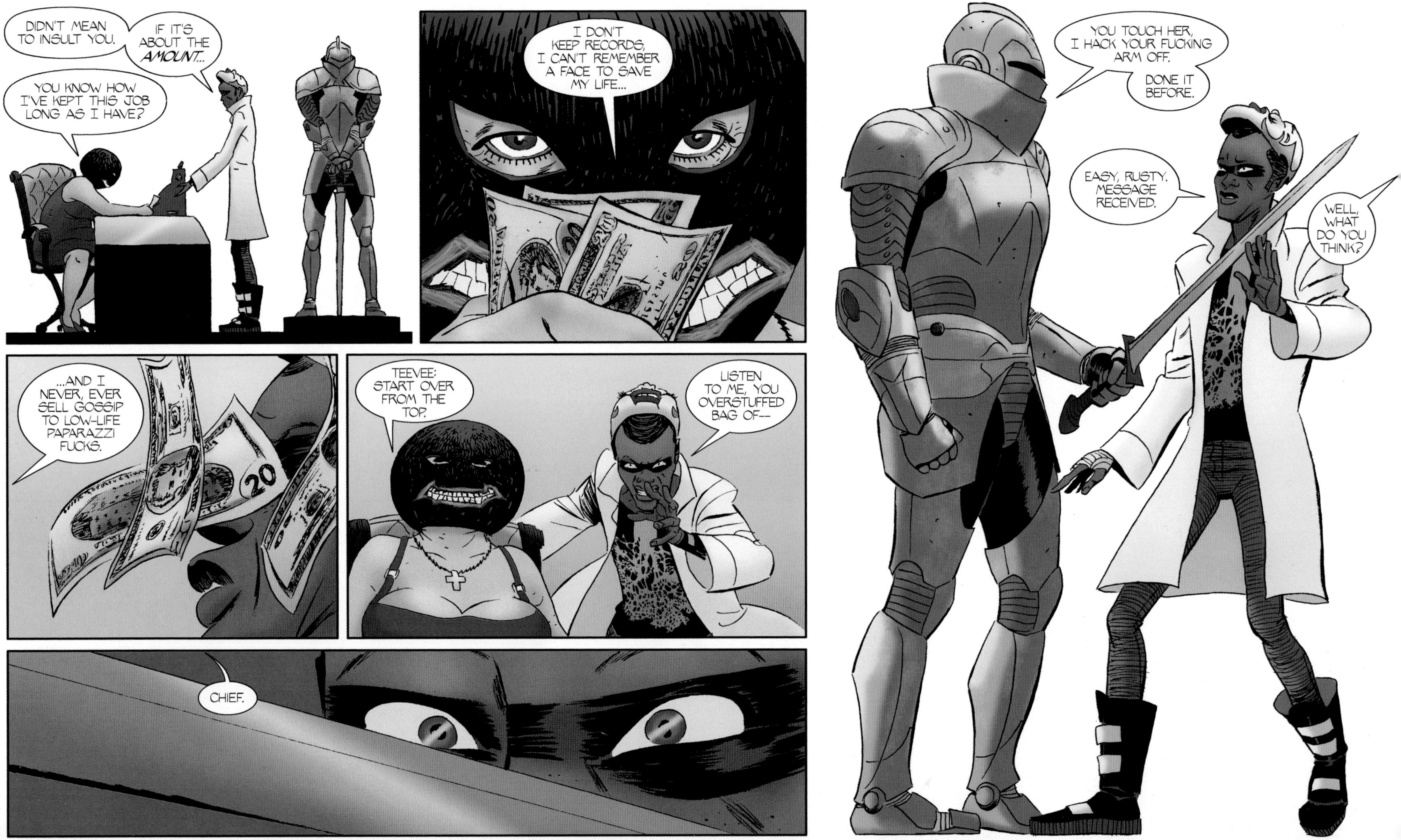
DIDN'T MEAN TO INSULT YOU.
IF IT'S ABOUT THE AMOUNT...
YOU KNOW HOW I'VE KEPT THIS JOB LONG AS I HAVE?
I DON'T KEEP RECORDS, I CAN'T REMEMBER A FACE TO SAVE MY LIFE...
...AND I NEVER, EVER SELL GOSSIP TO LOW-LIFE PAPARAZZI FUCKS.
TEEVEE: START OVER FROM THE TOP.
LISTEN TO ME, YOU OVERSTUFFED BAG OF--
CHIEF.
YOU TOUCH HER, I HACK YOUR FUCKING ARM OFF.
DONE IT BEFORE.
EASY, RUSTY. MESSAGE RECEIVED.
WELL, WHAT DO YOU THINK?

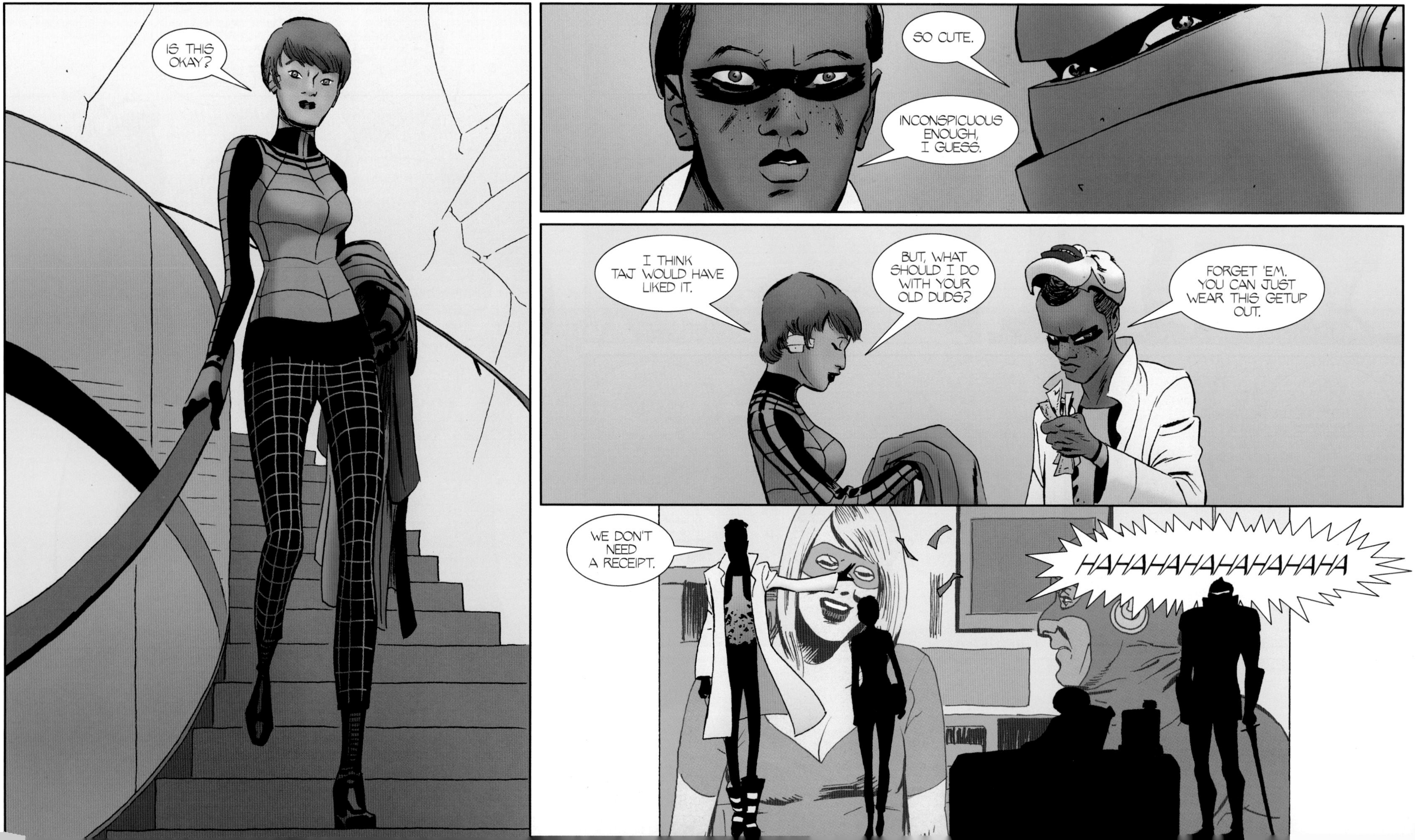
IS THIS OKAY?
SO CUTE.
INCONSPICUOUS ENOUGH, I GUESS.
I THINK TAJ WOULD HAVE LIKED IT.
BUT, WHAT SHOULD I DO WITH YOUR OLD DUDS?
FORGET 'EM. YOU CAN JUST WEAR THIS GETUP OUT.
WE DON'T NEED A RECEIPT.
HAHAHAHAHAHAHAHAHA

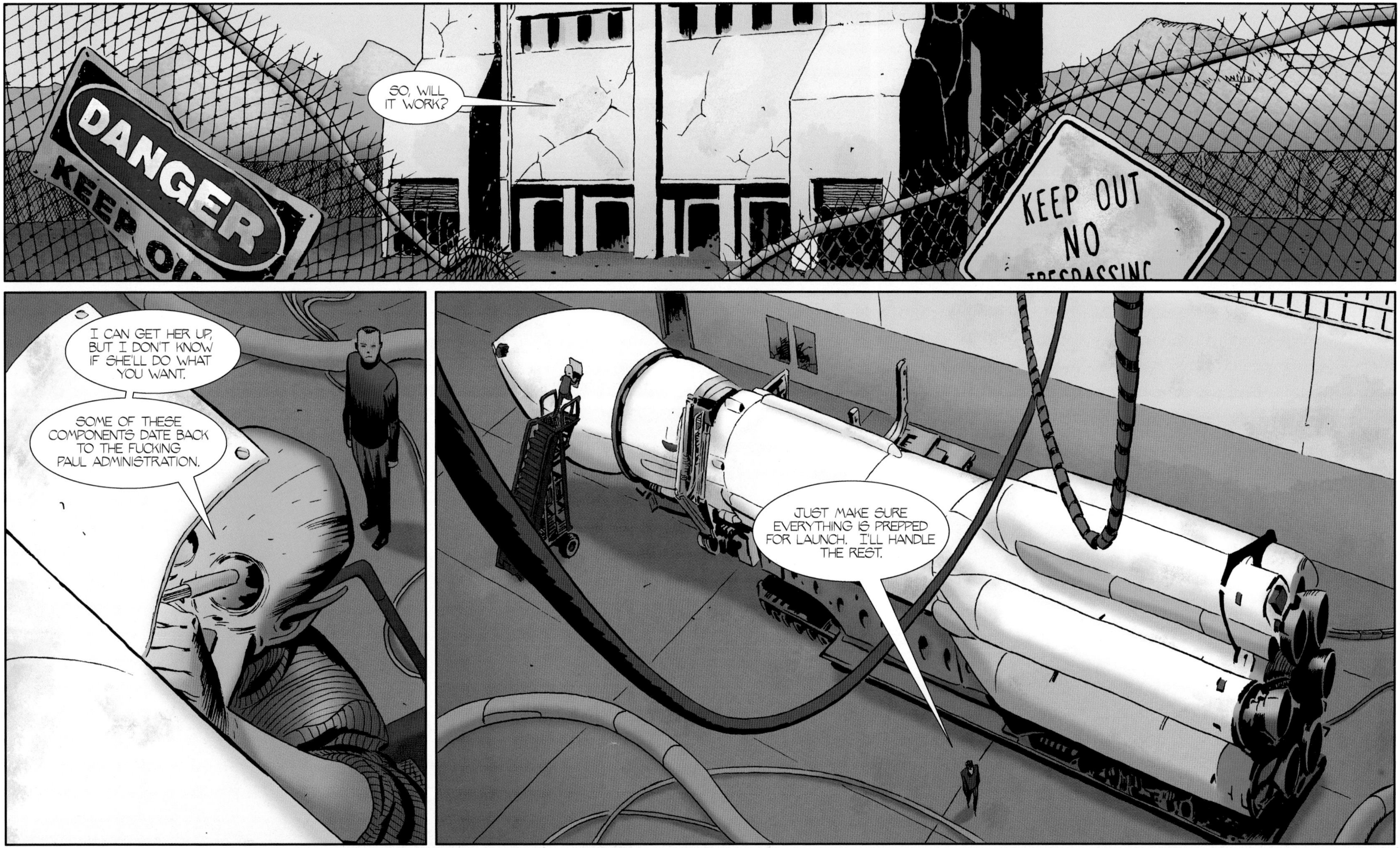
DANGER
KEEP OU
SO, WILL IT WORK?
KEEP OUT NO
I CAN GET HER UP, BUT I DON'T KNOW IF SHE'LL DO WHAT YOU WANT.
SOME OF THESE COMPONENTS DATE BACK TO THE FUCKING PAUL ADMINISTRATION.
JUST MAKE SURE EVERYTHING IS PREPPED FOR LAUNCH. I'LL HANDLE THE REST.

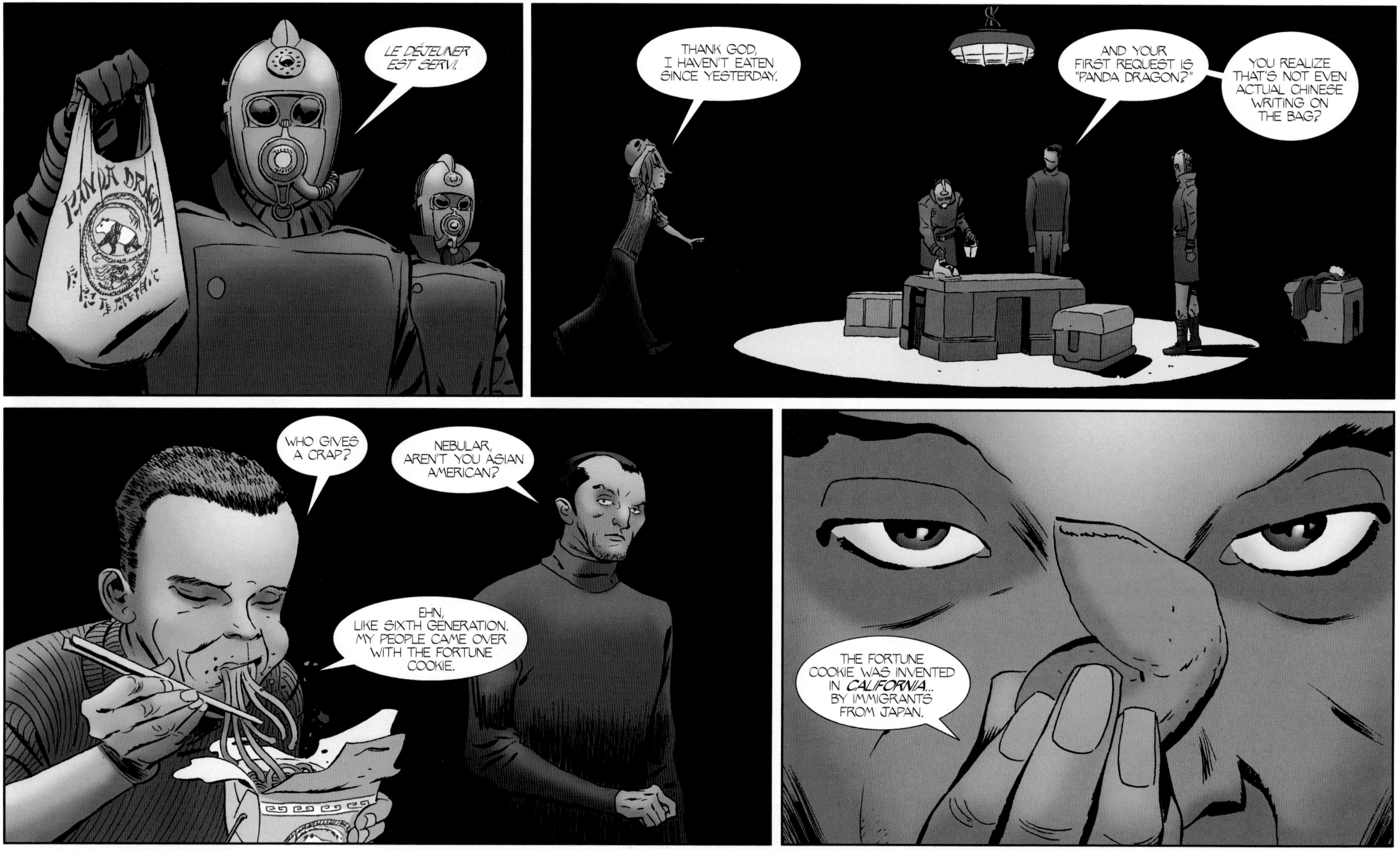
LE DÉJEUNER EST SERVI.
PANDA DRAGON
THANK GOD, I HAVEN'T EATEN SINCE YESTERDAY.
AND YOUR FIRST REQUEST IS "PANDA DRAGON?"
YOU REALIZE THAT'S NOT EVEN ACTUAL CHINESE WRITING ON THE BAG?
WHO GIVES A CRAP?
NEBULAR, AREN'T YOU ASIAN AMERICAN?
EHN, LIKE SIXTH GENERATION. MY PEOPLE CAME OVER WITH THE FORTUNE COOKIE.
THE FORTUNE COOKIE WAS INVENTED IN CALIFORNIA... BY IMMIGRANTS FROM JAPAN.

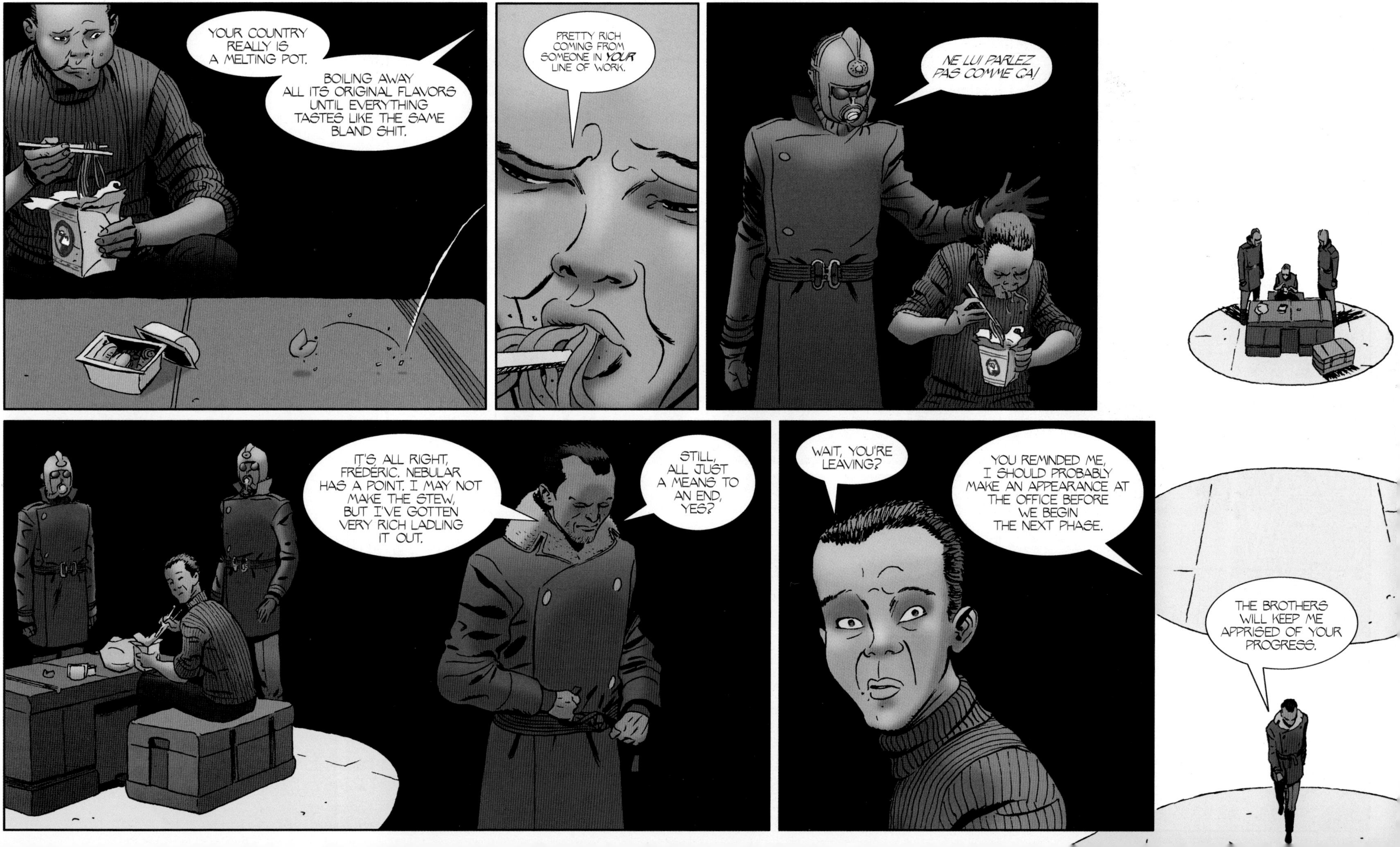
YOUR COUNTRY REALLY IS A MELTING POT.
BOILING AWAY ALL ITS ORIGINAL FLAVORS UNTIL EVERYTHING TASTES LIKE THE SAME BLAND SHIT.
PRETTY RICH COMING FROM SOMEONE IN *YOUR* LINE OF WORK.
NE LUI PARLEZ PAS COMME ÇA!
IT'S ALL RIGHT, FRÉDÉRIC. NEBULAR HAS A POINT. I MAY NOT MAKE THE STEW, BUT I'VE GOTTEN VERY RICH LADLING IT OUT.
STILL, ALL JUST A MEANS TO AN END, YES?
WAIT, YOU'RE LEAVING?
YOU REMINDED ME, I SHOULD PROBABLY MAKE AN APPEARANCE AT THE OFFICE BEFORE WE BEGIN THE NEXT PHASE.
THE BROTHERS WILL KEEP ME APPRISED OF YOUR PROGRESS.

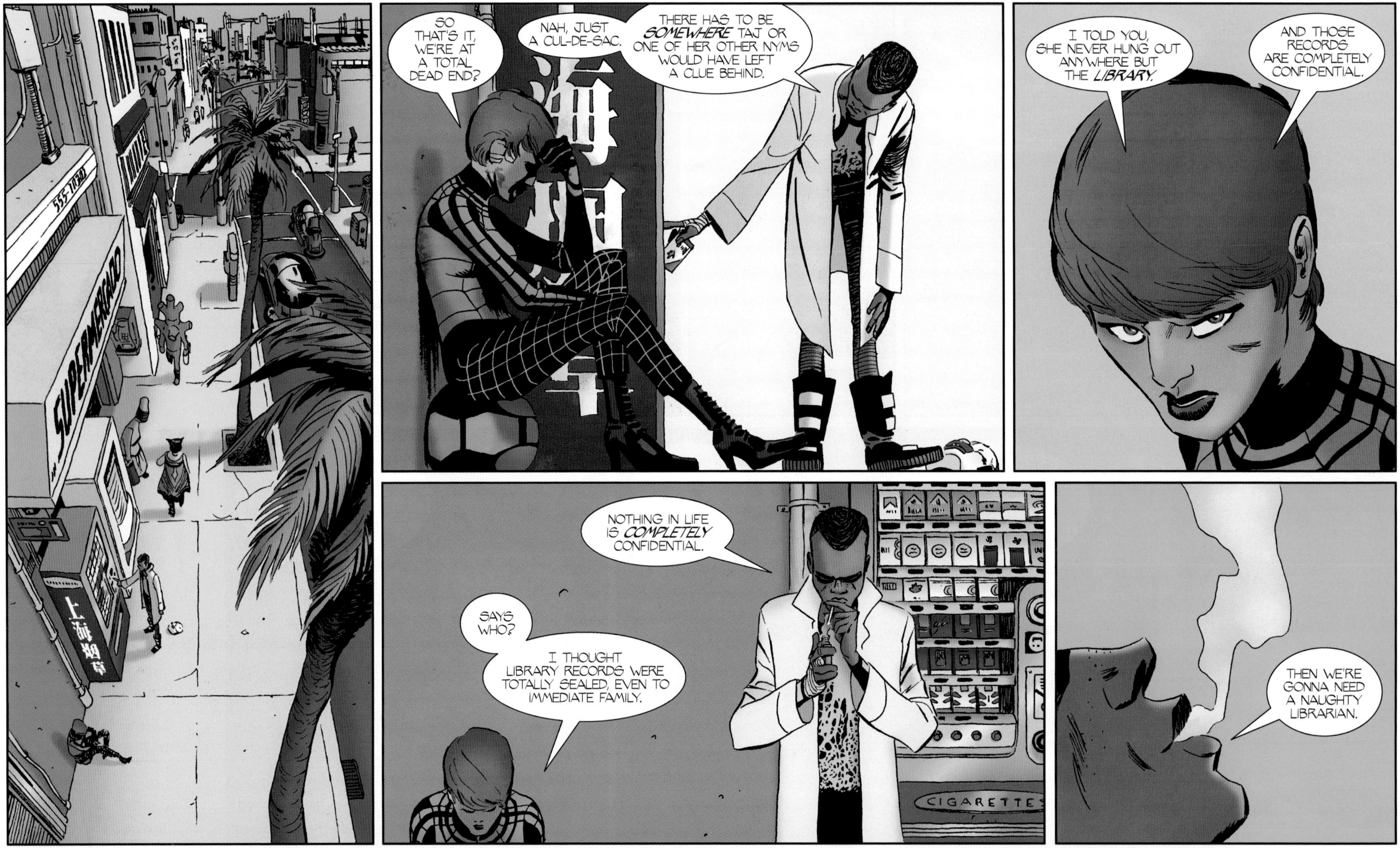
SUPERMERCADO
上海烟草
SO THAT'S IT, WE'RE AT A TOTAL DEAD END?
NAH, JUST A CUL-DE-SAC.
THERE HAS TO BE *SOMEWHERE* TAJ OR ONE OF HER OTHER NYMS WOULD HAVE LEFT A CLUE BEHIND.
I TOLD YOU, SHE NEVER HUNG OUT ANYWHERE BUT THE *LIBRARY.*
AND THOSE RECORDS ARE COMPLETELY CONFIDENTIAL.
NOTHING IN LIFE IS *COMPLETELY* CONFIDENTIAL.
SAYS WHO?
I THOUGHT LIBRARY RECORDS WERE TOTALLY SEALED, EVEN TO IMMEDIATE FAMILY.
CIGARETTES
THEN WE'RE GONNA NEED A NAUGHTY LIBRARIAN.

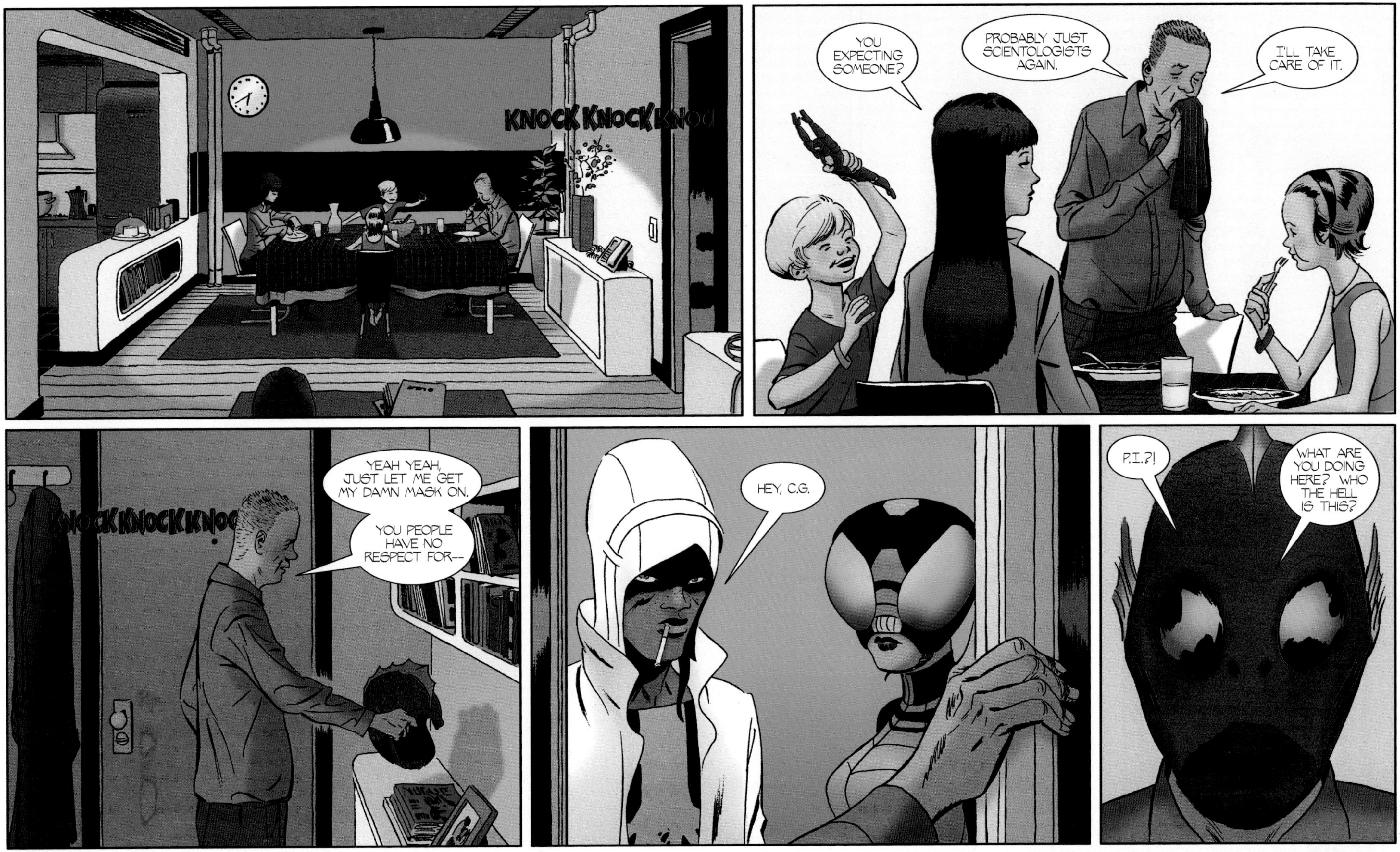
KNOCK KNOCK KNOC
YOU EXPECTING SOMEONE?
PROBABLY JUST SCIENTOLOGISTS AGAIN.
I'LL TAKE CARE OF IT.
KNOCK KNOCK KNOC
YEAH YEAH, JUST LET ME GET MY DAMN MASK ON.
YOU PEOPLE HAVE NO RESPECT FOR--
HEY, C.G.
P.I.?!
WHAT ARE YOU DOING HERE? WHO THE HELL IS THIS?

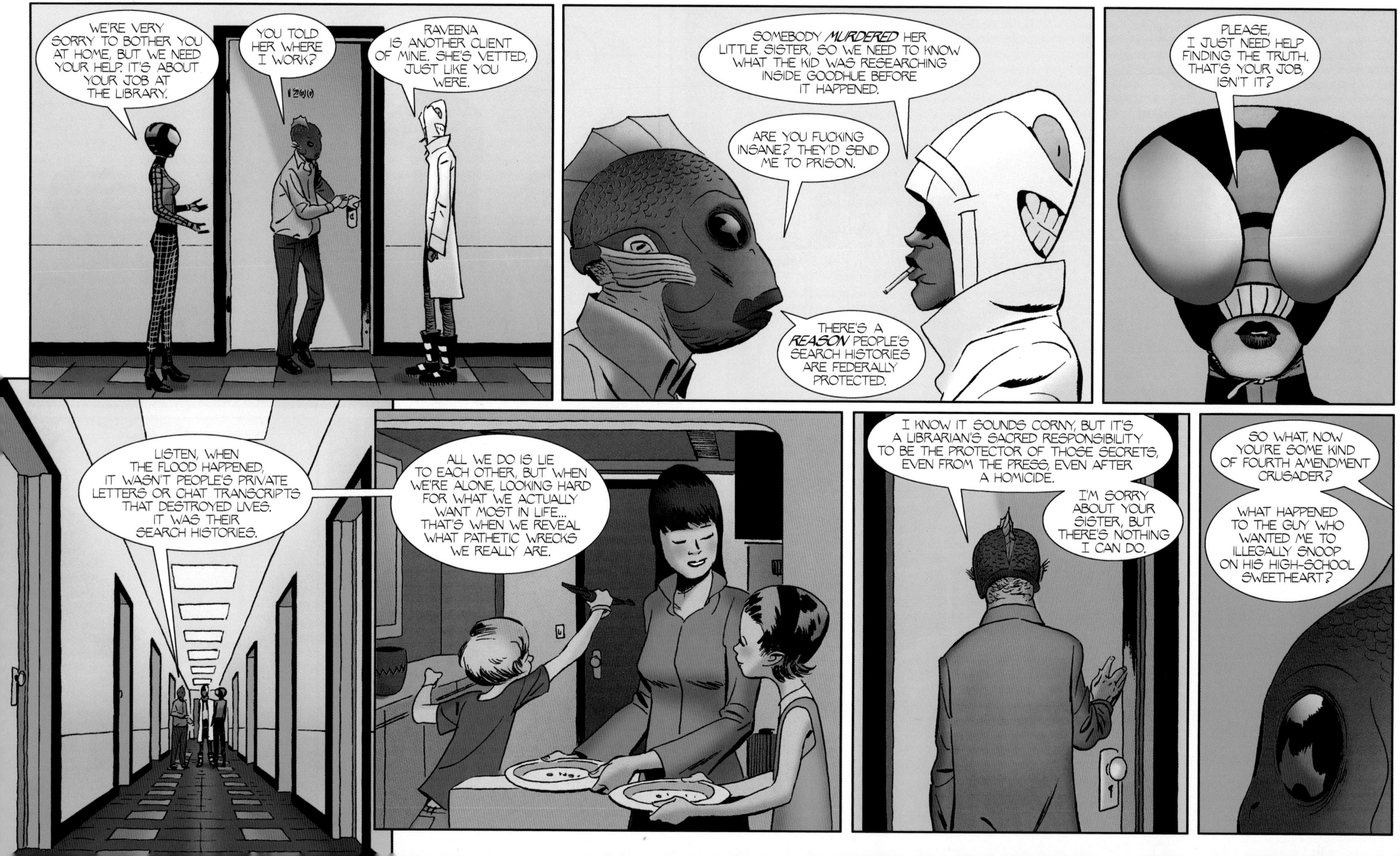
WE'RE VERY SORRY TO BOTHER YOU AT HOME, BUT WE NEED YOUR HELP. IT'S ABOUT YOUR JOB AT THE LIBRARY.
YOU TOLD HER WHERE I WORK?
RAVEENA IS ANOTHER CLIENT OF MINE. SHE'S VETTED, JUST LIKE YOU WERE.
SOMEBODY *MURDERED* HER LITTLE SISTER, SO WE NEED TO KNOW WHAT THE KID WAS RESEARCHING INSIDE GOODHUE BEFORE IT HAPPENED.
ARE YOU FUCKING INSANE? THEY'D SEND ME TO PRISON.
THERE'S A *REASON* PEOPLE'S SEARCH HISTORIES ARE FEDERALLY PROTECTED.
PLEASE, I JUST NEED HELP FINDING THE TRUTH. THAT'S YOUR JOB, ISN'T IT?
LISTEN, WHEN THE FLOOD HAPPENED, IT WASN'T PEOPLE'S PRIVATE LETTERS OR CHAT TRANSCRIPTS THAT DESTROYED LIVES. IT WAS THEIR SEARCH HISTORIES.
ALL WE DO IS LIE TO EACH OTHER, BUT WHEN WE'RE ALONE, LOOKING HARD FOR WHAT WE ACTUALLY WANT MOST IN LIFE... THAT'S WHEN WE REVEAL WHAT PATHETIC WRECKS WE REALLY ARE.
I KNOW IT SOUNDS CORNY, BUT IT'S A LIBRARIAN'S SACRED RESPONSIBILITY TO BE THE PROTECTOR OF THOSE SECRETS, EVEN FROM THE PRESS, EVEN AFTER A HOMICIDE.
I'M SORRY ABOUT YOUR SISTER, BUT THERE'S NOTHING I CAN DO.
SO WHAT, NOW YOU'RE SOME KIND OF FOURTH AMENDMENT CRUSADER?
WHAT HAPPENED TO THE GUY WHO WANTED ME TO ILLEGALLY SNOOP ON HIS HIGH-SCHOOL SWEETHEART?

THAT'S DIFFERENT AND YOU KNOW IT!

IS THAT WHAT THIS IS? I PAY YOU GOOD MONEY, AND NOW YOU'RE *BLACKMAILING* ME?

TELL IT TO YOUR ETHICS BOARD.

HOLD ON, YOU'RE STILL CRUSHED OUT ON AN OLD GIRLFRIEND? THAT IS SO *ROMANTIC*.

IT IS?

OH, TOTALLY.

THERE ARE JUST TONS OF GUYS FROM MY PAST I WISH HAD THE BALLS TO, YOU KNOW, SEEK ME OUT.

AND IF YOU HELP US JUST THIS ONCE, I PROMISE TO GIVE YOU EVERY LAST DETAIL ABOUT YOUR EX... HOME PHONE, ADDRESS, WHATEVER YOU NEED.

THE GUARD AT THE GATE HAS SEEN ME DRIVE IN AFTER HOURS BEFORE.

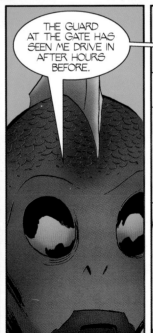

BUT JUST TO BE SAFE, YOU TWO SHOULD PROBABLY RIDE IN MY TRUNK.

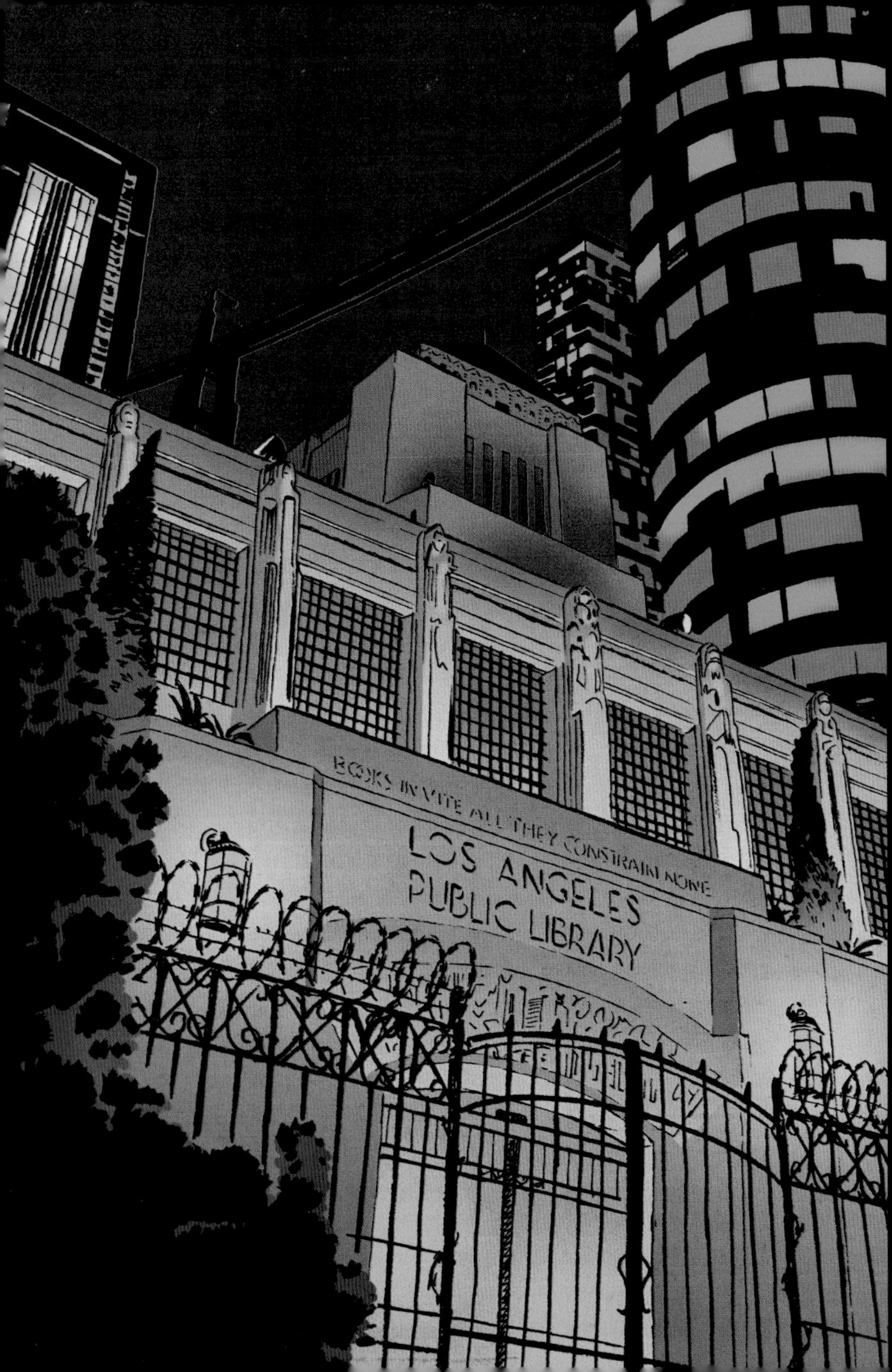
BOOKS INVITE ALL THEY CONSTRAIN NONE
LOS ANGELES
PUBLIC LIBRARY

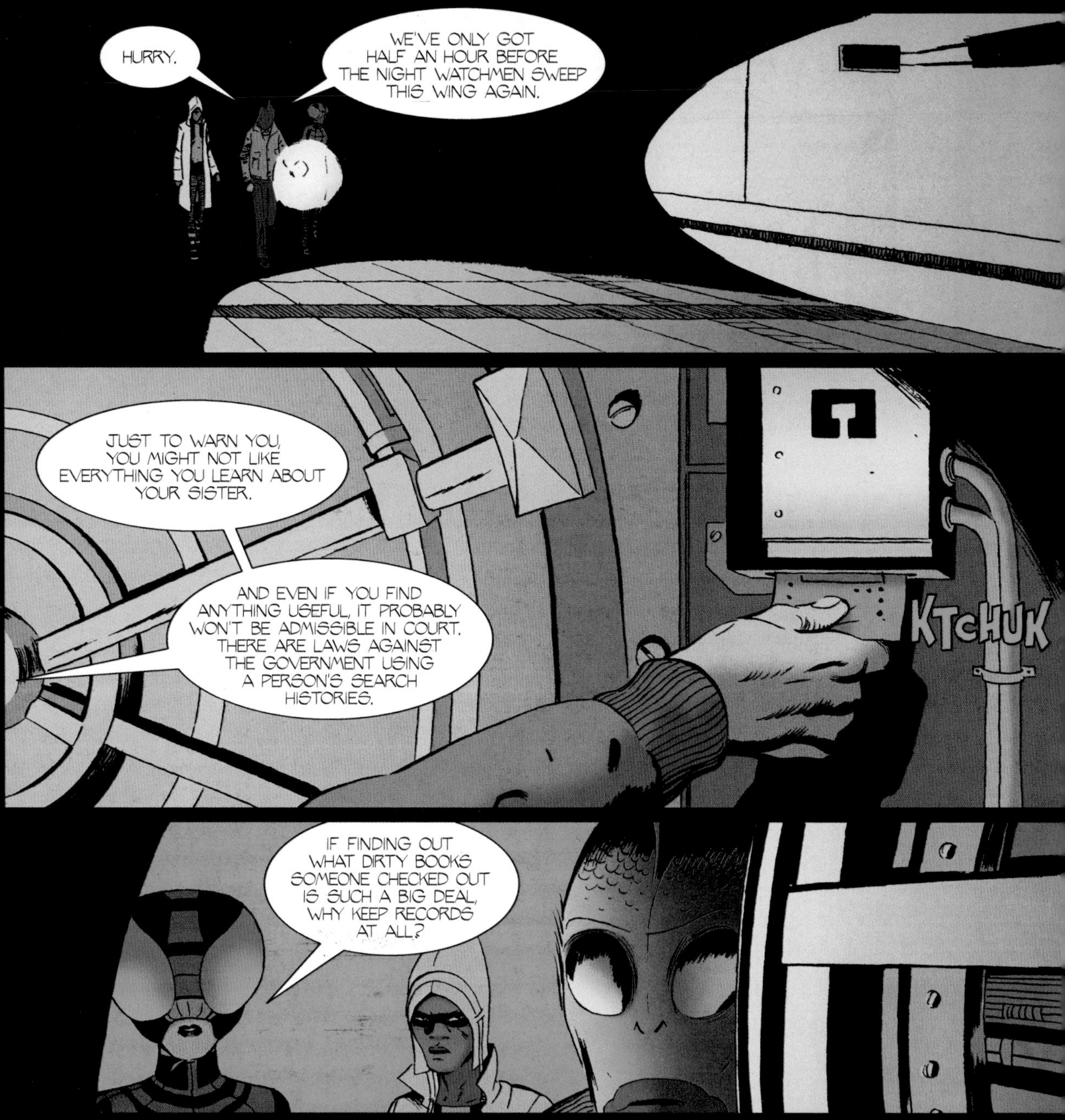
HURRY.
WE'VE ONLY GOT HALF AN HOUR BEFORE THE NIGHT WATCHMEN SWEEP THIS WING AGAIN.
JUST TO WARN YOU, YOU MIGHT NOT LIKE EVERYTHING YOU LEARN ABOUT YOUR SISTER.
AND EVEN IF YOU FIND ANYTHING USEFUL, IT PROBABLY WON'T BE ADMISSIBLE IN COURT. THERE ARE LAWS AGAINST THE GOVERNMENT USING A PERSON'S SEARCH HISTORIES.
KTCHUK
IF FINDING OUT WHAT DIRTY BOOKS SOMEONE CHECKED OUT IS SUCH A BIG DEAL, WHY KEEP RECORDS AT ALL?

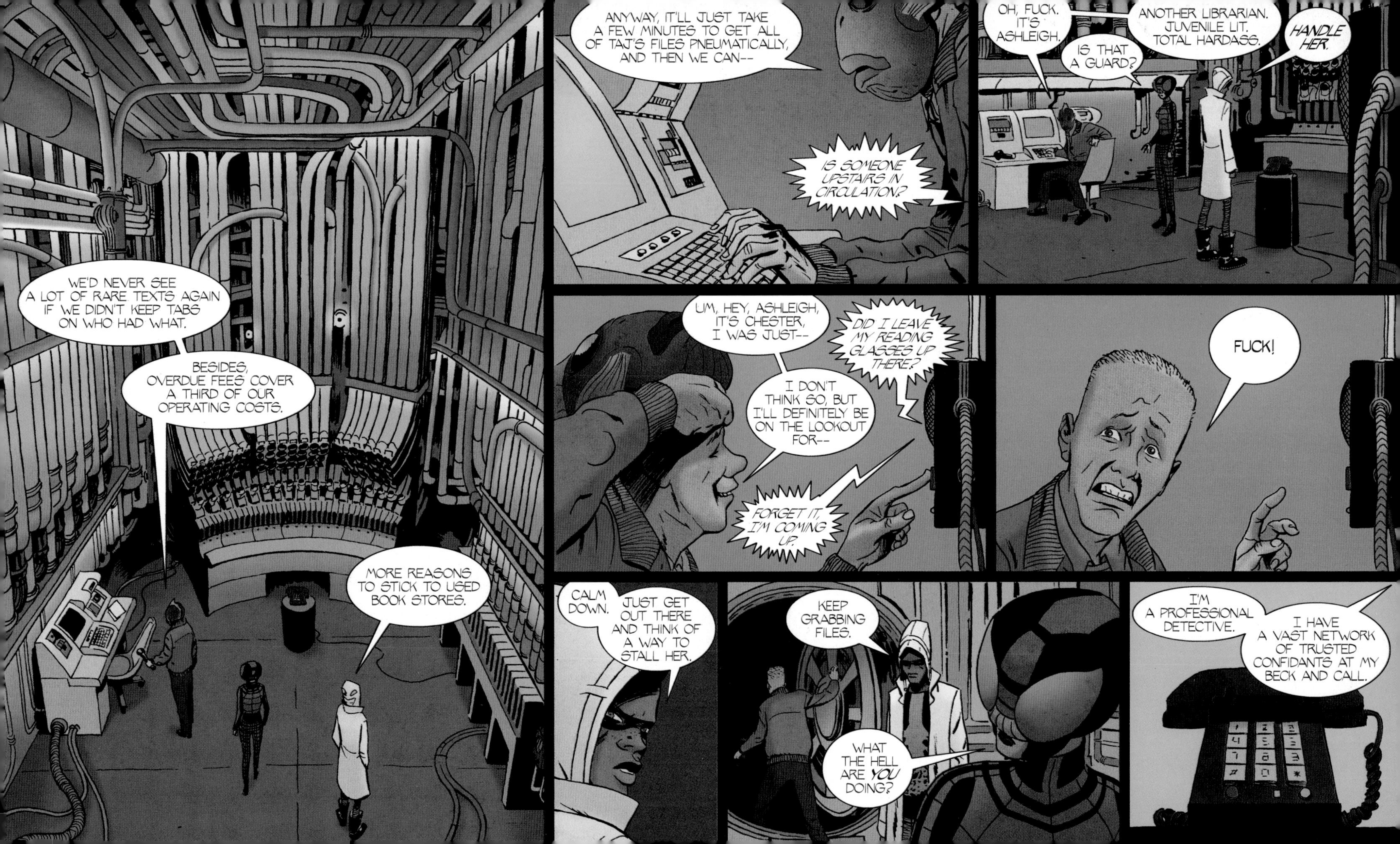
WE'D NEVER SEE A LOT OF RARE TEXTS AGAIN IF WE DIDN'T KEEP TABS ON WHO HAD WHAT.
BESIDES, OVERDUE FEES COVER A THIRD OF OUR OPERATING COSTS.
MORE REASONS TO STICK TO USED BOOK STORES.
ANYWAY, IT'LL JUST TAKE A FEW MINUTES TO GET ALL OF TAJ'S FILES PNEUMATICALLY, AND THEN WE CAN--
IS SOMEONE UPSTAIRS IN CIRCULATION?
OH, FUCK. IT'S ASHLEIGH.
IS THAT A GUARD?
ANOTHER LIBRARIAN. JUVENILE LIT. TOTAL HARDASS.
HANDLE HER.
UM, HEY, ASHLEIGH, IT'S CHESTER, I WAS JUST--
DID I LEAVE MY READING GLASSES UP THERE?
I DON'T THINK SO, BUT I'LL DEFINITELY BE ON THE LOOKOUT FOR--
FORGET IT, I'M COMING UP.
FUCK!
CALM DOWN.
JUST GET OUT THERE AND THINK OF A WAY TO STALL HER.
KEEP GRABBING FILES.
WHAT THE HELL ARE YOU DOING?
I'M A PROFESSIONAL DETECTIVE.
I HAVE A VAST NETWORK OF TRUSTED CONFIDANTS AT MY BECK AND CALL.

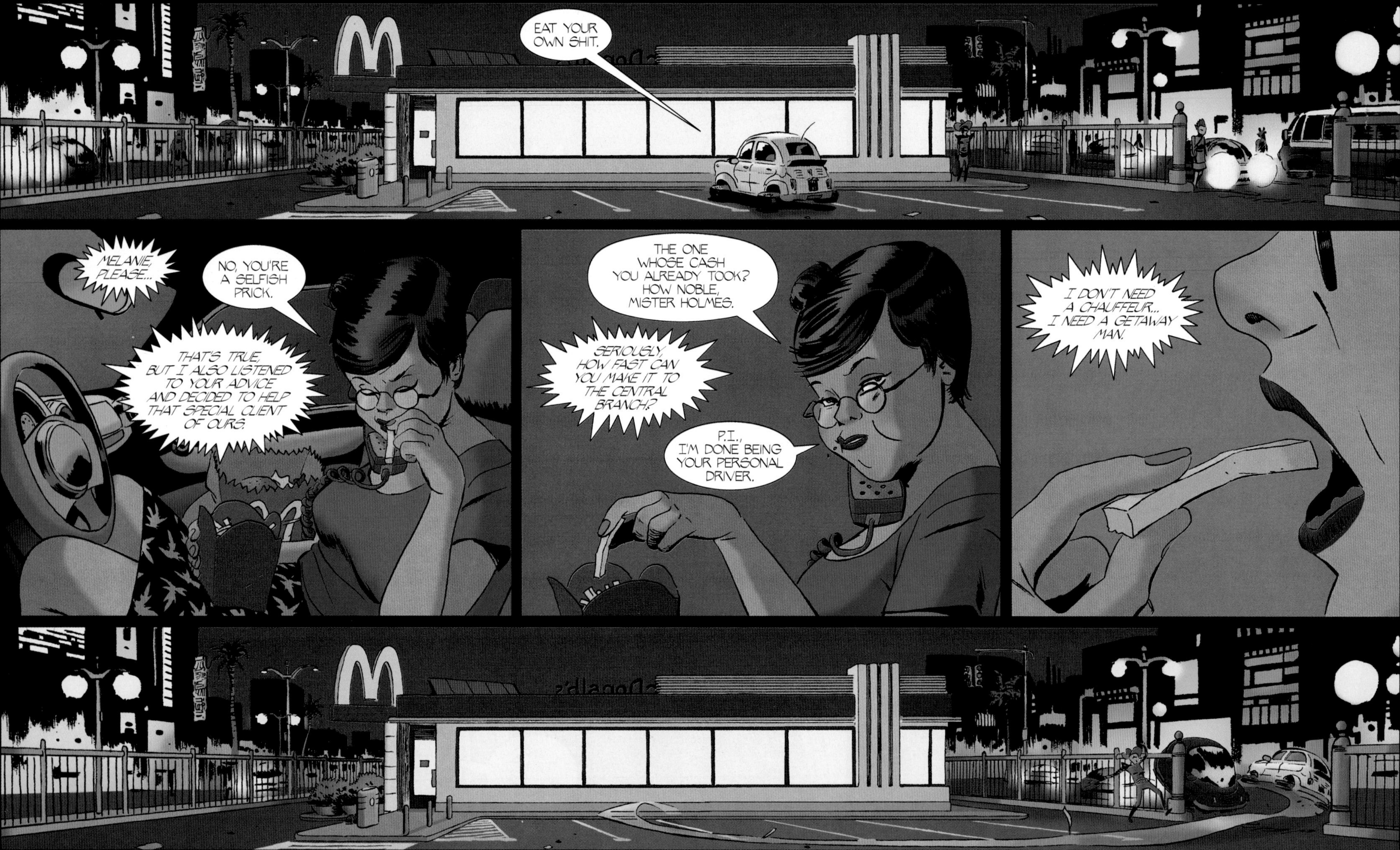
EAT YOUR OWN SHIT.
MELANIE, PLEASE...
NO, YOU'RE A SELFISH PRICK.
THAT'S TRUE, BUT I ALSO LISTENED TO YOUR ADVICE AND DECIDED TO HELP THAT SPECIAL CLIENT OF OURS.
THE ONE WHOSE CASH YOU ALREADY TOOK? HOW NOBLE, MISTER HOLMES.
SERIOUSLY, HOW FAST CAN YOU MAKE IT TO THE CENTRAL BRANCH?
P.I., I'M DONE BEING YOUR PERSONAL DRIVER.
I DON'T NEED A CHAUFFEUR... I NEED A GETAWAY MAN.

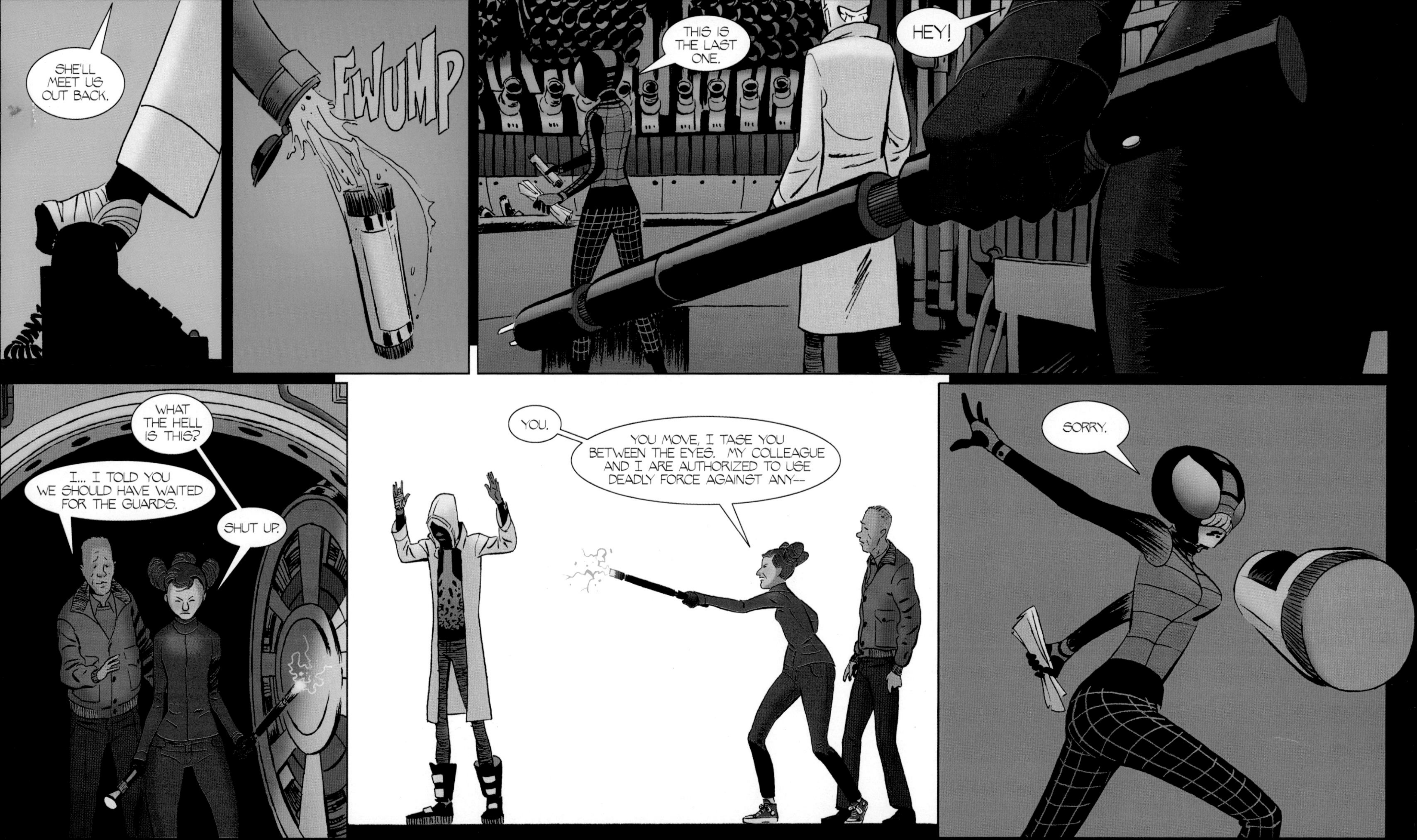

SHE'LL MEET US OUT BACK.
FWUMP
THIS IS THE LAST ONE.
HEY!
WHAT THE HELL IS THIS?
I... I TOLD YOU WE SHOULD HAVE WAITED FOR THE GUARDS.
SHUT UP.
YOU.
YOU MOVE, I TASE YOU BETWEEN THE EYES. MY COLLEAGUE AND I ARE AUTHORIZED TO USE DEADLY FORCE AGAINST ANY--
SORRY.

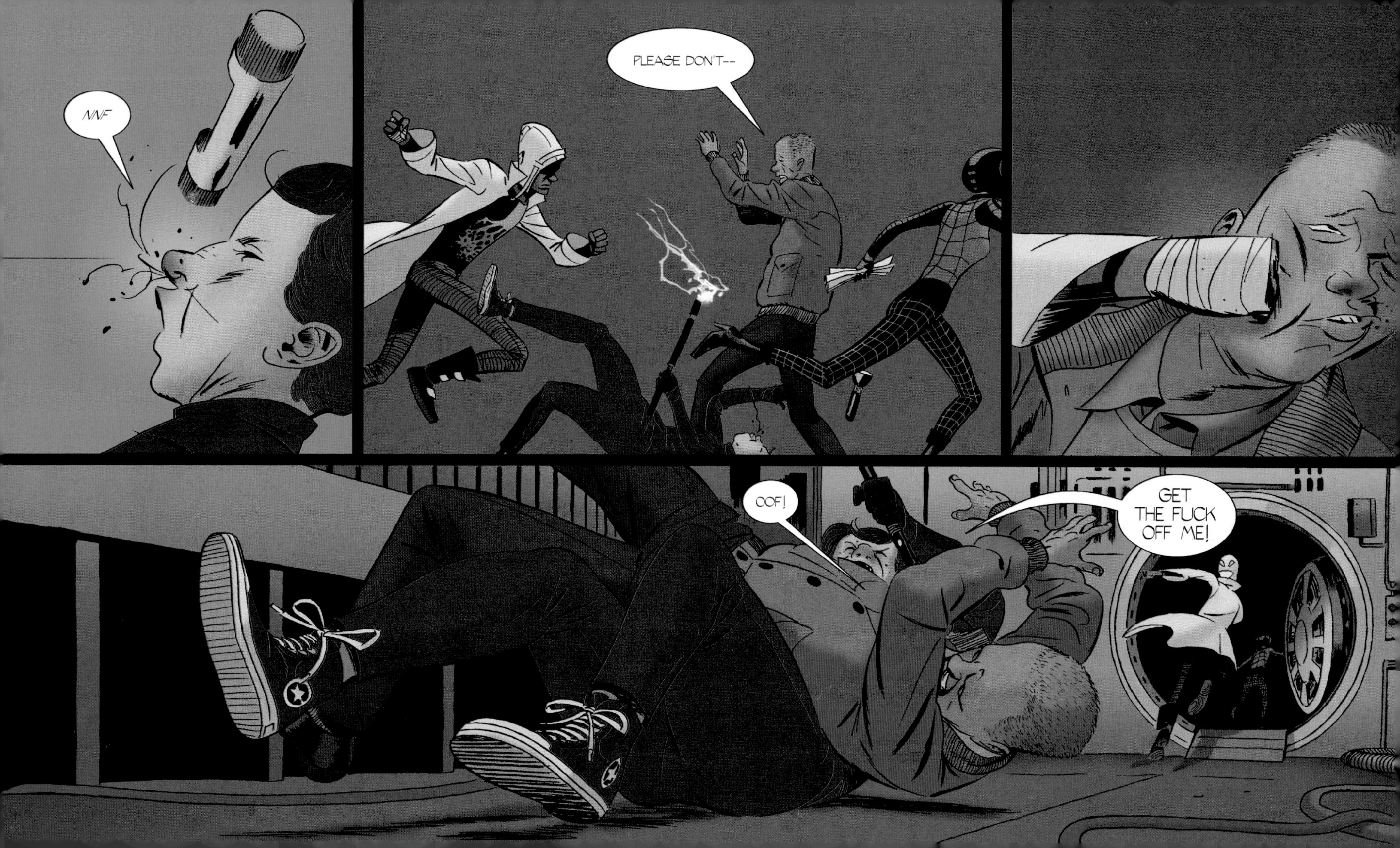
NNF
PLEASE DON'T--
OOF!
GET THE FUCK OFF ME!

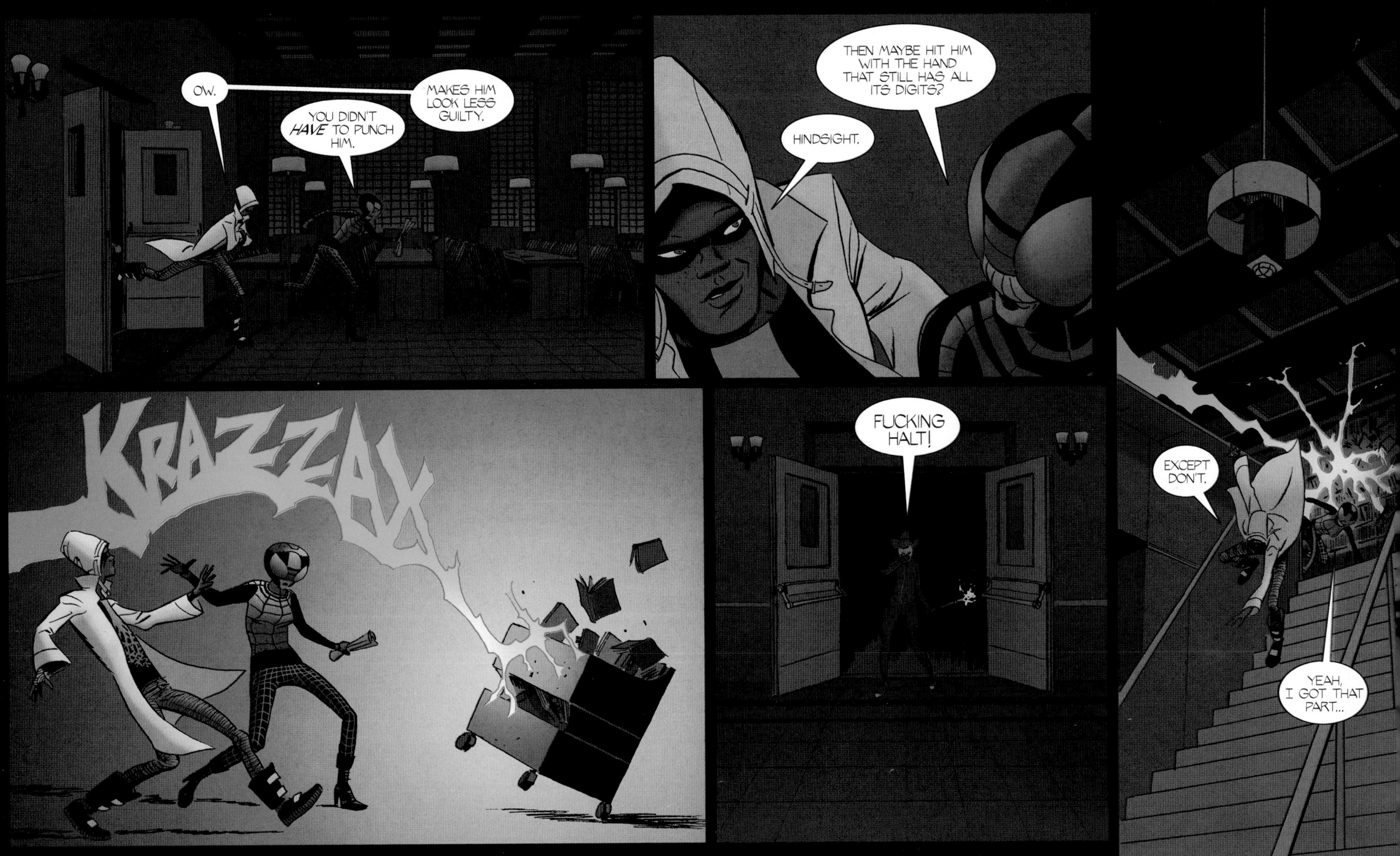
OW.
YOU DIDN'T HAVE TO PUNCH HIM.
MAKES HIM LOOK LESS GUILTY.
HINDSIGHT.
THEN MAYBE HIT HIM WITH THE HAND THAT STILL HAS ALL ITS DIGITS?
KRAZZAX
FUCKING HALT!
EXCEPT DON'T.
YEAH, I GOT THAT PART...

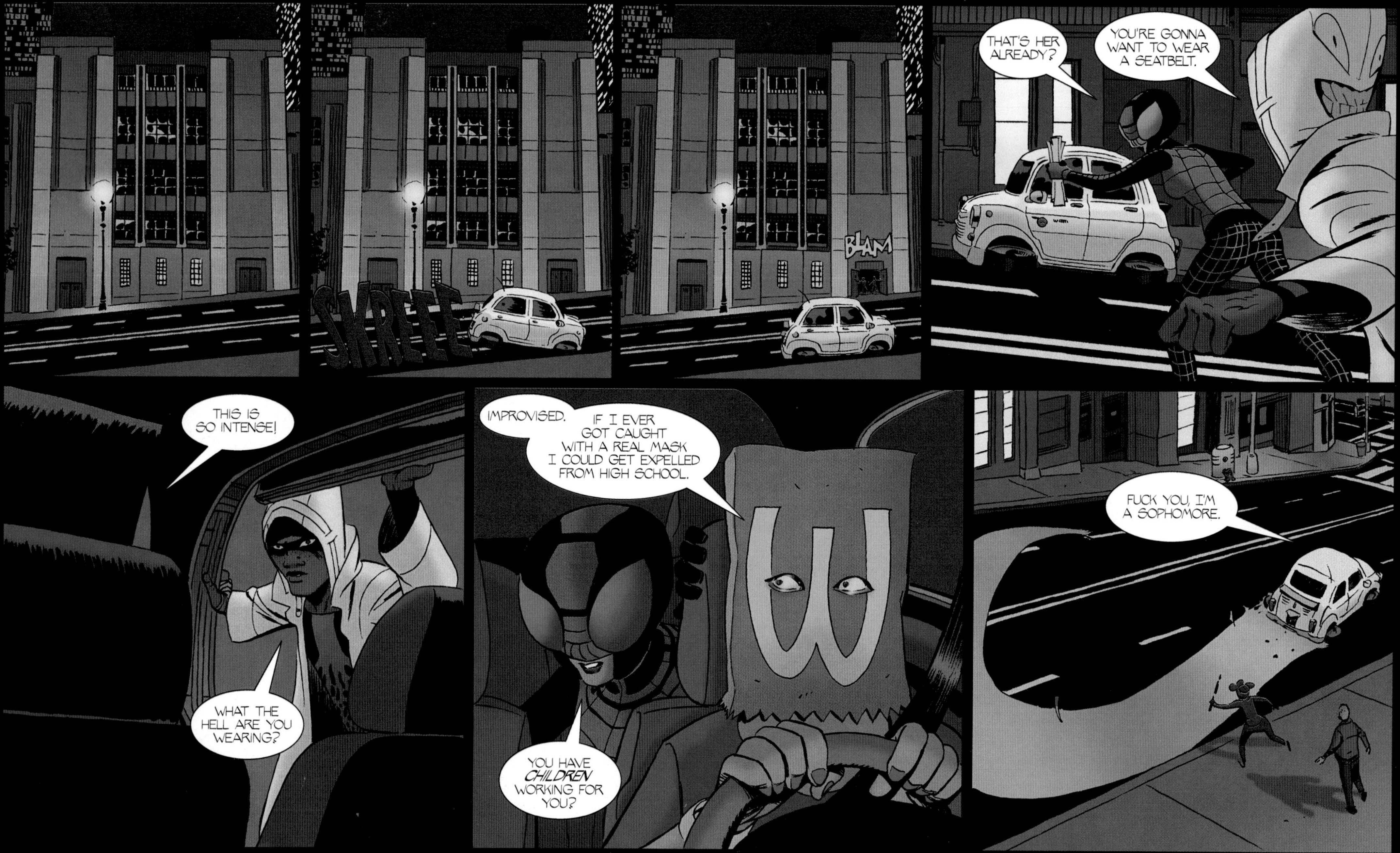
SKREEE
BLAM
THAT'S HER ALREADY?
YOU'RE GONNA WANT TO WEAR A SEATBELT.
THIS IS SO INTENSE!
WHAT THE HELL ARE YOU WEARING?
IMPROVISED.
IF I EVER GOT CAUGHT WITH A REAL MASK I COULD GET EXPELLED FROM HIGH SCHOOL.
YOU HAVE *CHILDREN* WORKING FOR YOU?
FUCK YOU, I'M A SOPHOMORE.

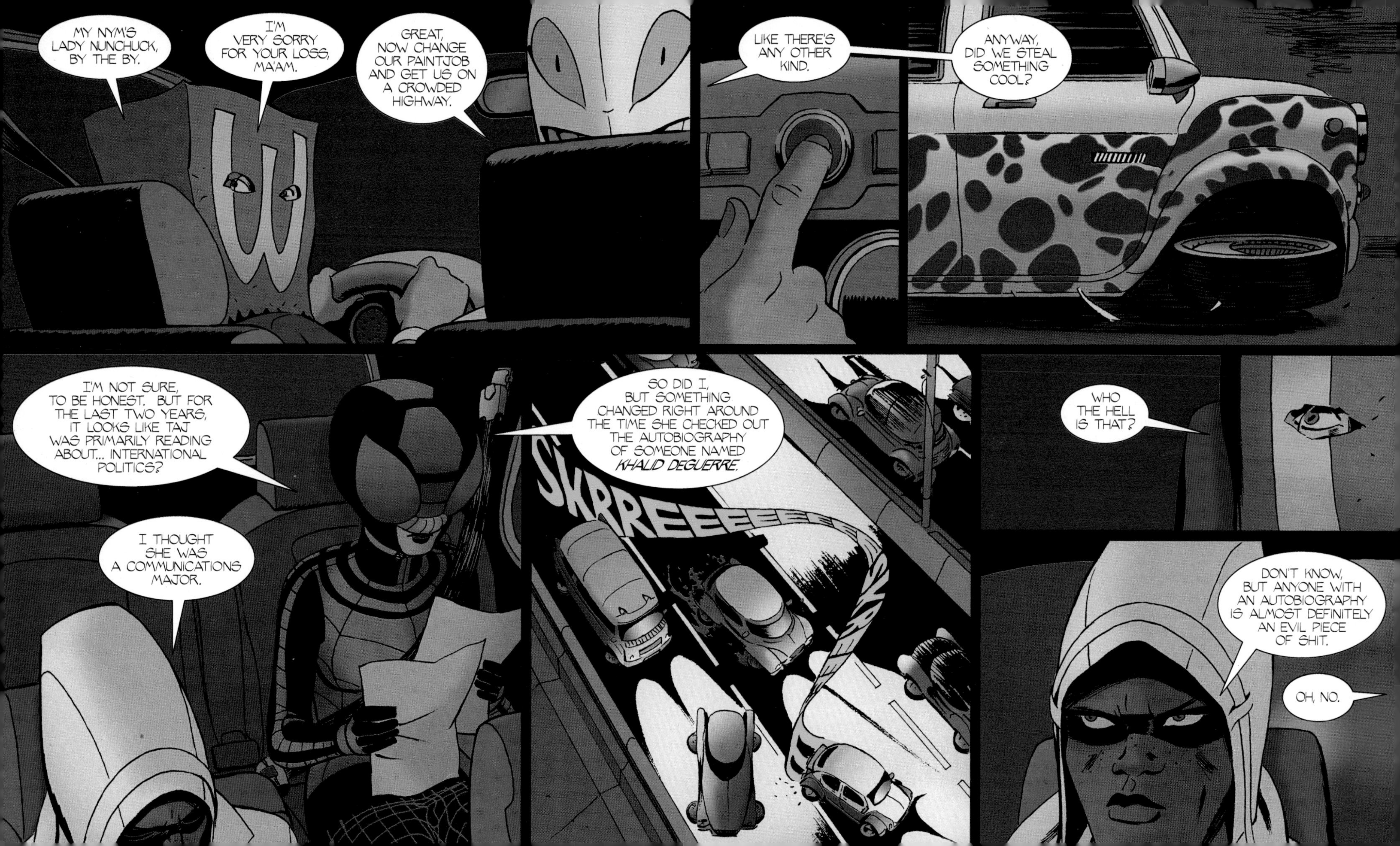

MY NYM'S LADY NUNCHUCK, BY THE BY.
I'M VERY SORRY FOR YOUR LOSS, MA'AM.
GREAT, NOW CHANGE OUR PAINTJOB AND GET US ON A CROWDED HIGHWAY.
LIKE THERE'S ANY OTHER KIND.
ANYWAY, DID WE STEAL SOMETHING COOL?
I'M NOT SURE, TO BE HONEST. BUT FOR THE LAST TWO YEARS, IT LOOKS LIKE TAJ WAS PRIMARILY READING ABOUT... INTERNATIONAL POLITICS?
I THOUGHT SHE WAS A COMMUNICATIONS MAJOR.
SO DID I, BUT SOMETHING CHANGED RIGHT AROUND THE TIME SHE CHECKED OUT THE AUTOBIOGRAPHY OF SOMEONE NAMED *KHALID DEGUERRE.*
SKRREEEEEEEEEE
WHO THE HELL IS THAT?
DON'T KNOW, BUT ANYONE WITH AN AUTOBIOGRAPHY IS ALMOST DEFINITELY AN EVIL PIECE OF SHIT.
OH, NO.

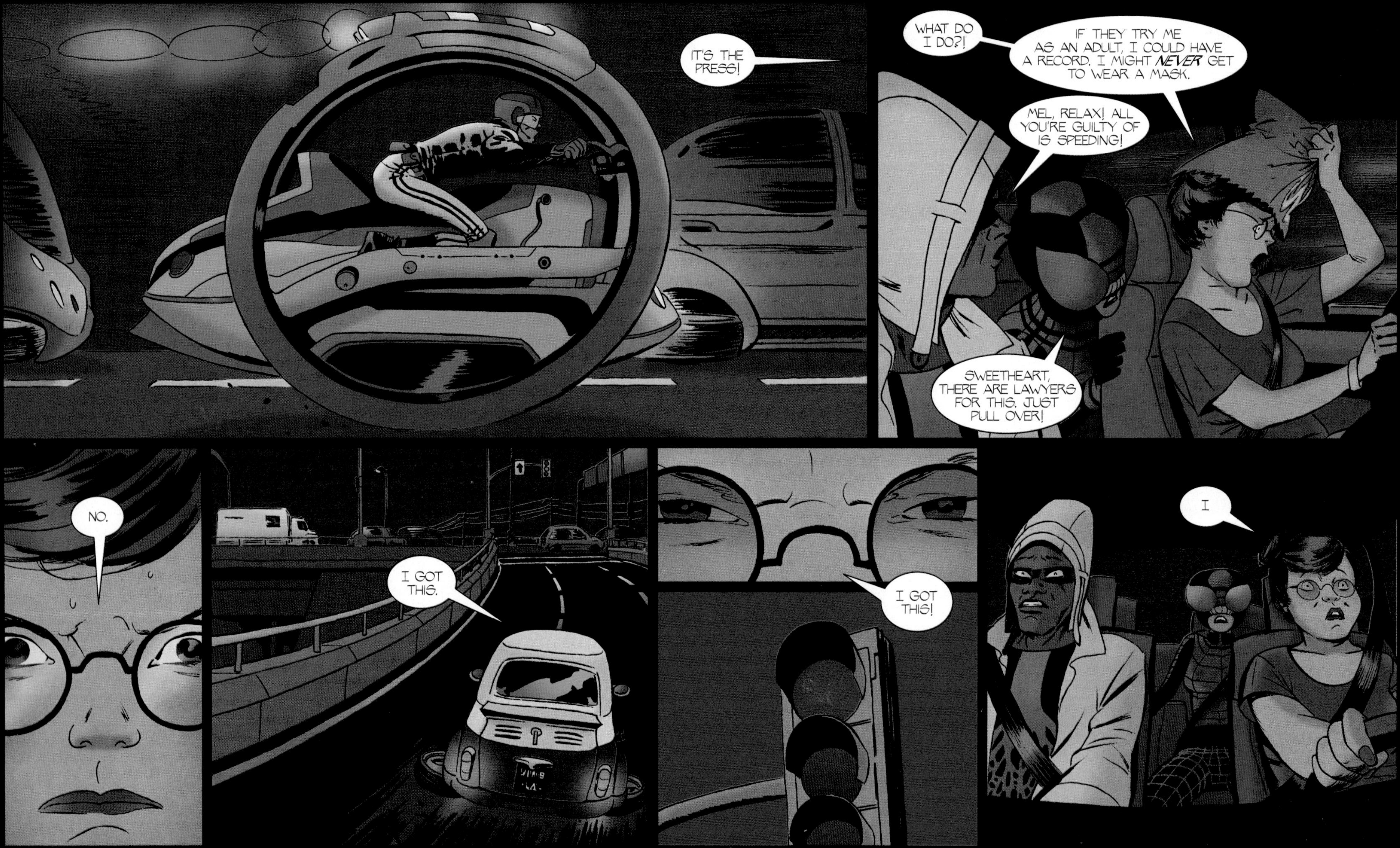
IT'S THE PRESS!
WHAT DO I DO?!
IF THEY TRY ME AS AN ADULT, I COULD HAVE A RECORD. I MIGHT *NEVER* GET TO WEAR A MASK.
MEL, RELAX! ALL YOU'RE GUILTY OF IS SPEEDING!
SWEETHEART, THERE ARE LAWYERS FOR THIS. JUST PULL OVER!
NO.
I GOT THIS.
I GOT THIS!
I

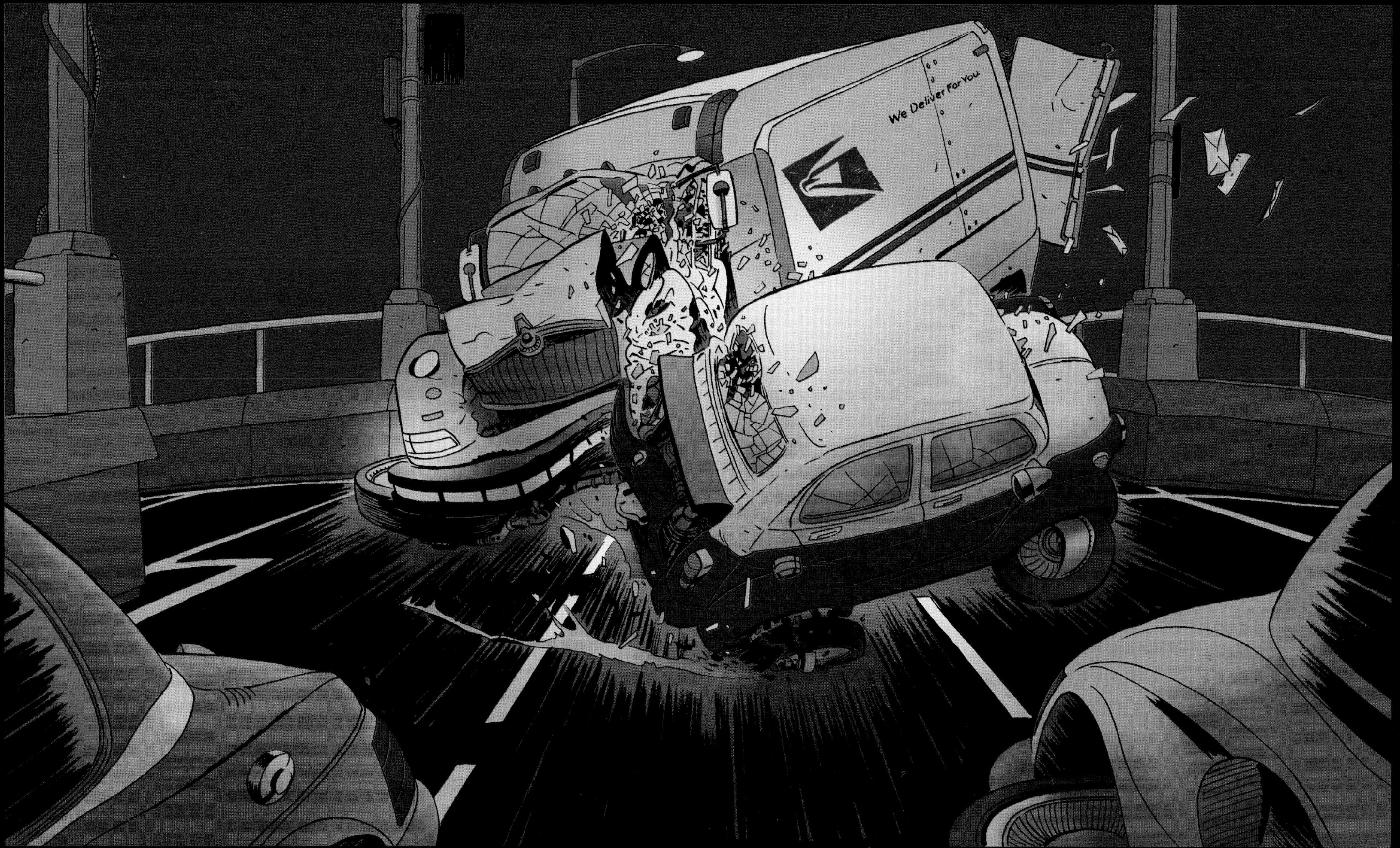
We Deliver For You.

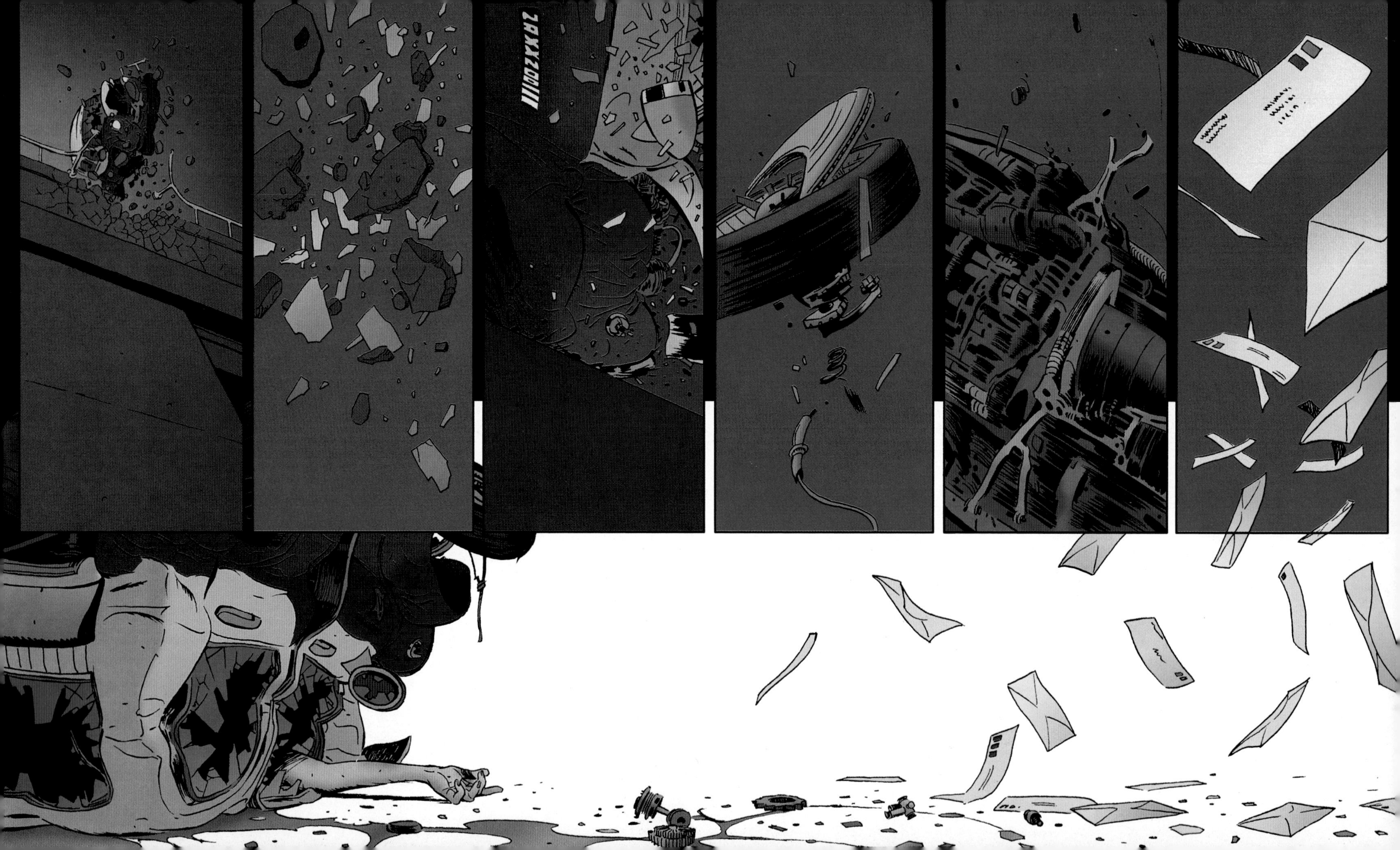

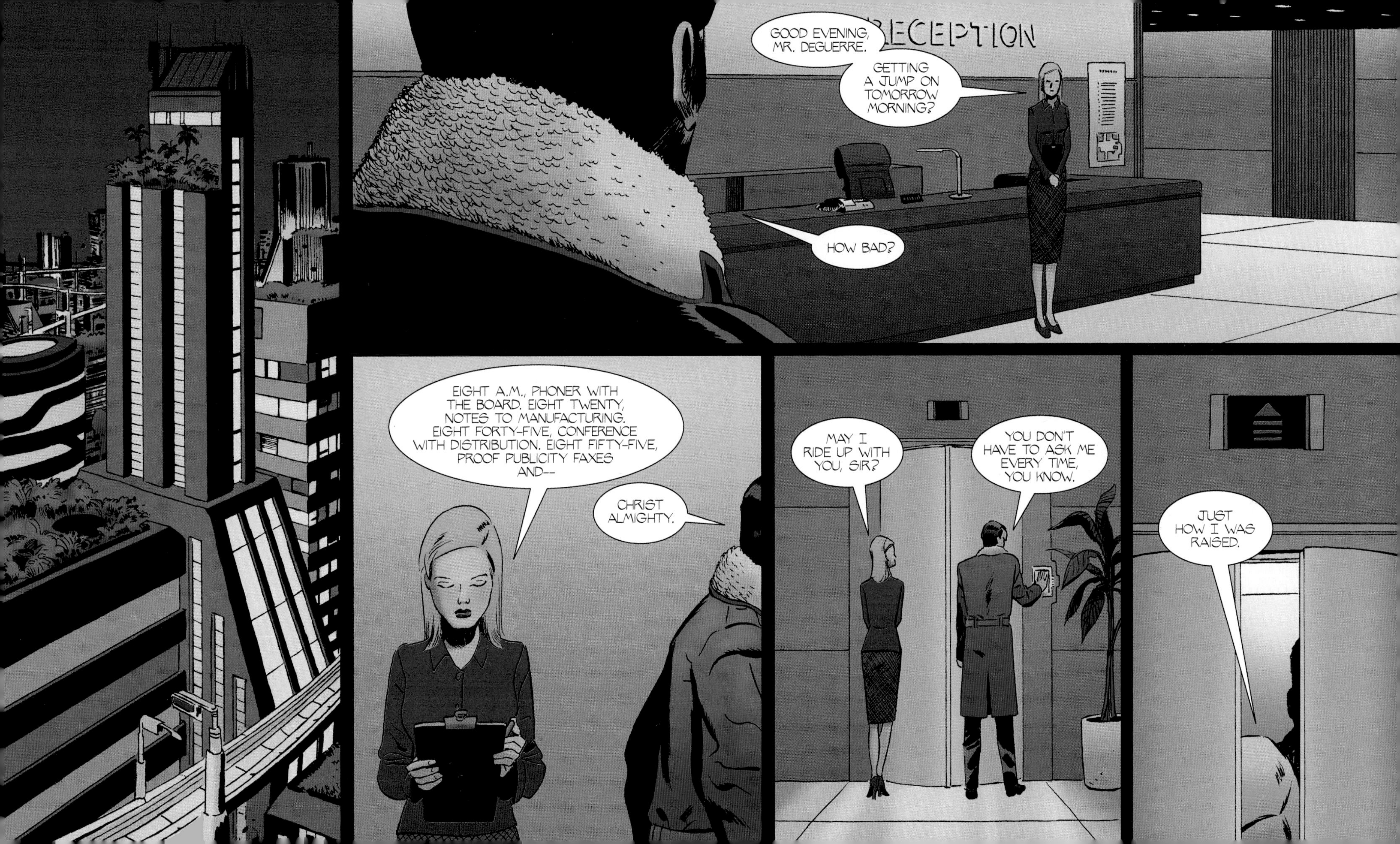
RECEPTION
GOOD EVENING, MR. DEGUERRE.
GETTING A JUMP ON TOMORROW MORNING?
HOW BAD?
EIGHT A.M., PHONER WITH THE BOARD. EIGHT TWENTY, NOTES TO MANUFACTURING. EIGHT FORTY-FIVE, CONFERENCE WITH DISTRIBUTION. EIGHT FIFTY-FIVE, PROOF PUBLICITY FAXES AND--
CHRIST ALMIGHTY.
MAY I RIDE UP WITH YOU, SIR?
YOU DON'T HAVE TO ASK ME EVERY TIME, YOU KNOW.
JUST HOW I WAS RAISED.

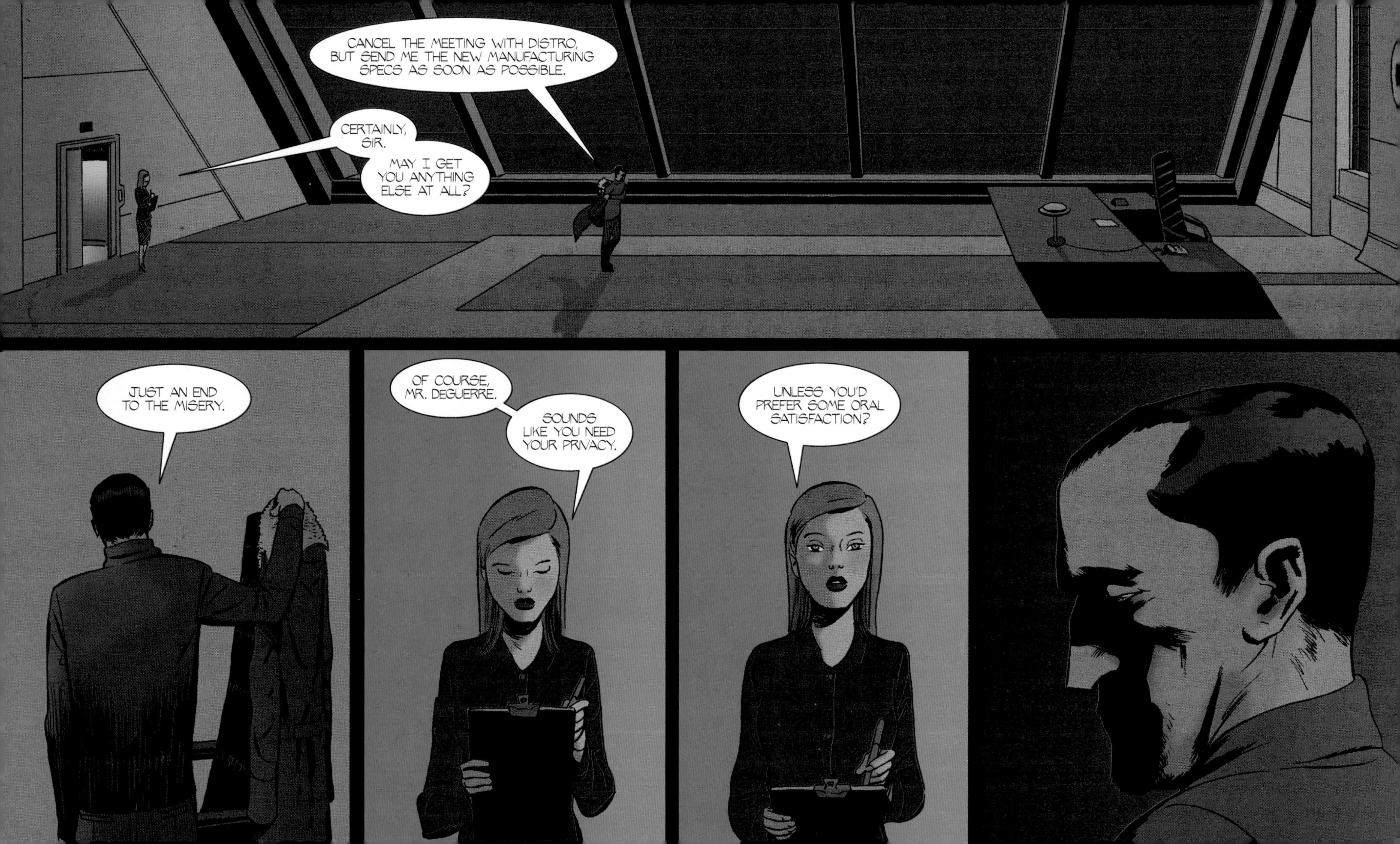

CANCEL THE MEETING WITH DISTRO, BUT SEND ME THE NEW MANUFACTURING SPECS AS SOON AS POSSIBLE.
CERTAINLY, SIR.
MAY I GET YOU ANYTHING ELSE AT ALL?
JUST AN END TO THE MISERY.
OF COURSE, MR. DEGUERRE.
SOUNDS LIKE YOU NEED YOUR PRIVACY.
UNLESS YOU'D PREFER SOME ORAL SATISFACTION?

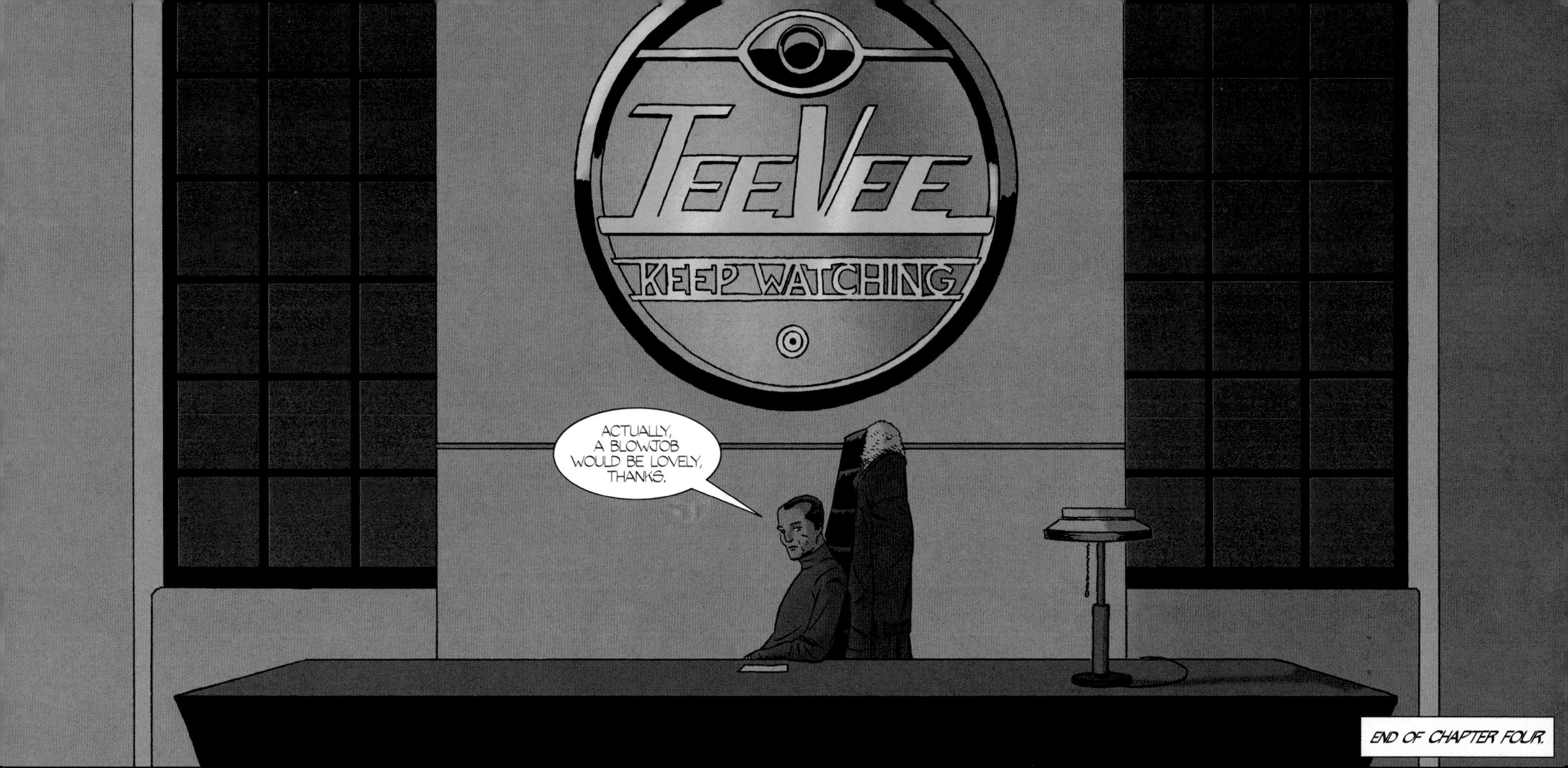
TEEVEE
KEEP WATCHING
ACTUALLY, A BLOWJOB WOULD BE LOVELY, THANKS.
END OF CHAPTER FOUR.

THE PRIVATE EYE

BRIAN K. VAUGHAN MARCOS MARTIN

WITH

MUNTSA VICENTE

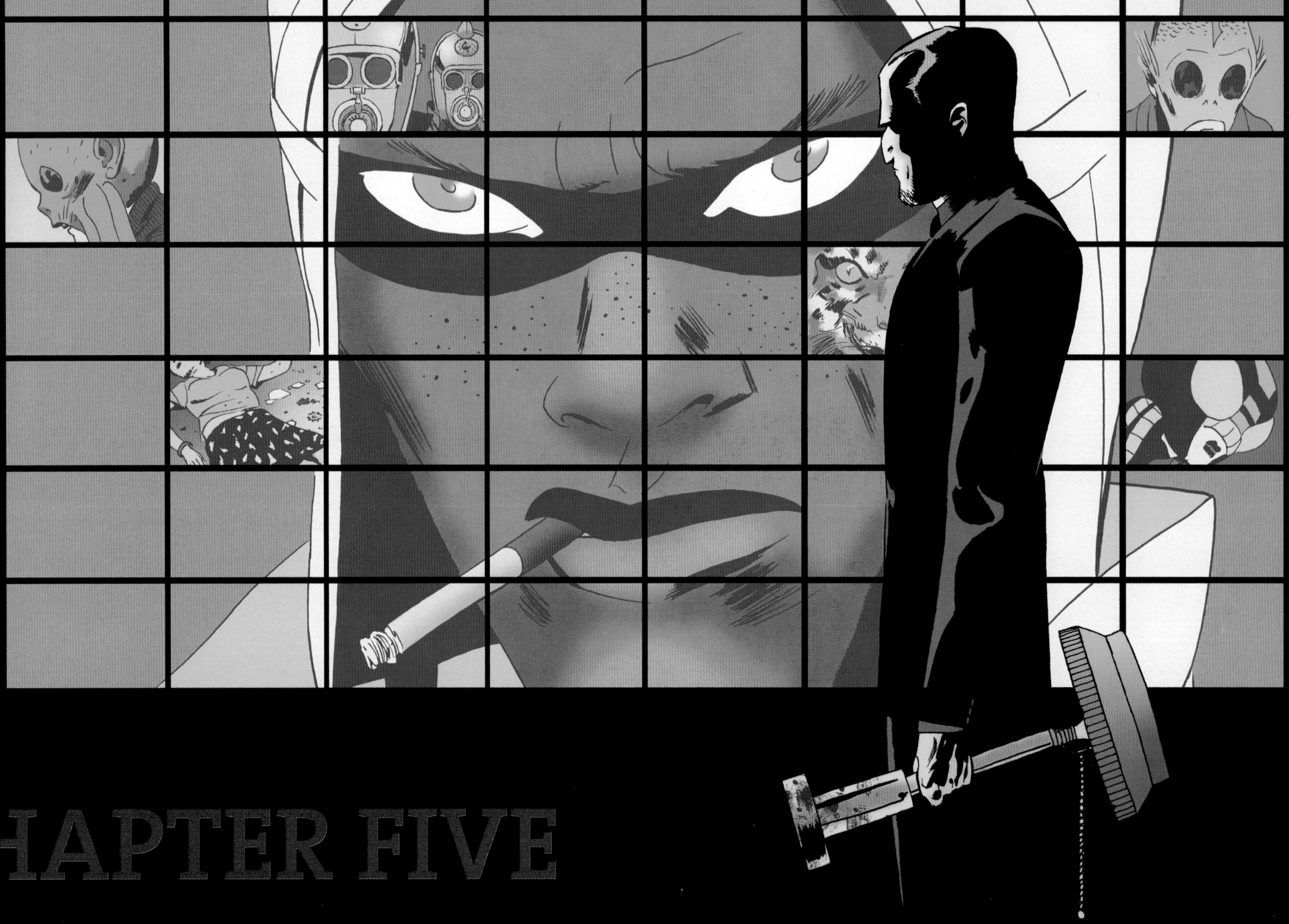

CHAPTER FIVE

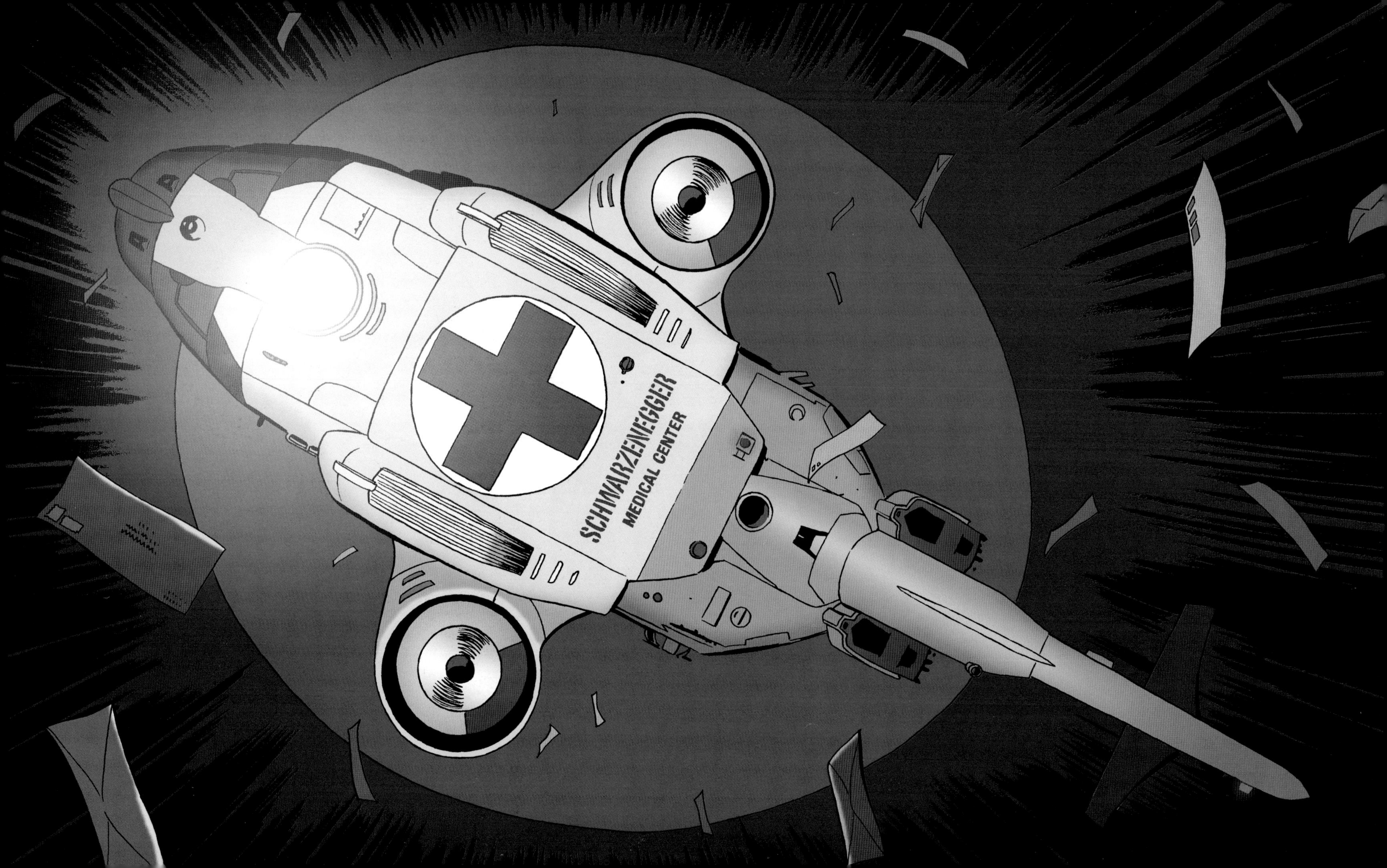

SCHWARZENEGGER
MEDICAL CENTER

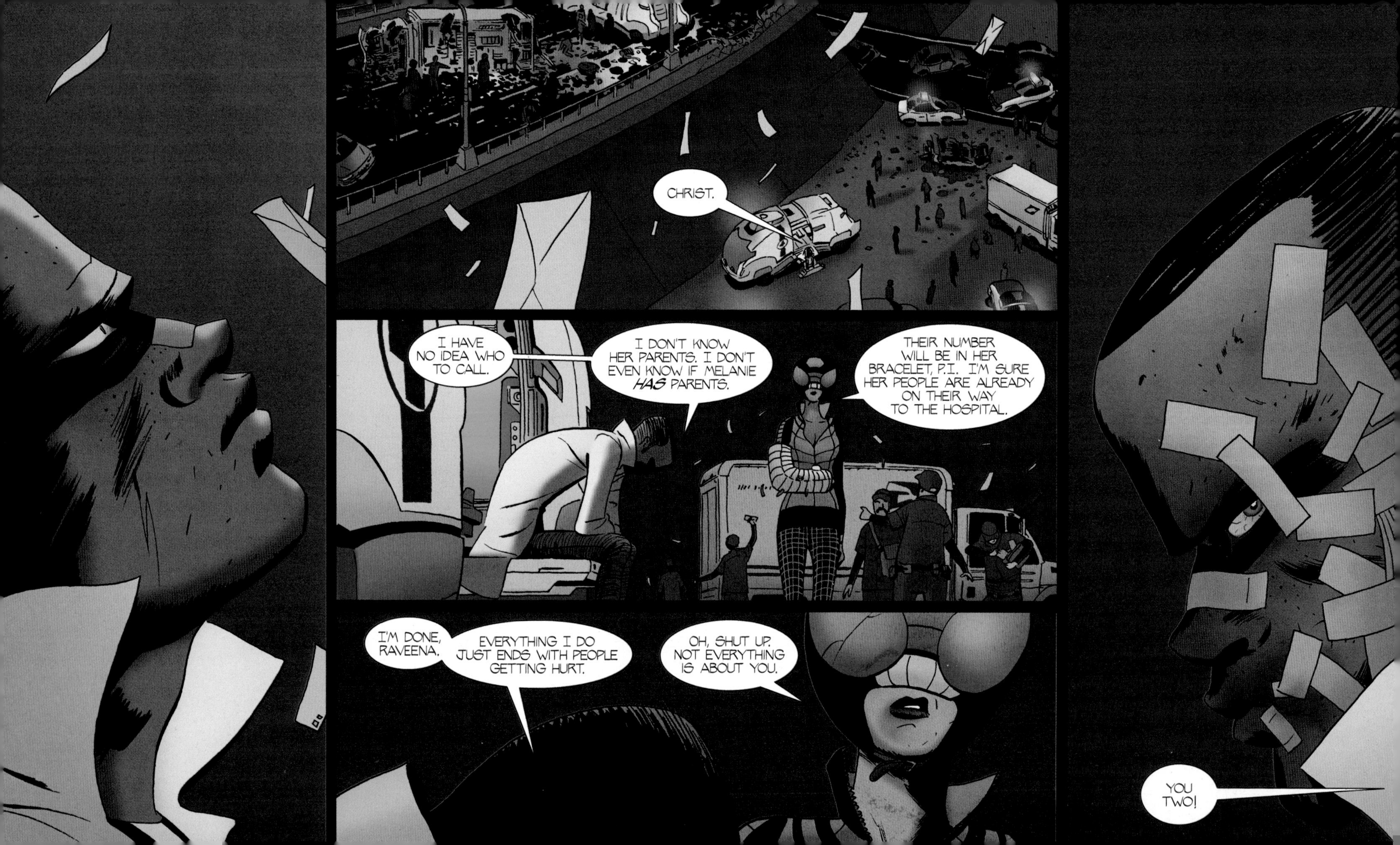
CHRIST.
I HAVE NO IDEA WHO TO CALL.
I DON'T KNOW HER PARENTS. I DON'T EVEN KNOW IF MELANIE *HAS* PARENTS.
THEIR NUMBER WILL BE IN HER BRACELET, P.I. I'M SURE HER PEOPLE ARE ALREADY ON THEIR WAY TO THE HOSPITAL.
I'M DONE, RAVEENA.
EVERYTHING I DO JUST ENDS WITH PEOPLE GETTING HURT.
OH, SHUT UP. NOT EVERYTHING IS ABOUT YOU.
YOU TWO!

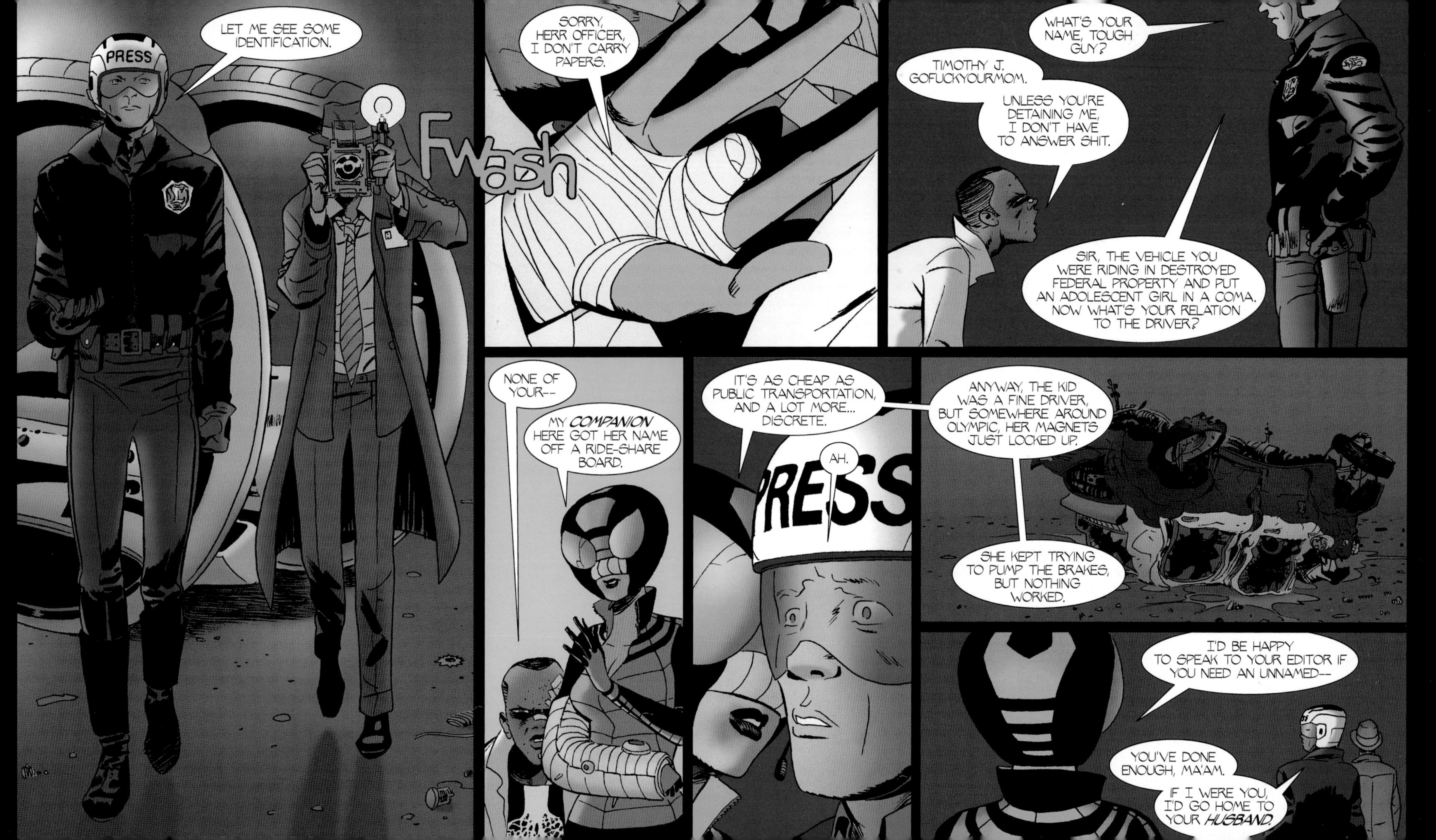
LET ME SEE SOME IDENTIFICATION.
PRESS
FWASH
SORRY, HERR OFFICER, I DON'T CARRY PAPERS.
WHAT'S YOUR NAME, TOUGH GUY?
TIMOTHY J. GOFUCKYOURMOM.
UNLESS YOU'RE DETAINING ME, I DON'T HAVE TO ANSWER SHIT.
SIR, THE VEHICLE YOU WERE RIDING IN DESTROYED FEDERAL PROPERTY AND PUT AN ADOLESCENT GIRL IN A COMA. NOW WHAT'S YOUR RELATION TO THE DRIVER?
NONE OF YOUR--
MY *COMPANION* HERE GOT HER NAME OFF A RIDE-SHARE BOARD.
IT'S AS CHEAP AS PUBLIC TRANSPORTATION, AND A LOT MORE... DISCRETE.
AH.
PRESS
ANYWAY, THE KID WAS A FINE DRIVER, BUT SOMEWHERE AROUND OLYMPIC, HER MAGNETS JUST LOCKED UP.
SHE KEPT TRYING TO PUMP THE BRAKES, BUT NOTHING WORKED.
I'D BE HAPPY TO SPEAK TO YOUR EDITOR IF YOU NEED AN UNNAMED--
YOU'VE DONE ENOUGH, MA'AM.
IF I WERE YOU, I'D GO HOME TO YOUR *HUSBAND*.

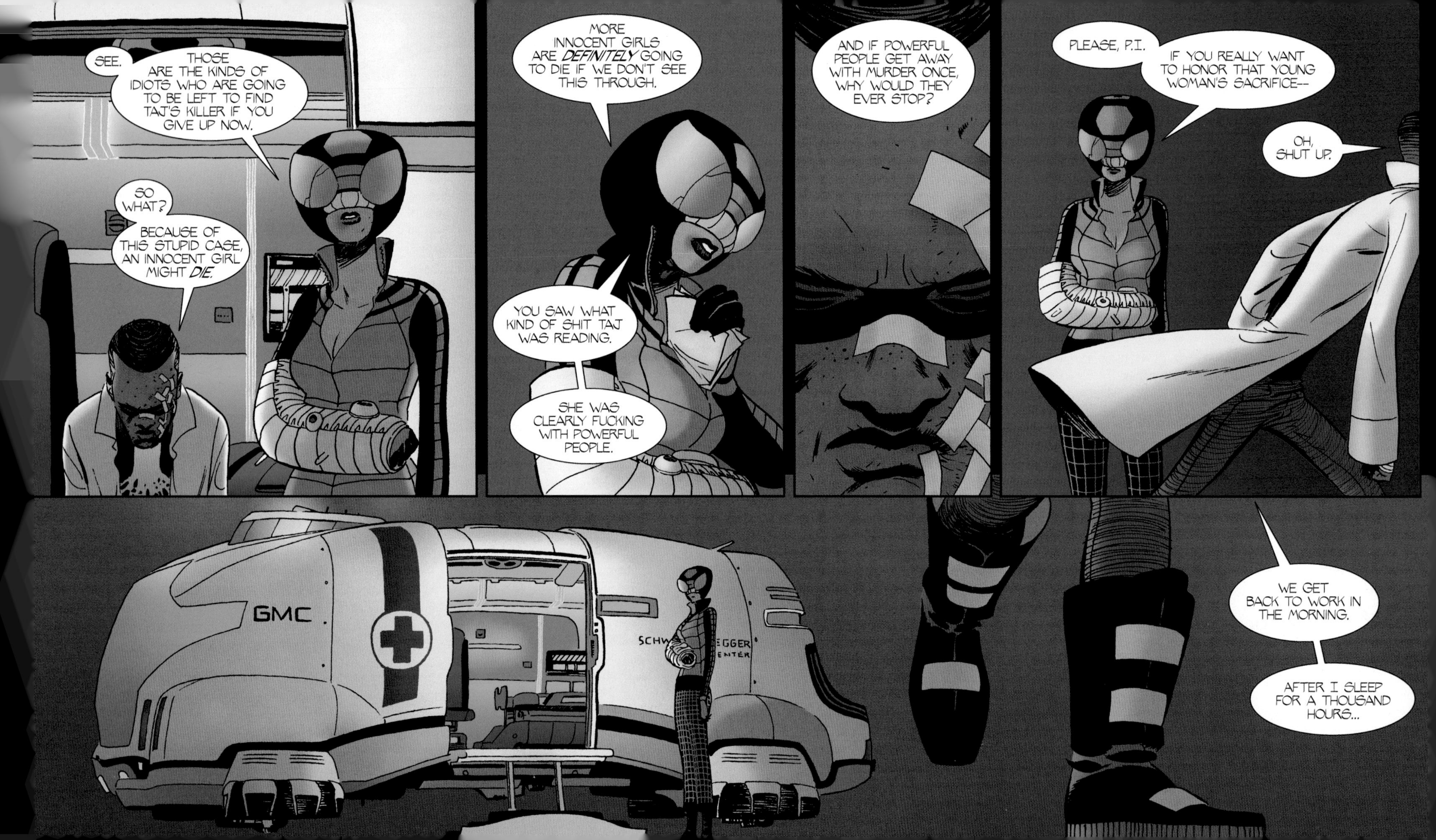
SEE.
THOSE ARE THE KINDS OF IDIOTS WHO ARE GOING TO BE LEFT TO FIND TAJ'S KILLER IF YOU GIVE UP NOW.
SO WHAT?
BECAUSE OF THIS STUPID CASE, AN INNOCENT GIRL MIGHT DIE.
MORE INNOCENT GIRLS ARE DEFINITELY GOING TO DIE IF WE DON'T SEE THIS THROUGH.
YOU SAW WHAT KIND OF SHIT TAJ WAS READING.
SHE WAS CLEARLY FUCKING WITH POWERFUL PEOPLE.
AND IF POWERFUL PEOPLE GET AWAY WITH MURDER ONCE, WHY WOULD THEY EVER STOP?
PLEASE, P.I.
IF YOU REALLY WANT TO HONOR THAT YOUNG WOMAN'S SACRIFICE--
OH, SHUT UP.
GMC
WE GET BACK TO WORK IN THE MORNING.
AFTER I SLEEP FOR A THOUSAND HOURS...

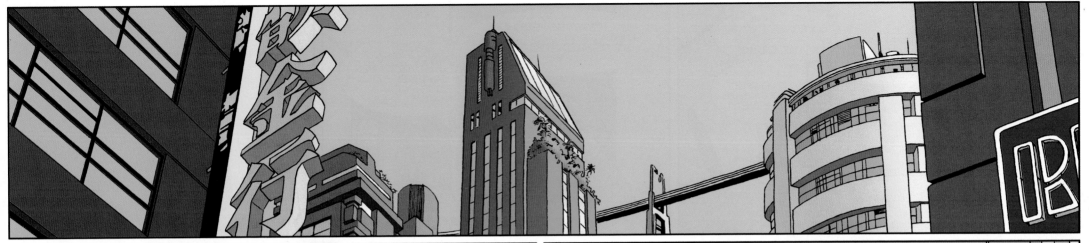

EXCUSE ME, MR. DEGUERRE.

MR. BRYANT FROM ENGINEERING DOESN'T HAVE AN APPOINTMENT, BUT HE SAYS IT'S URGENT.

IT IS, SIR.

EXTREMELY.

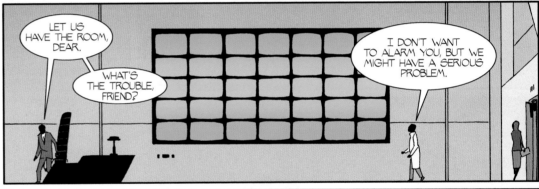

LET US HAVE THE ROOM, DEAR.

WHAT'S THE TROUBLE, FRIEND?

I DON'T WANT TO ALARM YOU, BUT WE MIGHT HAVE A SERIOUS PROBLEM.

I THINK A ROGUE ENGINEER INSIDE THE COMPANY MIGHT BE TRYING TO *SPY* ON OUR CUSTOMERS.

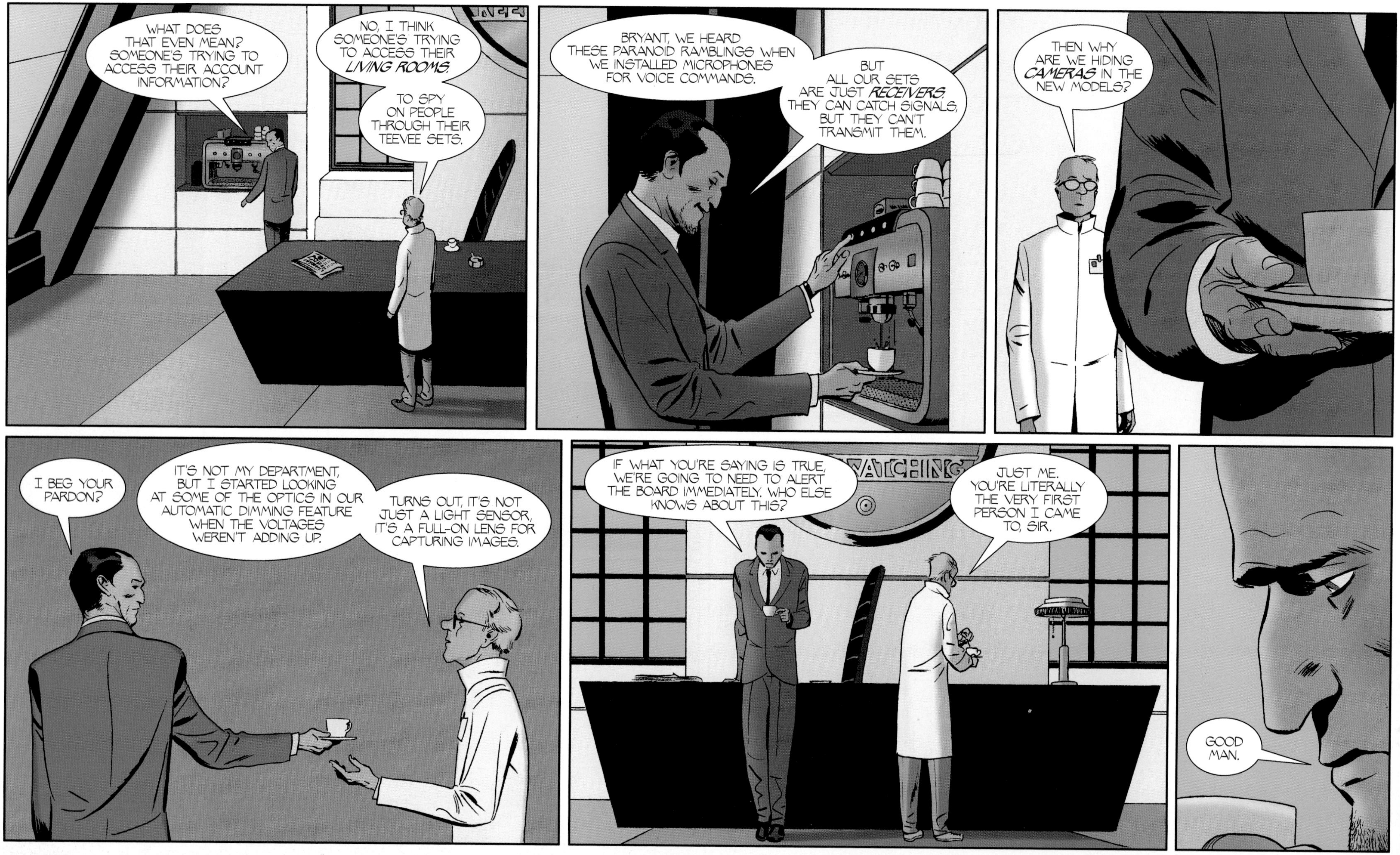
WHAT DOES THAT EVEN MEAN? SOMEONE'S TRYING TO ACCESS THEIR ACCOUNT INFORMATION?
NO, I THINK SOMEONE'S TRYING TO ACCESS THEIR *LIVING ROOMS.*
TO SPY ON PEOPLE THROUGH THEIR TEEVEE SETS.
BRYANT, WE HEARD THESE PARANOID RAMBLINGS WHEN WE INSTALLED MICROPHONES FOR VOICE COMMANDS.
BUT ALL OUR SETS ARE JUST *RECEIVERS.* THEY CAN CATCH SIGNALS, BUT THEY CAN'T TRANSMIT THEM.
THEN WHY ARE WE HIDING *CAMERAS* IN THE NEW MODELS?
I BEG YOUR PARDON?
IT'S NOT MY DEPARTMENT, BUT I STARTED LOOKING AT SOME OF THE OPTICS IN OUR AUTOMATIC DIMMING FEATURE WHEN THE VOLTAGES WEREN'T ADDING UP.
TURNS OUT, IT'S NOT JUST A LIGHT SENSOR, IT'S A FULL-ON LENS FOR CAPTURING IMAGES.
IF WHAT YOU'RE SAYING IS TRUE, WE'RE GOING TO NEED TO ALERT THE BOARD IMMEDIATELY. WHO ELSE KNOWS ABOUT THIS?
WATCHING
JUST ME. YOU'RE LITERALLY THE VERY FIRST PERSON I CAME TO, SIR.
GOOD MAN.

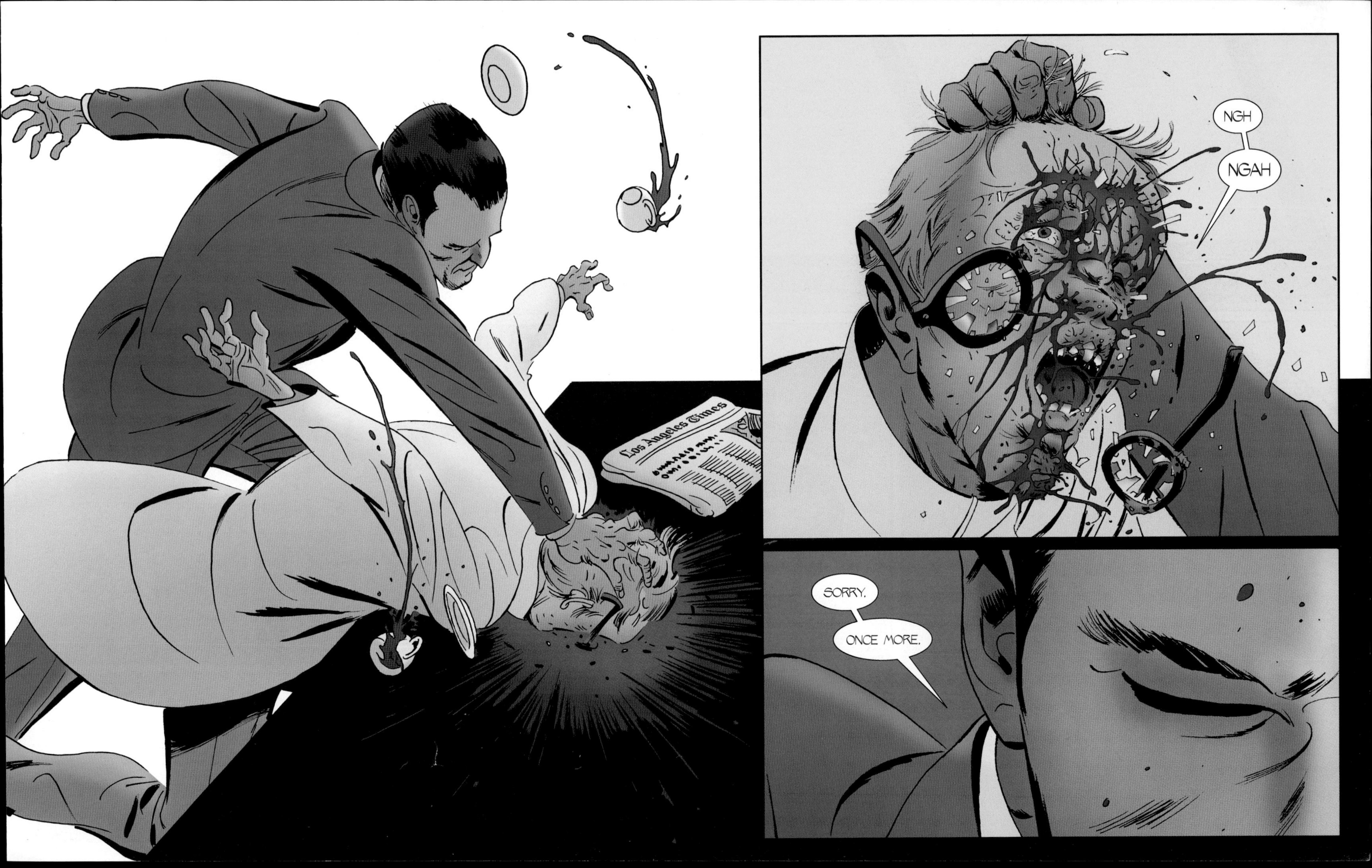
Los Angeles Times
NGH
NGAH
SORRY.
ONCE MORE.

TEEVEE
KEEP WATCHING
DAMMIT.
KEEP WATCHING

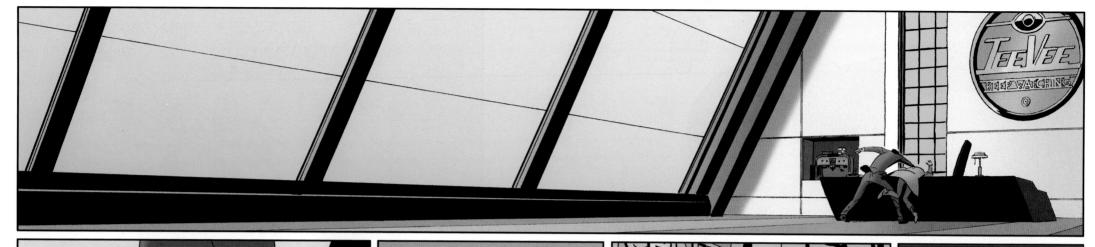

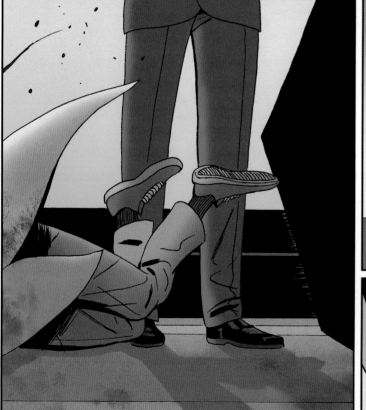

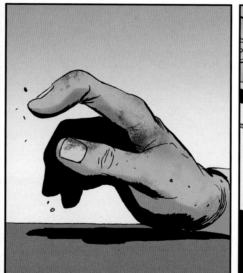

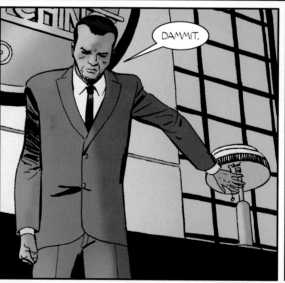

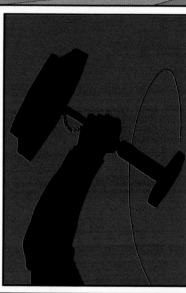

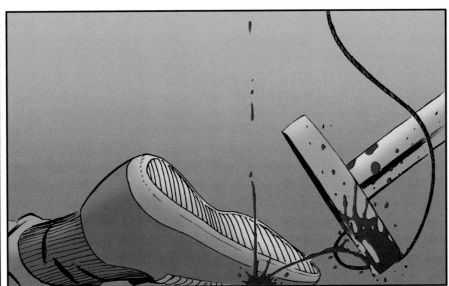

JOHANN, YOU ON?

OUI.

LEAVE FRÉDÉRIC WITH OUR GUEST AND GET OVER HERE NOW.

I NEED ANOTHER NEW MINI-FRIDGE FOR MY OFFICE.

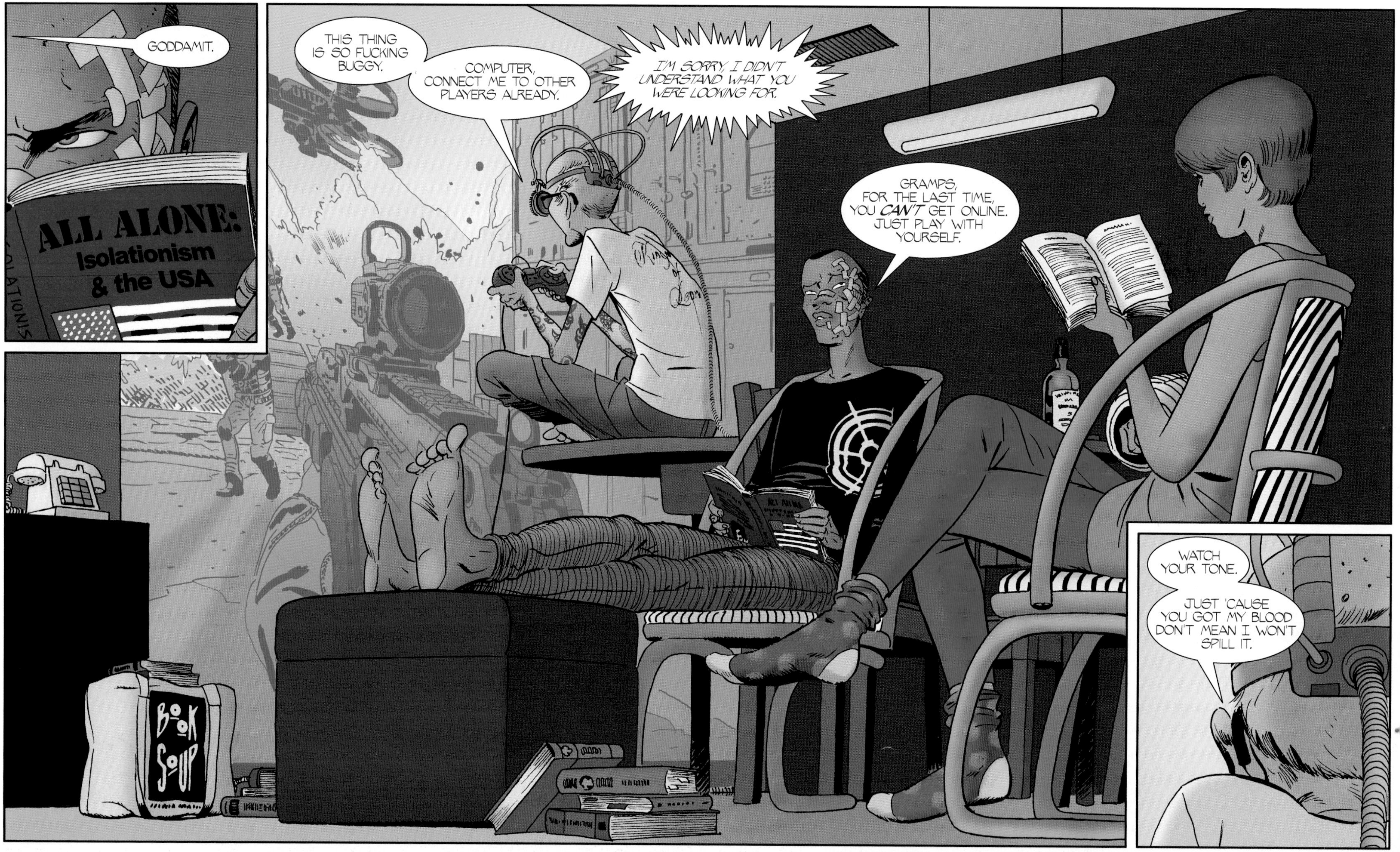
GODDAMIT.
ALL ALONE: Isolationism & the USA
THIS THING IS SO FUCKING BUGGY.
COMPUTER, CONNECT ME TO OTHER PLAYERS ALREADY.
I'M SORRY, I DIDN'T UNDERSTAND WHAT YOU WERE LOOKING FOR.
GRAMPS, FOR THE LAST TIME, YOU *CAN'T* GET ONLINE. JUST PLAY WITH YOURSELF.
WATCH YOUR TONE.
JUST 'CAUSE YOU GOT MY BLOOD DON'T MEAN I WON'T SPILL IT.
BOOK SOUP

WAIT, GRAMPS IS YOUR *ACTUAL* GRANDFATHER?

DUH.

KID LOOKS JUST LIKE ME.

HE STUCK AROUND TO HELP RAISE ME AFTER HIS PIECE-OF-WORK SON ABANDONED MOM AND ME.

ISOLATIONISM

WHERE'S YOUR MOTHER NOW?

CAN WE PLAY TWENTY QUESTIONS LATER?

I'VE GOT A DOZEN MORE OF TAJ'S SHITTY TEXTBOOKS TO SKIM.

PRACTICALLY EVERY SEARCH MY SISTER MADE GENERATED A RESPONSE THAT SOMEHOW CONNECTS TO THIS DeGUERRE GUY.

EYES ON THE PRIZE

KHALID
DeGUERRE

HE *MUST* BE INVOLVED IN ALL THIS SOMEHOW.

WELL, WE'RE NOT GOING TO FIND OUT THE TRUTH ABOUT HIM FROM HIS OWN WHITEWASHED P.R.

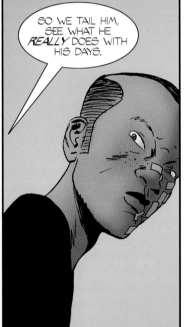

SO WE TAIL HIM, SEE WHAT HE *REALLY* DOES WITH HIS DAYS.

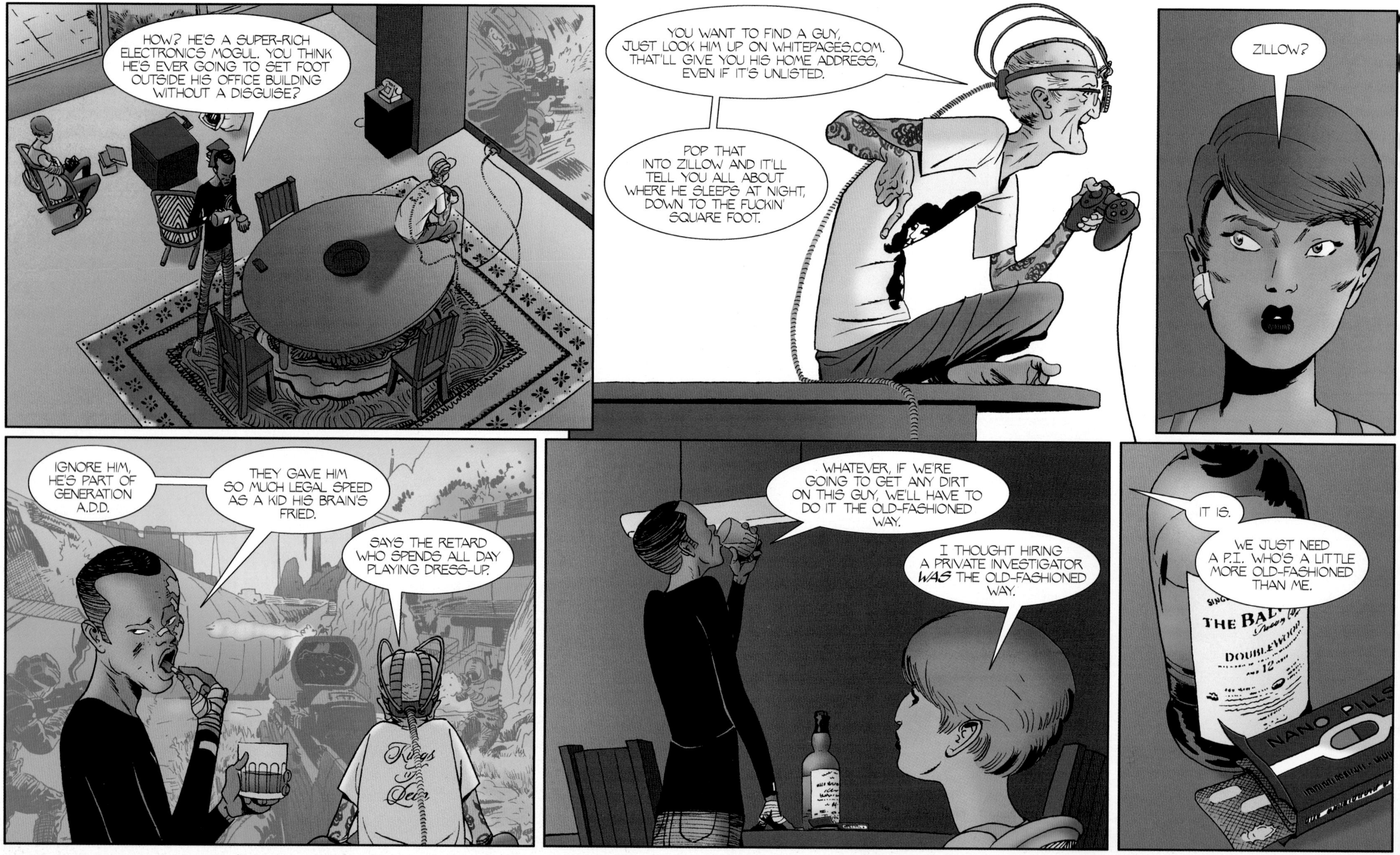
HOW? HE'S A SUPER-RICH ELECTRONICS MOGUL. YOU THINK HE'S EVER GOING TO SET FOOT OUTSIDE HIS OFFICE BUILDING WITHOUT A DISGUISE?
YOU WANT TO FIND A GUY, JUST LOOK HIM UP ON WHITEPAGES.COM. THAT'LL GIVE YOU HIS HOME ADDRESS, EVEN IF IT'S UNLISTED.
POP THAT INTO ZILLOW AND IT'LL TELL YOU ALL ABOUT WHERE HE SLEEPS AT NIGHT, DOWN TO THE FUCKIN' SQUARE FOOT.
ZILLOW?
IGNORE HIM, HE'S PART OF GENERATION A.D.D.
THEY GAVE HIM SO MUCH LEGAL SPEED AS A KID HIS BRAIN'S FRIED.
SAYS THE RETARD WHO SPENDS ALL DAY PLAYING DRESS-UP.
Kings of Leon
WHATEVER, IF WE'RE GOING TO GET ANY DIRT ON THIS GUY, WE'LL HAVE TO DO IT THE OLD-FASHIONED WAY.
I THOUGHT HIRING A PRIVATE INVESTIGATOR ***WAS*** THE OLD-FASHIONED WAY.
IT IS.
WE JUST NEED A P.I. WHO'S A LITTLE MORE OLD-FASHIONED THAN ME.
THE BAL
DOUBLEWOOD
12
NANO PILLS

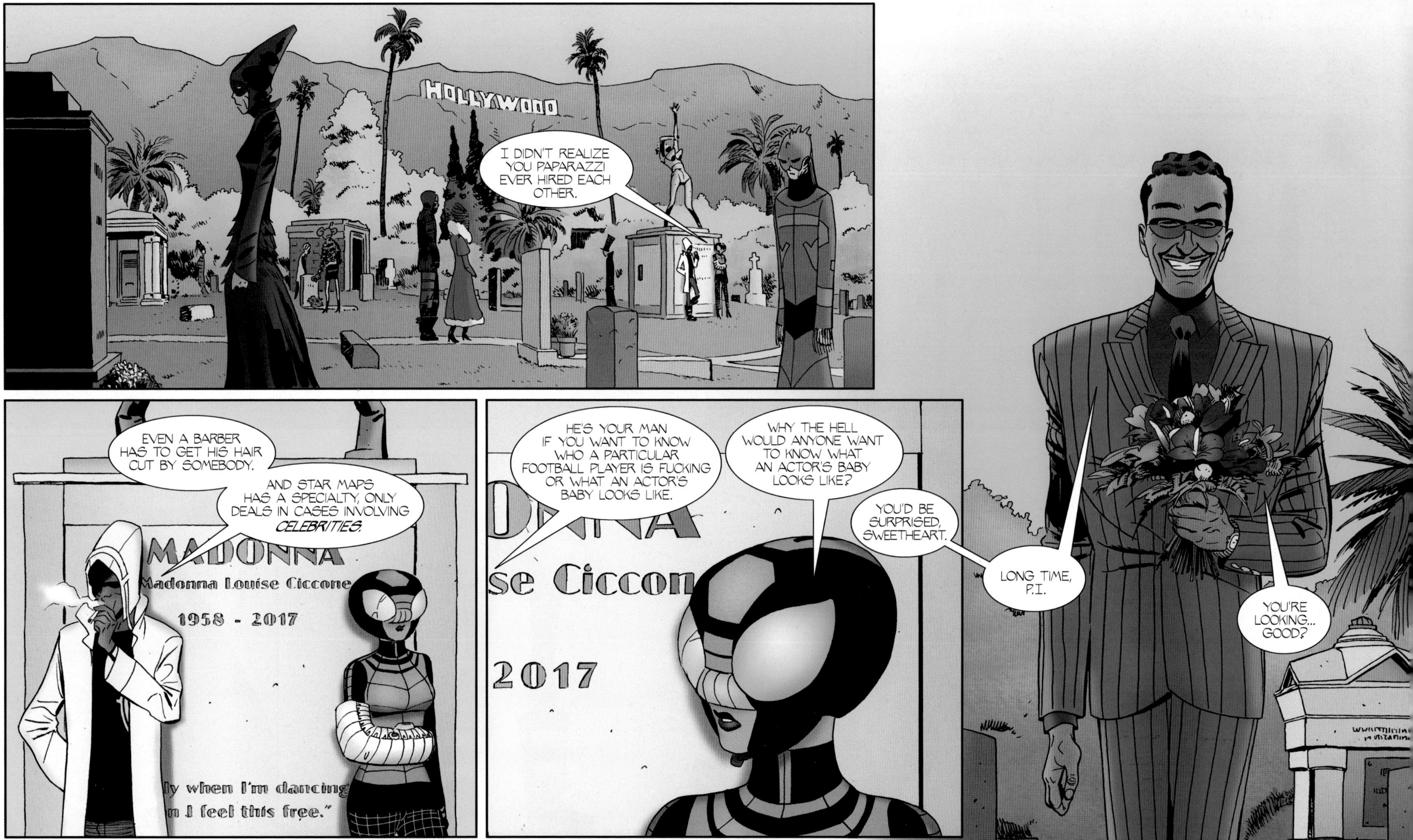
HOLLYWOOD
I DIDN'T REALIZE YOU PAPARAZZI EVER HIRED EACH OTHER.
EVEN A BARBER HAS TO GET HIS HAIR CUT BY SOMEBODY.
AND STAR MAPS HAS A SPECIALTY, ONLY DEALS IN CASES INVOLVING *CELEBRITIES*.
MADONNA
Madonna Louise Ciccone
1958 - 2017
ly when I'm dancing
n I feel this free."
HE'S YOUR MAN IF YOU WANT TO KNOW WHO A PARTICULAR FOOTBALL PLAYER IS FUCKING OR WHAT AN ACTOR'S BABY LOOKS LIKE.
WHY THE HELL WOULD ANYONE WANT TO KNOW WHAT AN ACTOR'S BABY LOOKS LIKE?
YOU'D BE SURPRISED, SWEETHEART.
LONG TIME, P.I.
YOU'RE LOOKING... GOOD?

YEAH, YEAH. LISTEN, MY CLIENT R.M. HERE COULD USE YOUR EXPERTISE.

SUCKING UP TO ME ALREADY? YOU TWO MUST REALLY BE UP SHIT CREEK.

MADONNA
Madonna Louise Ciccone
1958 - 2017

"By whom I'm dancing and I feel this free."

YOU'RE IN GOOD HANDS NOW, MY DEAR.

DID P.I. TELL YOU I TAUGHT HIM EVERYTHING HE KNOWS?

WELL, HE TOLD ME THOSE WOULD BE THE FIRST WORDS OUT OF YOUR MOUTH.

YOU HAVE ANY IDEA WHERE A MAN NAMED KHALID DeGUERRE LIVES?

THE TEEVEE GUY? OF COURSE. BUT IT WON'T DO YOU MUCH GOOD. HE'S ALMOST NEVER HOME.

THEN WHERE IS HE?

I'M SORRY, WERE YOU UNDER THE IMPRESSION THAT I WAS A NONPROFIT ORGANIZATION?

JUST TELL US WHAT YOU WANT, MAPS.

THE DREAMCOAT OFF YOUR BACK.

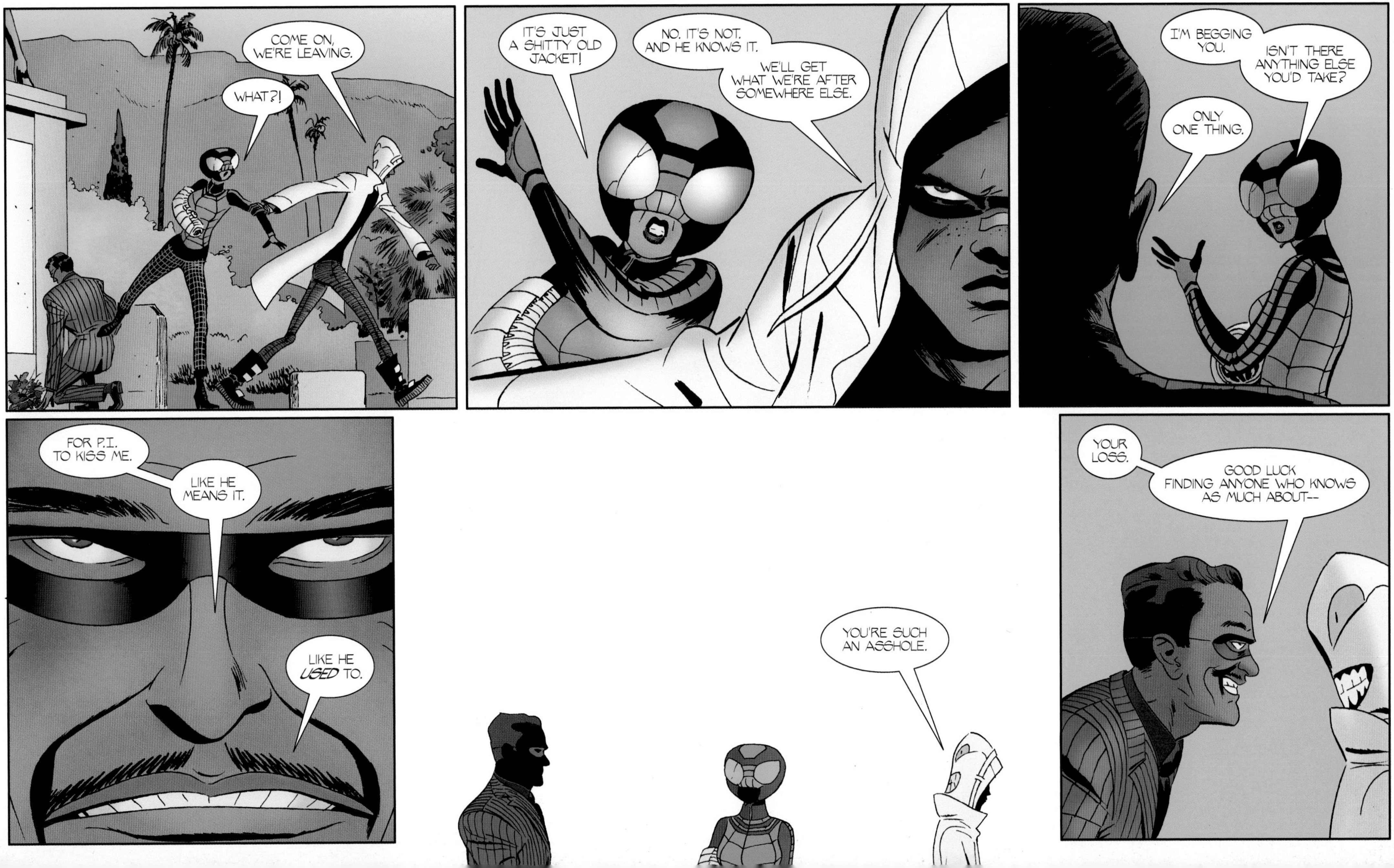
COME ON, WE'RE LEAVING.
WHAT?!
IT'S JUST A SHITTY OLD JACKET!
NO. IT'S NOT. AND HE KNOWS IT.
WE'LL GET WHAT WE'RE AFTER SOMEWHERE ELSE.
I'M BEGGING YOU.
ISN'T THERE ANYTHING ELSE YOU'D TAKE?
ONLY ONE THING.
FOR P.I. TO KISS ME.
LIKE HE MEANS IT.
LIKE HE USED TO.
YOU'RE SUCH AN ASSHOLE.
YOUR LOSS.
GOOD LUCK FINDING ANYONE WHO KNOWS AS MUCH ABOUT--

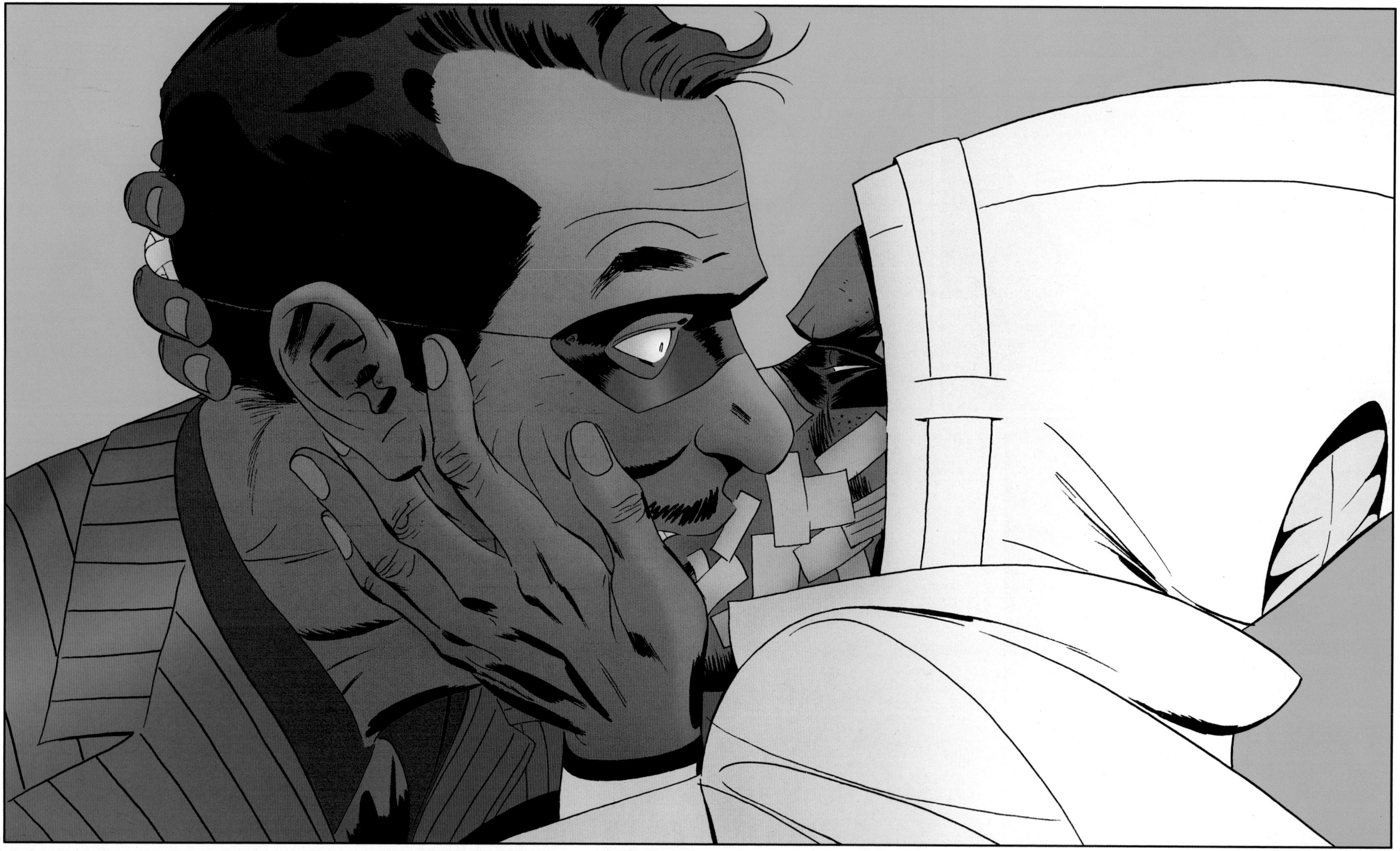

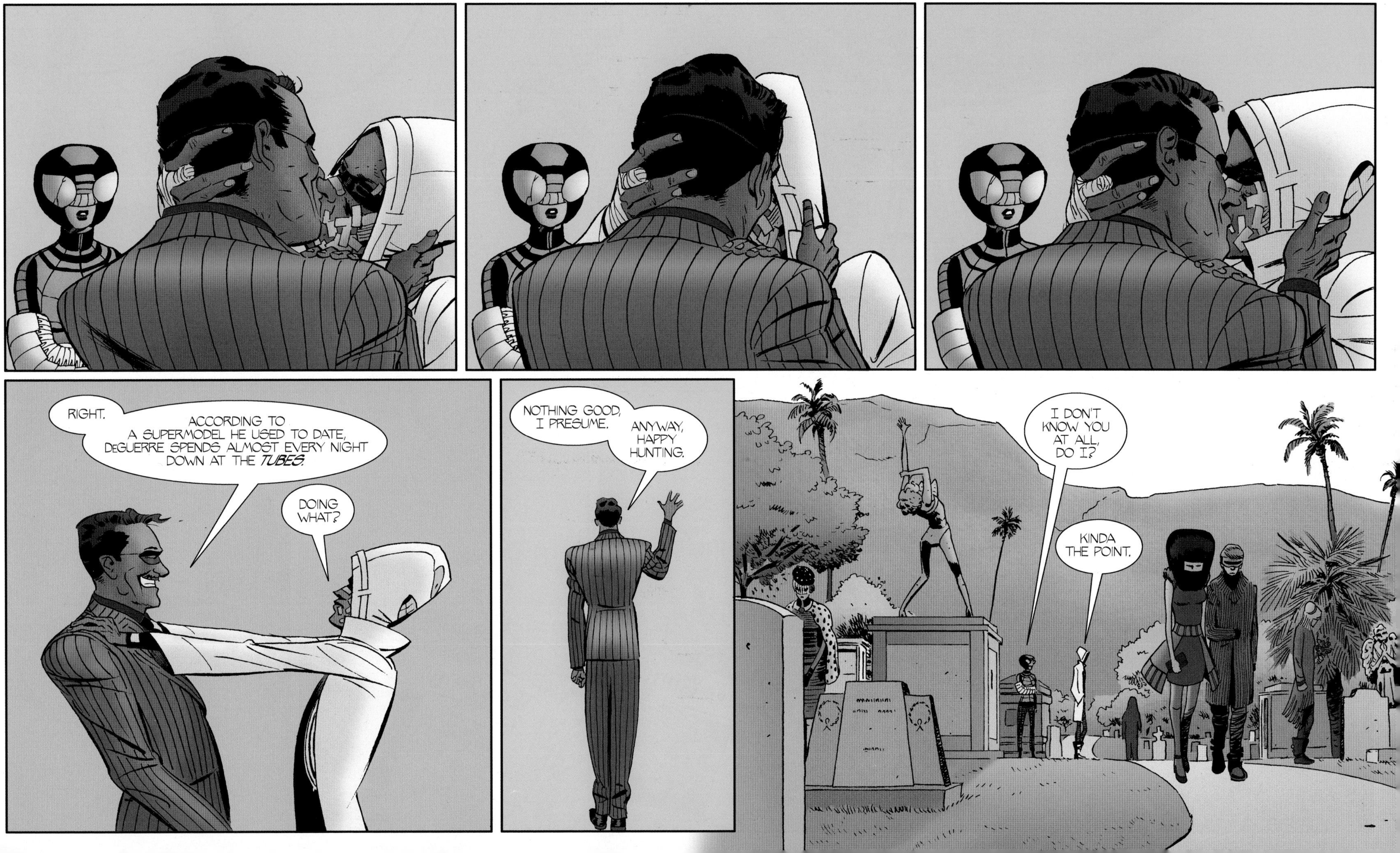
RIGHT.
ACCORDING TO A SUPERMODEL HE USED TO DATE, DEGUERRE SPENDS ALMOST EVERY NIGHT DOWN AT THE *TUBES.*
DOING WHAT?
NOTHING GOOD, I PRESUME.
ANYWAY, HAPPY HUNTING.
I DON'T KNOW YOU AT ALL, DO I?
KINDA THE POINT.

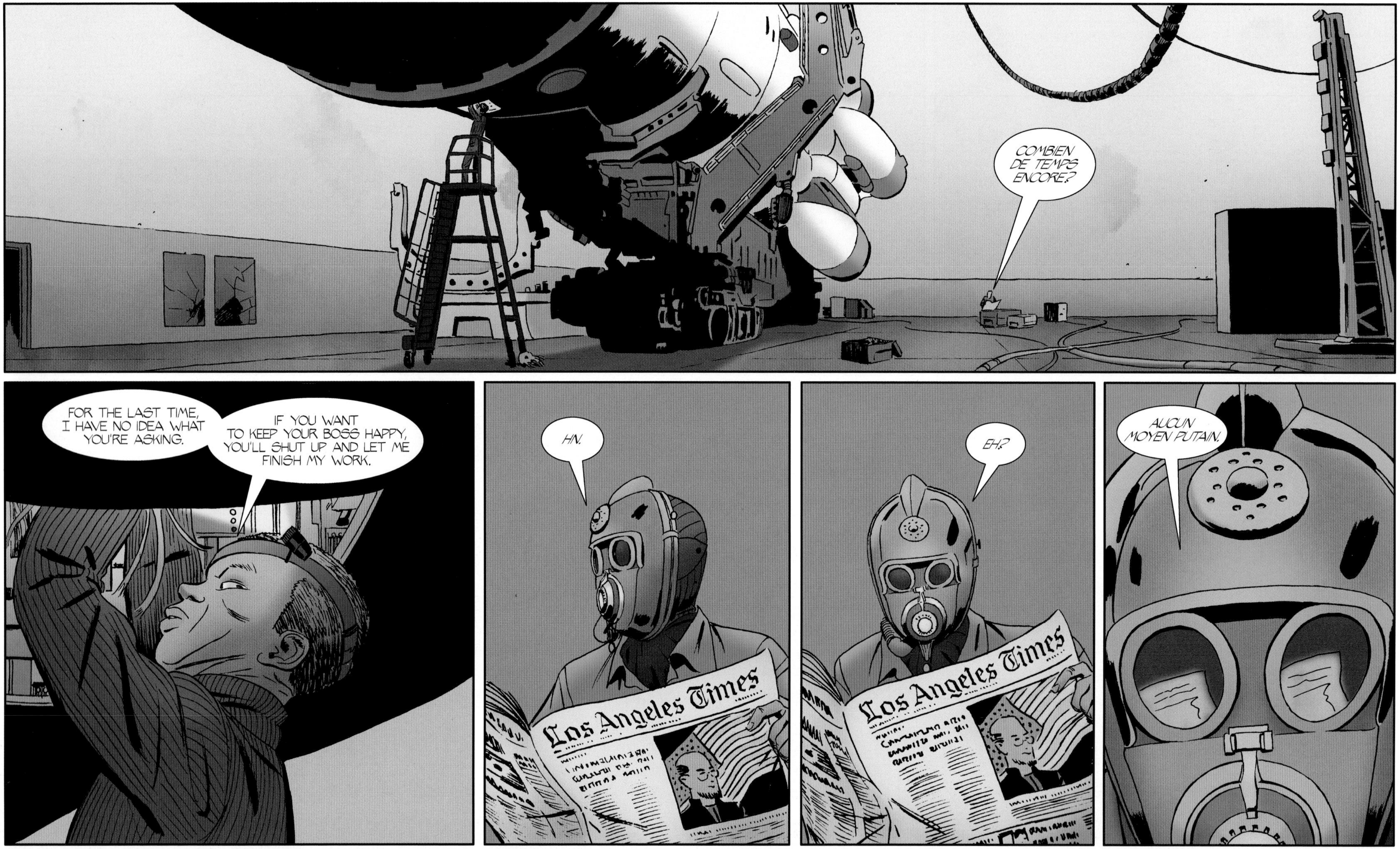
COMBIEN DE TEMPS ENCORE?
FOR THE LAST TIME, I HAVE NO IDEA WHAT YOU'RE ASKING.
IF YOU WANT TO KEEP YOUR BOSS HAPPY, YOU'LL SHUT UP AND LET ME FINISH MY WORK.
HN.
Los Angeles Times
EH?
Los Angeles Times
AUCUN MOYEN PUTAIN.

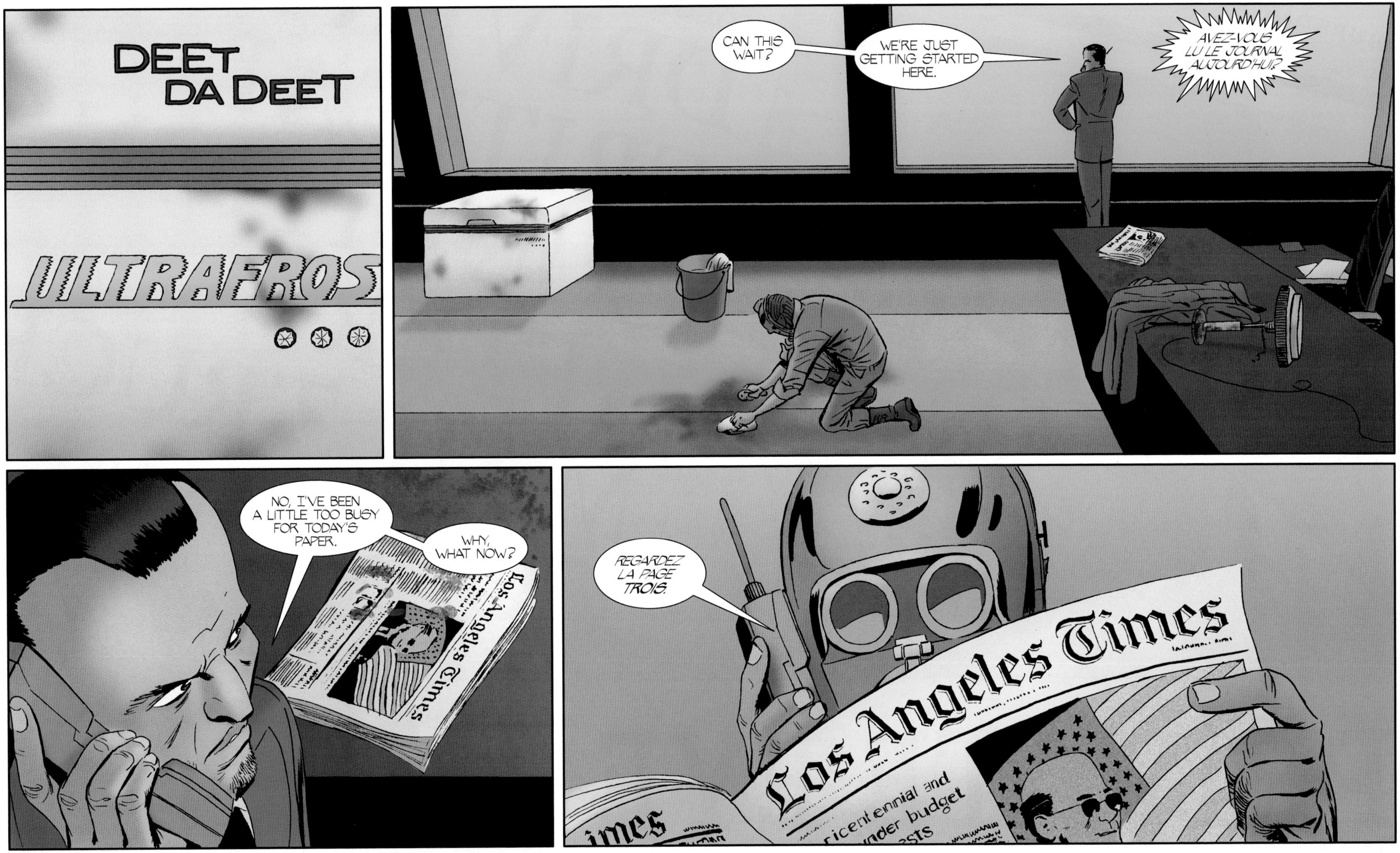
DEET DA DEET
ULTRAFROS
CAN THIS WAIT?
WE'RE JUST GETTING STARTED HERE.
AVEZ-VOUS LU LE JOURNAL AUJOURD'HUI?
NO, I'VE BEEN A LITTLE TOO BUSY FOR TODAY'S PAPER.
WHY, WHAT NOW?
Los Angeles Times
REGARDEZ LA PAGE TROIS.
Los Angeles Times

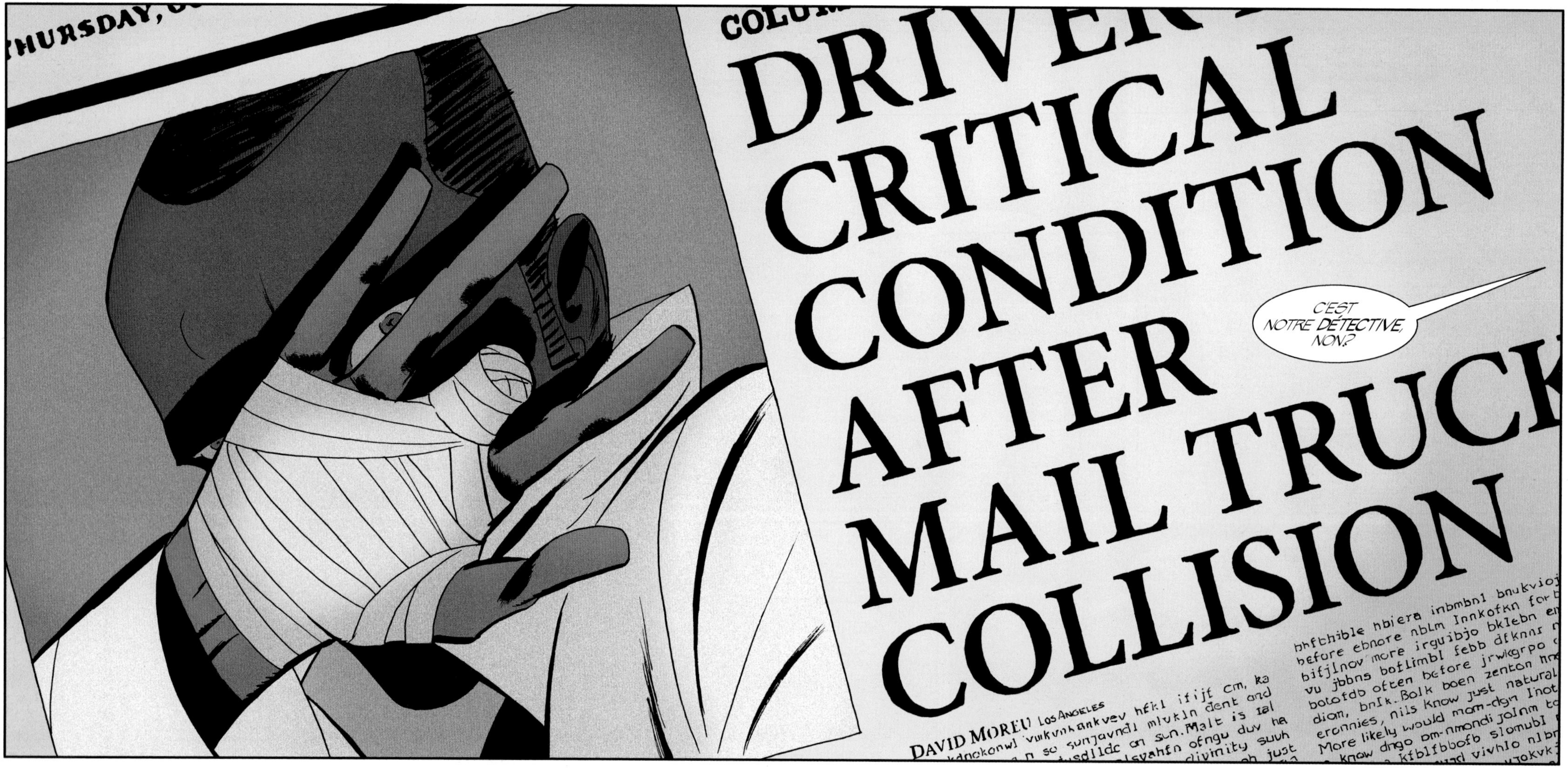
CRITICAL
CONDITION
AFTER
MAIL TRUCK
COLLISION
DAVID MOREU LOS ANGELES
C'EST NOTRE DÉTECTIVE, NON?

THE PRIVATE EYE

BRIAN K. VAUGHAN MARCOS MARTIN
WITH
MUNTSA VICENTE

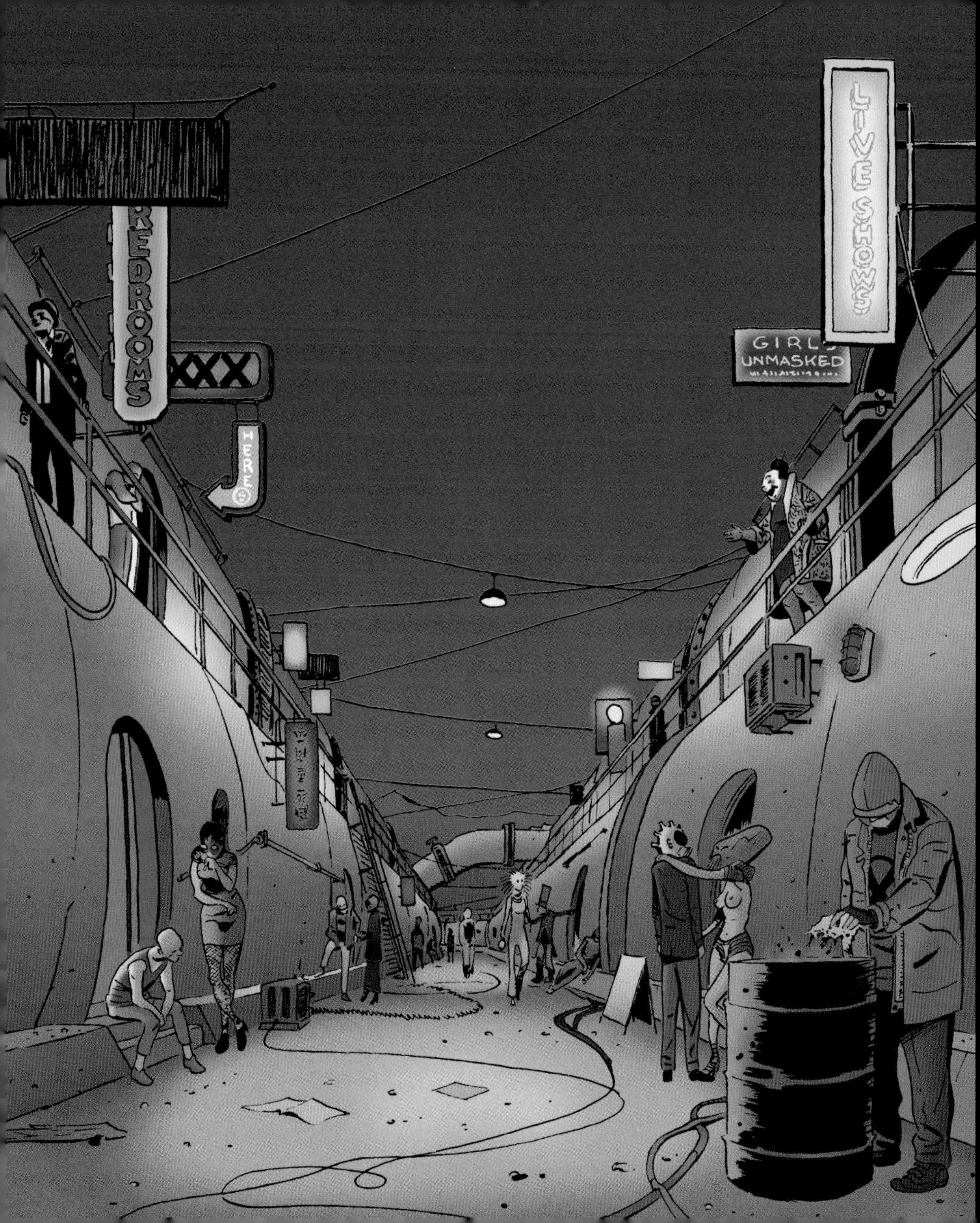
REDROOMS
XXX
HERE
LIVE SHOWS
UNMASKED

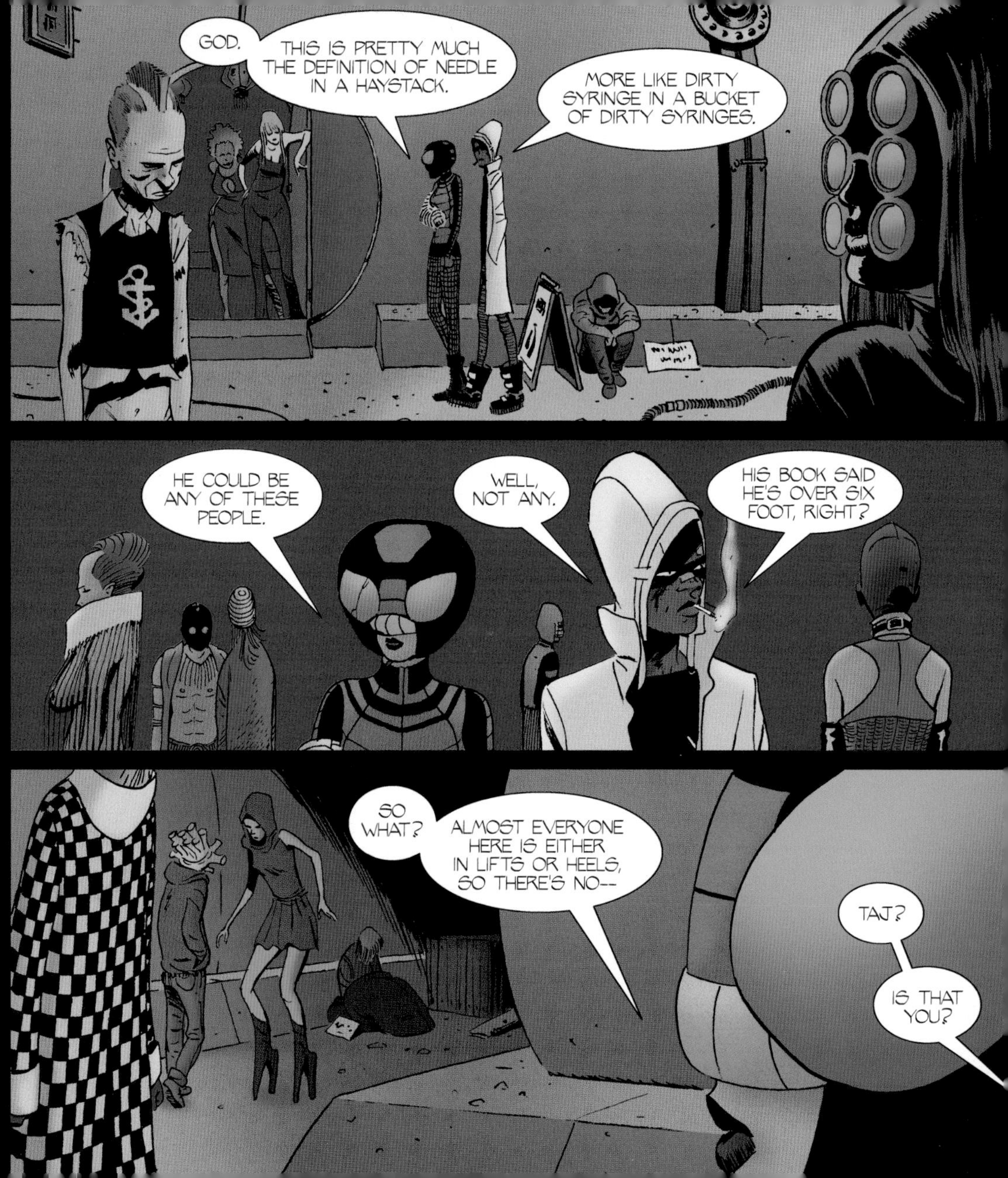
GOD.
THIS IS PRETTY MUCH THE DEFINITION OF NEEDLE IN A HAYSTACK.
MORE LIKE DIRTY SYRINGE IN A BUCKET OF DIRTY SYRINGES.
HE COULD BE ANY OF THESE PEOPLE.
WELL, NOT ANY.
HIS BOOK SAID HE'S OVER SIX FOOT, RIGHT?
SO WHAT?
ALMOST EVERYONE HERE IS EITHER IN LIFTS OR HEELS, SO THERE'S NO--
TAJ?
IS THAT YOU?

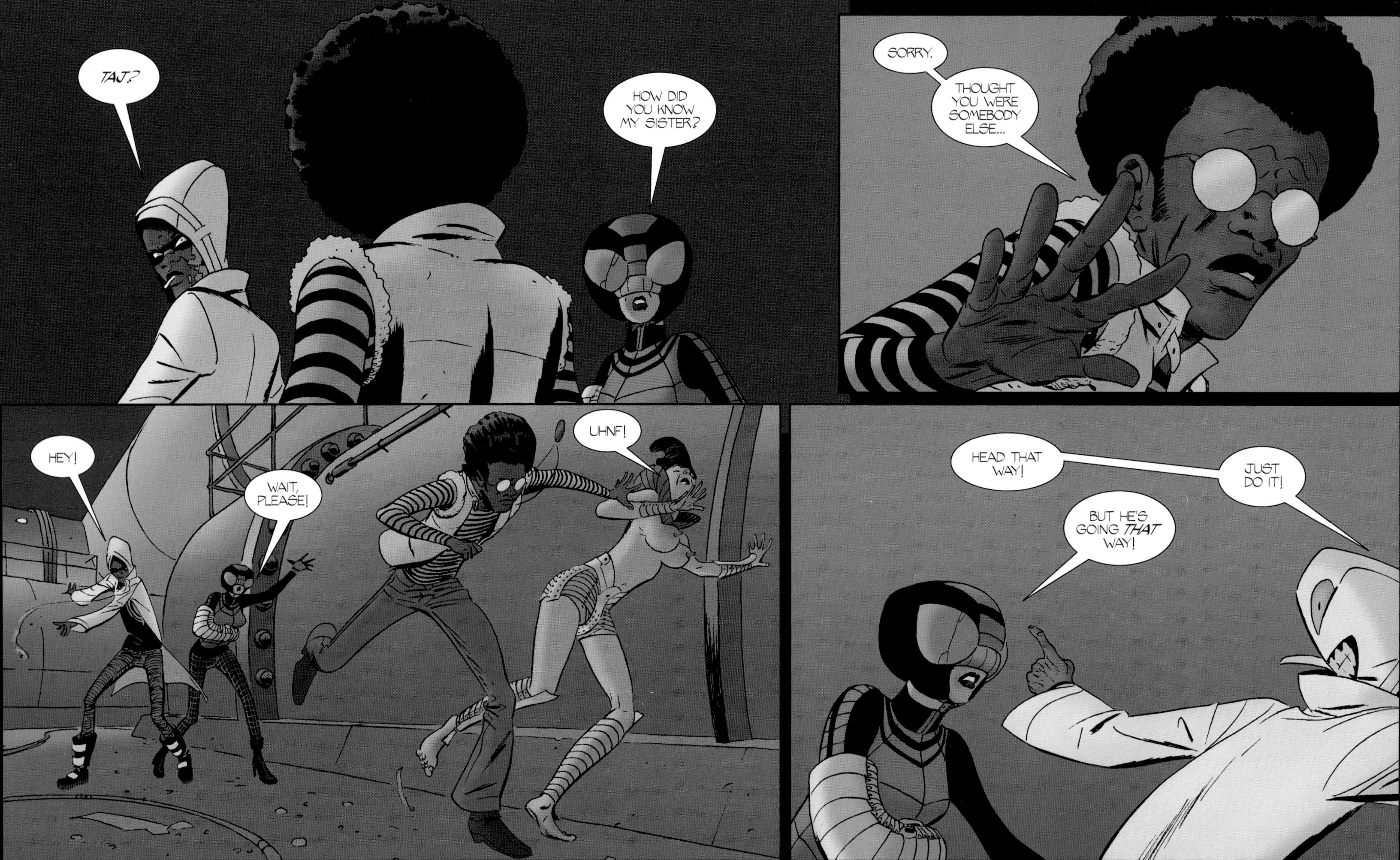
TAJ?
HOW DID YOU KNOW MY SISTER?
SORRY.
THOUGHT YOU WERE SOMEBODY ELSE...
HEY!
WAIT, PLEASE!
UHNF!
HEAD THAT WAY!
JUST DO IT!
BUT HE'S GOING *THAT* WAY!

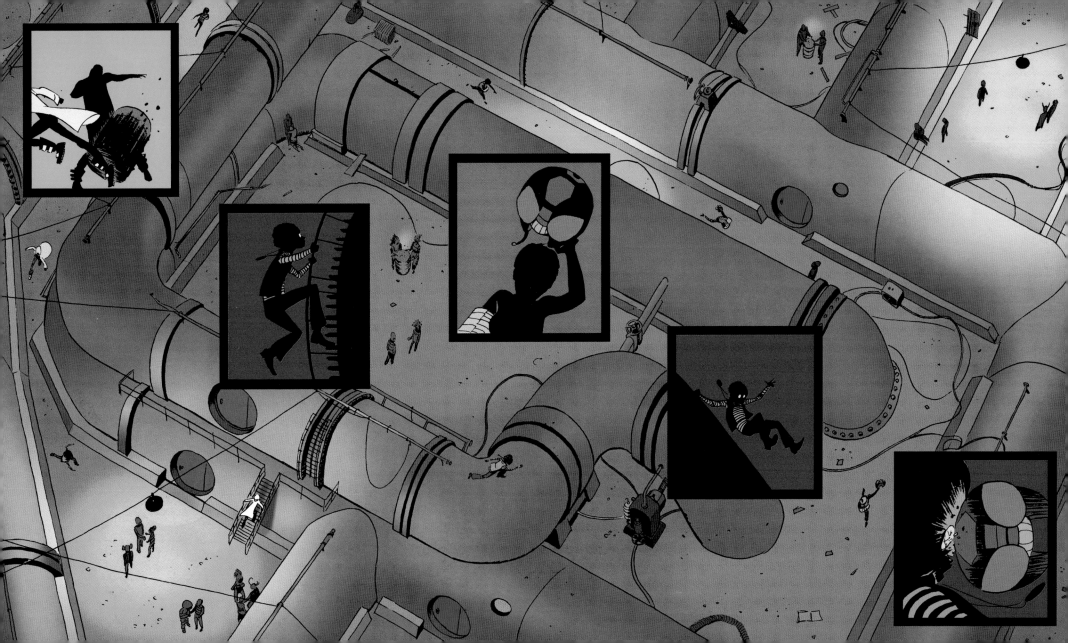

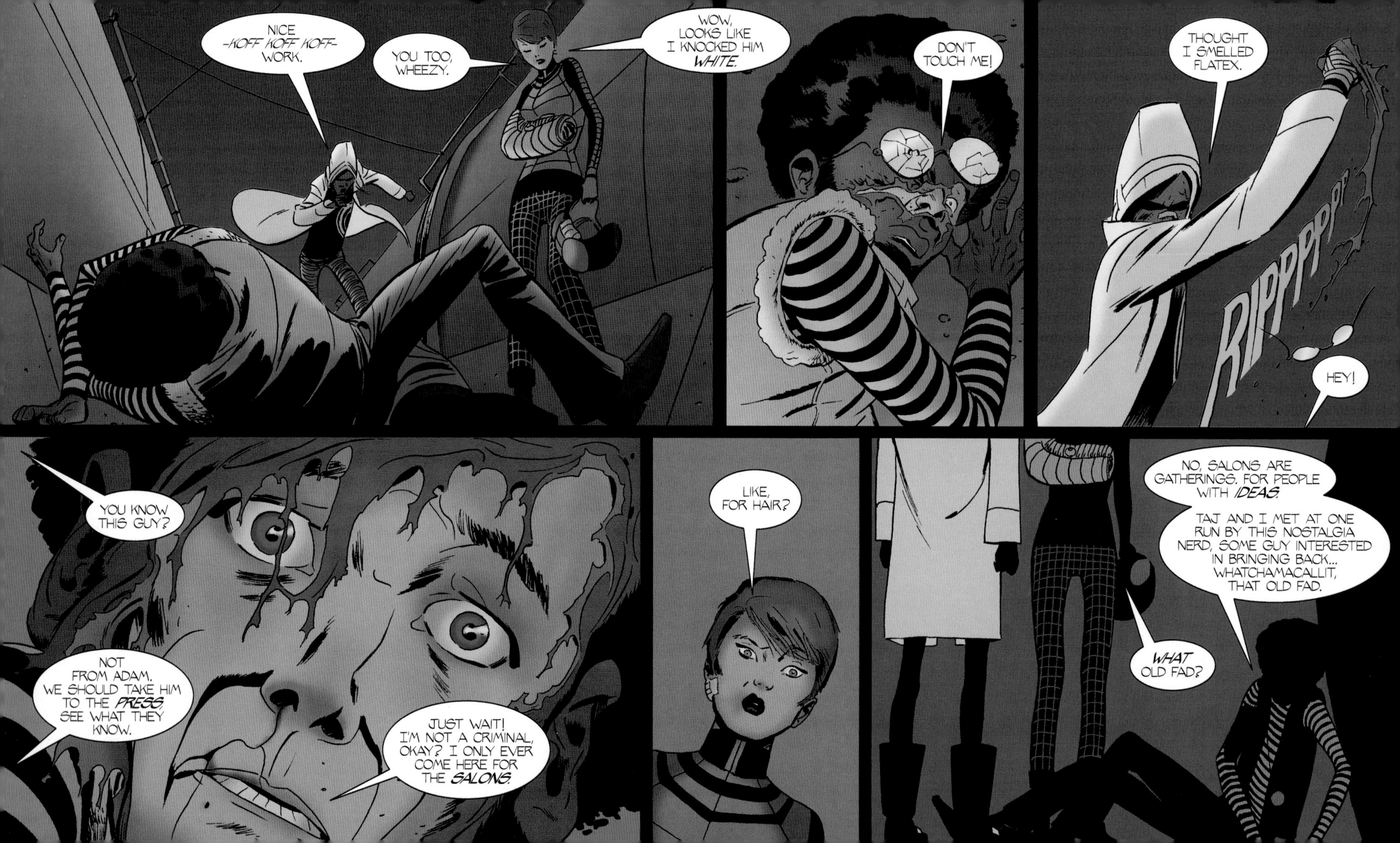
NICE -KOFF KOFF KOFF- WORK.
YOU TOO, WHEEZY.
WOW, LOOKS LIKE I KNOCKED HIM *WHITE.*
DON'T TOUCH ME!
THOUGHT I SMELLED FLATEX.
RIPPPPPP
HEY!
YOU KNOW THIS GUY?
NOT FROM ADAM. WE SHOULD TAKE HIM TO THE *PRESS,* SEE WHAT THEY KNOW.
JUST WAIT! I'M NOT A CRIMINAL, OKAY? I ONLY EVER COME HERE FOR THE *SALONS.*
LIKE, FOR HAIR?
NO, SALONS ARE GATHERINGS. FOR PEOPLE WITH *IDEAS.*
TAJ AND I MET AT ONE RUN BY THIS NOSTALGIA NERD, SOME GUY INTERESTED IN BRINGING BACK... WHATCHAMACALLIT, THAT OLD FAD.
WHAT OLD FAD?

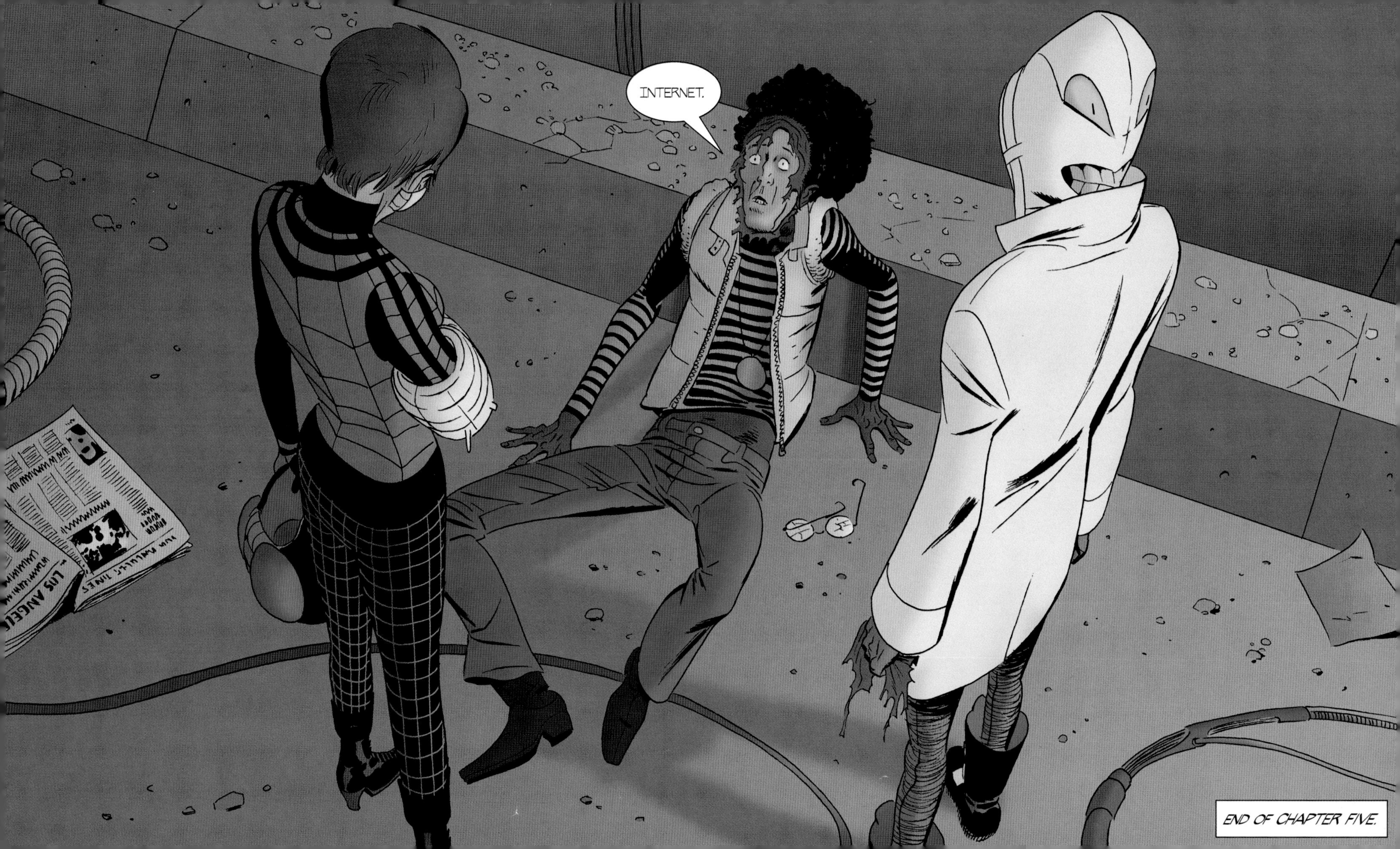
INTERNET.
END OF CHAPTER FIVE.

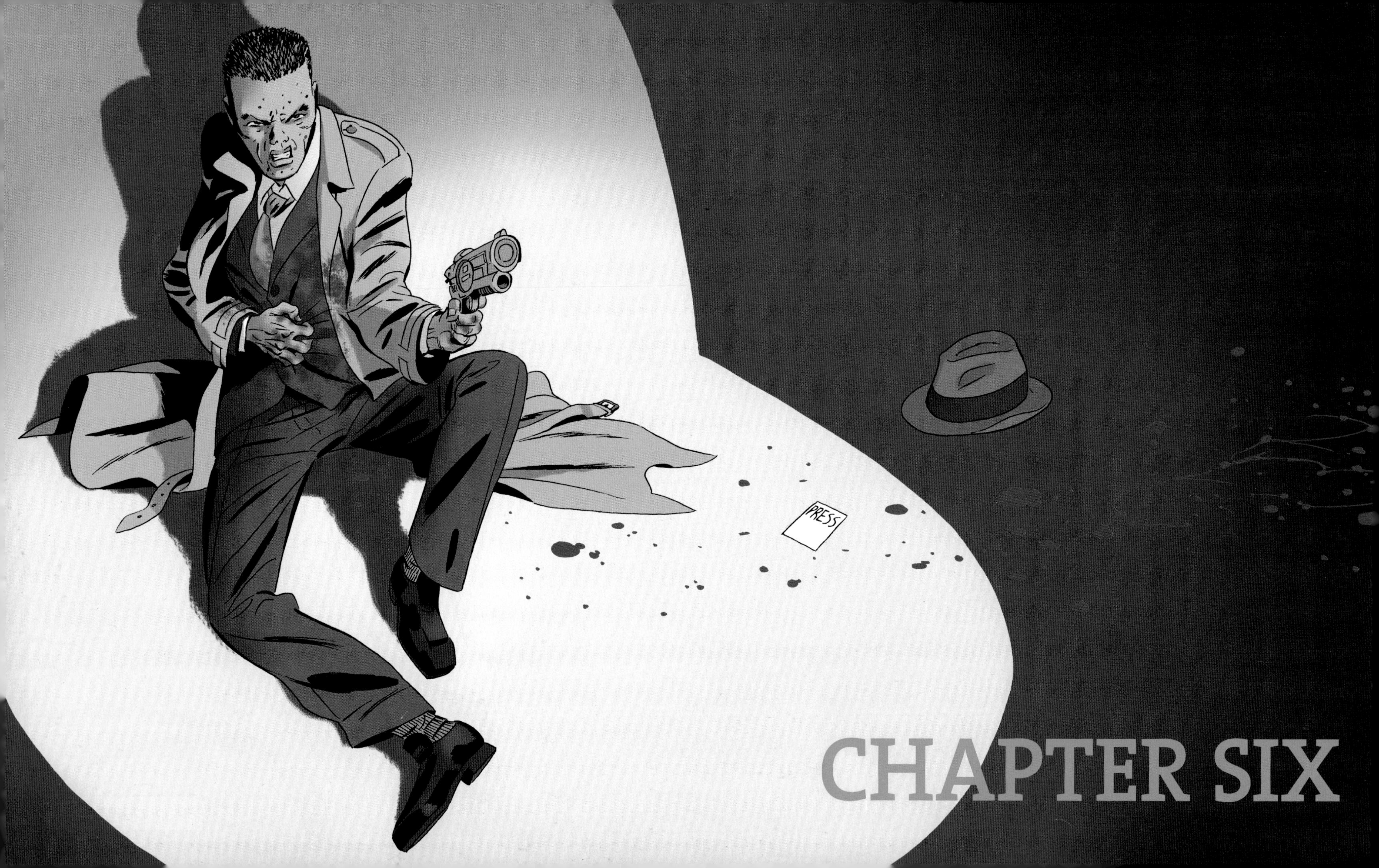
PRESS

CHAPTER SIX

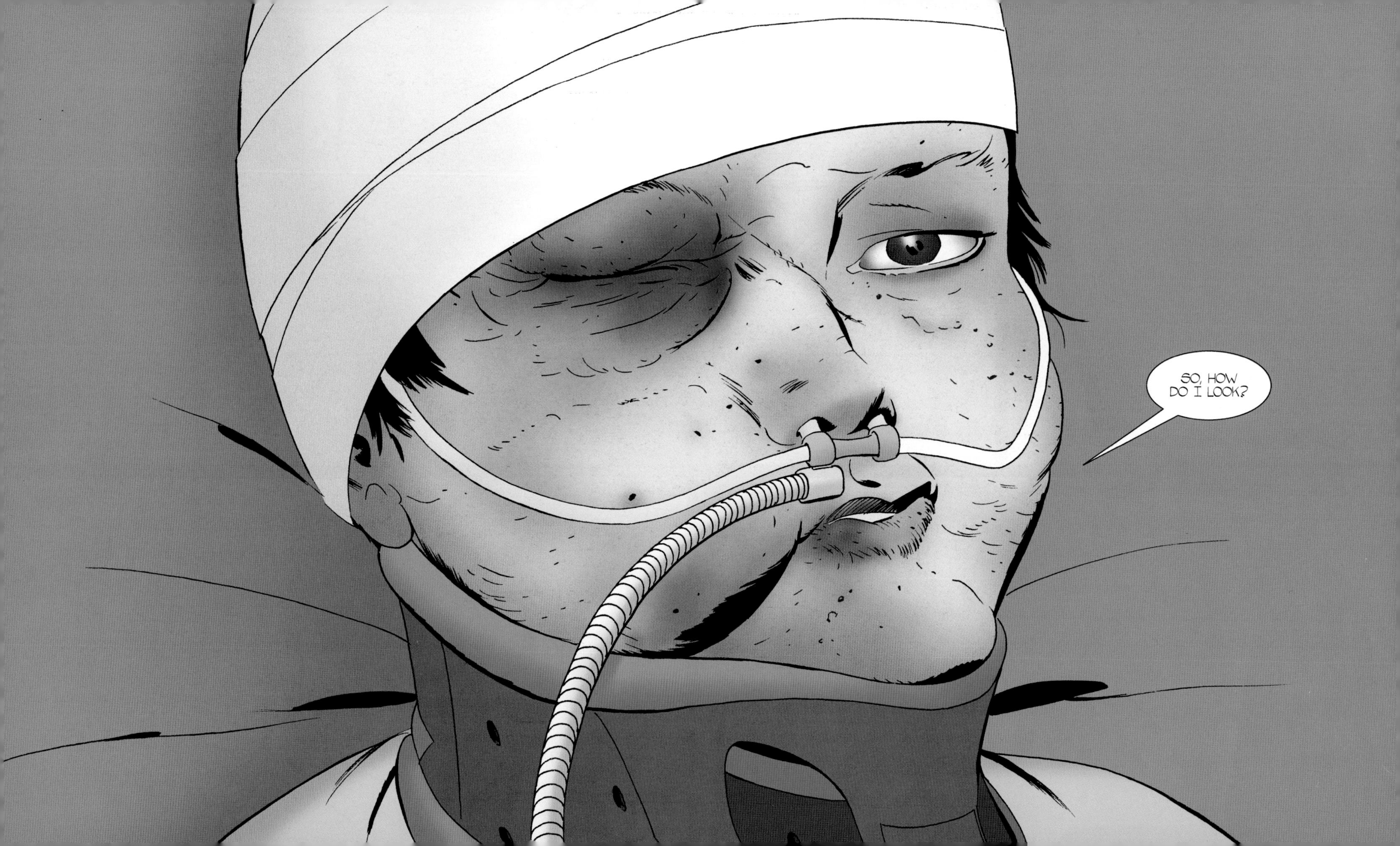
SO, HOW DO I LOOK?

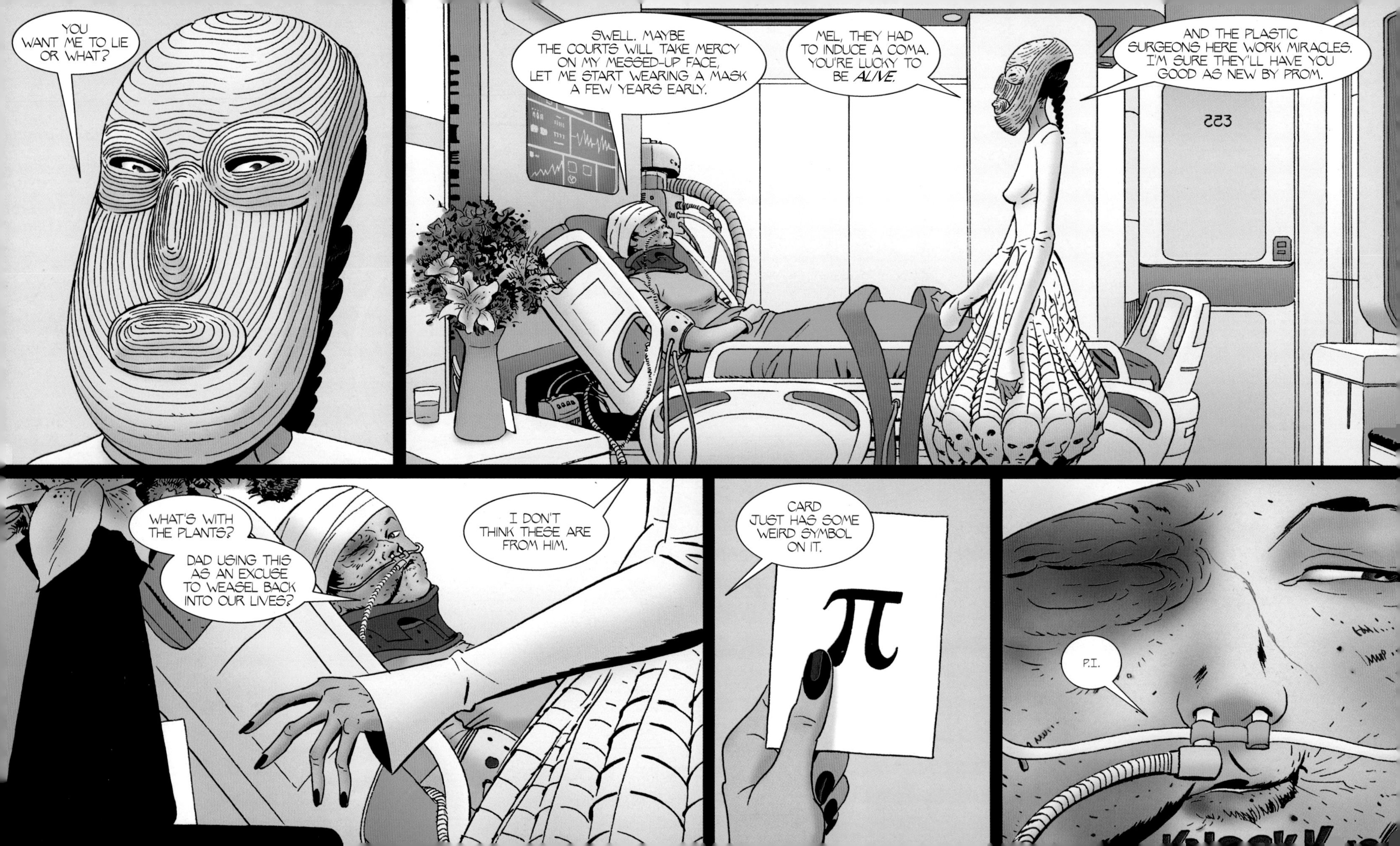
YOU WANT ME TO LIE OR WHAT?
SWELL. MAYBE THE COURTS WILL TAKE MERCY ON MY MESSED-UP FACE, LET ME START WEARING A MASK A FEW YEARS EARLY.
MEL, THEY HAD TO INDUCE A COMA. YOU'RE LUCKY TO BE *ALIVE.*
AND THE PLASTIC SURGEONS HERE WORK MIRACLES. I'M SURE THEY'LL HAVE YOU GOOD AS NEW BY PROM.
223
WHAT'S WITH THE PLANTS?
DAD USING THIS AS AN EXCUSE TO WEASEL BACK INTO OUR LIVES?
I DON'T THINK THESE ARE FROM HIM.
CARD JUST HAS SOME WEIRD SYMBOL ON IT.
π
P.I.

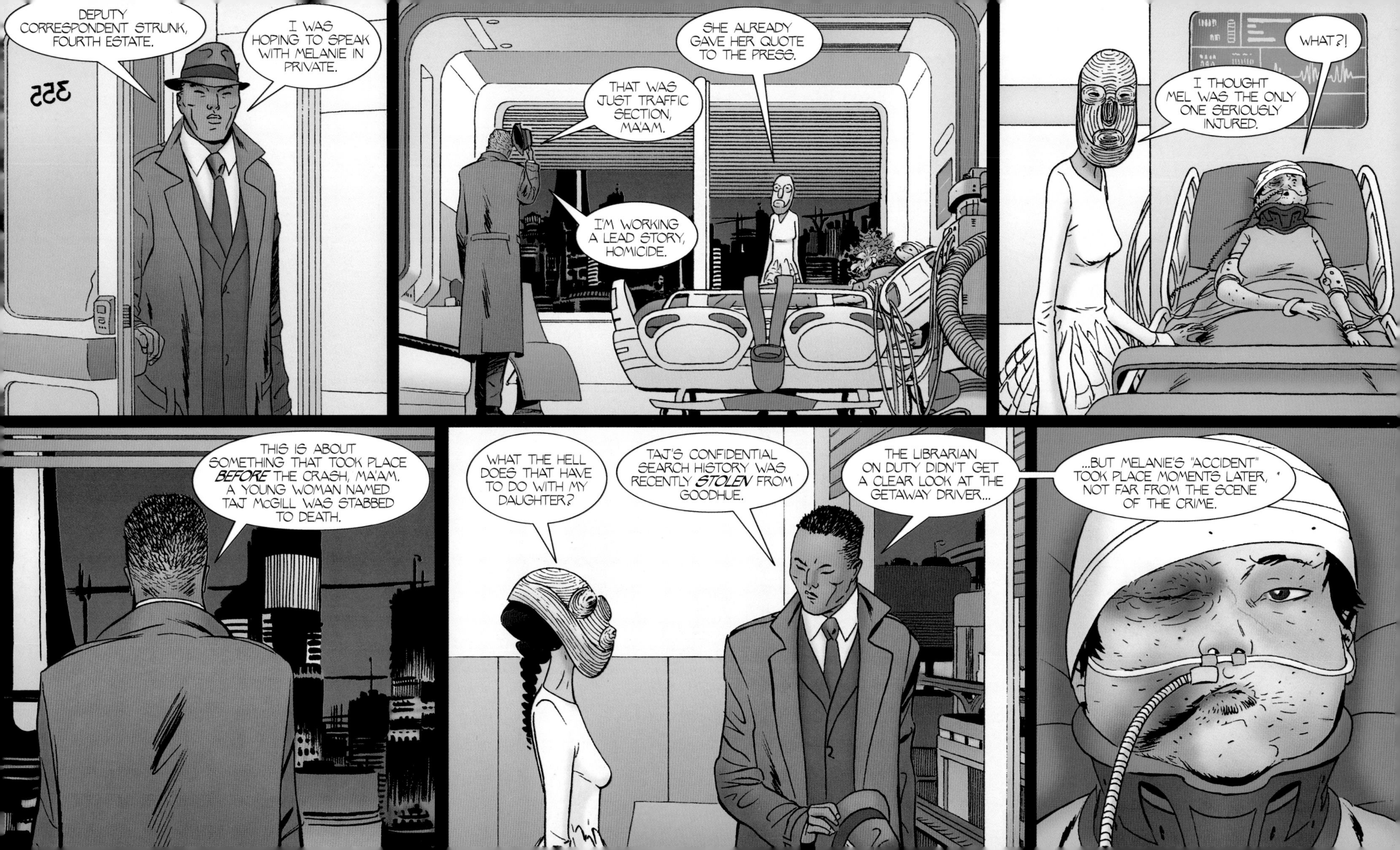

355
DEPUTY CORRESPONDENT STRUNK, FOURTH ESTATE.
I WAS HOPING TO SPEAK WITH MELANIE IN PRIVATE.
SHE ALREADY GAVE HER QUOTE TO THE PRESS.
THAT WAS JUST TRAFFIC SECTION, MA'AM.
I'M WORKING A LEAD STORY, HOMICIDE.
I THOUGHT MEL WAS THE ONLY ONE SERIOUSLY INJURED.
WHAT?!
THIS IS ABOUT SOMETHING THAT TOOK PLACE *BEFORE* THE CRASH, MA'AM. A YOUNG WOMAN NAMED TAJ McGILL WAS STABBED TO DEATH.
WHAT THE HELL DOES THAT HAVE TO DO WITH MY DAUGHTER?
TAJ'S CONFIDENTIAL SEARCH HISTORY WAS RECENTLY *STOLEN* FROM GOODHUE.
THE LIBRARIAN ON DUTY DIDN'T GET A CLEAR LOOK AT THE GETAWAY DRIVER...
...BUT MELANIE'S "ACCIDENT" TOOK PLACE MOMENTS LATER, NOT FAR FROM THE SCENE OF THE CRIME.

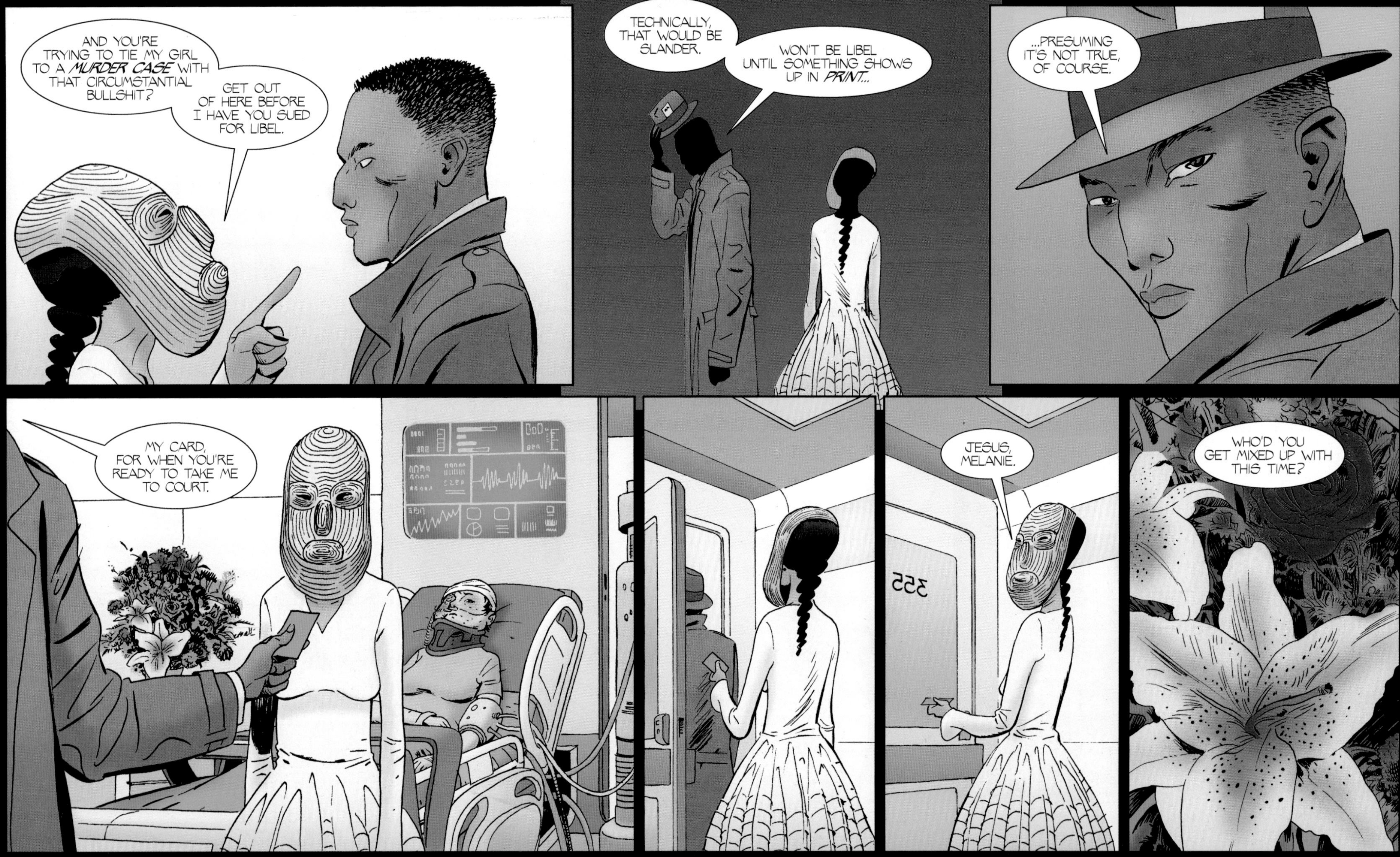
AND YOU'RE TRYING TO TIE MY GIRL TO A *MURDER CASE* WITH THAT CIRCUMSTANTIAL BULLSHIT?
GET OUT OF HERE BEFORE I HAVE YOU SUED FOR LIBEL.
TECHNICALLY, THAT WOULD BE SLANDER.
WON'T BE LIBEL UNTIL SOMETHING SHOWS UP IN *PRINT*...
...PRESUMING IT'S NOT TRUE, OF COURSE.
MY CARD, FOR WHEN YOU'RE READY TO TAKE ME TO COURT.
JESUS, MELANIE.
WHO'D YOU GET MIXED UP WITH THIS TIME?

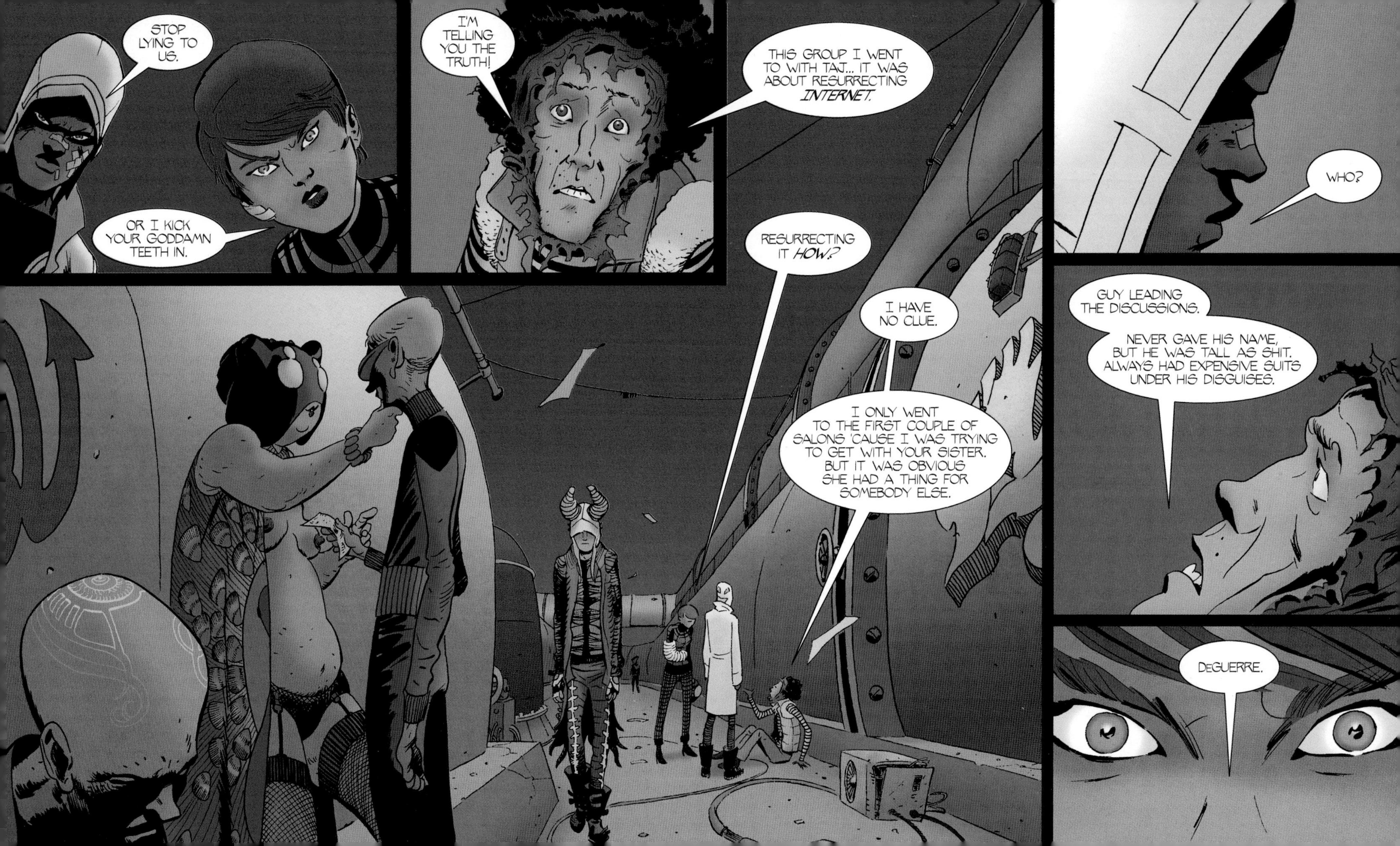
STOP LYING TO US.
OR I KICK YOUR GODDAMN TEETH IN.
I'M TELLING YOU THE TRUTH!
THIS GROUP I WENT TO WITH TAJ... IT WAS ABOUT RESURRECTING *INTERNET.*
RESURRECTING IT *HOW?*
I HAVE NO CLUE.
I ONLY WENT TO THE FIRST COUPLE OF SALONS 'CAUSE I WAS TRYING TO GET WITH YOUR SISTER. BUT IT WAS OBVIOUS SHE HAD A THING FOR SOMEBODY ELSE.
WHO?
GUY LEADING THE DISCUSSIONS.
NEVER GAVE HIS NAME, BUT HE WAS TALL AS SHIT. ALWAYS HAD EXPENSIVE SUITS UNDER HIS DISGUISES.
DEGUERRE.

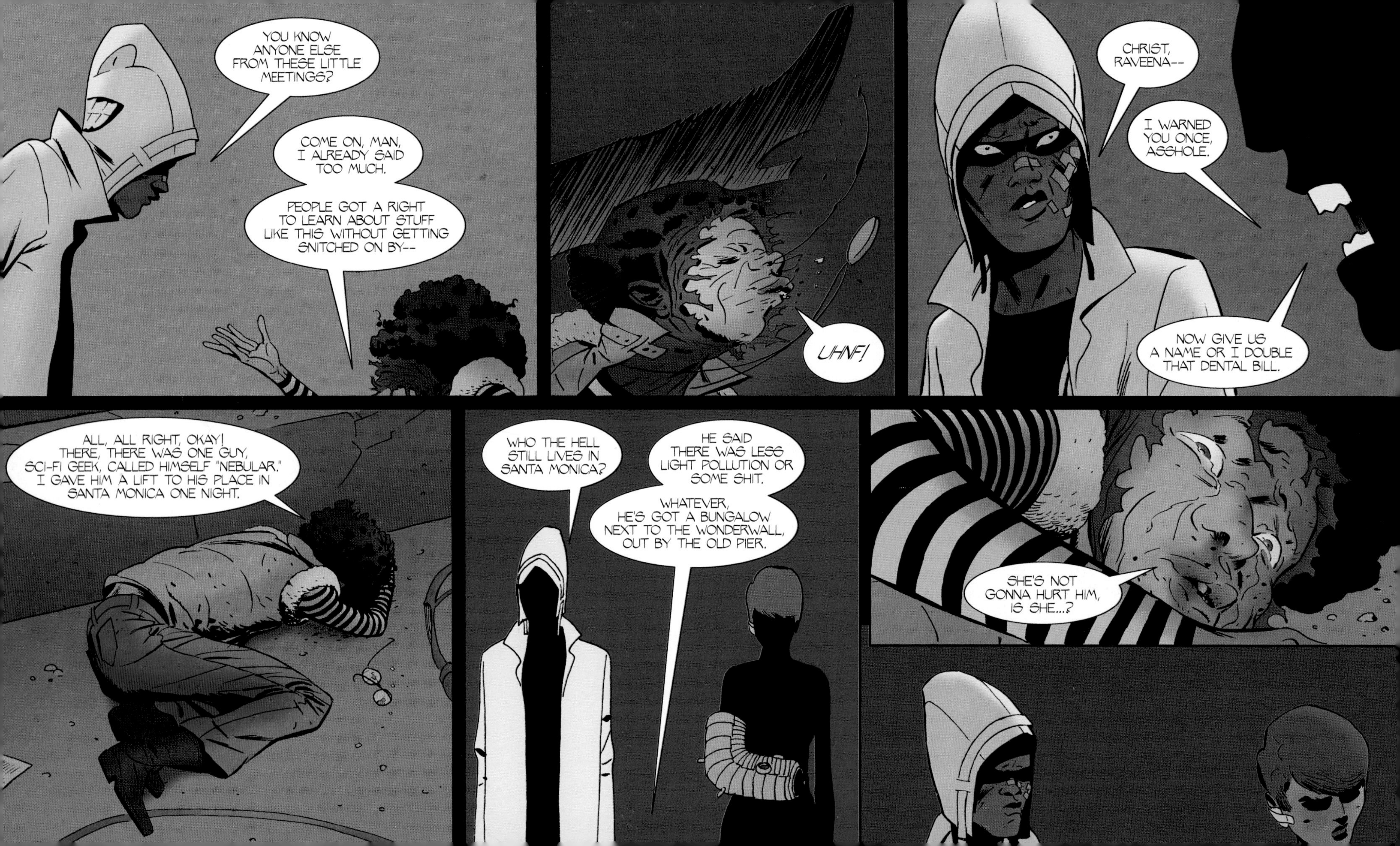
YOU KNOW ANYONE ELSE FROM THESE LITTLE MEETINGS?
COME ON, MAN, I ALREADY SAID TOO MUCH.
PEOPLE GOT A RIGHT TO LEARN ABOUT STUFF LIKE THIS WITHOUT GETTING SNITCHED ON BY--
UHNF!
CHRIST, RAVEENA--
I WARNED YOU ONCE, ASSHOLE.
NOW GIVE US A NAME OR I DOUBLE THAT DENTAL BILL.
ALL, ALL RIGHT, OKAY! THERE, THERE WAS ONE GUY, SCI-FI GEEK, CALLED HIMSELF "NEBULAR." I GAVE HIM A LIFT TO HIS PLACE IN SANTA MONICA ONE NIGHT.
WHO THE HELL STILL LIVES IN SANTA MONICA?
HE SAID THERE WAS LESS LIGHT POLLUTION OR SOME SHIT.
WHATEVER, HE'S GOT A BUNGALOW NEXT TO THE WONDERWALL, OUT BY THE OLD PIER.
SHE'S NOT GONNA HURT HIM, IS SHE...?

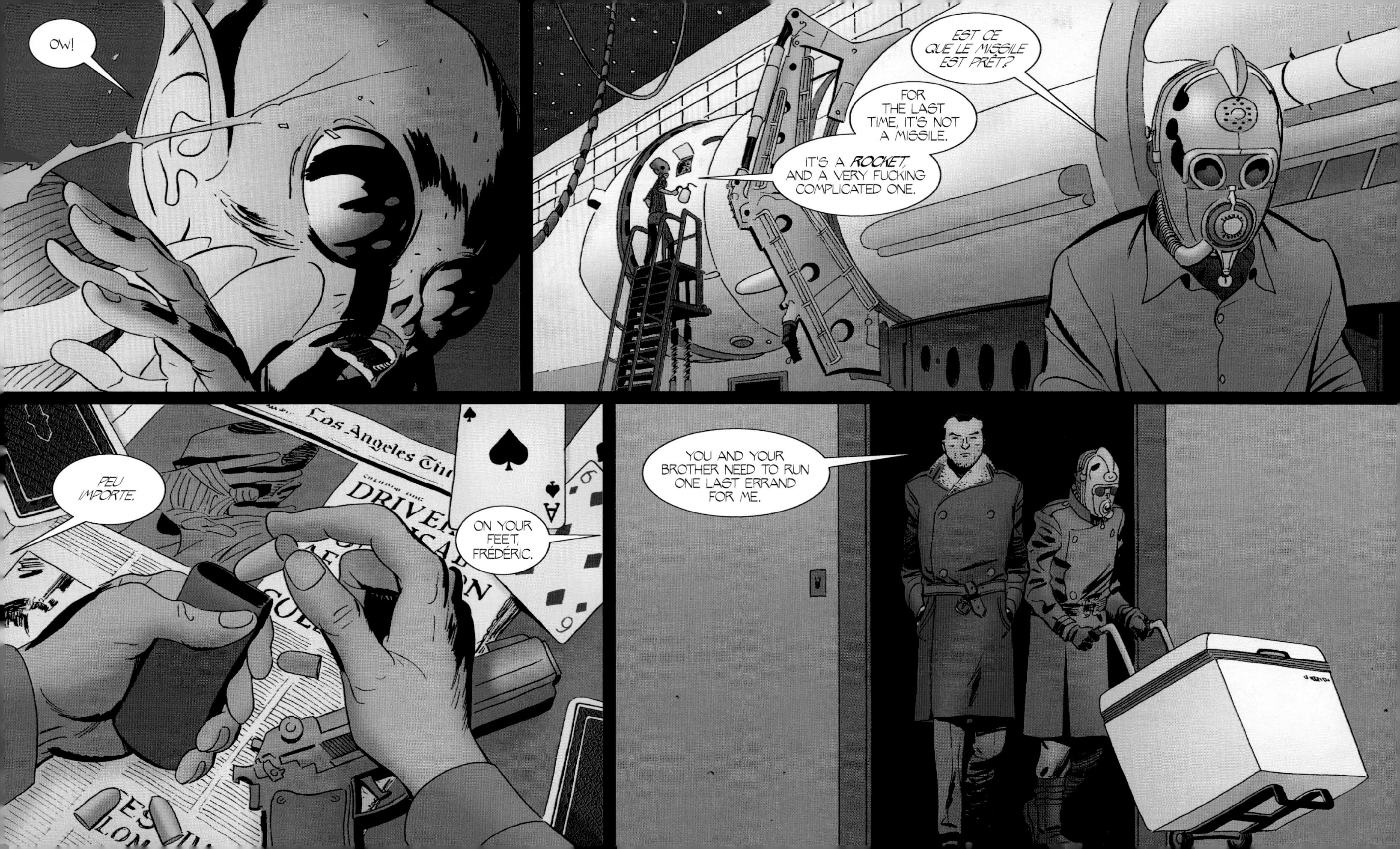
OW!
EST CE QUE LE MISSILE EST PRÊT?
FOR THE LAST TIME, IT'S NOT A MISSILE.
IT'S A *ROCKET*, AND A VERY FUCKING COMPLICATED ONE.
PEU IMPORTE.
ON YOUR FEET, FRÉDÉRIC.
YOU AND YOUR BROTHER NEED TO RUN ONE LAST ERRAND FOR ME.
Los Angeles Times
DRIVEN

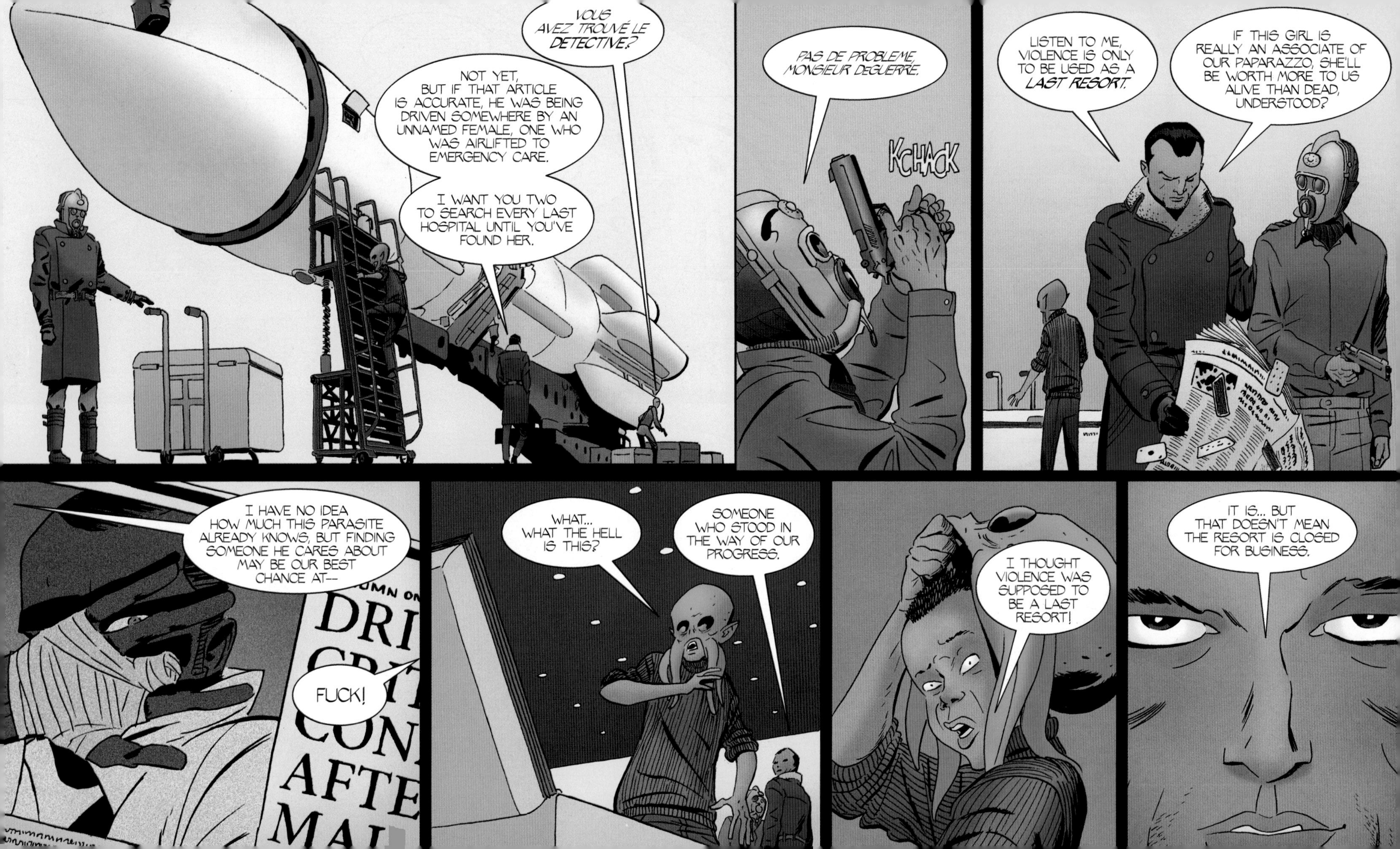
VOUS AVEZ TROUVÉ LE DETECTIVE?
NOT YET, BUT IF THAT ARTICLE IS ACCURATE, HE WAS BEING DRIVEN SOMEWHERE BY AN UNNAMED FEMALE, ONE WHO WAS AIRLIFTED TO EMERGENCY CARE.
I WANT YOU TWO TO SEARCH EVERY LAST HOSPITAL UNTIL YOU'VE FOUND HER.
PAS DE PROBLEME, MONSIEUR DEGUERRE.
KCHACK
LISTEN TO ME, VIOLENCE IS ONLY TO BE USED AS A LAST RESORT.
IF THIS GIRL IS REALLY AN ASSOCIATE OF OUR PAPARAZZO, SHE'LL BE WORTH MORE TO US ALIVE THAN DEAD, UNDERSTOOD?
I HAVE NO IDEA HOW MUCH THIS PARASITE ALREADY KNOWS, BUT FINDING SOMEONE HE CARES ABOUT MAY BE OUR BEST CHANCE AT--
FUCK!
WHAT... WHAT THE HELL IS THIS?
SOMEONE WHO STOOD IN THE WAY OF OUR PROGRESS.
I THOUGHT VIOLENCE WAS SUPPOSED TO BE A LAST RESORT!
IT IS... BUT THAT DOESN'T MEAN THE RESORT IS CLOSED FOR BUSINESS.

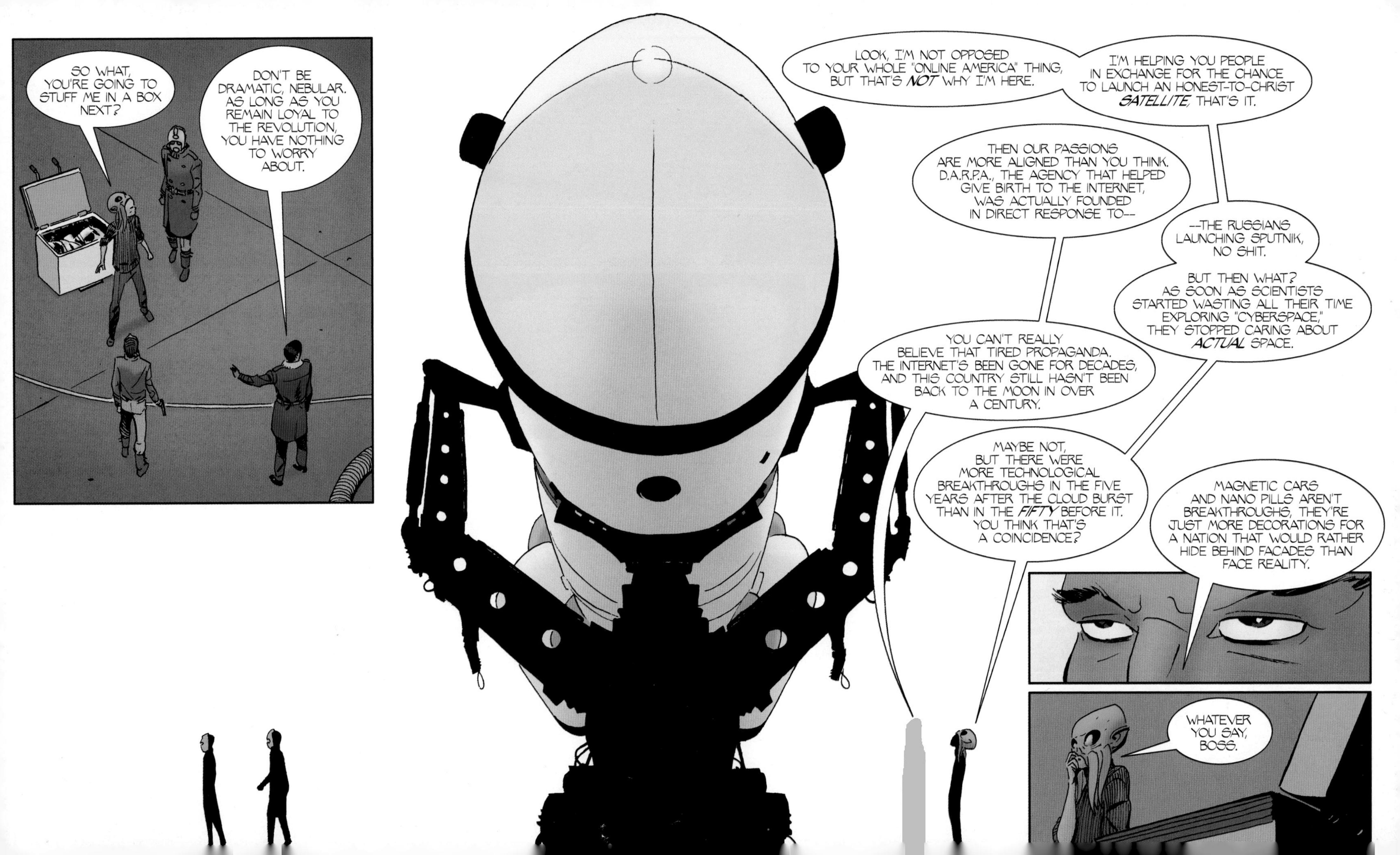
SO WHAT, YOU'RE GOING TO STUFF ME IN A BOX NEXT?
DON'T BE DRAMATIC, NEBULAR. AS LONG AS YOU REMAIN LOYAL TO THE REVOLUTION, YOU HAVE NOTHING TO WORRY ABOUT.
LOOK, I'M NOT OPPOSED TO YOUR WHOLE "ONLINE AMERICA" THING, BUT THAT'S *NOT* WHY I'M HERE.
I'M HELPING YOU PEOPLE IN EXCHANGE FOR THE CHANCE TO LAUNCH AN HONEST-TO-CHRIST *SATELLITE*, THAT'S IT.
THEN OUR PASSIONS ARE MORE ALIGNED THAN YOU THINK. D.A.R.P.A., THE AGENCY THAT HELPED GIVE BIRTH TO THE INTERNET, WAS ACTUALLY FOUNDED IN DIRECT RESPONSE TO--
--THE RUSSIANS LAUNCHING SPUTNIK, NO SHIT.
BUT THEN WHAT? AS SOON AS SCIENTISTS STARTED WASTING ALL THEIR TIME EXPLORING "CYBERSPACE," THEY STOPPED CARING ABOUT *ACTUAL* SPACE.
YOU CAN'T REALLY BELIEVE THAT TIRED PROPAGANDA. THE INTERNET'S BEEN GONE FOR DECADES, AND THIS COUNTRY STILL HASN'T BEEN BACK TO THE MOON IN OVER A CENTURY.
MAYBE NOT, BUT THERE WERE MORE TECHNOLOGICAL BREAKTHROUGHS IN THE FIVE YEARS AFTER THE CLOUD BURST THAN IN THE *FIFTY* BEFORE IT. YOU THINK THAT'S A COINCIDENCE?
MAGNETIC CARS AND NANO PILLS AREN'T BREAKTHROUGHS, THEY'RE JUST MORE DECORATIONS FOR A NATION THAT WOULD RATHER HIDE BEHIND FACADES THAN FACE REALITY.
WHATEVER YOU SAY, BOSS.

INTERNET?

FUCKING INTERNET.

I GUESS PART OF ME IS RELIEVED.

AT LEAST MY SISTER WASN'T MIXED UP IN HARD DRUGS OR ILLEGAL ARMS SMUGGLING.

I WOULD'VE PREFERRED EITHER.

WHY, JUST BECAUSE THIS PIPEDREAM WOULD PUT YOU OUT OF A JOB?

INTERNET USED TO RUN ON, LIKE, PERSONAL COMPUTERS, RIGHT? HOW MANY AMERICANS EVEN *HAVE* THOSE ANYMORE? THESE DAYS, PEOPLE ARE WAY MORE INTERESTED IN...

RAVEENA, THE WEB NEARLY DESTROYED THIS COUNTRY ONCE. IF DEGUERRE'S SECRET CLUB IS REALLY CLOSE TO BRINGING IT BACK--

HOW WOULD THAT EVEN BE POSSIBLE?

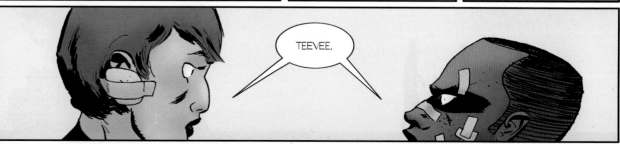

TEEVEE.

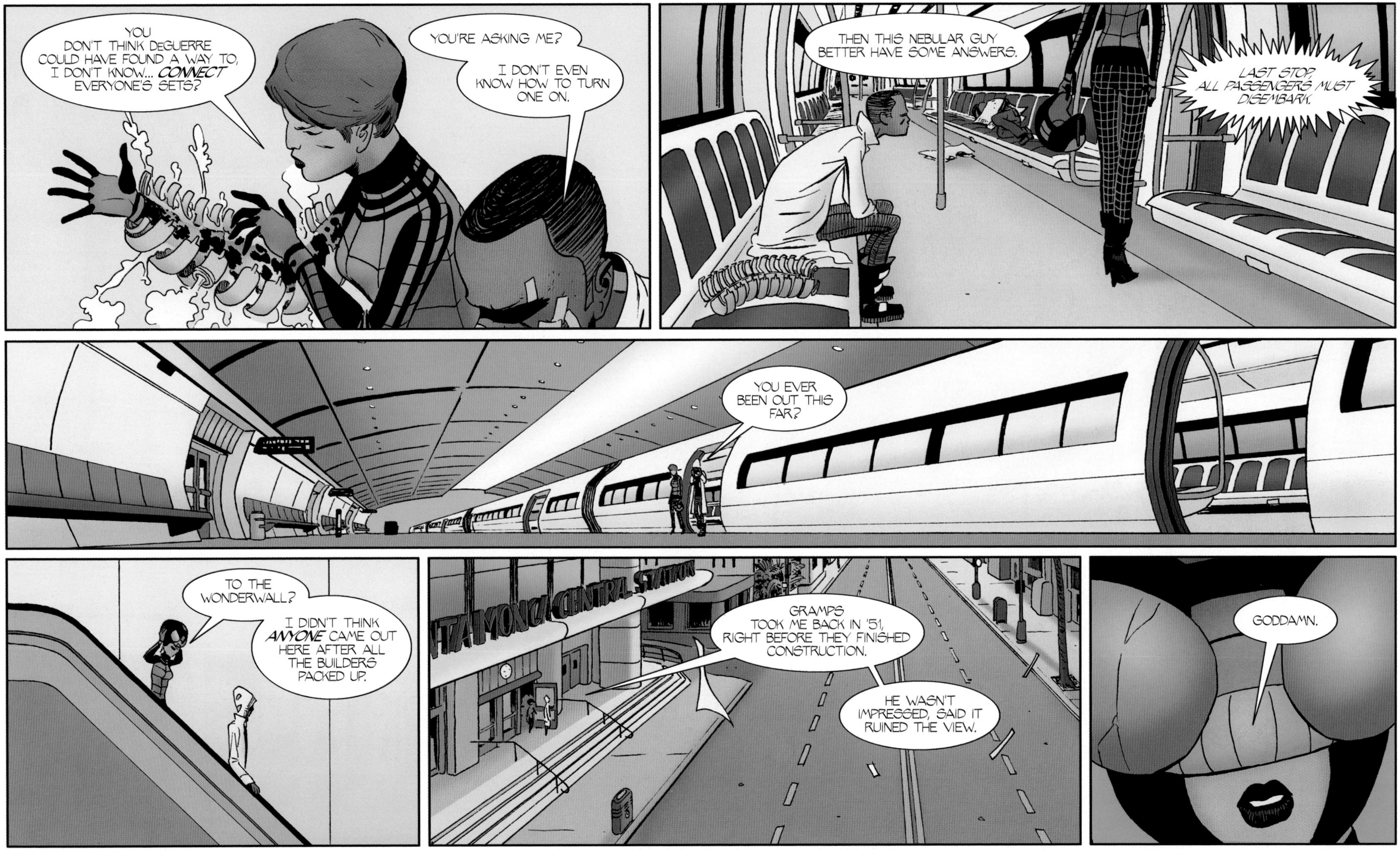
YOU DON'T THINK DeGUERRE COULD HAVE FOUND A WAY TO, I DON'T KNOW... CONNECT EVERYONE'S SETS?
YOU'RE ASKING ME?
I DON'T EVEN KNOW HOW TO TURN ONE ON.
THEN THIS NEBULAR GUY BETTER HAVE SOME ANSWERS.
LAST STOP. ALL PASSENGERS MUST DISEMBARK.
YOU EVER BEEN OUT THIS FAR?
TO THE WONDERWALL?
I DIDN'T THINK ANYONE CAME OUT HERE AFTER ALL THE BUILDERS PACKED UP.
NTA MONICA CENTRAL STATION
GRAMPS TOOK ME BACK IN '51, RIGHT BEFORE THEY FINISHED CONSTRUCTION.
HE WASN'T IMPRESSED, SAID IT RUINED THE VIEW.
GODDAMN.

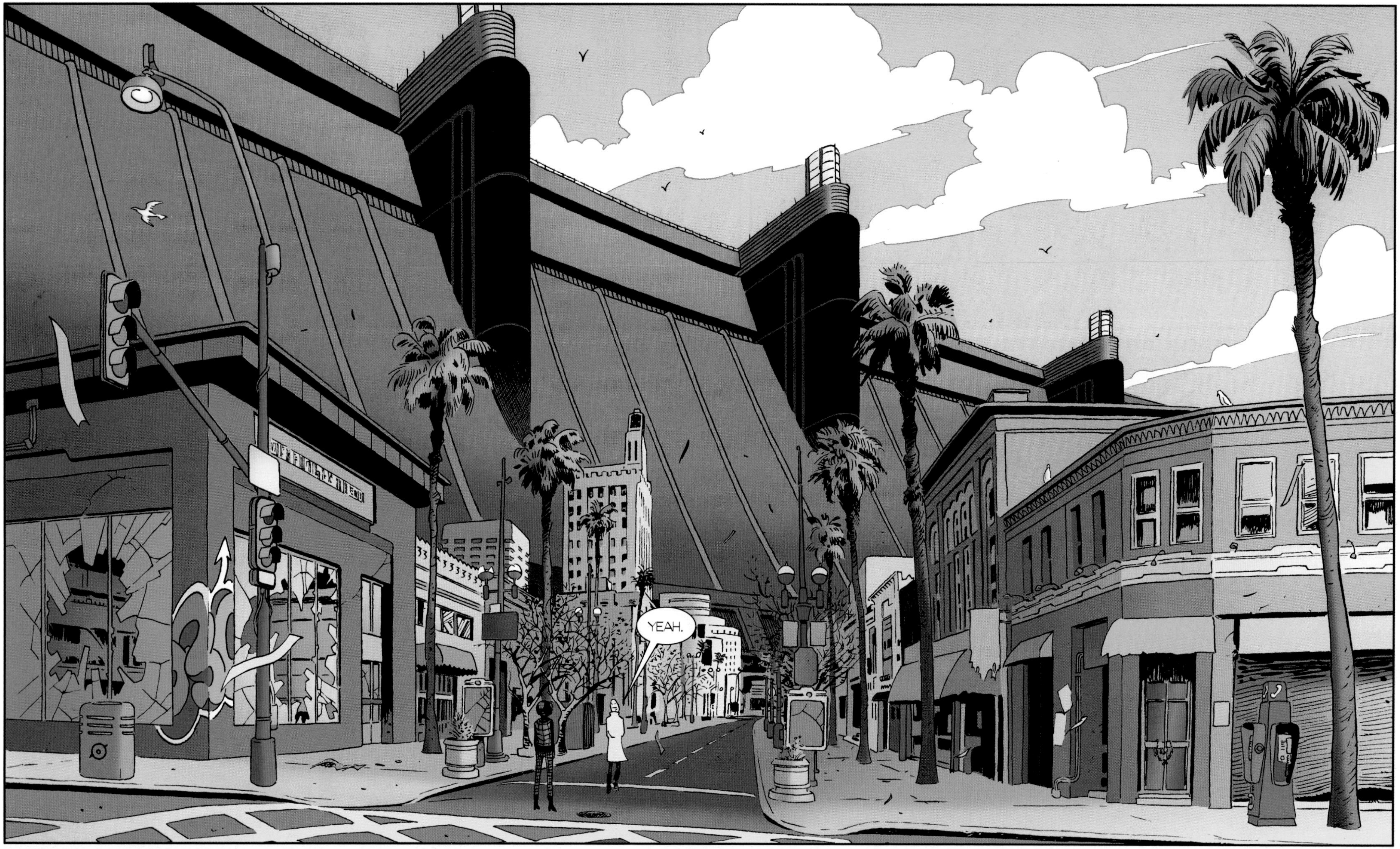
YEAH.

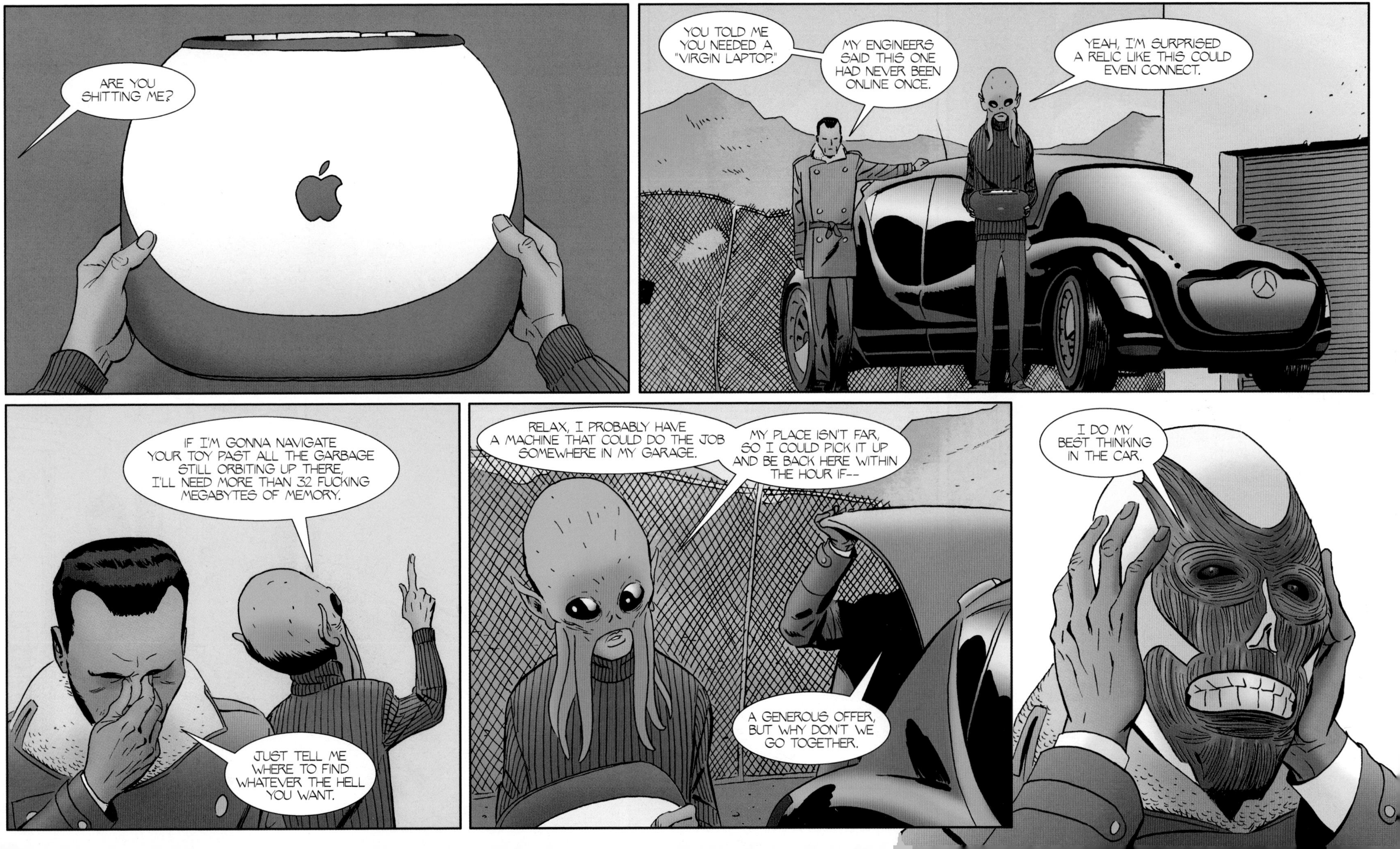
ARE YOU SHITTING ME?
YOU TOLD ME YOU NEEDED A "VIRGIN LAPTOP."
MY ENGINEERS SAID THIS ONE HAD NEVER BEEN ONLINE ONCE.
YEAH, I'M SURPRISED A RELIC LIKE THIS COULD EVEN CONNECT.
IF I'M GONNA NAVIGATE YOUR TOY PAST ALL THE GARBAGE STILL ORBITING UP THERE, I'LL NEED MORE THAN 32 FUCKING MEGABYTES OF MEMORY.
JUST TELL ME WHERE TO FIND WHATEVER THE HELL YOU WANT.
RELAX, I PROBABLY HAVE A MACHINE THAT COULD DO THE JOB SOMEWHERE IN MY GARAGE.
MY PLACE ISN'T FAR, SO I COULD PICK IT UP AND BE BACK HERE WITHIN THE HOUR IF--
A GENEROUS OFFER, BUT WHY DON'T WE GO TOGETHER.
I DO MY BEST THINKING IN THE CAR.

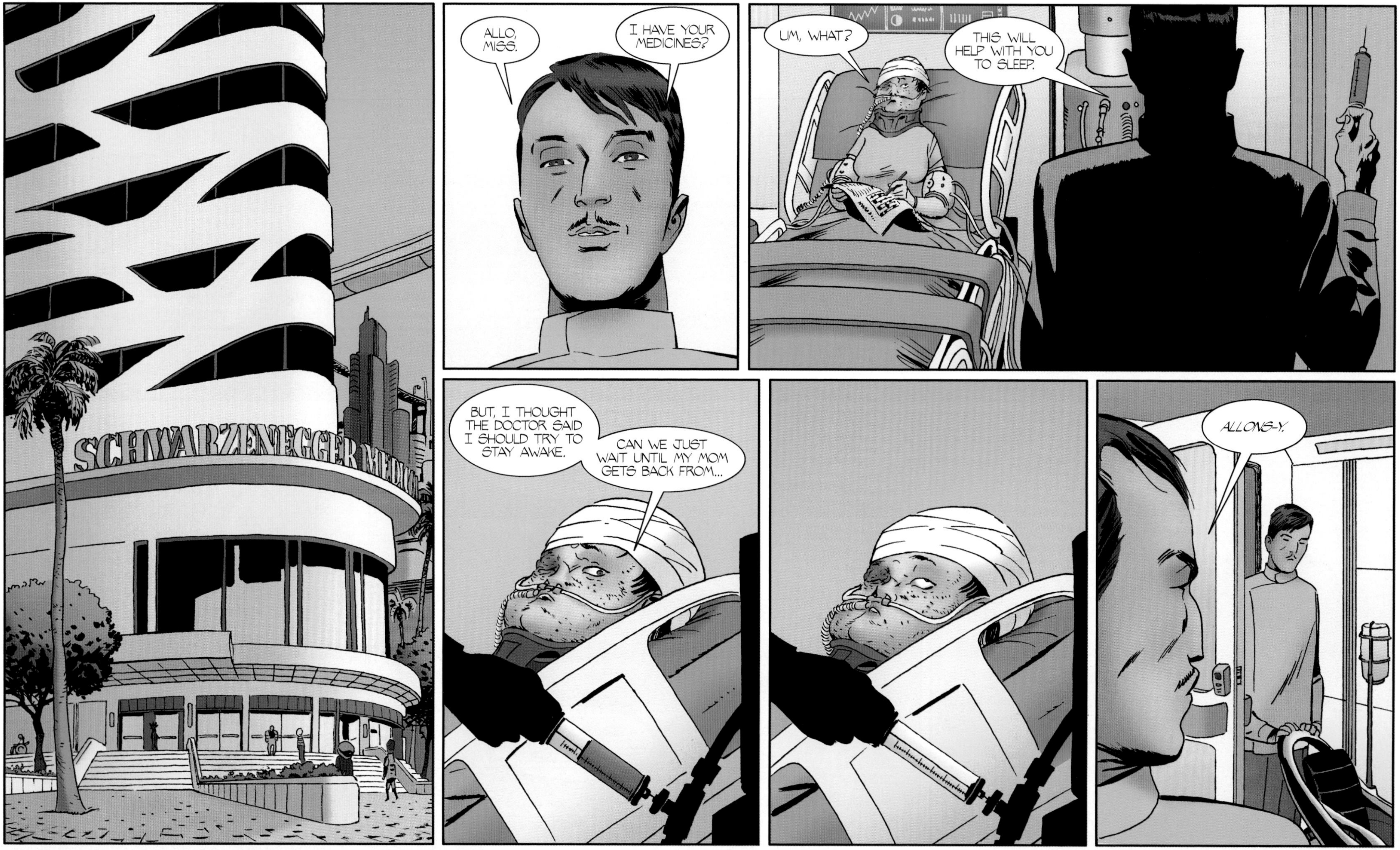
SCHWARZENEGGER MEDICA
ALLO, MISS.
I HAVE YOUR MEDICINES?
UM, WHAT?
THIS WILL HELP WITH YOU TO SLEEP.
BUT, I THOUGHT THE DOCTOR SAID I SHOULD TRY TO STAY AWAKE.
CAN WE JUST WAIT UNTIL MY MOM GETS BACK FROM...
ALLONS-Y.

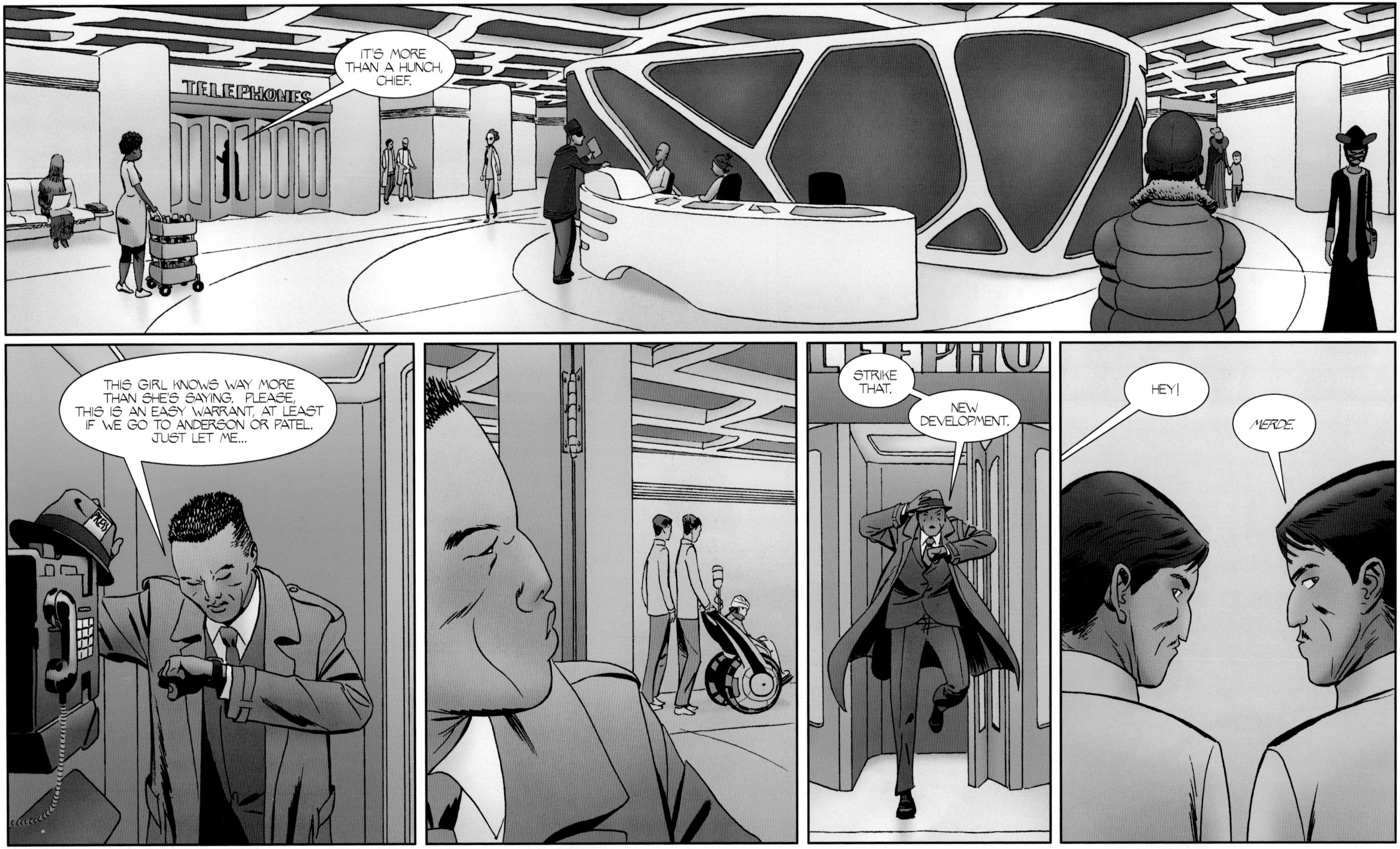
TELEPHONES
IT'S MORE THAN A HUNCH, CHIEF.
THIS GIRL KNOWS WAY MORE THAN SHE'S SAYING. PLEASE, THIS IS AN EASY WARRANT, AT LEAST IF WE GO TO ANDERSON OR PATEL. JUST LET ME...
PRESS
STRIKE THAT.
NEW DEVELOPMENT.
HEY!
MERDE.

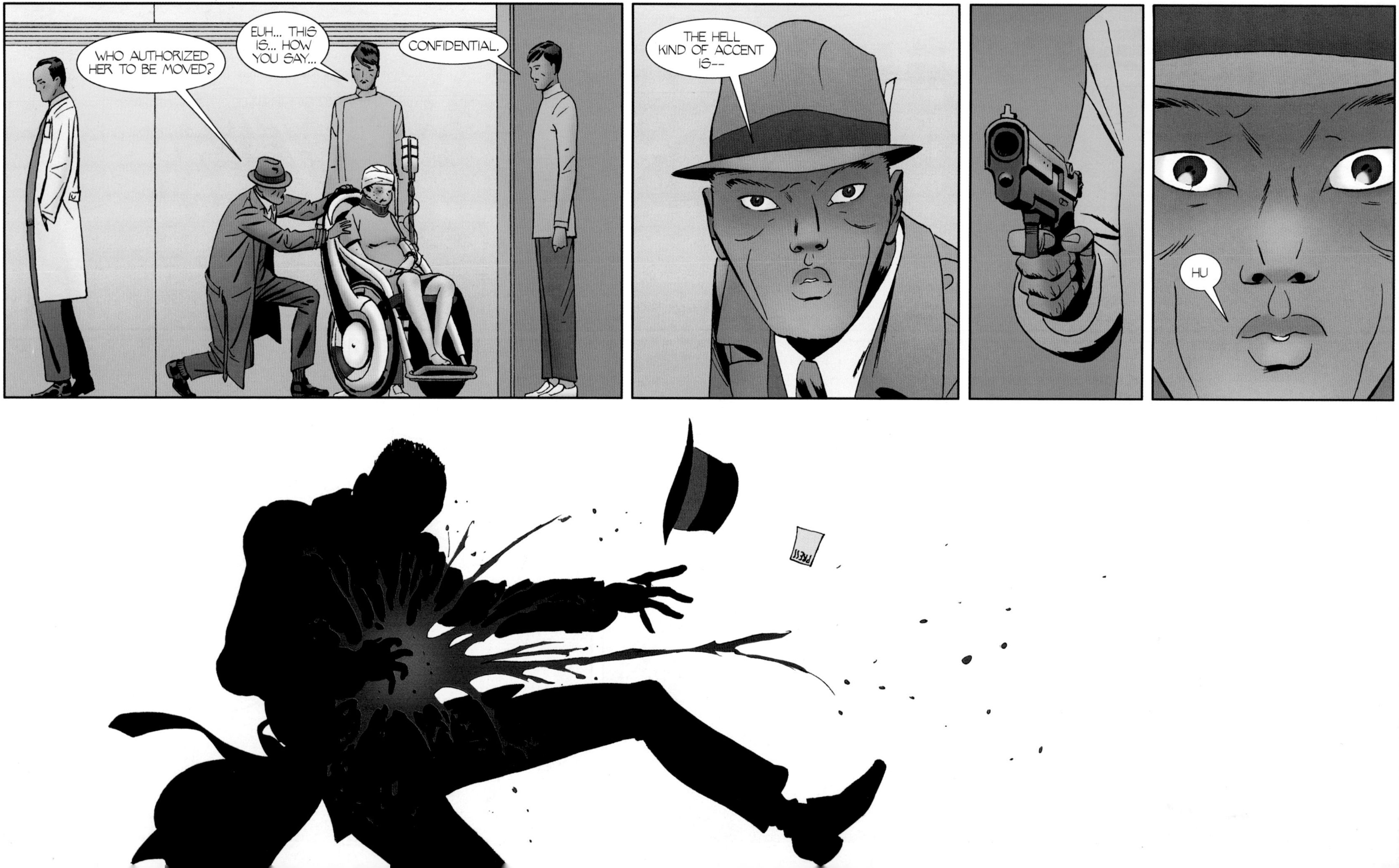
WHO AUTHORIZED HER TO BE MOVED?
EUH... THIS IS... HOW YOU SAY...
CONFIDENTIAL.
THE HELL KIND OF ACCENT IS--
HU

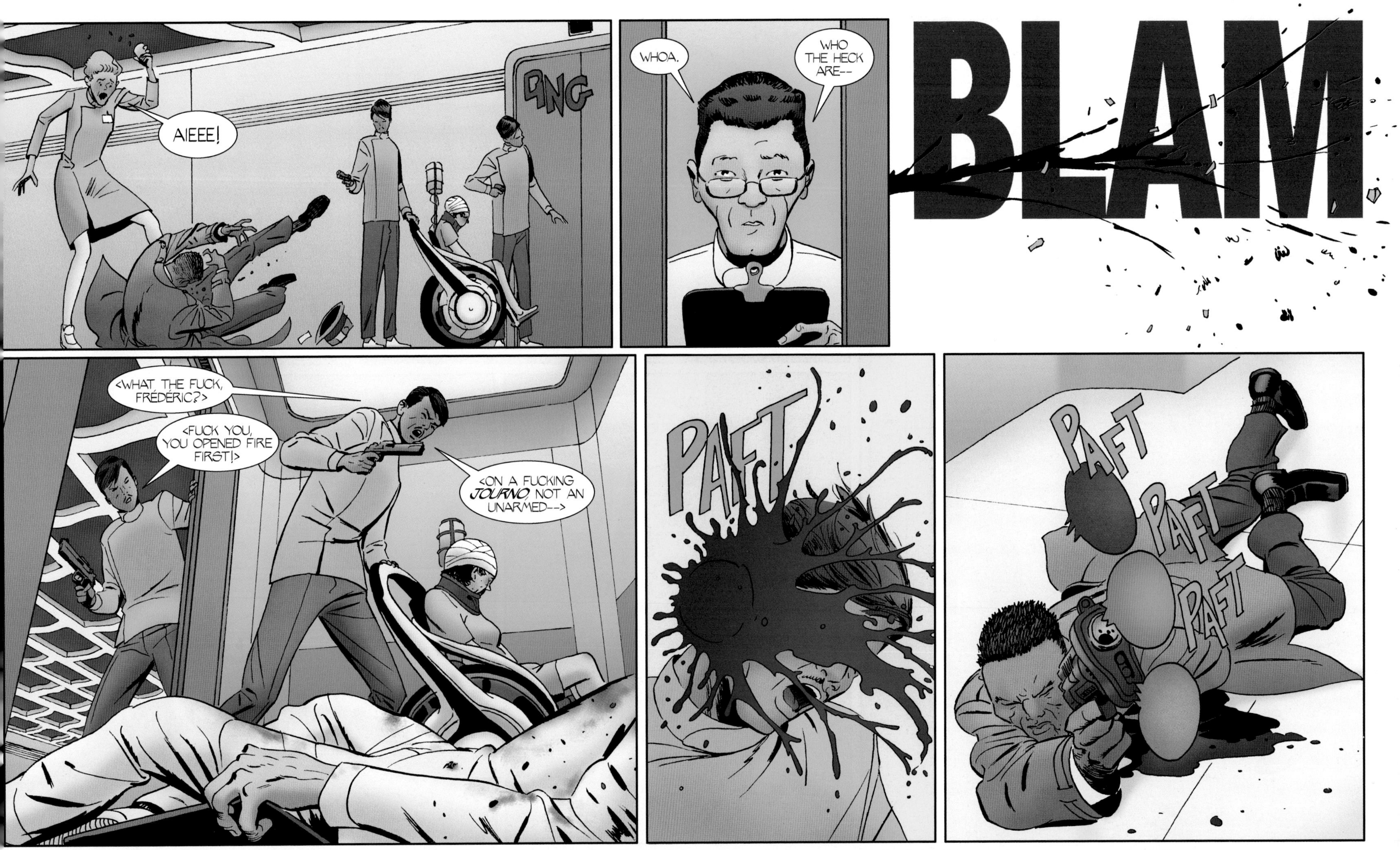
AIEEE!
PING
WHOA.
WHO THE HECK ARE--
BLAM
<WHAT THE FUCK, FRÉDÉRIC?>
<FUCK YOU, YOU OPENED FIRE FIRST!>
<ON A FUCKING *JOURNO*, NOT AN UNARMED-->
PAFT
PAFT
PAFT
PAFT

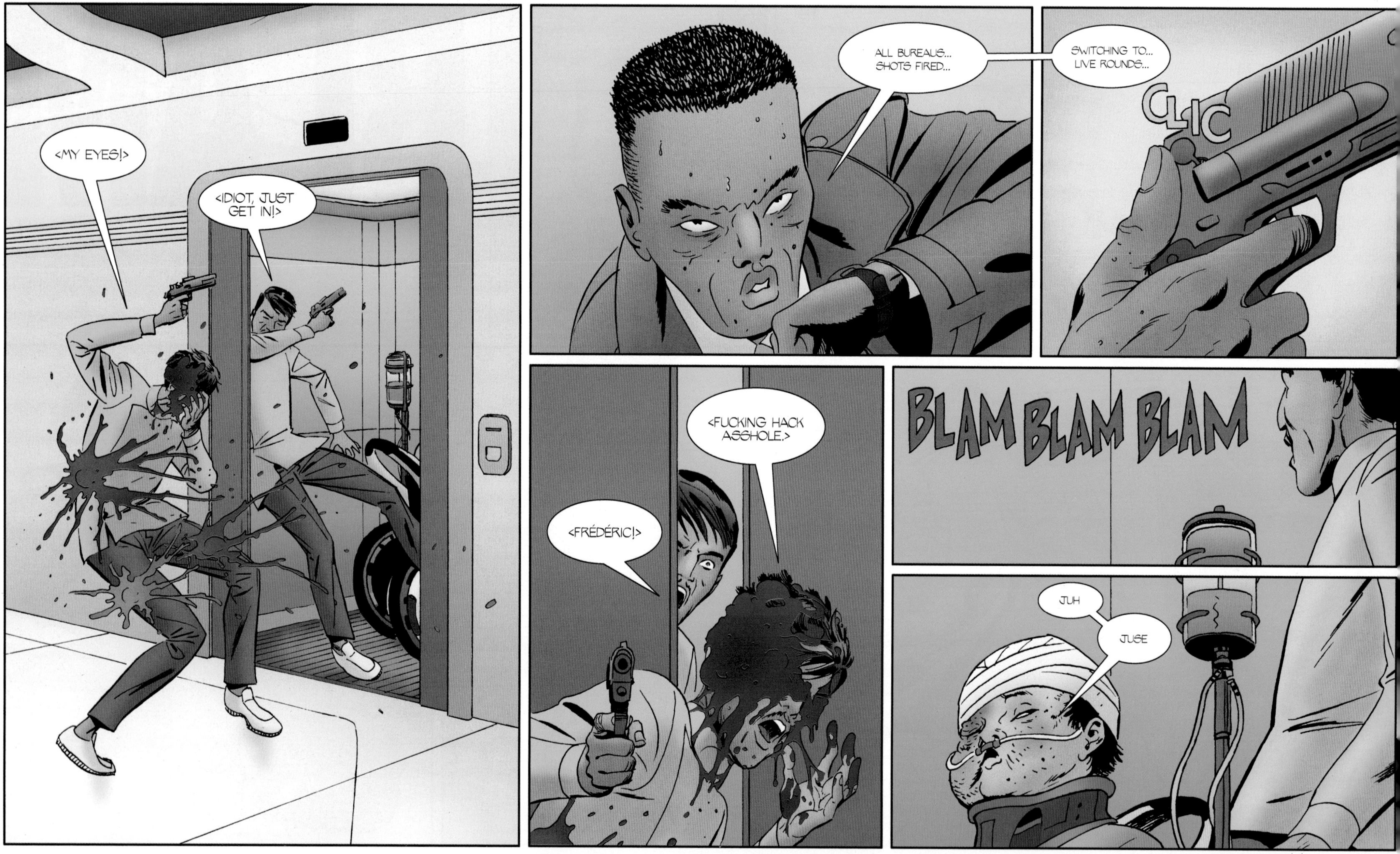
<MY EYES!>
<IDIOT, JUST GET IN!>
ALL BUREAUS... SHOTS FIRED...
SWITCHING TO... LIVE ROUNDS...
CLIC
<FUCKING HACK ASSHOLE.>
<FRÉDÉRIC!>
BLAM BLAM BLAM
JUH
JUSE

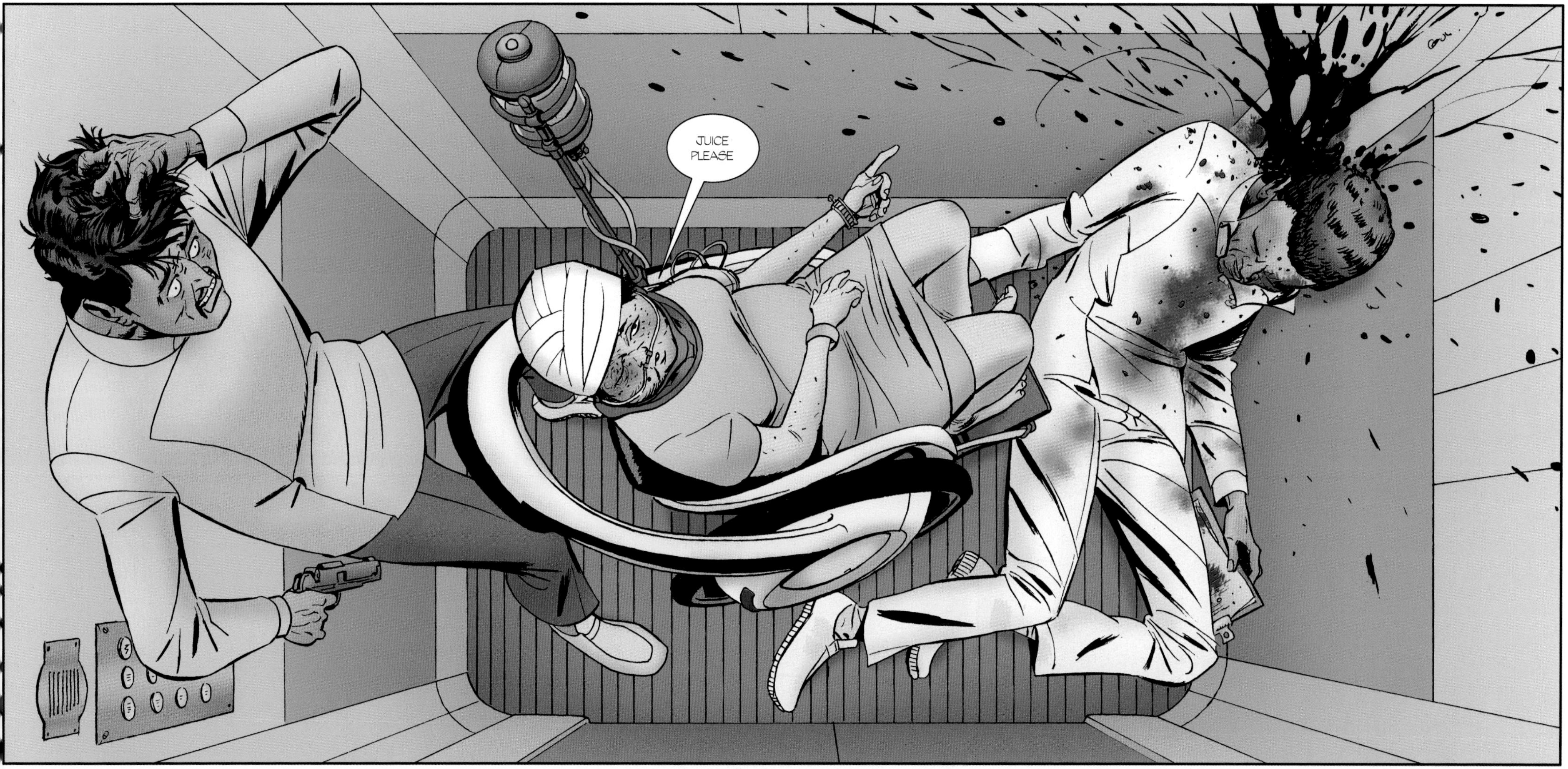

JUICE
PLEASE

THE PRIVATE EYE

BRIAN K. VAUGHAN MARCOS MARTIN
WITH
MUNTSA VICENTE

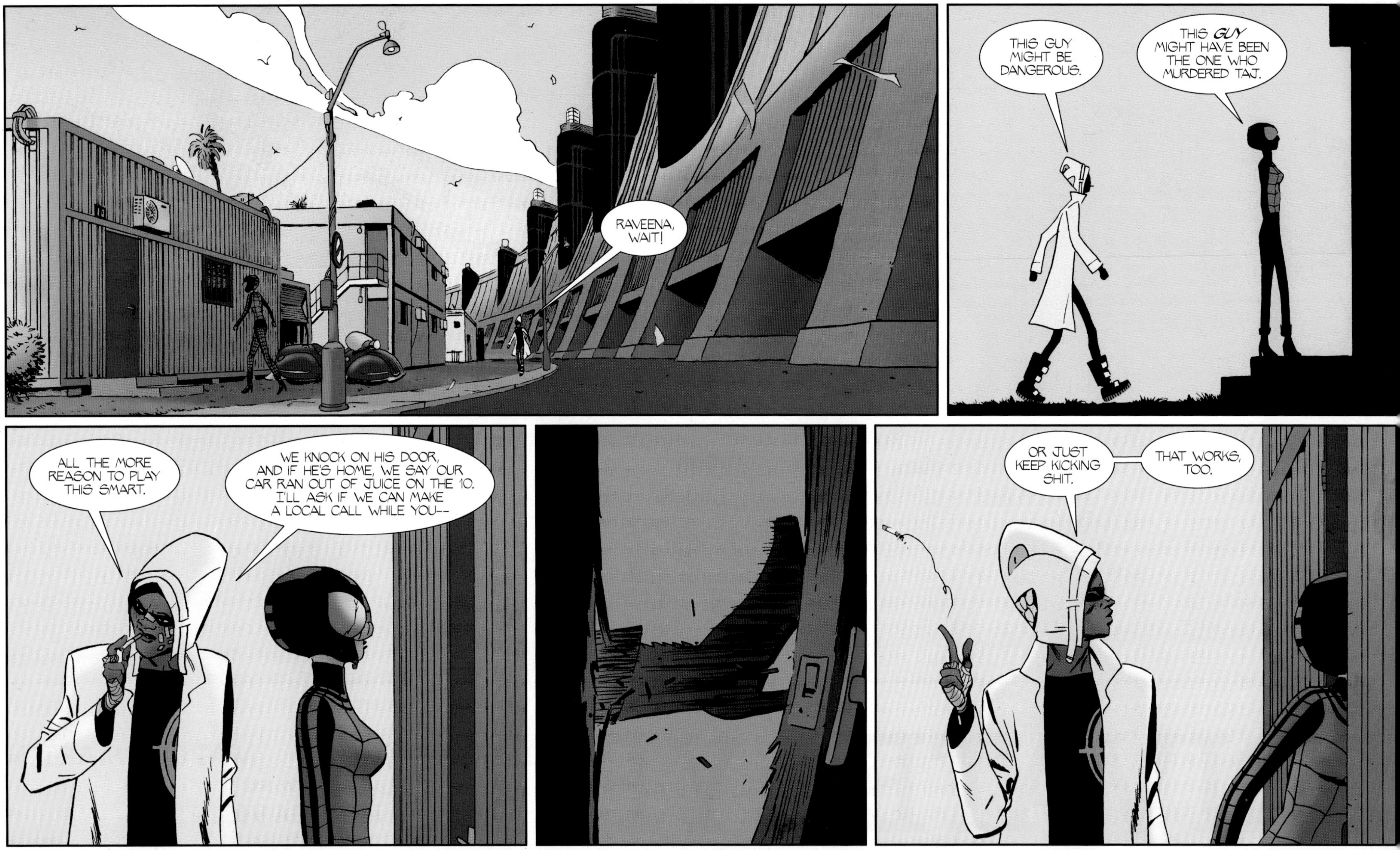
RAVEENA, WAIT!
THIS GUY MIGHT BE DANGEROUS.
THIS GUY MIGHT HAVE BEEN THE ONE WHO MURDERED TAJ.
ALL THE MORE REASON TO PLAY THIS SMART.
WE KNOCK ON HIS DOOR, AND IF HE'S HOME, WE SAY OUR CAR RAN OUT OF JUICE ON THE 10. I'LL ASK IF WE CAN MAKE A LOCAL CALL WHILE YOU--
OR JUST KEEP KICKING SHIT.
THAT WORKS, TOO.

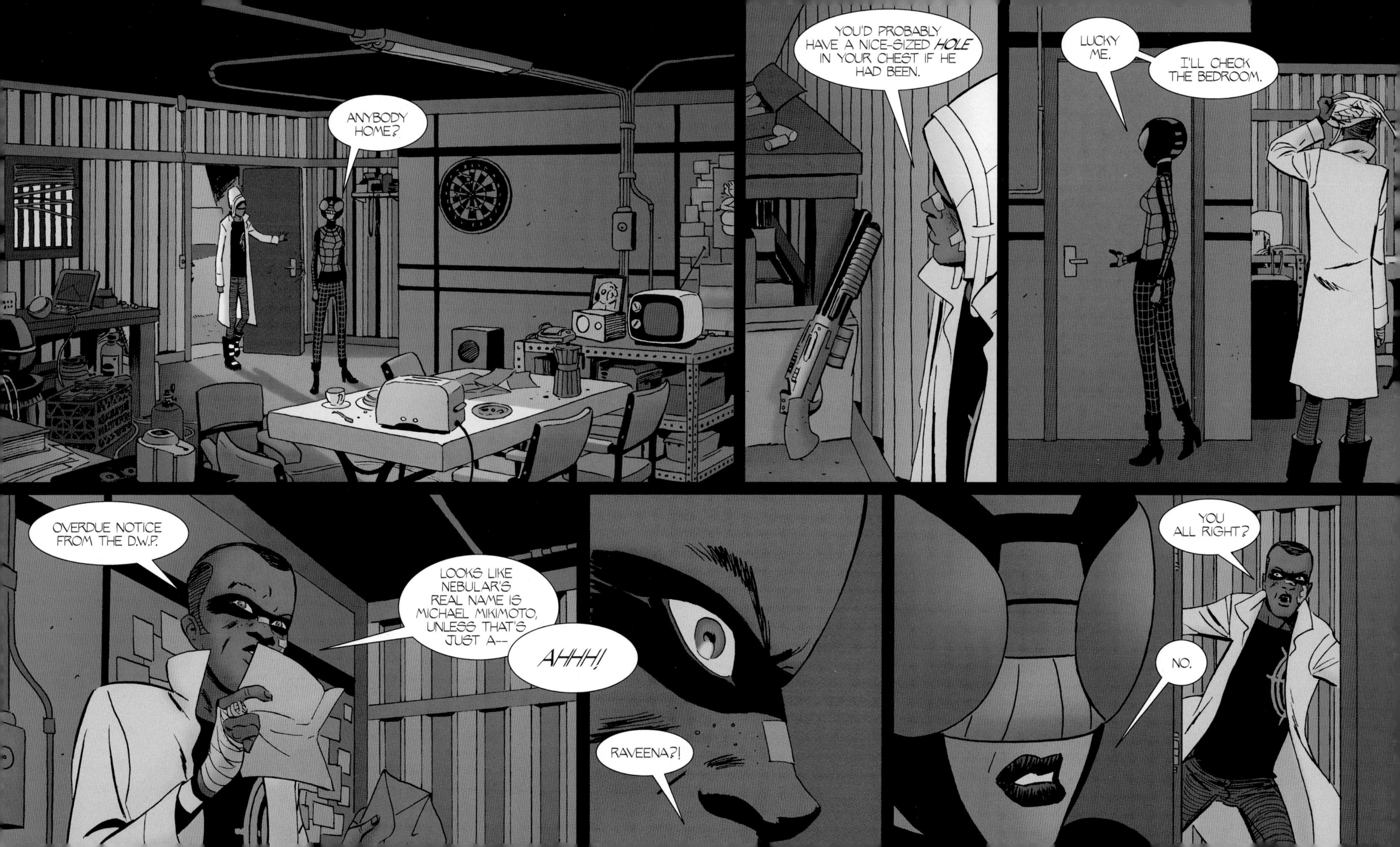
ANYBODY HOME?
YOU'D PROBABLY HAVE A NICE-SIZED *HOLE* IN YOUR CHEST IF HE HAD BEEN.
LUCKY ME.
I'LL CHECK THE BEDROOM.
OVERDUE NOTICE FROM THE D.W.P.
LOOKS LIKE NEBULAR'S REAL NAME IS MICHAEL MIKIMOTO, UNLESS THAT'S JUST A--
AHHH!
RAVEENA?!
YOU ALL RIGHT?
NO.

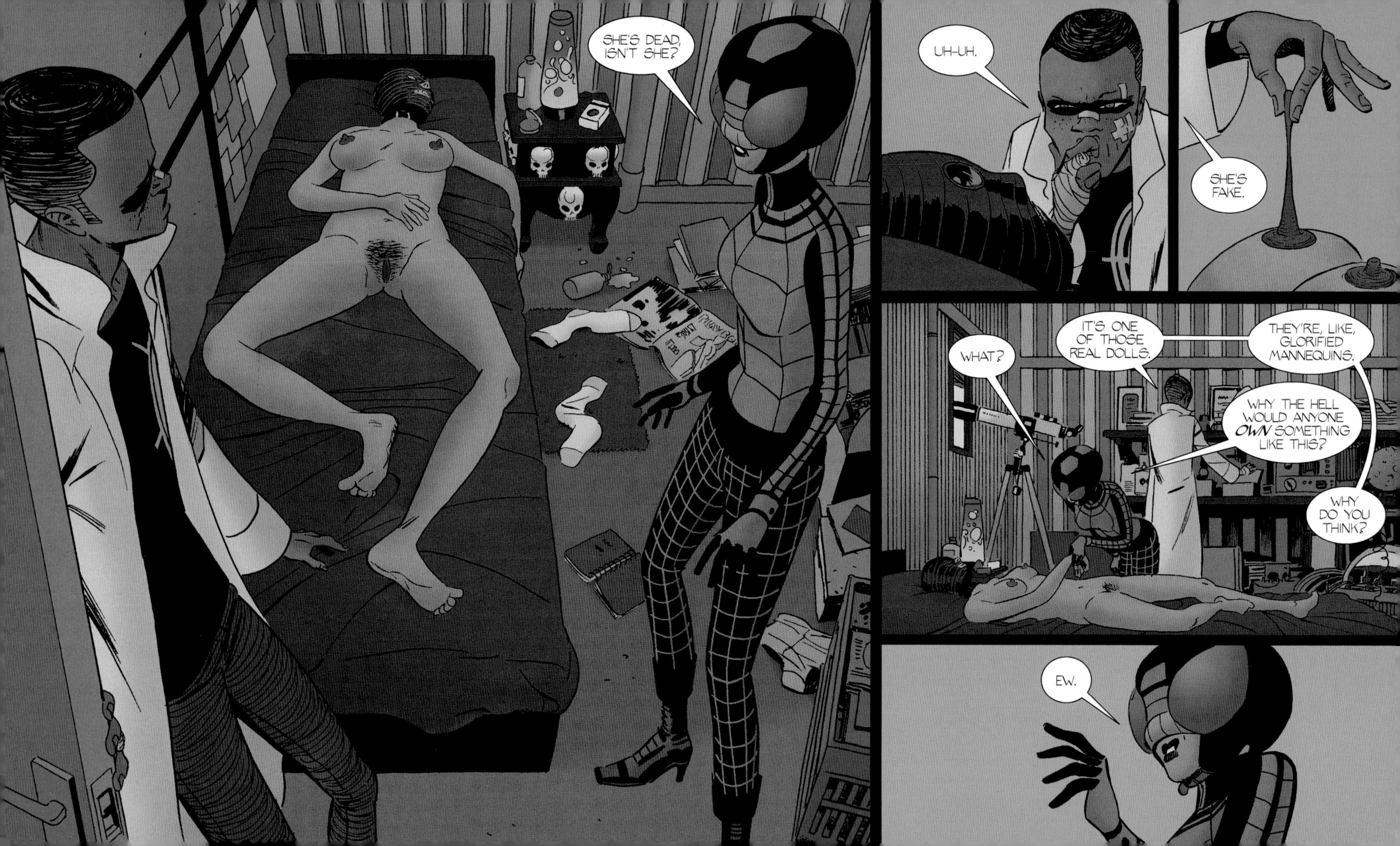
SHE'S DEAD, ISN'T SHE?
UH-UH.
SHE'S FAKE.
WHAT?
IT'S ONE OF THOSE REAL DOLLS.
THEY'RE, LIKE, GLORIFIED MANNEQUINS.
WHY THE HELL WOULD ANYONE *OWN* SOMETHING LIKE THIS?
WHY DO YOU THINK?
EW.

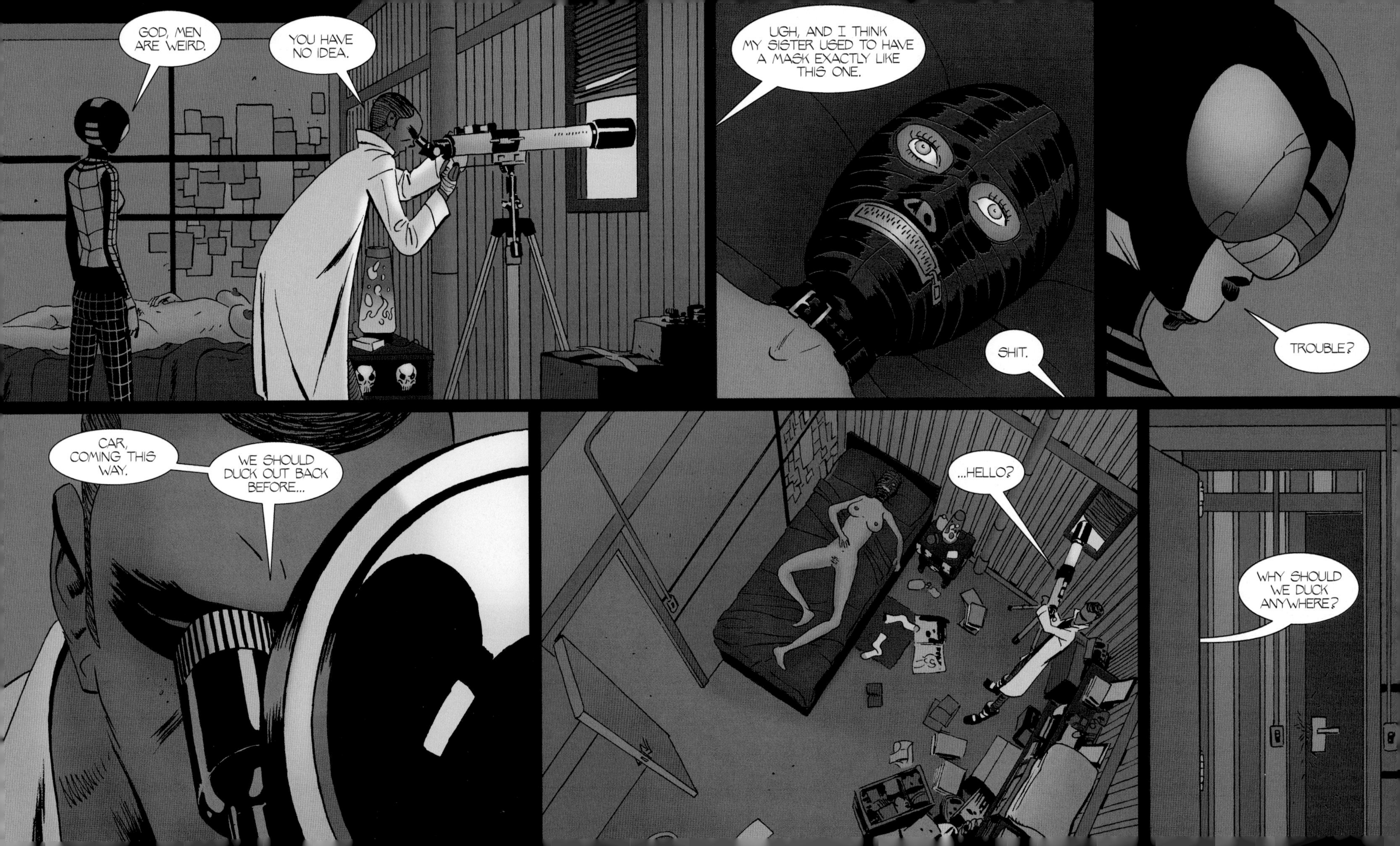
GOD, MEN ARE WEIRD.
YOU HAVE NO IDEA.
UGH, AND I THINK MY SISTER USED TO HAVE A MASK EXACTLY LIKE THIS ONE.
SHIT.
TROUBLE?
CAR, COMING THIS WAY.
WE SHOULD DUCK OUT BACK BEFORE...
...HELLO?
WHY SHOULD WE DUCK ANYWHERE?

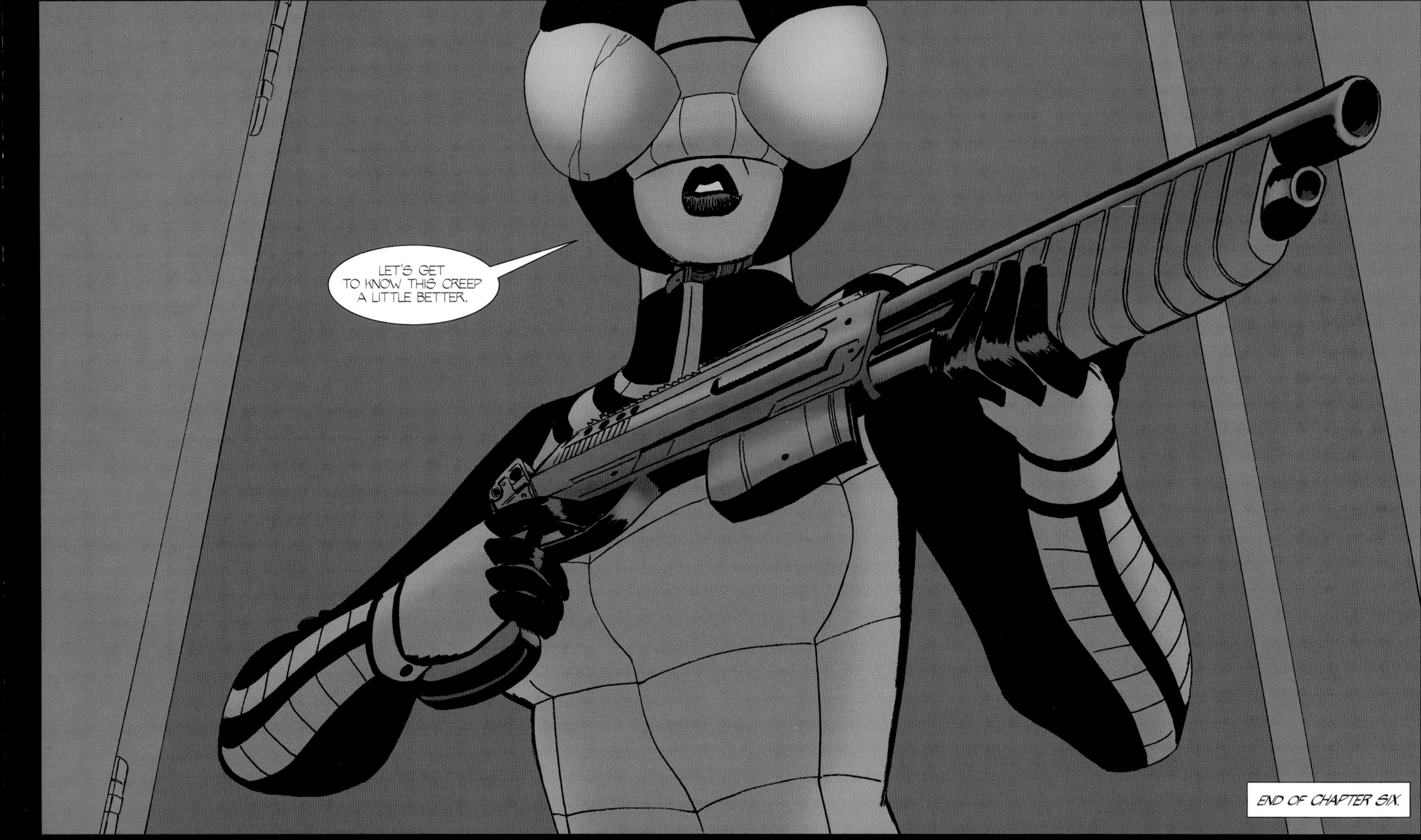
LET'S GET
TO KNOW THIS CREEP
A LITTLE BETTER.
END OF CHAPTER SIX.

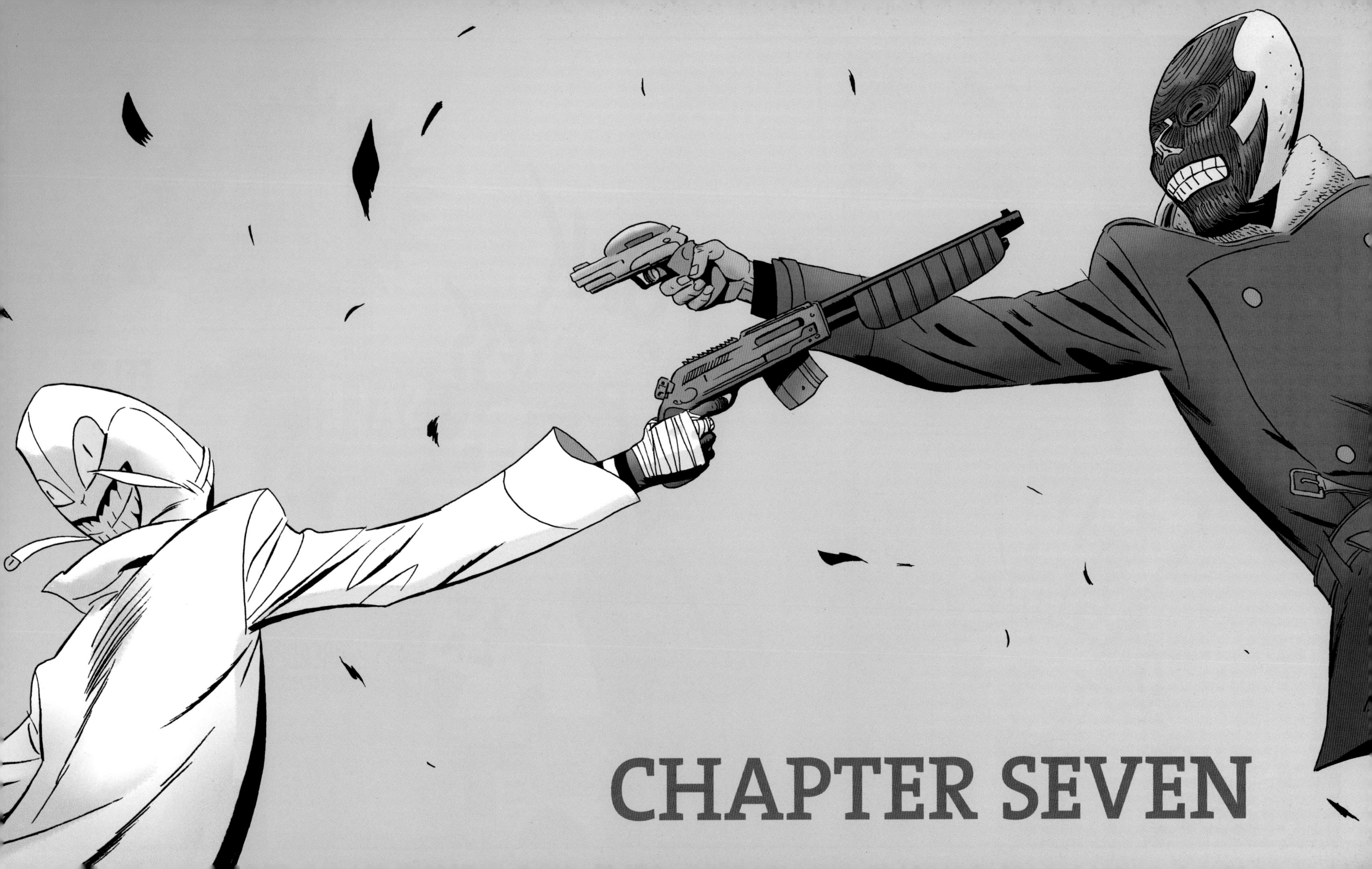

CHAPTER SEVEN

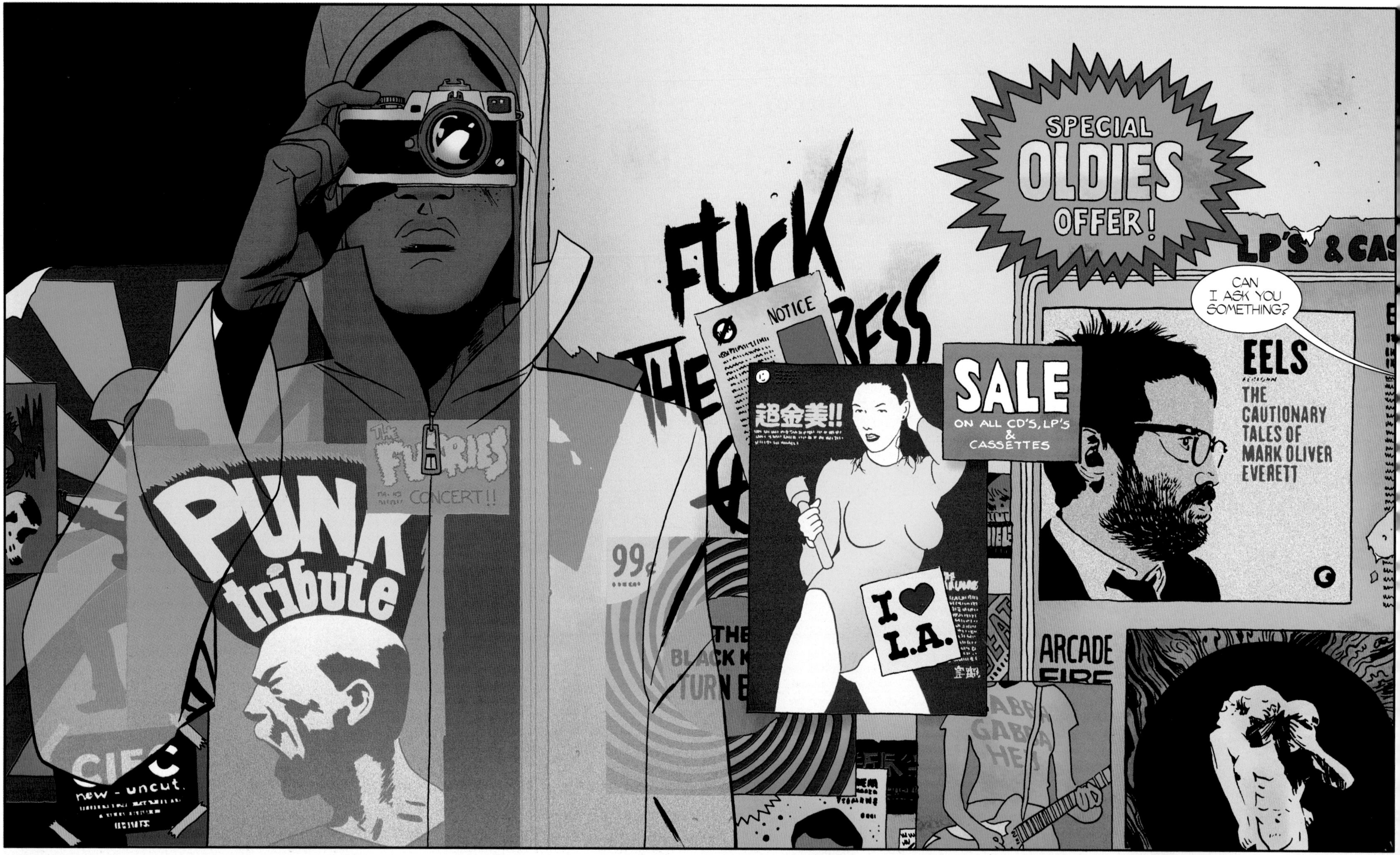

CAN I ASK YOU SOMETHING?
SPECIAL OLDIES OFFER!
SALE ON ALL CD'S, LP'S & CASSETTES
EELS
THE CAUTIONARY TALES OF MARK OLIVER EVERETT
NOTICE
超金美!!
I ♥ L.A.
THE FURIES
CONCERT!!
PUNK tribute
99¢
ARCADE
new - uncut.

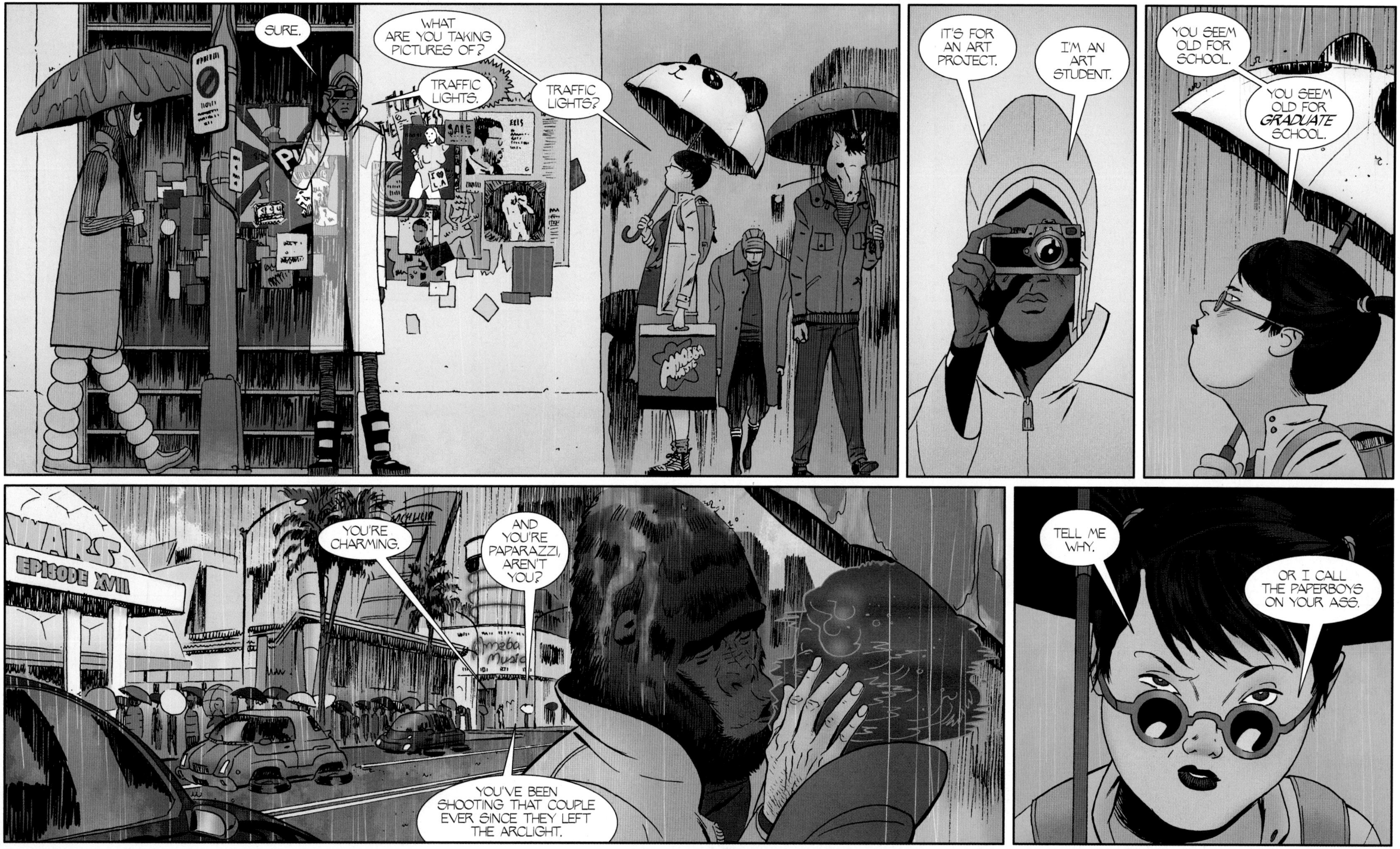
SURE.
WHAT ARE YOU TAKING PICTURES OF?
TRAFFIC LIGHTS.
TRAFFIC LIGHTS?
IT'S FOR AN ART PROJECT.
I'M AN ART STUDENT.
YOU SEEM OLD FOR SCHOOL.
YOU SEEM OLD FOR *GRADUATE* SCHOOL.
WARS
EPISODE XVIII
Ameba Music
YOU'RE CHARMING.
AND YOU'RE PAPARAZZI, AREN'T YOU?
YOU'VE BEEN SHOOTING THAT COUPLE EVER SINCE THEY LEFT THE ARCLIGHT.
TELL ME WHY.
OR I CALL THE PAPERBOYS ON YOUR ASS.

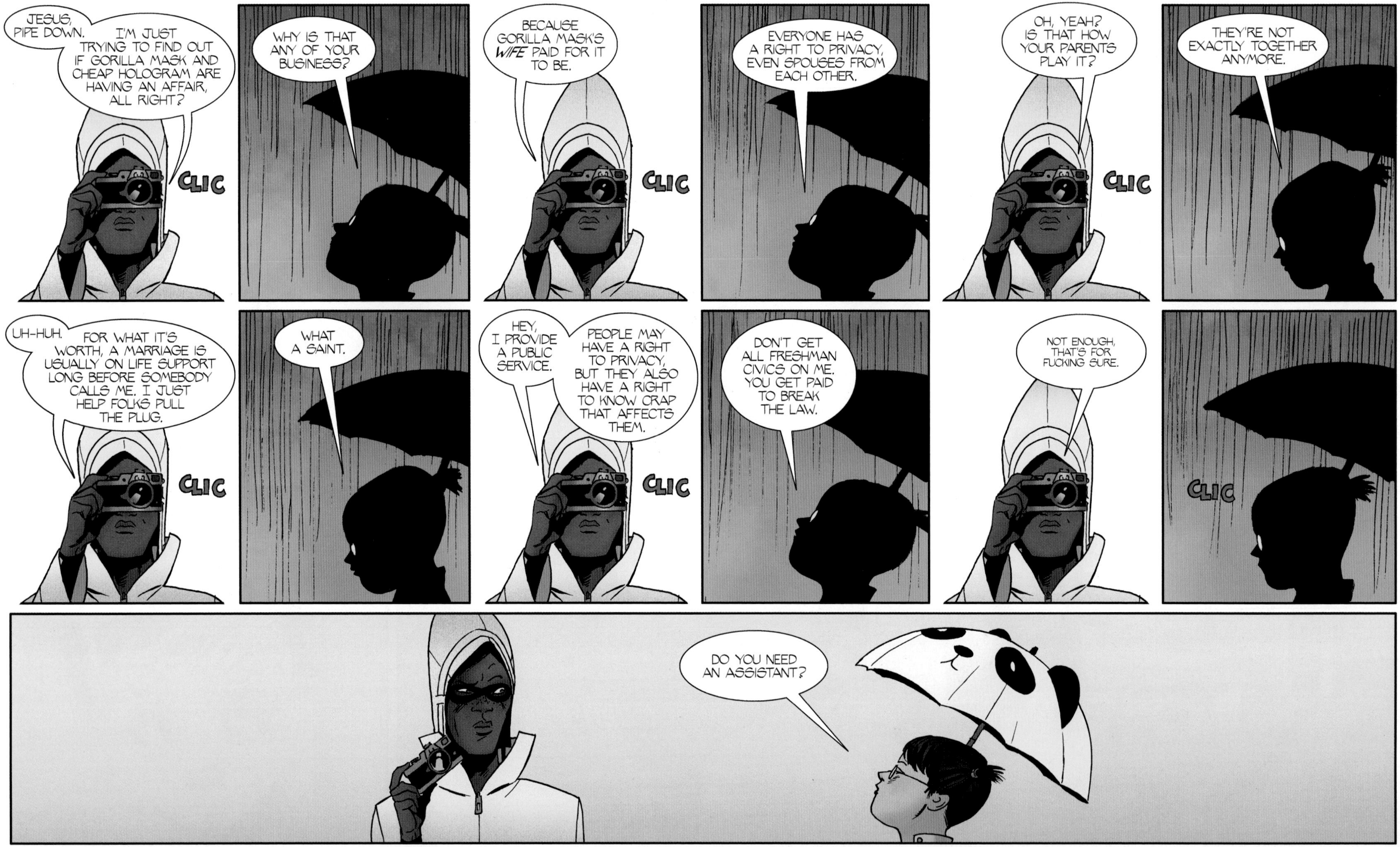
JESUS, PIPE DOWN.
I'M JUST TRYING TO FIND OUT IF GORILLA MASK AND CHEAP HOLOGRAM ARE HAVING AN AFFAIR, ALL RIGHT?
CLIC
WHY IS THAT ANY OF YOUR BUSINESS?
BECAUSE GORILLA MASK'S *WIFE* PAID FOR IT TO BE.
CLIC
EVERYONE HAS A RIGHT TO PRIVACY, EVEN SPOUSES FROM EACH OTHER.
OH, YEAH? IS THAT HOW YOUR PARENTS PLAY IT?
CLIC
THEY'RE NOT EXACTLY TOGETHER ANYMORE.
UH-HUH.
FOR WHAT IT'S WORTH, A MARRIAGE IS USUALLY ON LIFE SUPPORT LONG BEFORE SOMEBODY CALLS ME. I JUST HELP FOLKS PULL THE PLUG.
CLIC
WHAT A SAINT.
HEY, I PROVIDE A PUBLIC SERVICE.
PEOPLE MAY HAVE A RIGHT TO PRIVACY, BUT THEY ALSO HAVE A RIGHT TO KNOW CRAP THAT AFFECTS THEM.
CLIC
DON'T GET ALL FRESHMAN CIVICS ON ME. YOU GET PAID TO BREAK THE LAW.
NOT ENOUGH, THAT'S FOR FUCKING SURE.
CLIC
DO YOU NEED AN ASSISTANT?

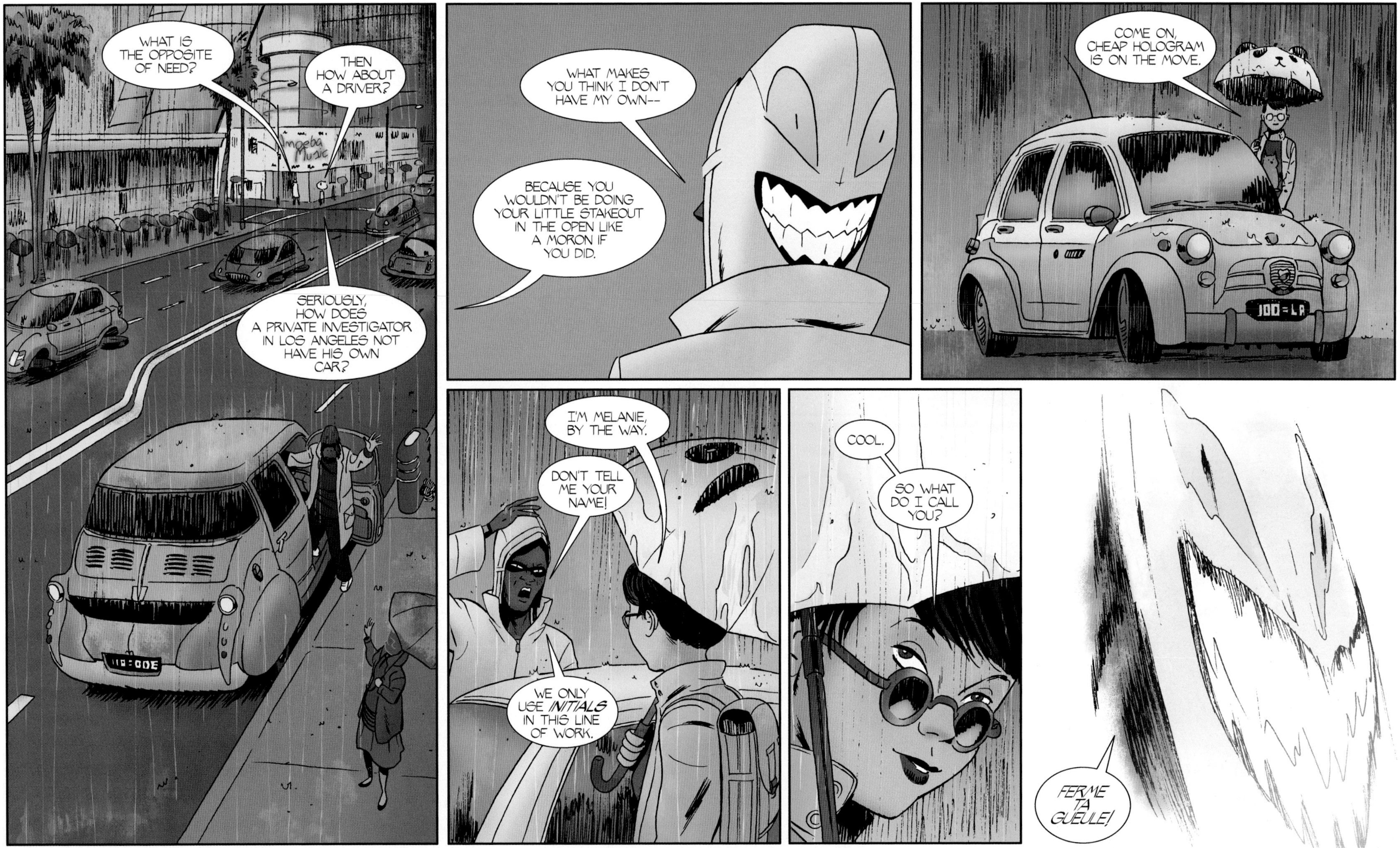

WHAT IS THE OPPOSITE OF NEED?
THEN HOW ABOUT A DRIVER?
SERIOUSLY, HOW DOES A PRIVATE INVESTIGATOR IN LOS ANGELES NOT HAVE HIS OWN CAR?
WHAT MAKES YOU THINK I DON'T HAVE MY OWN--
BECAUSE YOU WOULDN'T BE DOING YOUR LITTLE STAKEOUT IN THE OPEN LIKE A MORON IF YOU DID.
COME ON, CHEAP HOLOGRAM IS ON THE MOVE.
I'M MELANIE, BY THE WAY.
DON'T TELL ME YOUR NAME!
WE ONLY USE *INITIALS* IN THIS LINE OF WORK.
COOL.
SO WHAT DO I CALL YOU?
FERME TA GUEULE!

WHA...?

I SAY SHUT YOUR FUCKING MOUTH!

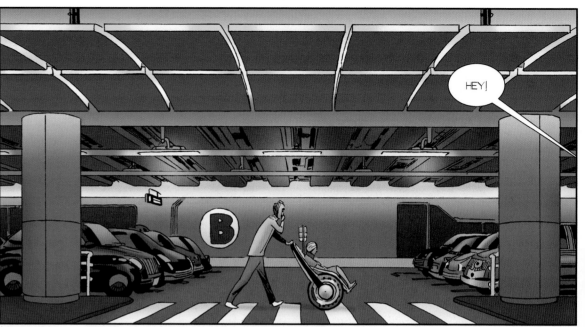

HEY!

SECURITY!

STEP AWAY FROM THE PATIENT RIGHT

<FUCK!>

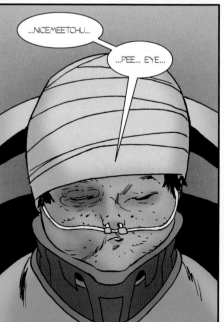

...NICEMEETCHU...

...PEE... EYE...

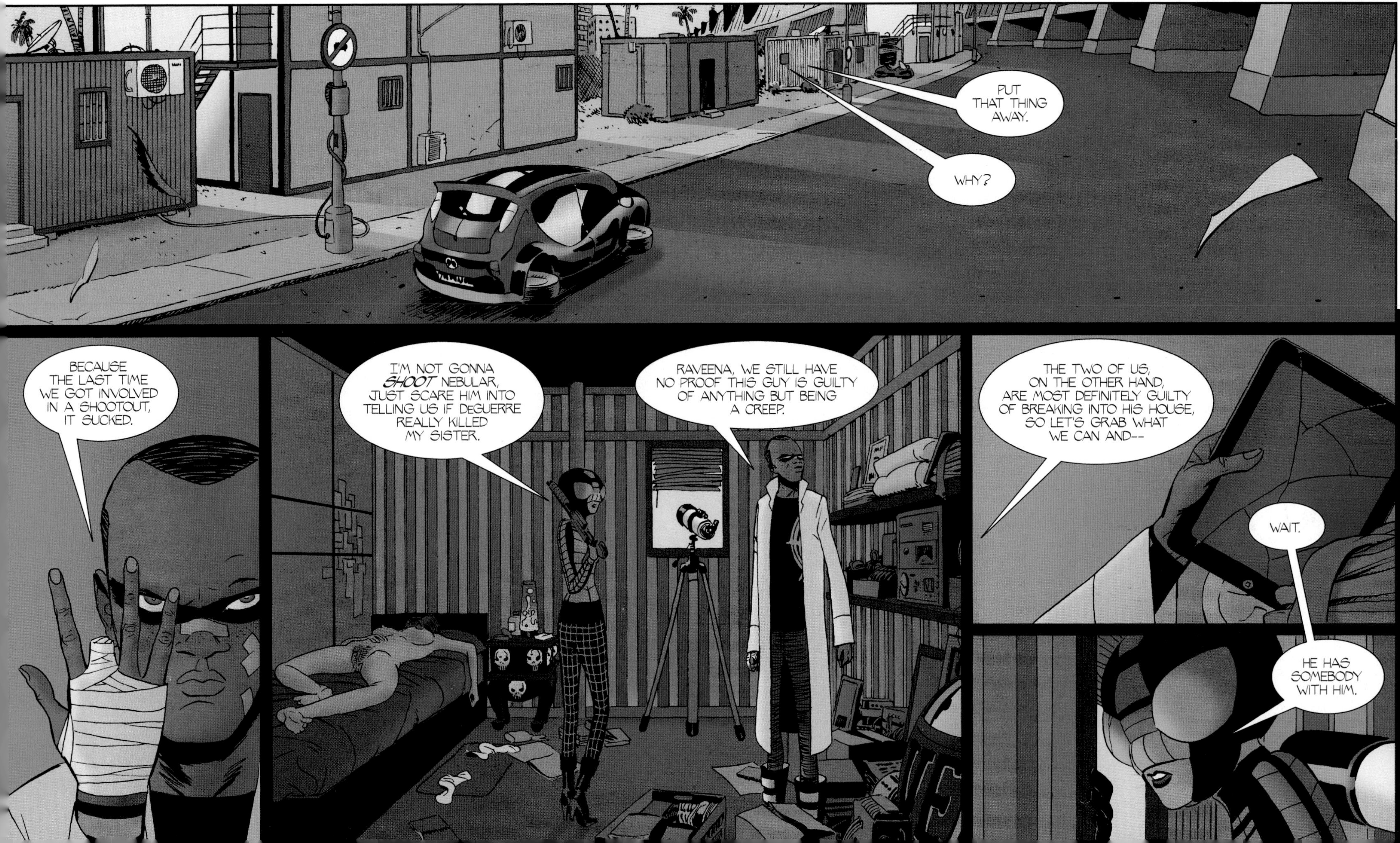
PUT THAT THING AWAY.
WHY?
BECAUSE THE LAST TIME WE GOT INVOLVED IN A SHOOTOUT, IT SUCKED.
I'M NOT GONNA *SHOOT* NEBULAR, JUST SCARE HIM INTO TELLING US IF DEGUERRE REALLY KILLED MY SISTER.
RAVEENA, WE STILL HAVE NO PROOF THIS GUY IS GUILTY OF ANYTHING BUT BEING A CREEP.
THE TWO OF US, ON THE OTHER HAND, ARE MOST DEFINITELY GUILTY OF BREAKING INTO HIS HOUSE, SO LET'S GRAB WHAT WE CAN AND--
WAIT.
HE HAS SOMEBODY WITH HIM.

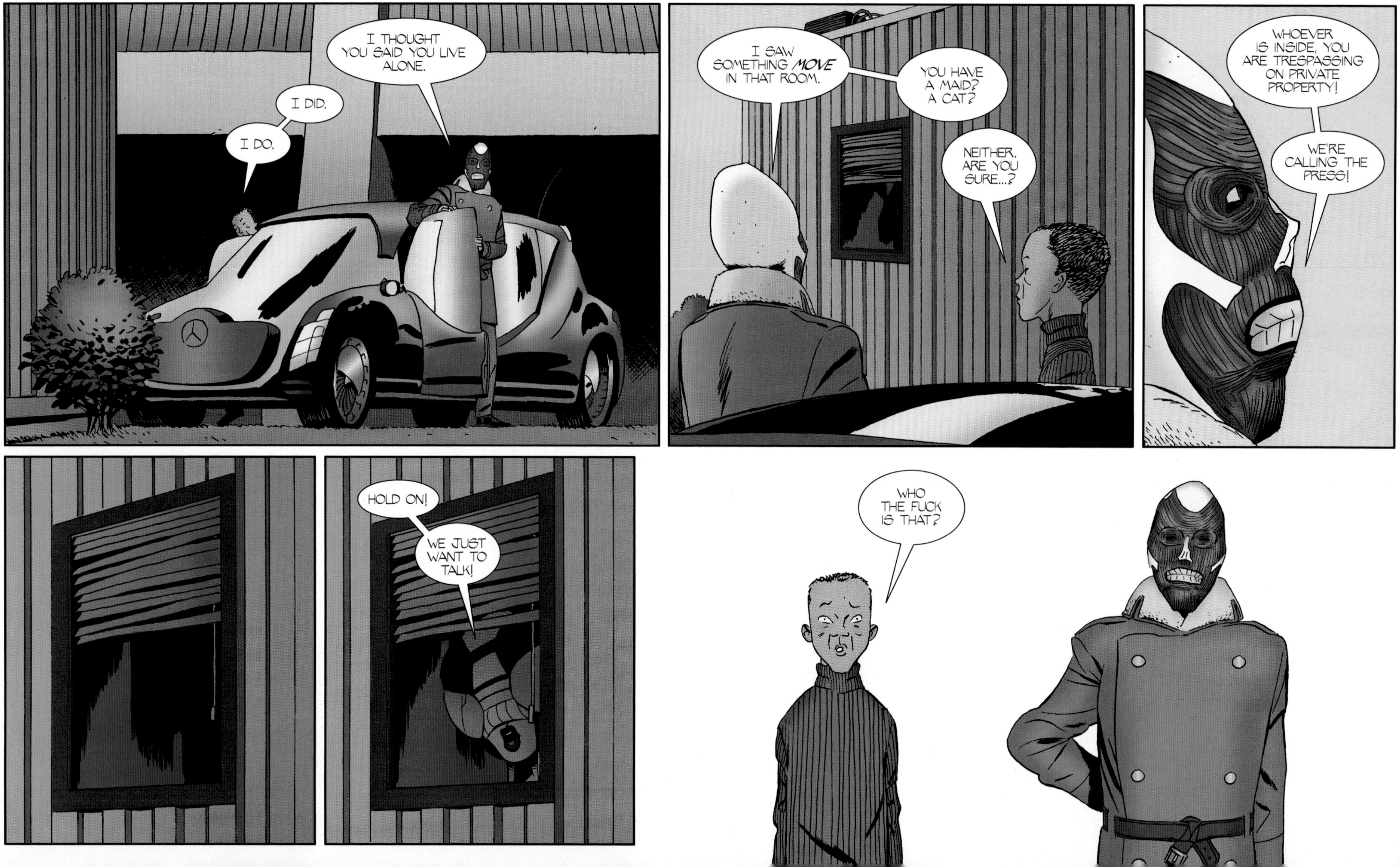
I THOUGHT YOU SAID YOU LIVE ALONE.
I DID.
I DO.
I SAW SOMETHING *MOVE* IN THAT ROOM.
YOU HAVE A MAID? A CAT?
NEITHER. ARE YOU SURE...?
WHOEVER IS INSIDE, YOU ARE TRESPASSING ON PRIVATE PROPERTY!
WE'RE CALLING THE PRESS!
HOLD ON!
WE JUST WANT TO TALK!
WHO THE FUCK IS THAT?

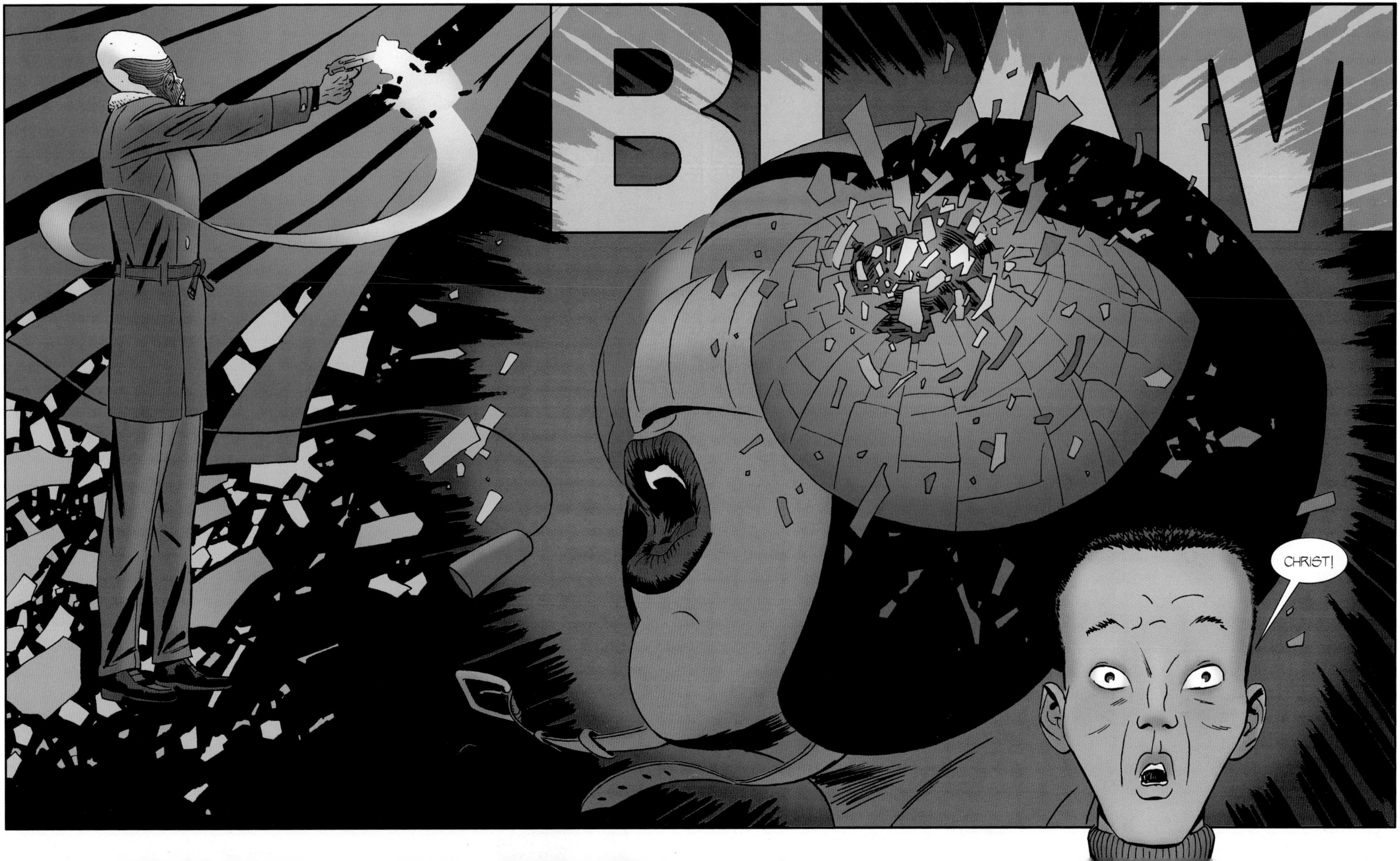
BLAM
CHRIST!

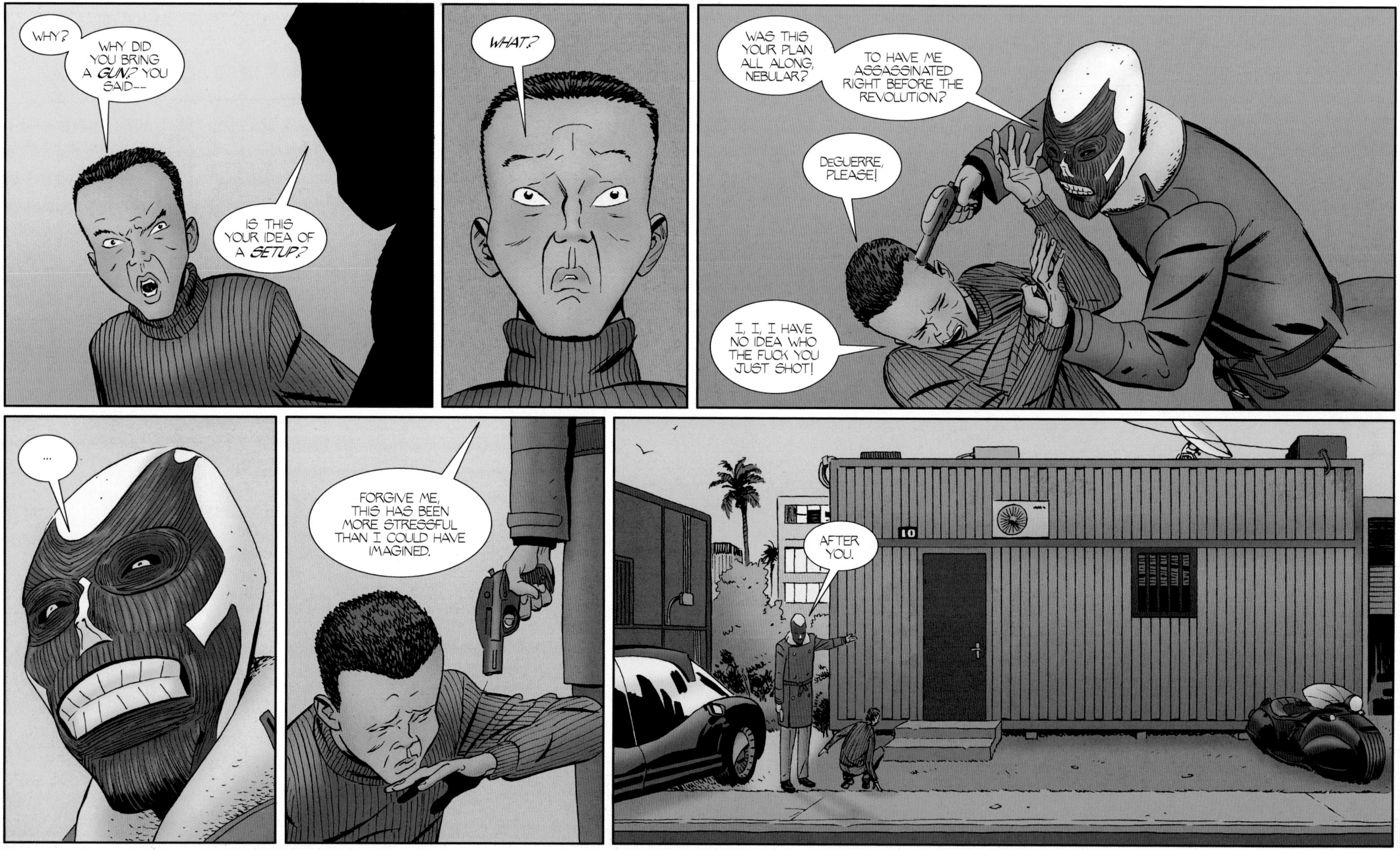
WHY?
WHY DID YOU BRING A GUN? YOU SAID--
IS THIS YOUR IDEA OF A SETUP?
WHAT?
WAS THIS YOUR PLAN ALL ALONG, NEBULAR?
TO HAVE ME ASSASSINATED RIGHT BEFORE THE REVOLUTION?
DEGUERRE, PLEASE!
I, I, I HAVE NO IDEA WHO THE FUCK YOU JUST SHOT!
...
FORGIVE ME, THIS HAS BEEN MORE STRESSFUL THAN I COULD HAVE IMAGINED.
10
AFTER YOU.

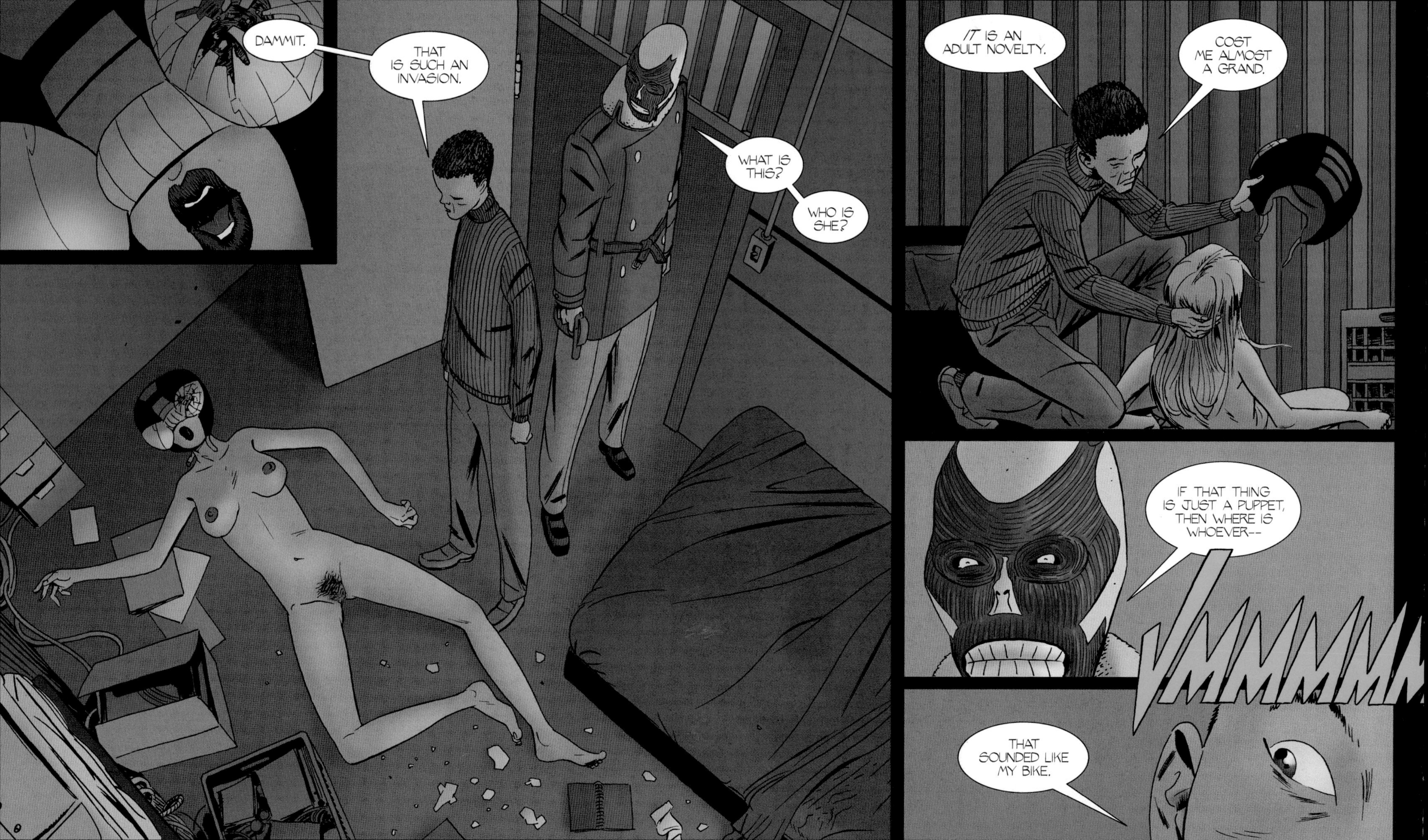
DAMMIT.
THAT IS SUCH AN INVASION.
WHAT IS THIS?
WHO IS SHE?
IT IS AN ADULT NOVELTY.
COST ME ALMOST A GRAND.
IF THAT THING IS JUST A PUPPET, THEN WHERE IS WHOEVER--
VMMMMM
THAT SOUNDED LIKE MY BIKE.

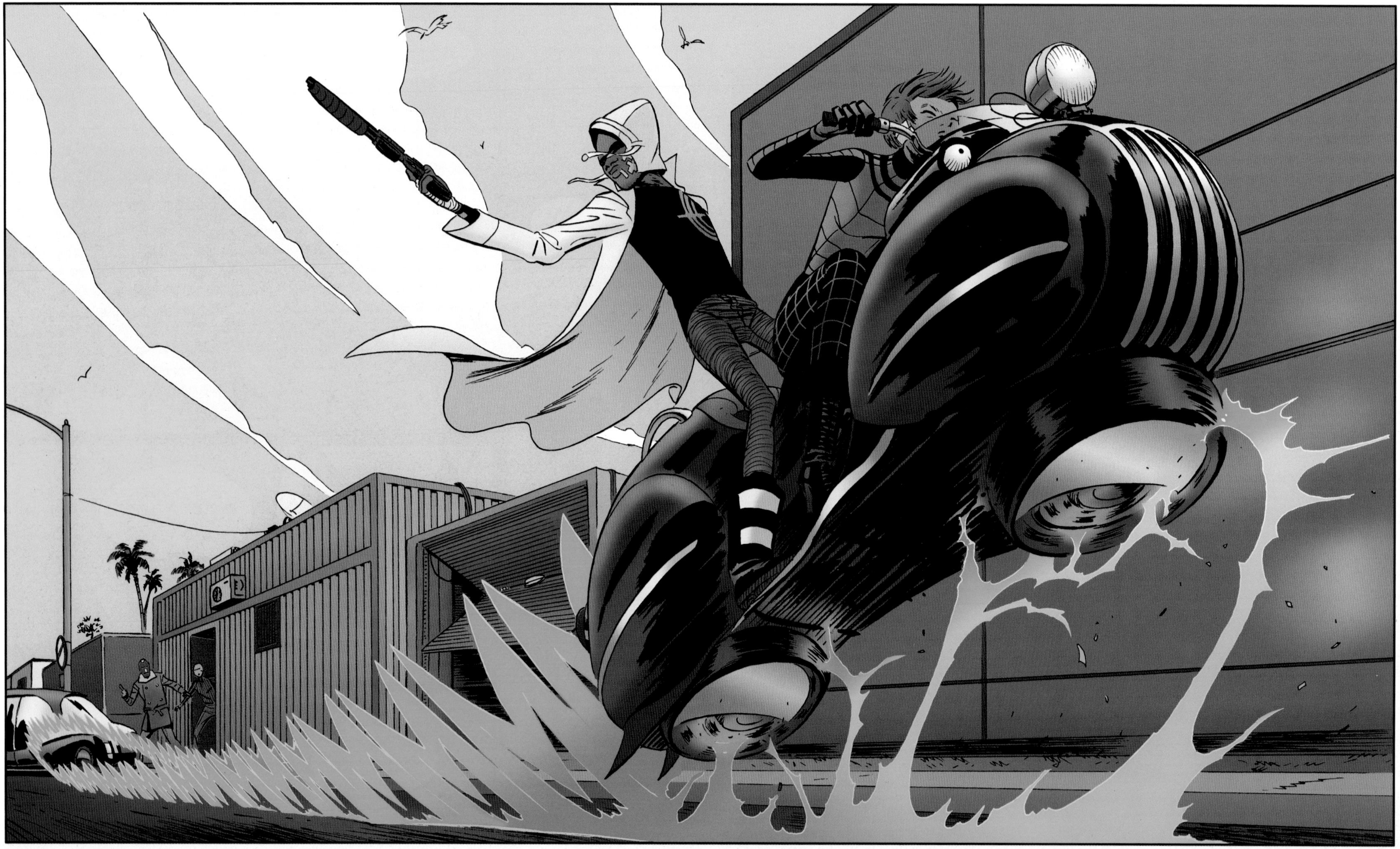

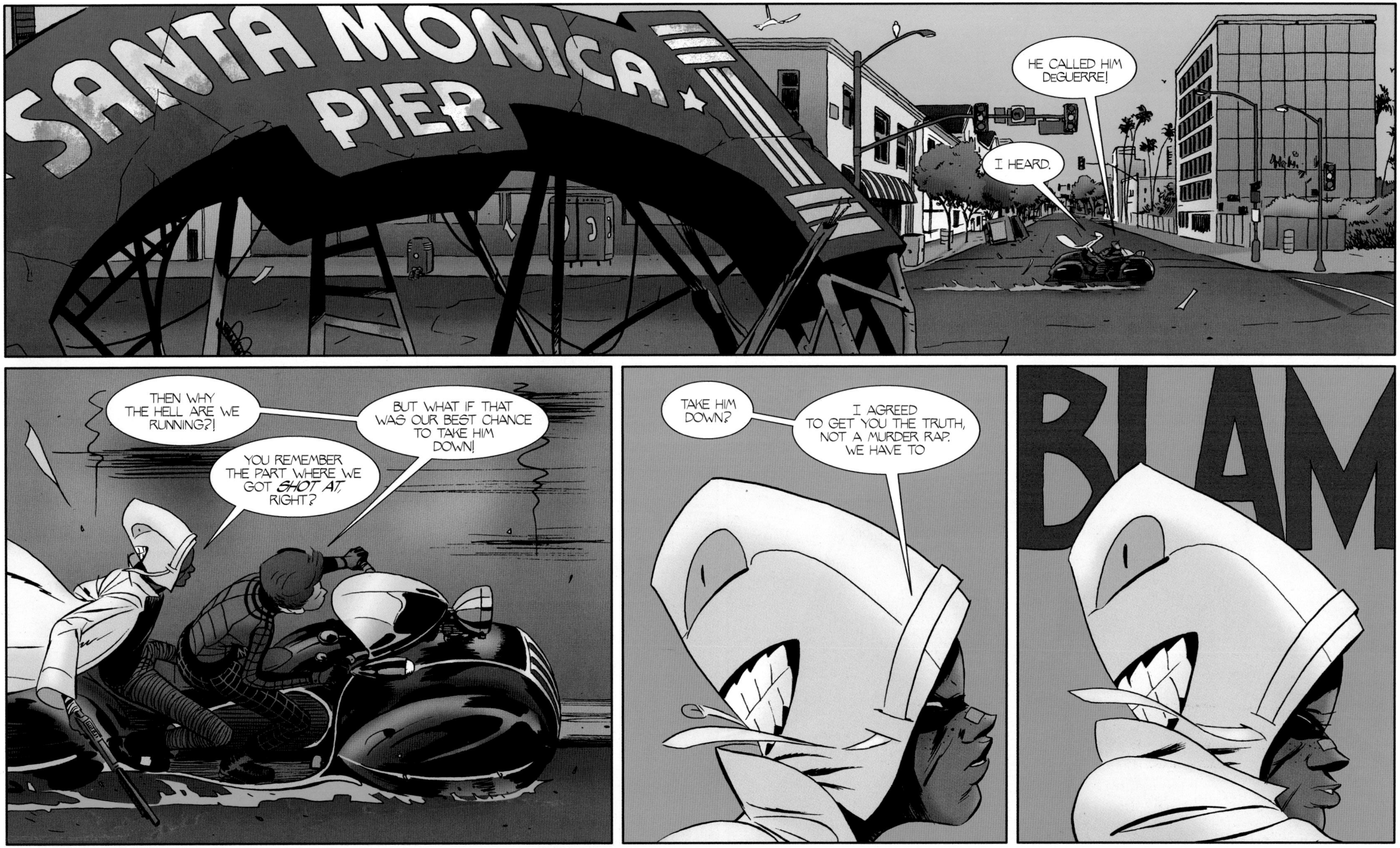
SANTA MONICA PIER
HE CALLED HIM DeGUERRE!
I HEARD.
THEN WHY THE HELL ARE WE RUNNING?!
BUT WHAT IF THAT WAS OUR BEST CHANCE TO TAKE HIM DOWN!
YOU REMEMBER THE PART WHERE WE GOT *SHOT AT*, RIGHT?
TAKE HIM DOWN?
I AGREED TO GET YOU THE TRUTH, NOT A MURDER RAP. WE HAVE TO
BLAM

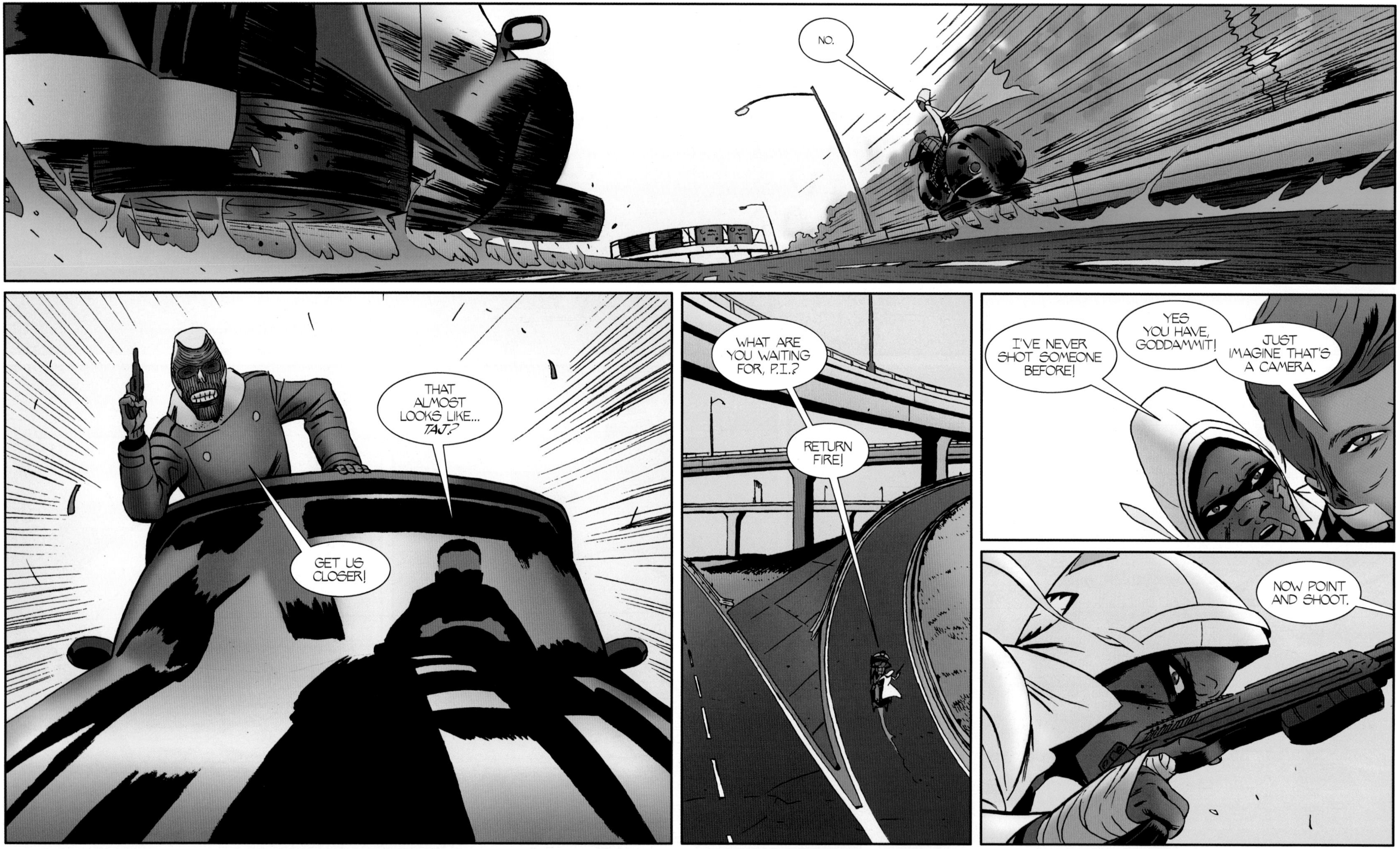
NO.
THAT ALMOST LOOKS LIKE... *TAJ?*
GET US CLOSER!
WHAT ARE YOU WAITING FOR, P.I.?
RETURN FIRE!
I'VE NEVER SHOT SOMEONE BEFORE!
YES YOU HAVE, GODDAMMIT!
JUST IMAGINE THAT'S A CAMERA.
NOW POINT AND SHOOT.

HE TOOK MY GUN!

DON'T SLOW DOWN.

ROAD CLOSED

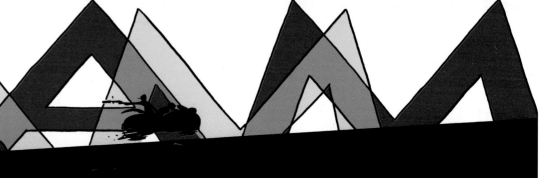

BBLAAAM

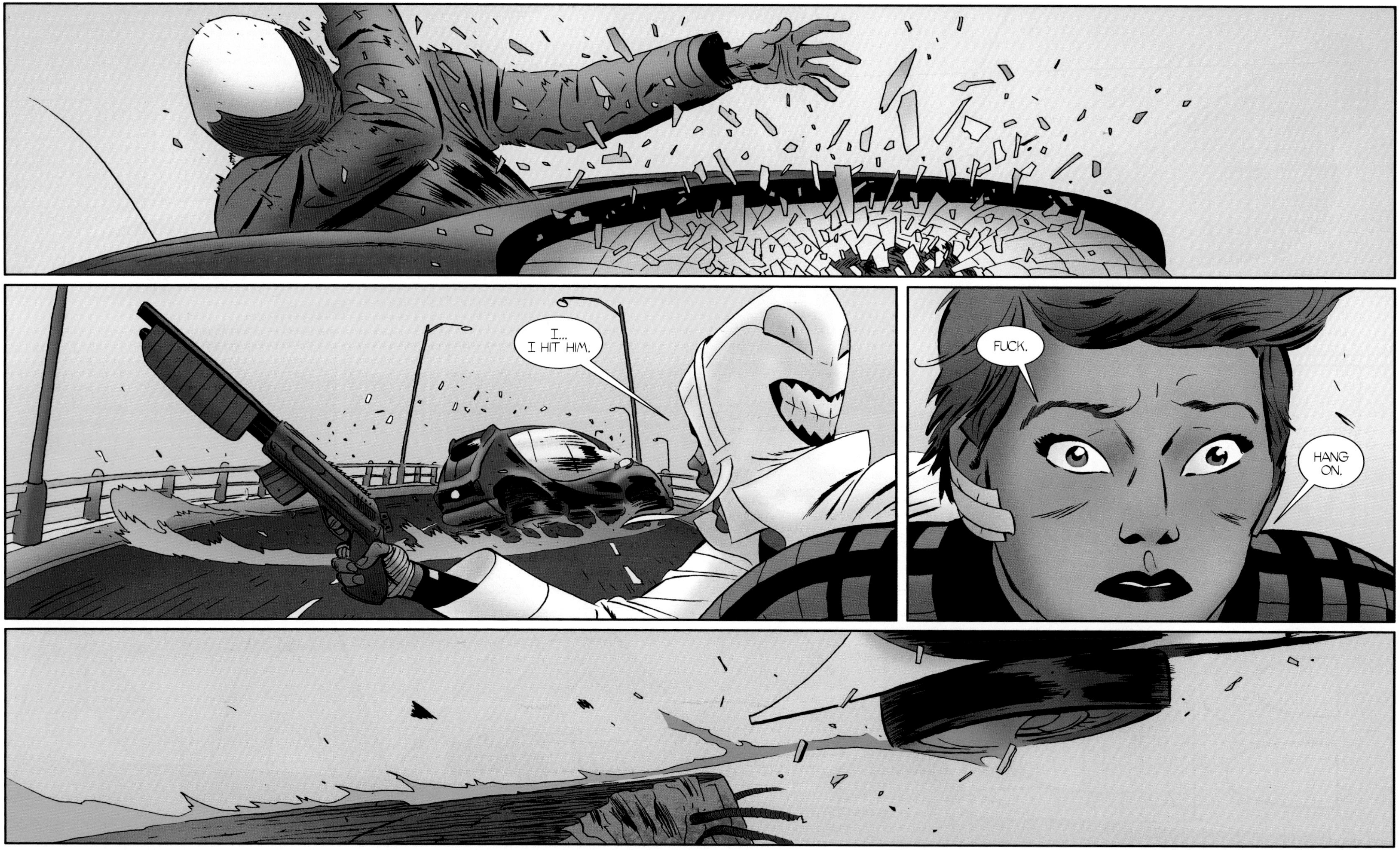
I...
I HIT HIM.
FUCK.
HANG ON.

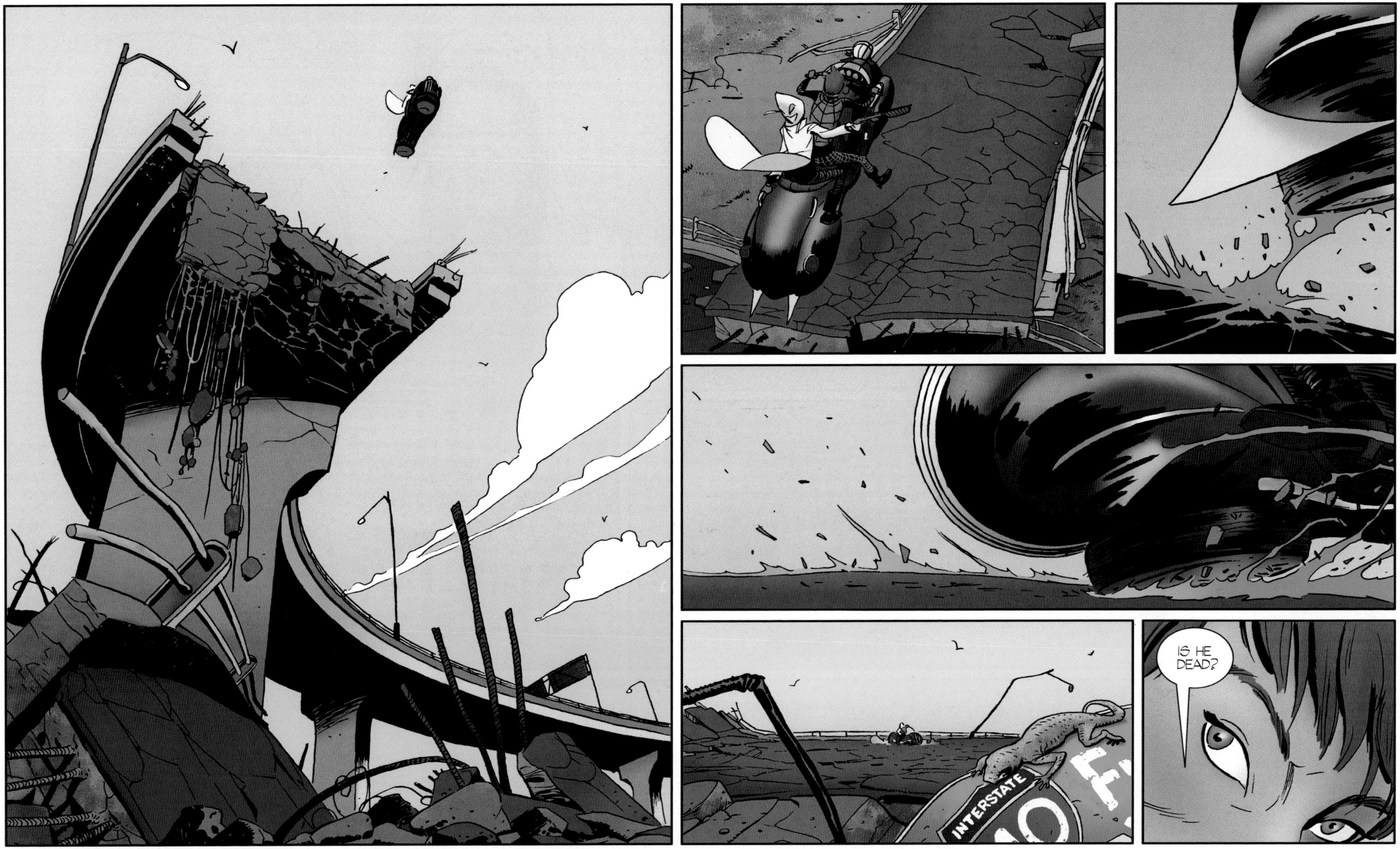
IS HE DEAD?
INTERSTATE

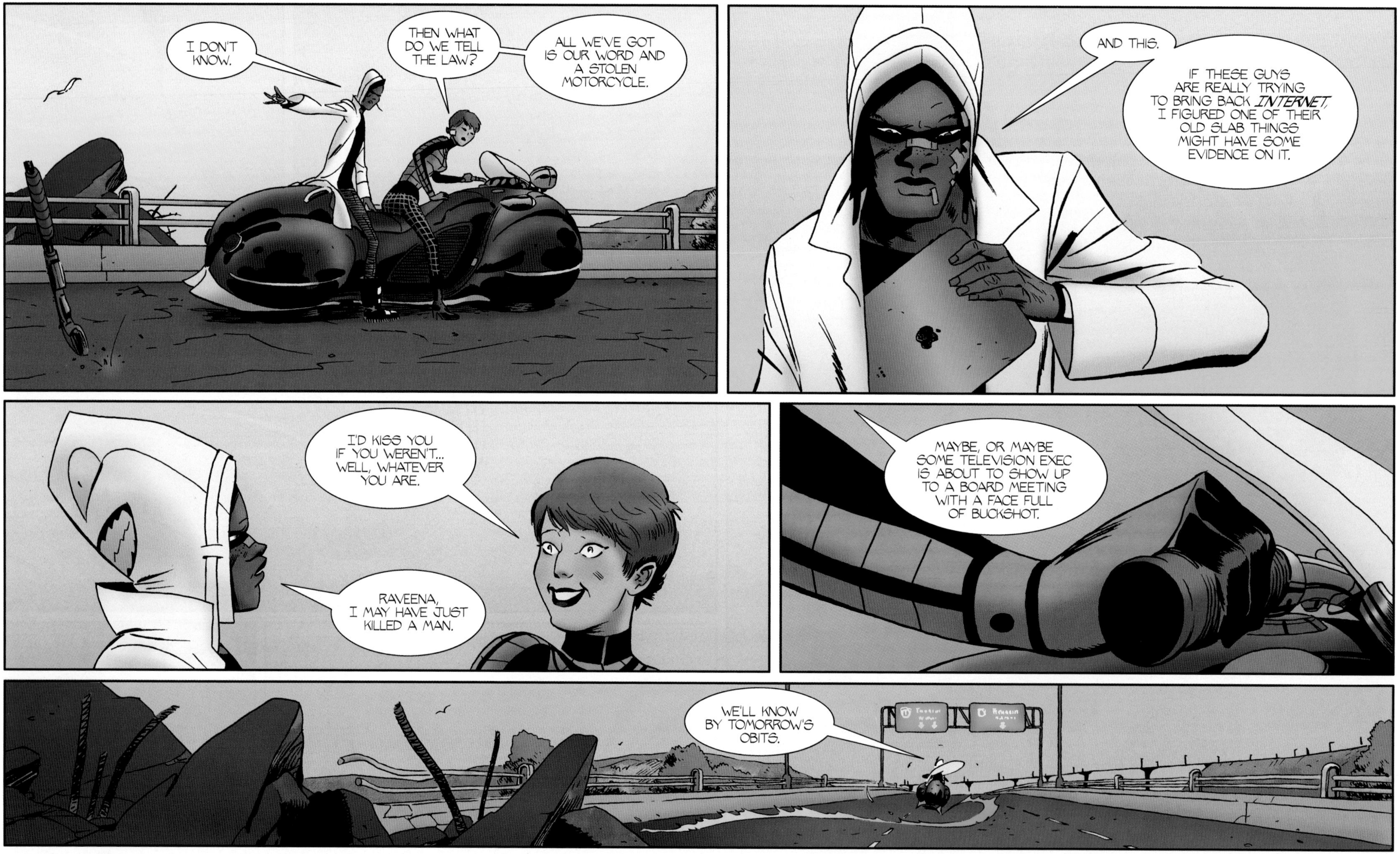
I DON'T KNOW.
THEN WHAT DO WE TELL THE LAW?
ALL WE'VE GOT IS OUR WORD AND A STOLEN MOTORCYCLE.
AND THIS.
IF THESE GUYS ARE REALLY TRYING TO BRING BACK *INTERNET*, I FIGURED ONE OF THEIR OLD SLAB THINGS MIGHT HAVE SOME EVIDENCE ON IT.
I'D KISS YOU IF YOU WEREN'T... WELL, WHATEVER YOU ARE.
RAVEENA, I MAY HAVE JUST KILLED A MAN.
MAYBE, OR MAYBE SOME TELEVISION EXEC IS ABOUT TO SHOW UP TO A BOARD MEETING WITH A FACE FULL OF BUCKSHOT.
WE'LL KNOW BY TOMORROW'S OBITS.

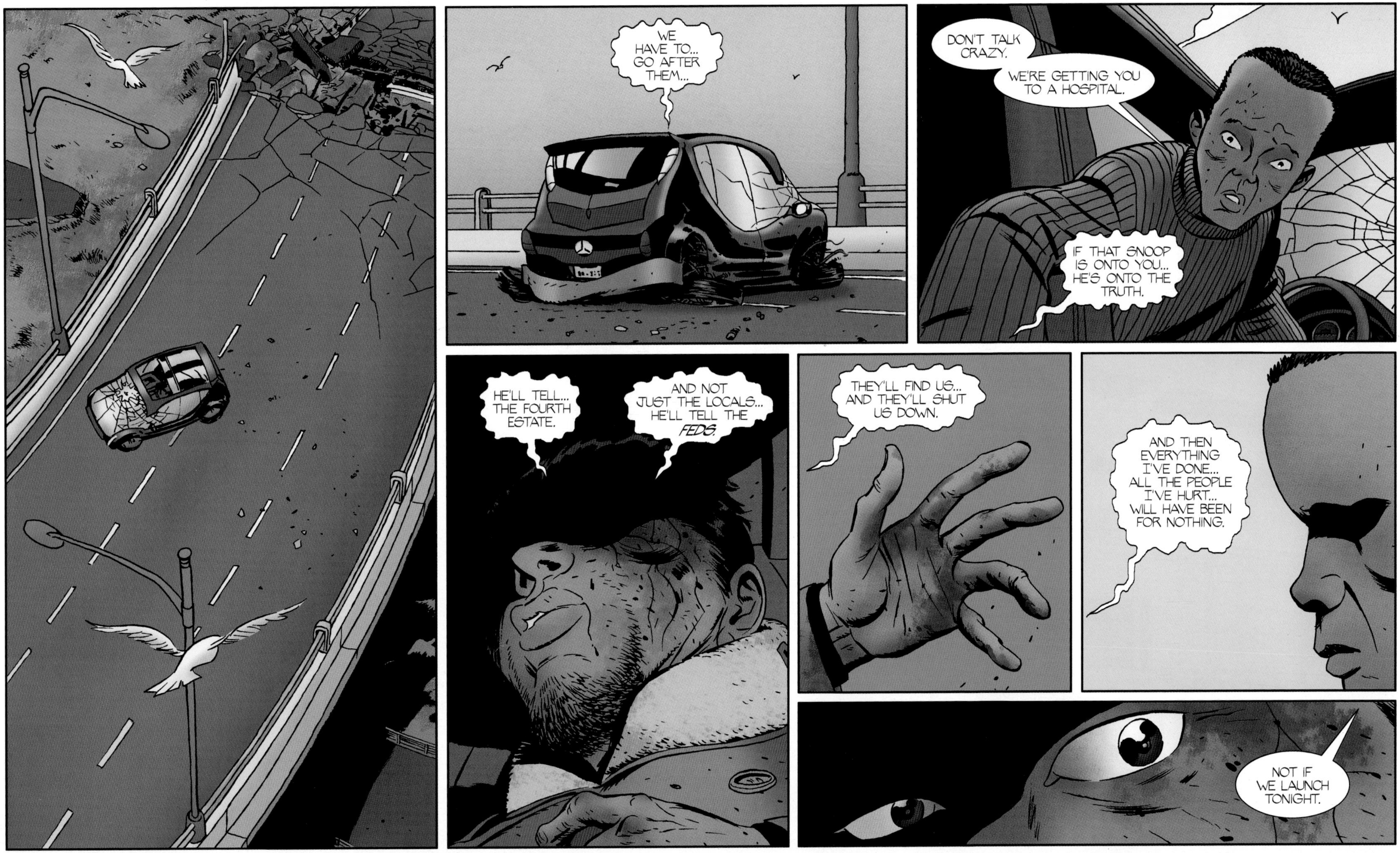
WE HAVE TO... GO AFTER THEM...
DON'T TALK CRAZY.
WE'RE GETTING YOU TO A HOSPITAL.
IF THAT SNOOP IS ONTO YOU... HE'S ONTO THE TRUTH.
HE'LL TELL... THE FOURTH ESTATE.
AND NOT JUST THE LOCALS... HE'LL TELL THE FEDS.
THEY'LL FIND US... AND THEY'LL SHUT US DOWN.
AND THEN EVERYTHING I'VE DONE... ALL THE PEOPLE I'VE HURT... WILL HAVE BEEN FOR NOTHING.
NOT IF WE LAUNCH TONIGHT.

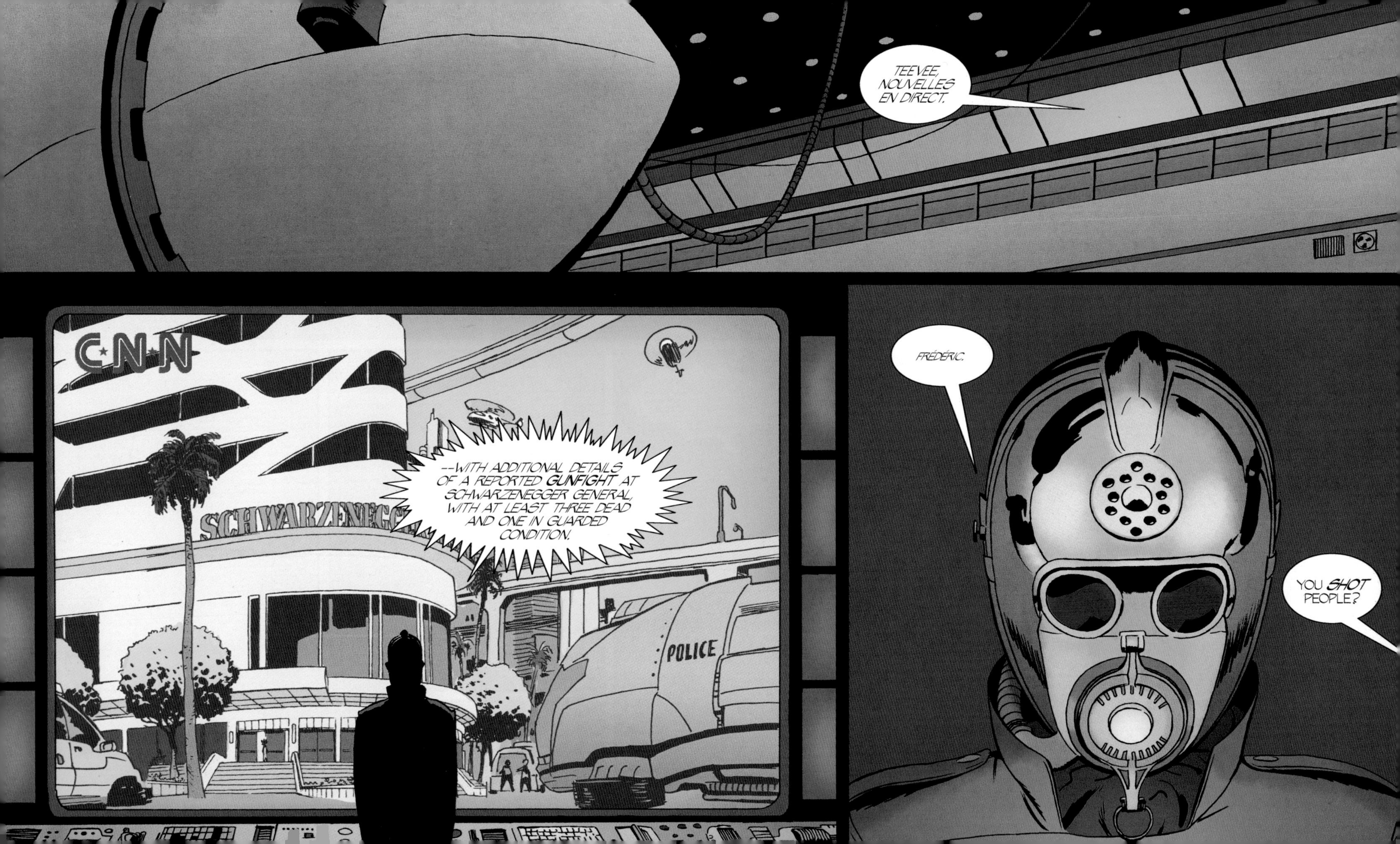
TEEVEE, NOUVELLES EN DIRECT.
CNN
--WITH ADDITIONAL DETAILS OF A REPORTED **GUNFIGHT** AT SCHWARZENEGGER GENERAL, WITH AT LEAST THREE DEAD AND ONE IN GUARDED CONDITION.
POLICE
FRÉDÉRIC.
YOU ***SHOT*** PEOPLE?

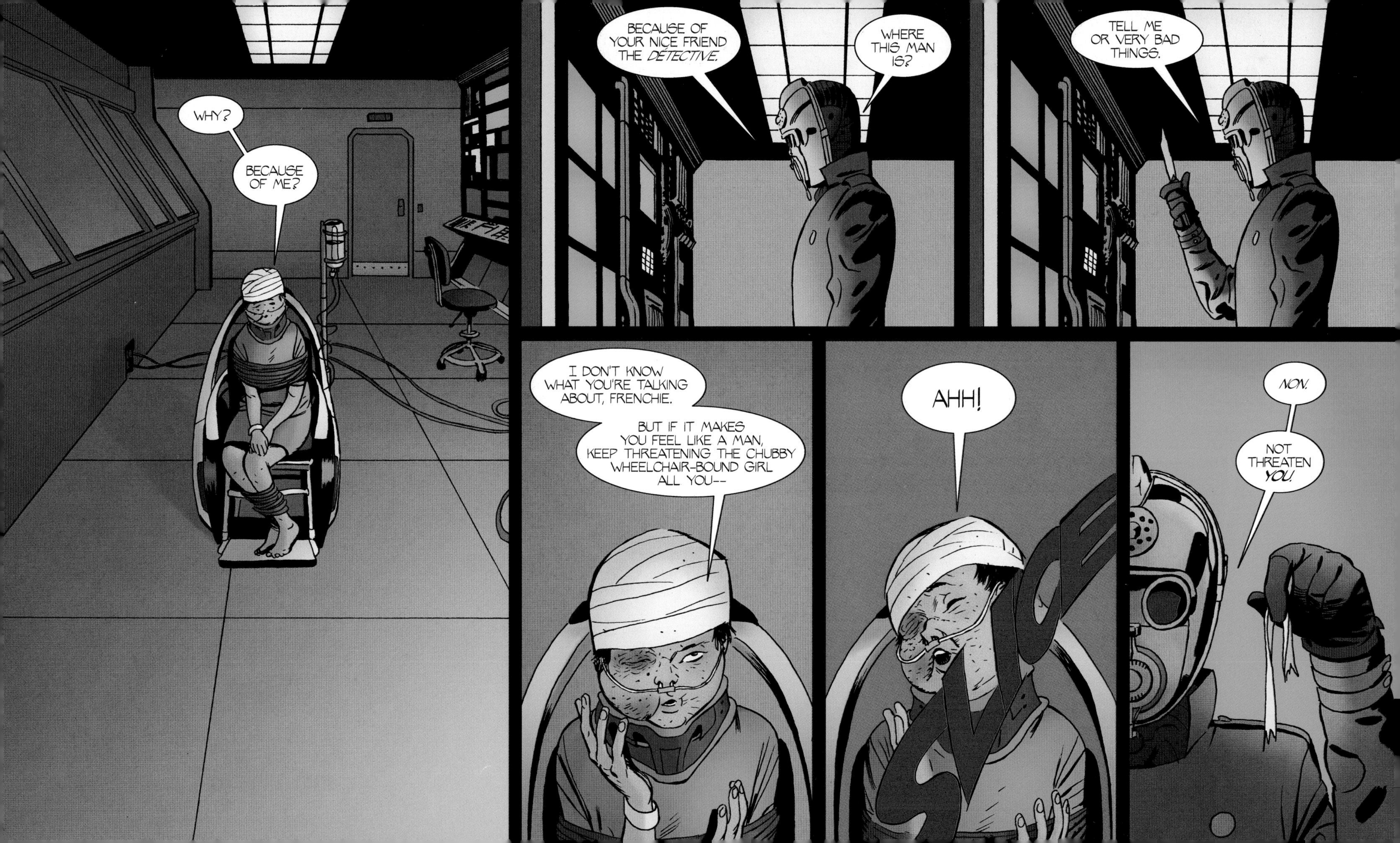
WHY?
BECAUSE OF ME?
BECAUSE OF YOUR NICE FRIEND THE *DÉTECTIVE.*
WHERE THIS MAN IS?
TELL ME OR VERY BAD THINGS.
I DON'T KNOW WHAT YOU'RE TALKING ABOUT, FRENCHIE.
BUT IF IT MAKES YOU FEEL LIKE A MAN, KEEP THREATENING THE CHUBBY WHEELCHAIR-BOUND GIRL ALL YOU--
AHH!
NON.
NOT THREATEN *YOU.*

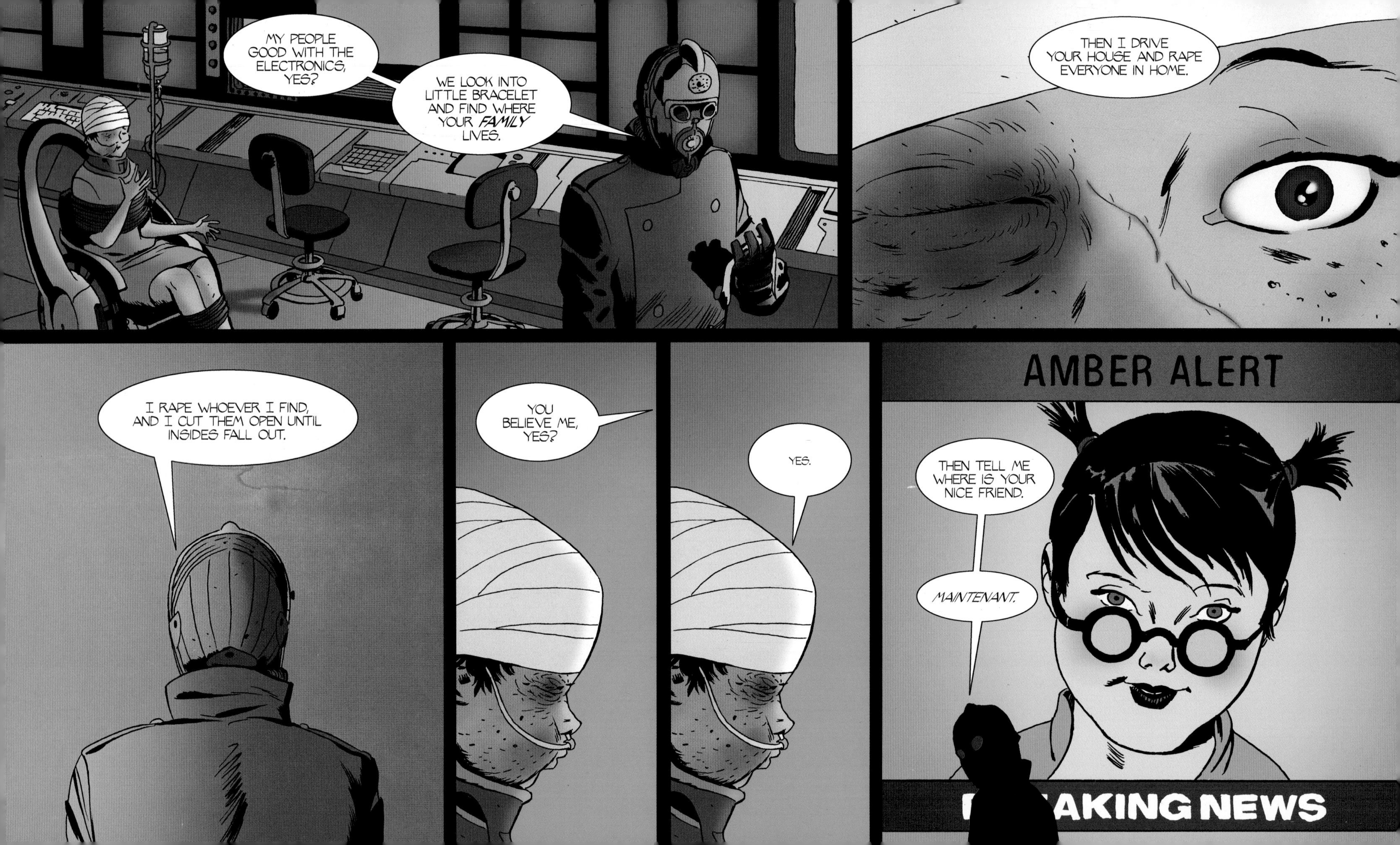
MY PEOPLE GOOD WITH THE ELECTRONICS, YES?
WE LOOK INTO LITTLE BRACELET AND FIND WHERE YOUR *FAMILY* LIVES.
THEN I DRIVE YOUR HOUSE AND RAPE EVERYONE IN HOME.
I RAPE WHOEVER I FIND, AND I CUT THEM OPEN UNTIL INSIDES FALL OUT.
YOU BELIEVE ME, YES?
YES.
AMBER ALERT
THEN TELL ME WHERE IS YOUR NICE FRIEND.
MAINTENANT.
AKING NEWS

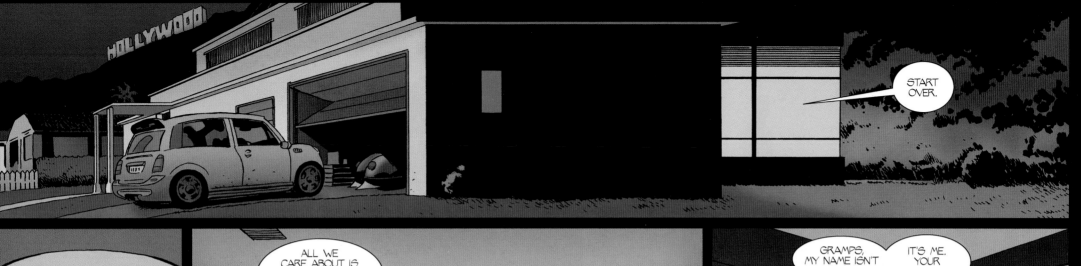

START OVER.

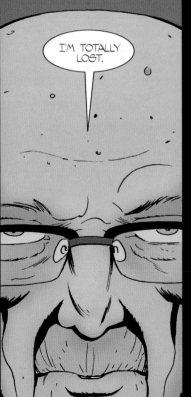

I'M TOTALLY LOST.

ALL WE CARE ABOUT IS WHATEVER YOU CALL THIS OVERSIZED OLD PHONE.

CAN YOU GET IT WORKING?

DAMMIT, JIM, I'M A DOCTOR, NOT A SOFTWARE ENGINEER.

GRAMPS, MY NAME ISN'T JIM.

IT'S ME. YOUR GRANDSON.

I KNOW YOU DIMWIT, IT WAS JUST A...

KIDS TODAY GOT NO CULTURE.

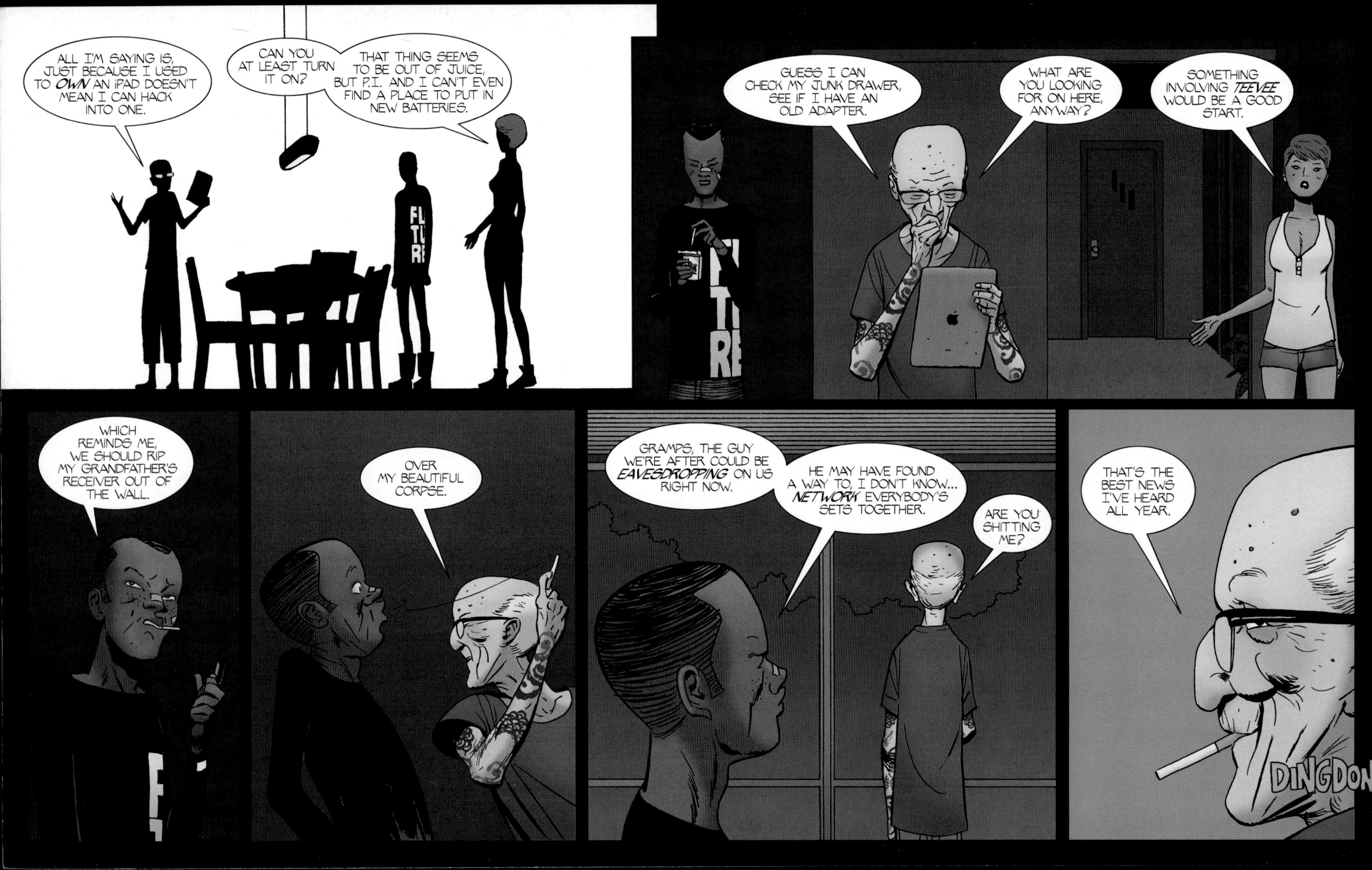
ALL I'M SAYING IS, JUST BECAUSE I USED TO OWN AN iPAD DOESN'T MEAN I CAN HACK INTO ONE.
CAN YOU AT LEAST TURN IT ON?
THAT THING SEEMS TO BE OUT OF JUICE, BUT P.I. AND I CAN'T EVEN FIND A PLACE TO PUT IN NEW BATTERIES.
GUESS I CAN CHECK MY JUNK DRAWER, SEE IF I HAVE AN OLD ADAPTER.
WHAT ARE YOU LOOKING FOR ON HERE, ANYWAY?
SOMETHING INVOLVING TEEVEE WOULD BE A GOOD START.
WHICH REMINDS ME, WE SHOULD RIP MY GRANDFATHER'S RECEIVER OUT OF THE WALL.
OVER MY BEAUTIFUL CORPSE.
GRAMPS, THE GUY WE'RE AFTER COULD BE EAVESDROPPING ON US RIGHT NOW.
HE MAY HAVE FOUND A WAY TO, I DON'T KNOW... NETWORK EVERYBODY'S SETS TOGETHER.
ARE YOU SHITTING ME?
THAT'S THE BEST NEWS I'VE HEARD ALL YEAR.
DINGDON

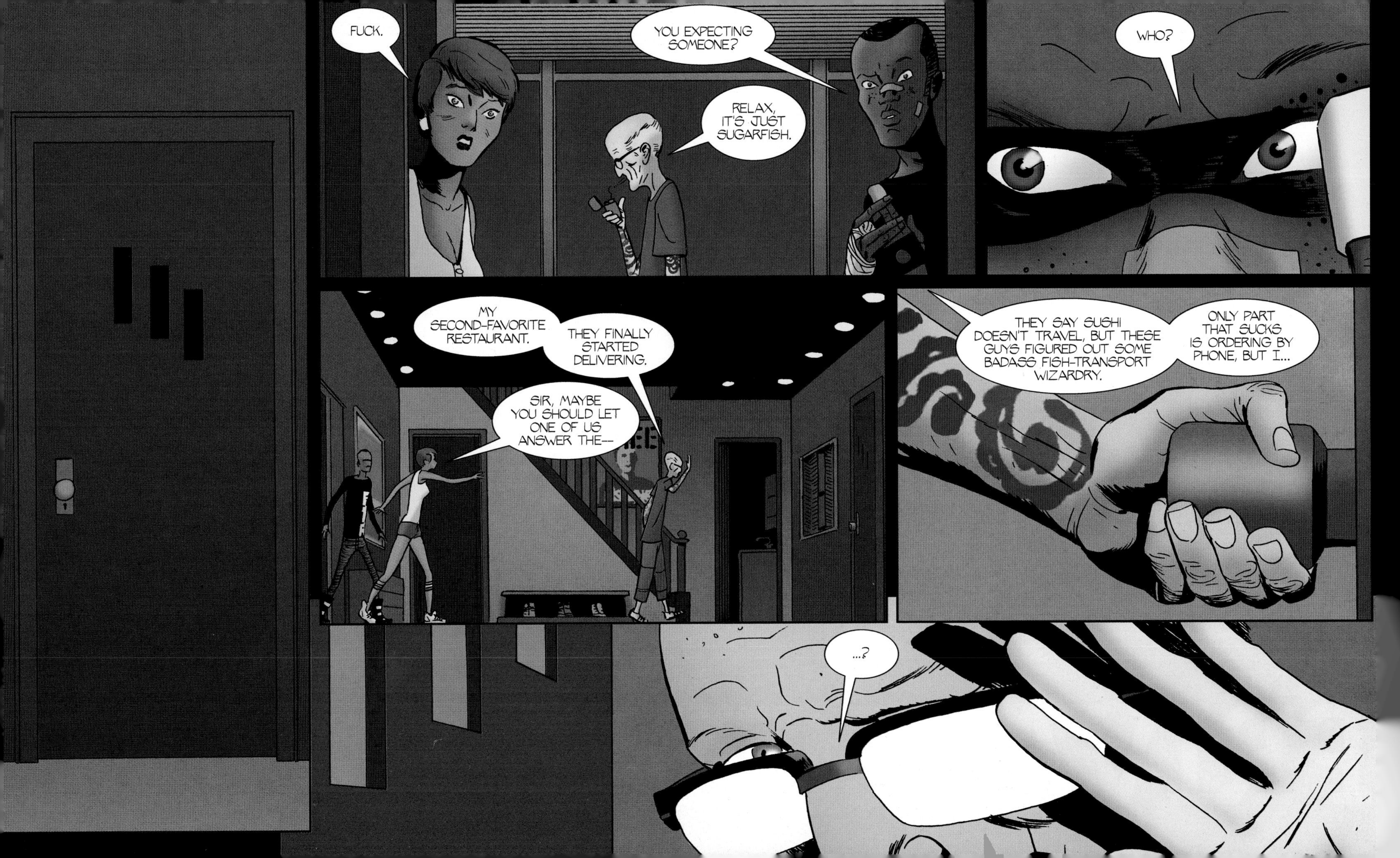
FUCK.
YOU EXPECTING SOMEONE?
RELAX, IT'S JUST SUGARFISH.
WHO?
MY SECOND-FAVORITE RESTAURANT.
THEY FINALLY STARTED DELIVERING.
SIR, MAYBE YOU SHOULD LET ONE OF US ANSWER THE--
THEY SAY SUSHI DOESN'T TRAVEL, BUT THESE GUYS FIGURED OUT SOME BADASS FISH-TRANSPORT WIZARDRY.
ONLY PART THAT SUCKS IS ORDERING BY PHONE, BUT I...
...?

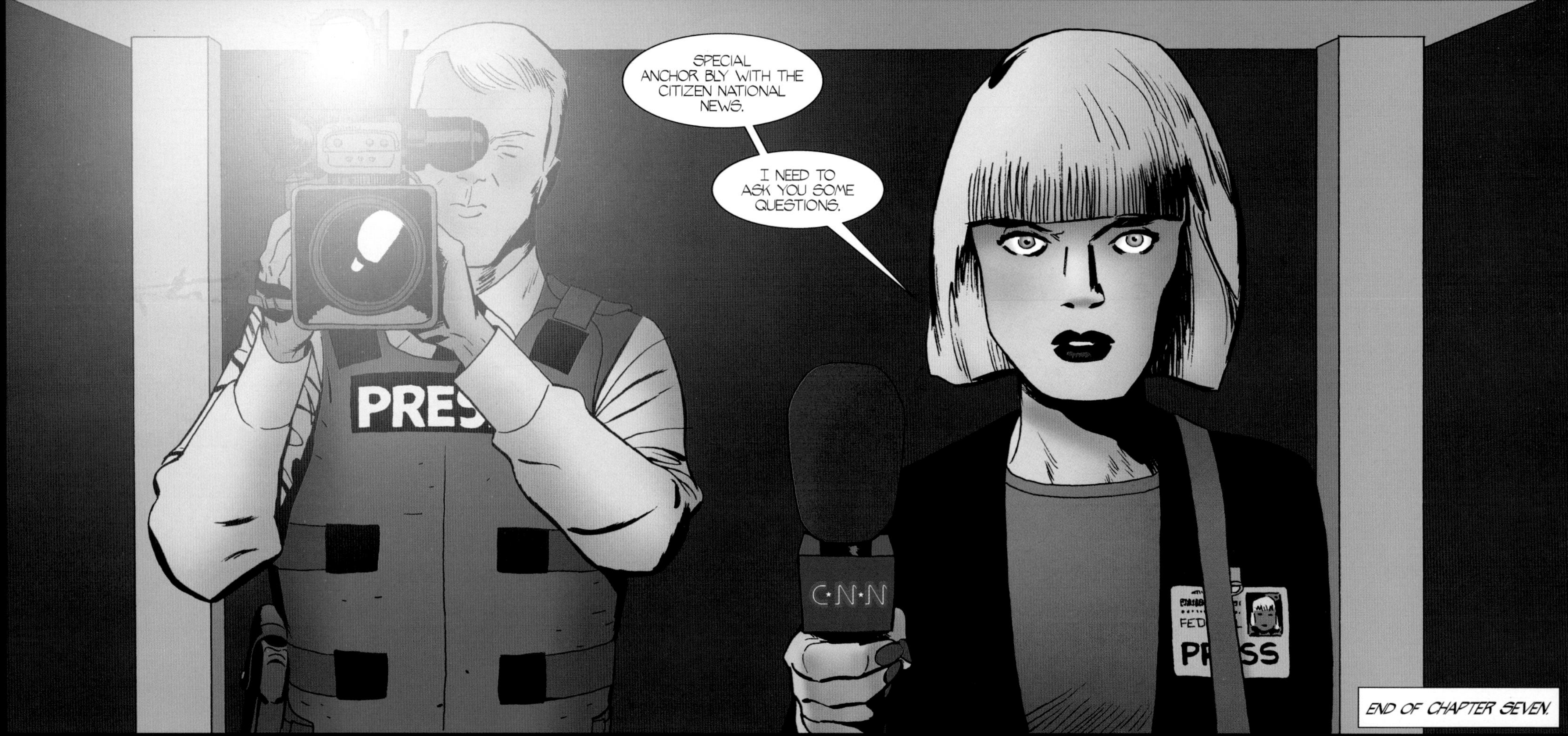
SPECIAL ANCHOR BLY WITH THE CITIZEN NATIONAL NEWS.
I NEED TO ASK YOU SOME QUESTIONS.
PRES
C·N·N
END OF CHAPTER SEVEN.

THE PRIVATE EYE

BRIAN K. VAUGHAN MARCOS MARTIN
WITH
MUNTSA VICENTE

CHAPTER EIGHT

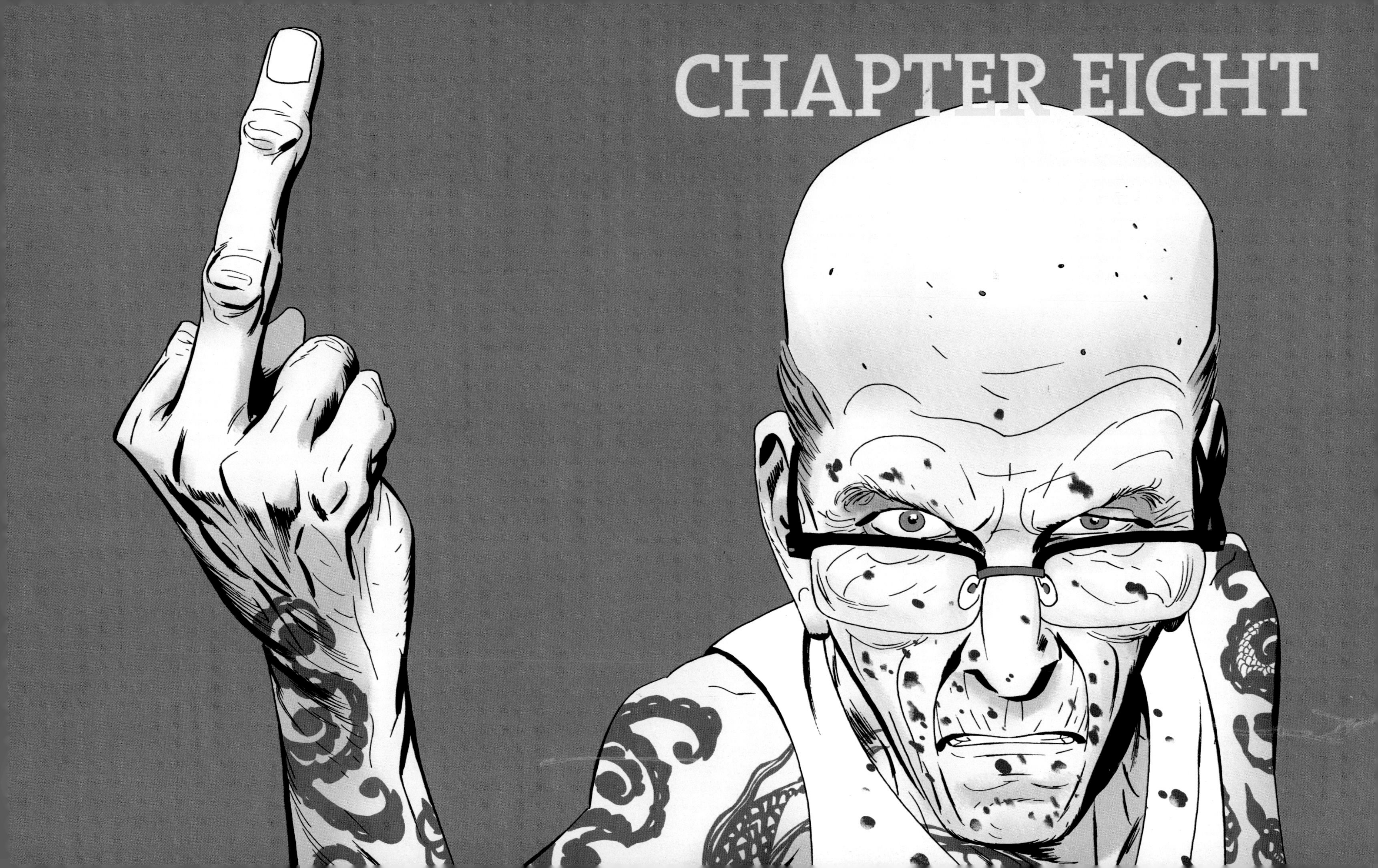

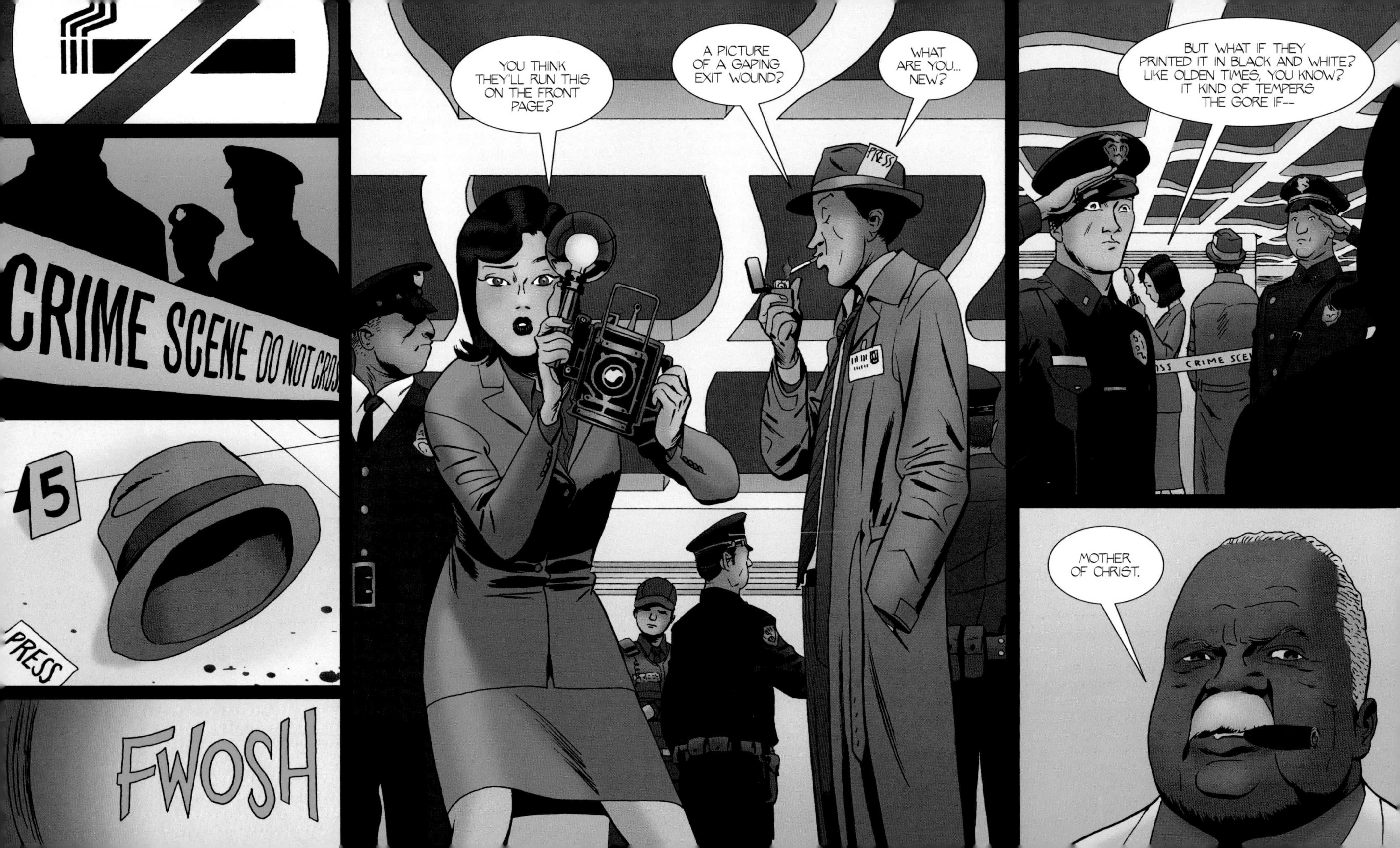
CRIME SCENE DO NOT CROSS
5
PRESS
FWOSH
YOU THINK THEY'LL RUN THIS ON THE FRONT PAGE?
A PICTURE OF A GAPING EXIT WOUND?
WHAT ARE YOU... NEW?
PRESS
BUT WHAT IF THEY PRINTED IT IN BLACK AND WHITE? LIKE OLDEN TIMES, YOU KNOW? IT KIND OF TEMPERS THE GORE IF--
CRIME SCE
MOTHER OF CHRIST.

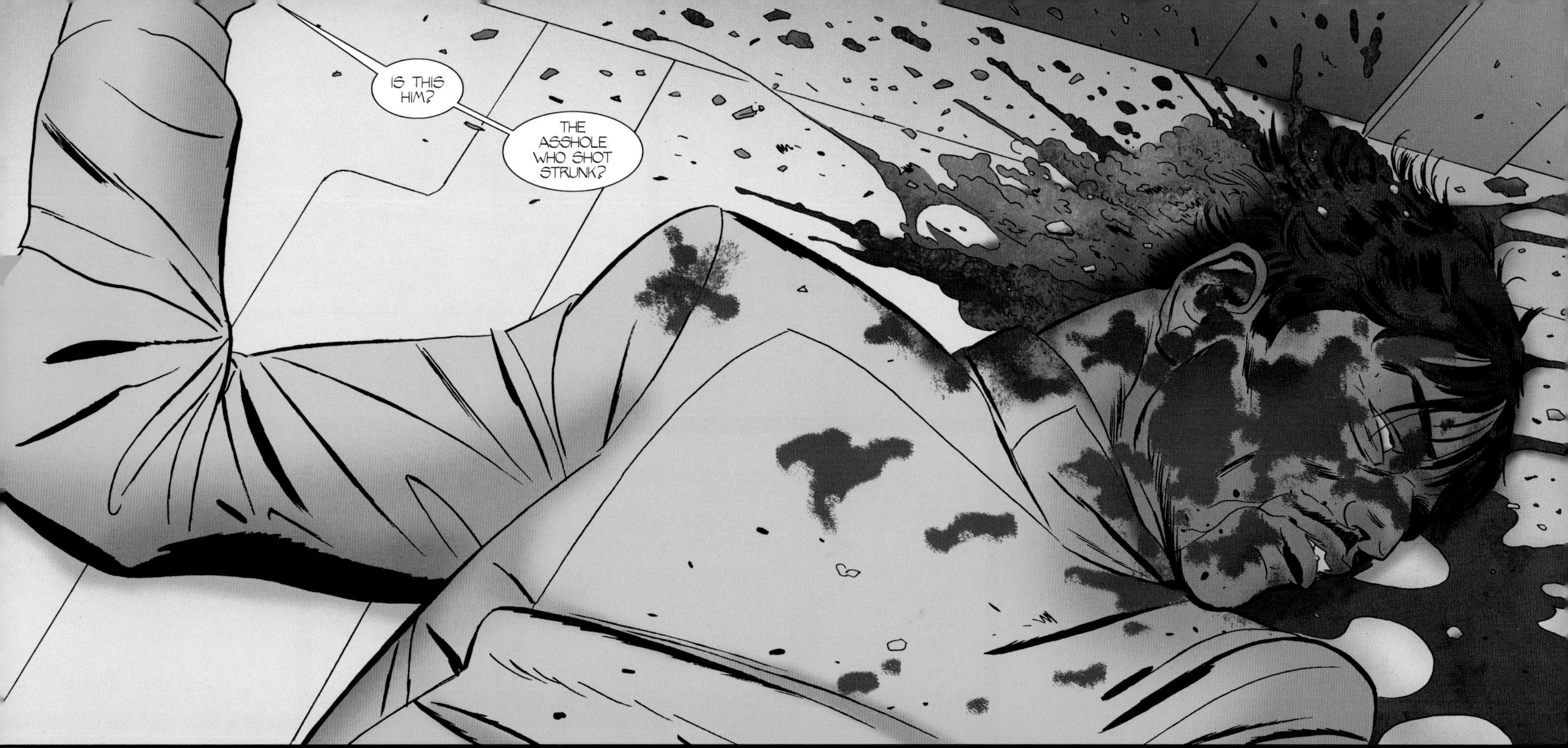
IS THIS HIM?
THE ASSHOLE WHO SHOT STRUNK?

THE PRIVATE EYE

BRIAN K. VAUGHAN
MARCOS MARTIN
WITH
MUNTSA VICENTE

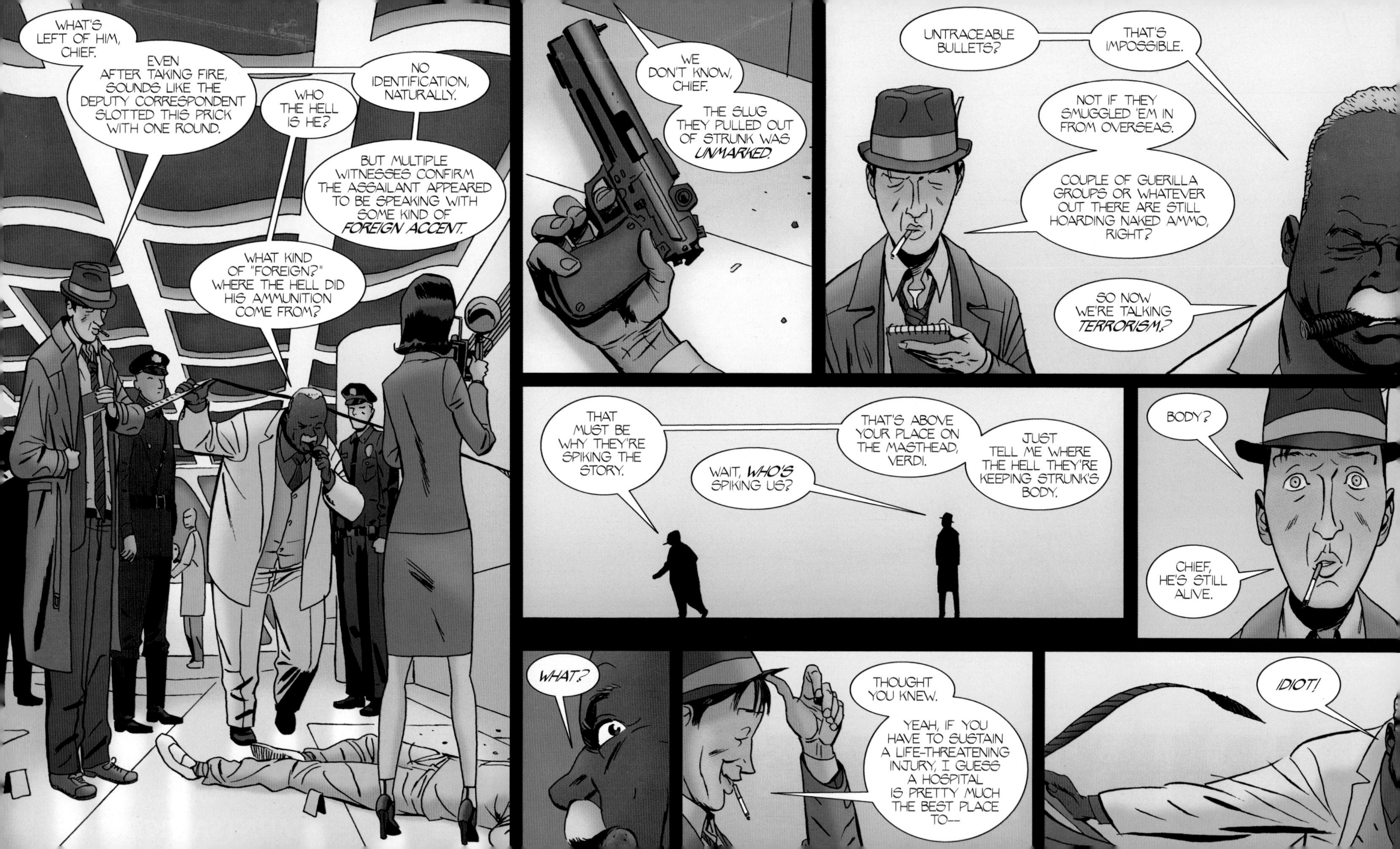
WHAT'S LEFT OF HIM, CHIEF.
EVEN AFTER TAKING FIRE, SOUNDS LIKE THE DEPUTY CORRESPONDENT SLOTTED THIS PRICK WITH ONE ROUND.
NO IDENTIFICATION, NATURALLY.
WHO THE HELL IS HE?
BUT MULTIPLE WITNESSES CONFIRM THE ASSAILANT APPEARED TO BE SPEAKING WITH SOME KIND OF *FOREIGN ACCENT.*
WHAT KIND OF "FOREIGN?" WHERE THE HELL DID HIS AMMUNITION COME FROM?
WE DON'T KNOW, CHIEF.
THE SLUG THEY PULLED OUT OF STRUNK WAS *UNMARKED.*
UNTRACEABLE BULLETS?
THAT'S IMPOSSIBLE.
NOT IF THEY SMUGGLED 'EM IN FROM OVERSEAS.
COUPLE OF GUERILLA GROUPS OR WHATEVER OUT THERE ARE STILL HOARDING NAKED AMMO, RIGHT?
SO NOW WE'RE TALKING *TERRORISM?*
THAT MUST BE WHY THEY'RE SPIKING THE STORY.
WAIT, *WHO'S* SPIKING US?
THAT'S ABOVE YOUR PLACE ON THE MASTHEAD, VERDI.
JUST TELL ME WHERE THE HELL THEY'RE KEEPING STRUNK'S BODY.
BODY?
CHIEF, HE'S STILL ALIVE.
WHAT?
THOUGHT YOU KNEW.
YEAH, IF YOU HAVE TO SUSTAIN A LIFE-THREATENING INJURY, I GUESS A HOSPITAL IS PRETTY MUCH THE BEST PLACE TO--
IDIOT!

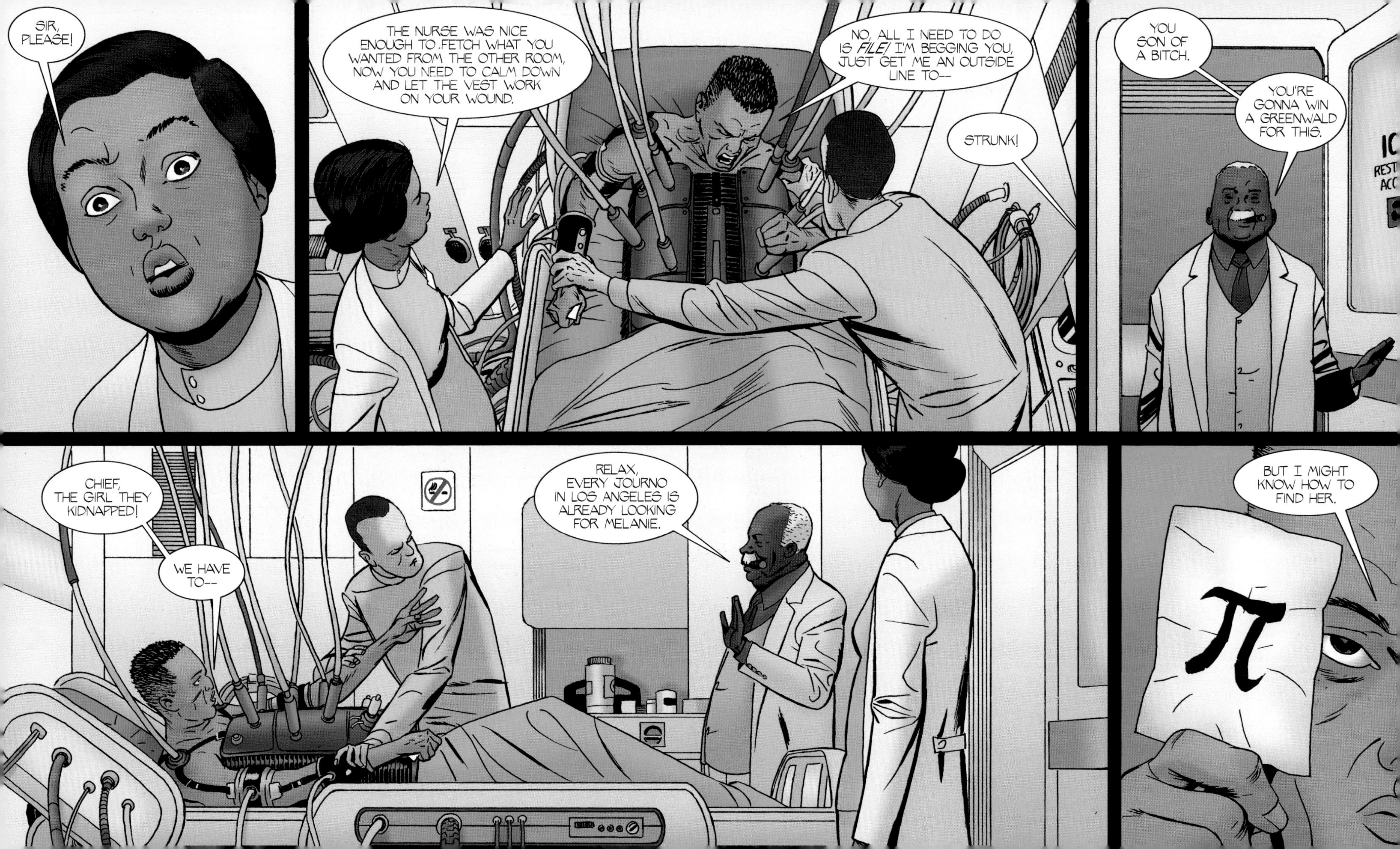
SIR, PLEASE!
THE NURSE WAS NICE ENOUGH TO FETCH WHAT YOU WANTED FROM THE OTHER ROOM, NOW YOU NEED TO CALM DOWN AND LET THE VEST WORK ON YOUR WOUND.
NO, ALL I NEED TO DO IS *FILE!* I'M BEGGING YOU, JUST GET ME AN OUTSIDE LINE TO--
STRUNK!
YOU SON OF A BITCH.
YOU'RE GONNA WIN A GREENWALD FOR THIS.
CHIEF, THE GIRL THEY KIDNAPPED!
WE HAVE TO--
RELAX, EVERY JOURNO IN LOS ANGELES IS ALREADY LOOKING FOR MELANIE.
BUT I MIGHT KNOW HOW TO FIND HER.

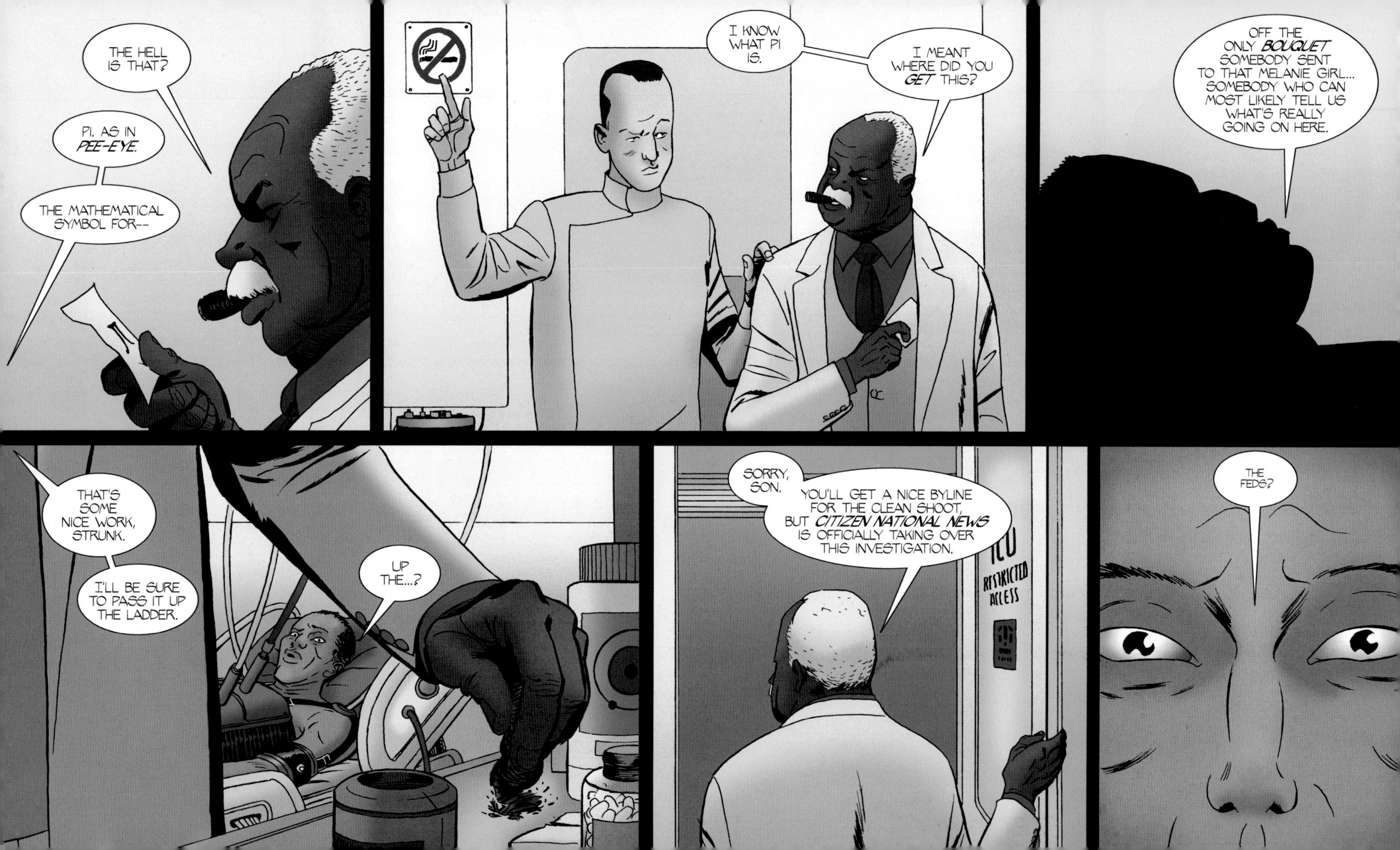

THE HELL IS THAT?
PI. AS IN PEE-EYE.
THE MATHEMATICAL SYMBOL FOR--
I KNOW WHAT PI IS.
I MEANT WHERE DID YOU GET THIS?
OFF THE ONLY BOUQUET SOMEBODY SENT TO THAT MELANIE GIRL... SOMEBODY WHO CAN MOST LIKELY TELL US WHAT'S REALLY GOING ON HERE.
THAT'S SOME NICE WORK, STRUNK.
I'LL BE SURE TO PASS IT UP THE LADDER.
UP THE...?
SORRY, SON.
YOU'LL GET A NICE BYLINE FOR THE CLEAN SHOOT, BUT CITIZEN NATIONAL NEWS IS OFFICIALLY TAKING OVER THIS INVESTIGATION.
ICU
RESTRICTED ACCESS
THE FEDS?

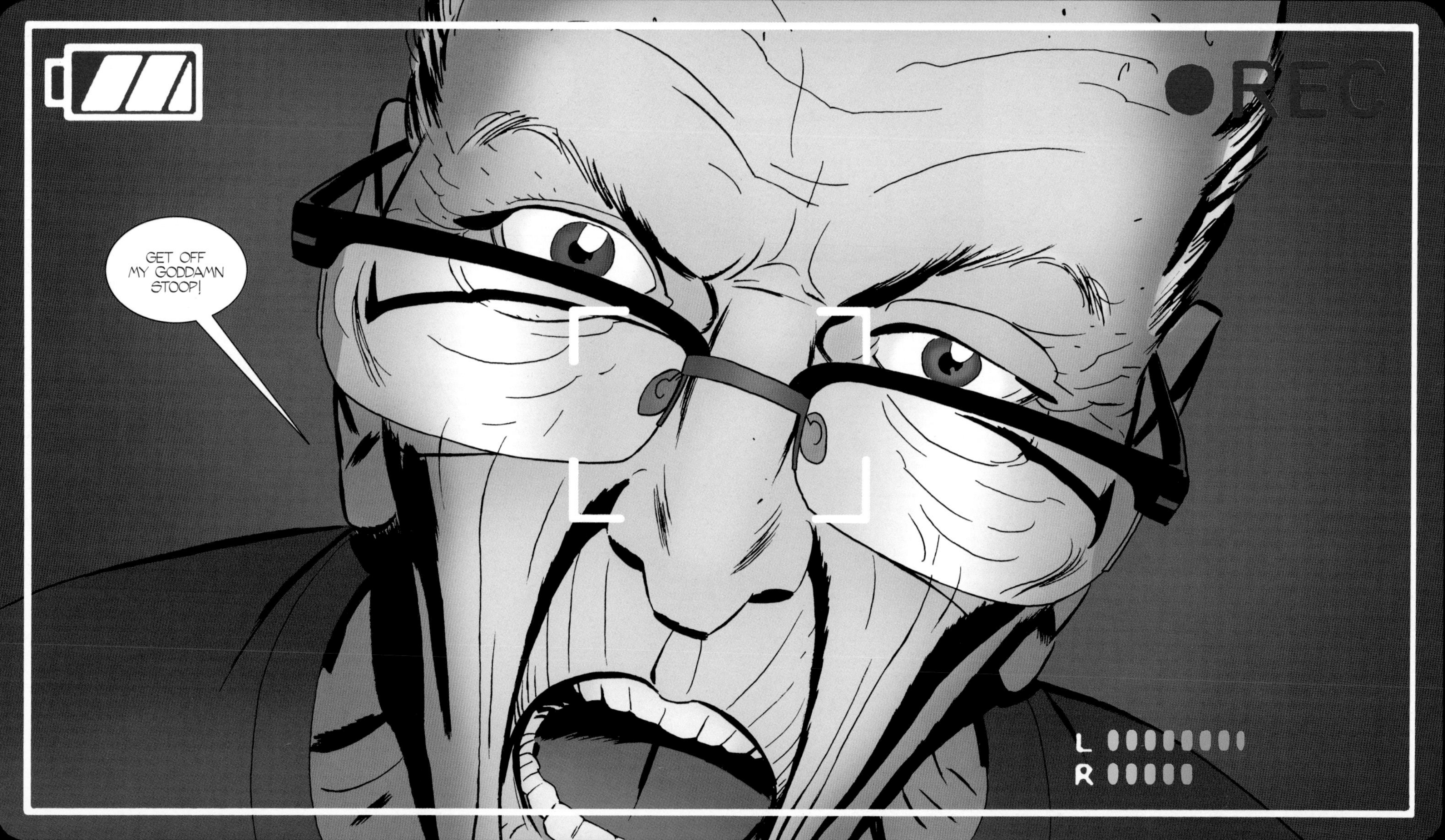
REC
GET OFF MY GODDAMN STOOP!
L
R

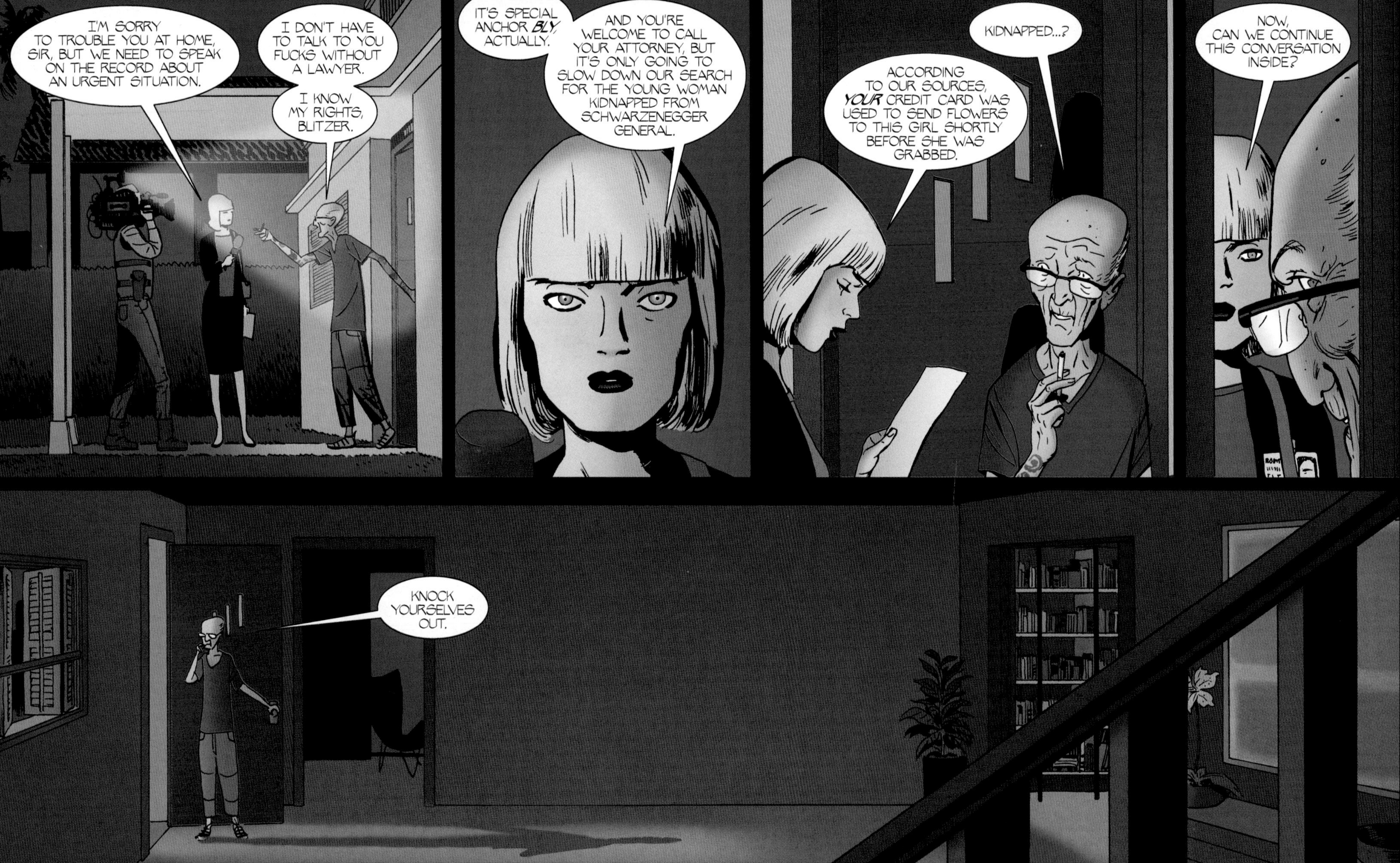

I'M SORRY TO TROUBLE YOU AT HOME, SIR, BUT WE NEED TO SPEAK ON THE RECORD ABOUT AN URGENT SITUATION.
I DON'T HAVE TO TALK TO YOU FUCKS WITHOUT A LAWYER.
I KNOW MY RIGHTS, BLITZER.
IT'S SPECIAL ANCHOR BLY, ACTUALLY.
AND YOU'RE WELCOME TO CALL YOUR ATTORNEY, BUT IT'S ONLY GOING TO SLOW DOWN OUR SEARCH FOR THE YOUNG WOMAN KIDNAPPED FROM SCHWARZENEGGER GENERAL.
ACCORDING TO OUR SOURCES, YOUR CREDIT CARD WAS USED TO SEND FLOWERS TO THIS GIRL SHORTLY BEFORE SHE WAS GRABBED.
KIDNAPPED...?
NOW, CAN WE CONTINUE THIS CONVERSATION INSIDE?
KNOCK YOURSELVES OUT.

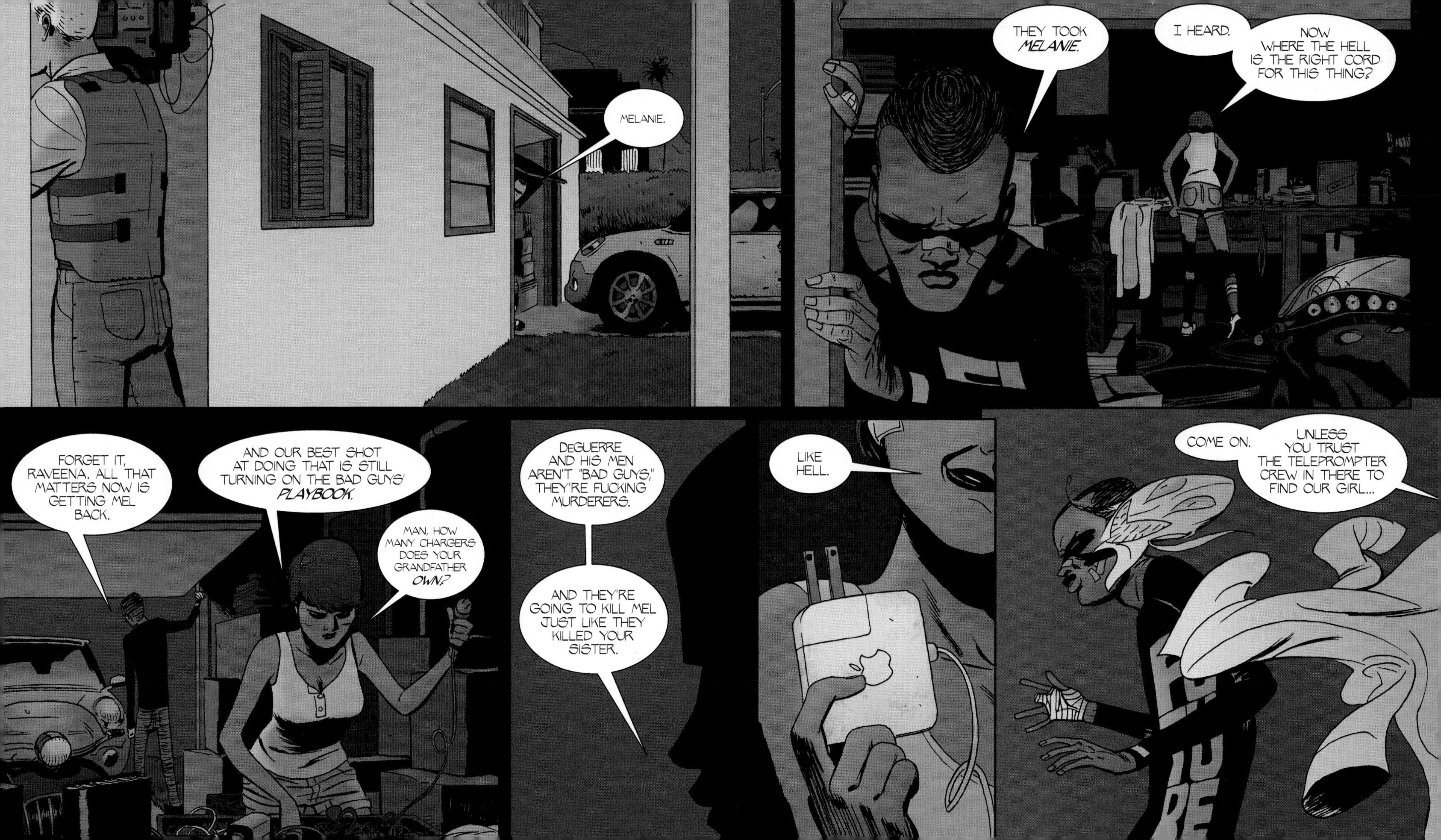
MELANIE.
THEY TOOK *MELANIE.*
I HEARD.
NOW WHERE THE HELL IS THE RIGHT CORD FOR THIS THING?
FORGET IT, RAVEENA. ALL THAT MATTERS NOW IS GETTING MEL BACK.
AND OUR BEST SHOT AT DOING THAT IS STILL TURNING ON THE BAD GUYS' *PLAYBOOK.*
MAN, HOW MANY CHARGERS DOES YOUR GRANDFATHER *OWN?*
DeGUERRE AND HIS MEN AREN'T "BAD GUYS," THEY'RE FUCKING MURDERERS.
AND THEY'RE GOING TO KILL MEL JUST LIKE THEY KILLED YOUR SISTER.
LIKE HELL.
COME ON.
UNLESS YOU TRUST THE TELEPROMPTER CREW IN THERE TO FIND OUR GIRL...

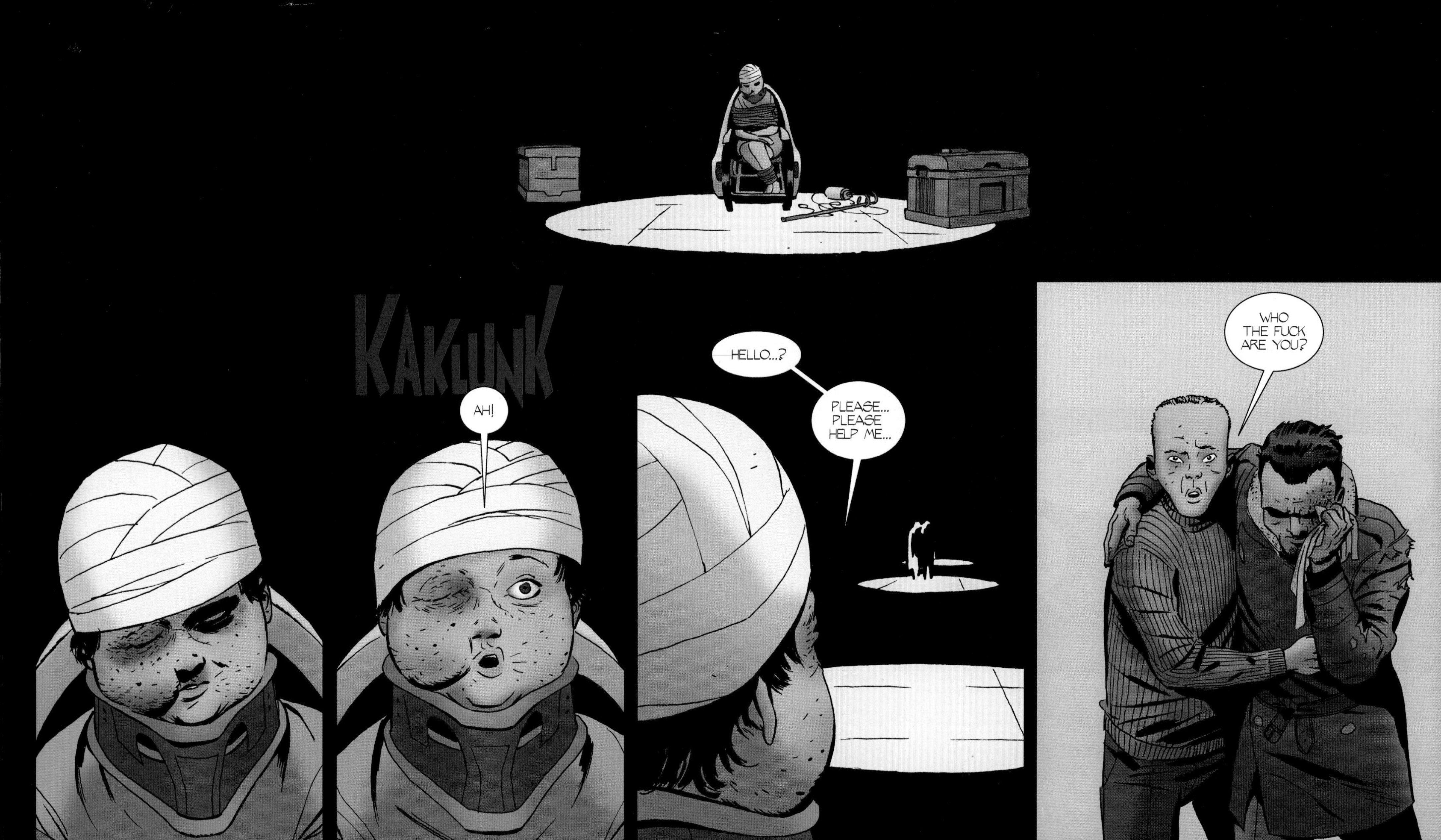
KAKLUNK
AH!
HELLO...?
PLEASE... PLEASE HELP ME...
WHO THE FUCK ARE YOU?

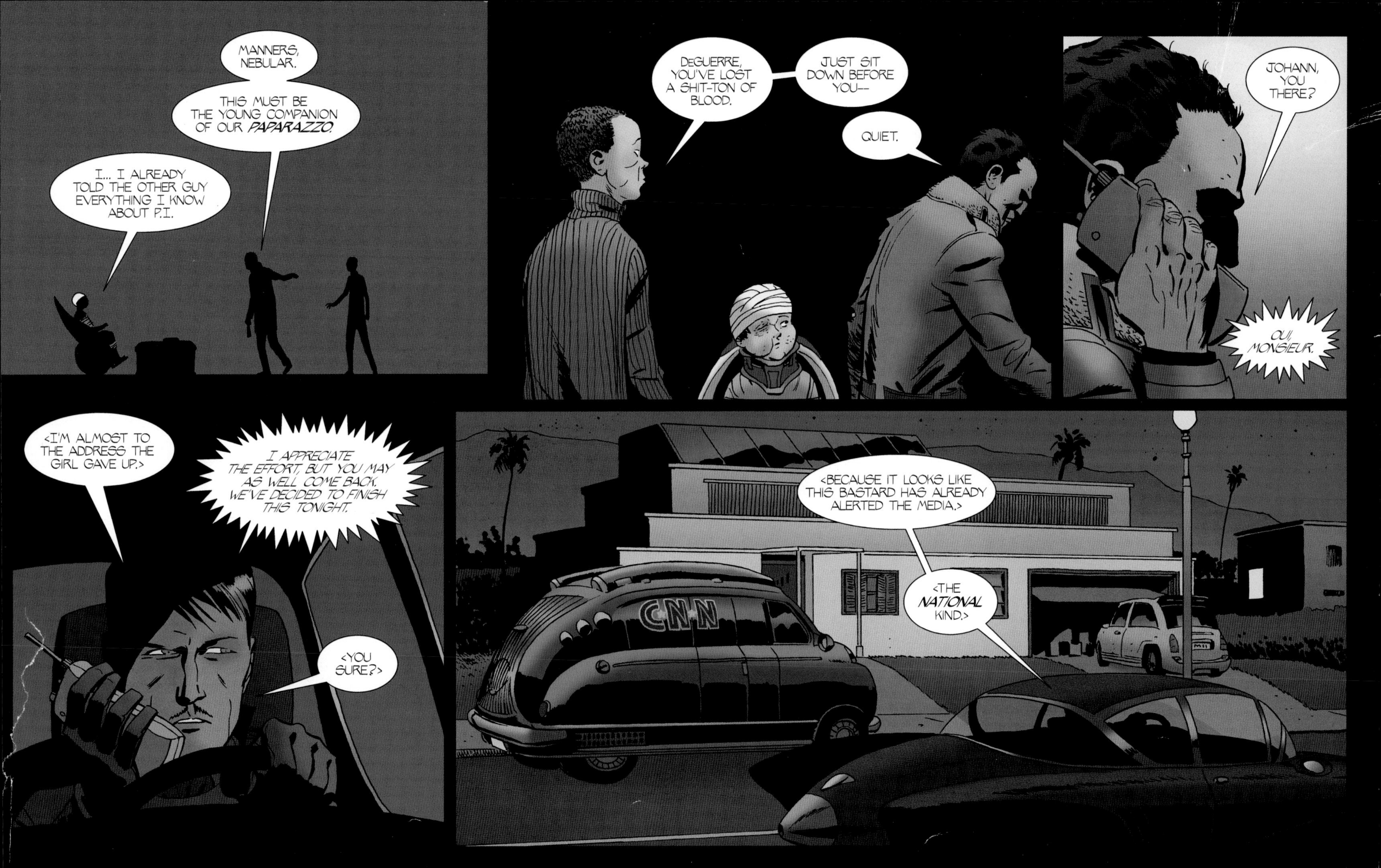
MANNERS, NEBULAR.
THIS MUST BE THE YOUNG COMPANION OF OUR *PAPARAZZO.*
I... I ALREADY TOLD THE OTHER GUY EVERYTHING I KNOW ABOUT P.I.
DEGUERRE, YOU'VE LOST A SHIT-TON OF BLOOD.
JUST SIT DOWN BEFORE YOU--
QUIET.
JOHANN, YOU THERE?
OUI, MONSIEUR.
<I'M ALMOST TO THE ADDRESS THE GIRL GAVE UP.>
I APPRECIATE THE EFFORT, BUT YOU MAY AS WELL COME BACK. WE'VE DECIDED TO FINISH THIS TONIGHT.
<YOU SURE?>
<BECAUSE IT LOOKS LIKE THIS BASTARD HAS ALREADY ALERTED THE MEDIA.>
<THE *NATIONAL* KIND.>
CNN

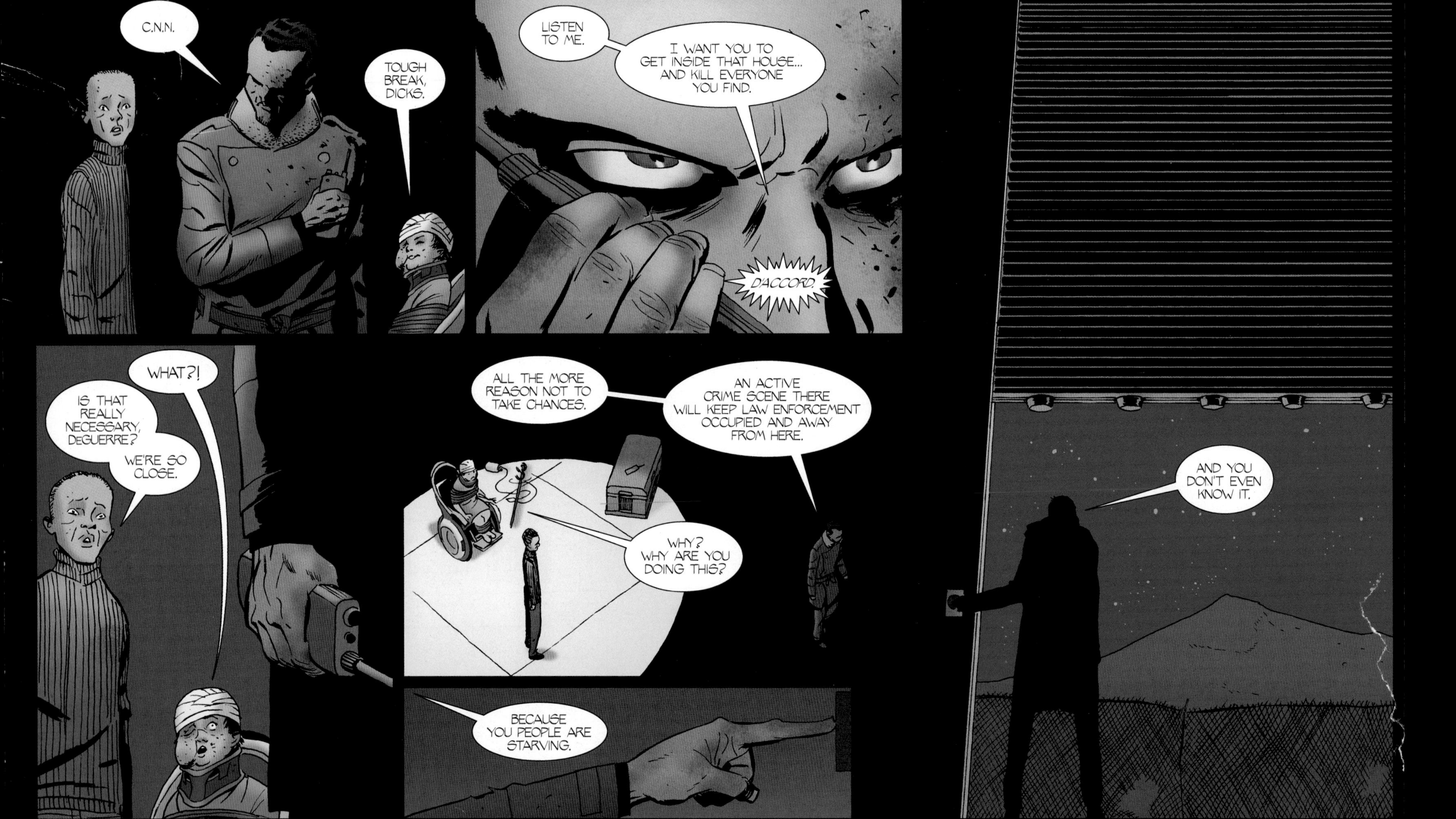
C.N.N.
TOUGH BREAK, DICKS.
LISTEN TO ME.
I WANT YOU TO GET INSIDE THAT HOUSE... AND KILL EVERYONE YOU FIND.
D'ACCORD.
WHAT?!
IS THAT REALLY NECESSARY, DEGUERRE?
WE'RE SO CLOSE.
ALL THE MORE REASON NOT TO TAKE CHANCES.
AN ACTIVE CRIME SCENE THERE WILL KEEP LAW ENFORCEMENT OCCUPIED AND AWAY FROM HERE.
WHY? WHY ARE YOU DOING THIS?
BECAUSE YOU PEOPLE ARE STARVING.
AND YOU DON'T EVEN KNOW IT.

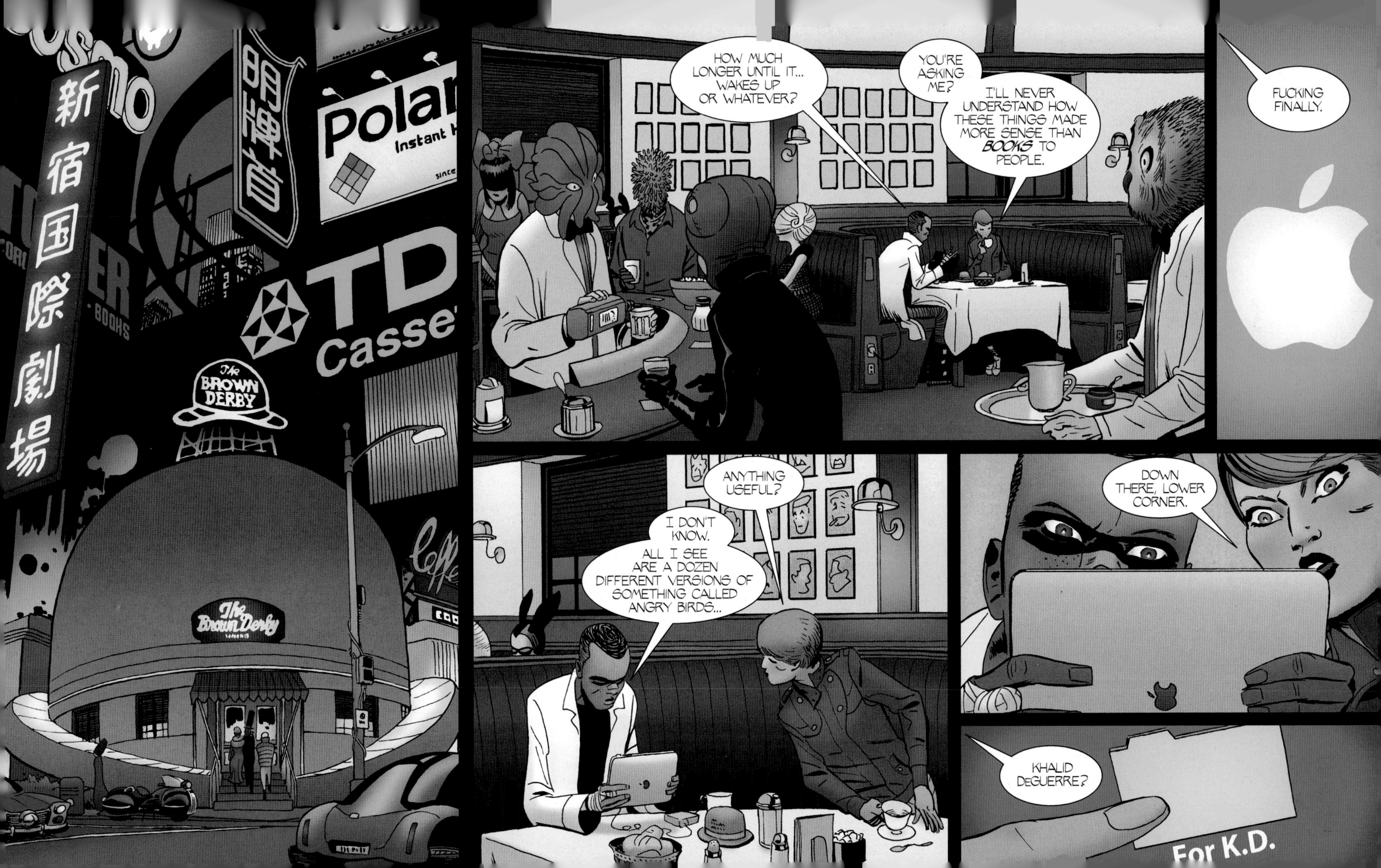
新宿国際劇場
The BROWN DERBY
The Brown Derby
HOW MUCH LONGER UNTIL IT... WAKES UP OR WHATEVER?
YOU'RE ASKING ME?
I'LL NEVER UNDERSTAND HOW THESE THINGS MADE MORE SENSE THAN *BOOKS* TO PEOPLE.
FUCKING FINALLY.
ANYTHING USEFUL?
I DON'T KNOW.
ALL I SEE ARE A DOZEN DIFFERENT VERSIONS OF SOMETHING CALLED ANGRY BIRDS...
DOWN THERE, LOWER CORNER.
KHALID DeGUERRE?
For K.D.

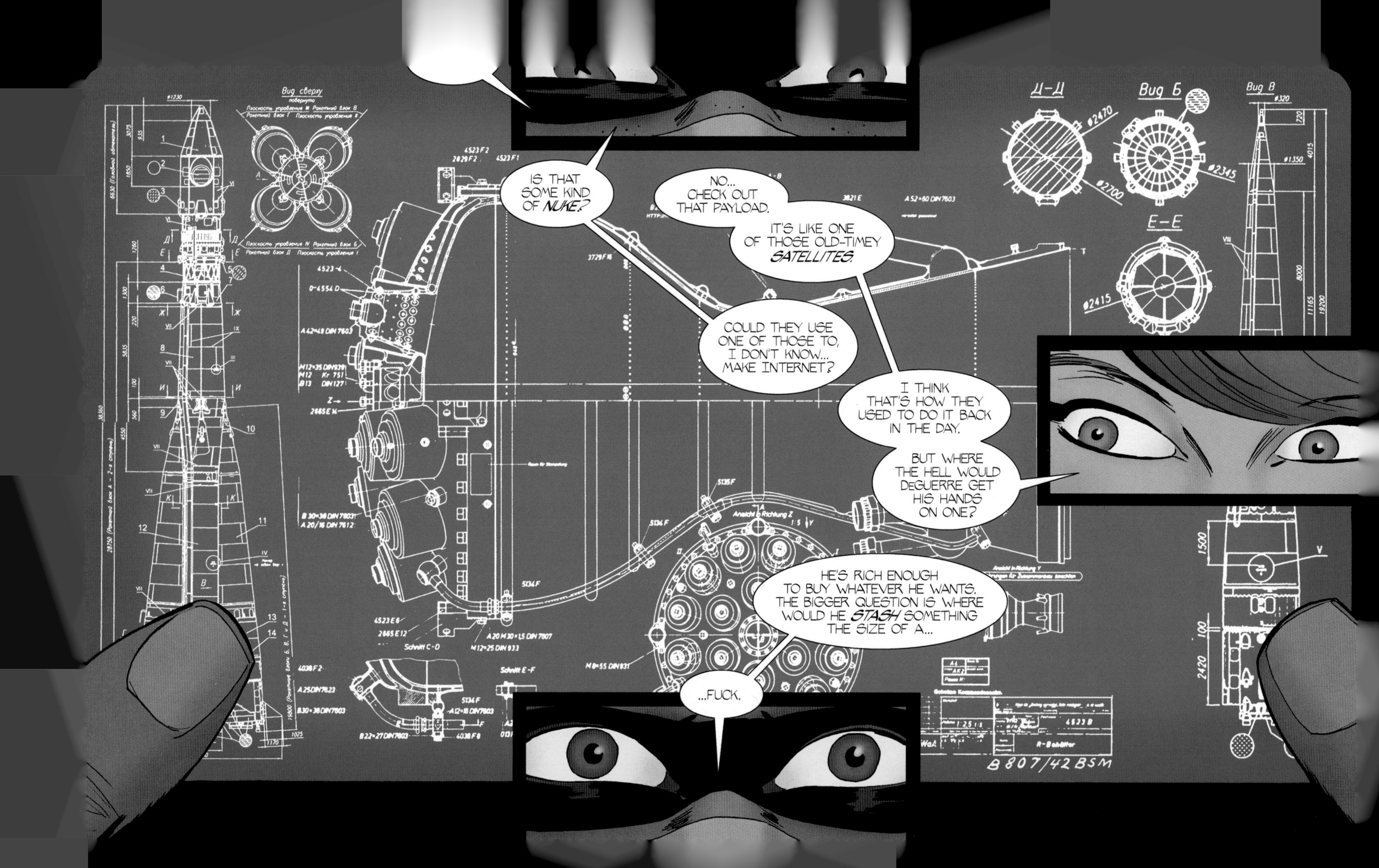
IS THAT SOME KIND OF NUKE?
NO... CHECK OUT THAT PAYLOAD.
IT'S LIKE ONE OF THOSE OLD-TIMEY SATELLITES.
COULD THEY USE ONE OF THOSE TO, I DON'T KNOW... MAKE INTERNET?
I THINK THAT'S HOW THEY USED TO DO IT BACK IN THE DAY.
BUT WHERE THE HELL WOULD DeGUERRE GET HIS HANDS ON ONE?
HE'S RICH ENOUGH TO BUY WHATEVER HE WANTS. THE BIGGER QUESTION IS WHERE WOULD HE STASH SOMETHING THE SIZE OF A...
...FUCK.

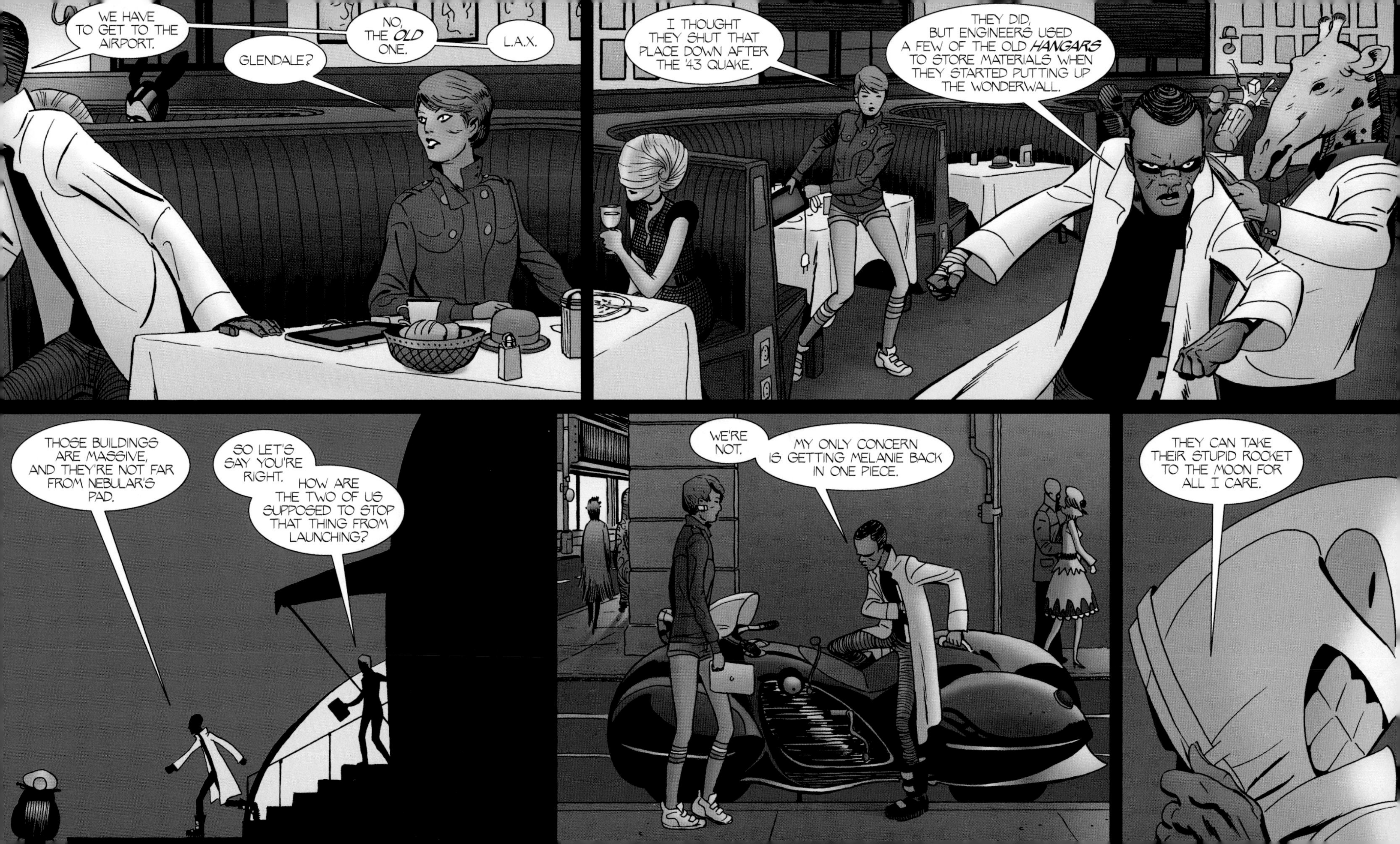
WE HAVE TO GET TO THE AIRPORT.
GLENDALE?
NO, THE OLD ONE.
L.A.X.
I THOUGHT THEY SHUT THAT PLACE DOWN AFTER THE '43 QUAKE.
THEY DID, BUT ENGINEERS USED A FEW OF THE OLD HANGARS TO STORE MATERIALS WHEN THEY STARTED PUTTING UP THE WONDERWALL.
THOSE BUILDINGS ARE MASSIVE, AND THEY'RE NOT FAR FROM NEBULAR'S PAD.
SO LET'S SAY YOU'RE RIGHT.
HOW ARE THE TWO OF US SUPPOSED TO STOP THAT THING FROM LAUNCHING?
WE'RE NOT.
MY ONLY CONCERN IS GETTING MELANIE BACK IN ONE PIECE.
THEY CAN TAKE THEIR STUPID ROCKET TO THE MOON FOR ALL I CARE.

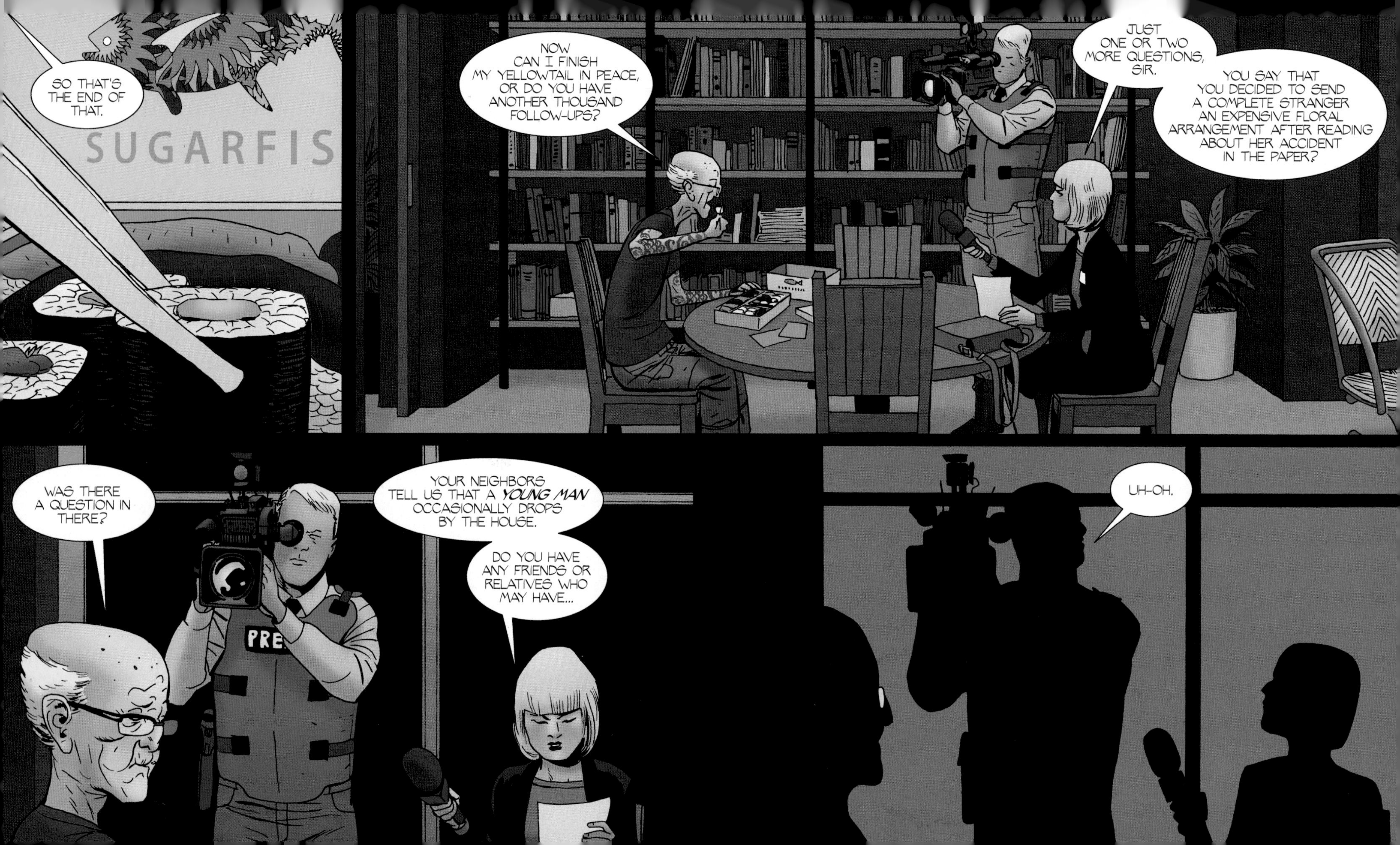
SO THAT'S THE END OF THAT.
SUGARFIS
NOW CAN I FINISH MY YELLOWTAIL IN PEACE, OR DO YOU HAVE ANOTHER THOUSAND FOLLOW-UPS?
JUST ONE OR TWO MORE QUESTIONS, SIR.
YOU SAY THAT YOU DECIDED TO SEND A COMPLETE STRANGER AN EXPENSIVE FLORAL ARRANGEMENT AFTER READING ABOUT HER ACCIDENT IN THE PAPER?
WAS THERE A QUESTION IN THERE?
PRE
YOUR NEIGHBORS TELL US THAT A *YOUNG MAN* OCCASIONALLY DROPS BY THE HOUSE.
DO YOU HAVE ANY FRIENDS OR RELATIVES WHO MAY HAVE...
UH-OH.

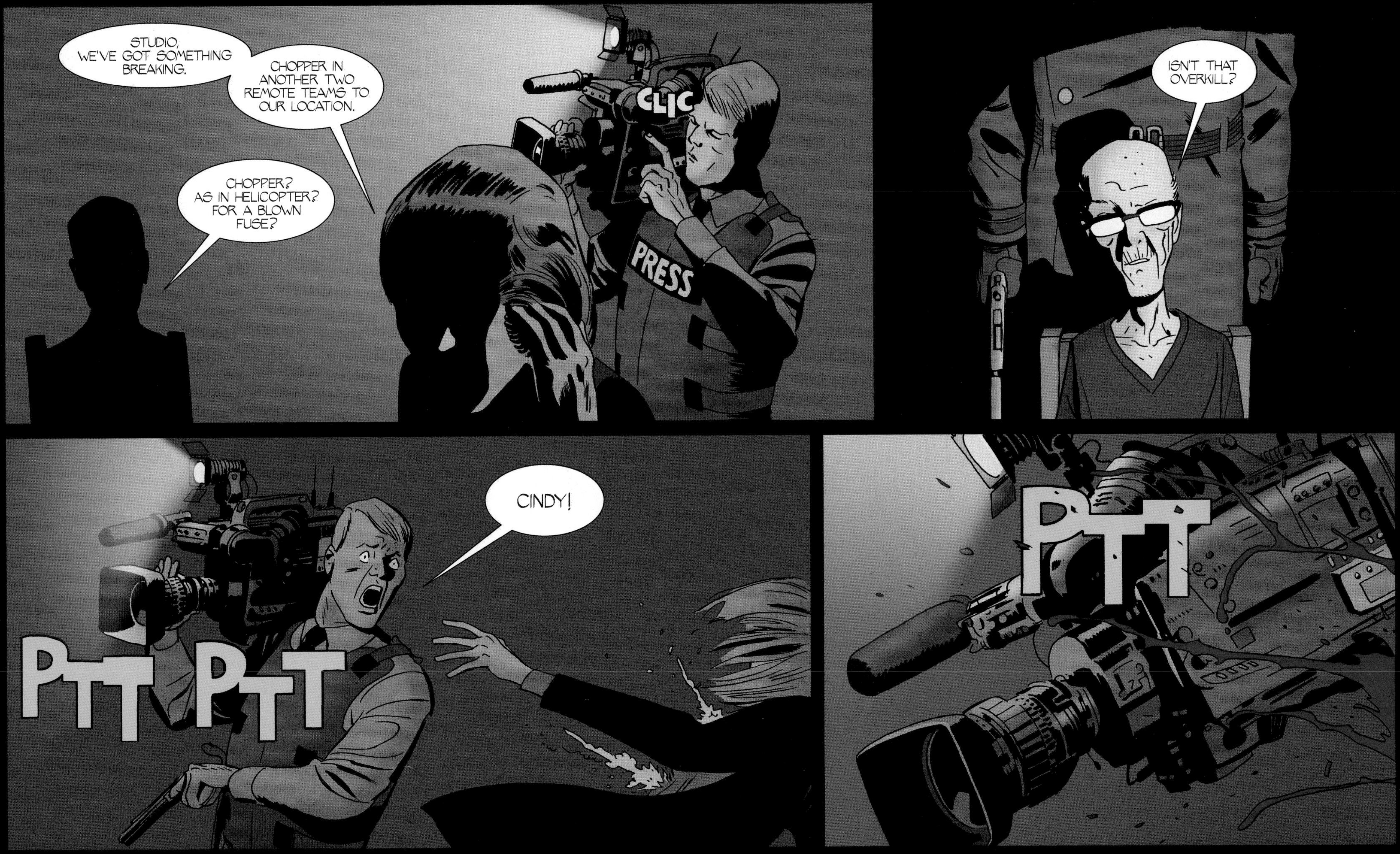
STUDIO, WE'VE GOT SOMETHING BREAKING.
CHOPPER IN ANOTHER TWO REMOTE TEAMS TO OUR LOCATION.
CLIC
CHOPPER? AS IN HELICOPTER? FOR A BLOWN FUSE?
PRESS
ISN'T THAT OVERKILL?
CINDY!
PTT PTT
PTT

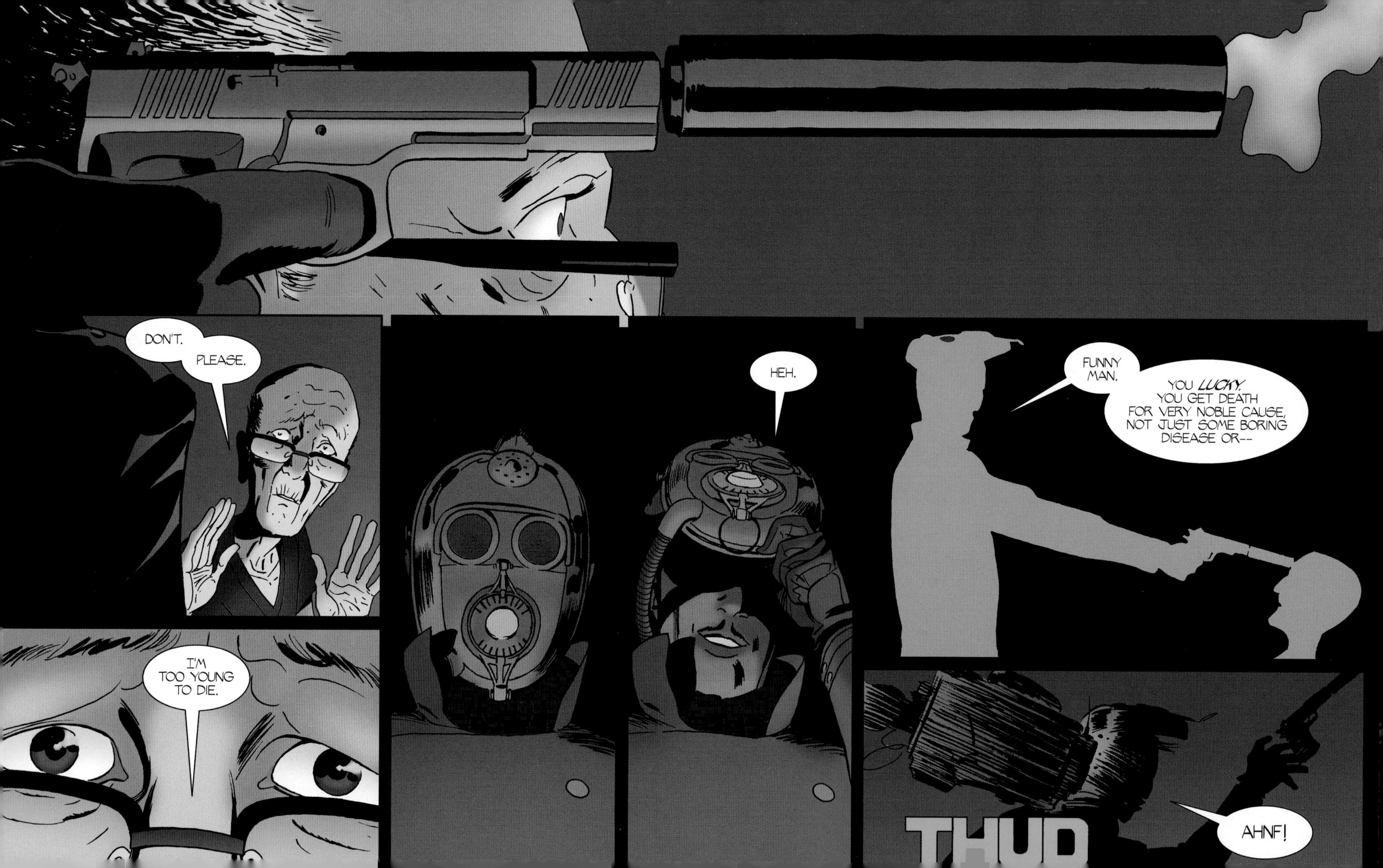
DON'T.
PLEASE.
I'M TOO YOUNG TO DIE.
HEH.
FUNNY MAN.
YOU *LUCKY.* YOU GET DEATH FOR VERY NOBLE CAUSE, NOT JUST SOME BORING DISEASE OR--
THUD
AHNF!

OOF!

WAIT OUTSIDE FOR MY BACKUP.

BUT YOU—

NOW.

AHN!

THE GIRL.

TELL ME WHERE SHE IS.

YOU THINK YOU TOUGH INTERVIEW?

I GIVE YOU NOTHING, CUNT.

"WE'LL SEE."

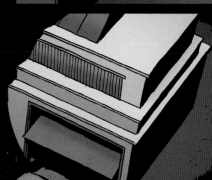

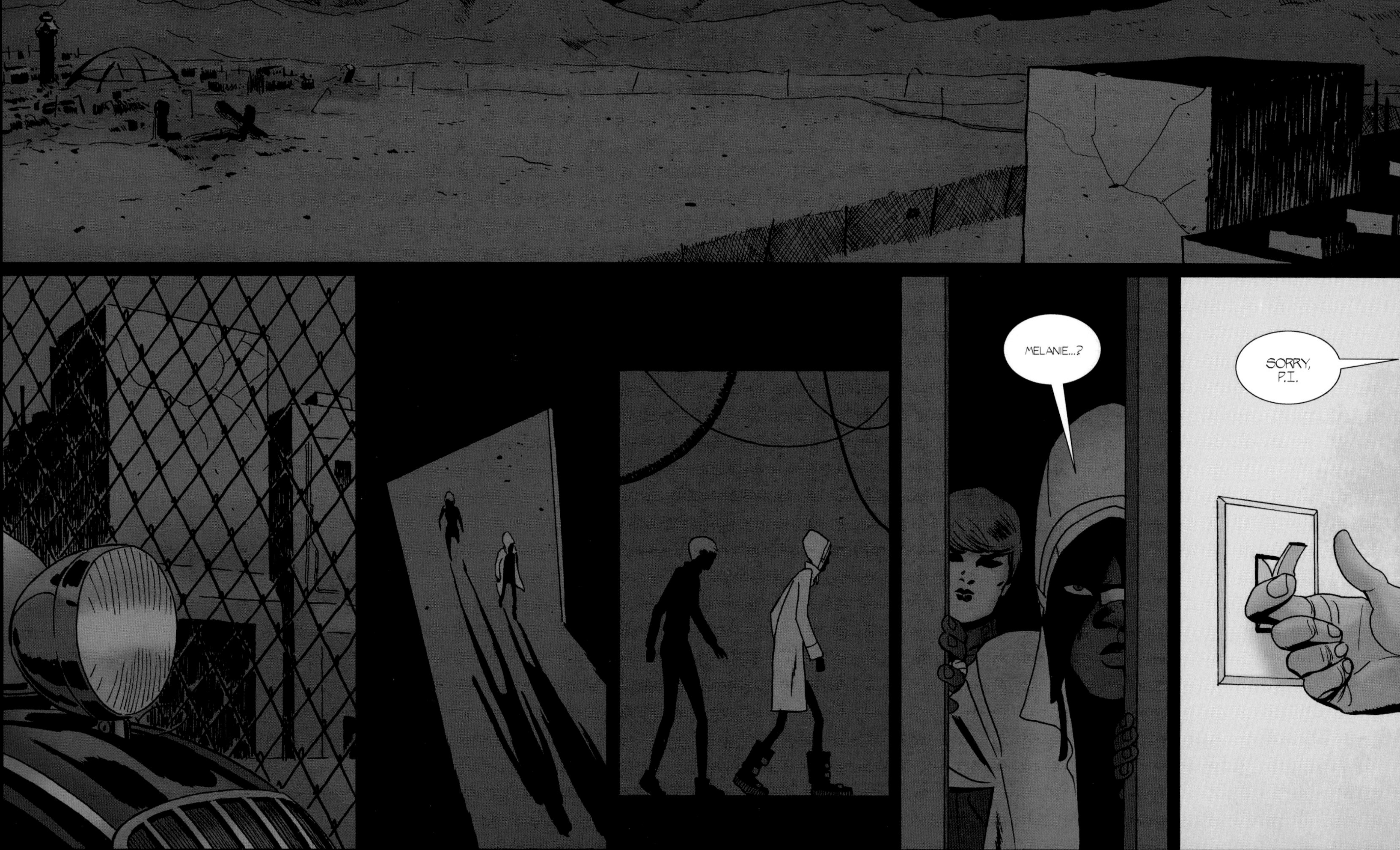
MELANIE...?
SORRY, P.I.

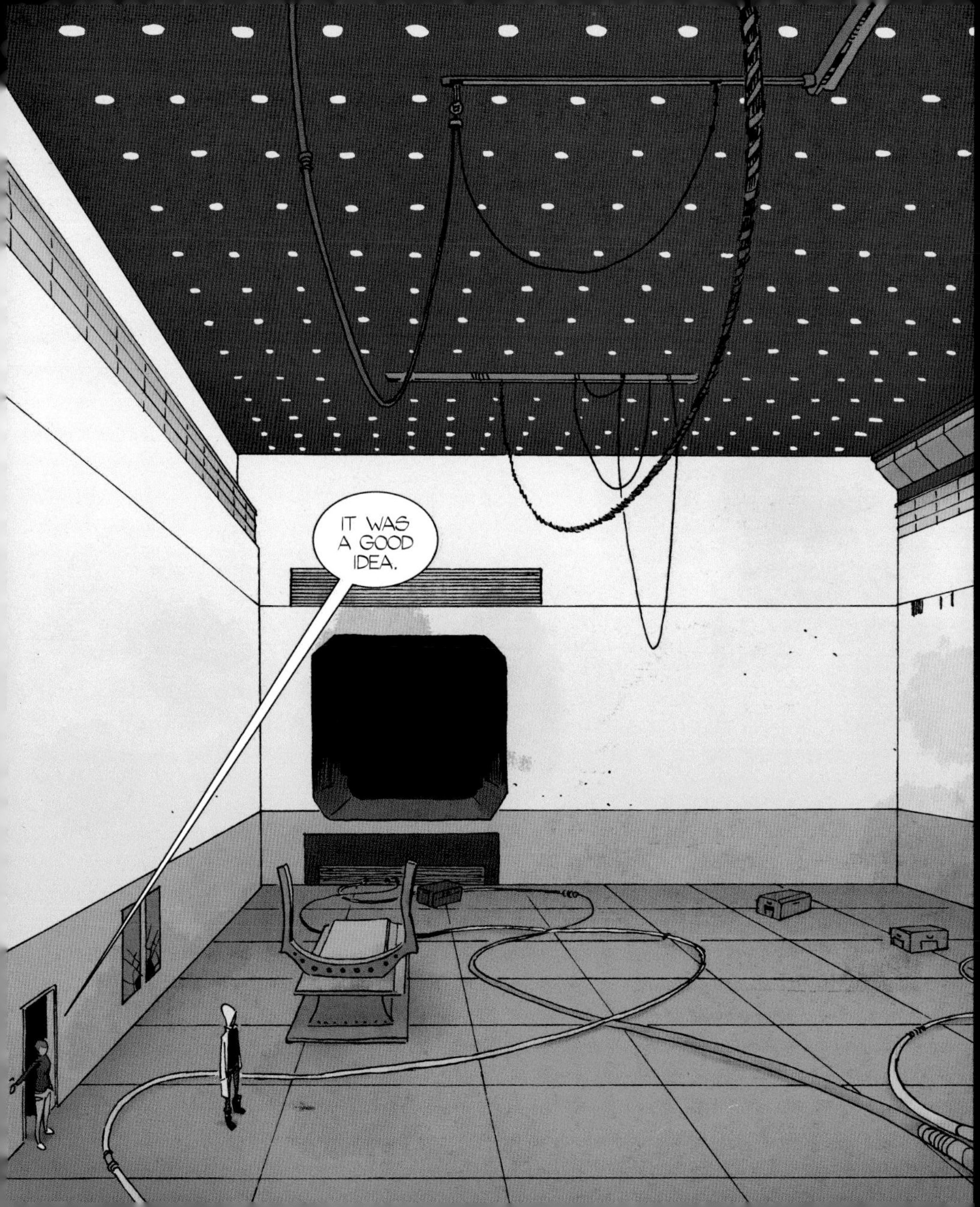
IT WAS A GOOD IDEA.

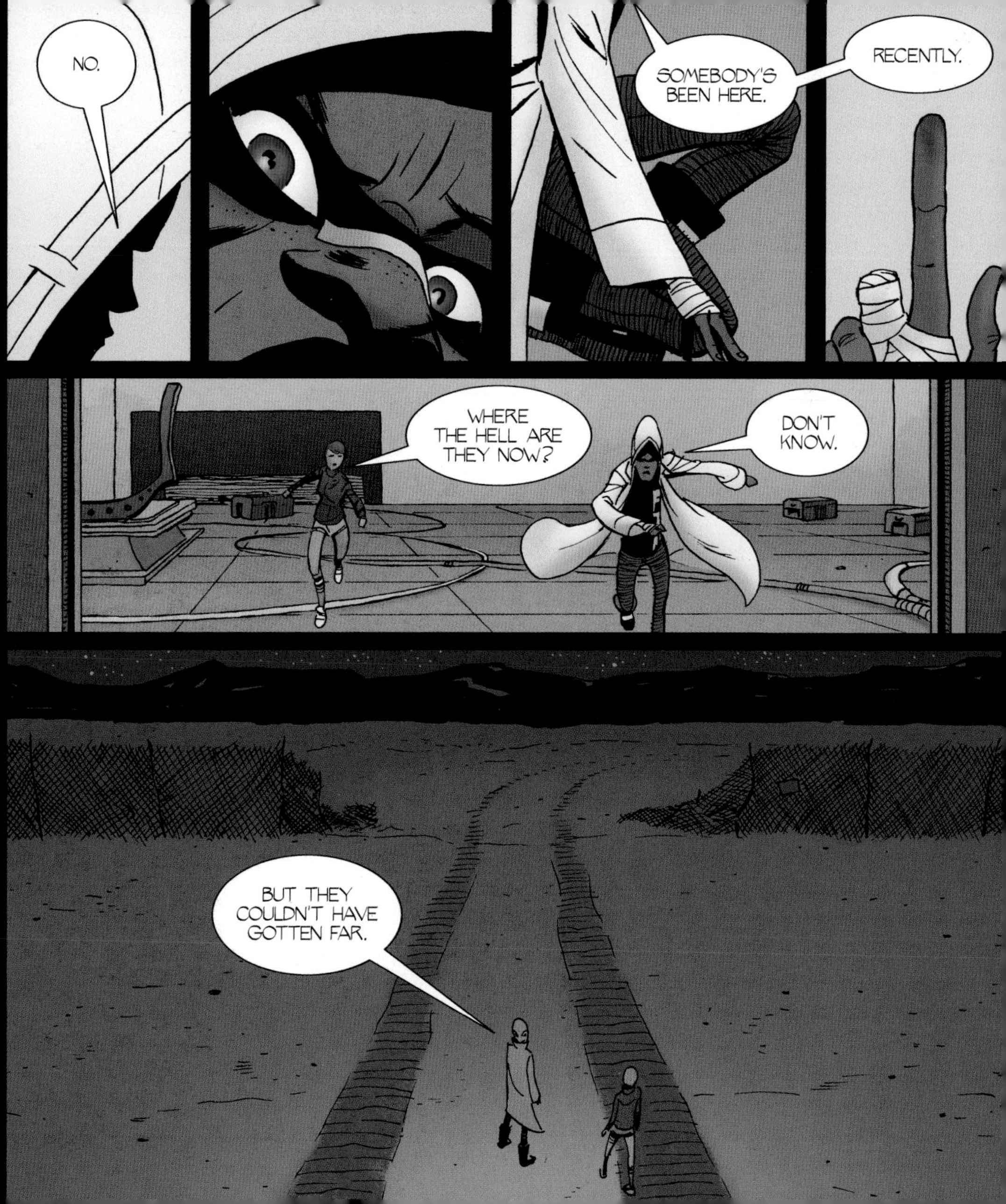
NO.
SOMEBODY'S BEEN HERE.
RECENTLY.
WHERE THE HELL ARE THEY NOW?
DON'T KNOW.
BUT THEY COULDN'T HAVE GOTTEN FAR.

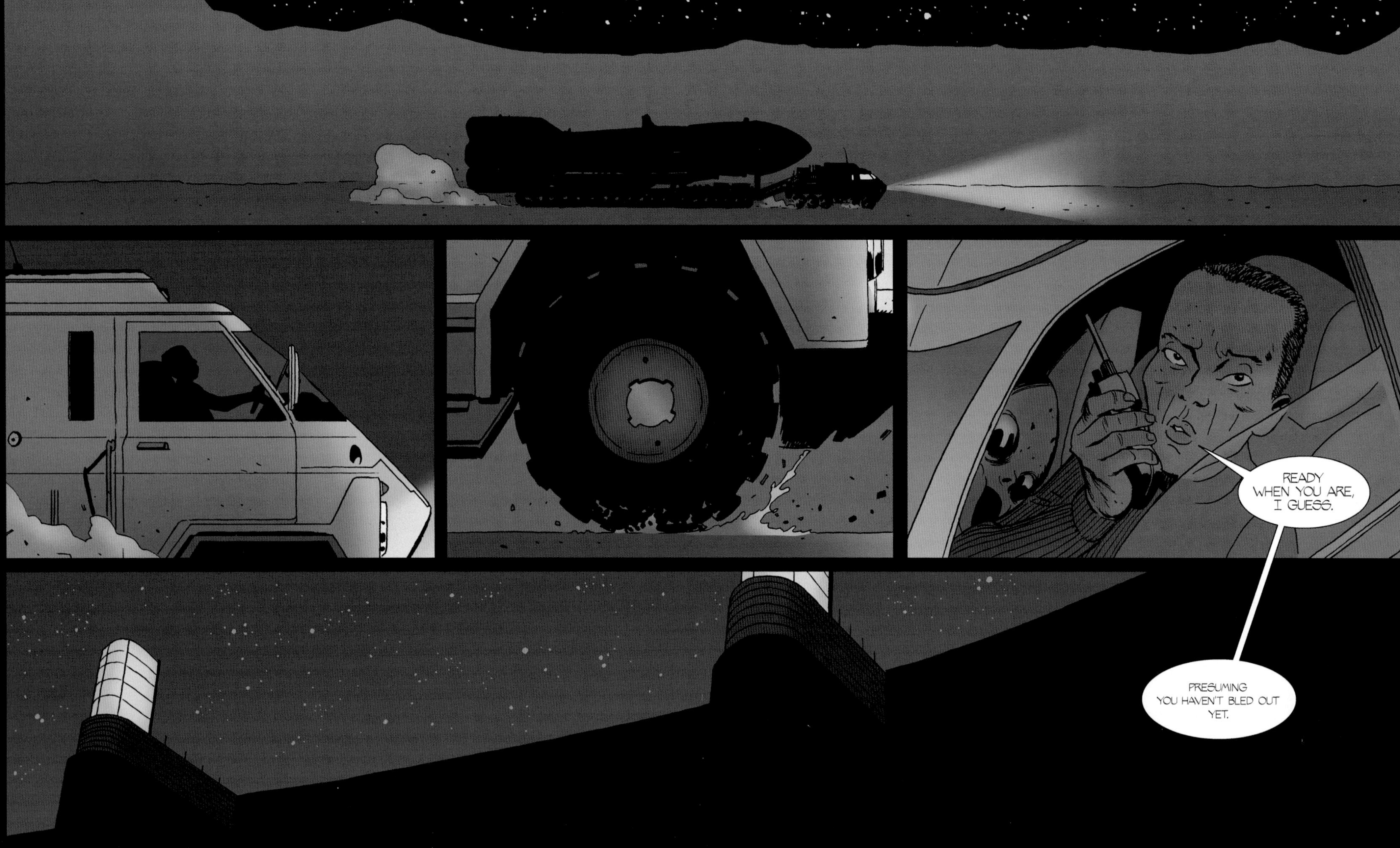
READY WHEN YOU ARE, I GUESS.
PRESUMING YOU HAVEN'T BLED OUT YET.

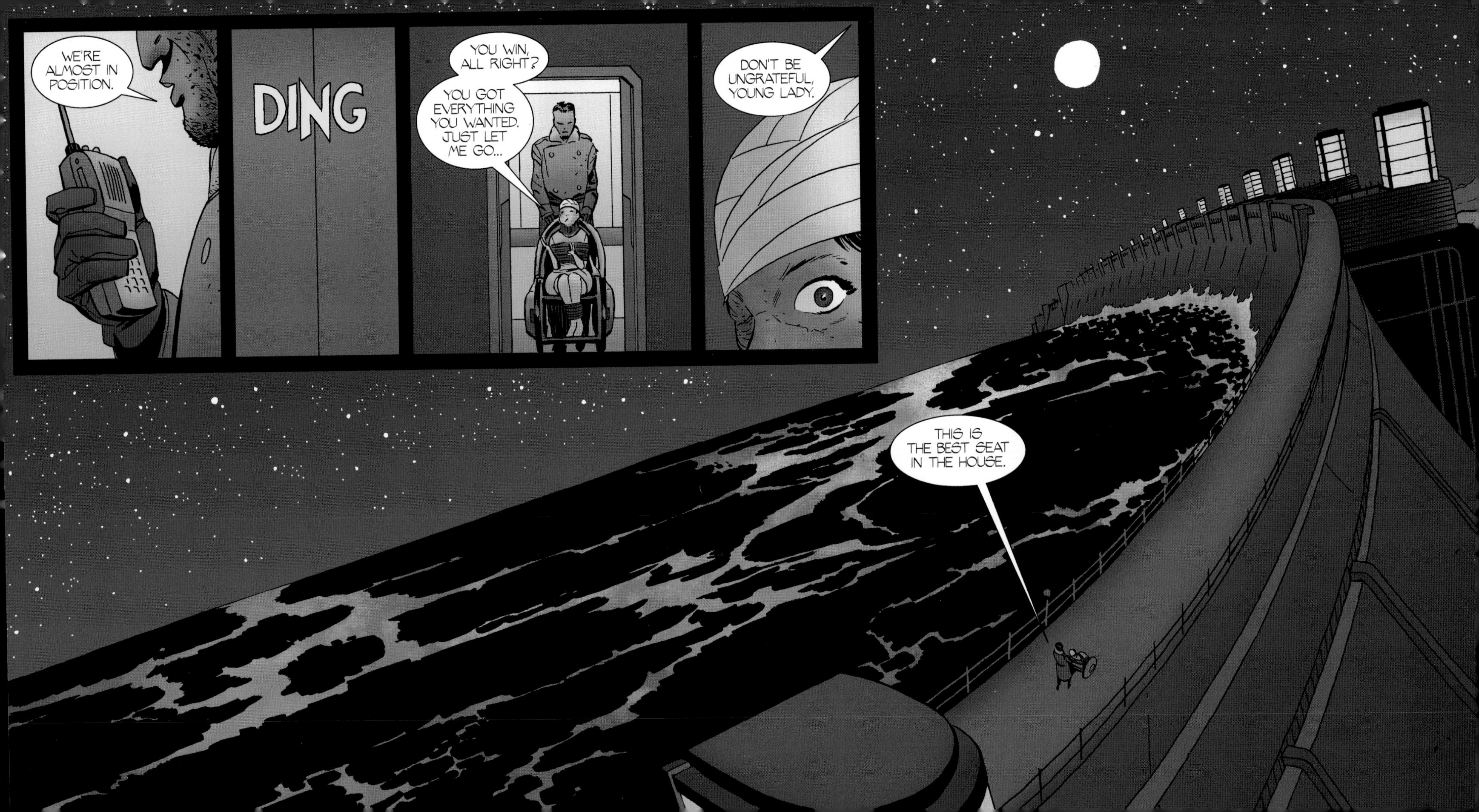
WE'RE ALMOST IN POSITION.
DING
YOU WIN, ALL RIGHT?
YOU GOT EVERYTHING YOU WANTED. JUST LET ME GO...
DON'T BE UNGRATEFUL, YOUNG LADY.
THIS IS THE BEST SEAT IN THE HOUSE.

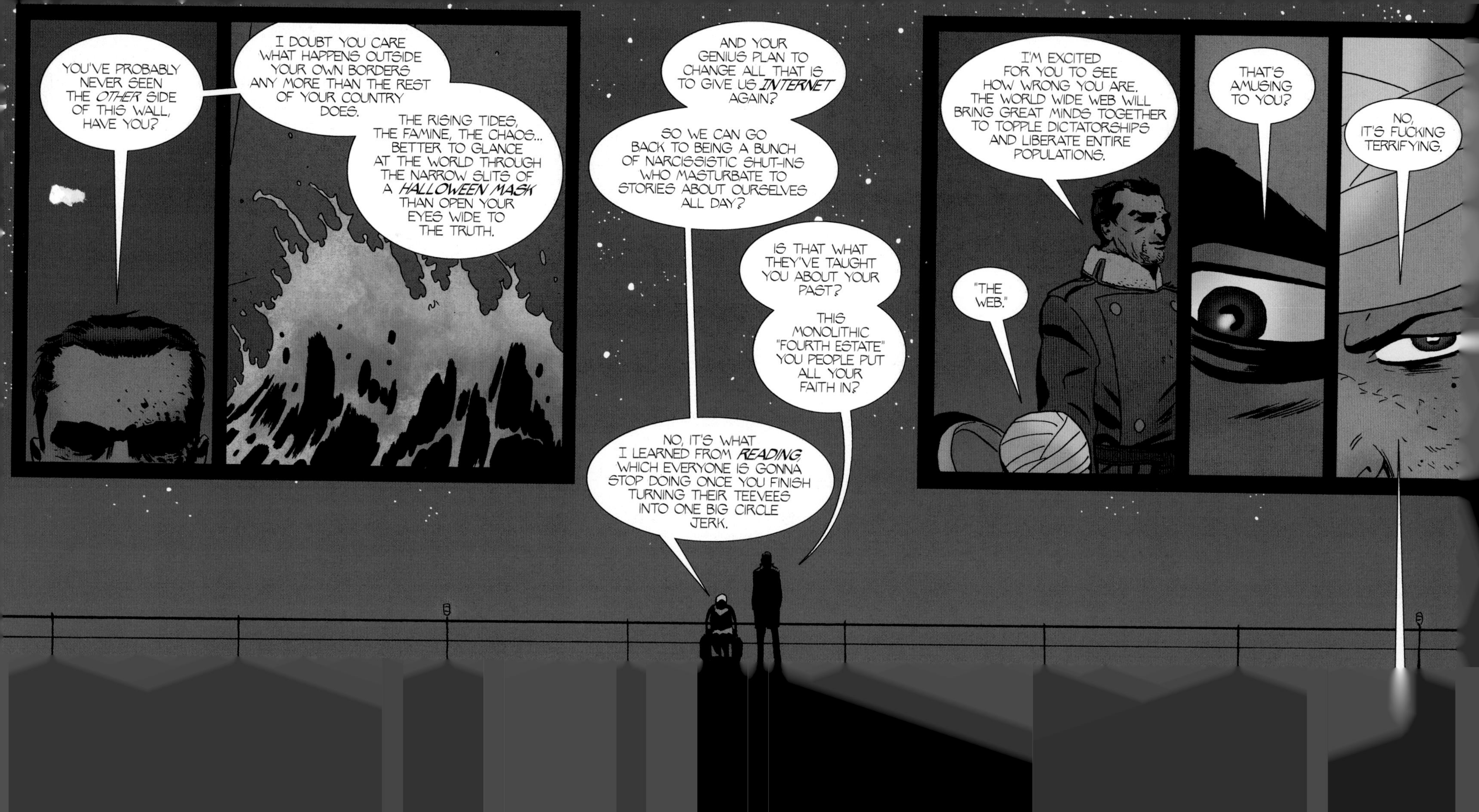
YOU'VE PROBABLY NEVER SEEN THE OTHER SIDE OF THIS WALL, HAVE YOU?
I DOUBT YOU CARE WHAT HAPPENS OUTSIDE YOUR OWN BORDERS ANY MORE THAN THE REST OF YOUR COUNTRY DOES.
THE RISING TIDES, THE FAMINE, THE CHAOS... BETTER TO GLANCE AT THE WORLD THROUGH THE NARROW SLITS OF A HALLOWEEN MASK THAN OPEN YOUR EYES WIDE TO THE TRUTH.
AND YOUR GENIUS PLAN TO CHANGE ALL THAT IS TO GIVE US INTERNET AGAIN?
SO WE CAN GO BACK TO BEING A BUNCH OF NARCISSISTIC SHUT-INS WHO MASTURBATE TO STORIES ABOUT OURSELVES ALL DAY?
IS THAT WHAT THEY'VE TAUGHT YOU ABOUT YOUR PAST?
THIS MONOLITHIC "FOURTH ESTATE" YOU PEOPLE PUT ALL YOUR FAITH IN?
NO, IT'S WHAT I LEARNED FROM READING, WHICH EVERYONE IS GONNA STOP DOING ONCE YOU FINISH TURNING THEIR TEEVEES INTO ONE BIG CIRCLE JERK.
I'M EXCITED FOR YOU TO SEE HOW WRONG YOU ARE. THE WORLD WIDE WEB WILL BRING GREAT MINDS TOGETHER TO TOPPLE DICTATORSHIPS AND LIBERATE ENTIRE POPULATIONS.
"THE WEB."
THAT'S AMUSING TO YOU?
NO, IT'S FUCKING TERRIFYING.

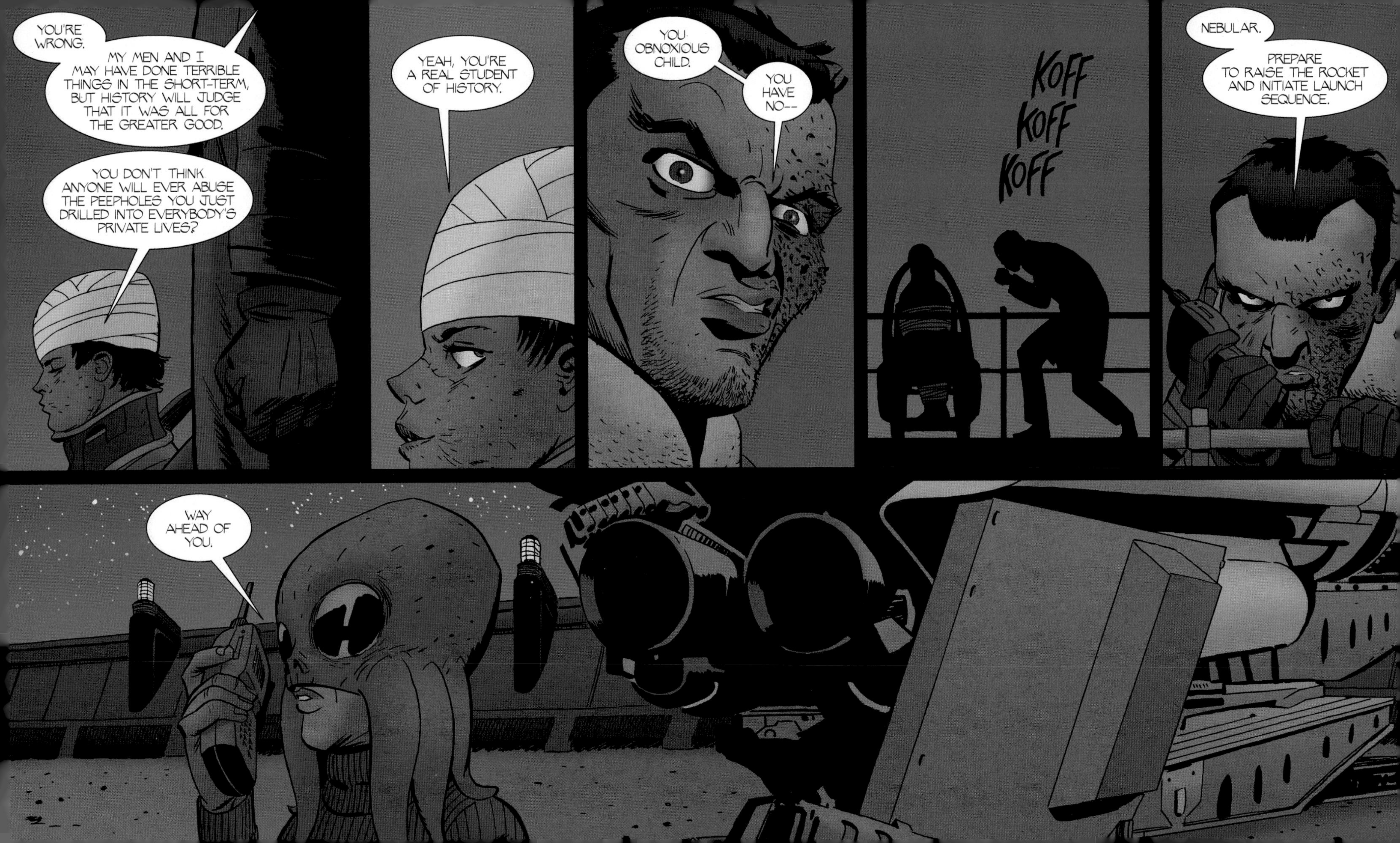
YOU'RE WRONG.
MY MEN AND I MAY HAVE DONE TERRIBLE THINGS IN THE SHORT-TERM, BUT HISTORY WILL JUDGE THAT IT WAS ALL FOR THE GREATER GOOD.
YOU DON'T THINK ANYONE WILL EVER ABUSE THE PEEPHOLES YOU JUST DRILLED INTO EVERYBODY'S PRIVATE LIVES?
YEAH, YOU'RE A REAL STUDENT OF HISTORY.
YOU OBNOXIOUS CHILD.
YOU HAVE NO--
KOFF KOFF KOFF
NEBULAR.
PREPARE TO RAISE THE ROCKET AND INITIATE LAUNCH SEQUENCE.
WAY AHEAD OF YOU.

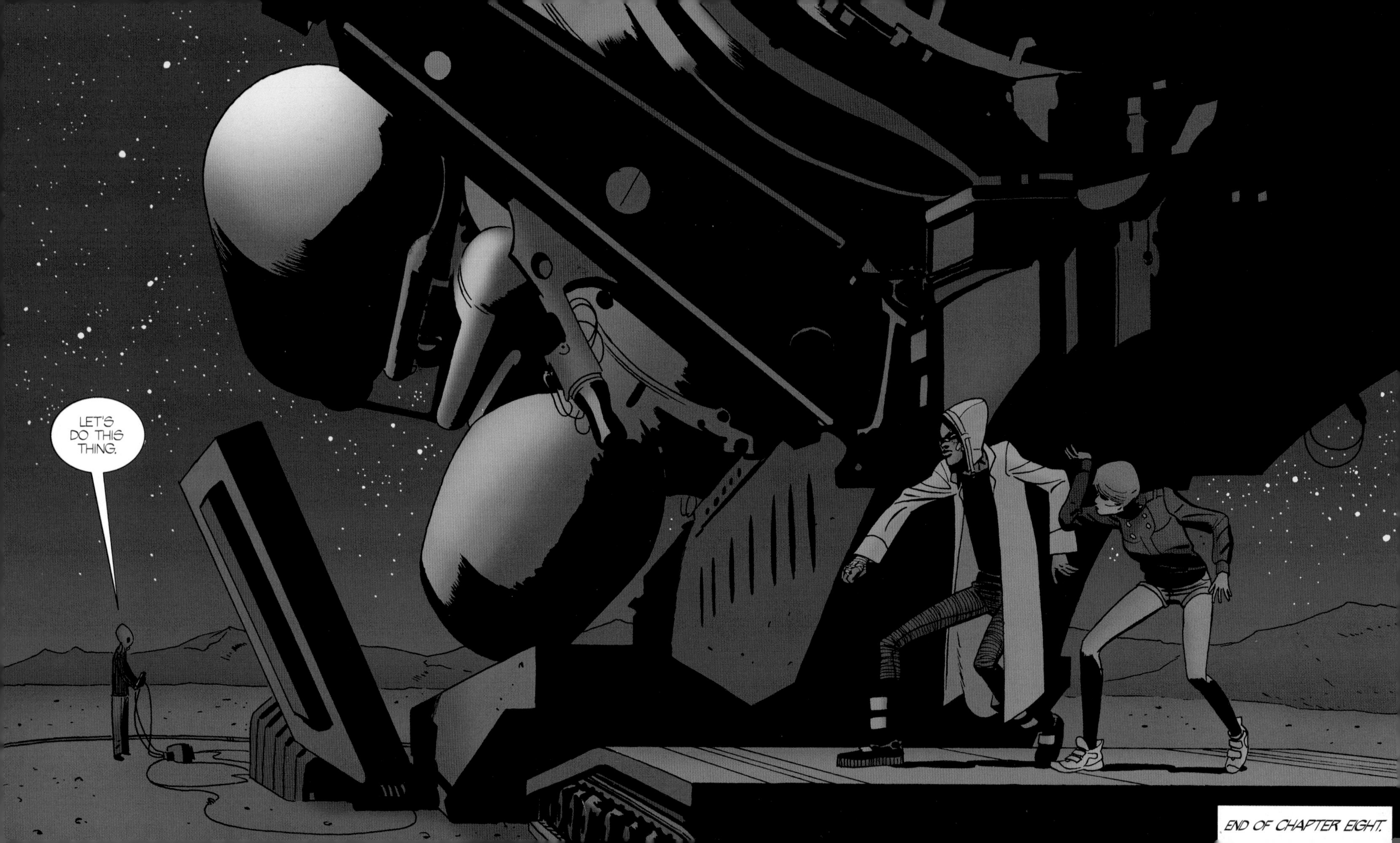
LET'S DO THIS THING.
END OF CHAPTER EIGHT.

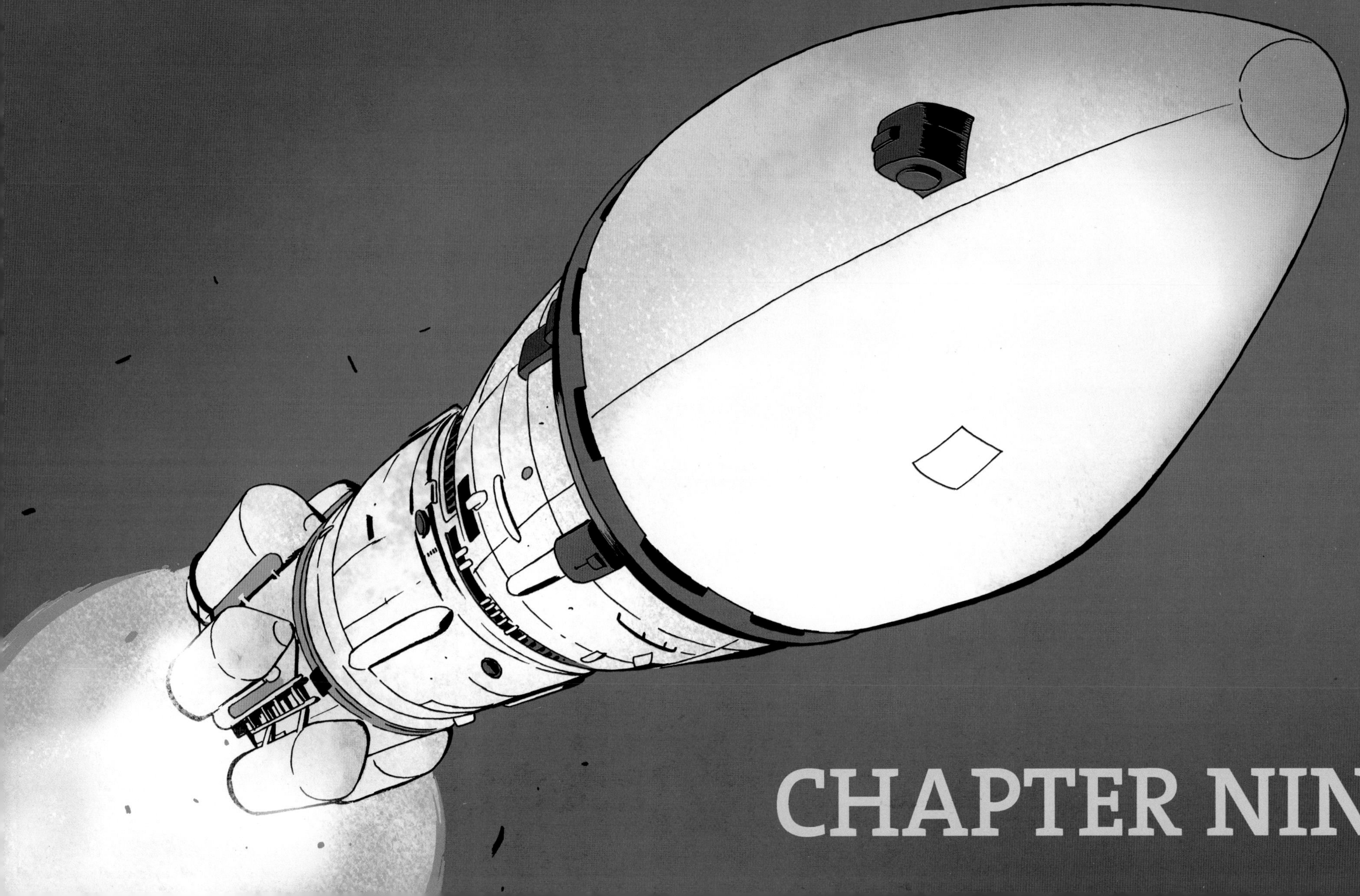

CHAPTER NINE

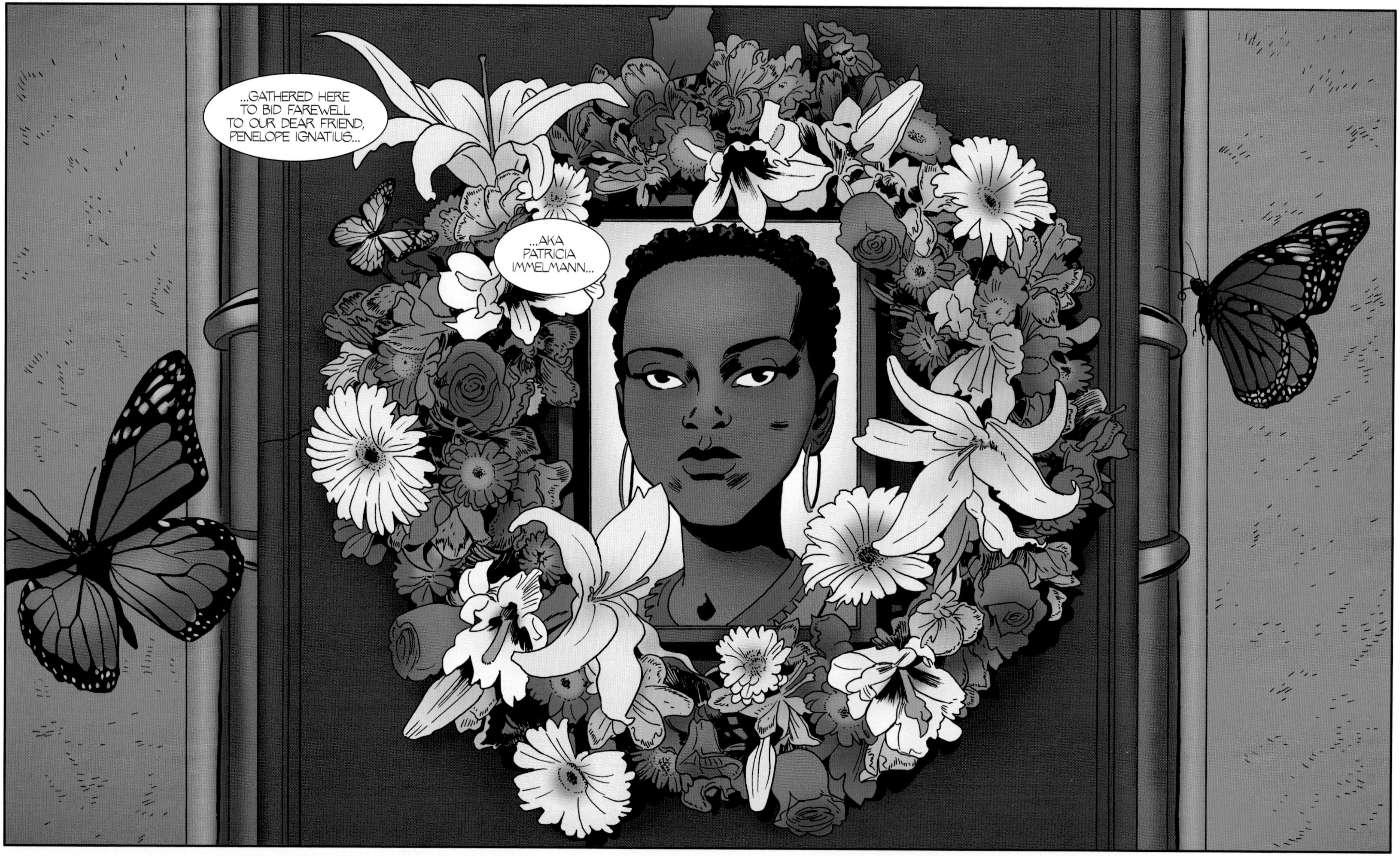
...GATHERED HERE TO BID FAREWELL TO OUR DEAR FRIEND, PENELOPE IGNATIUS...
...AKA PATRICIA IMMELMANN...

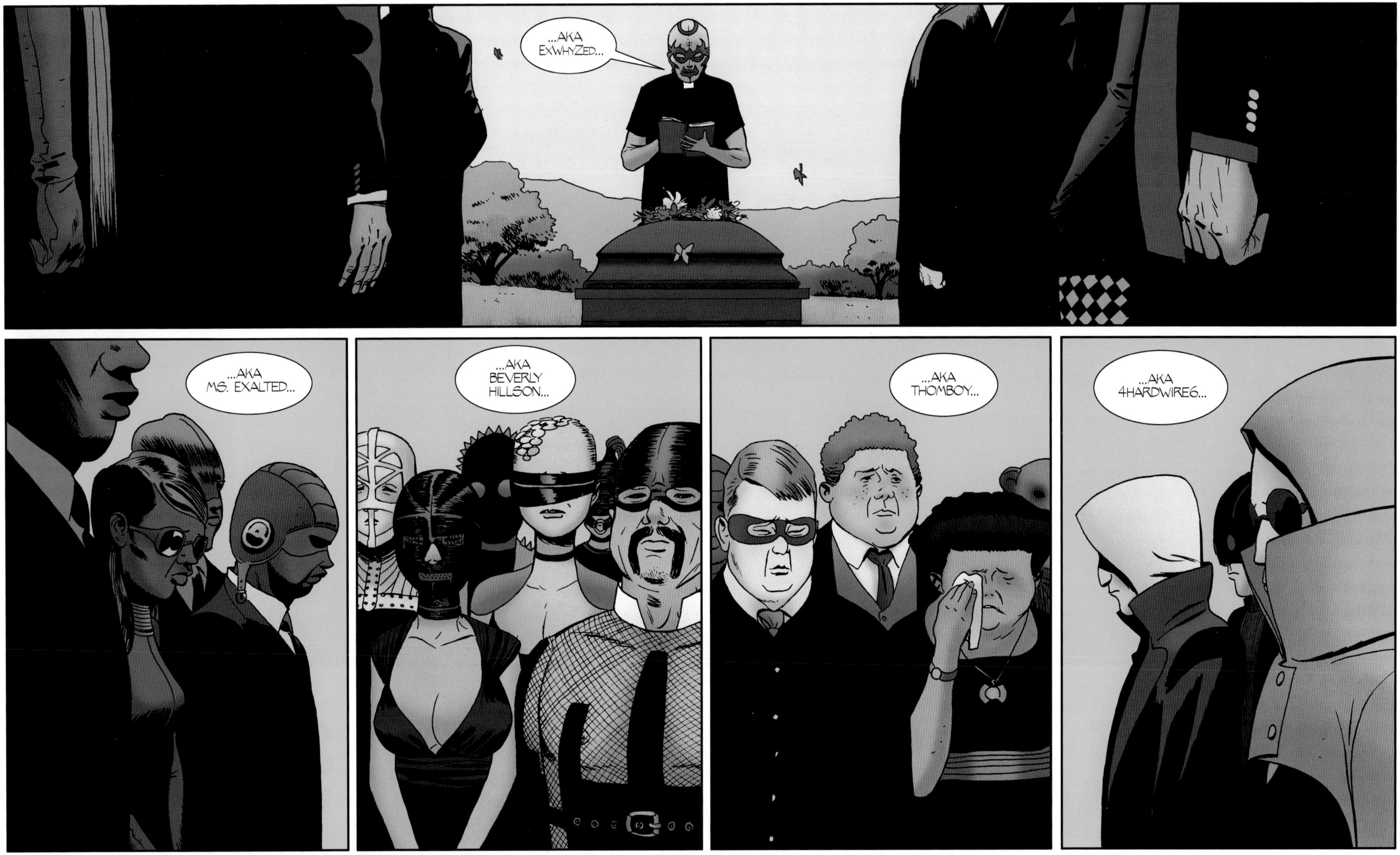
...AKA EXWHYZED...
...AKA MS. EXALTED...
...AKA BEVERLY HILLSON...
...AKA THOMBOY...
...AKA 4HARDWIRE6...

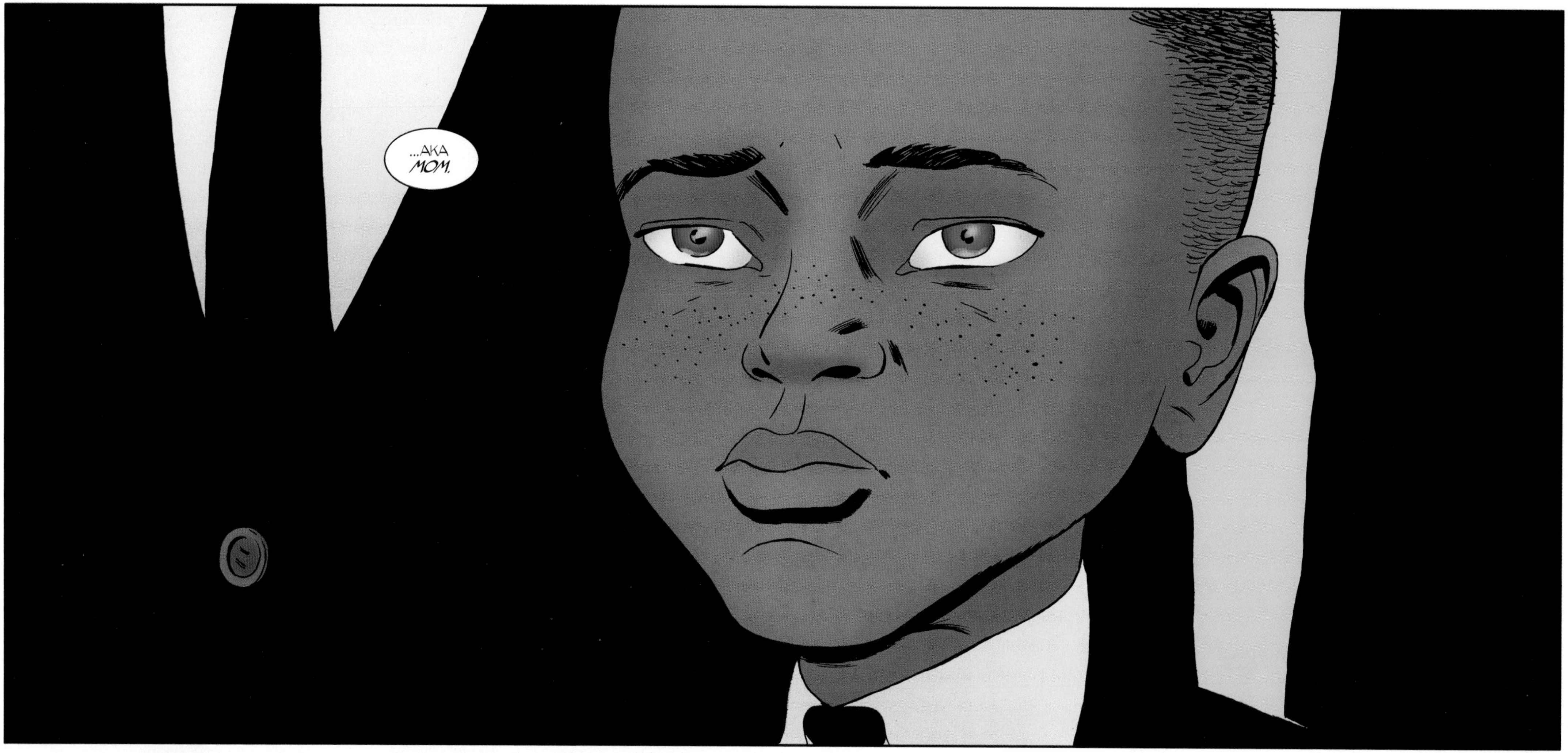
...AKA MOM.

THE PRIVATE EYE

BRIAN K. VAUGHAN

MARCOS MARTIN

WITH

MUNTSA VICENTE

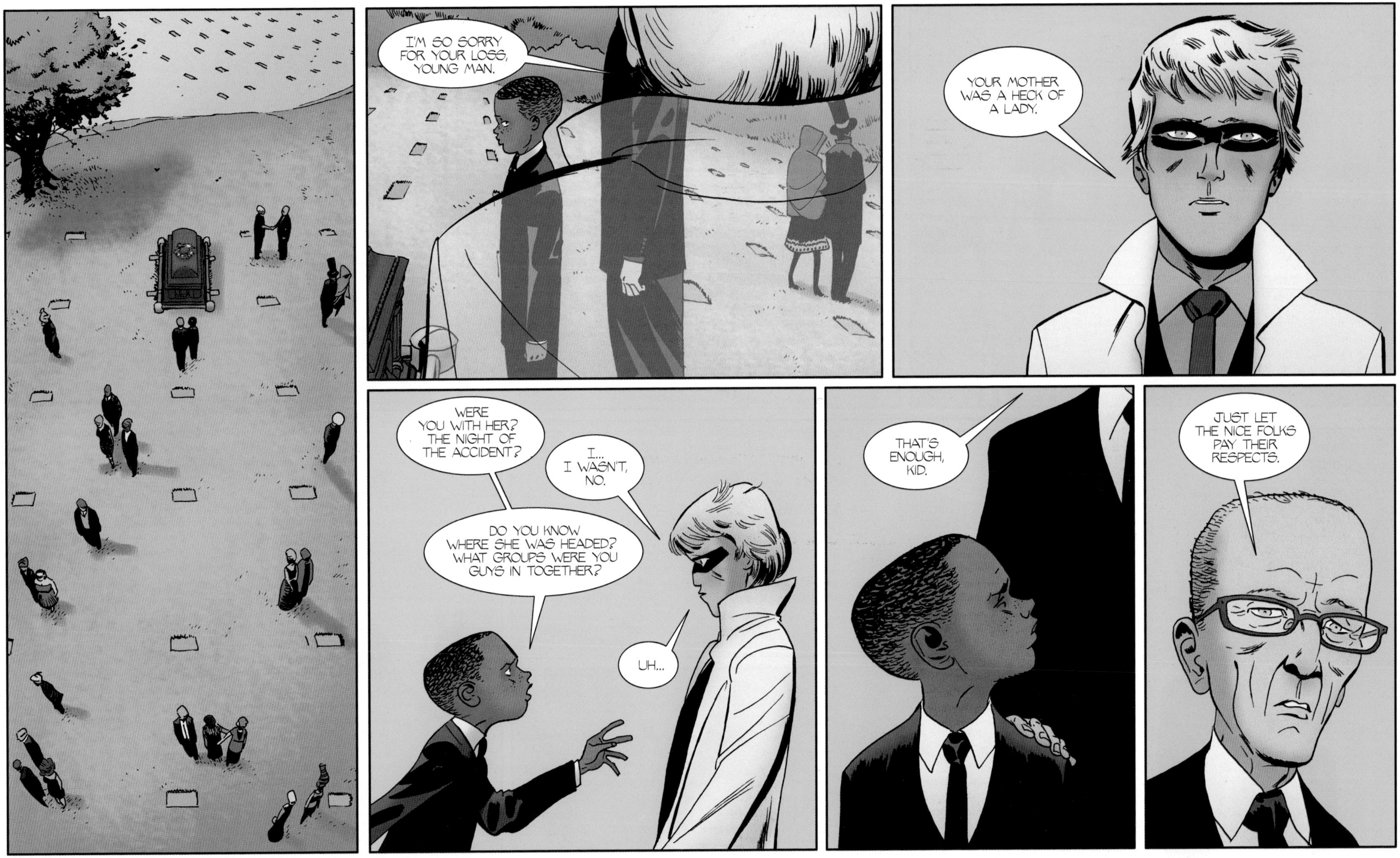
I'M SO SORRY FOR YOUR LOSS, YOUNG MAN.
YOUR MOTHER WAS A HECK OF A LADY.
WERE YOU WITH HER? THE NIGHT OF THE ACCIDENT?
I... I WASN'T, NO.
DO YOU KNOW WHERE SHE WAS HEADED? WHAT GROUPS WERE YOU GUYS IN TOGETHER?
UH...
THAT'S ENOUGH, KID.
JUST LET THE NICE FOLKS PAY THEIR RESPECTS.

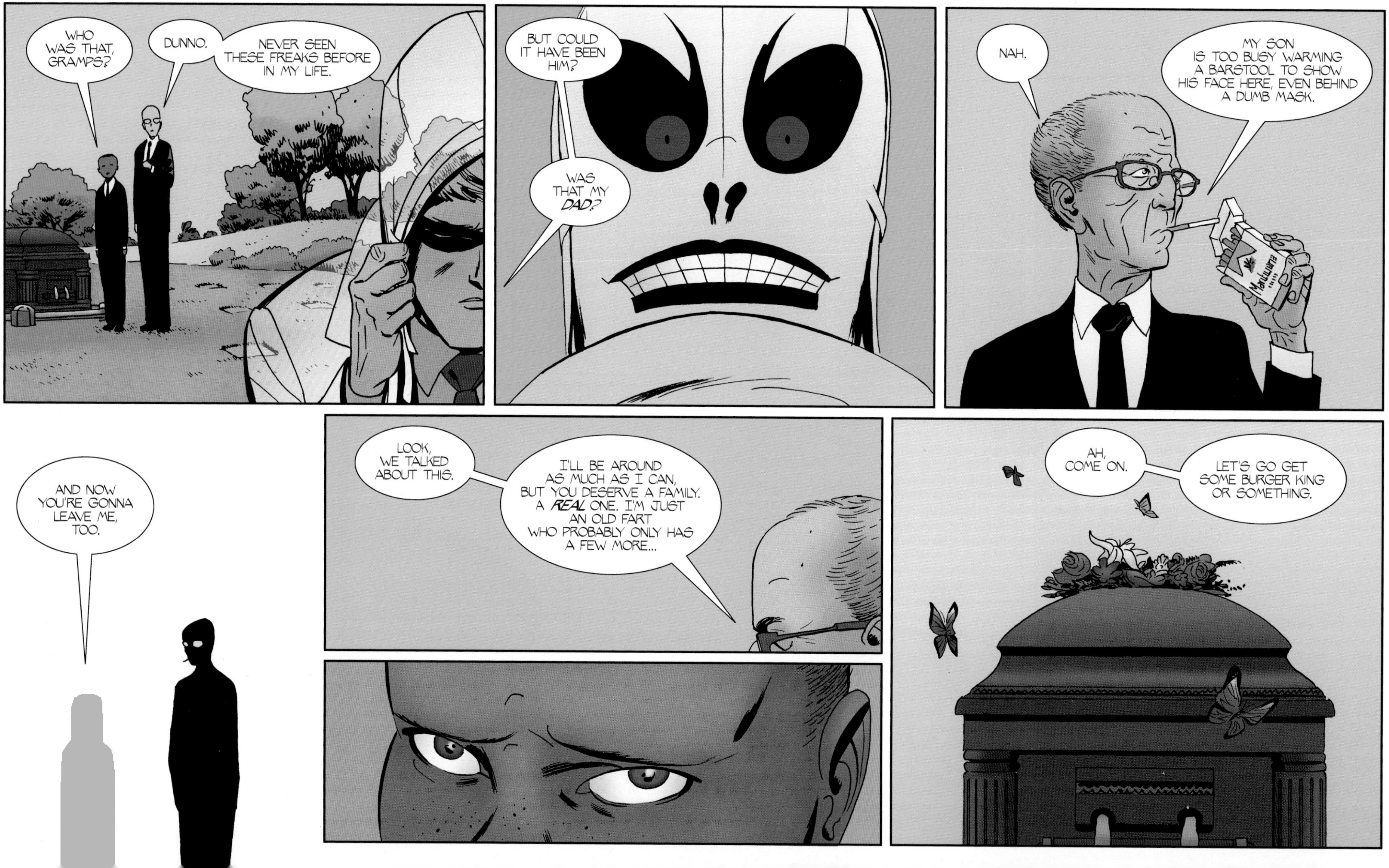
WHO WAS THAT, GRAMPS?
DUNNO.
NEVER SEEN THESE FREAKS BEFORE IN MY LIFE.
BUT COULD IT HAVE BEEN HIM?
WAS THAT MY DAD?
NAH.
MY SON IS TOO BUSY WARMING A BARSTOOL TO SHOW HIS FACE HERE, EVEN BEHIND A DUMB MASK.
AND NOW YOU'RE GONNA LEAVE ME, TOO.
LOOK, WE TALKED ABOUT THIS.
I'LL BE AROUND AS MUCH AS I CAN, BUT YOU DESERVE A FAMILY. A REAL ONE. I'M JUST AN OLD FART WHO PROBABLY ONLY HAS A FEW MORE...
AH, COME ON.
LET'S GO GET SOME BURGER KING OR SOMETHING.

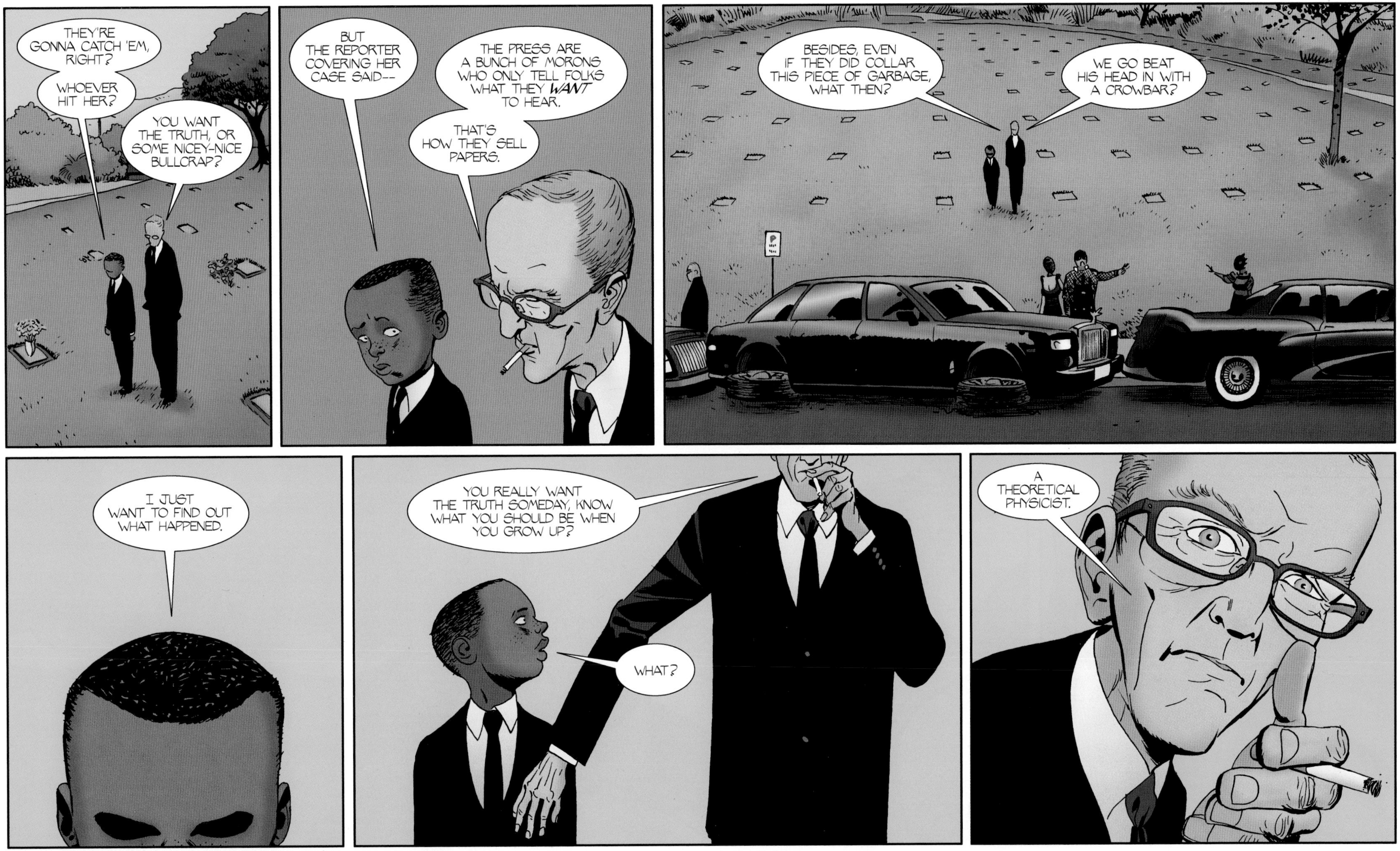
THEY'RE GONNA CATCH 'EM, RIGHT?
WHOEVER HIT HER?
YOU WANT THE TRUTH, OR SOME NICEY-NICE BULLCRAP?
BUT THE REPORTER COVERING HER CASE SAID--
THE PRESS ARE A BUNCH OF MORONS WHO ONLY TELL FOLKS WHAT THEY WANT TO HEAR.
THAT'S HOW THEY SELL PAPERS.
BESIDES, EVEN IF THEY DID COLLAR THIS PIECE OF GARBAGE, WHAT THEN?
WE GO BEAT HIS HEAD IN WITH A CROWBAR?
I JUST WANT TO FIND OUT WHAT HAPPENED.
YOU REALLY WANT THE TRUTH SOMEDAY, KNOW WHAT YOU SHOULD BE WHEN YOU GROW UP?
WHAT?
A THEORETICAL PHYSICIST.

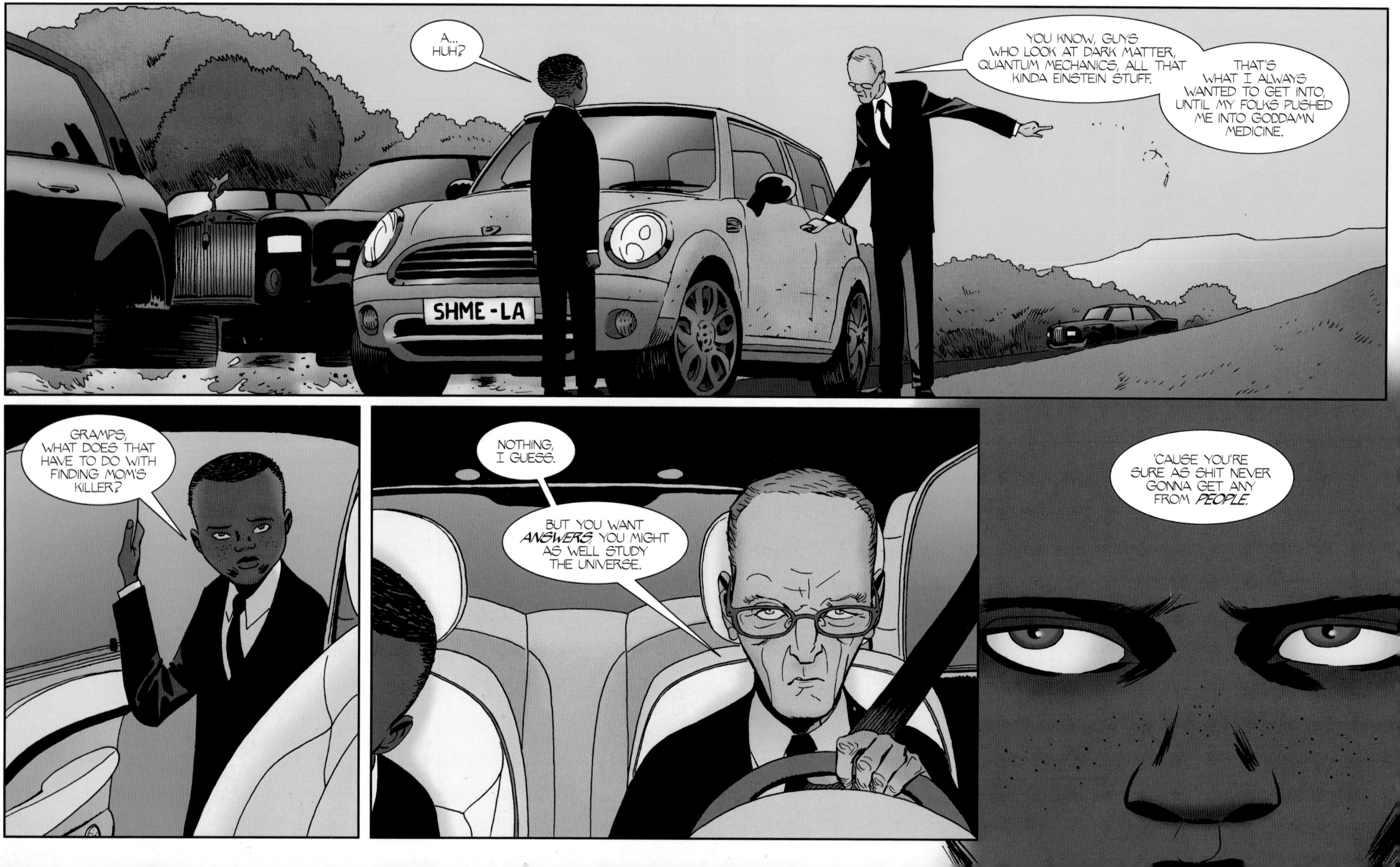
A... HUH?
YOU KNOW, GUYS WHO LOOK AT DARK MATTER, QUANTUM MECHANICS, ALL THAT KINDA EINSTEIN STUFF.
THAT'S WHAT I ALWAYS WANTED TO GET INTO, UNTIL MY FOLKS PUSHED ME INTO GODDAMN MEDICINE.
SHME-LA
GRAMPS, WHAT DOES THAT HAVE TO DO WITH FINDING MOM'S KILLER?
NOTHING, I GUESS.
BUT YOU WANT *ANSWERS*, YOU MIGHT AS WELL STUDY THE UNIVERSE.
'CAUSE YOU'RE SURE AS SHIT NEVER GONNA GET ANY FROM *PEOPLE*.

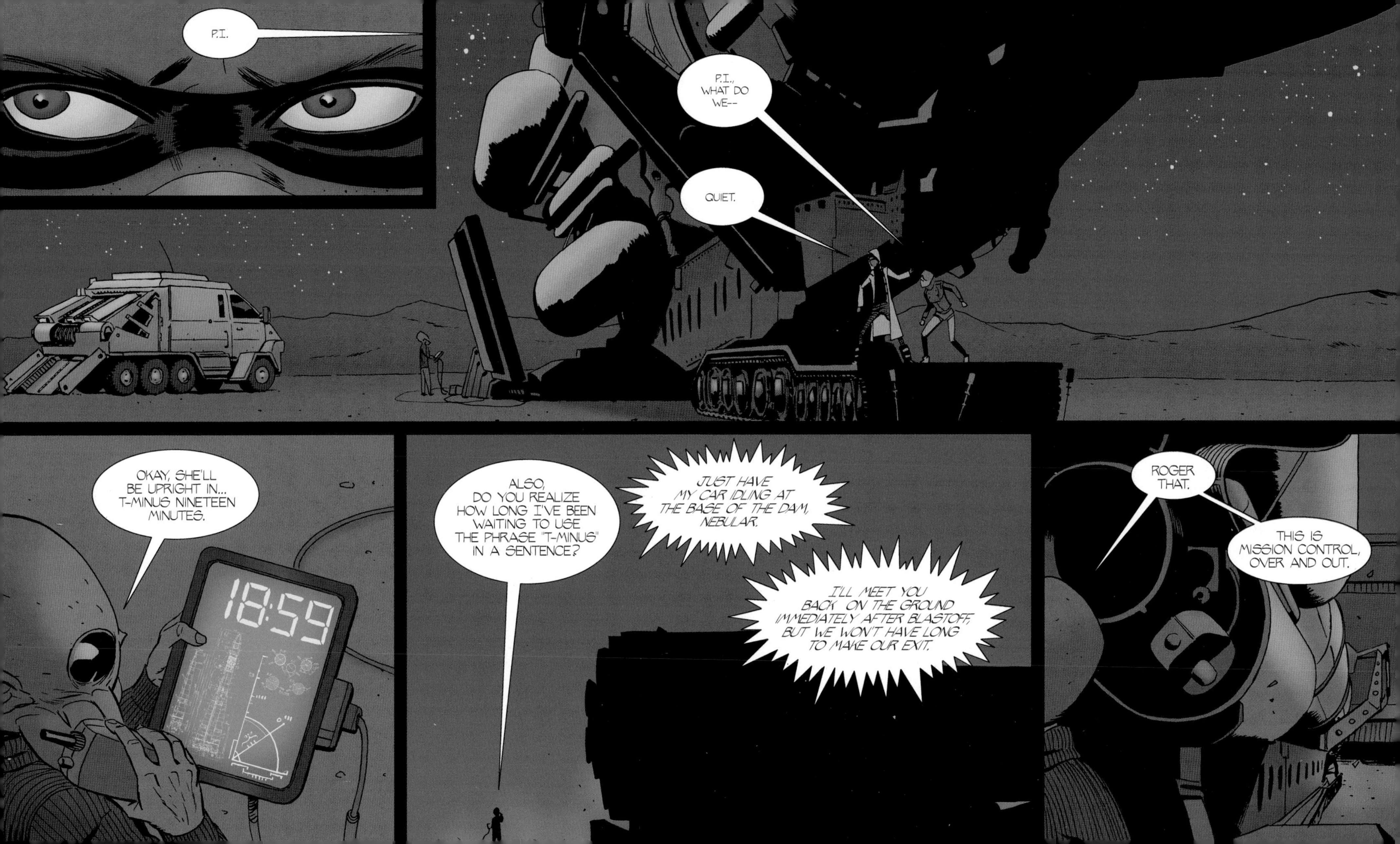
P.I.
P.I., WHAT DO WE--
QUIET.
OKAY, SHE'LL BE UPRIGHT IN... T-MINUS NINETEEN MINUTES.
18:59
ALSO, DO YOU REALIZE HOW LONG I'VE BEEN WAITING TO USE THE PHRASE "T-MINUS" IN A SENTENCE?
JUST HAVE MY CAR IDLING AT THE BASE OF THE DAM, NEBULAR.
I'LL MEET YOU BACK ON THE GROUND IMMEDIATELY AFTER BLASTOFF, BUT WE WON'T HAVE LONG TO MAKE OUR EXIT.
ROGER THAT.
THIS IS MISSION CONTROL, OVER AND OUT.

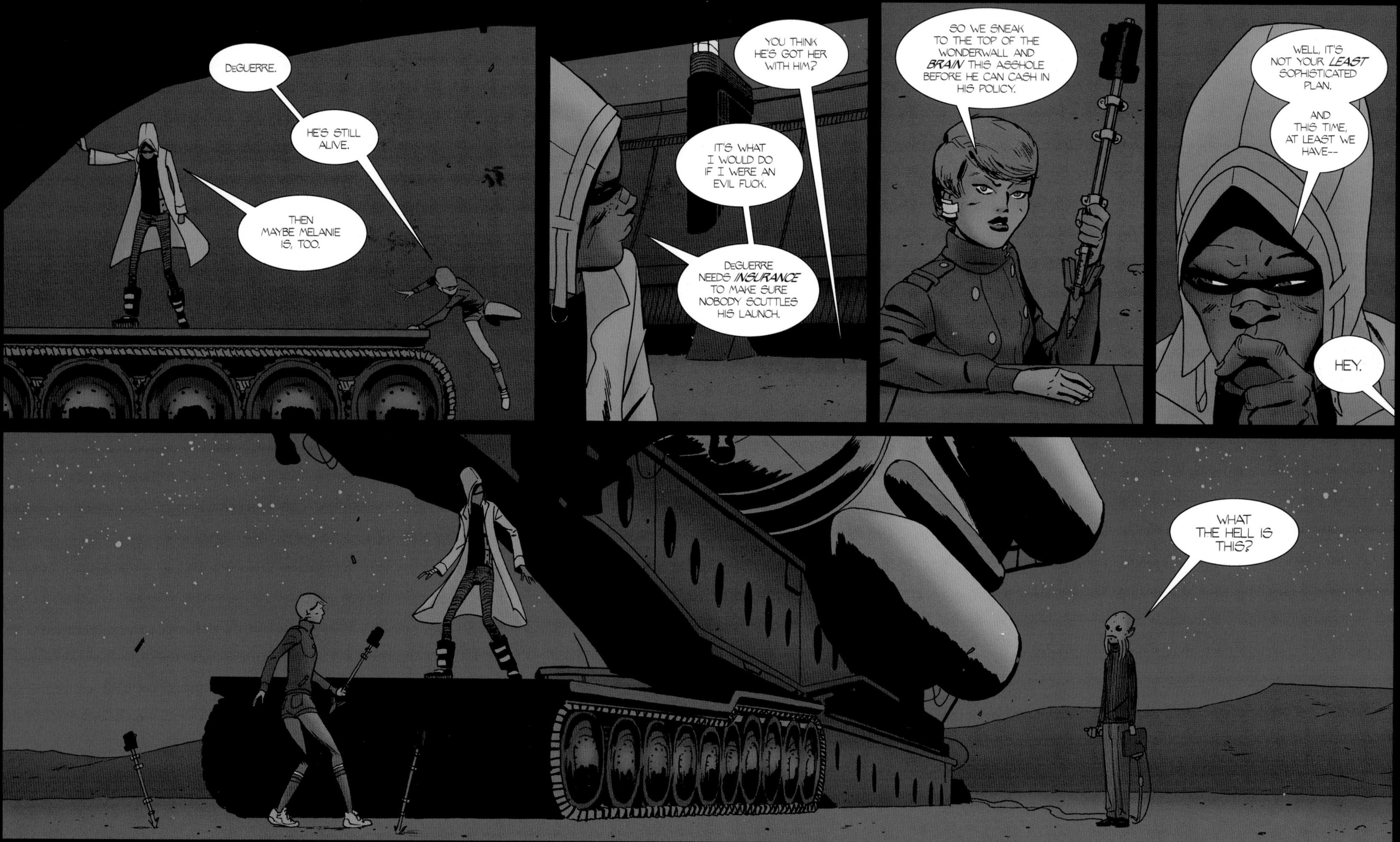
DeGUERRE.
HE'S STILL ALIVE.
THEN MAYBE MELANIE IS, TOO.
YOU THINK HE'S GOT HER WITH HIM?
IT'S WHAT I WOULD DO IF I WERE AN EVIL FUCK.
DeGUERRE NEEDS *INSURANCE* TO MAKE SURE NOBODY SCUTTLES HIS LAUNCH.
SO WE SNEAK TO THE TOP OF THE WONDERWALL AND *BRAIN* THIS ASSHOLE BEFORE HE CAN CASH IN HIS POLICY.
WELL, IT'S NOT YOUR *LEAST* SOPHISTICATED PLAN.
AND THIS TIME, AT LEAST WE HAVE--
HEY.
WHAT THE HELL IS THIS?

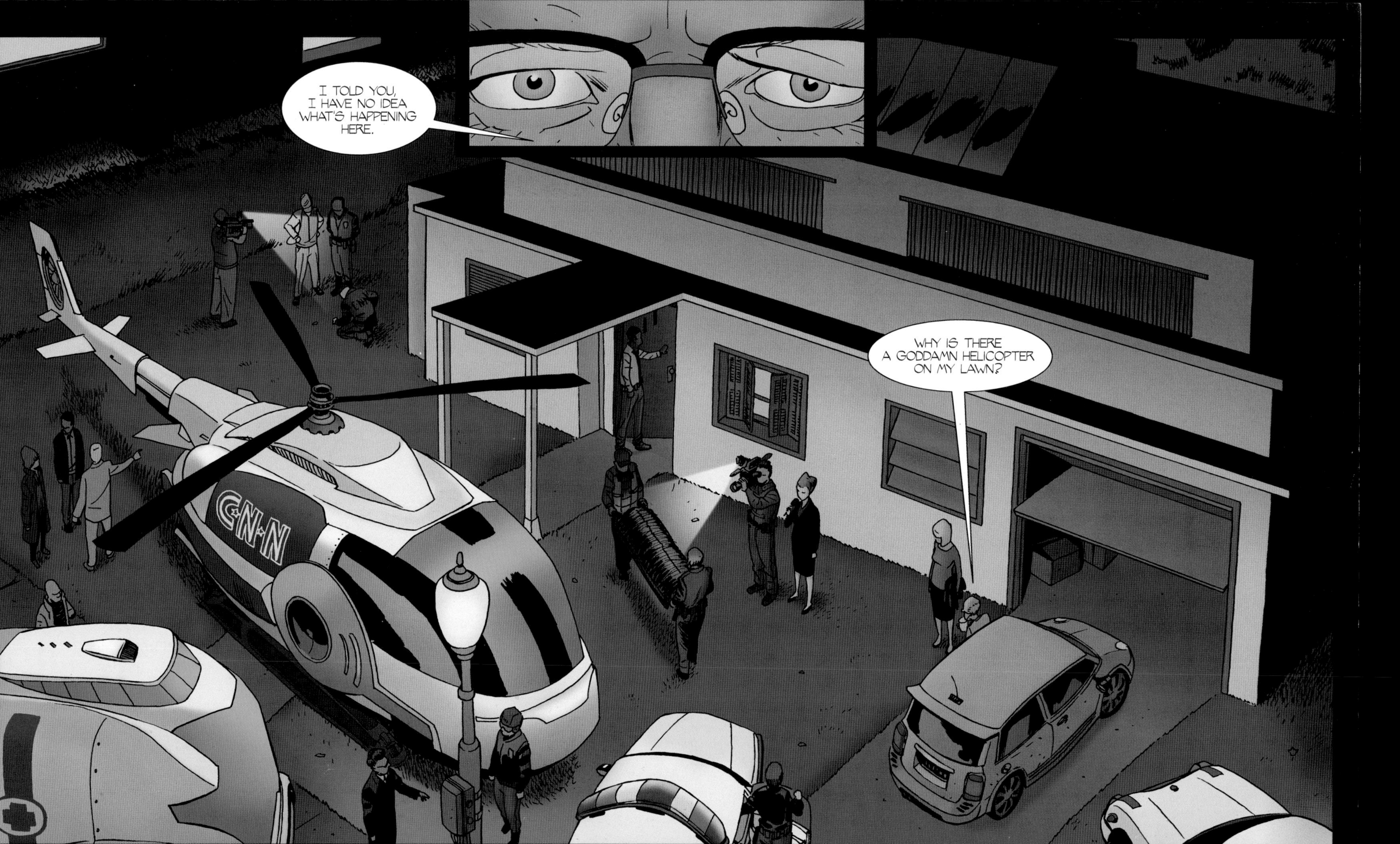
I TOLD YOU, I HAVE NO IDEA WHAT'S HAPPENING HERE.
WHY IS THERE A GODDAMN HELICOPTER ON MY LAWN?
CNN

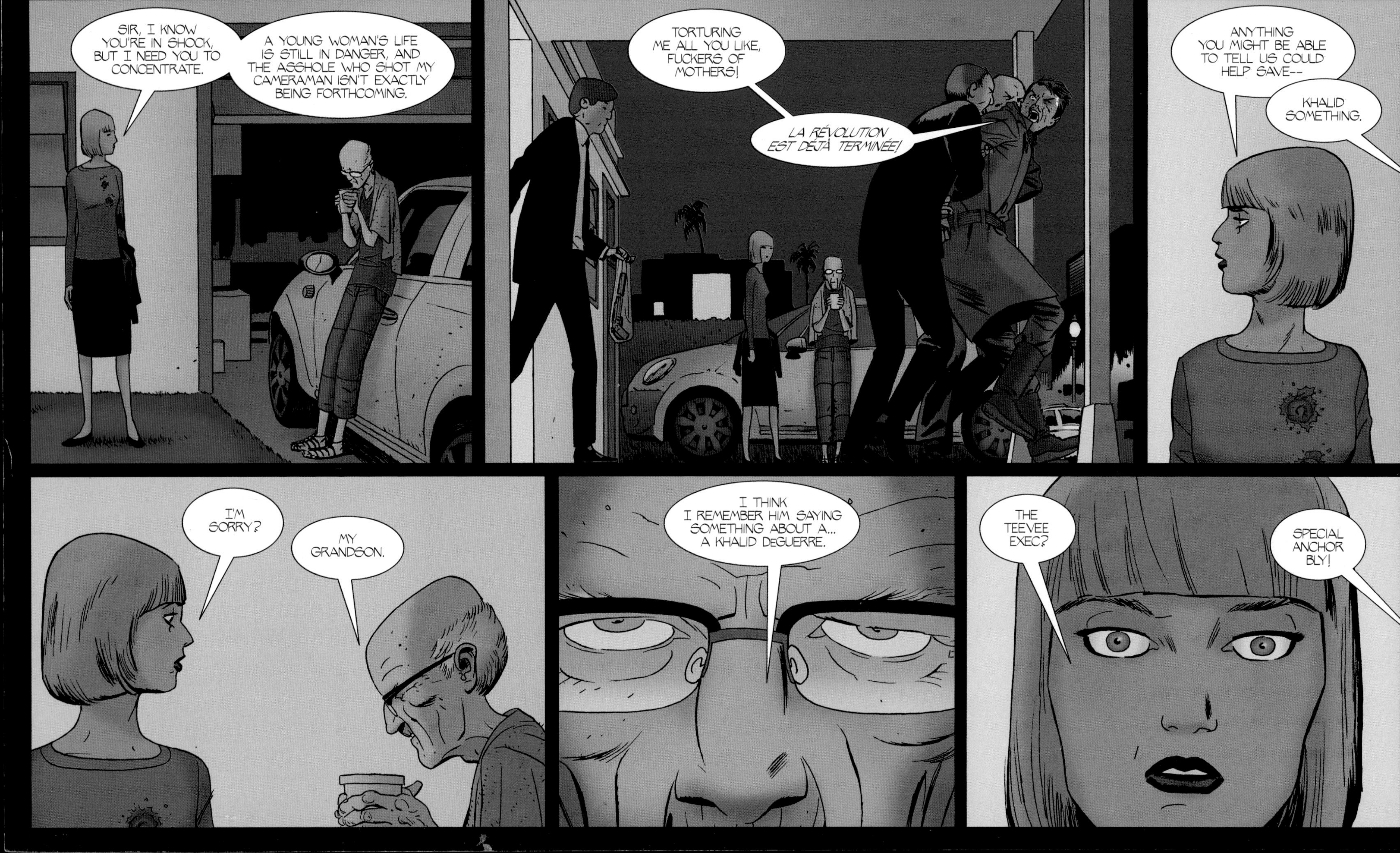

SIR, I KNOW YOU'RE IN SHOCK, BUT I NEED YOU TO CONCENTRATE.
A YOUNG WOMAN'S LIFE IS STILL IN DANGER, AND THE ASSHOLE WHO SHOT MY CAMERAMAN ISN'T EXACTLY BEING FORTHCOMING.
TORTURING ME ALL YOU LIKE, FUCKERS OF MOTHERS!
LA RÉVOLUTION EST DÉJÀ TERMINÉE!
ANYTHING YOU MIGHT BE ABLE TO TELL US COULD HELP SAVE--
KHALID SOMETHING.
I'M SORRY?
MY GRANDSON.
I THINK I REMEMBER HIM SAYING SOMETHING ABOUT A... A KHALID DeGUERRE.
THE TEEVEE EXEC?
SPECIAL ANCHOR BLY!

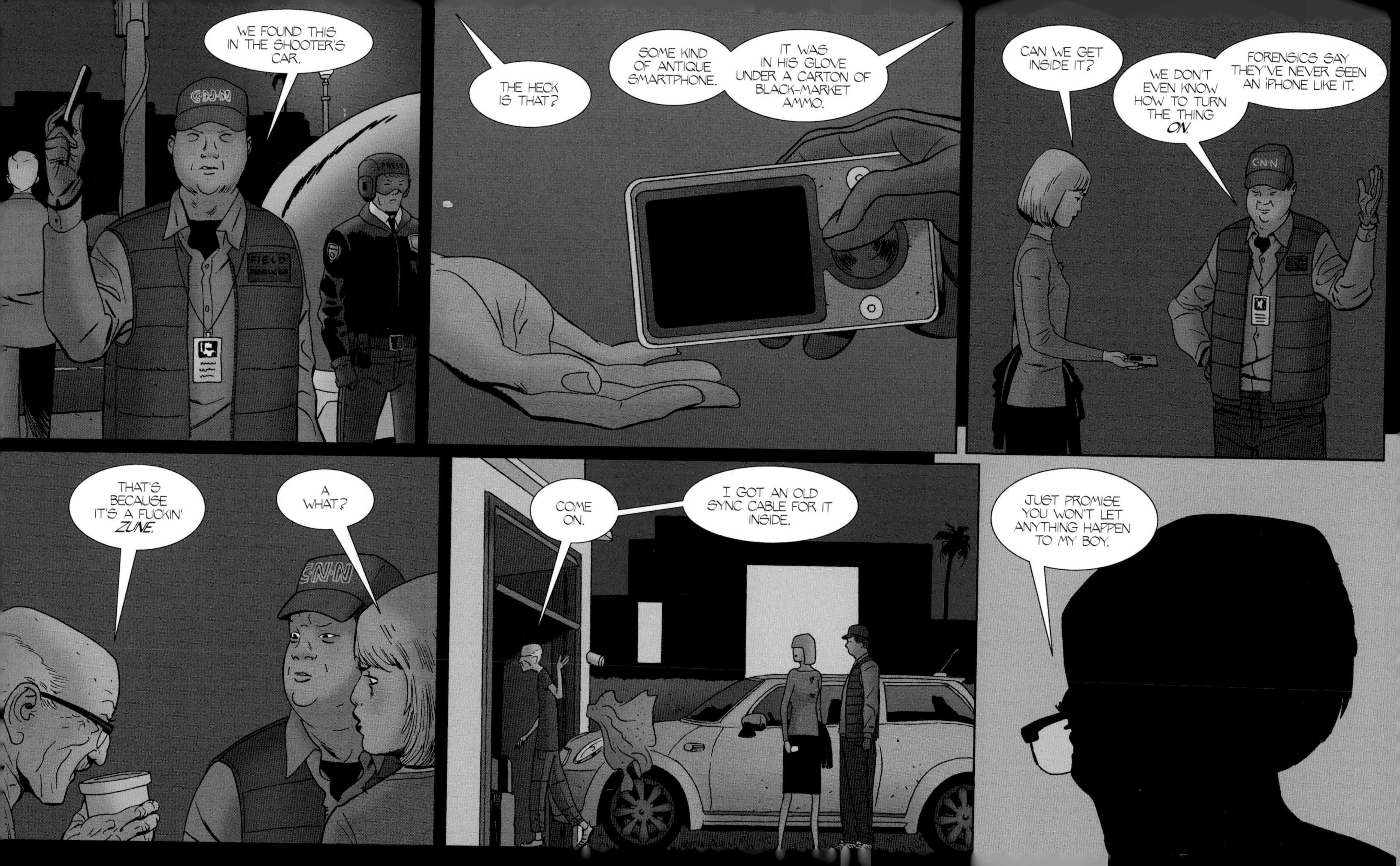
WE FOUND THIS IN THE SHOOTER'S CAR.
THE HECK IS THAT?
SOME KIND OF ANTIQUE SMARTPHONE.
IT WAS IN HIS GLOVE UNDER A CARTON OF BLACK-MARKET AMMO.
CAN WE GET INSIDE IT?
FORENSICS SAY THEY'VE NEVER SEEN AN iPHONE LIKE IT.
WE DON'T EVEN KNOW HOW TO TURN THE THING *ON*.
THAT'S BECAUSE IT'S A FUCKIN' *ZUNE*.
A WHAT?
COME ON.
I GOT AN OLD SYNC CABLE FOR IT INSIDE.
JUST PROMISE YOU WON'T LET ANYTHING HAPPEN TO MY BOY.

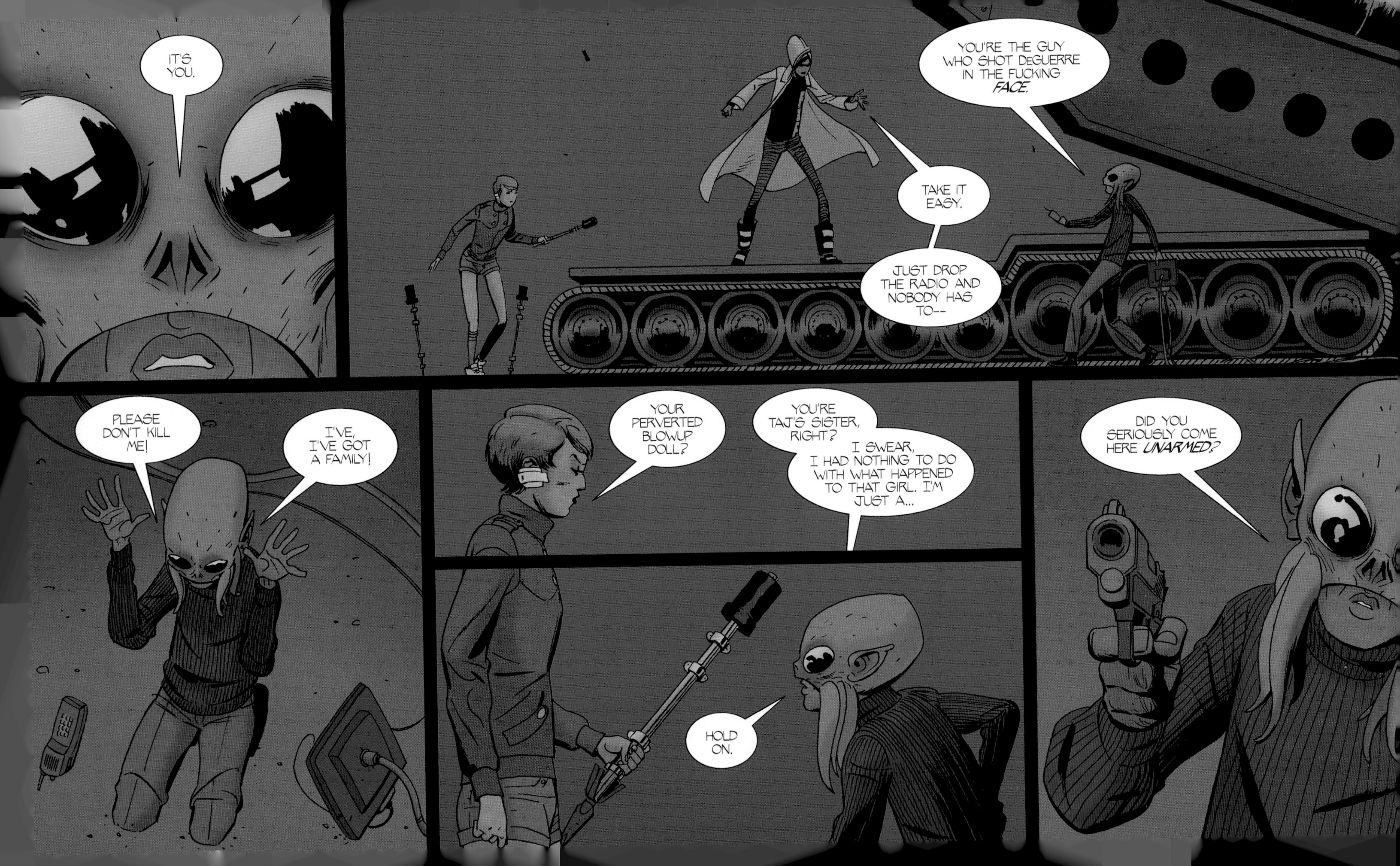
IT'S YOU.
YOU'RE THE GUY WHO SHOT DEGUERRE IN THE FUCKING FACE.
TAKE IT EASY.
JUST DROP THE RADIO AND NOBODY HAS TO--
PLEASE DON'T KILL ME!
I'VE, I'VE GOT A FAMILY!
YOUR PERVERTED BLOWUP DOLL?
YOU'RE TAJ'S SISTER, RIGHT?
I SWEAR, I HAD NOTHING TO DO WITH WHAT HAPPENED TO THAT GIRL. I'M JUST A...
HOLD ON.
DID YOU SERIOUSLY COME HERE UNARMED?

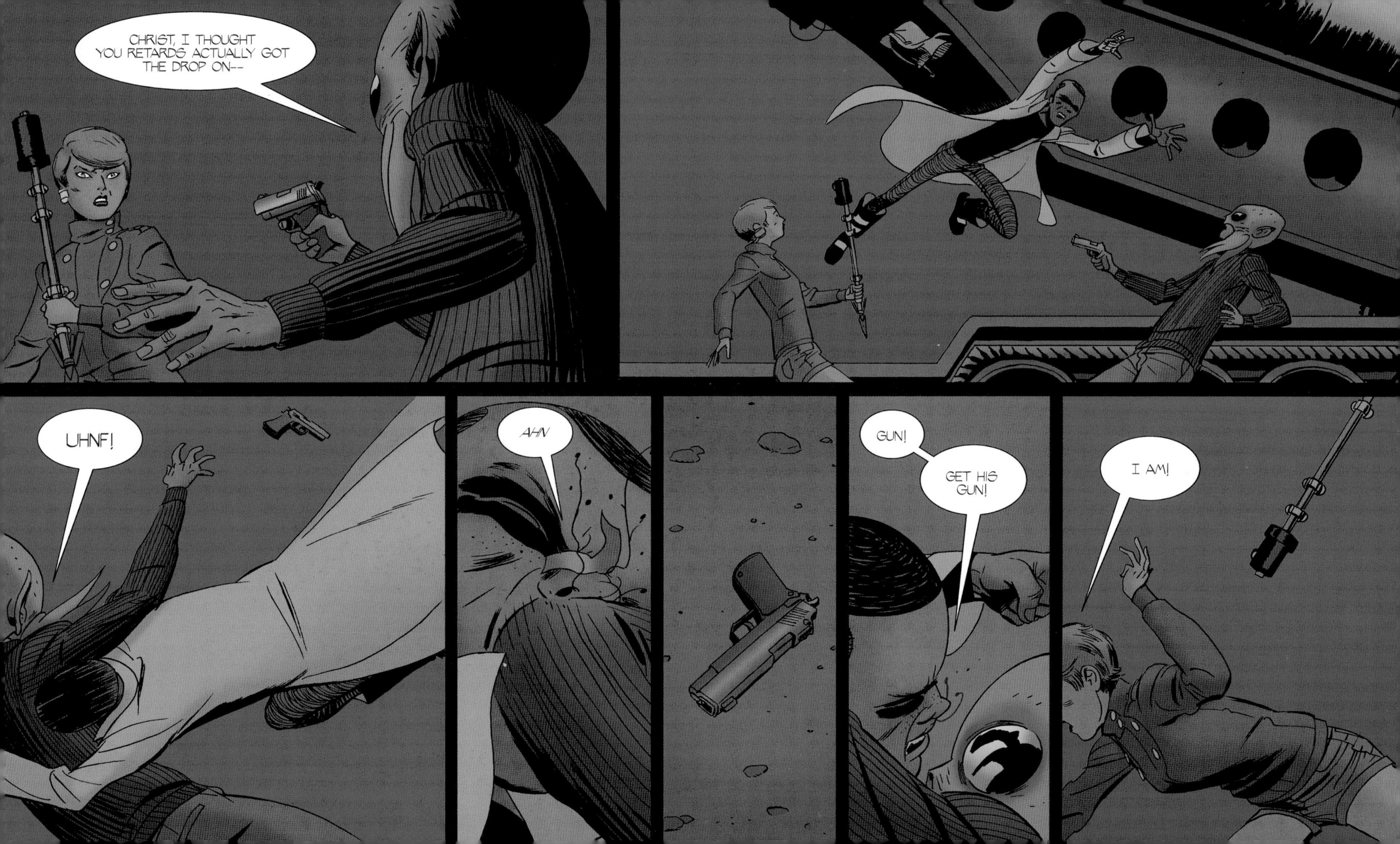
CHRIST, I THOUGHT YOU RETARDS ACTUALLY GOT THE DROP ON--
UHNF!
AHN
GUN!
GET HIS GUN!
I AM!

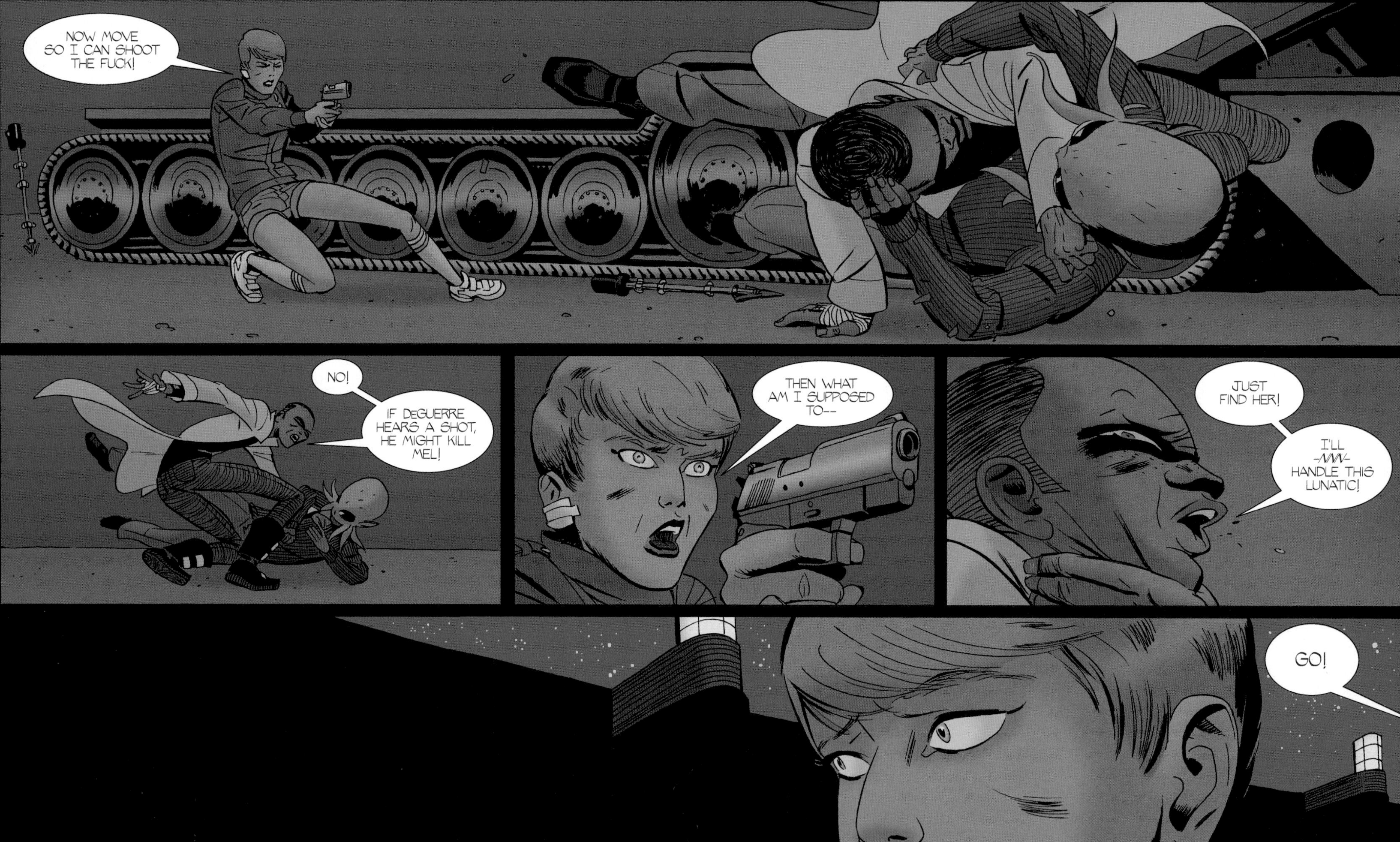
NOW MOVE SO I CAN SHOOT THE FUCK!
NO!
IF DeGUERRE HEARS A SHOT, HE MIGHT KILL MEL!
THEN WHAT AM I SUPPOSED TO--
JUST FIND HER!
I'LL -NNN- HANDLE THIS LUNATIC!
GO!

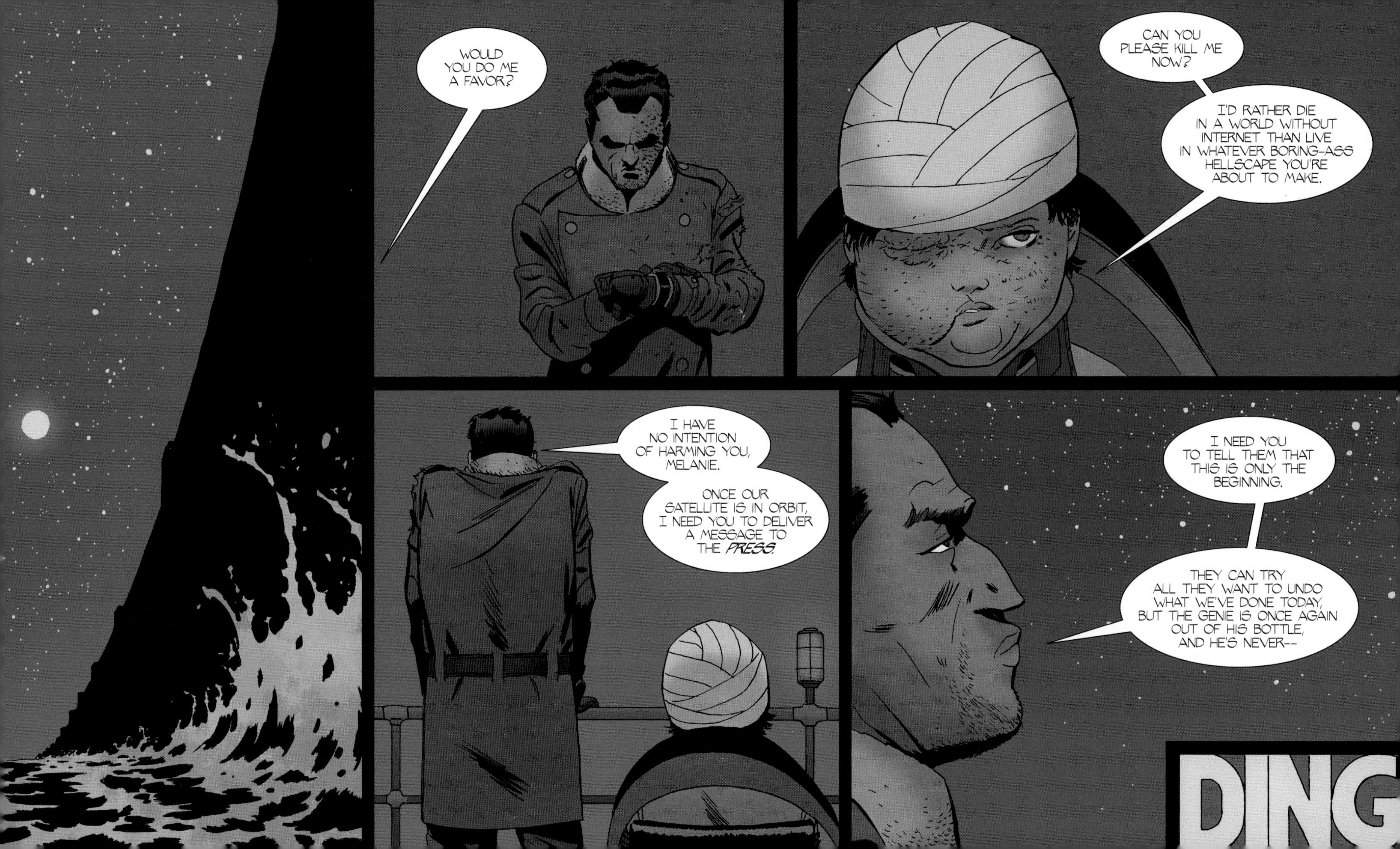
WOULD YOU DO ME A FAVOR?
CAN YOU PLEASE KILL ME NOW?
I'D RATHER DIE IN A WORLD WITHOUT INTERNET THAN LIVE IN WHATEVER BORING-ASS HELLSCAPE YOU'RE ABOUT TO MAKE.
I HAVE NO INTENTION OF HARMING YOU, MELANIE.
ONCE OUR SATELLITE IS IN ORBIT, I NEED YOU TO DELIVER A MESSAGE TO THE *PRESS.*
I NEED YOU TO TELL THEM THAT THIS IS ONLY THE BEGINNING.
THEY CAN TRY ALL THEY WANT TO UNDO WHAT WE'VE DONE TODAY, BUT THE GENIE IS ONCE AGAIN OUT OF HIS BOTTLE, AND HE'S NEVER--
DING

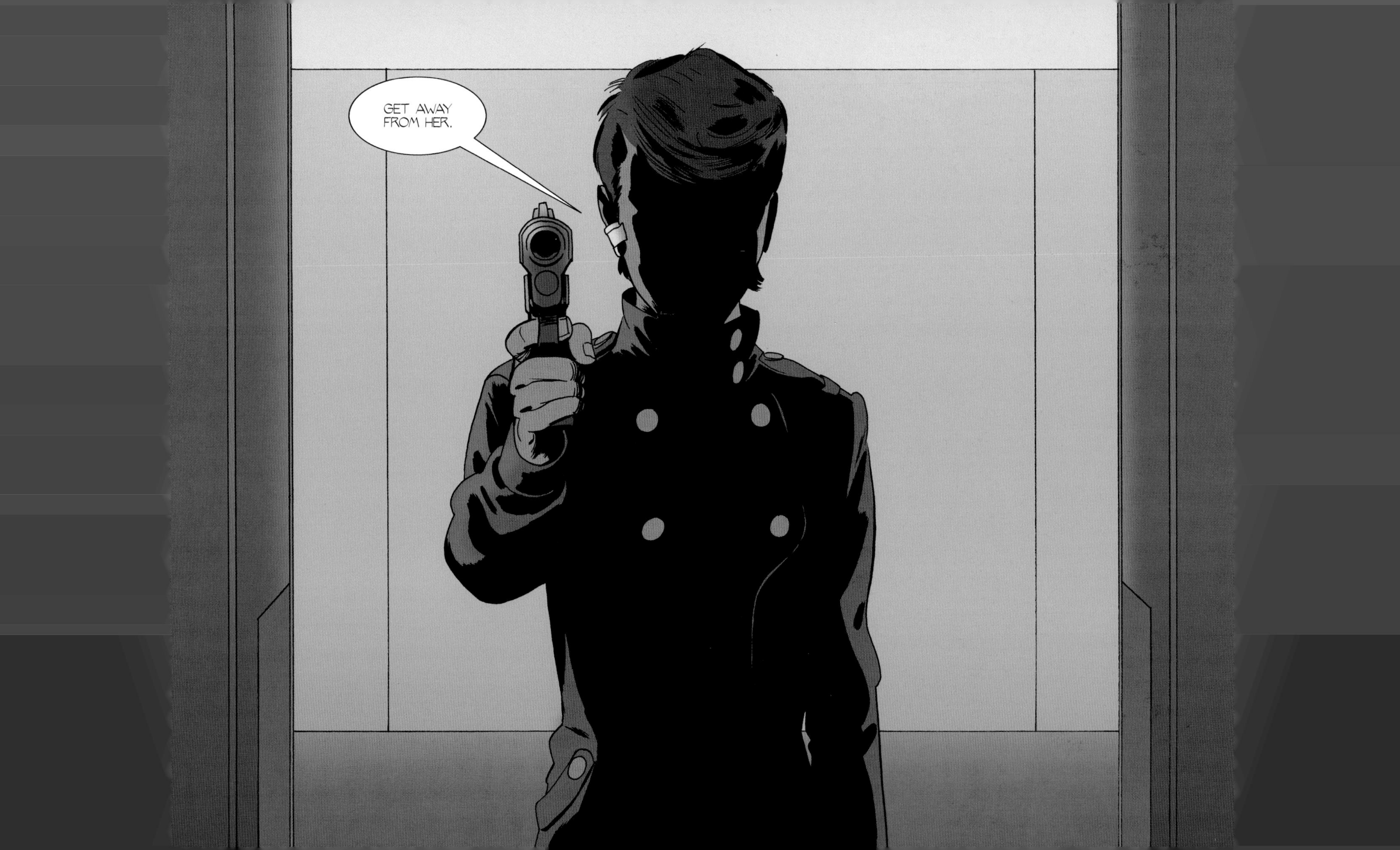
GET AWAY FROM HER.

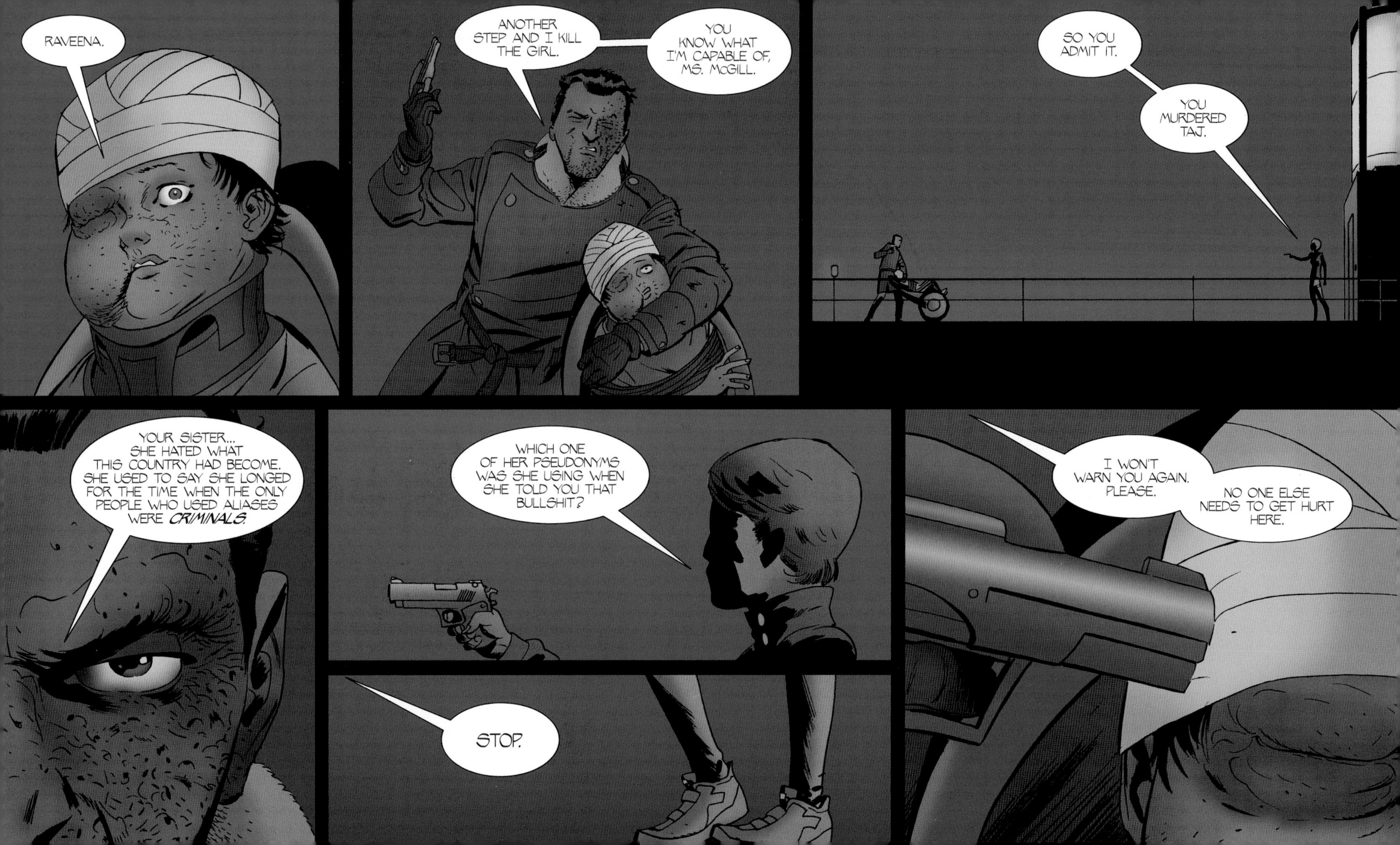
RAVEENA.
ANOTHER STEP AND I KILL THE GIRL.
YOU KNOW WHAT I'M CAPABLE OF, MS. McGILL.
SO YOU ADMIT IT.
YOU MURDERED TAJ.
YOUR SISTER... SHE HATED WHAT THIS COUNTRY HAD BECOME. SHE USED TO SAY SHE LONGED FOR THE TIME WHEN THE ONLY PEOPLE WHO USED ALIASES WERE *CRIMINALS*.
WHICH ONE OF HER PSEUDONYMS WAS SHE USING WHEN SHE TOLD YOU THAT BULLSHIT?
STOP.
I WON'T WARN YOU AGAIN. PLEASE.
NO ONE ELSE NEEDS TO GET HURT HERE.

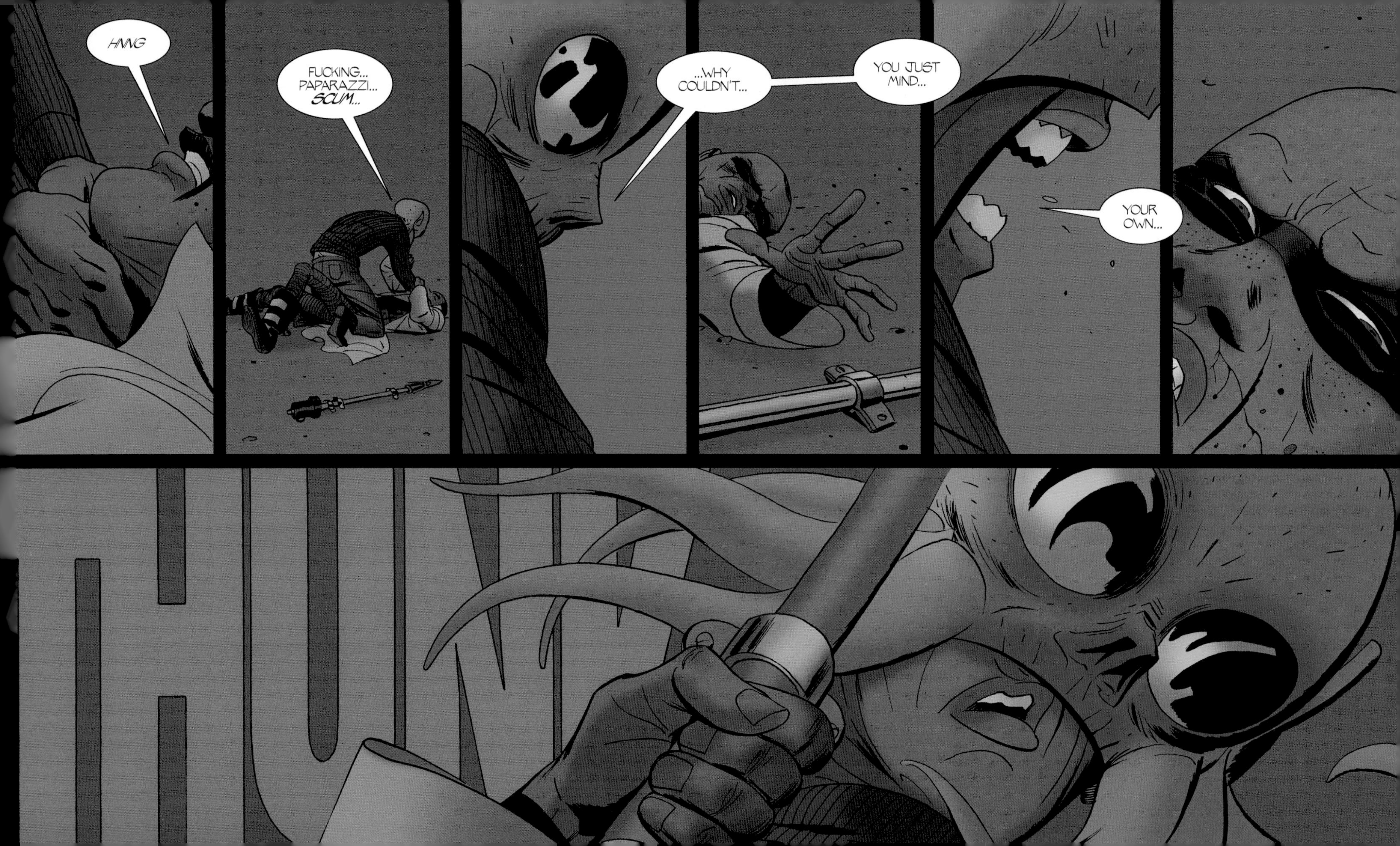
HNNG
FUCKING... PAPARAZZI... SCUM...
...WHY COULDN'T...
YOU JUST MIND...
YOUR OWN...
THU

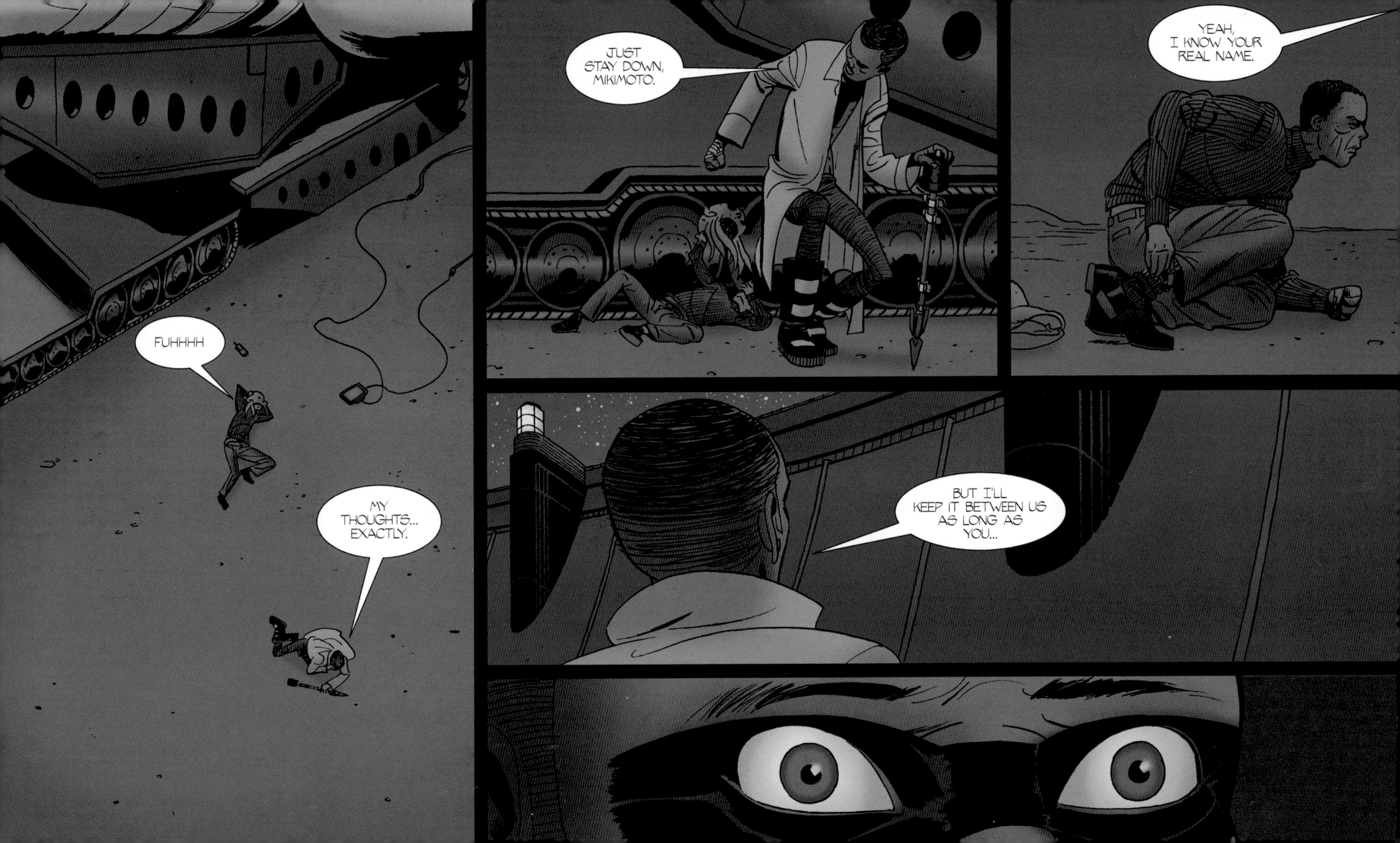
FUHHHH
MY THOUGHTS... EXACTLY.
JUST STAY DOWN, MIKIMOTO.
YEAH, I KNOW YOUR REAL NAME.
BUT I'LL KEEP IT BETWEEN US AS LONG AS YOU...

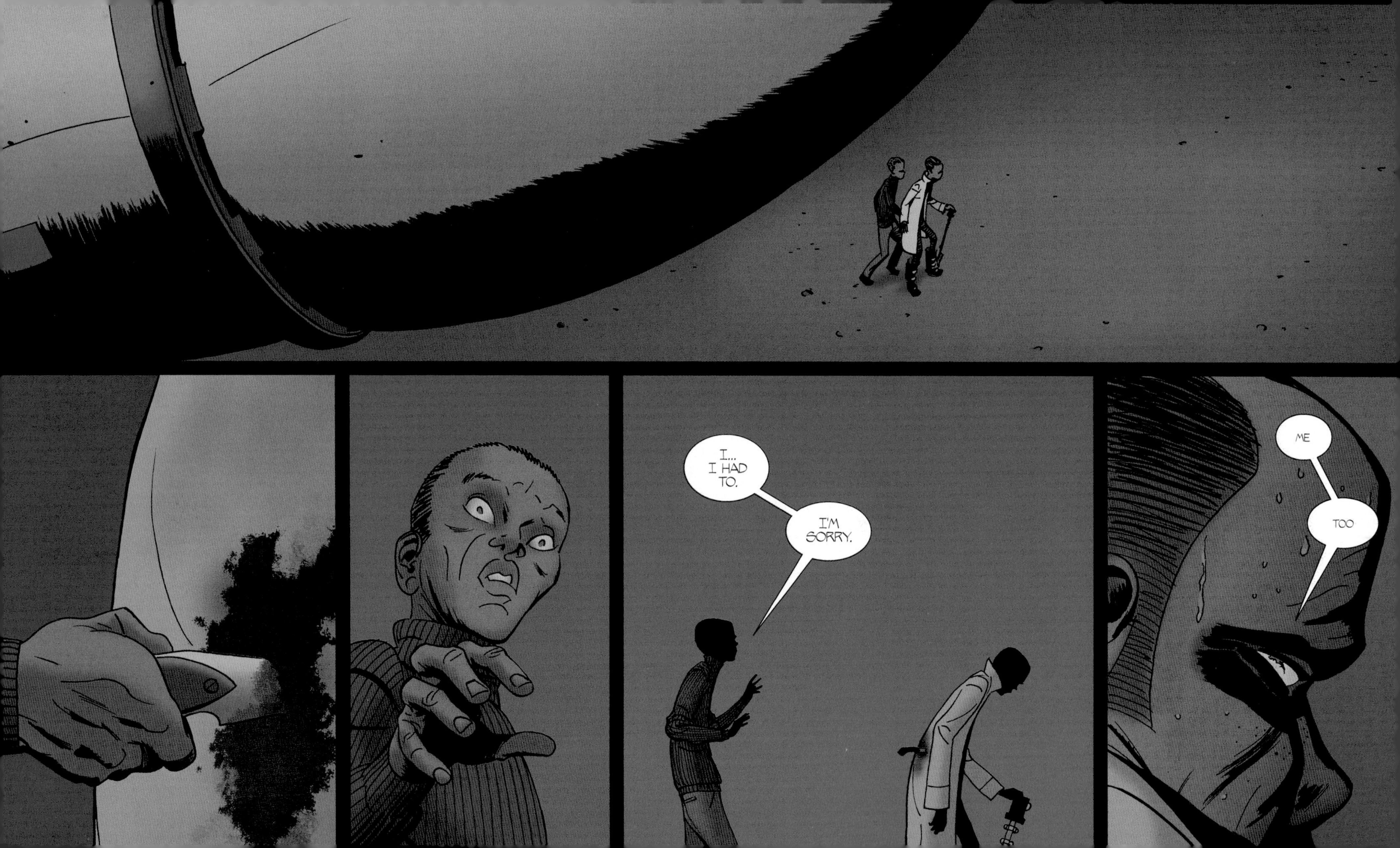

I...
I HAD
TO.
I'M
SORRY.
ME
TOO

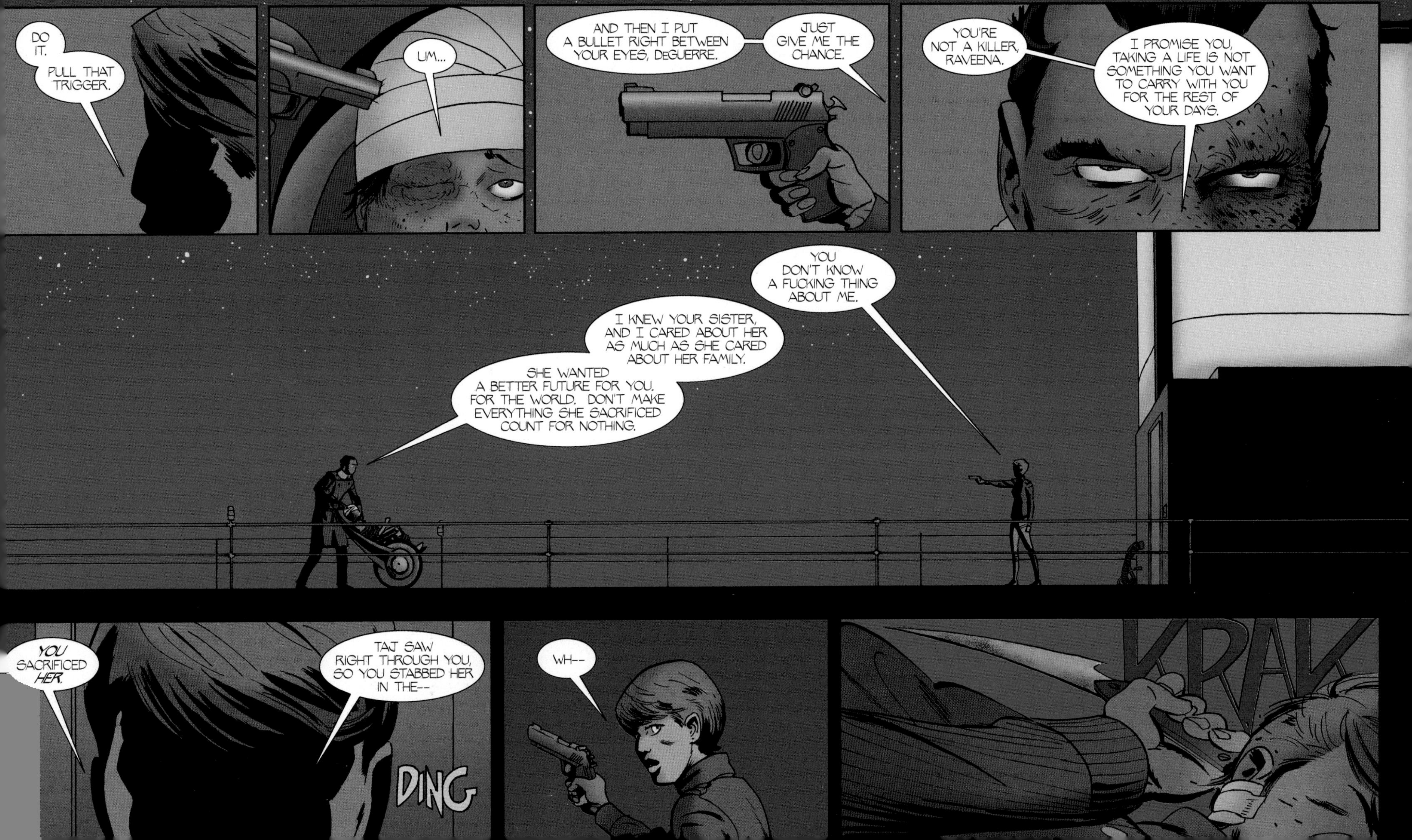
DO IT.
PULL THAT TRIGGER.
UM...
AND THEN I PUT A BULLET RIGHT BETWEEN YOUR EYES, DEGUERRE.
JUST GIVE ME THE CHANCE.
YOU'RE NOT A KILLER, RAVEENA.
I PROMISE YOU, TAKING A LIFE IS NOT SOMETHING YOU WANT TO CARRY WITH YOU FOR THE REST OF YOUR DAYS.
YOU DON'T KNOW A FUCKING THING ABOUT ME.
I KNEW YOUR SISTER, AND I CARED ABOUT HER AS MUCH AS SHE CARED ABOUT HER FAMILY.
SHE WANTED A BETTER FUTURE FOR YOU. FOR THE WORLD. DON'T MAKE EVERYTHING SHE SACRIFICED COUNT FOR NOTHING.
YOU SACRIFICED *HER*.
TAJ SAW RIGHT THROUGH YOU, SO YOU STABBED HER IN THE--
DING
WH--
KRAK

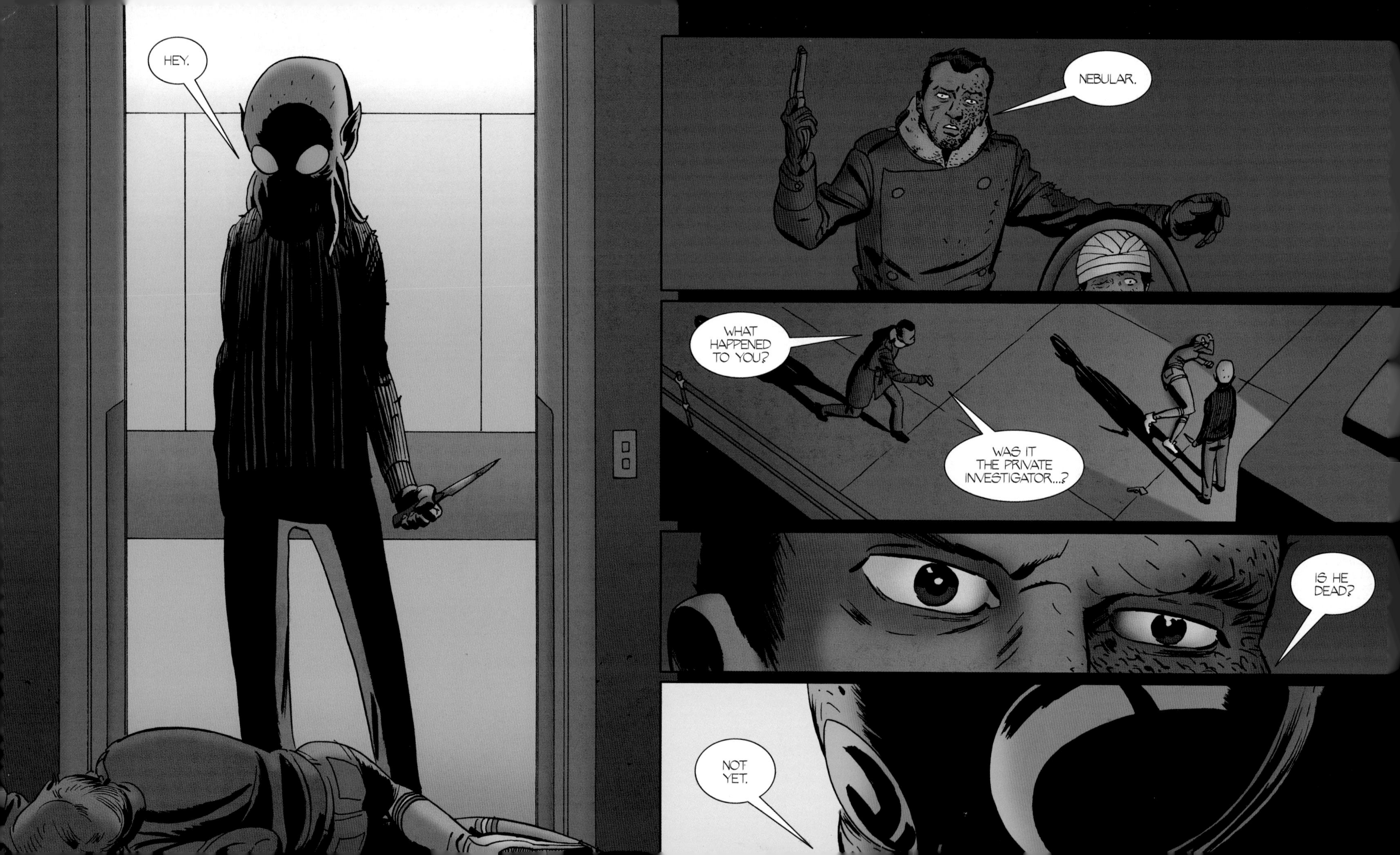
HEY.
NEBULAR.
WHAT HAPPENED TO YOU?
WAS IT THE PRIVATE INVESTIGATOR...?
IS HE DEAD?
NOT YET.

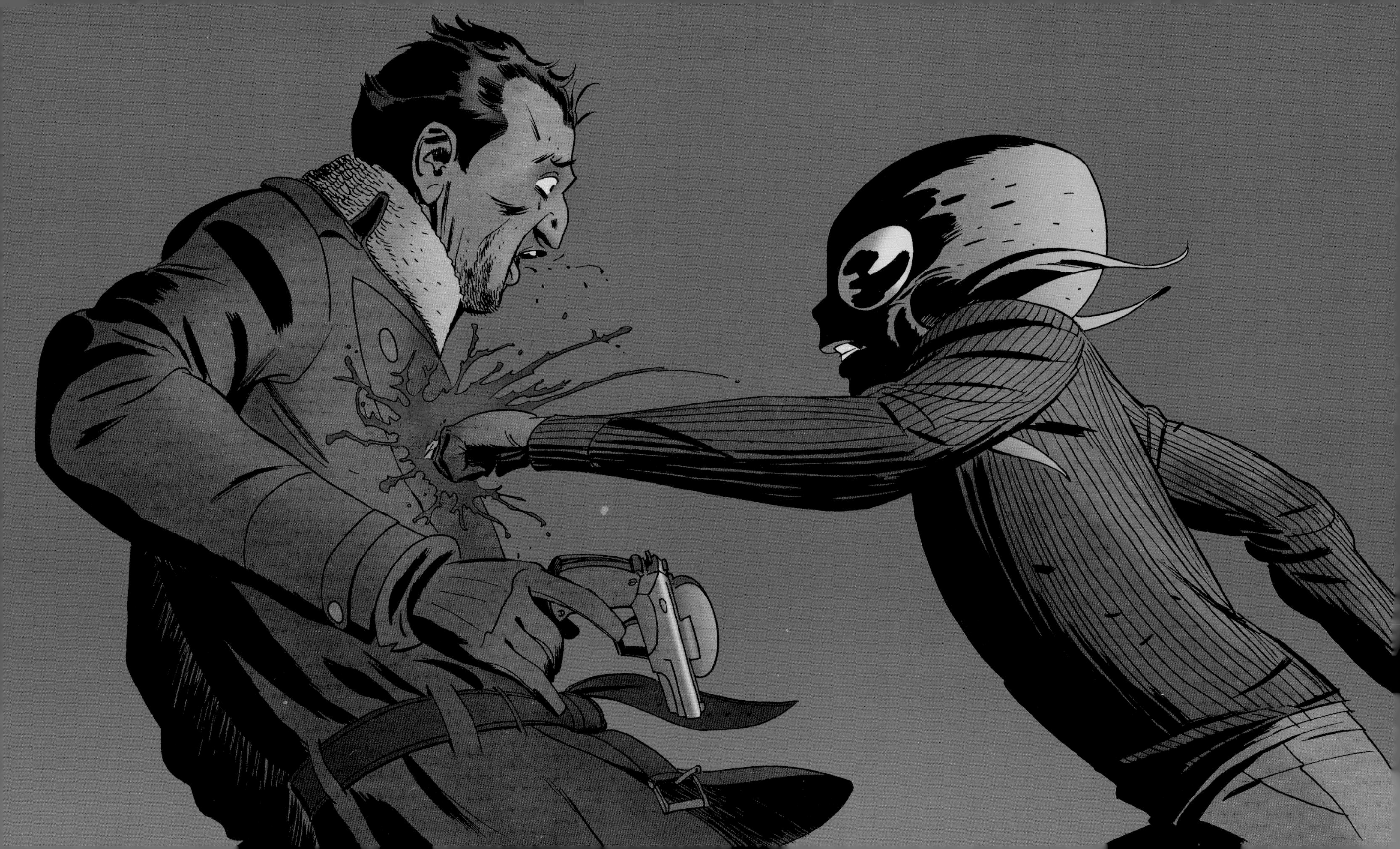

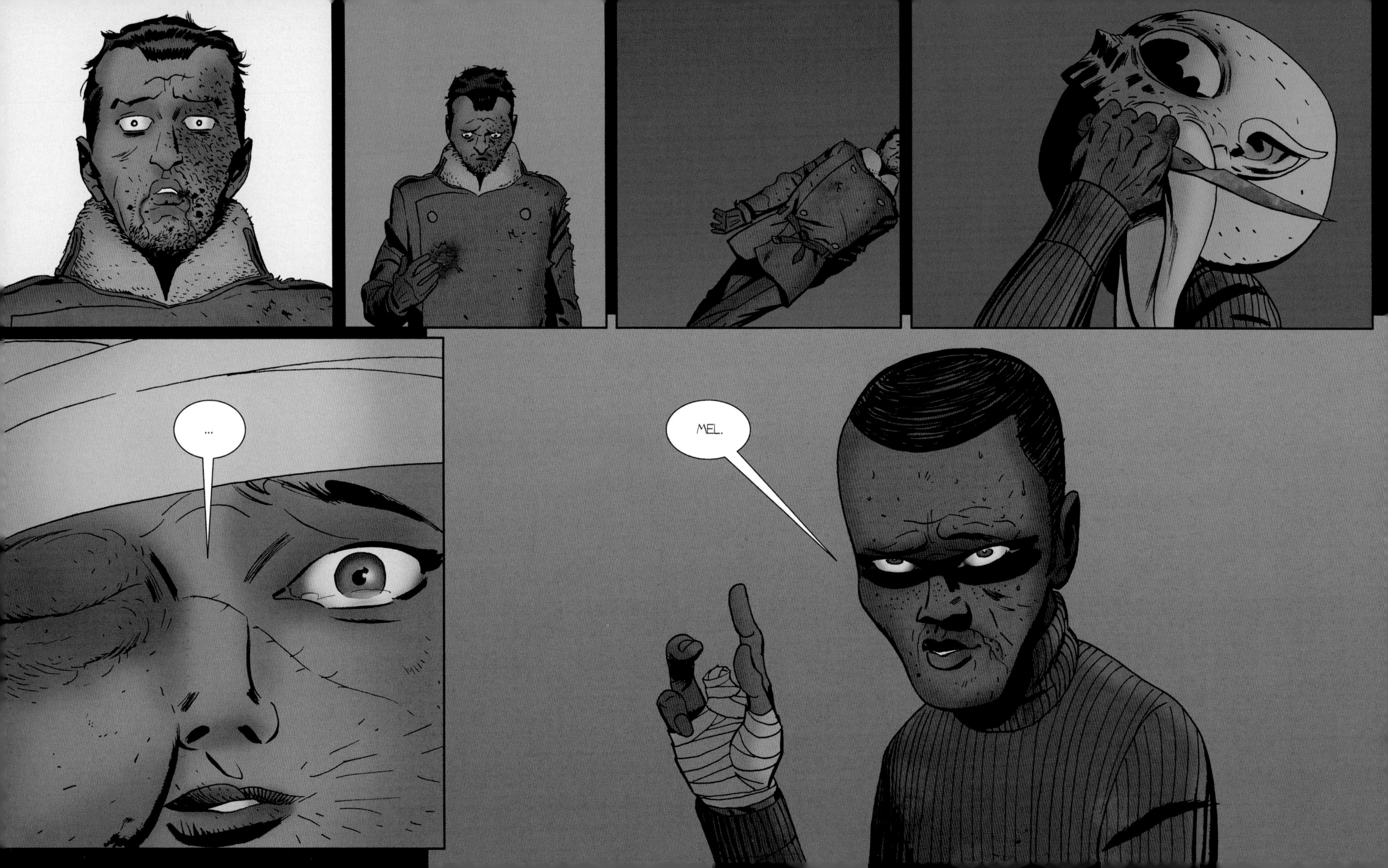
...
MEL.

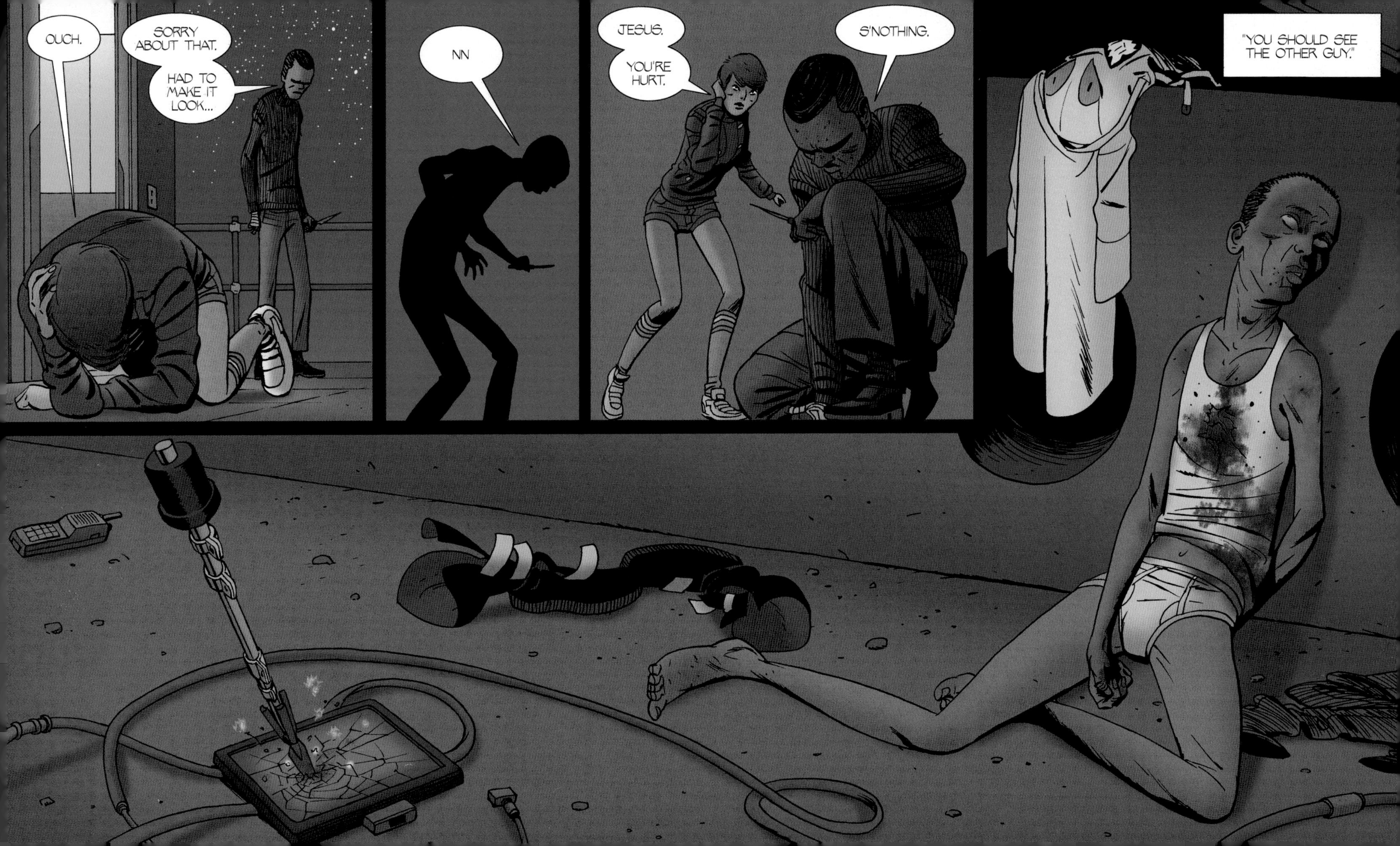

OUCH.
SORRY ABOUT THAT.
HAD TO MAKE IT LOOK...
NN
JESUS.
YOU'RE HURT.
S'NOTHING.
"YOU SHOULD SEE THE OTHER GUY."

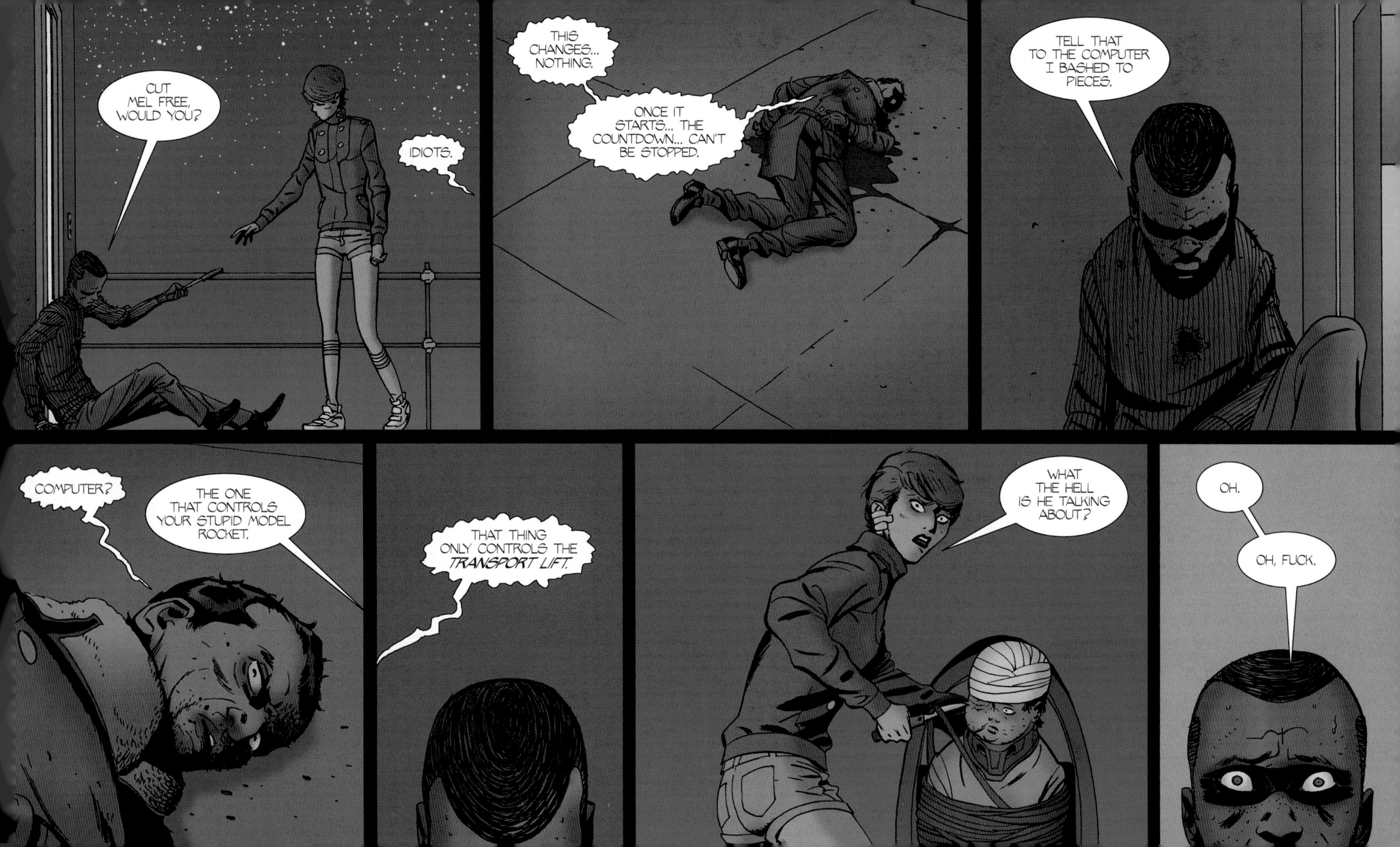
CUT MEL FREE, WOULD YOU?
IDIOTS.
THIS CHANGES... NOTHING.
ONCE IT STARTS... THE COUNTDOWN... CAN'T BE STOPPED.
TELL THAT TO THE COMPUTER I BASHED TO PIECES.
COMPUTER?
THE ONE THAT CONTROLS YOUR STUPID MODEL ROCKET.
THAT THING ONLY CONTROLS THE *TRANSPORT LIFT.*
WHAT THE HELL IS HE TALKING ABOUT?
OH.
OH, FUCK.

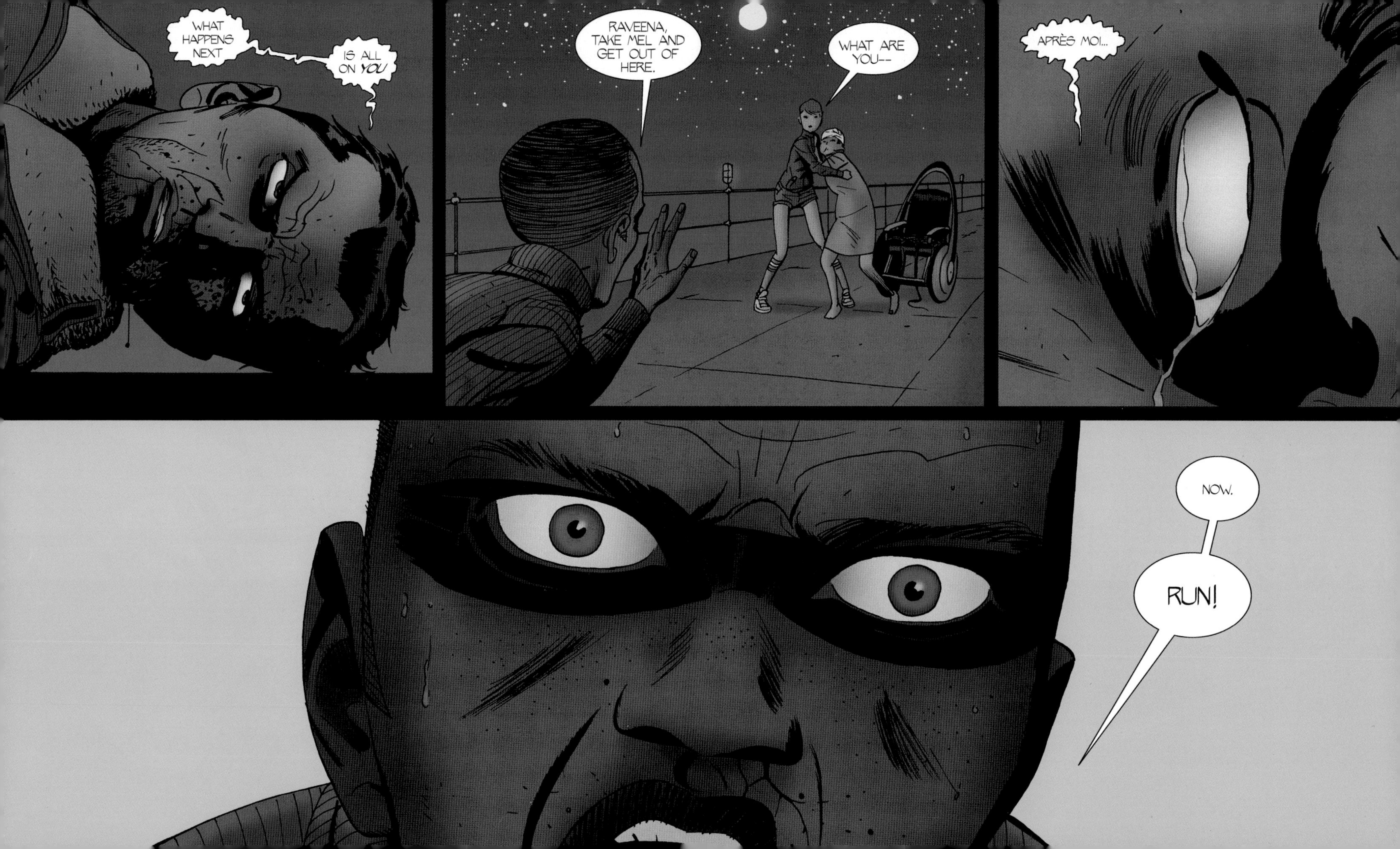
WHAT HAPPENS NEXT
IS ALL ON YOU
RAVEENA, TAKE MEL AND GET OUT OF HERE.
WHAT ARE YOU--
APRÈS MOI...
NOW.
RUN!

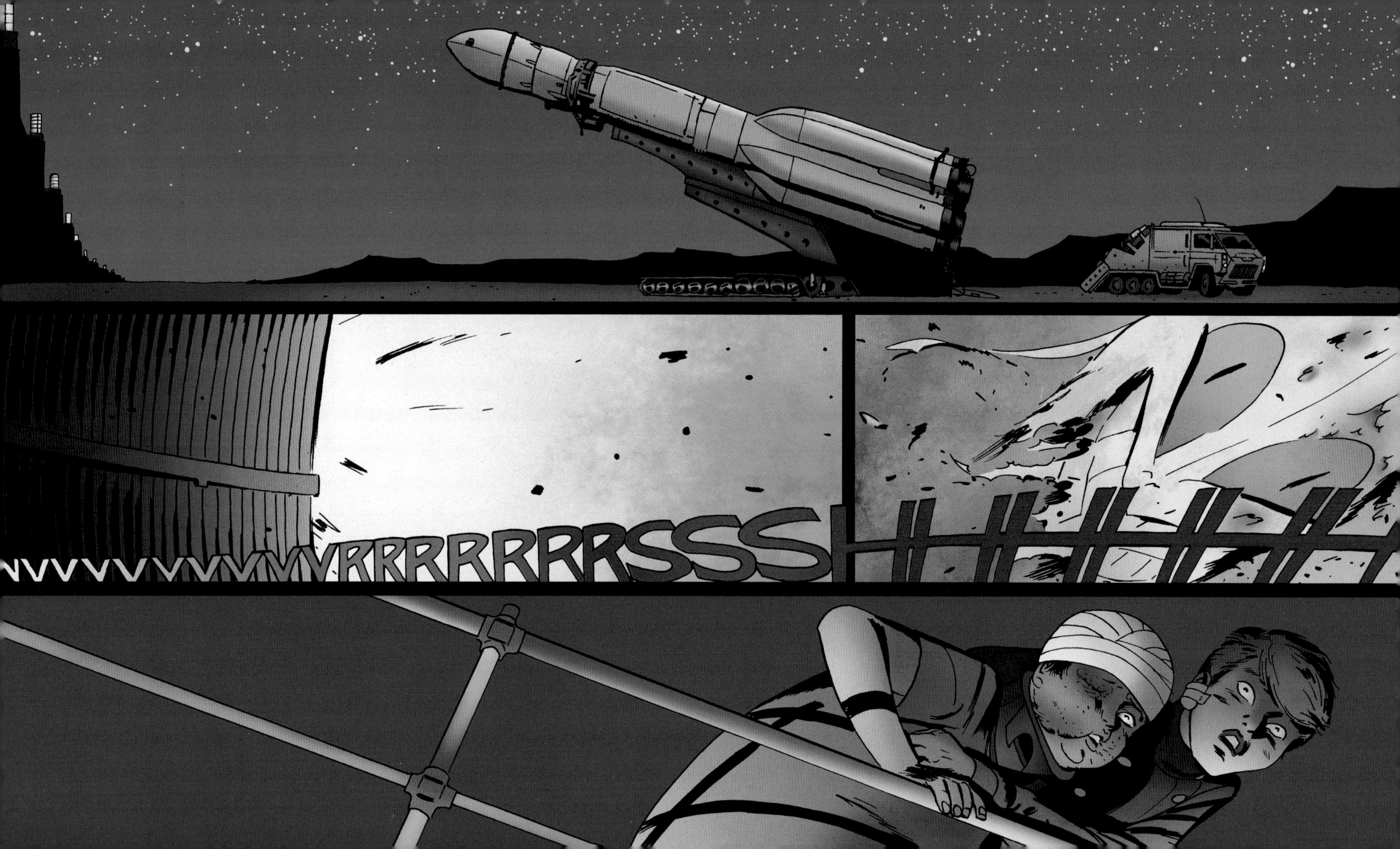
VVVVVVVVVVVVVRRRRRRRRSSSSHHHHHHHHHH

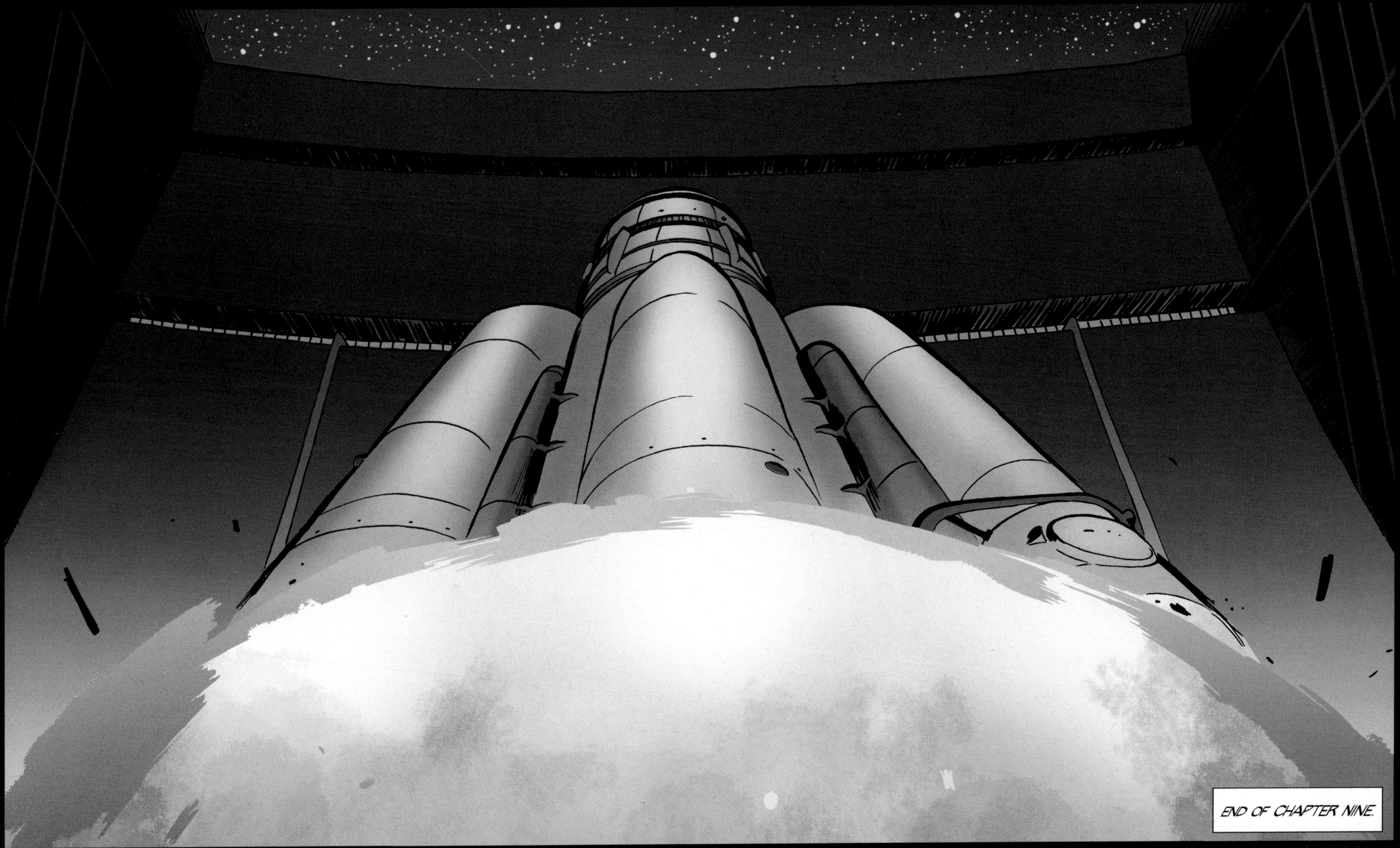
END OF CHAPTER NINE.

CHAPTER TEN

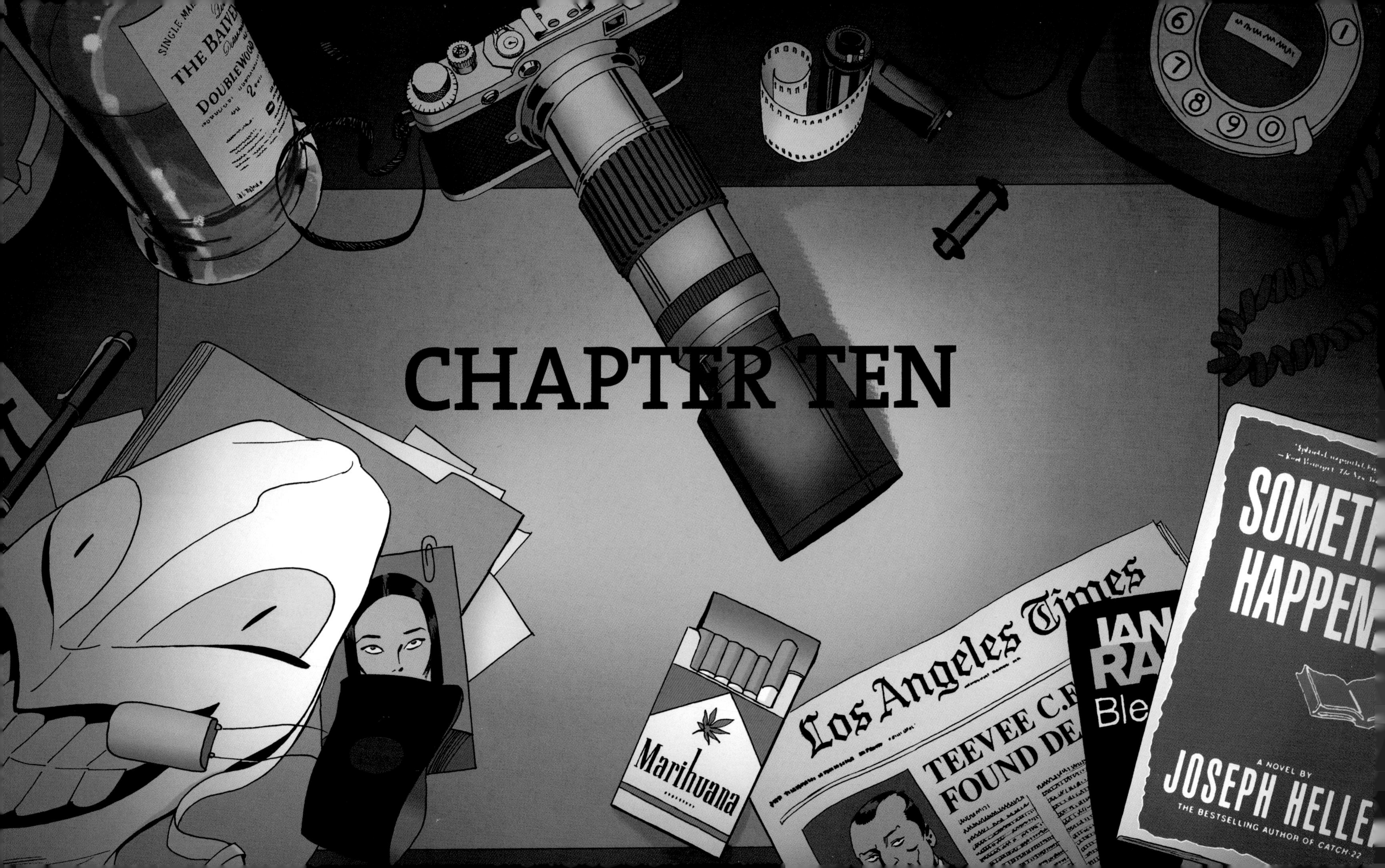
DOUBLEWOOD
Los Angeles Times
Marihuana
A NOVEL BY
THE BESTSELLING AUTHOR OF CATCH-22

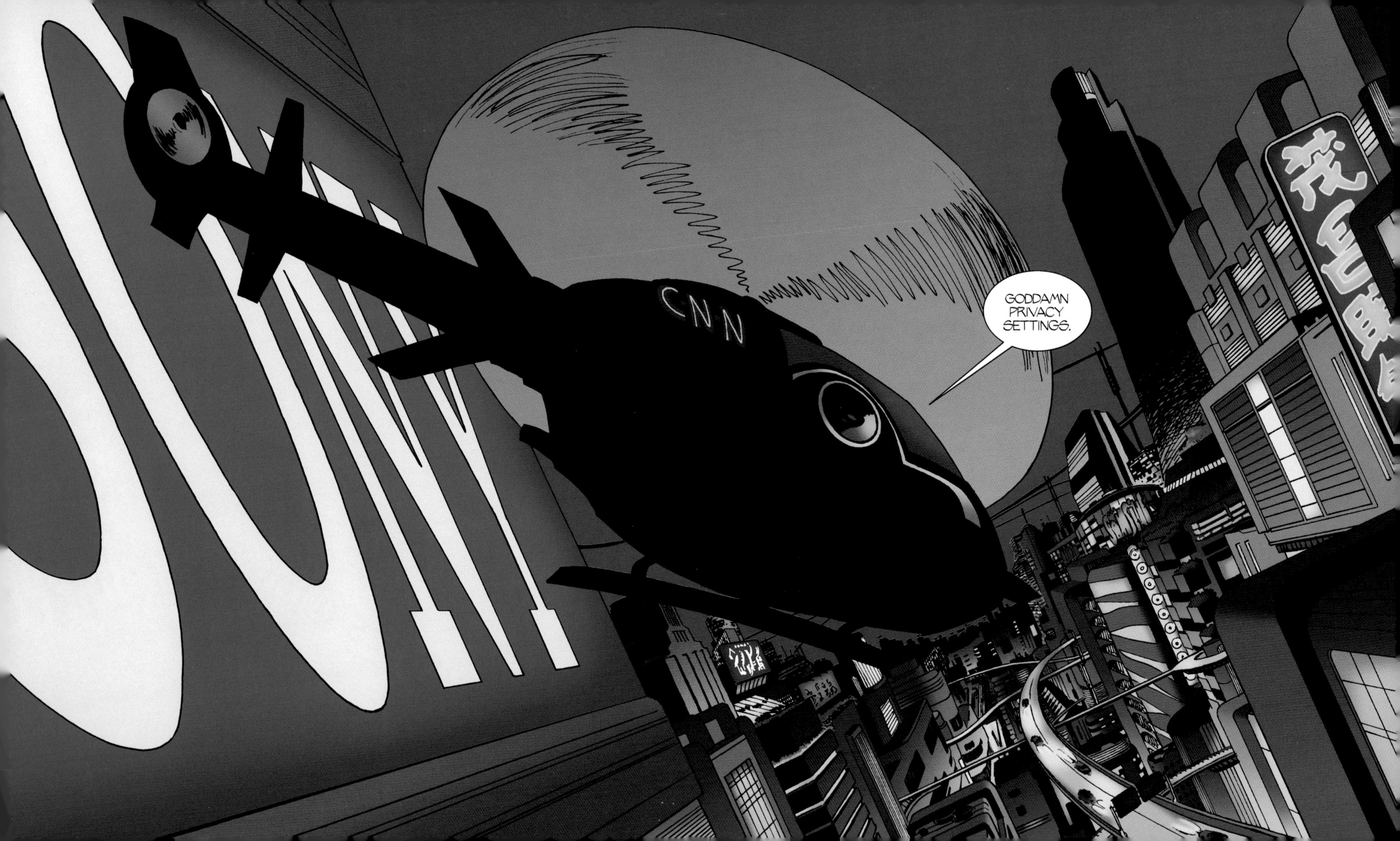
CNN
GODDAMN PRIVACY SETTINGS.

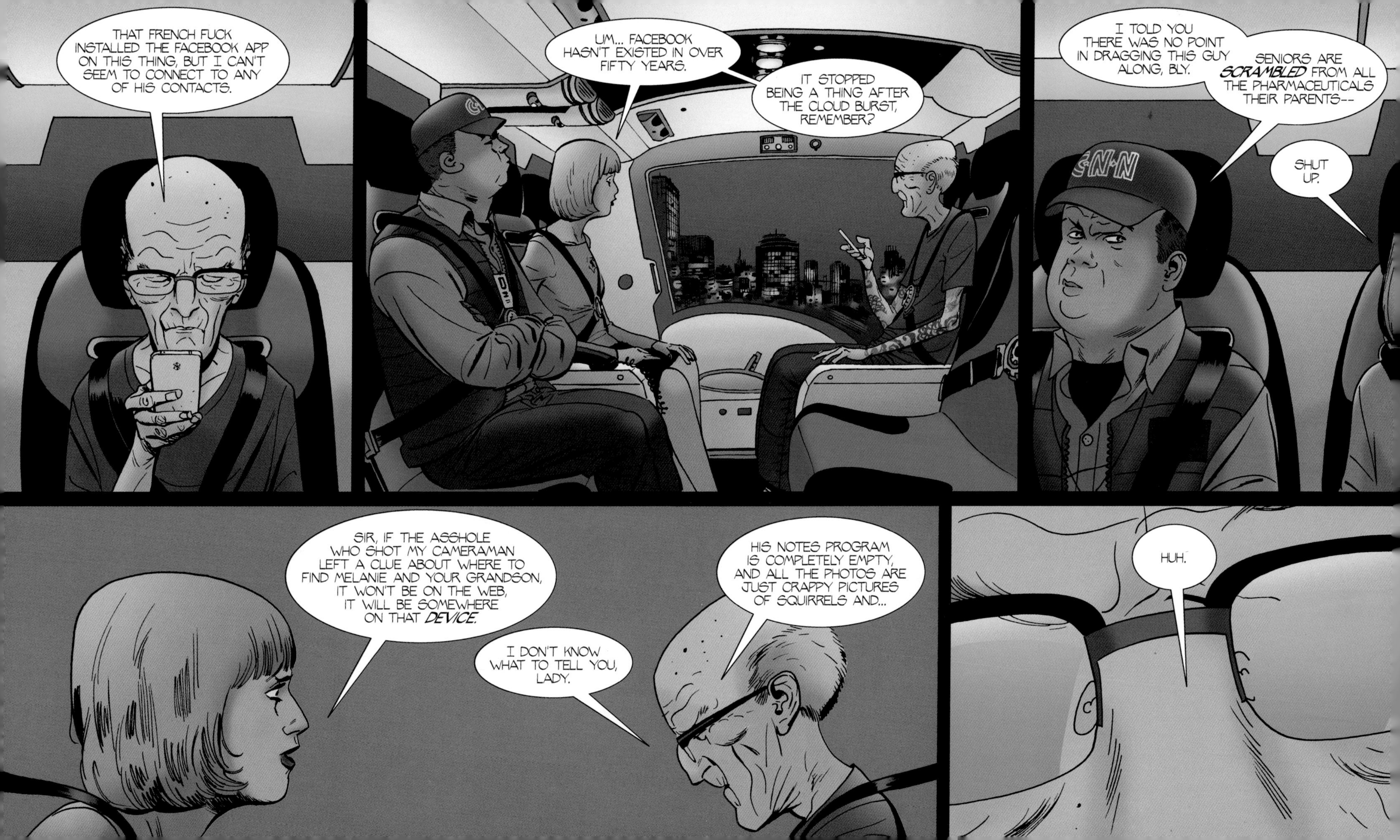

THAT FRENCH FUCK INSTALLED THE FACEBOOK APP ON THIS THING, BUT I CAN'T SEEM TO CONNECT TO ANY OF HIS CONTACTS.
UM... FACEBOOK HASN'T EXISTED IN OVER FIFTY YEARS.
IT STOPPED BEING A THING AFTER THE CLOUD BURST, REMEMBER?
I TOLD YOU THERE WAS NO POINT IN DRAGGING THIS GUY ALONG, BLY.
SENIORS ARE *SCRAMBLED* FROM ALL THE PHARMACEUTICALS THEIR PARENTS--
SHUT UP.
CNN
SIR, IF THE ASSHOLE WHO SHOT MY CAMERAMAN LEFT A CLUE ABOUT WHERE TO FIND MELANIE AND YOUR GRANDSON, IT WON'T BE ON THE WEB, IT WILL BE SOMEWHERE ON THAT *DEVICE.*
I DON'T KNOW WHAT TO TELL YOU, LADY.
HIS NOTES PROGRAM IS COMPLETELY EMPTY, AND ALL THE PHOTOS ARE JUST CRAPPY PICTURES OF SQUIRRELS AND...
HUH.

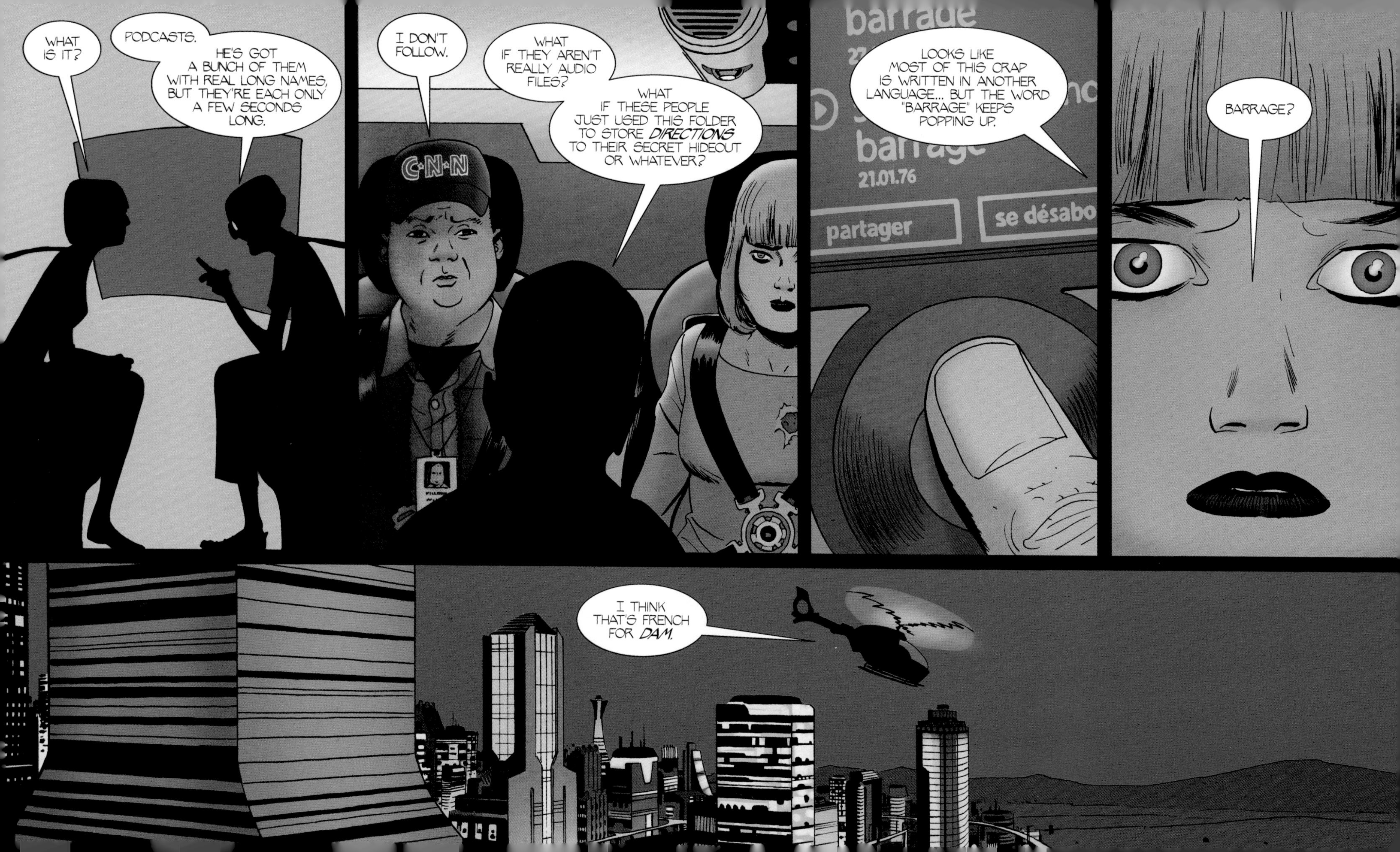
WHAT IS IT?
PODCASTS.
HE'S GOT A BUNCH OF THEM WITH REAL LONG NAMES, BUT THEY'RE EACH ONLY A FEW SECONDS LONG.
I DON'T FOLLOW.
C·N·N
WHAT IF THEY AREN'T REALLY AUDIO FILES?
WHAT IF THESE PEOPLE JUST USED THIS FOLDER TO STORE *DIRECTIONS* TO THEIR SECRET HIDEOUT OR WHATEVER?
barrage
barrage
21.01.76
partager
se désabo
LOOKS LIKE MOST OF THIS CRAP IS WRITTEN IN ANOTHER LANGUAGE... BUT THE WORD "BARRAGE" KEEPS POPPING UP.
BARRAGE?
I THINK THAT'S FRENCH FOR *DAM*.

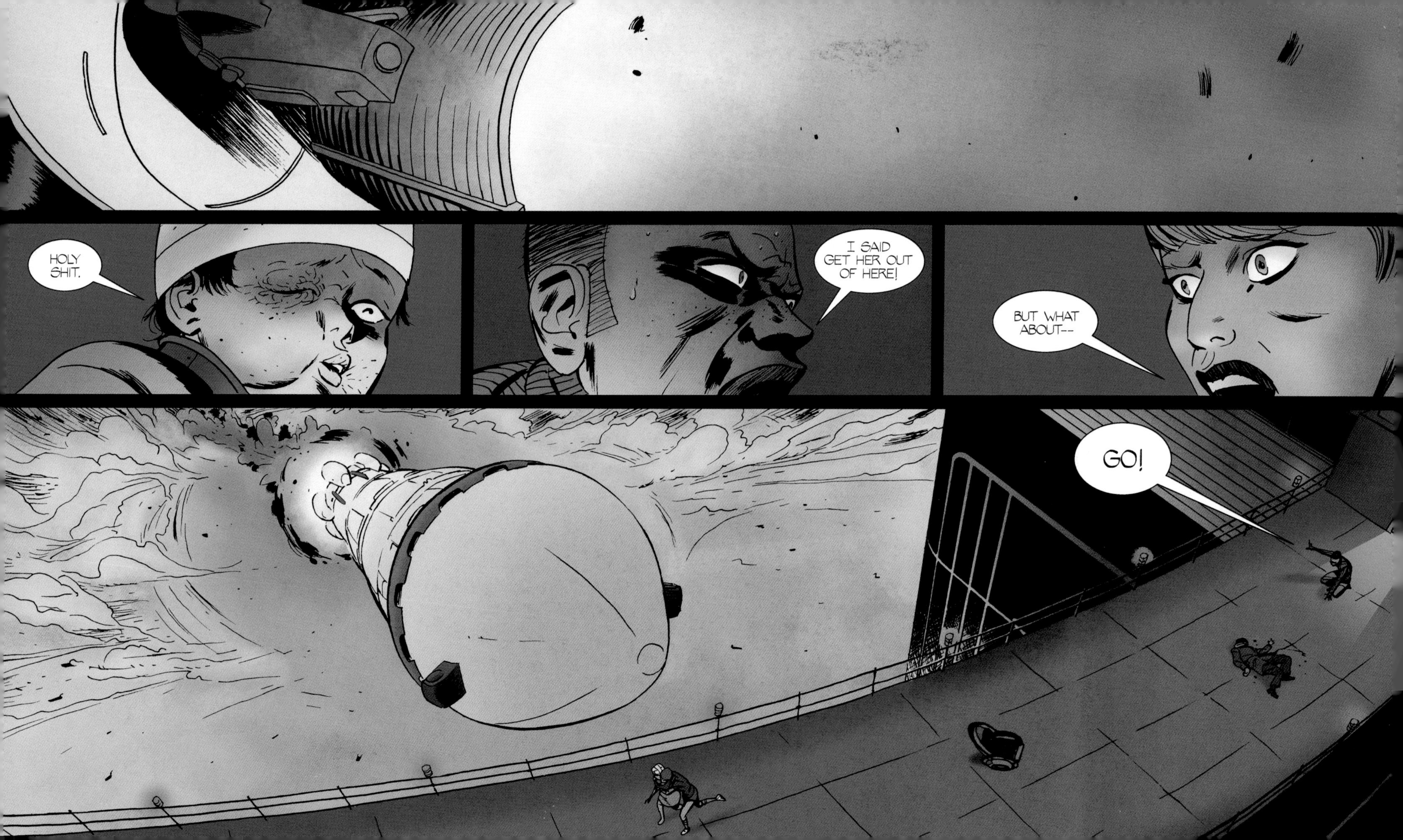
HOLY SHIT.
I SAID GET HER OUT OF HERE!
BUT WHAT ABOUT--
GO!

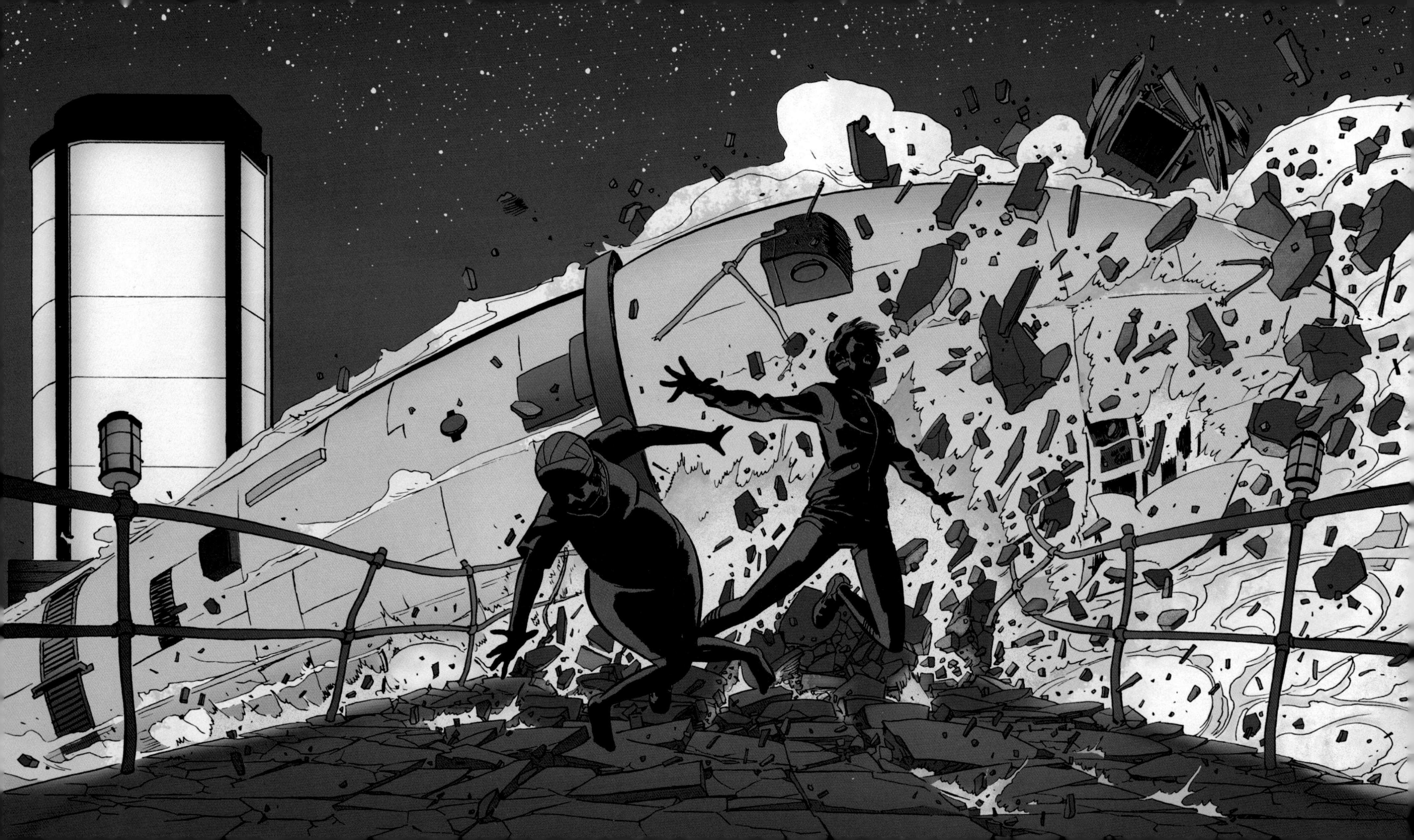

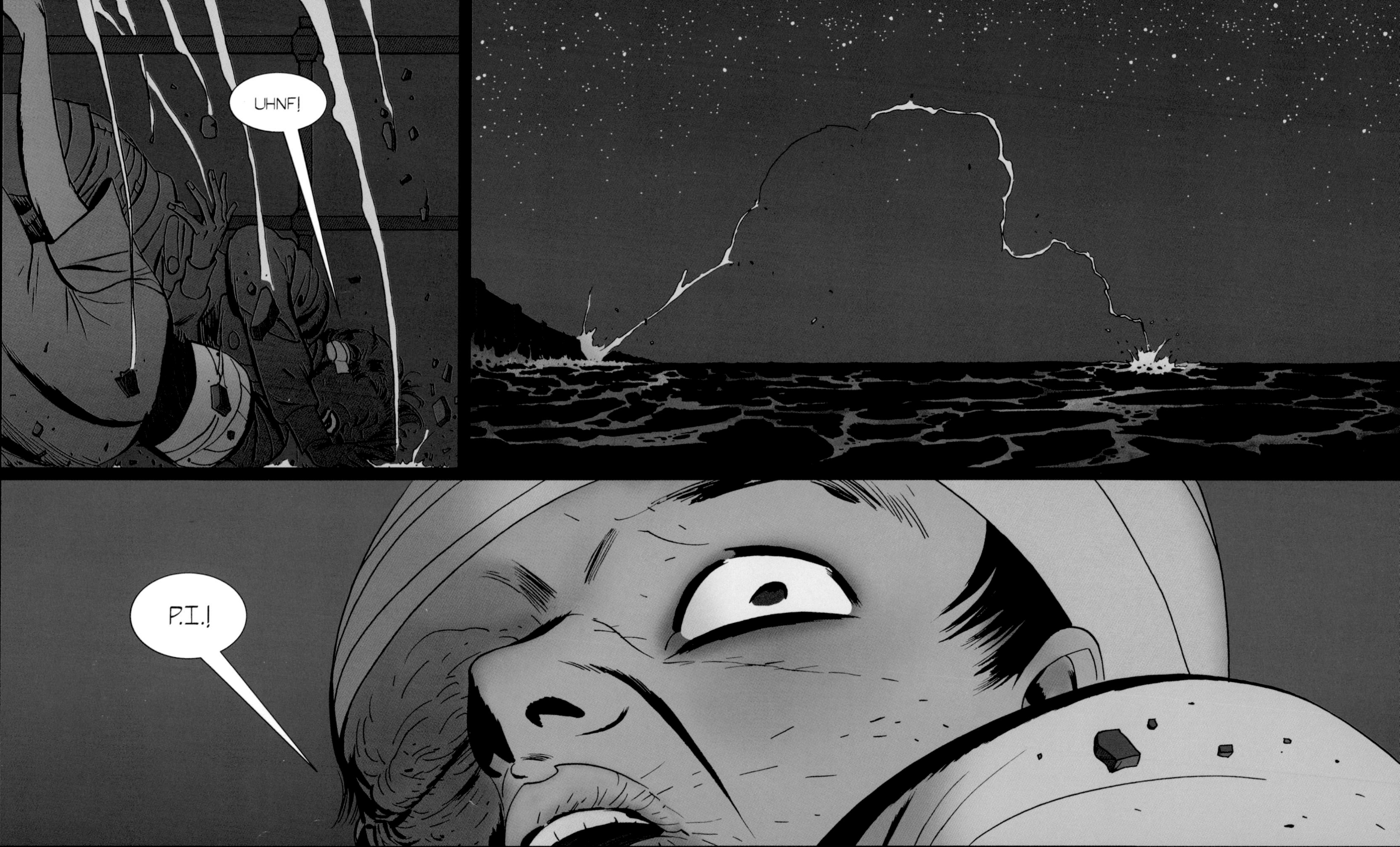
UHNF!
P.I.!

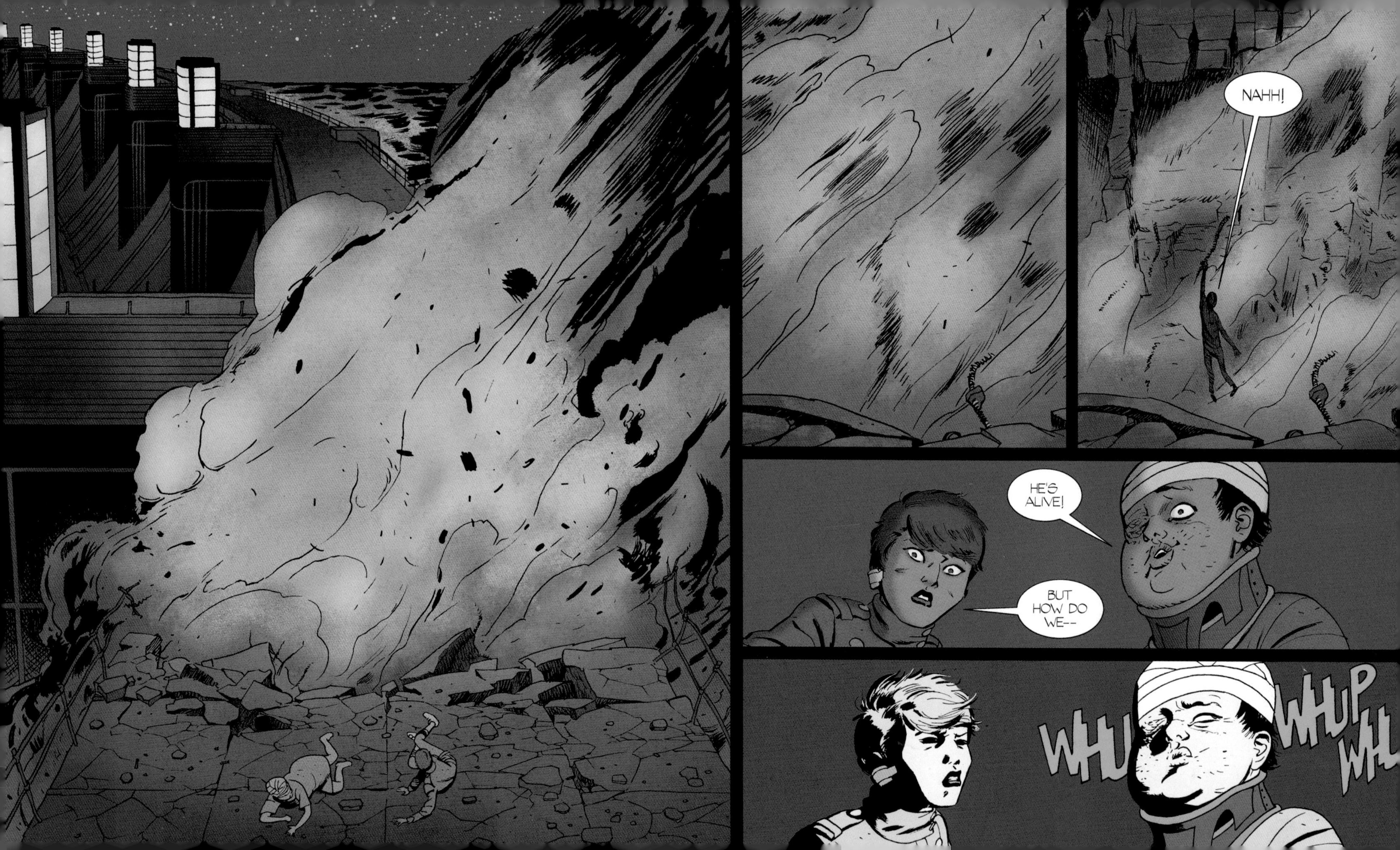
NAHH!
HE'S ALIVE!
BUT HOW DO WE--
WHUP
WHUP
WHU
WHU

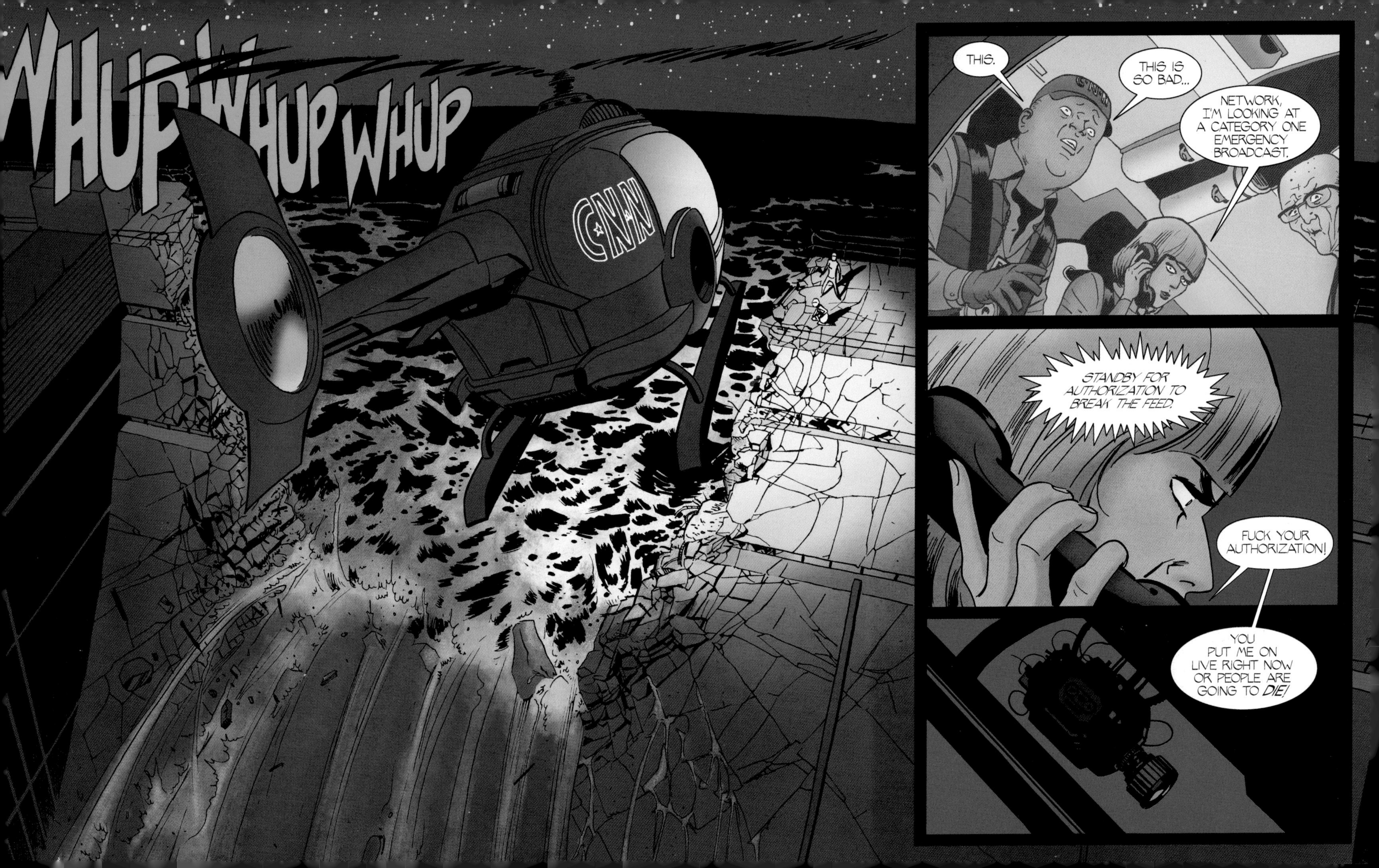
WHUP WHUP WHUP WHUP
THIS.
THIS IS SO BAD...
NETWORK, I'M LOOKING AT A CATEGORY ONE EMERGENCY BROADCAST.
STANDBY FOR AUTHORIZATION TO BREAK THE FEED.
FUCK YOUR AUTHORIZATION!
YOU PUT ME ON LIVE RIGHT NOW OR PEOPLE ARE GOING TO *DIE!*

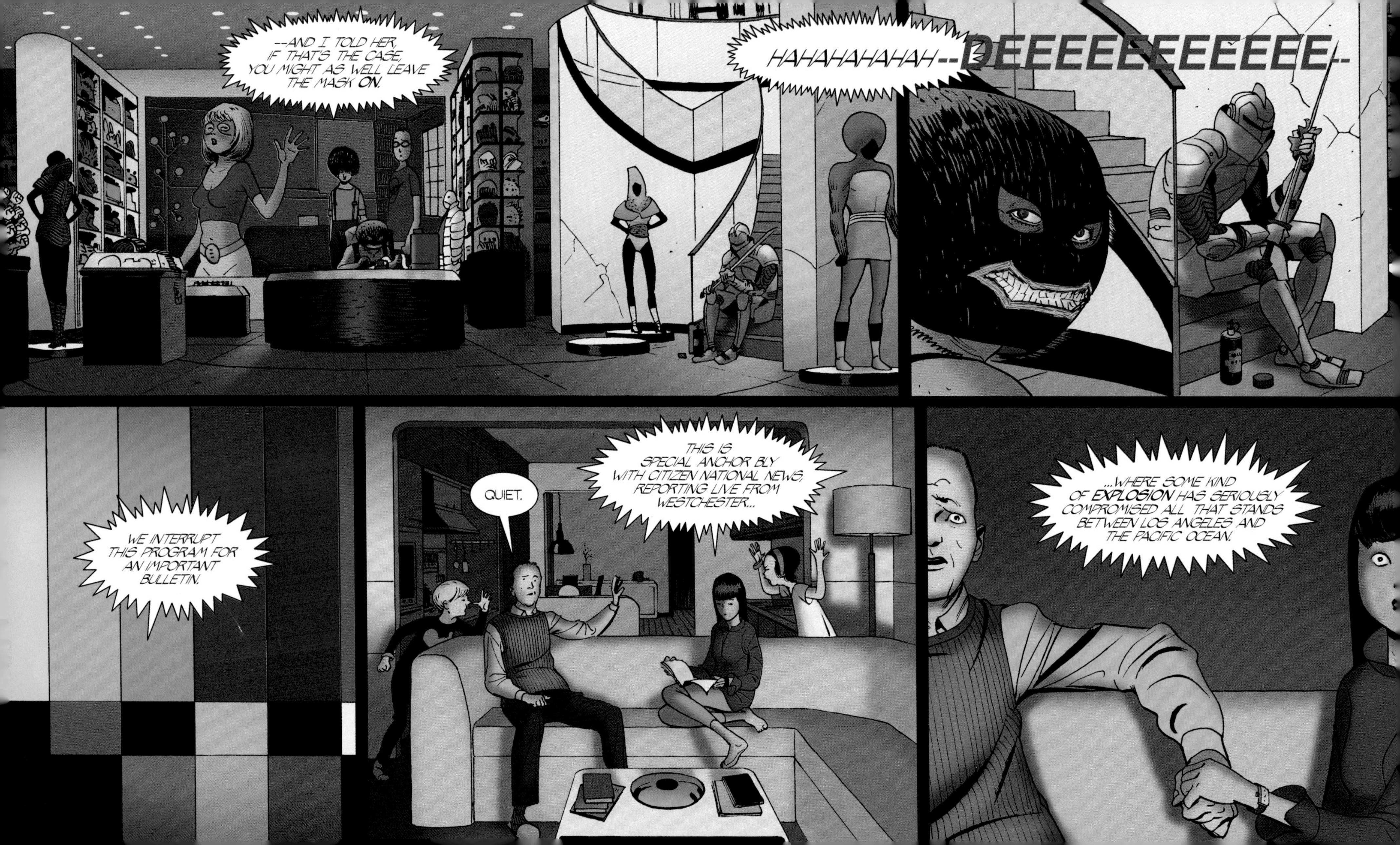
--AND I TOLD HER, IF THAT'S THE CASE, YOU MIGHT AS WELL LEAVE THE MASK ON.
HAHAHAHAHAH--DEEEEEEEEEEEE--
WE INTERRUPT THIS PROGRAM FOR AN IMPORTANT BULLETIN.
QUIET.
THIS IS SPECIAL ANCHOR BLY WITH CITIZEN NATIONAL NEWS, REPORTING LIVE FROM WESTCHESTER...
...WHERE SOME KIND OF EXPLOSION HAS SERIOUSLY COMPROMISED ALL THAT STANDS BETWEEN LOS ANGELES AND THE PACIFIC OCEAN.

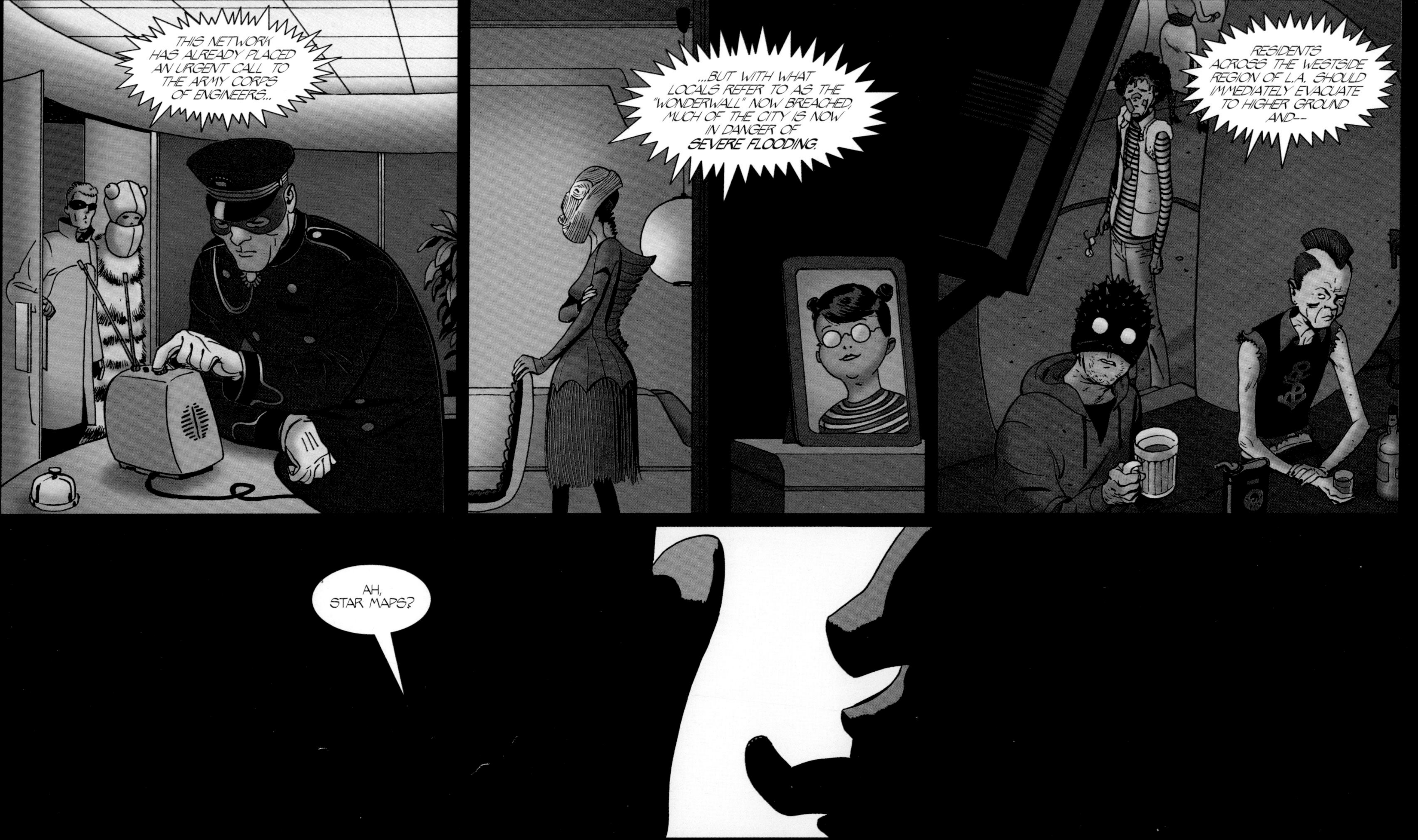
THIS NETWORK HAS ALREADY PLACED AN URGENT CALL TO THE ARMY CORPS OF ENGINEERS...
...BUT WITH WHAT LOCALS REFER TO AS THE "WONDERWALL" NOW BREACHED, MUCH OF THE CITY IS NOW IN DANGER OF SEVERE FLOODING.
RESIDENTS ACROSS THE WESTSIDE REGION OF L.A. SHOULD IMMEDIATELY EVACUATE TO HIGHER GROUND AND--
AH, STAR MAPS?

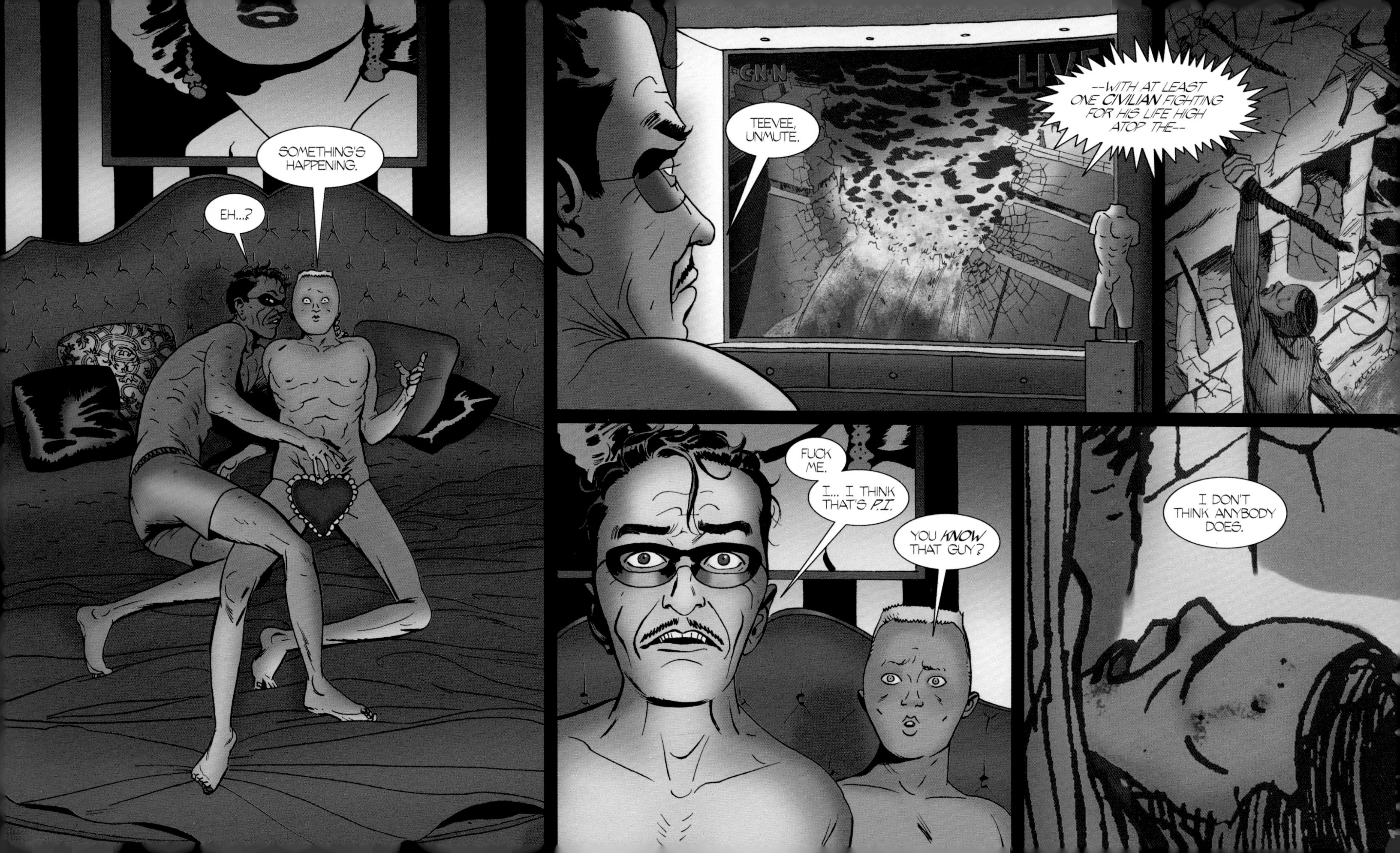
SOMETHING'S HAPPENING.
EH...?
TEEVEE, UNMUTE.
CNN
LIVE
--WITH AT LEAST ONE *CIVILIAN* FIGHTING FOR HIS LIFE HIGH ATOP THE--
FUCK ME.
I... I THINK THAT'S *P.I.*
YOU *KNOW* THAT GUY?
I DON'T THINK ANYBODY DOES.

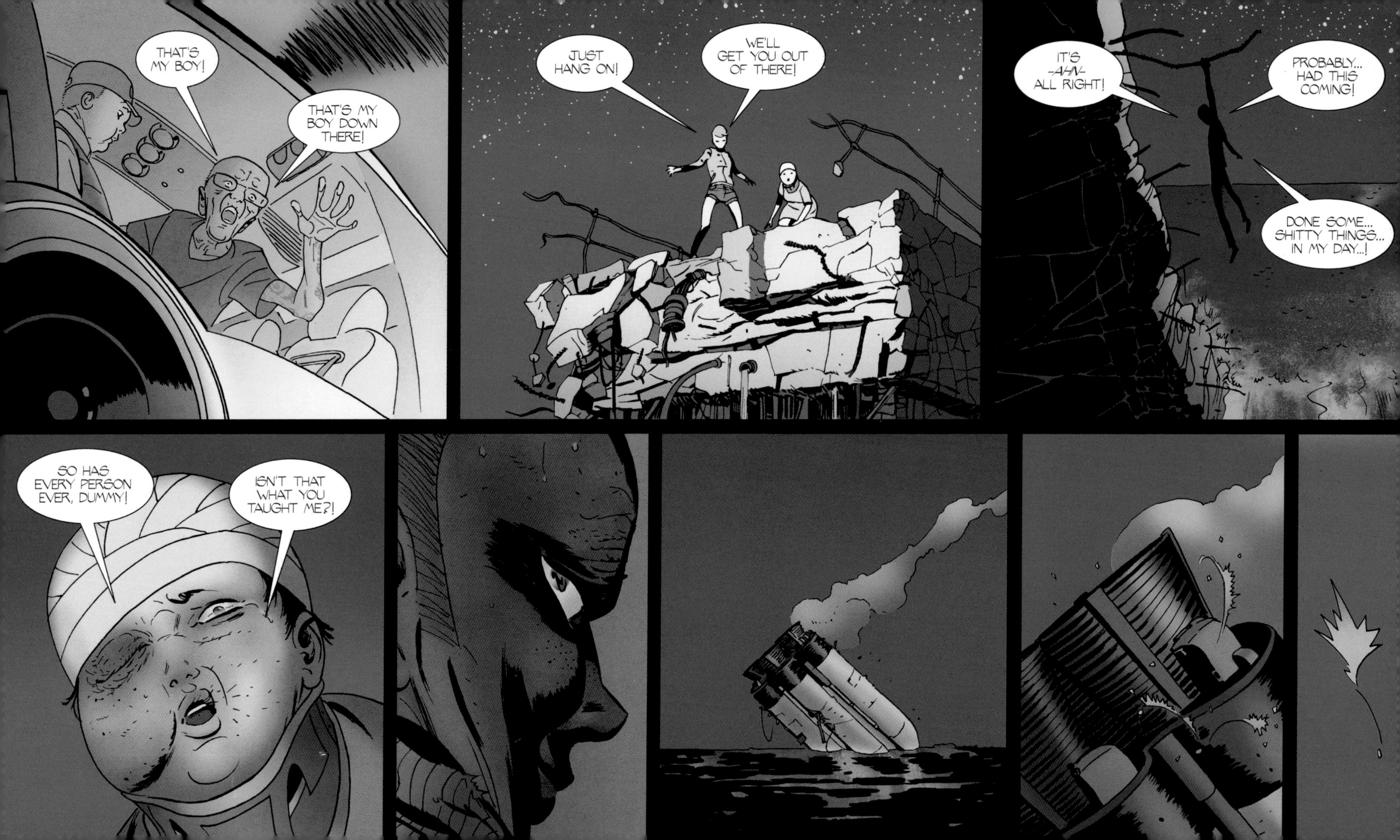
THAT'S MY BOY!
THAT'S MY BOY DOWN THERE!
JUST HANG ON!
WE'LL GET YOU OUT OF THERE!
IT'S -AHN- ALL RIGHT!
PROBABLY... HAD THIS COMING!
DONE SOME... SHITTY THINGS... IN MY DAY...!
SO HAS EVERY PERSON EVER, DUMMY!
ISN'T THAT WHAT YOU TAUGHT ME?!

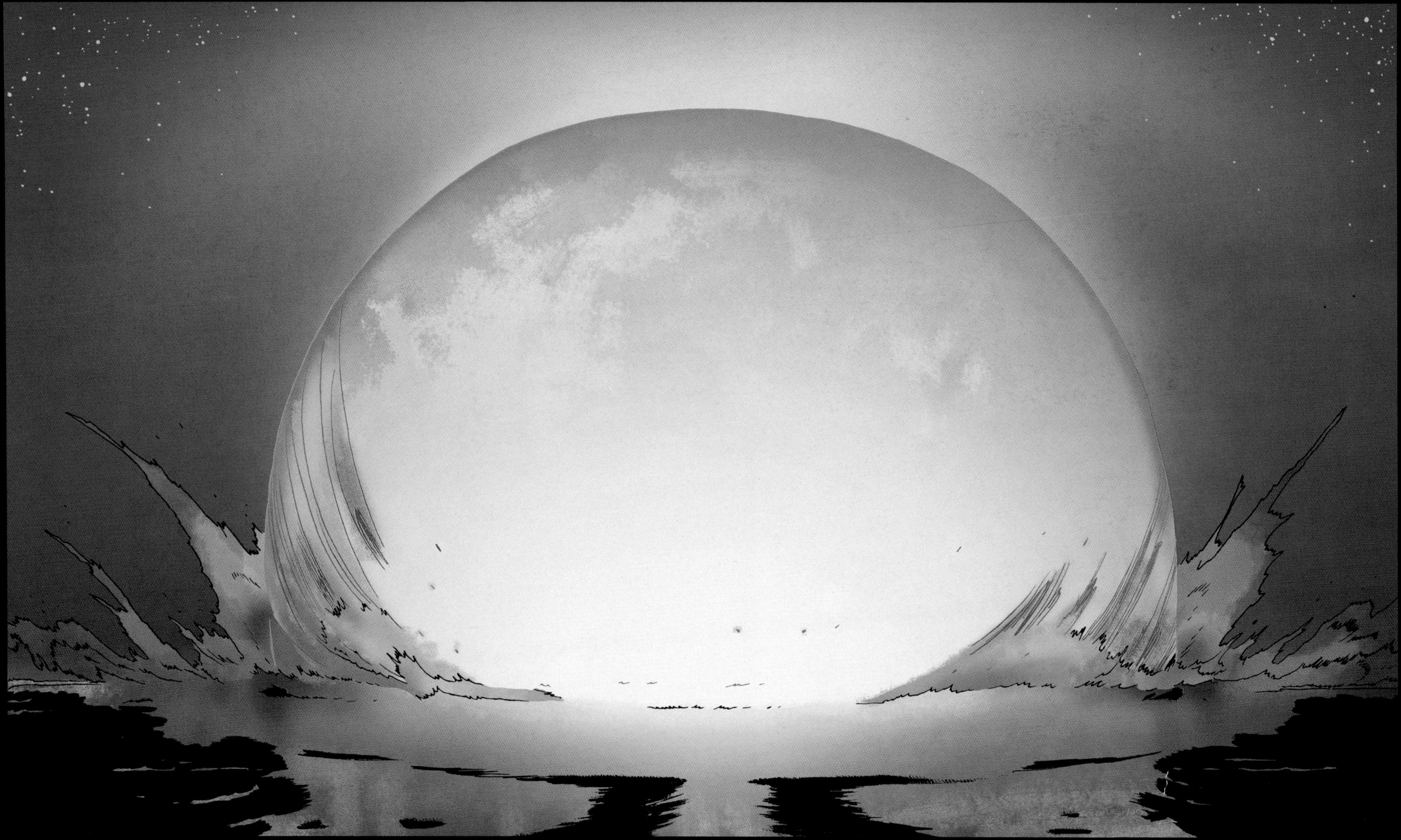

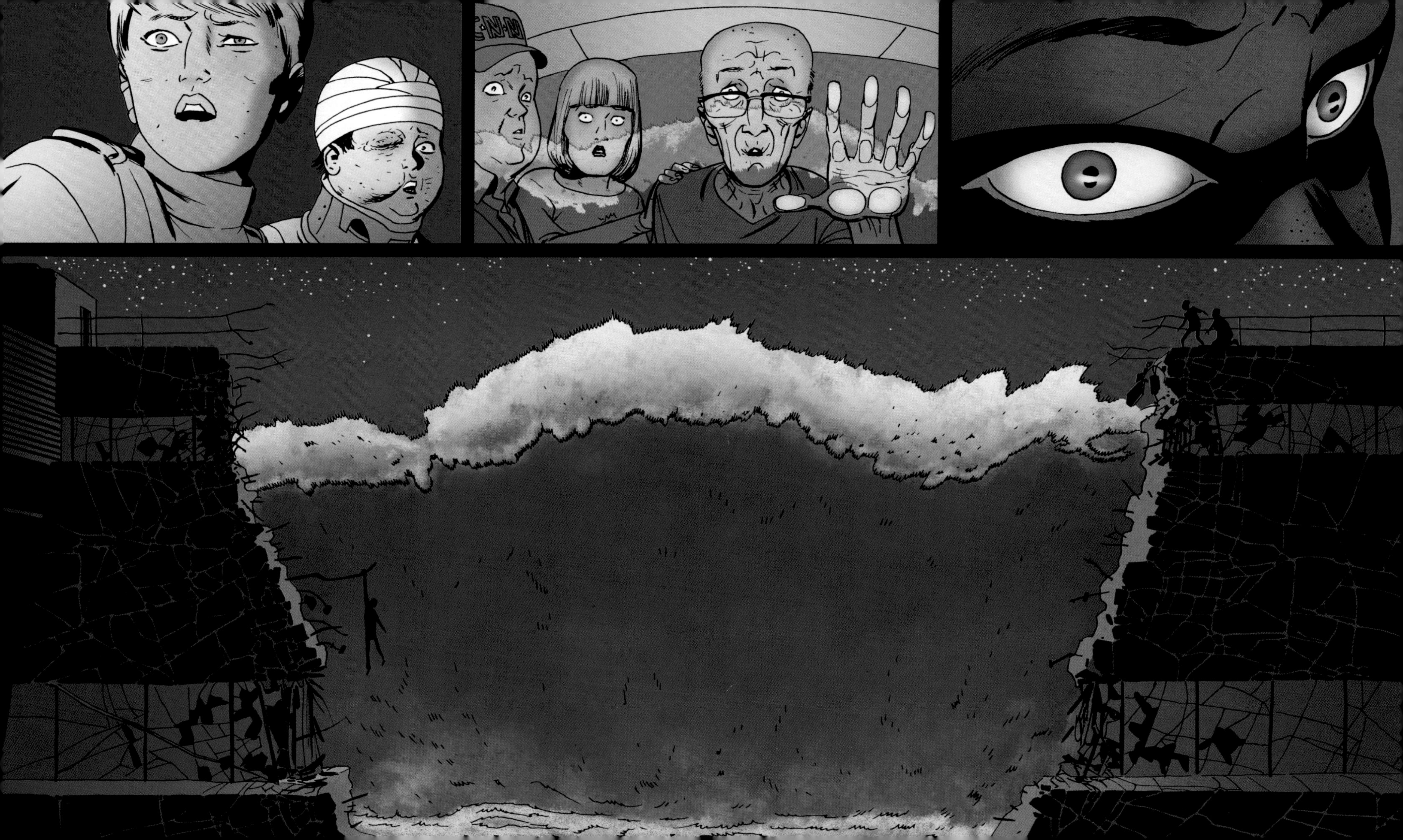

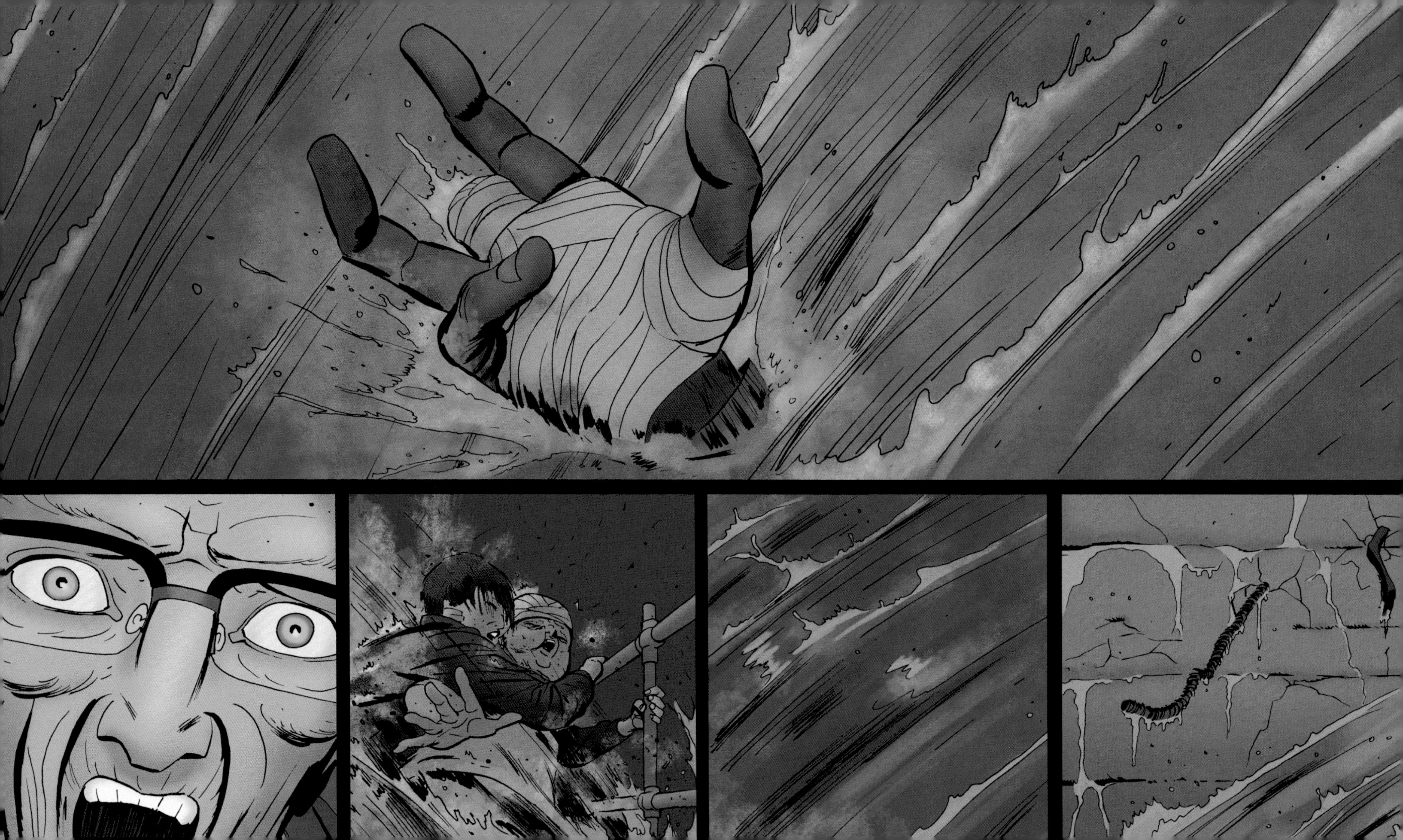

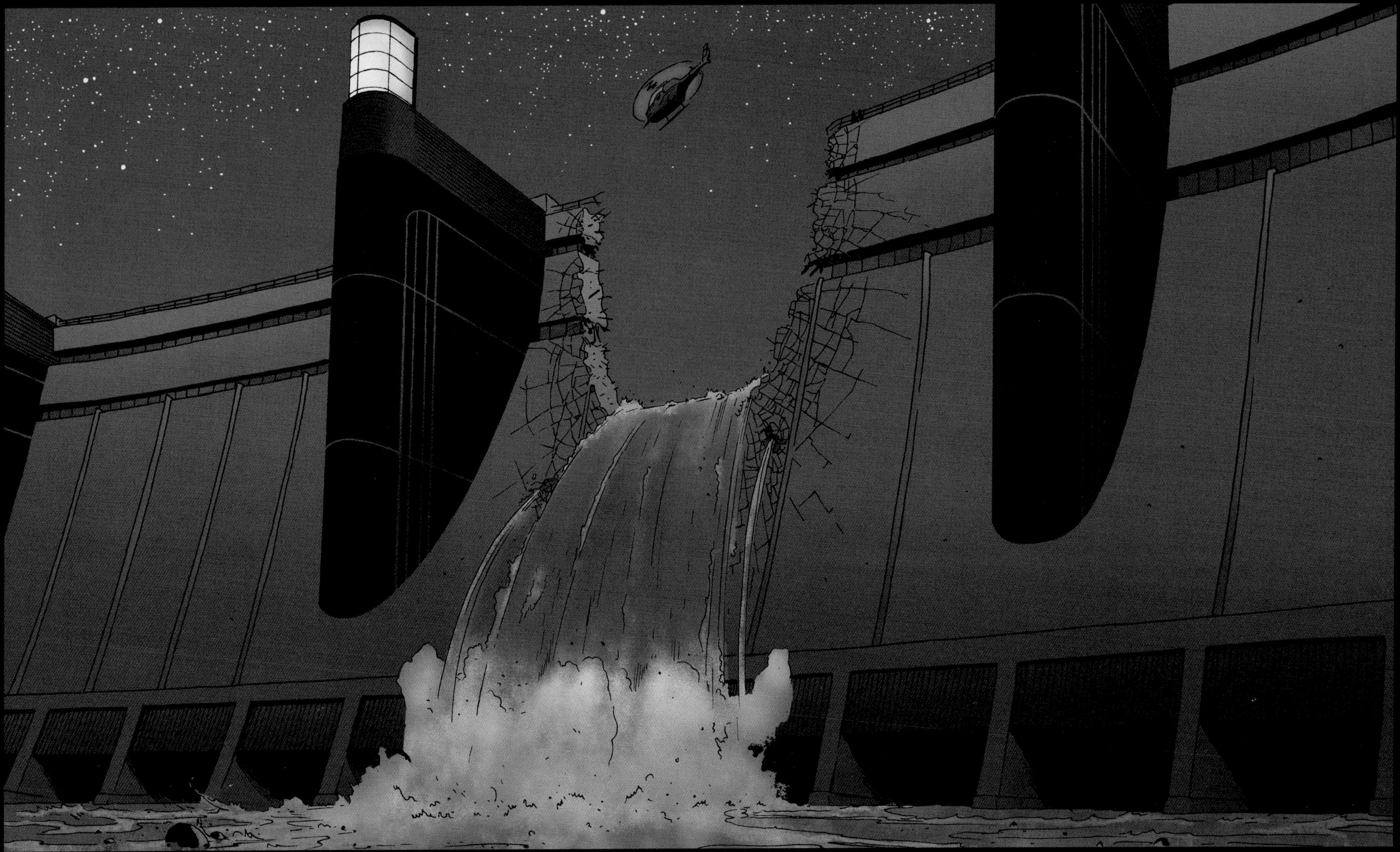

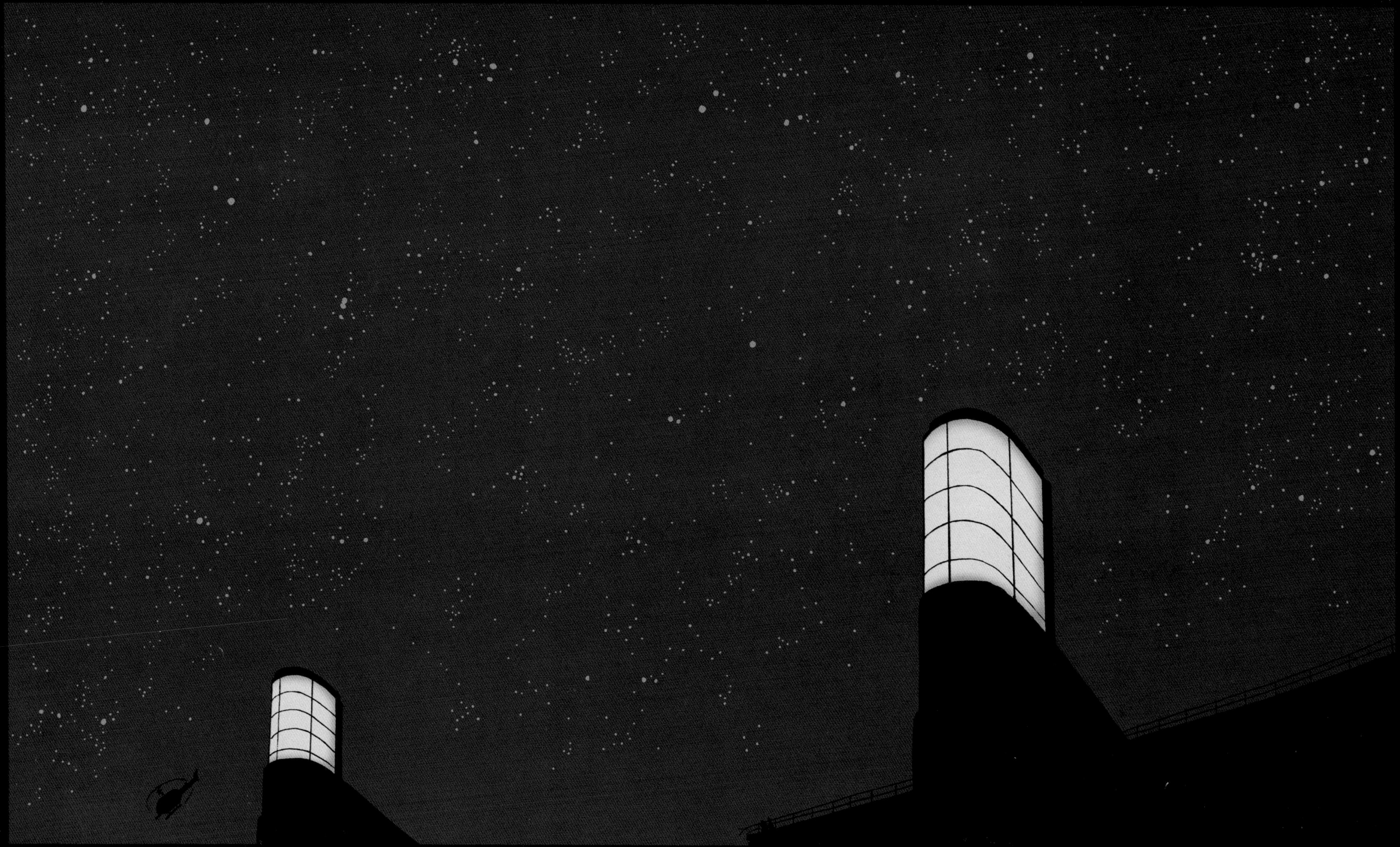

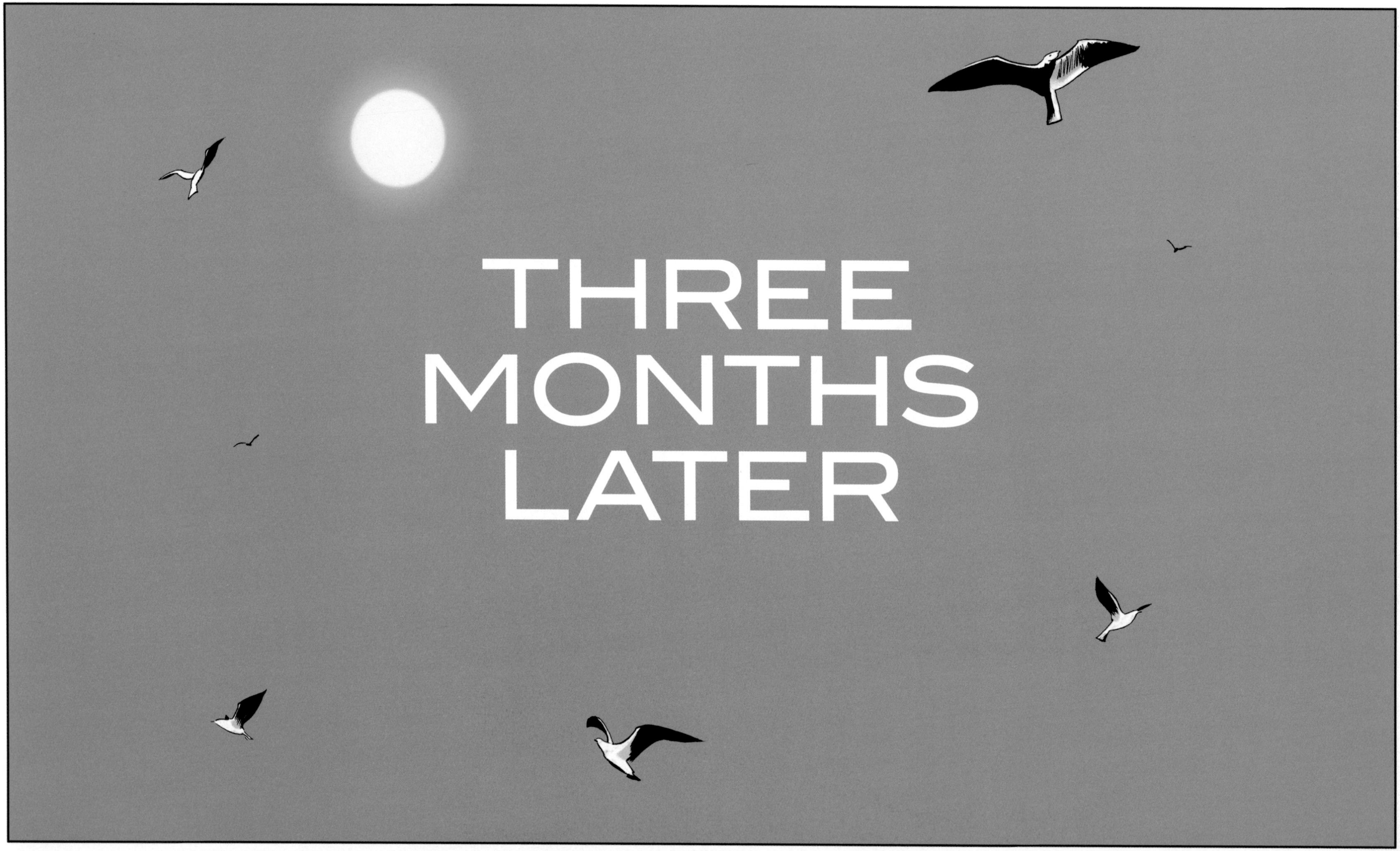
THREE MONTHS LATER

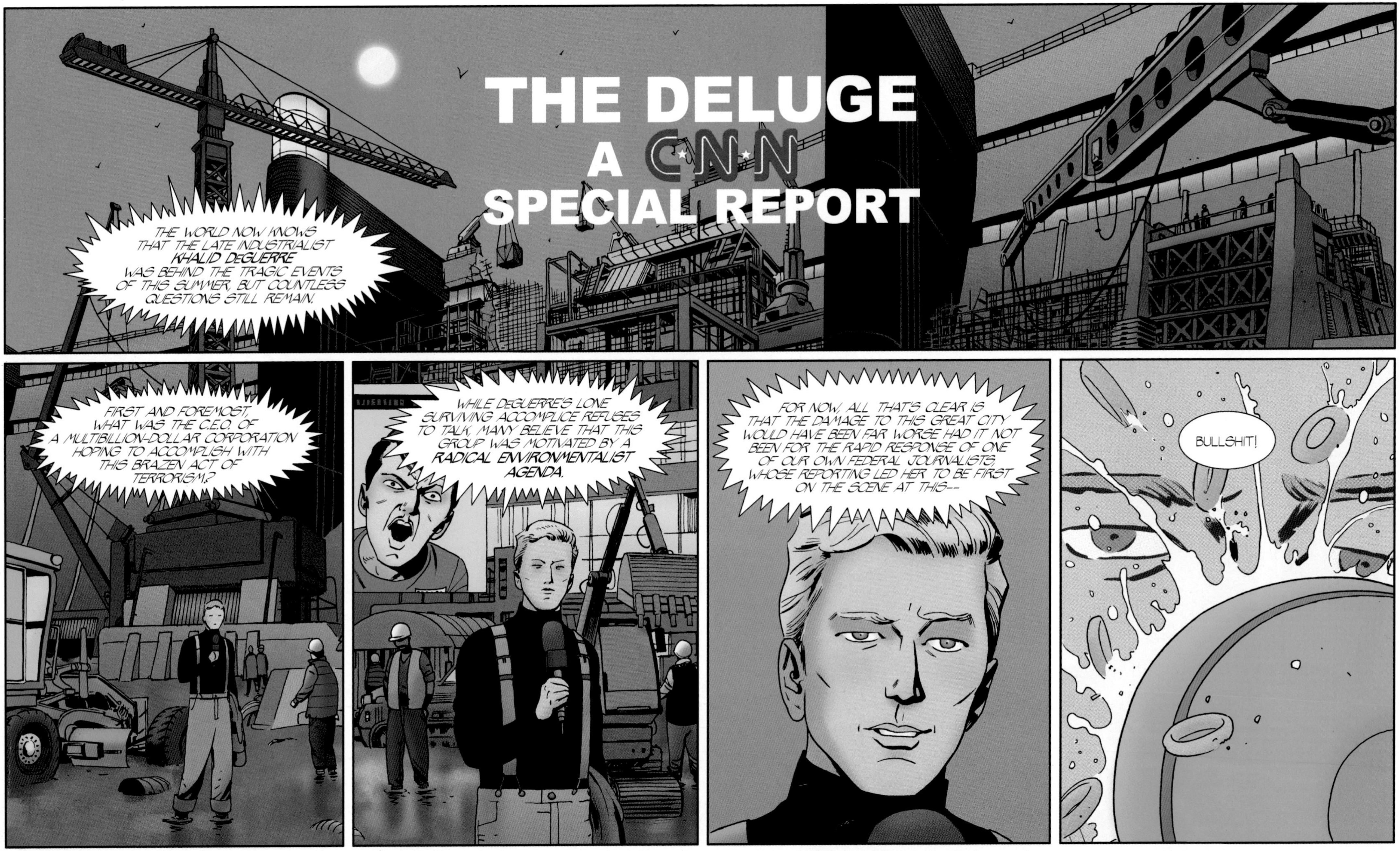
THE DELUGE
A CNN SPECIAL REPORT
THE WORLD NOW KNOWS THAT THE LATE INDUSTRIALIST KHALID DeGUERRE WAS BEHIND THE TRAGIC EVENTS OF THIS SUMMER, BUT COUNTLESS QUESTIONS STILL REMAIN.
FIRST AND FOREMOST, WHAT WAS THE C.E.O. OF A MULTIBILLION-DOLLAR CORPORATION HOPING TO ACCOMPLISH WITH THIS BRAZEN ACT OF TERRORISM?
WHILE DeGUERRE'S LONE SURVIVING ACCOMPLICE REFUSES TO TALK, MANY BELIEVE THAT THIS GROUP WAS MOTIVATED BY A RADICAL ENVIRONMENTALIST AGENDA.
FOR NOW, ALL THAT'S CLEAR IS THAT THE DAMAGE TO THIS GREAT CITY WOULD HAVE BEEN FAR WORSE HAD IT NOT BEEN FOR THE RAPID RESPONSE OF ONE OF OUR OWN FEDERAL JOURNALISTS, WHOSE REPORTING LED HER TO BE FIRST ON THE SCENE AT THIS--
BULLSHIT!

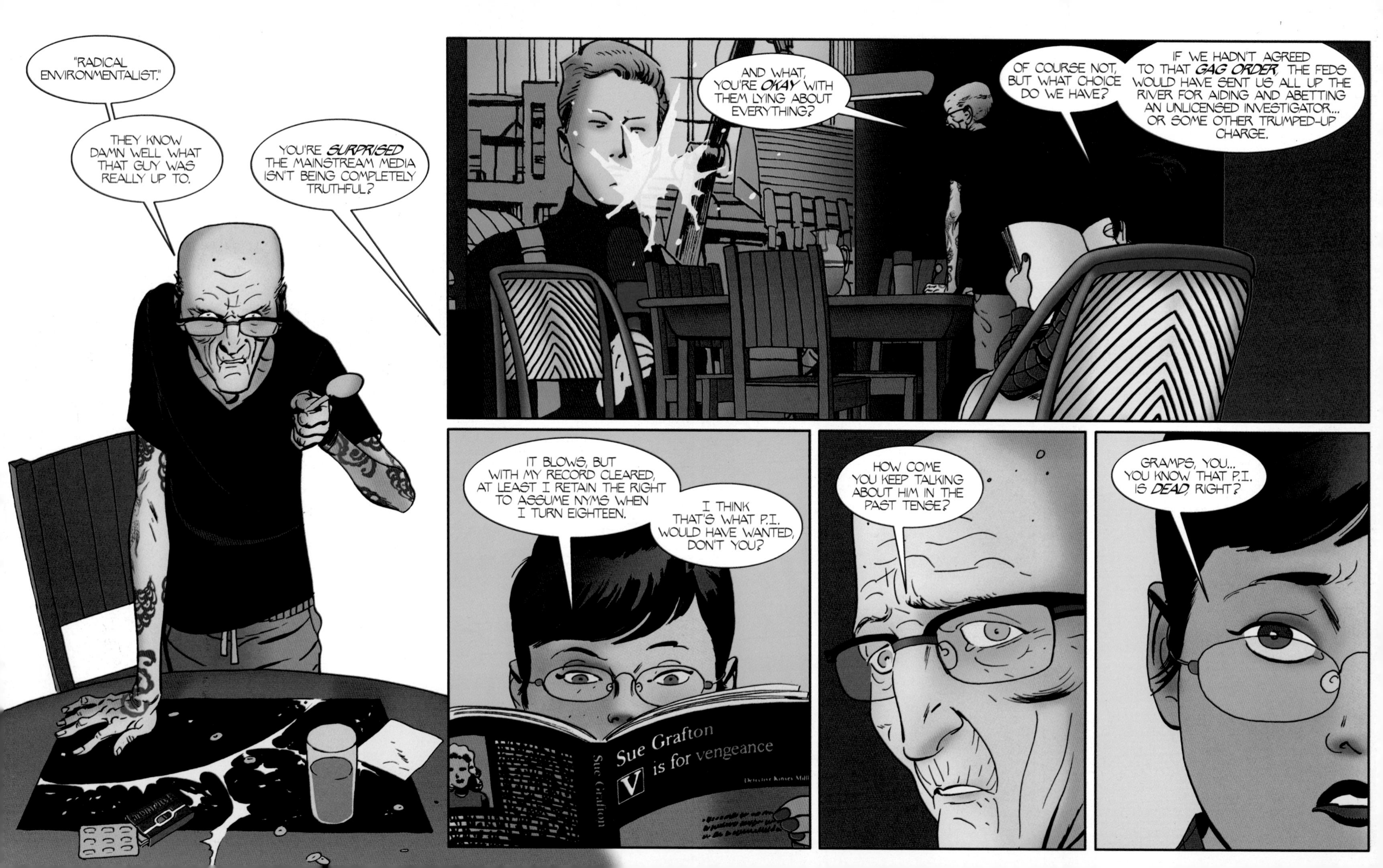
"RADICAL ENVIRONMENTALIST."
THEY KNOW DAMN WELL WHAT THAT GUY WAS REALLY UP TO.
YOU'RE SURPRISED THE MAINSTREAM MEDIA ISN'T BEING COMPLETELY TRUTHFUL?
AND WHAT, YOU'RE OKAY WITH THEM LYING ABOUT EVERYTHING?
OF COURSE NOT, BUT WHAT CHOICE DO WE HAVE?
IF WE HADN'T AGREED TO THAT GAG ORDER, THE FEDS WOULD HAVE SENT US ALL UP THE RIVER FOR AIDING AND ABETTING AN UNLICENSED INVESTIGATOR... OR SOME OTHER TRUMPED-UP CHARGE.
IT BLOWS, BUT WITH MY RECORD CLEARED, AT LEAST I RETAIN THE RIGHT TO ASSUME NYMS WHEN I TURN EIGHTEEN.
I THINK THAT'S WHAT P.I. WOULD HAVE WANTED, DON'T YOU?
Sue Grafton
V is for vengeance
Sue Grafton
HOW COME YOU KEEP TALKING ABOUT HIM IN THE PAST TENSE?
GRAMPS, YOU... YOU KNOW THAT P.I. IS DEAD, RIGHT?

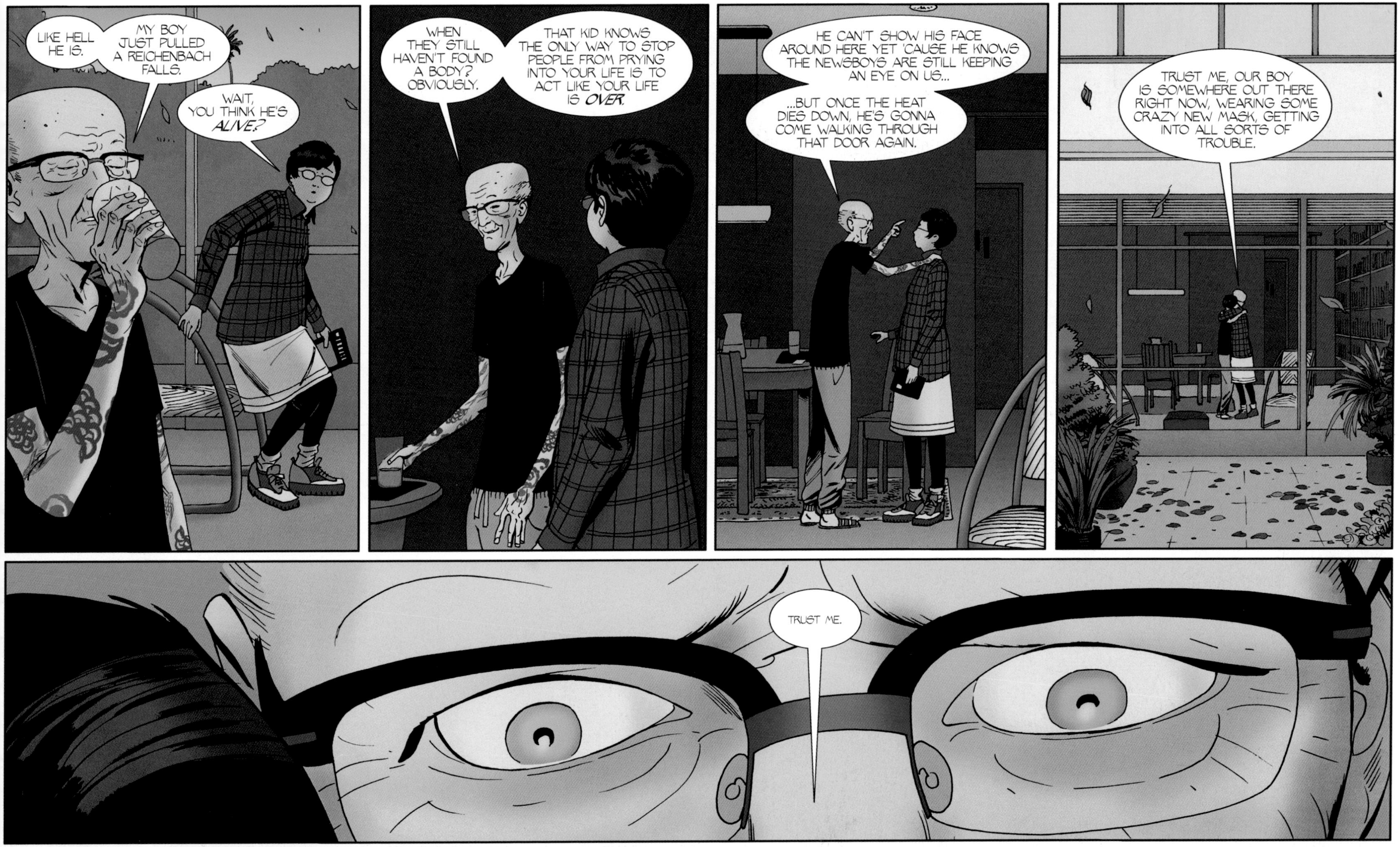
LIKE HELL HE IS.
MY BOY JUST PULLED A REICHENBACH FALLS.
WAIT, YOU THINK HE'S *ALIVE?*
WHEN THEY STILL HAVEN'T FOUND A BODY? OBVIOUSLY.
THAT KID KNOWS THE ONLY WAY TO STOP PEOPLE FROM PRYING INTO YOUR LIFE IS TO ACT LIKE YOUR LIFE IS *OVER.*
HE CAN'T SHOW HIS FACE AROUND HERE YET 'CAUSE HE KNOWS THE NEWSBOYS ARE STILL KEEPING AN EYE ON US...
...BUT ONCE THE HEAT DIES DOWN, HE'S GONNA COME WALKING THROUGH THAT DOOR AGAIN.
TRUST ME, OUR BOY IS SOMEWHERE OUT THERE RIGHT NOW, WEARING SOME CRAZY NEW MASK, GETTING INTO ALL SORTS OF TROUBLE.
TRUST ME.

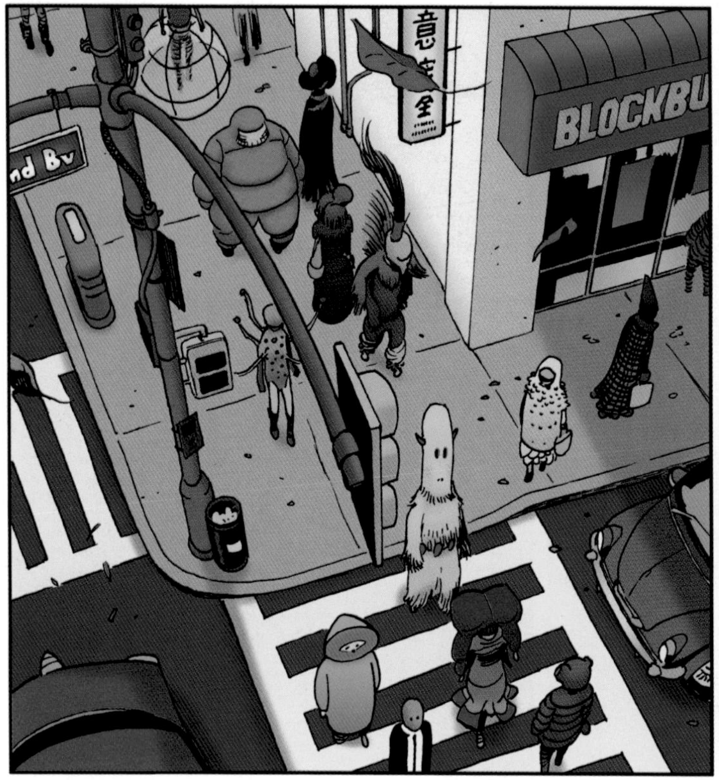
nd Bv
BLOCKBU

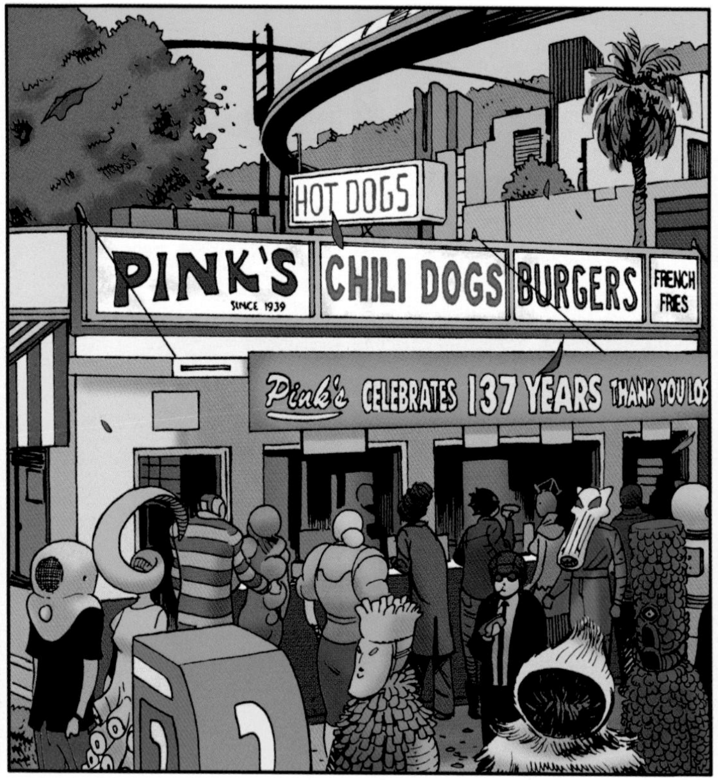
HOT DOGS
PINK'S
SINCE 1939
CHILI DOGS
BURGERS
FRENCH FRIES
Pink's CELEBRATES 137 YEARS THANK YOU LOS

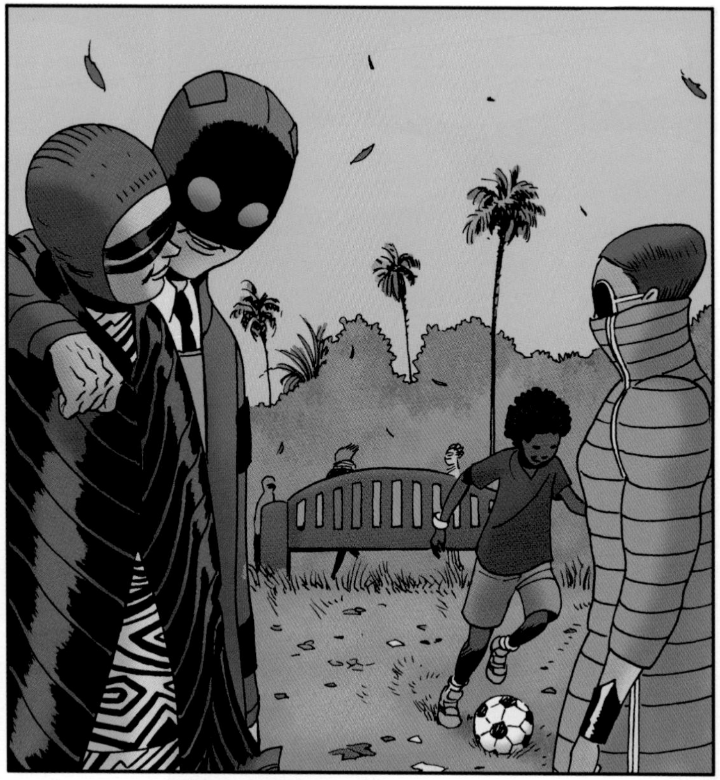

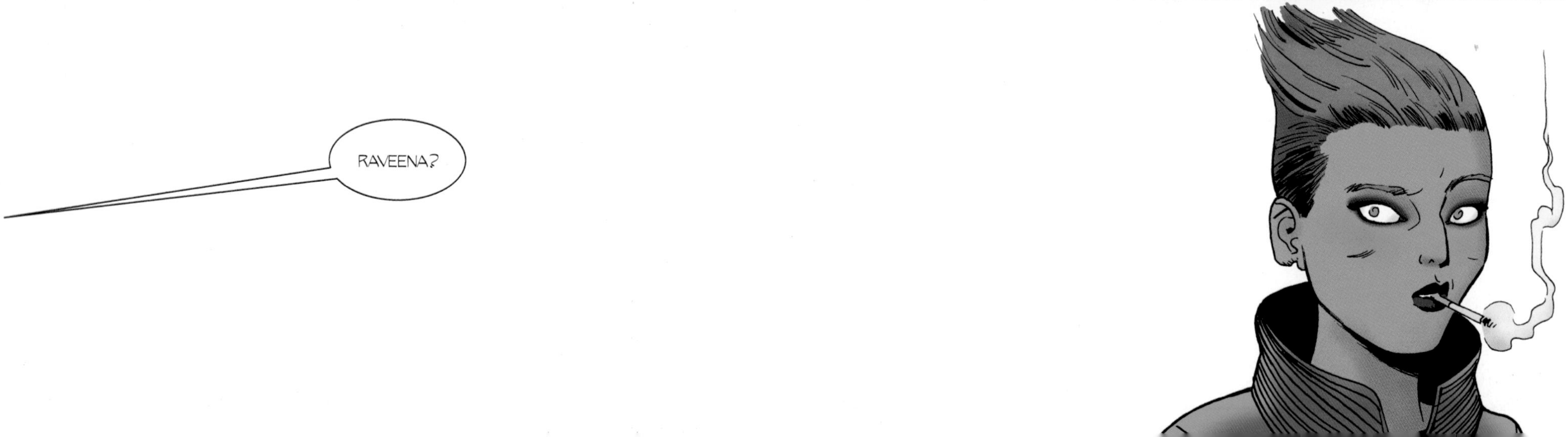
RAVEENA?

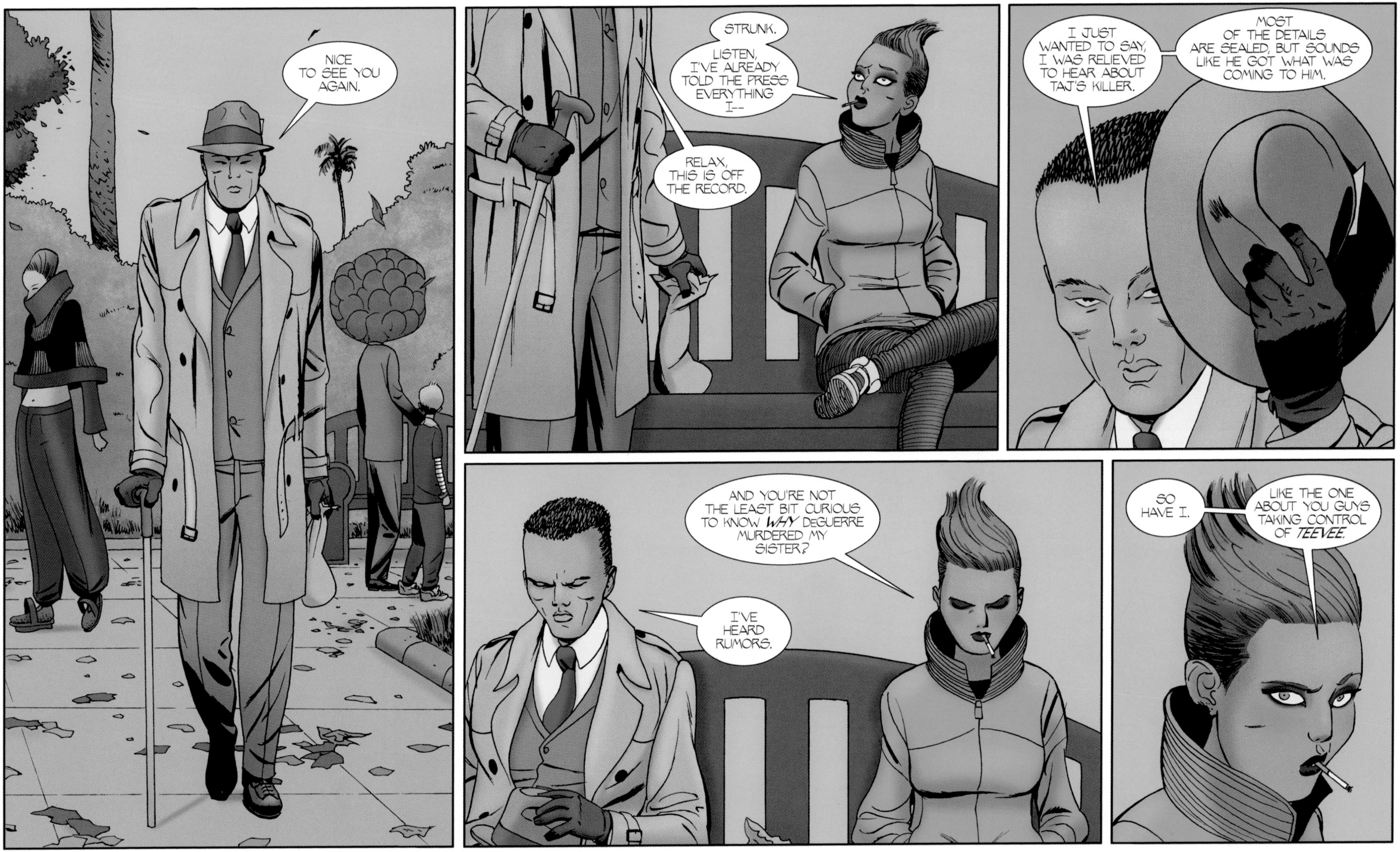
NICE TO SEE YOU AGAIN.
STRUNK.
LISTEN, I'VE ALREADY TOLD THE PRESS EVERYTHING I--
RELAX, THIS IS OFF THE RECORD.
I JUST WANTED TO SAY, I WAS RELIEVED TO HEAR ABOUT TAJ'S KILLER.
MOST OF THE DETAILS ARE SEALED, BUT SOUNDS LIKE HE GOT WHAT WAS COMING TO HIM.
AND YOU'RE NOT THE LEAST BIT CURIOUS TO KNOW *WHY* DEGUERRE MURDERED MY SISTER?
I'VE HEARD RUMORS.
SO HAVE I.
LIKE THE ONE ABOUT YOU GUYS TAKING CONTROL OF *TEEVEE*.

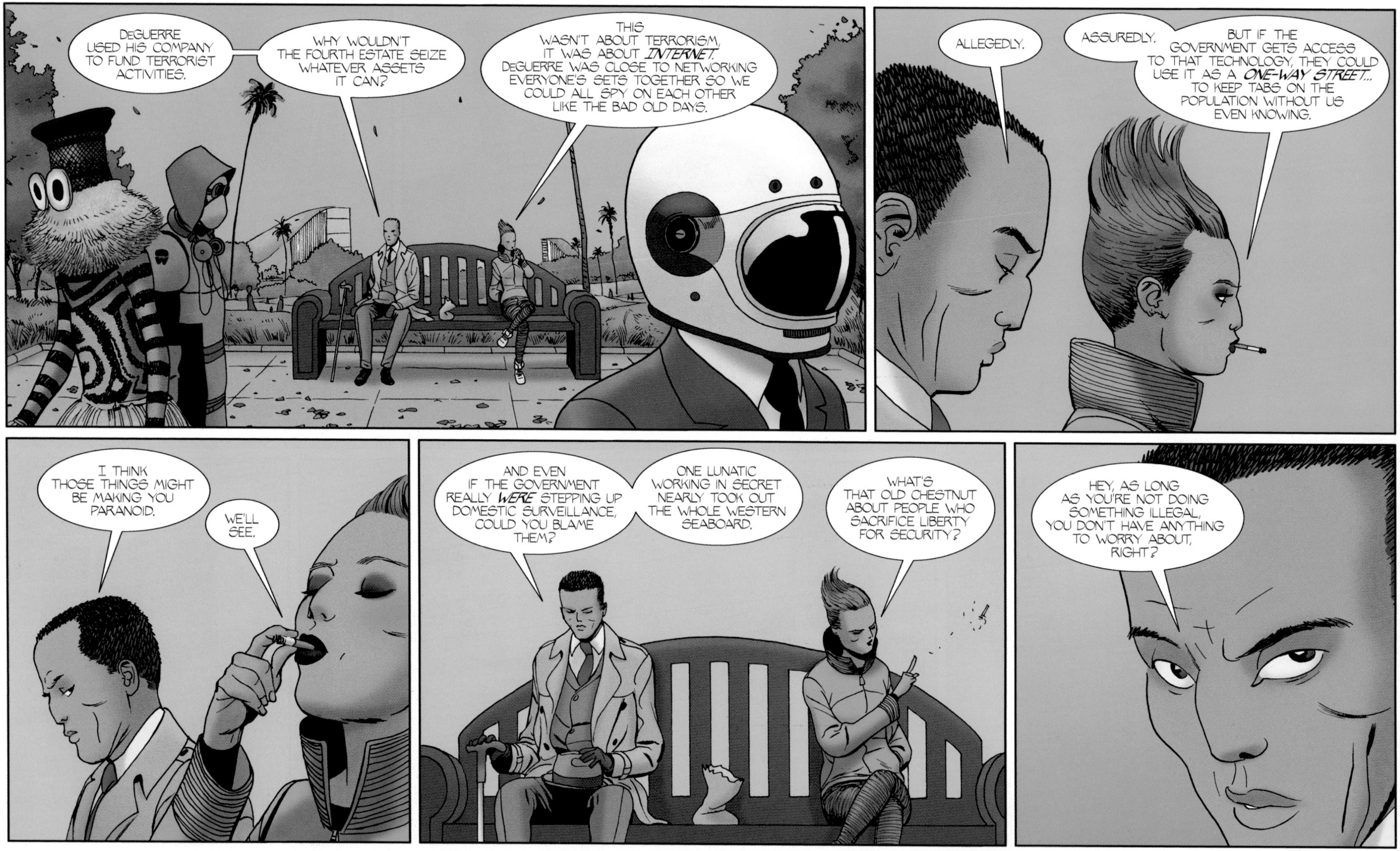
DeGUERRE USED HIS COMPANY TO FUND TERRORIST ACTIVITIES.
WHY WOULDN'T THE FOURTH ESTATE SEIZE WHATEVER ASSETS IT CAN?
THIS WASN'T ABOUT TERRORISM, IT WAS ABOUT *INTERNET.* DeGUERRE WAS CLOSE TO NETWORKING EVERYONE'S SETS TOGETHER SO WE COULD ALL SPY ON EACH OTHER LIKE THE BAD OLD DAYS.
ALLEGEDLY.
ASSUREDLY.
BUT IF THE GOVERNMENT GETS ACCESS TO THAT TECHNOLOGY, THEY COULD USE IT AS A *ONE-WAY STREET...* TO KEEP TABS ON THE POPULATION WITHOUT US EVEN KNOWING.
I THINK THOSE THINGS MIGHT BE MAKING YOU PARANOID.
WE'LL SEE.
AND EVEN IF THE GOVERNMENT REALLY *WERE* STEPPING UP DOMESTIC SURVEILLANCE, COULD YOU BLAME THEM?
ONE LUNATIC WORKING IN SECRET NEARLY TOOK OUT THE WHOLE WESTERN SEABOARD.
WHAT'S THAT OLD CHESTNUT ABOUT PEOPLE WHO SACRIFICE LIBERTY FOR SECURITY?
HEY, AS LONG AS YOU'RE NOT DOING SOMETHING ILLEGAL, YOU DON'T HAVE ANYTHING TO WORRY ABOUT, RIGHT?

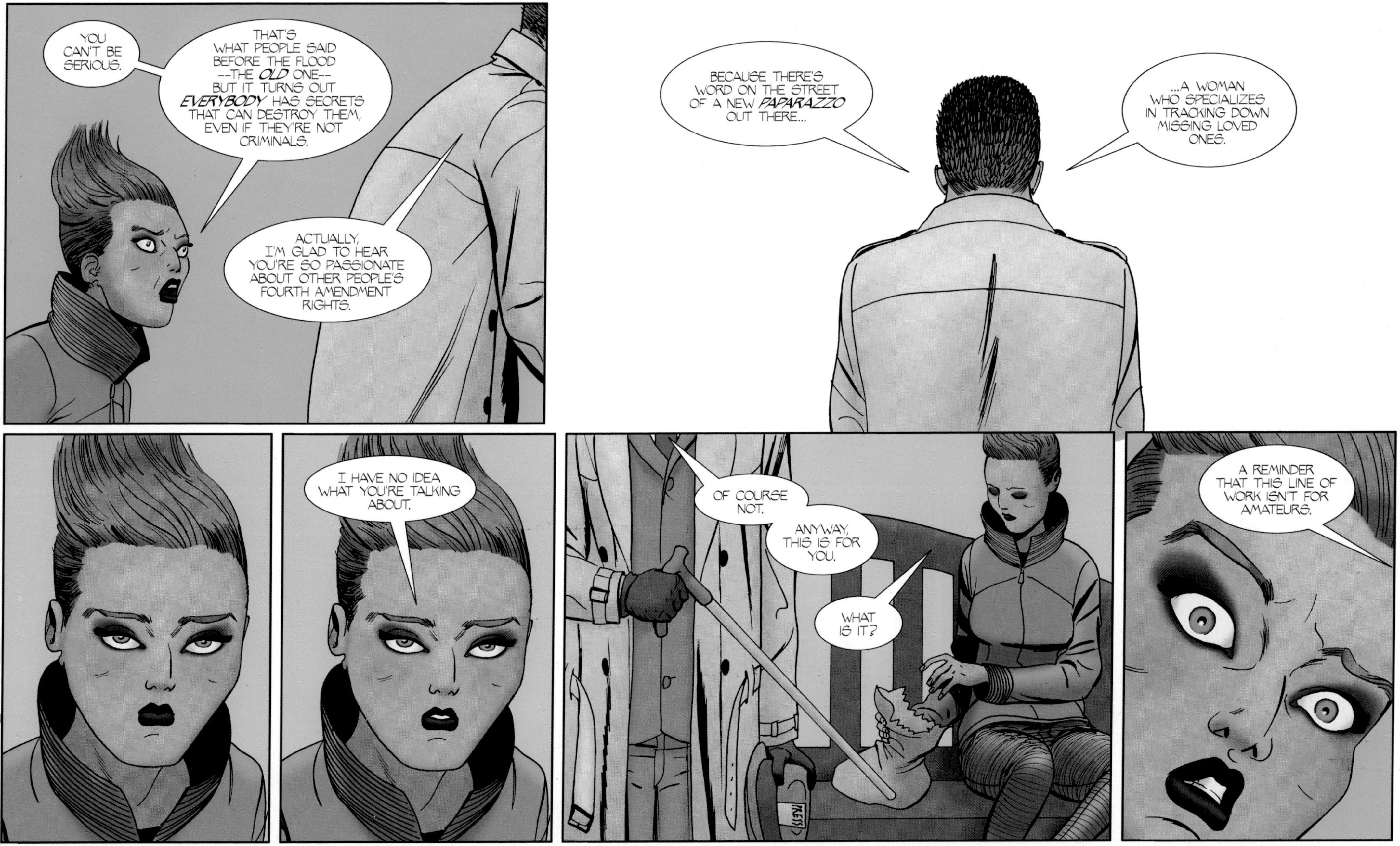
YOU CAN'T BE SERIOUS.
THAT'S WHAT PEOPLE SAID BEFORE THE FLOOD --THE OLD ONE-- BUT IT TURNS OUT EVERYBODY HAS SECRETS THAT CAN DESTROY THEM, EVEN IF THEY'RE NOT CRIMINALS.
ACTUALLY, I'M GLAD TO HEAR YOU'RE SO PASSIONATE ABOUT OTHER PEOPLE'S FOURTH AMENDMENT RIGHTS.
BECAUSE THERE'S WORD ON THE STREET OF A NEW PAPARAZZO OUT THERE...
...A WOMAN WHO SPECIALIZES IN TRACKING DOWN MISSING LOVED ONES.
I HAVE NO IDEA WHAT YOU'RE TALKING ABOUT.
OF COURSE NOT.
ANYWAY, THIS IS FOR YOU.
WHAT IS IT?
A REMINDER THAT THIS LINE OF WORK ISN'T FOR AMATEURS.

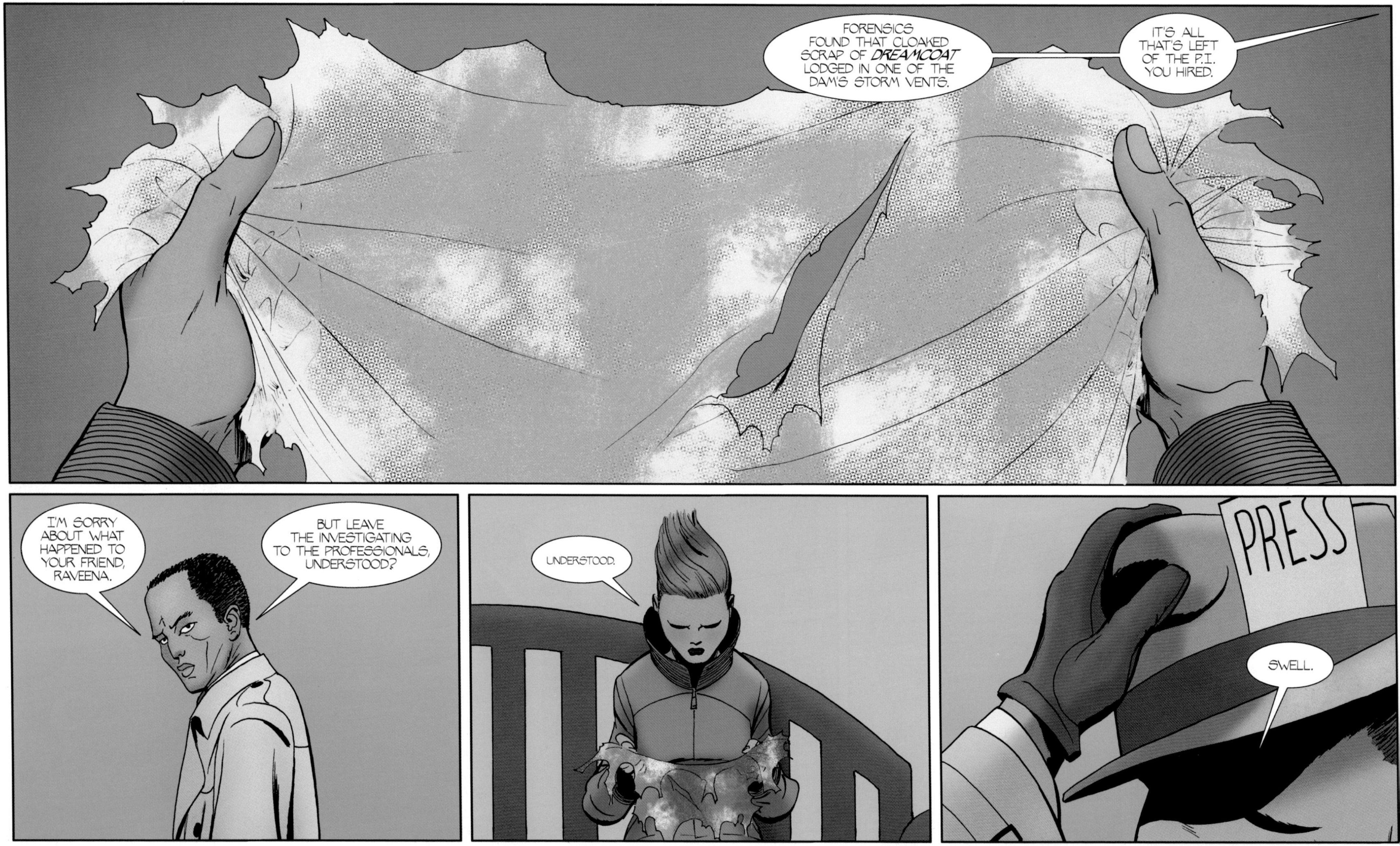
FORENSICS FOUND THAT CLOAKED SCRAP OF DREAMCOAT LODGED IN ONE OF THE DAM'S STORM VENTS.
IT'S ALL THAT'S LEFT OF THE P.I. YOU HIRED.
I'M SORRY ABOUT WHAT HAPPENED TO YOUR FRIEND, RAVEENA.
BUT LEAVE THE INVESTIGATING TO THE PROFESSIONALS, UNDERSTOOD?
UNDERSTOOD.
PRESS
SWELL.

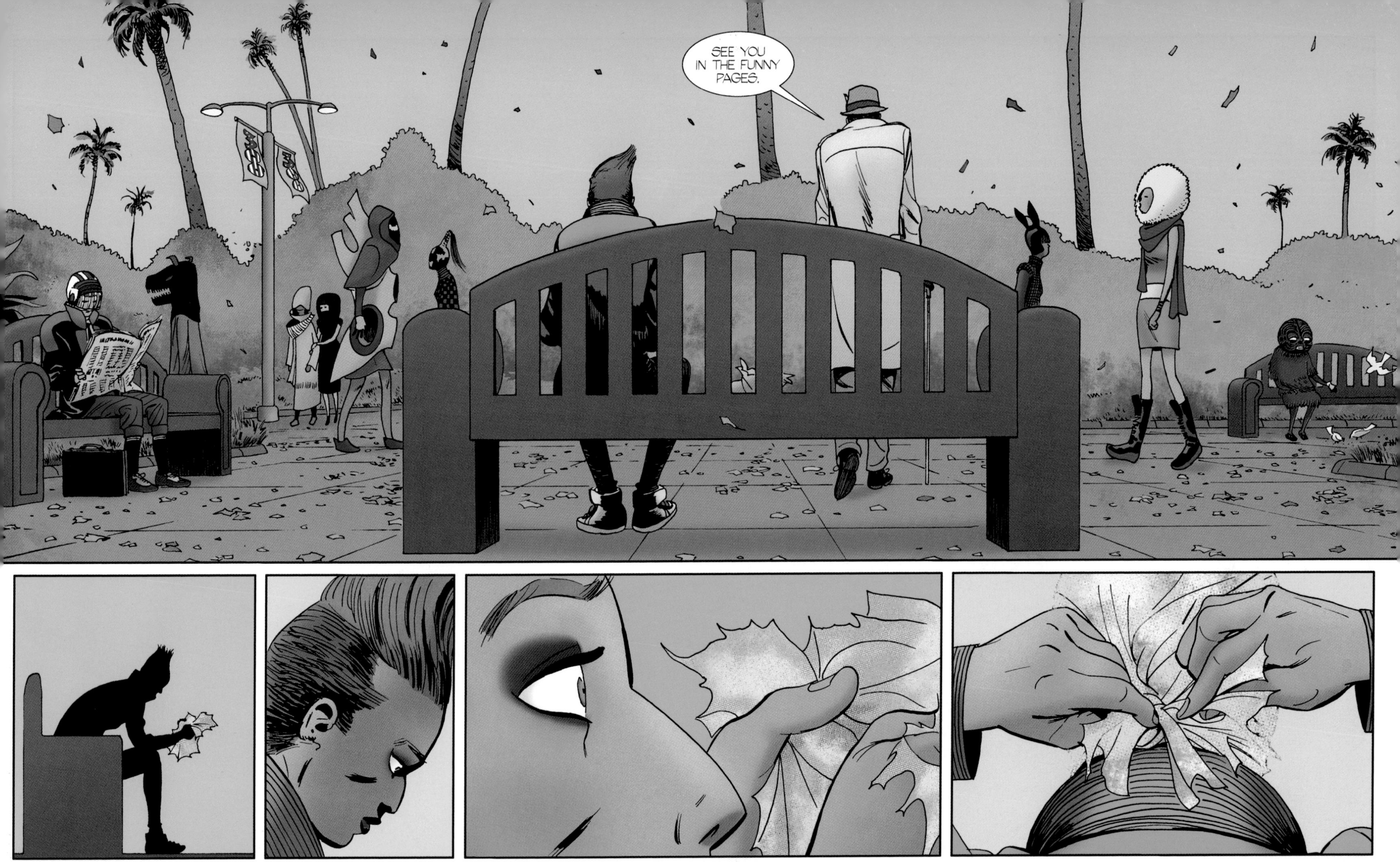
SEE YOU IN THE FUNNY PAGES.

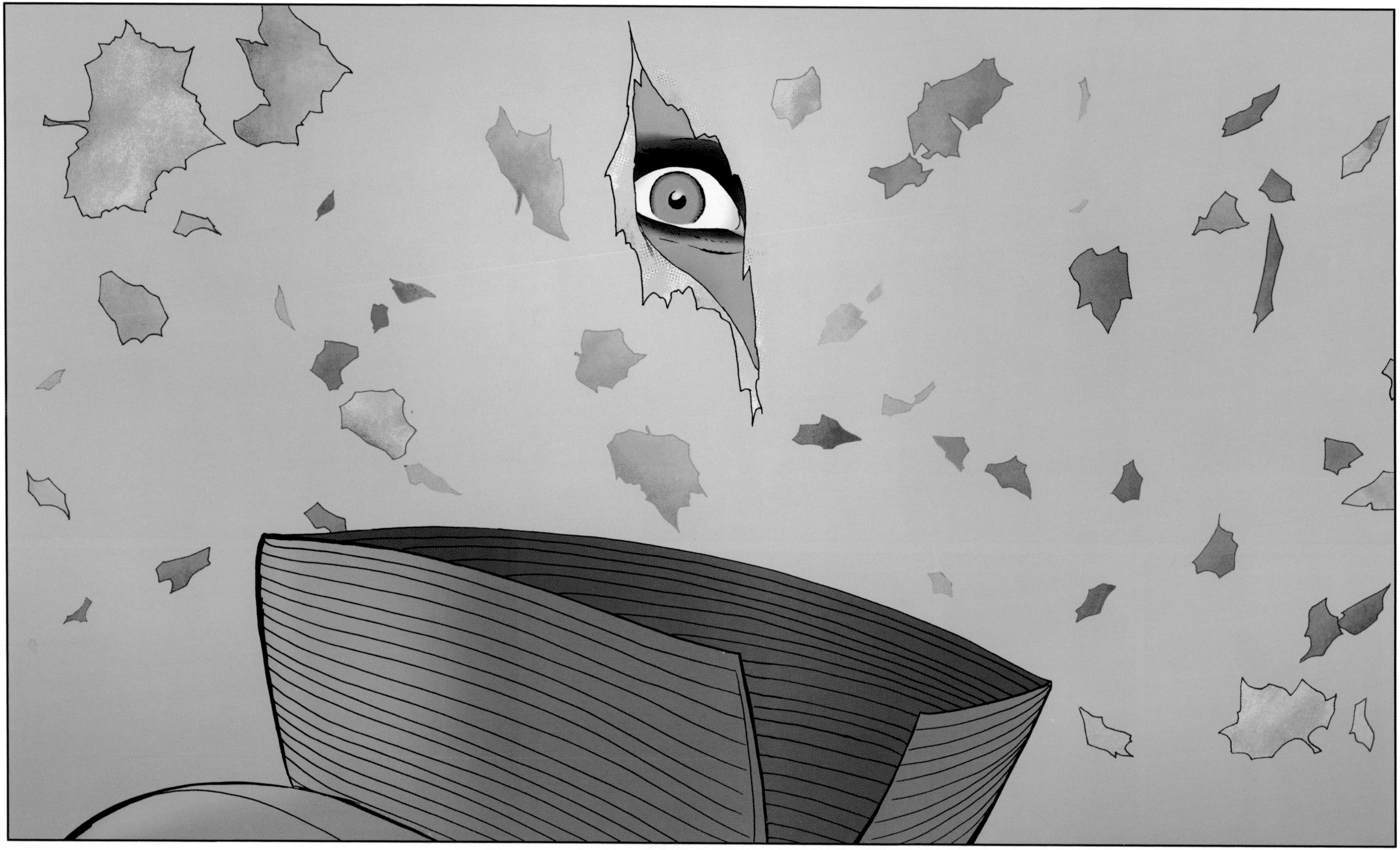

THE PRIVATE EYE

BRIAN K. VAUGHAN   MARCOS MARTIN

WITH

MUNTSA VICENTE

THE BIRTH OF PANEL SYNDICATE & THE PRIVATE EYE

When I told Marcos I was thinking about a comic set in a futuristic United States that no longer used the internet, his first suggestion was that we should make the story exclusively available online.

This is what it's like collaborating with Marcos Martin.

I first met Marcos and his stunningly talented better half Muntsa way back in the 20th century, when they were crashing around the corner from my old studio apartment on 10th Street in Manhattan. From the beginning, it was clear that Marcos--along with being one of the best artists in the history of comics--was also a grumpy, stubborn contrarian.

We got along fucking great.

Marcos and I worked on some fun projects at DC and Marvel, but we always wanted to do something much more independently, with as little interference as possible between readers and creators.

I will always love print comics--their look, their feel, their *smell*--but I was intrigued by Marcos' idea of a place where we could offer our new work to readers around the world the second it was finished, DRM-free, in multiple languages, for whatever price each reader thought was fair (including nothing!).

Marcos has always said that comics used to be an affordable medium for everyone, but it's instead become a very expensive hobby for a few relatively affluent fans. He believed that we could use the internet to help reverse that… and so, PanelSyndicate.com was born.

I was 100% confident that this experiment would lead to financial ruin for everyone involved, but against all odds, the site was a massive success from the day we went live, and even more unbelievably, readers continued to show up for the duration of our entire series, graciously paying what they could each and every chapter.

Our dream was just to be able to tell P.I.'s entire ten-part story, but our *secret* dream was that Panel Syndicate might eventually be able to expand beyond us, hosting work from other creators. That's already started with renowned Spanish cartoonist Albert Monteys, whose hilarious/traumatizing UNIVERSE! is available right now, and Marcos and I are hard at work at our own new project, which you should be able to find at PanelSyndicate.com right this second if everything has gone according to plan.

For now, Marcos came up with the horrible idea of voluntarily violating our own privacy with the following collection of "leaked" emails and other behind-the-scenes material. We hope you'll enjoy this warts-and-all look at how an original comic like *The Private Eye* (which you'll see went through about a dozen different working titles) actually comes into existence. And if you're really into "sausage making," you can find even more exclusive sketches and extras in our "Making Of" issue, also available at Panelsyndicate.com.

Thanks so much to Eric Stephenson, Robert Kirkman, and all of our friends at Image Comics for making this long-requested print edition of our story a reality. If this was your first time reading *The Private Eye* and you'd like to share your thoughts with us, you can always reach Marcos and me through the helpful contact link at PanelSyndicate.com, but we may print your email in a future edition, so please let us know if it's okay to use your real name.

Your privacy is important to us.

Confidentially,
BKV
Somewhere in California
September, 2015

From: Brian K. Vaughan
Re: Hola!
Date: July 2nd 2011 02:16:20 GMT+02:00

Great to hear from you, especially because I just today finally finished the attached document for SECRET SOCIETY! It's more a loose collection of my rambling thoughts than an official pitch, but it'll hopefully give you a slightly better idea what I'm thinking about. The document is long and boring, but I promise the comic would be fast-paced and fun. And every day it seems like I read another privacy-related story in the paper, so the subject matter feels especially topical.
Anyway, curious to hear your thoughts, but obviously take your time reading it, Pops. I bet you almost forgot how rough these first couple of sleepless nights can be, huh?

From: Marcos Martín
Re: Hola!
Date: July 2nd 2011 21:37:53 GMT+02:00

Brian,

I was excited about the project but after reading the pitch I can only say: FUCK YEAH!
This just sounds fantastic to me. I've got a few thoughts but it'll probably be better to discuss them over the phone when you have the time (sorry, it just takes me forever to sit down and type anything coherent). For example, I have a completely crazy idea about format that I know you'll hate but that I'd like to share anyway. But I really can't express how incredibly excited I am right now. And you've given me enough info to start working on some more specific visuals.

From: Brian K. Vaughan
Re: Hola!
Date: July 6th 2011 01:36:39 GMT+02:00

Whew! Very excited you dug it. And yes, I'm not married to anything in that document, so eager to hear any/all ideas, especially about format.

SECRET SOCIETY

A brief summary by Brian K. Vaughan
for Marcos Martin
June 20, 2011

The Premise

In the not-too-distant future, everyone will have a secret identity.

The Theme

This is a story about **privacy**, and whether our generation's ongoing campaign against it will ultimately be good or bad for society. I don't know the answer to that yet, so I want to make a comic to find out.

The Tone

Futuristic noir, but more bright and poppy than the dreary dystopia of *Blade Runner*. And while there are masks and even some colorful costumes in our world, there are no mythical super-powers, just plausible (though fun and wildly imaginative!) science fiction. It's a cool mystery with action, sex, and some two-fisted social commentary.

The Backstory

Once upon a time, Americans trusted their most precious information to something called the Cloud. And whether or not they knew it, this Cloud also contained detailed information about their darkest secrets and most hidden desires.

Then, one day, the Cloud burst.

No one knew if it was an accident or a declaration of war or an act of God, but for forty days and forty nights, the Cloud rained down its entire contents across the country. The ensuing flood hurt everyone. Digital assets were completely wiped out and vast online libraries were lost forever, but it was the slow and steady leak of individuals' personal information that destroyed the most lives.

If our parents had feared Big Brother, we had *become* him, a generation of exhibitionists willfully sharing every detail of our private lives with each other. But the Great Flood revealed that we were all only ever sharing one *version* of ourselves, a fantasy as ethereal as the Cloud itself. Hoisted by our own petard, the network we created to preserve and share our daily triumphs also remembered and revealed our worst failings.

Like a WikiLeaks dump on humanity itself, all of our medical records, credit card bills, email accounts, financial passwords, high school transcripts, political donations, cell phone messages, GPS-tracked movements, Facebook photos, anonymous Amazon reviews, online search histories, embarrassing playlists, tax returns, half-finished novels, abandoned Photoshop projects, Twitter direct messages, dating site profiles, sex tapes, angry message board posts, Craigslist ads, and pathetic late-night drunk texts to your ex-girlfriend were all instantly available to anyone and everyone -- employers, neighbors, loved ones, or just curious strangers.

Careers were lost, reputations were ruined, friendships were ended, and families were scarred forever.

Forty days later, the Great Flood finally ended, and those left standing knew that it was time to rebuild. Things could never again be like they were, and maybe that was okay.

The Cloud was gone, but for the first time in a long time, people could see the sky.

Our Brave New World

Our story takes place in 2076, several decades after the Great Flood. The setting is LOS ANGELES, a city that's always had a complex relationship with both celebrity and secrecy.

If Freedom is my country's current love affair, I think her next obsession will be her old flame Privacy, specifically the Fourth Amendment's guarantee of "the right of the people to be secure in their persons, houses, papers and effects against unreasonable searches and seizures."

Former Google CEO Eric Schmidt once said (jokingly?), *"Every young person one day will be entitled automatically to change his or her name on reaching adulthood in order to disown youthful hijinks stored on their friends' social media sites."*

But what if a single name change were only the beginning? What if, just like women in some fundamentalist Islamic societies donning burqas before leaving the house, nearly every adult American put on some form of DISGUISE before stepping outside. But unlike burqas, these masked costumes are extremely varied, ranging from drab and conservative to vibrant and hyper-sexual. Everyone has at least one, most have many.

In short, Americans are now allowed to safely and anonymously explore new ideas and new identities in the REAL WORLD, in the same way we could *online* way back in 2011.

Every part of daily life is now focused towards discretion, with most commuters slipping out of their underground garages in nondescript cars with tinted black windows. While workers normally "unmask" once they're at the office with their trusted colleagues, they each slip back into one of their multiple secret identities as they leave work separately in private elevators.

What you do outside of your place of business is no longer your *employer's* business.

And because the internet no longer exists and all of its precious contents were lost, there's a renewed interest in the beauty and permanence of physical objects like books and records and buildings. Digital communication is no longer trusted, so we're back to the good-old days of Clark Kent-style PHONE BOOTHS and old-school PNEUMATIC TUBES delivering flash-paper messages that are burned after reading.

As a matter of fact, without an internet, the world has become a *literal* "series of tubes," with futuristic automobiles traveling through transparent tunnels that now crisscross high above the city, ultra-overpasses connecting the diverse neighborhoods of Los Angeles like never before.

With the end of the virtual world, engineers have stopped building websites, and started once again making THINGS. Untethered from the glowing screens that turned their visions inwards, inventors started looking at new ways to transform the world around them, and a revived industrial workforce eventually erected the kind of retro-futuristic wonderland that guys like Walt Disney always dreamed of.

Masked citizens regularly sample new political meetings, cultural events, sex clubs, and places of worship, no longer afraid of being judged by their community. Some alternate identities are revealed to like-minded friends, while others are kept even from significant others. Rather than destroying marriage, this new union of liberty and discretion has only strengthened the institution, bringing divorce rates to new lows.

Actors, professional athletes, and other celebrities can now don masks and freely interact with the rest of the world, famous only for their achievements, not the mundanely sordid details of their private lives.

Still, because there are times when people legitimately need to be investigated, the most powerful law enforcement agents are now JOURNALISTS, federal operatives who work for a new independent and citizen-reviewed branch of government called The Fourth Estate.

In the future, not every kid with a blog gets to be a reporter. Journalists are all highly trained men and women, who use their skills, sidearms and search warrants to inform and protect the citizenry. But because of their added powers and responsibilities, journalists--like other elected officials--aren't allowed to wear masks, only dark sunglasses and old-school fedoras clearly identifying them as "PRESS."

Beyond the daily papers provided by The Fourth Estate, when citizens need fast, free and accurate information, they turn to LIBRARIANS, whose places of work are now treated like temples.

Librarians are the rock stars of our future, wildly talented professionals with sex appeal and a high-paying, highly coveted gig. Reliable and trustworthy, Librarians will discreetly help you find exactly what you're looking for... as long as it's safe, legal and doesn't infringe on the privacy of others.

The "Hero"

But what if you want to know what happened to that high school sweetheart who's not listed in the Yellow Pages? Or if you're just curious about whether or not your favorite movie star is gay? What if you're worried your child's teacher used to be a porn star?

That's when you turn to the gray market and hire a member of the PAPARAZZI, unlicensed private investigators willing to get you sensitive information by any means necessary... for a price.

Our protagonist is a twenty-something paparazzo who goes by the initials **P.I.** (he even uses the "π" symbol for *pi* on his cryptic business cards). Like most Americans in the year 2076, P.I. is multi-racial, a mix of Black and Irish and Spanish.

Usually sporting a Ninja Turtles-style eyemask tied around his head, I imagine P.I. also wearing a hooded poncho called a DREAMCOAT, only a slightly more advanced version of these early crappy Japanese "invisibility cloaks": http://www.cuteandweird.com/2010/01/photos-invisibility-cloak-coat-makes-you-invisible/

While it doesn't actually make you invisible, the coat's optics constantly match its wearer's surroundings, helping them to always blend in to the background and never stand out. This, and the fact that lots of other Angelenos wear this exact same brand of "urban camouflage," makes it easy for P.I. to stay lost in a crowd.

P.I.'s main weapon is his old school Nikon film camera, which he uses to secretly snap candid photos of misbehaving workers, long-lost relatives, potential suitors, etc. He doesn't carry a gun, but because P.I. has a vast network of clients across Los Angeles who owe him favors, it wouldn't be hard for him to get one.

Unlike some of his more radical peers, P.I. isn't ideologically opposed to America's new obsession with privacy. He's just a a benevolent opportunist who gets off knowing things he's not supposed to know. If you've got enough cash, he'll get you your story, whether it's an easy "puff piece" or a more challenging "hatchet job."

When we first meet him, P.I. is essentially amoral, happy to switch ethics with each new outfit. That all begins to change the night a **FEMME FATALE** walks through his door wearing a tight black dress and the kind of ANIMATRONIC ANIMAL MASK that only the super-wealthy can afford...

The Case

"I want you to find out everything you can about someone," the masked woman tells P.I.

"Who?"

Lighting a cigarette, she replies, "<u>Me</u>."

The alluring woman explains that she's just applied for one of the few occupations that still requires a background check (making P.I. suspect she might be *military*). Our femme fatale is pretty sure she's covered her tracks from some "youthful indiscretions," but if there's any dirt to be found, she wants P.I. to get to it before her potential employers do.

P.I. agrees to take the case, and a voyeuristic investigation begins. But when this masked woman eventually DISAPPEARS, our hero will be dragged into a massive conspiracy that reaches to the highest levels of government, and threatens to alter society even more permanently than the Great Flood.

Lots of bullets, fishnet stockings and rooftop chases ensue.

Other Characters

CATHERINE WHEEL: Taking her new name from the medieval torture device used to kill Saint Catherine (patron saint of librarians), Catherine Wheel works for a large Public Library in the San Fernando Valley. P.I. is obsessed with this alluring librarian, but the openly gay Catherine doesn't swing his way. Still, she likes this strange guy who occasionally offers her cigarettes on her walk home. Normally a by-the-books professional, Catherine sometimes slips her friend snippets of information, even though P.I.'s library card was revoked years ago. Every librarian has to be naughty sometime.

THE OLD MAN: P.I. was raised by his Irish grandfather, a 90-something-year-old man who currently resides in a skyscraper-like nursing facility for the scores of elderly living in Los Angeles. The last of the Facebook generation, the Old Man is an ancient hipster with rusted piercings and faded tattoos. Addled by the long-term effects of a lifetime of attention deficit disorder drugs, he still clutches a Blackberry that hasn't been networked in ages. Refusing to ever wear a goddamn mask, the Old Man loves to regale his loyal grandson with tales from the long-gone days of the Information Age.

DEPUTY EDITOR STRUNK: A high-ranking journalist in The Fourth Estate, Strunk is a straight-laced older male investigator obsessed with apprehending and unmasking the unlicensed P.I. Strunk is an expert marksman and an even better typist.

CLIENT IX: P.I. is kept on retainer by several repeat customers, including Client IX, an overweight masked Malibu millionaire who is obsessed with knowing how much other neighboring millionaires paid for their homes/weddings/etc. In exchange for this info, the heavyset Client IX often gives P.I. tools and resources to use on other cases.

MELANIE: Only sixteen years old, Melanie isn't yet old enough to legally wear a mask (a right granted at the age of 18), but she can drive a car, something the teen often does for P.I. (who's too paranoid to have his real photo taken for a driver's license). Acting as his personal chauffeur in exchange for gas money, Melanie also provides her boss with inside information about the secretive world inside Los Angeles' very private public schools.

THE FOREIGNERS: Gas masks are a relatively common fashion accessory in 2076, but P.I. thinks there's something particularly strange about the men wearing old Russian gas masks he keeps running into following the Femme Fatale's disappearance. It's their whispered voices... it sounds like they have *accents*. As we'll learn, one of the Secret Society's dirty secrets is that it's also a very *closed* society, one that's less welcoming to immigrants than at almost any other time in America's often dark history. Still, P.I. is unsure if these strange visitors are enemies or potential assets...

The Format

What do you feel up to, Marcos? I'd love to swing for the fences with a cool maxi-series (maybe even a full twelve issues?), a rich, epic, dramatically satisfying mystery that could eventually be collected into one beautiful hardcover.

The End

Whew. So those are my initial ramblings. I have lots more ideas, but I wanted to see if you sparked to any of this craziness before I got too far ahead of myself. If you're up for it, I think I could write you some very detailed scripts that would still give you a lot of freedom to build this world and design these characters and tell this story exactly the way you want to, as only you and your ridiculous artistic talents can.

There are no guarantees in this marketplace, obviously, but I think this is the kind of topical big idea that will have a lot of resonance with mainstream audiences, but it's also got enough cool genre trappings to appeal to more traditional comics readers. Anyway, I think it'd be a hit.

More importantly, I think we'd make a great book, one that we'd both be proud to have on the shelves of our quaint new homes in France, where we and our families can retire like R. Crumb after our oversized *Secret Society* albums become beloved bestsellers there.

What do you think?

From: Brian K. Vaughan
Re: Project poverty
Date: September 13th 2011 18:07:52 GMT+02:00

1) Seriously, how long are you okay with not getting paid? We both know this is a gamble, but I don't want your family to suffer because of your decision to do something creator-owned. If we really want to go the digital-only route first, you wouldn't see a dime until at least after our entire first "chapter" was completed. And again, there are no guarantees even then. Our other option is to try pitching this idea to traditional book publishers. I bet all we would need would be a few sketches from you or maybe even just a cool sample cover to accompany that overview I wrote. If a publisher were interested, we might be able to secure a generous advance that would keep the lights on for you as you drew the book at a respectable pace. Plus, unlikedoing this for most comics publishers, we'd probably still be able to maintain all our media/toy/whatever rights. I know an old-school graphic novel isn't as exciting as a self-published digital series, but it's still an option if money is a concern...

2) I think you said that you were interested in doing a lot of double-page spreads, but in reading the new DC launch books online, I've noticed that spreads are really hard to read on tablets and laptops (and phones obviously). On all the most popular comics-reading apps, books seem to flow best when readers just look at one panel at a time, swiping from one to the next (as opposed to first taking in the page or pages as a whole).

Anyway, no worries, wherever we decide to tell this and in whatever format, I'm still incredibly excited to make this story with you. I'm 100% confident it will be a hit, I just don't want your babies to go hungry as we're making it!

More soon,
Brian

From: Marcos Martín
Re: Project poverty
Date: September 14th 2011 22:14:03 GMT+02:00

Right now, I think I should be ok for about a year without a steady income. That should give us enough time to produce a few issues (fingers crossed). Also, I might keep doing occasional covers here and there and Muntsa will probably do some color work, too, so that should help a bit.
You're absolutely right about the digital-only route. And we shouldn't get our hopes too high about seeing much money, especially with the first issue. But still, I'm convinced this is the way to go even if there's a huge chance it won't work.
Book publishers are a good idea and it'd guarantee some money but we'd be back to the usual business. I believe this is the time to try something new, no matter how unlikely it is to succeed. And again, even if it's a complete disaster and we failmiserably, we'll still be able to go back to the traditional route.
I've given this plenty of thought so let's discuss it further when we Skype.

You're right about double spreads but you have to keep in mind we'd be doing PDFs while Comixology uses an entirely different technology (I think). Also, I really wasn't thinking of doing double spreads as much as adapting to the 16:9 format of most computer monitors nowadays. It's just a different format that will require us to come up with a different creative approach to the page.

Likewise! I feel above everything else our only worry should be to turn out a good a product as we can possibly can. Let's worry about food later!

MM

From: Brian K. Vaughan
Re: Project poverty
Date: September 16th 2011 19:12:42 GMT+02:00

Excellent, your passion and crazed confidence fills me with strength. This PDF plan still sounds a little batshit to me, but you're absolutely right that the old way is no longer working for anyone, so why not roll the dice on something new? If we tell a great story (which we will), people will find it. I'm excited.

And sounds like you have a sense of how to tell our story visually in this new "aspect ratio," so I'm just going to write an old-fashioned script and trust you to translate it into the 21st Century. Like I said, it'll hopefully be more detailed than a Marvel plot, but less constrictive (and good?) than an Alan Moore full script--lots of details for you to use when you need them, but also plenty of freedom to pace the story your unique way. I just started writing the opening scene, and it's pretty fucking cool. You'll probably hate it.

From: Brian K. Vaughan
Re: Advance Bleeding Cool
Date: November 28th 2011 17:45:53 GMT+01:00

Okay, about to proofread the whole script one last time. Will send shortly. Sorry again this took forever, I forgot how much work first issues are!

And yeah, the rooftop chase goes vertical pretty quickly, but as you'll see, I give you all the dialogue but also lots of leeway to execute it however you want. I hope. We'll see. Oh, and your Pipes idea is genius. Expect our hero to be visiting them soon.

On the digital front, I don't know if you know comedian Louis C.K., but he's been doing an amazing job creating and promoting this excellent new show of his almost entirely independently of the studio system. Anyway, Louis is doing a new standup special that he's marketing directly to his fans via the internet: http://www.louisck.net/

I love the simplicity of that box on the front page. "Digital download available exclusively here on 12/10/11. Just enter your email for updates." And there are two little buttons for fans to share the news via Facebook or Twitter. Anyway, I think it might be a good model for what we're trying to accomplish, too...

More soon,
Brian

From: Marcos Martín
Re: A SECRET SOCIETY - Part One
Date: November 29th 2011 18:26:15 GMT+01:00

Brian,

I've only given this one read but I can already tell you this is BRUTAL. Brutally good, that is.
My only concern right now is how the hell am I going to make this justice! In any case, I want to go over this a few more times and then we can set up a time to Skype and discuss.

This is the shit.

Congrats, man.

Marcos - So it begins! As you'll see, because I'm a hopeless creature of habit, I'm still using terms like "splash" and "panel one," etc., but I really do trust you (implore you!) to have the story unfold in <u>any way you see fit</u>. This is just a rough guide to help convey what general kind of pacing I was feeling for each moment, but obviously feel free to expand/delete/change however you see fit. If anyone can think of a way to make reading a comic online a beautiful experience, it's you. With that in mind, now here's a story where the Internet is the villain...

Page One

Page One, SPLASH

Look, I learned how to import photos directly into documents, so now I can be even lazier about describing stuff! So you know this shot from *Rear Window*?

It's kind of what I'm picturing for our opening splash, but instead of Jimmy Stewart behind the old-school still camera, it's our protagonist, a 33-year-old African-American male who goes by the initials **P.I.** I picture him wearing a simple Ninja Turtles-style PURPLE CLOTH EYEMASK and a "DREAMCOAT," a hooded poncho that helps its wearer blend into his or her surroundings by constantly projecting a digital image of the background (it's not true invisibility, but this old-school Japanese tech is cheap and popular with people who want to remain anonymous): http://tinyurl.com/7nd659h

And instead of Raymond Burr in the reflection of the telephoto lens, we can see an ATTRACTIVELY TANNED BLONDE WOMAN wearing a low-cut EVENING GOWN and LONG BLACK GLOVES. She's just arrived home at her apartment, and she's taking of her little cape-like shrug, revealing her ample CLEAVAGE. P.I. SMILES lasciviously.

Oh, and instead of being stuck inside, P.I. is actually on the ROOFTOP of an office building in DOWNTOWN LOS ANGELES, across the street from the blonde. In the background behind him, maybe we can see hints of our transformed future, with its criss-crossing network of COVERED HIGH-SPEED OVERPASSES that now arc above the city, connecting it like a literal "series of tubes" (again, just a suggestion; I leave the architecture of Future L.A. to you, but I picture it always appearing TACTILE, FORWARD-THINKING and, most importantly, PRIVATE).

   1) <u>P.I.</u>: That's it.
   2) <u>P.I.</u>: Take it off.

Page Two

Page Two, Panel One

Change angles on P.I., maybe cutting to profile shot, so we can clearly see that he's leaning over the edge of this rooftop to SNAP PHOTOS with his long lens. It's NIGHT in Los Angeles, and other skyscrapers glisten in the distance.

   1) <u>SFX</u>: *click click click*

Page Two, Panel Two

Now cut BEHIND P.I. He continues to shoot the woman across the street, as she tosses her little shrug on a couch in her tastefully decorated apartment.

   2) <u>SFX</u>: *click click click*

Page Two, Panel Three

And now we jump INSIDE the woman's apartment, framed so that we can subtly see P.I. on the roof of the dark and otherwise uninhabited-at-this-hour office building across the way. In the foreground, the woman is saying something aloud as she starts to seductively peel off her gloves.

   3) <u>Woman</u>: Teevee: Channel Five.

Page Three

Page Three, Panel One

As the woman then UNZIPS the back of her tight dress, ONE ENTIRE WALL in her apartment comes to life as a giant TELEVISION SCREEN, on which a man dressed as a loose approximation of UNCLE SAM stands in a SALES LOT of nearly IDENTICAL BLACK CARS, all futuristic midsize hydrogen fuel personal vehicles with DARK WINDOW TINTING.

1) Tailless (electronic): *--join us for next week's Tricentennial Triumph, and save an extra $2076 on the purchase of any American-made car or--*

Page Three, Panel Two

The woman again speaks aloud as she starts to pull her dress down past plain undergarments, which we can now see are covering a slightly OLDER, PASTIER, FLABBIER body than the highly supportive dress might have led us to believe.

2) Woman: Teevee: Mute through break.

Page Three, Panel Three

Cut back to P.I., frustrated that he hasn't gotten what he needs yet.

3) P.I.: Come on, beautiful.
4) P.I.: Make yourself at home, already...

Page Three, Panel Four

Now we're watching the woman through P.I.'s VIEWFINDER, as she starts to tug at a flab of LOOSE TAN SKIN around her neck. Gross.

5) P.I. (from off): Yeah, just like that.

Page Three, Panel Five

And now our payoff, as the attractive young blonde woman with a tan PEELS OFF HER LIFELIKE MASK AND WIG, revealing a plain-looking 43-year-old woman with short red hair and a mess of freckles.

6) P.I. (from off): There's the money shot.

7) SFX: *click*

A SECRET SOCIETY - Part One - November 28, 2011

Page Four

Page Four, Panel One

Cut back to P.I., who's still excitedly snapping pics on this rooftop when someone yells at him from off-panel.

1) Another Voice (from off): Hey!

Page Four, Panel Two

Cut to the normally locked entrance to the roof of this office building, where a heavyset BUILDING MANAGER wearing an old-school DOMINO MASK is holding the door open for the law enforcement/journalism agent he called here. Like most reporters in our future, DEPUTY CORRESPONDENT STRUNK is an unmasked professional in peak physical condition. A Japanese-American man, Strunk is dressed in a decent suit and tie (probably not black), and he's wearing a brown FEDORA with his clearly labelled PRESS credentials tucked inside the brim. He's wearing a retro-futuristic RADIO WATCH on his left wrist, and wielding a non-lethal stun-gun called a KICKER in his right hand. The weapon is lowered at his side... for now.

2) Strunk: Fourth Estate.
3) Strunk: Keep your hands where I can see them.

Page Four, Panel Three

Cut back to P.I., who smiles nervously as he subtly raises his hood over his head...

4) P.I.: No problem!
5) P.I.: I was just taking some pictures of the architecture down here for my...

Page Four, Panel Four

...before P.I. goes LEAPING over the side of the office building! Behind him, a screaming Strunk is already running after him.

6) P.I.: ...fuck it.

7) Strunk: NO!

Pages Five through Nine

The Chase Goes Vertical!

Okay, so of course P.I. didn't commit suicide, he's just leaping down some network of lower roofs and fire escapes on his way to a back alley and eventually street level. He's not Daredevil or some highly trained gymnast, just a slightly crazy dude who knows this city very well and is willing to use its quirks to his advantage. I imagine him encountering things like futuristic SOLAR CELL ARRAYS or maybe ROOFTOP MINI-FORESTS, but mostly, I just want you to enjoy drawing this, Marcos, so let me know if you need more details.

Regardless, P.I. is going to keep his mouth shut (no wisecracks!), so the only person talking will be Strunk, who's having a breathless conversation with his BUREAU CHIEF via radio watch. Here's more or less how that dialogue will play out as you let the action unfold:

1) <u>Strunk (at P.I.)</u>: FREEZE!

2) <u>Strunk (into his watch)</u>: Bureau Chief, this is Deputy Correspondent Strunk.

3) <u>From Watch (electronic)</u>: Go ahead, Strunk.

4) <u>Strunk</u>: Sir, after receiving a tip from an anonymous source, this reporter witnessed a possible Fourth Amendment violation, specifically photographing a citizen in her place of home or business without prior consent.

5) <u>Strunk</u>: Subject appears to be an adult male wearing an old-fashioned **Dreamcoat**. He's currently fleeing on foot across Upper Wilshire Boulevard.

6) <u>From Watch (electronic)</u>: Well, that's the first four Ws on our Peeping Tom, how about a **why**? Sexual gratification?

7) <u>Strunk</u>: I don't believe so, subject is armed with an illegally modified telephoto lens.
8) <u>Strunk</u>: Sir, I think he's **paparazzi**.

9) <u>From Watch (electronic)</u>: Christ, way to bury the lede, Strunk. I'm authorizing an immediate search warrant. **Paint his ass**.

10) <u>Strunk</u>: Copy.

((Strunk uses his Kicker to unleash a series of paintball-like EXPLODING DYE PACKS, but P.I. manages to DODGE them as he makes his way down a fire escape. Strunk continues to follow as P.I. races down a DARK ALLEY and out to the street...))

11) <u>From Watch (electronic)</u>: Strunk? File already! Did you get him?

12) <u>Strunk</u>: Sorry, sir.

Pages Ten and Eleven

Pages Ten and Eleven, DOUBLE-PAGE SPREAD

And now for *our* money shot, as the winded reporter steps out of the dark alley and onto WILSHIRE BOULEVARD (or any other PALM TREE-LINED major downtown L.A. thoroughfare you might prefer). It's night, but the street is PACKED with as many revelers, merchants, and pedestrians as you can humanly draw.

At this late hour, they're all adults, and most importantly, they're ALL WEARING VARIOUS MASKS, COSTUMES & DISGUISES, many of them accented with ever-changing DREAMCOATS exactly like P.I.'s. If our hero is somewhere in this vast crowd of pseudonyms and aliases, we can't see him.

Again, the disguises range from simple to elaborate, drab to vibrant, conservative to hyper-sexual. In our future, <u>nearly everyone has at least one alternate identity</u>, so we should a huge variety on display here.

1) <u>Strunk (into watch)</u>: He's gone to ground.

From: Marcos Martín
Subject: Sketches
Date: February 1st 2012 19:50:27 GMT+01:00

Brian!

I'm sorry it's taken me forever to get these done. I blame Christmas' holidays, my children, the IMF and the world in general for throwing stuff at my face just to distract me!

Anyway, I'm sending a batch of sketches with my take on Pi for your review. There's a bunch of things I'm not sure about, yet -- I'm having trouble with the specific design of the coat but I know I don't want it to be a poncho (I'm afraid I'm not too fond of them). And I prefer to have the hood as a separate element. Also, I've added a smiling face on the back of the hood (again, still working on the exact design). I thought it might be cool to create a sort of Cheshire cat effect when he uses the invisibility properties of the coat/hood. I feel painting a mocking grin on the back of his head suits the character's nature. By the way, I started with a more conventional hood design but I gradually exaggerated its shape and ended up with something closer to a Moebius character. I think the ones in the last pic are probably my favorite.

About the mask, I'm afraid I haven't been able to solve it, yet. I couldn't make the initial idea of the TMNT style mask work at all. Dark glasses is an option and I've also tried with just a streak of black paint across the eyes. I'm not crazy about any of these but they might work. Personally, I prefer having him without the mask and using the hood as his identifying trait.

About the face I think he should have blue or green eyes and freckles. And I'd like him to have slighly oriental eyes to further add to the mixed race idea. I picture him with a very short haircut, almost shaved but I've added a couple of other options just in case.

The character is basically going to be black and white (white coat, black t-shirt and boots and dark pants). I think this will work well against the rest of the characters which I'm imagining to be very colorful. The t-shirt design is completely arbitrary so I'm open to any suggestions.

Gramps is still in the early stages but I'm sending you what I've got so far in case you've got any ideas you want me to work with.

End of part 1. More sketches with the costume design look for the series coming up in a bit.

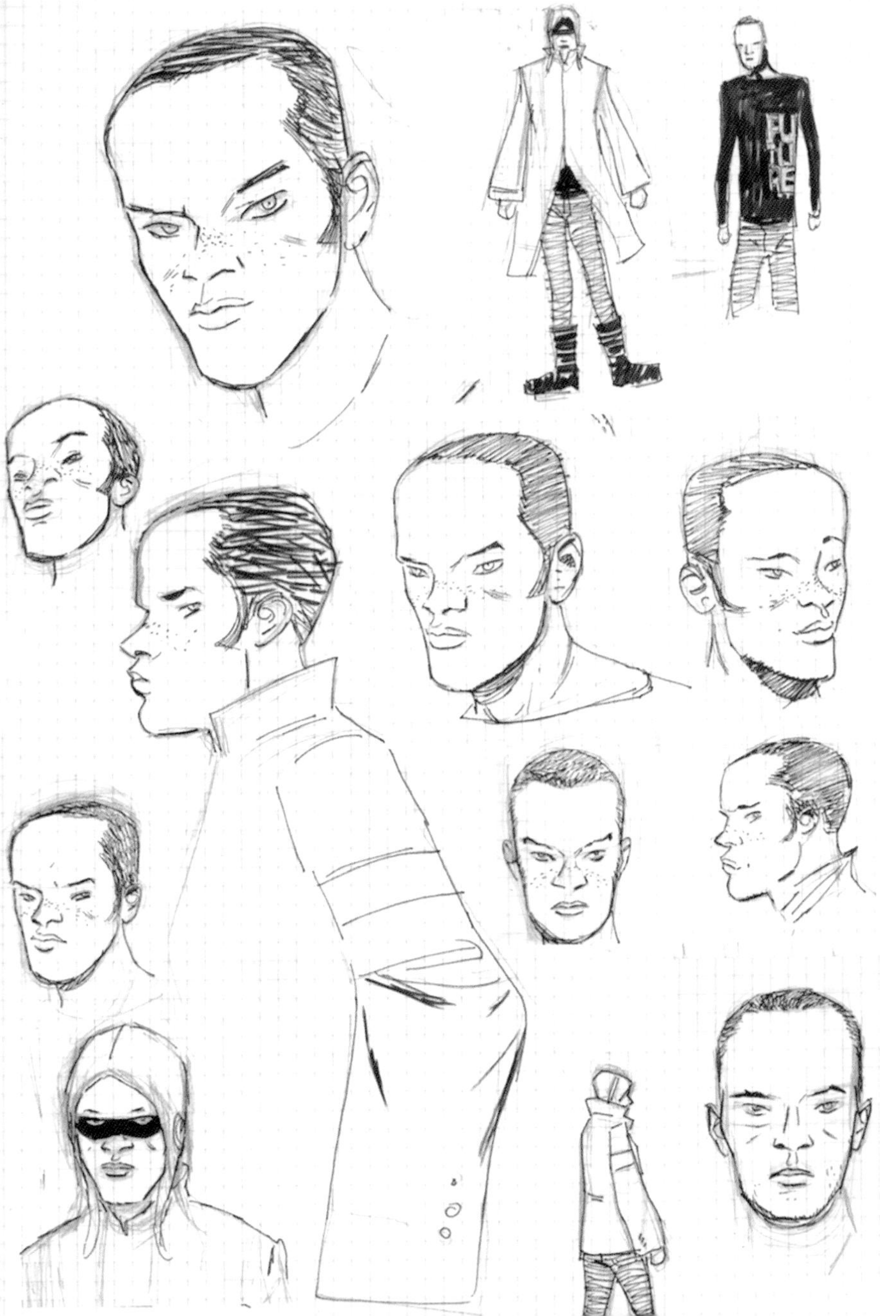
FUTURE

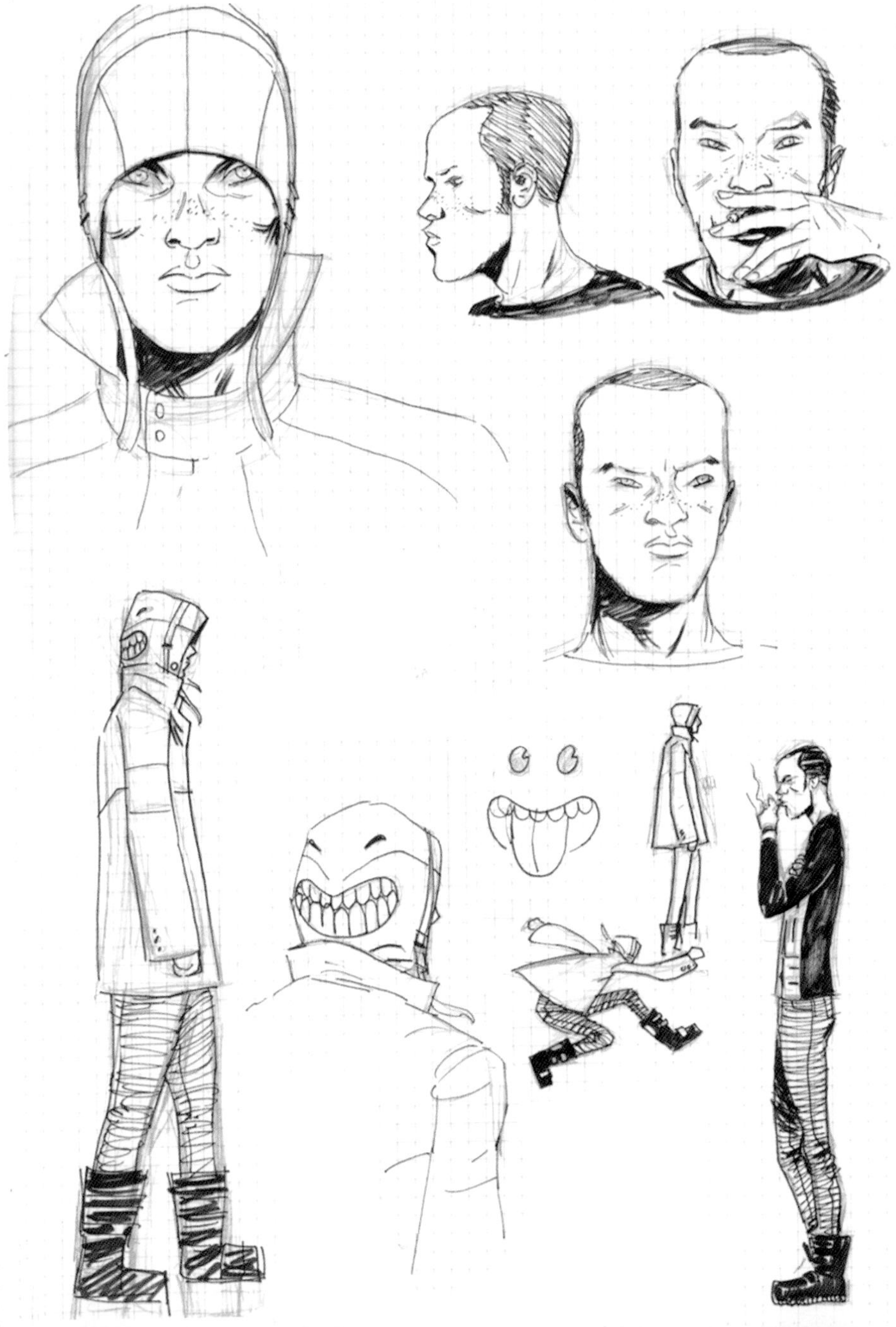

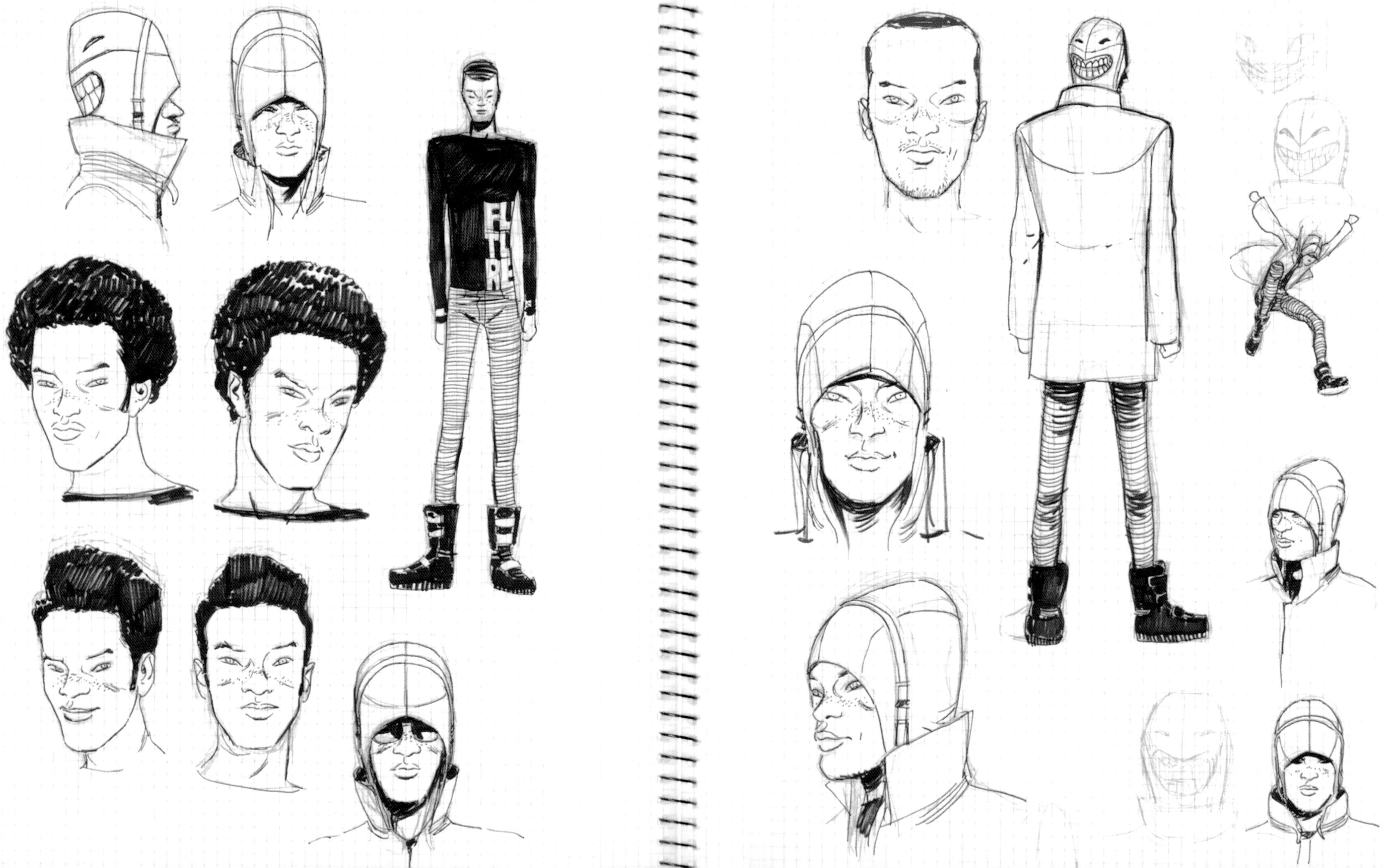
FU
TU
RE

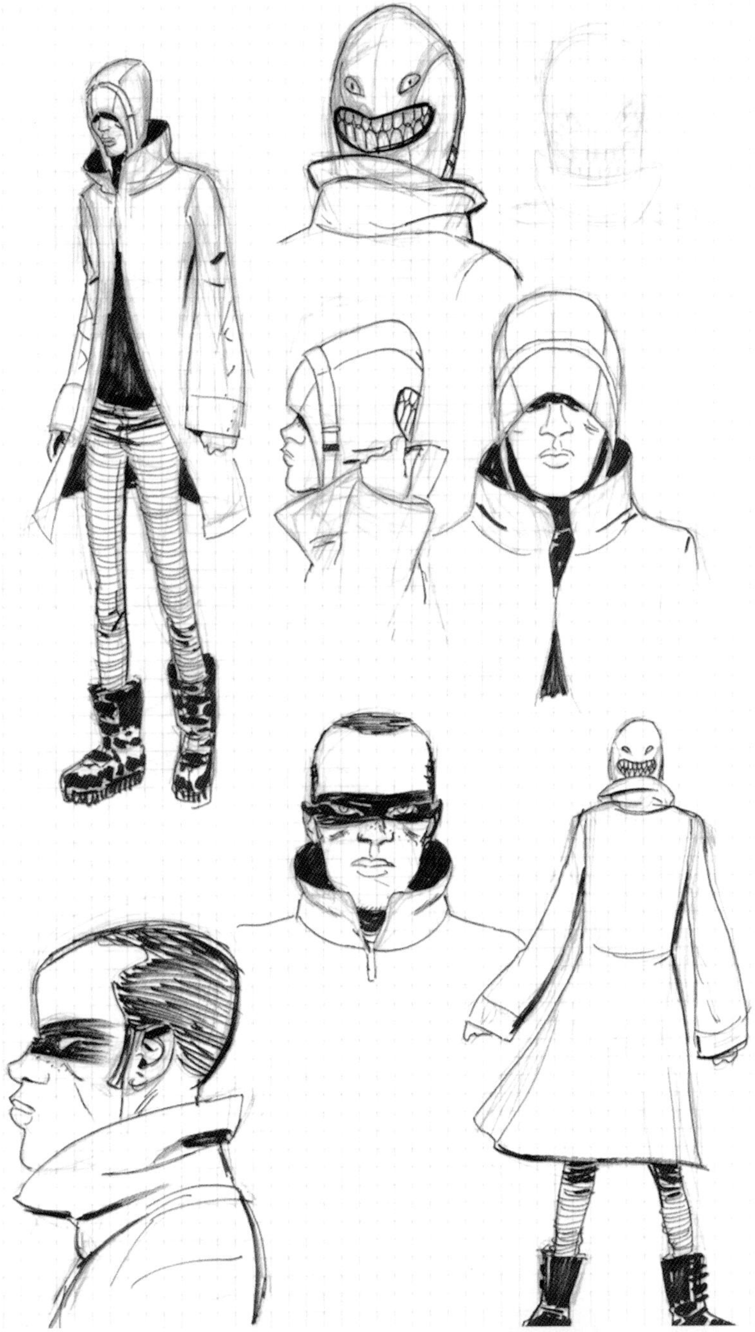

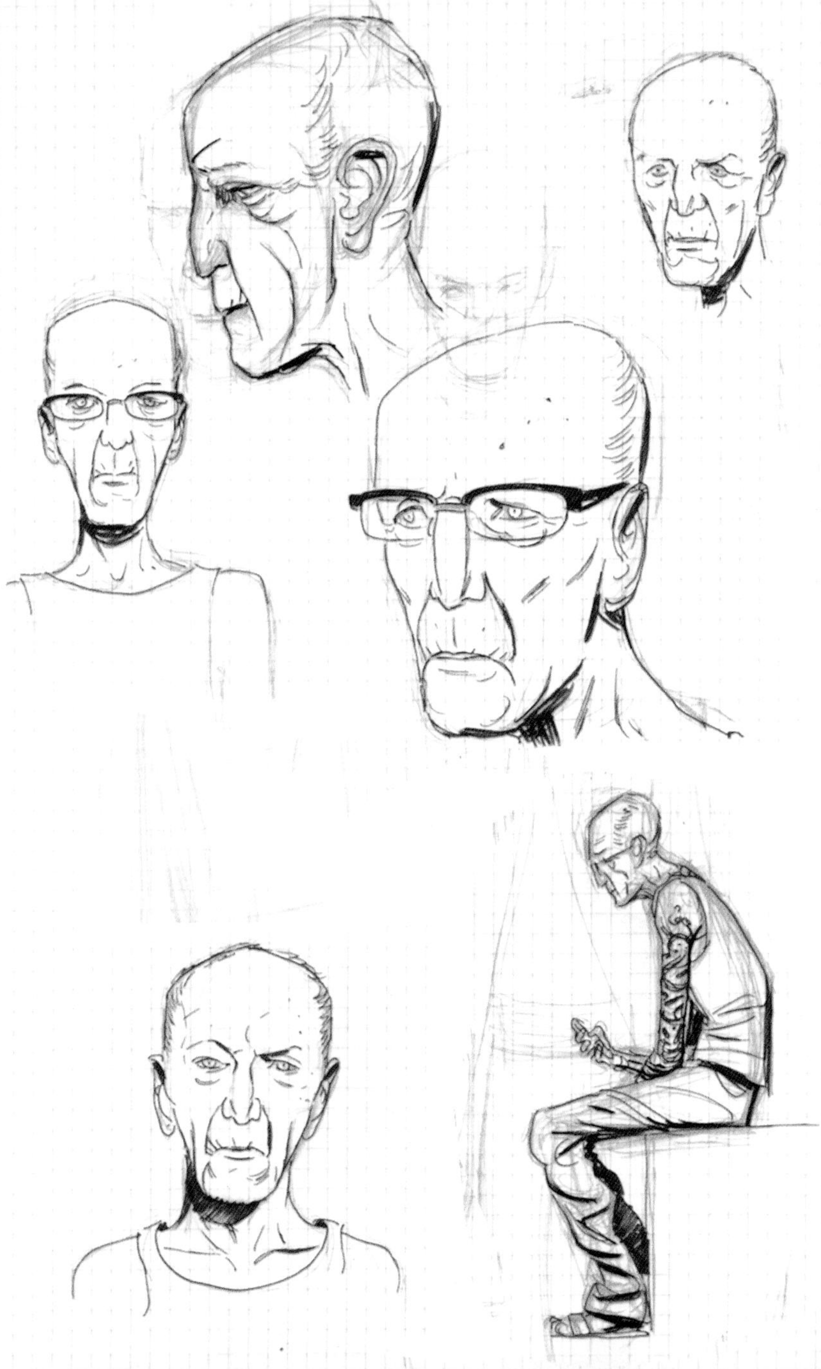

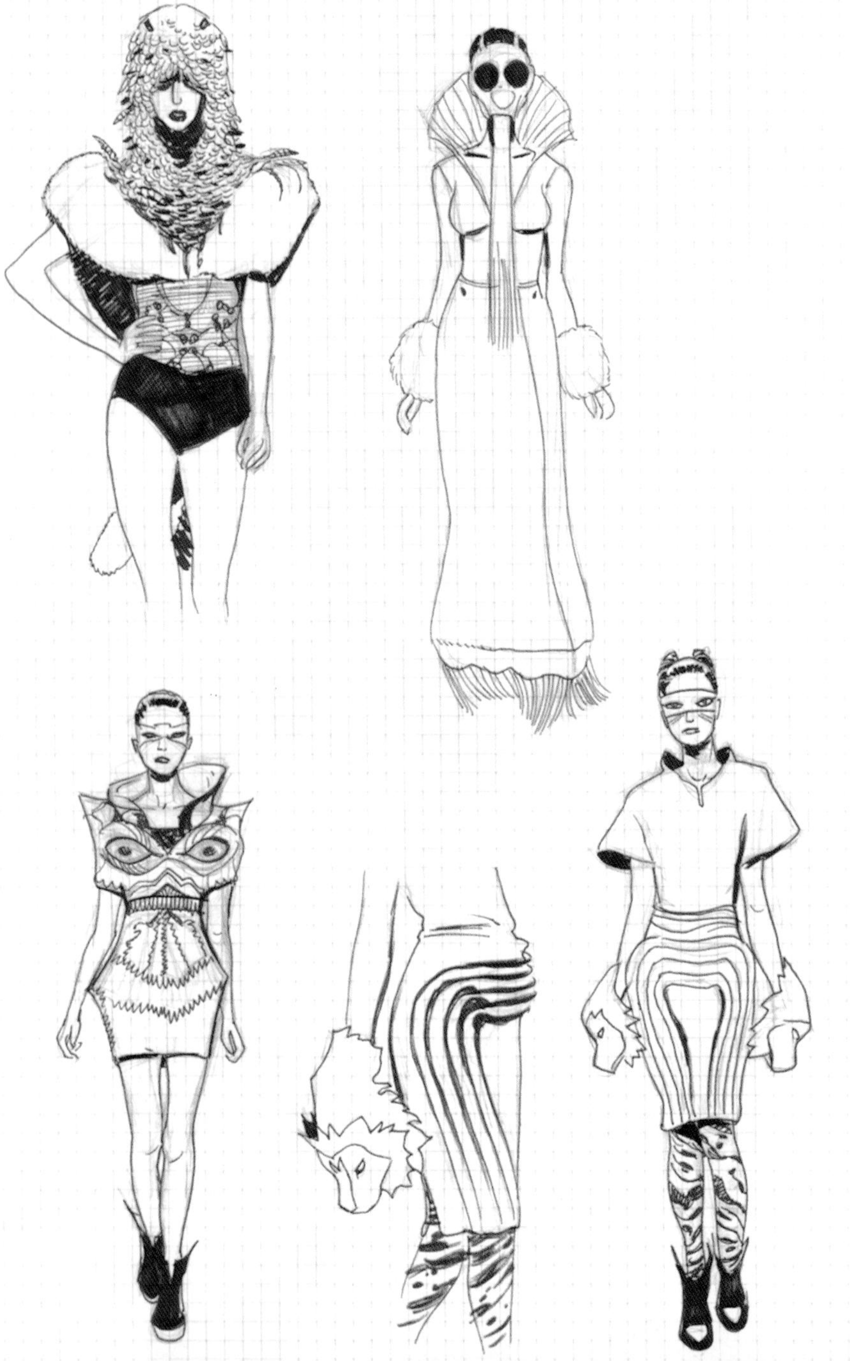
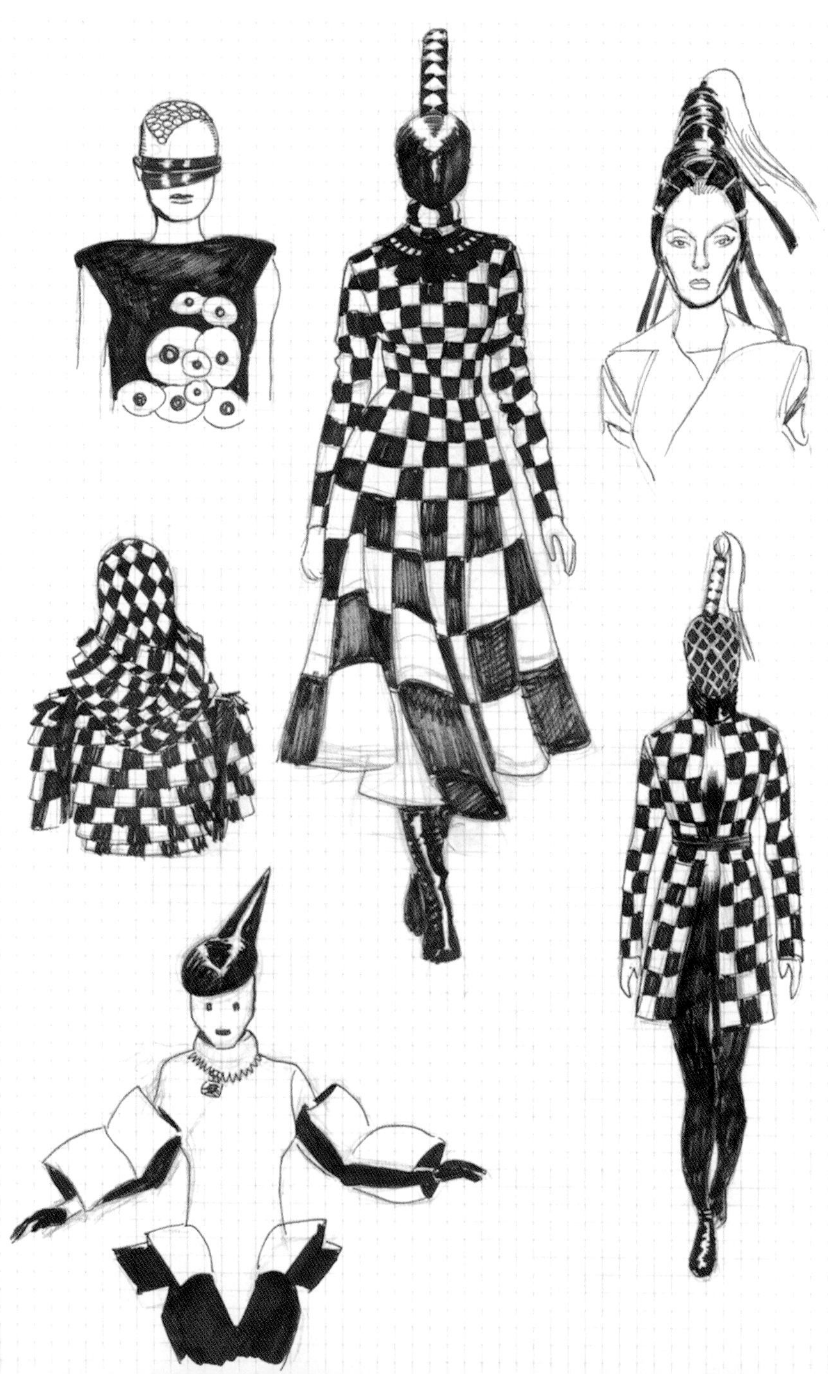

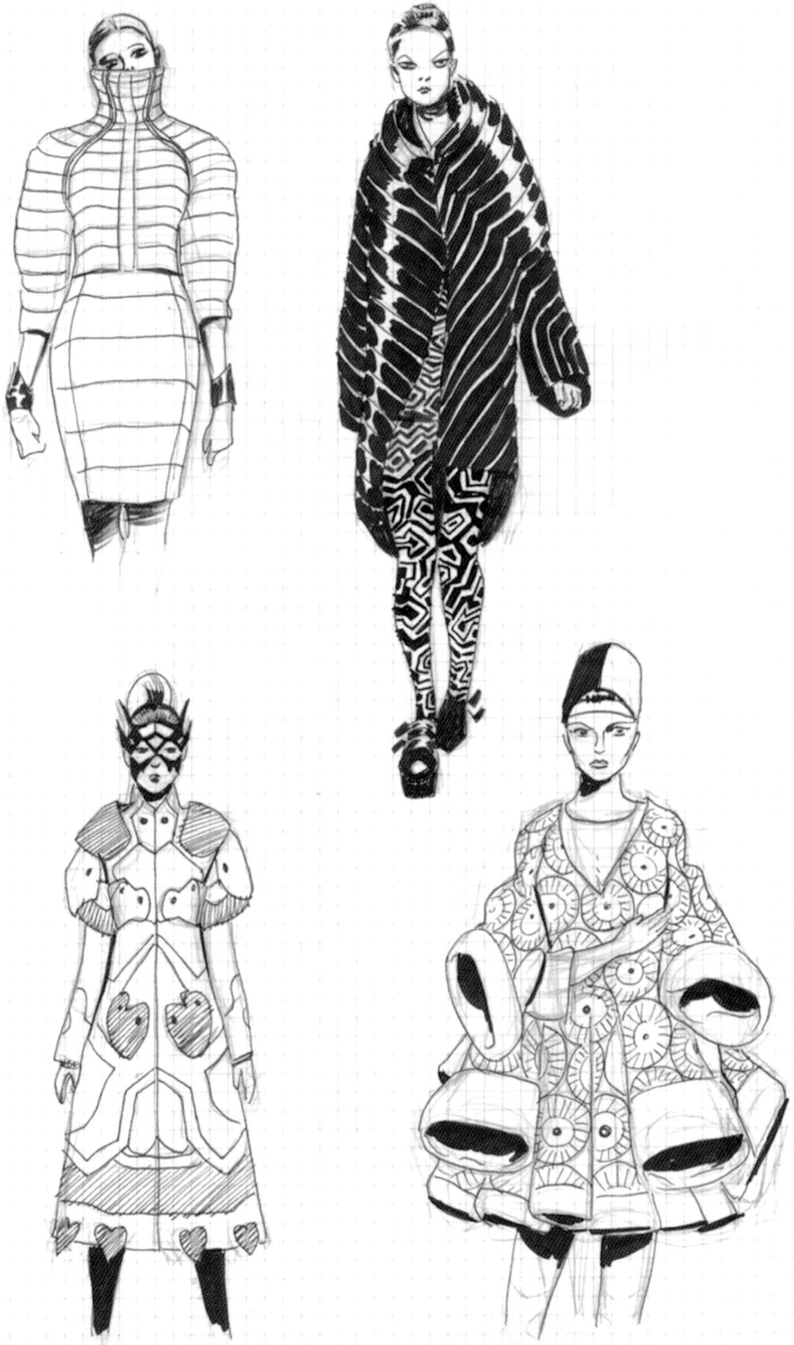

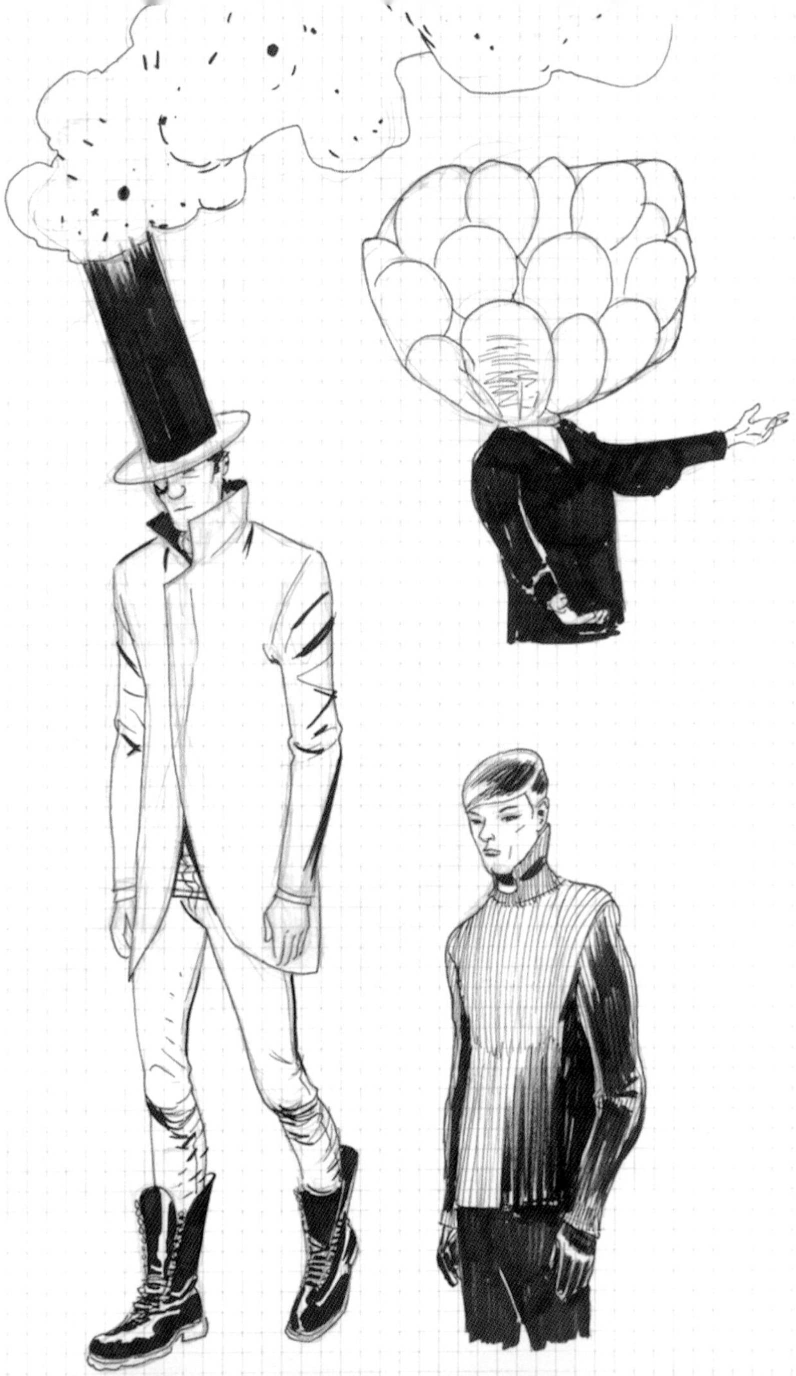

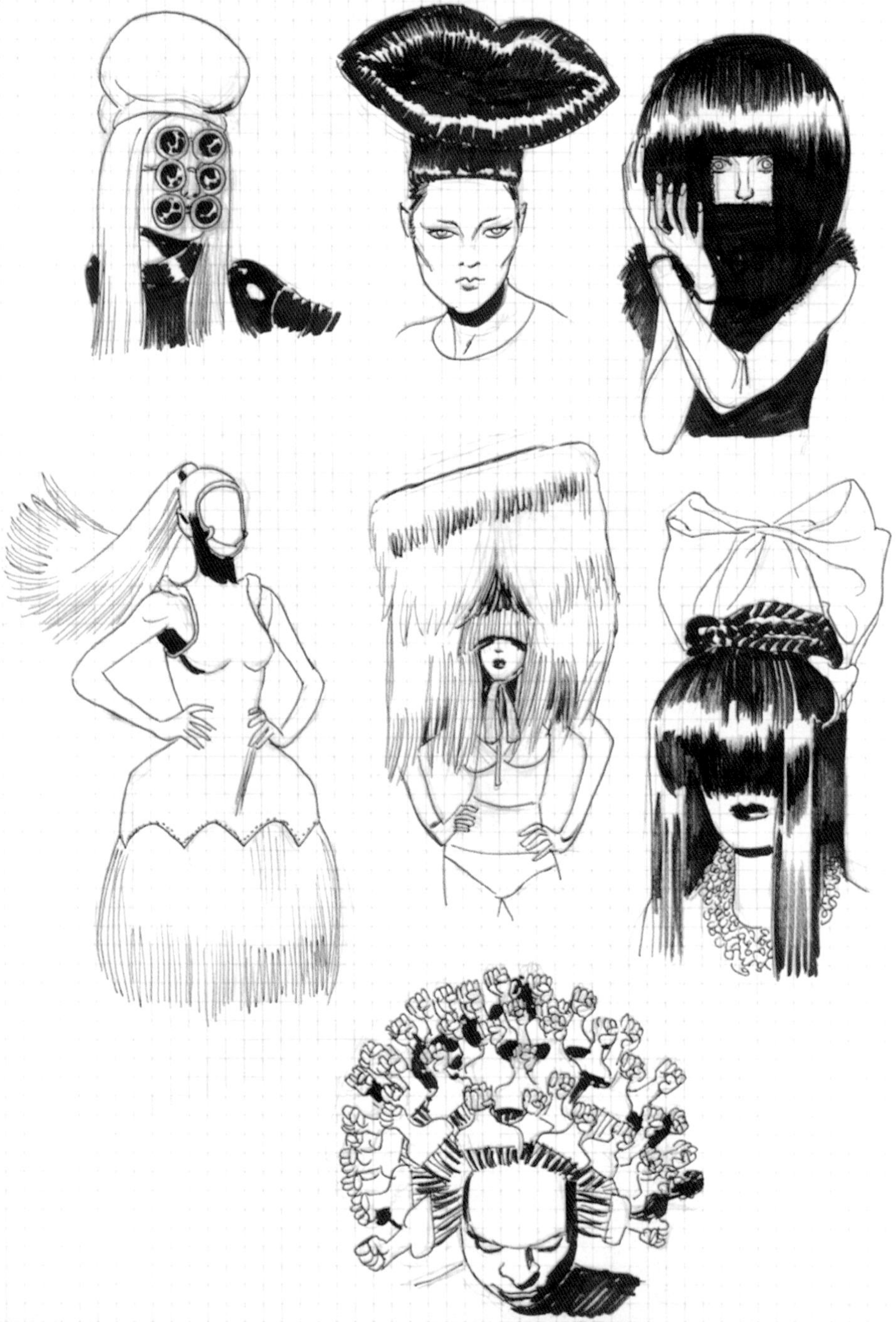

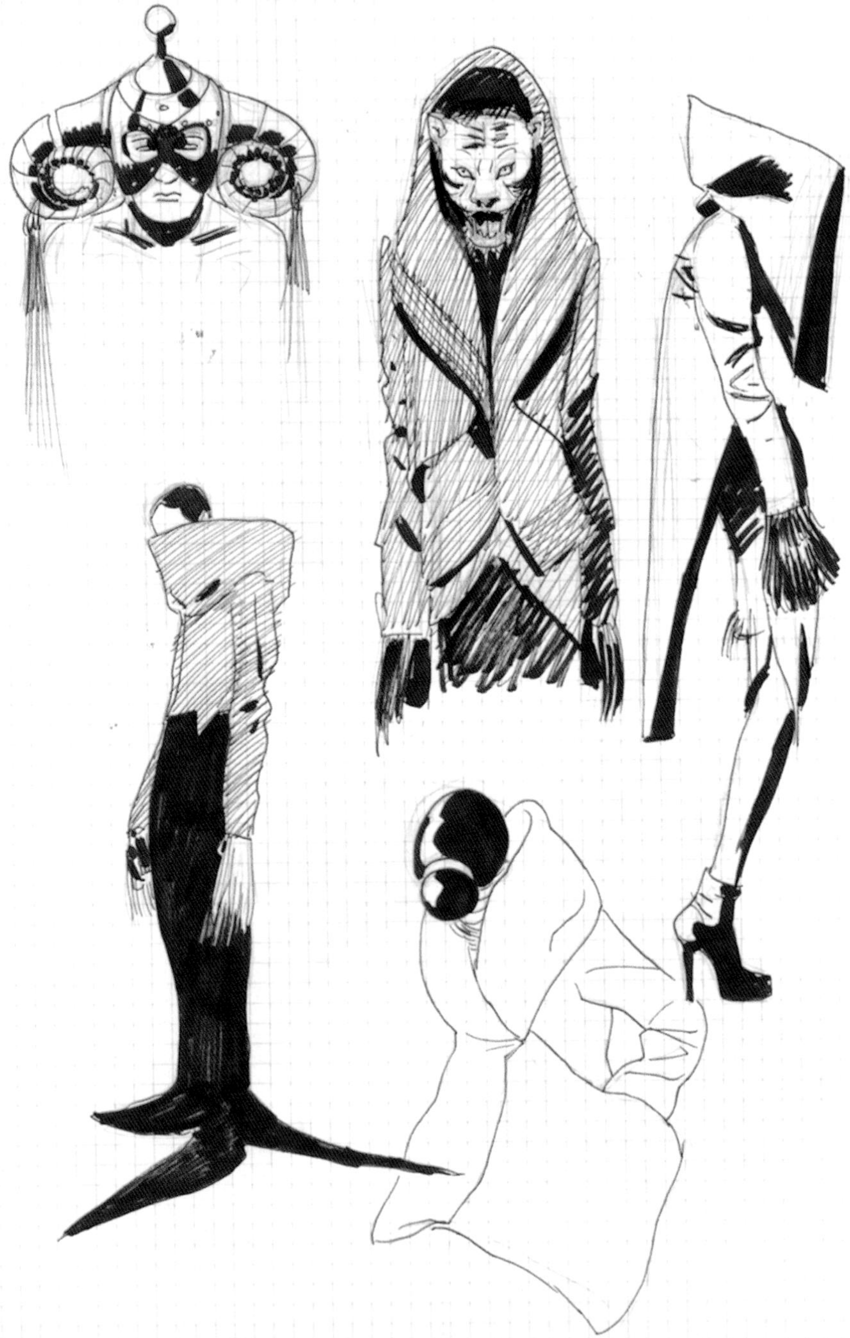

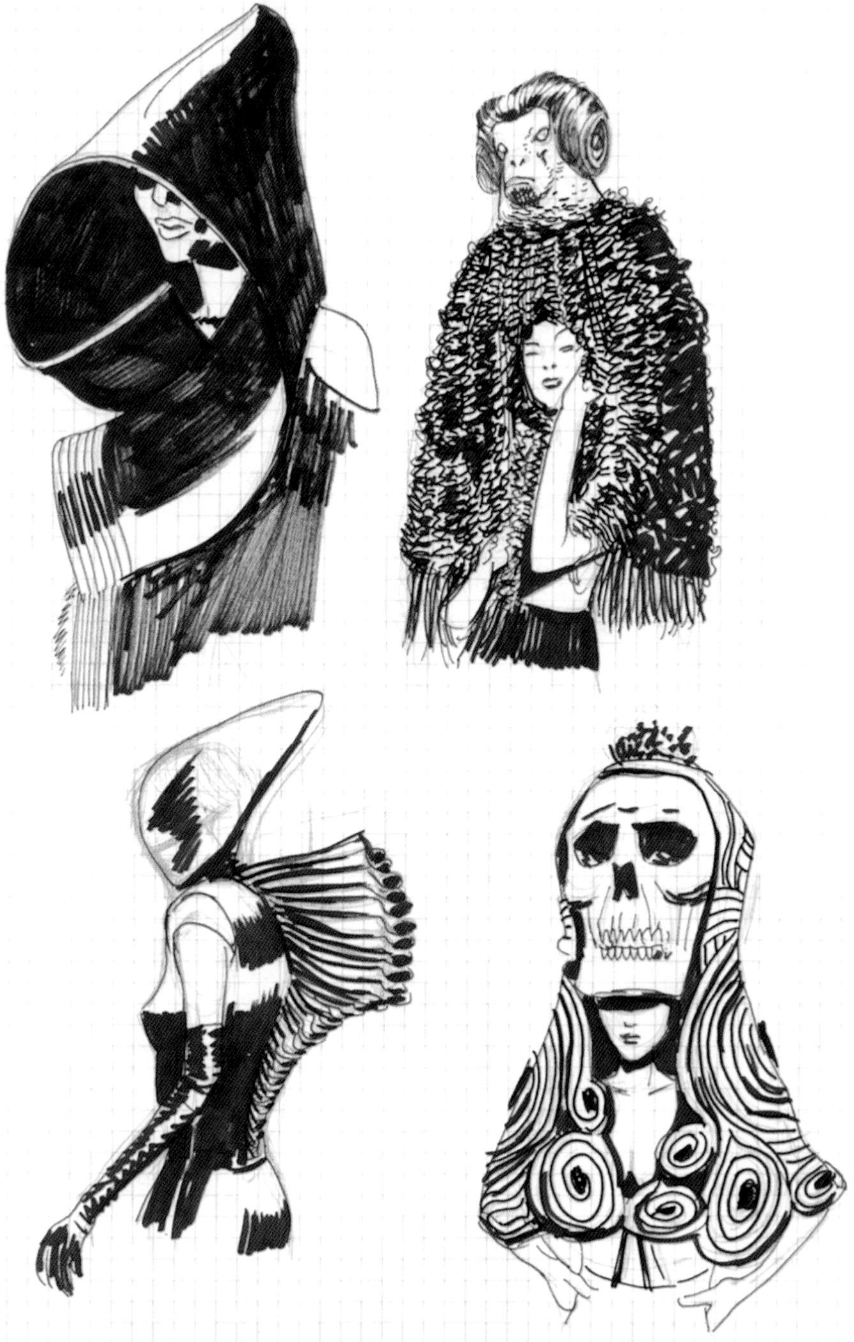

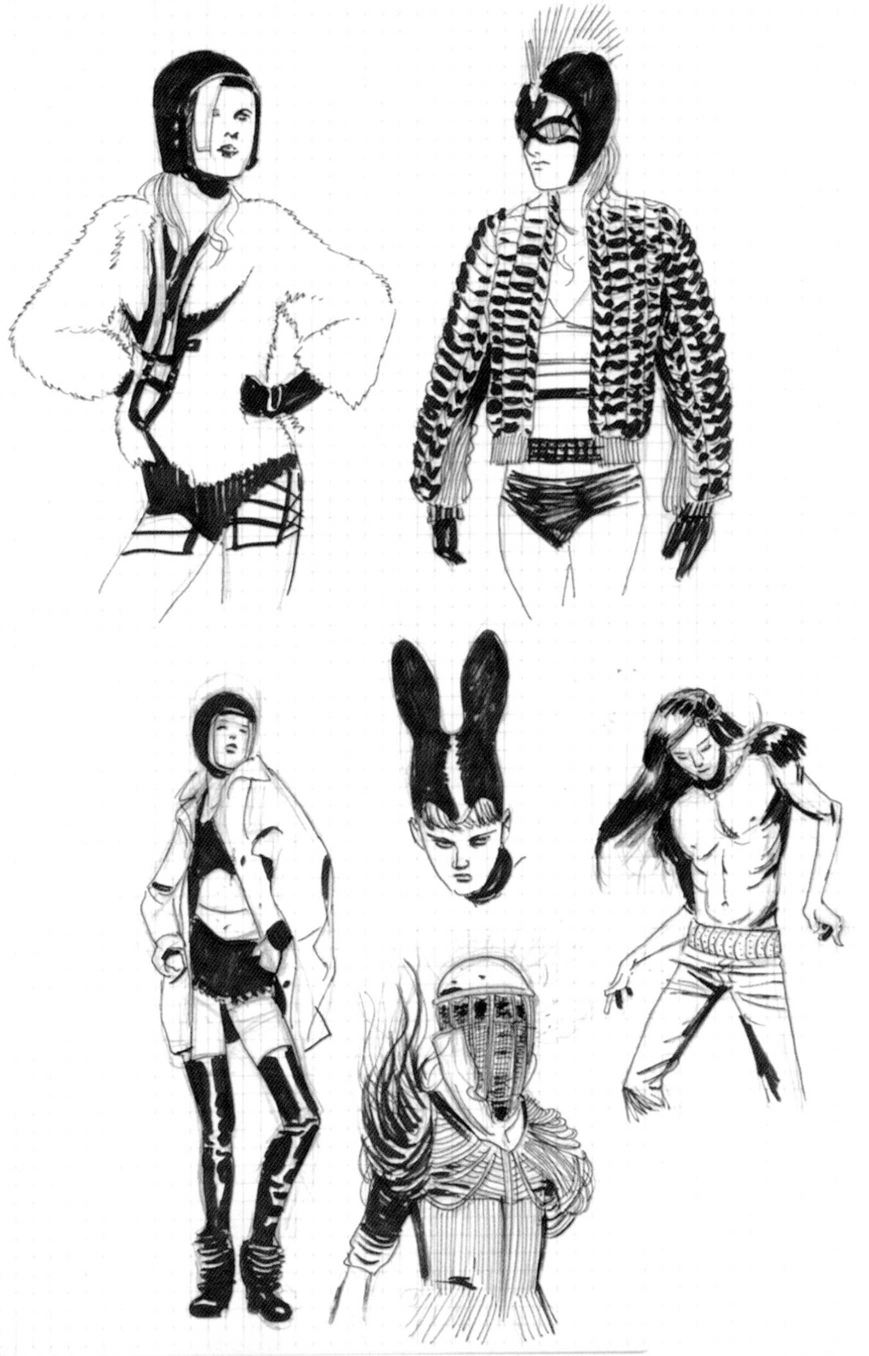

From: Marcos Martín
Subject: Architecture
Date: February 8th 2012 13:52:37 GMT+01:00

Hola!

I'm sending a few more sketches, this time outlining a few ideas on the architectural front. Once again, none of these are original designs just different examples I've gathered that reflect some of the possibilities I'm looking into.

First of all, I think we should try to reflect a new eco-friendly city, with self sustainable buildings, capable of generating their own energy. Perhaps even growing their own farms like it's starting to happen in some builings nowadays but at a much greater scale. Also, some of these buildings could even be covered by a thick carpet of grass and plants, half hidden underneath this natural skin (not so much in the city center, but on the suburbs or around parks or big green areas).

Also, we should emphasize the use of what are now alternative sources of energy. I can see huge solar plates as an integral part of the buildings' structure (perfect for PI to slide down). Magnetism should probably play a big part in the future, too. I'm thinking elevated magnetic trains running through the city at high speeds. Cars could also be powered with magnetism and run through especially prepared highways.
As any present-day city there should be a landscape of billboards but sporting unexpected brand names like "Kodak" (the only one I could think of but I'm sure you can come up with more:)).
Something I think could also reflect this society's newfound sense of privacy would be "bunker-looking", "windowless" buildings. However, it's hard to imagine anyone living like that besides the fact it conflicts with our opening scene. So another option would be to have tinted window glasses on all buildings. That way we could give PI some kind of special infrarred camera (or some other high-tech gadget) to peep through them.

Ideally, the chase scene should serve as the perfect, organic way to present the reader with some of these ideas.

I've also added a couple of initial sketches for my Pipes idea I told you about.

Anyway, plenty more to talk about as I'm about to start with the layouts. Let's see if we can Skype sometime this week or the next.

MM

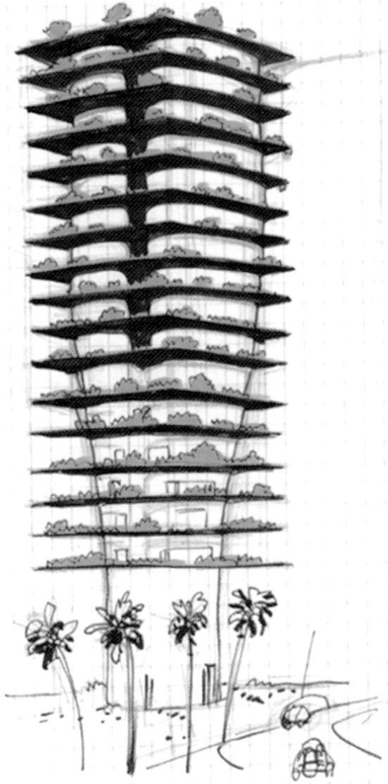
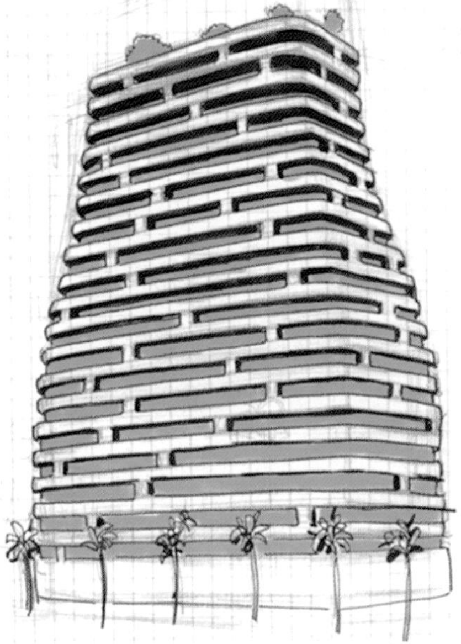
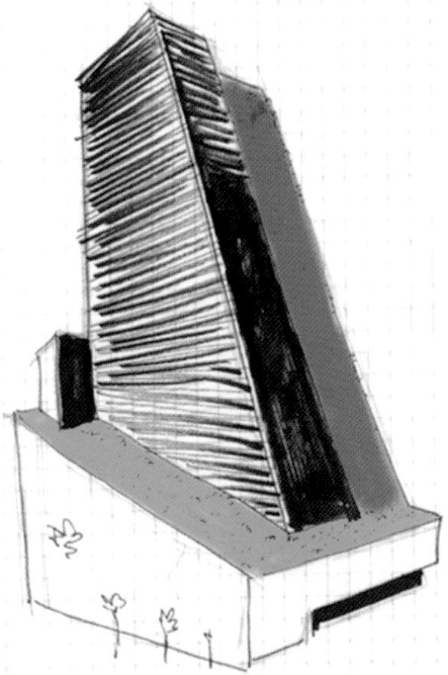
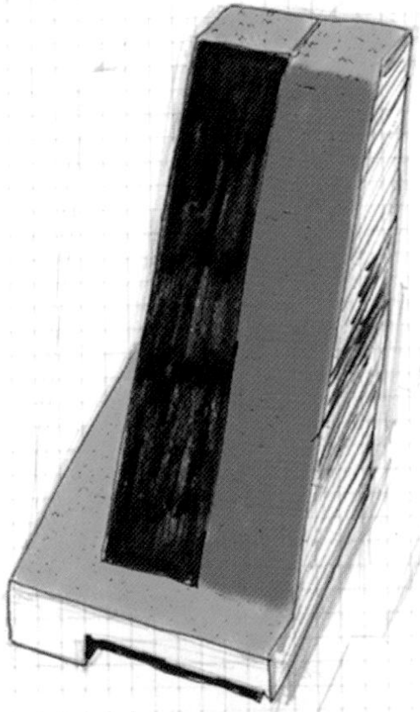
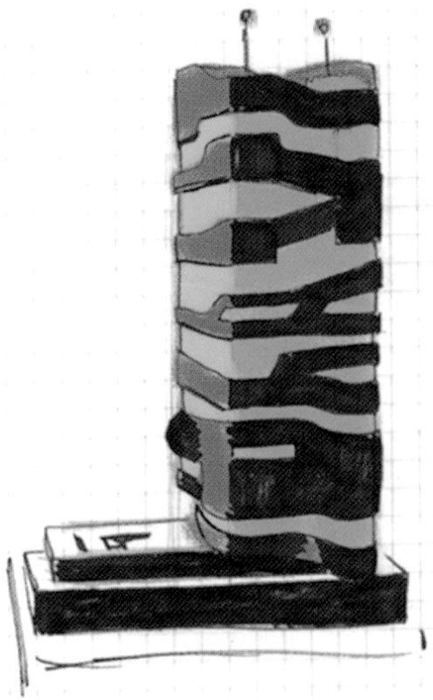
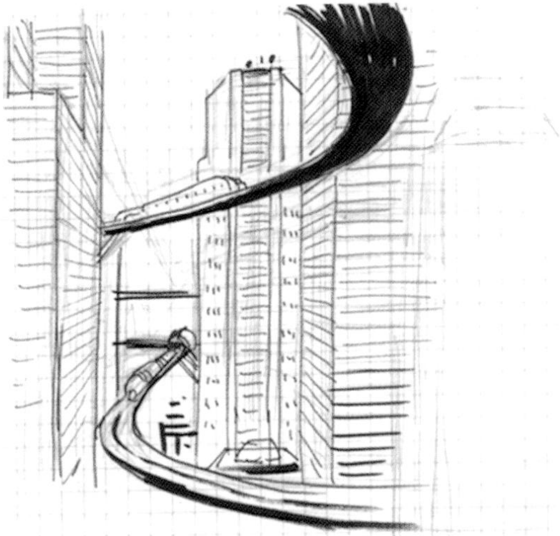
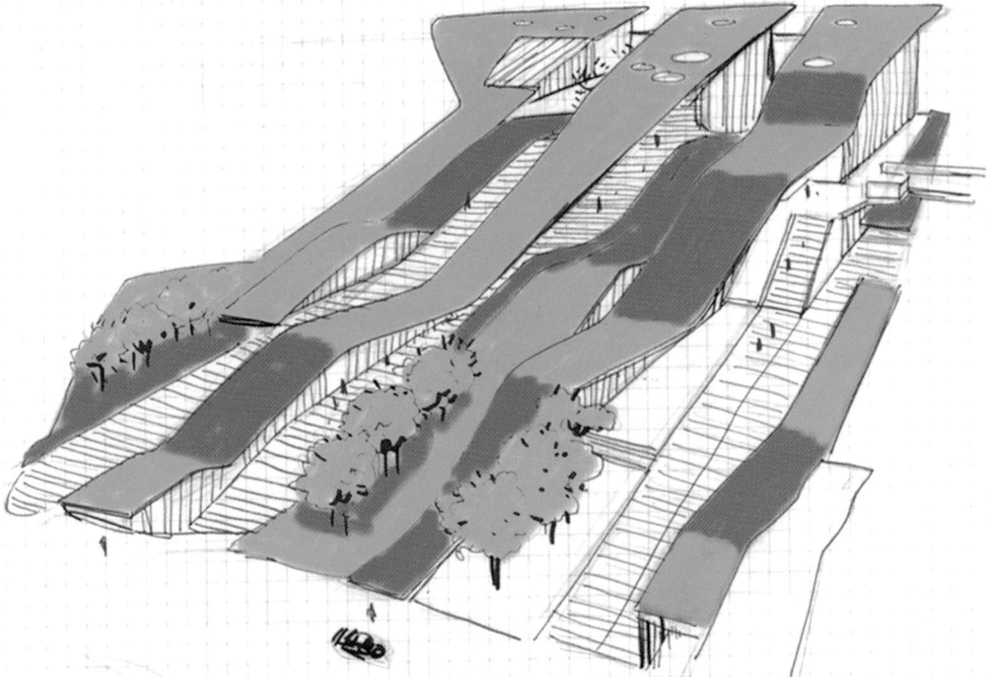

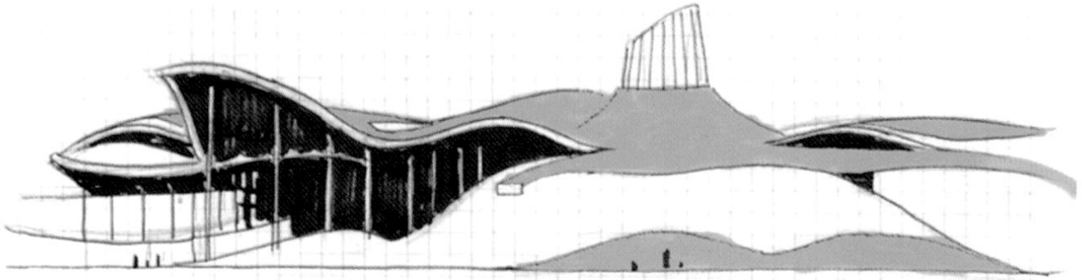
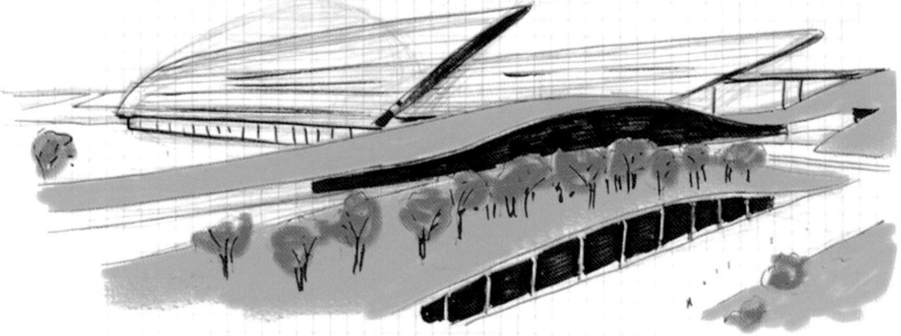
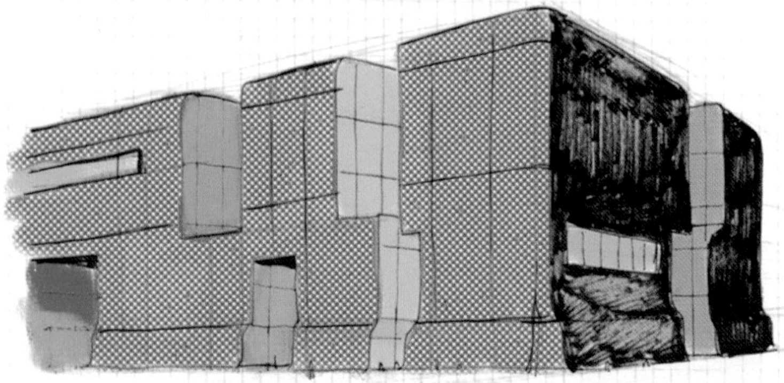
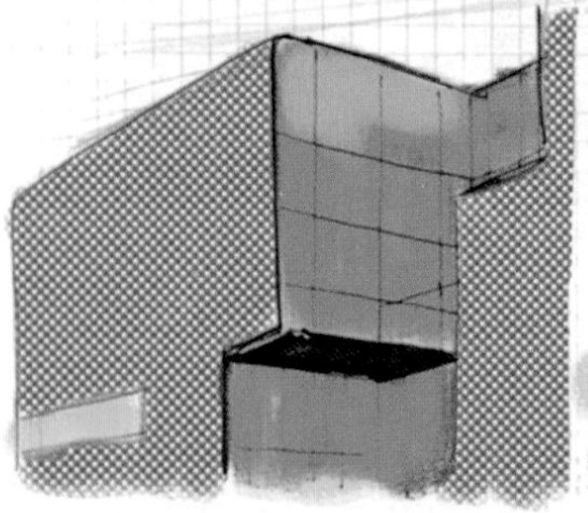
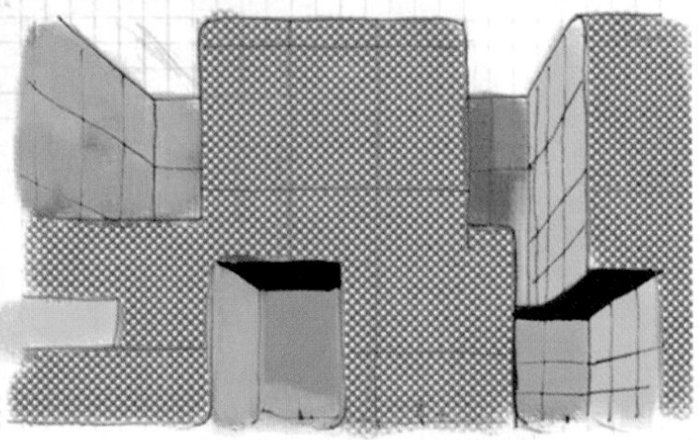
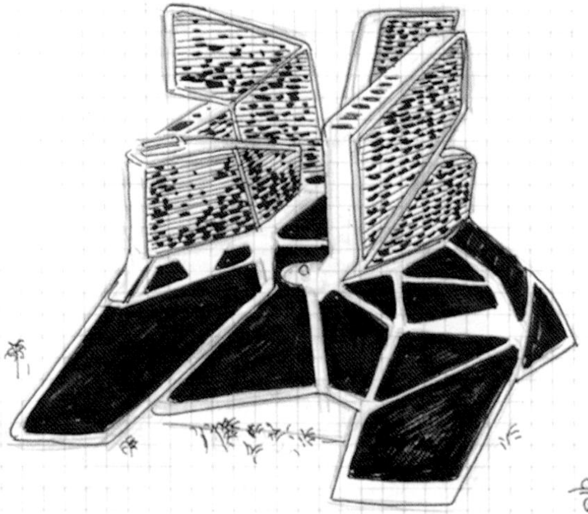
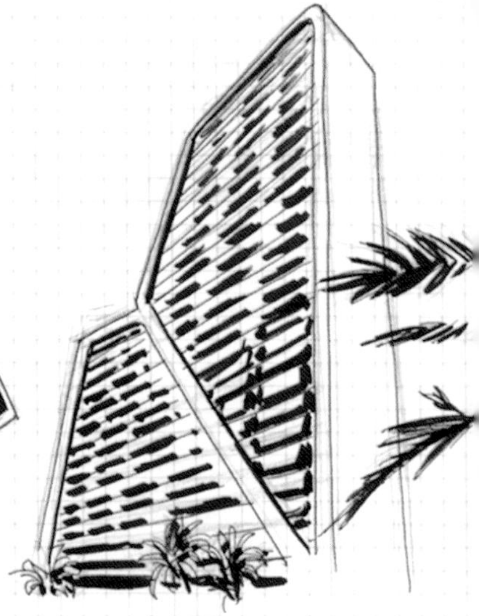
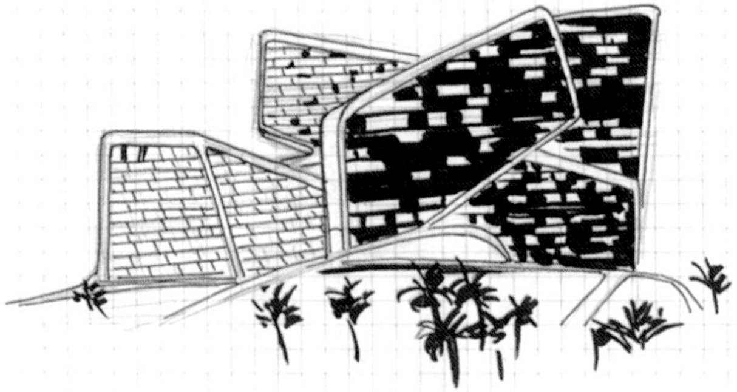
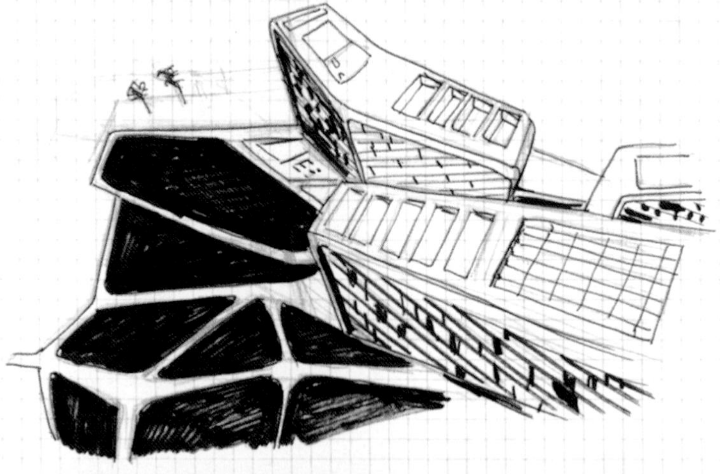

From: Marcos Martín
Subject: So...
Date: March 8th 2012 18:14:37 GMT+01:00

Here are the layouts for the first 11 pages... finally! Again, my apologies for taking so long with this. It's been really tough figuring out the whole chase scene and the change of format has taken a bit to adjust to. I'm still working on it, actually.
In any case, here it is for your review. There will probably be things you might not agree with, you're not sure of or places where you simply can't figure out my crappy doodlings. I usually add a ton of notes to explain but I think it'll be better if we just Skype and go over the whole thing. I guess the sooner, the better so I can get started with the actual drawing. However, in the meantime I'll just keep working on the layouts for the rest of the issue.

Oh, I've also added some copy through the chase scene just to give you an idea of what I had in mind while I was planning it.
And finally, don't be too scared.. yet. The finished pages should look slightly better.

From: Marcos Martín
Re: So...
Date: March 12th 2012 19:12:53 GMT+01:00

My plan is to letter the whole thing myself, including the title. We'll see how that works. It won't be perfect but it'll look more organic, at least.

PAGE 1

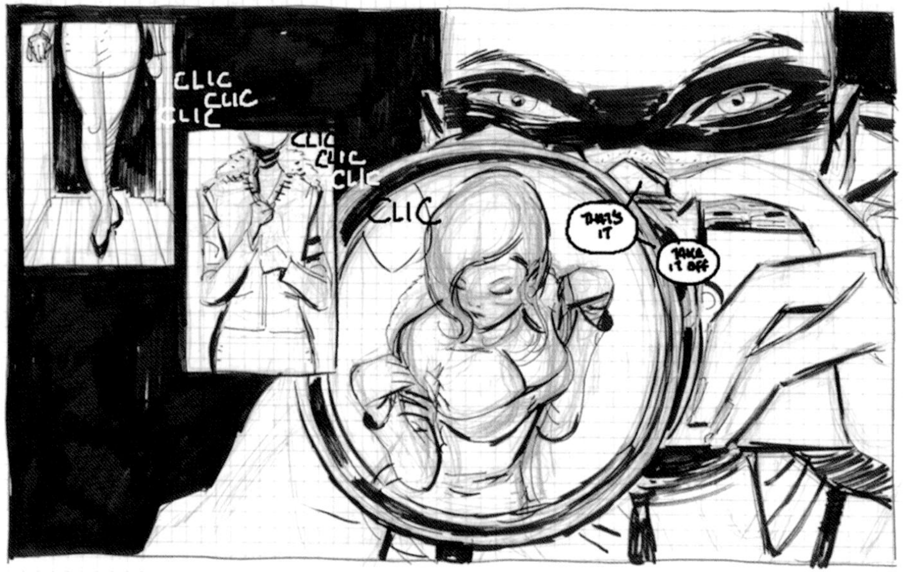
CLIC
CLIC
CLIC
CLIC
CLIC
CLIC
CLIC
THAT'S IT
TAKE IT OFF

PAGE 2

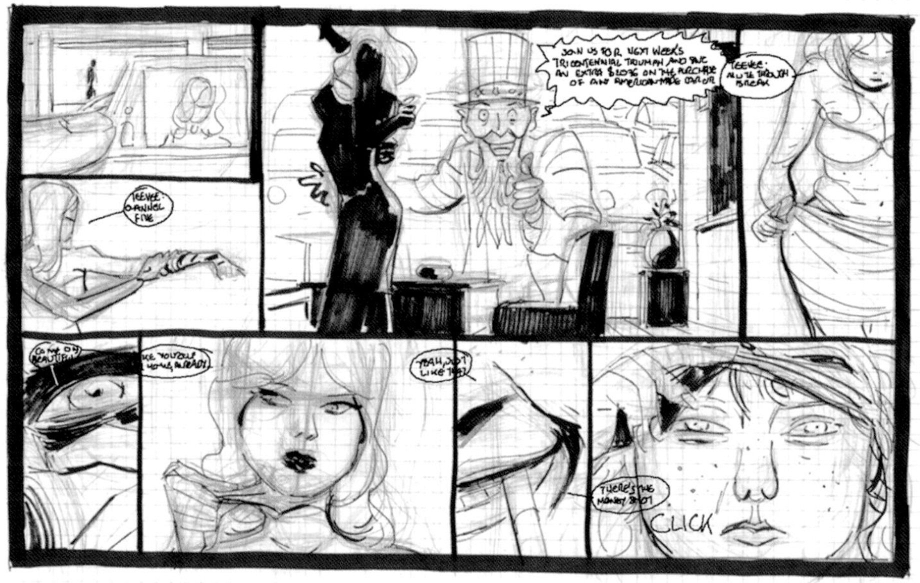
TEEVEE: CHANNEL FIVE
TEEVEE: MUTE THROUGH BREAK
YEAH, JUST LIKE THAT
THERE'S THE MONEY SHOT
CLICK

PAGE 3

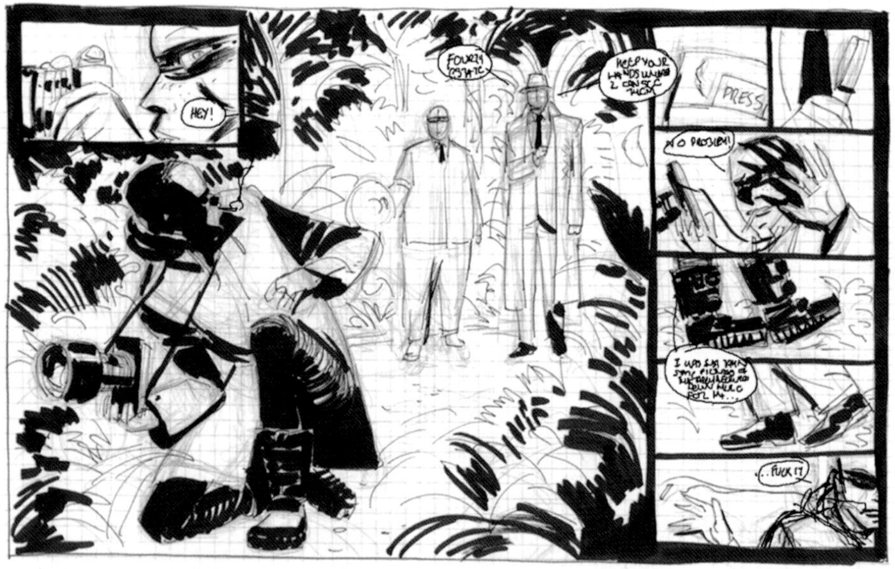
HEY!
KEEP YOUR HANDS WHERE I CAN SEE THEM
PRESS
NO PROBLEM!
...FUCK IT

PAGE 4

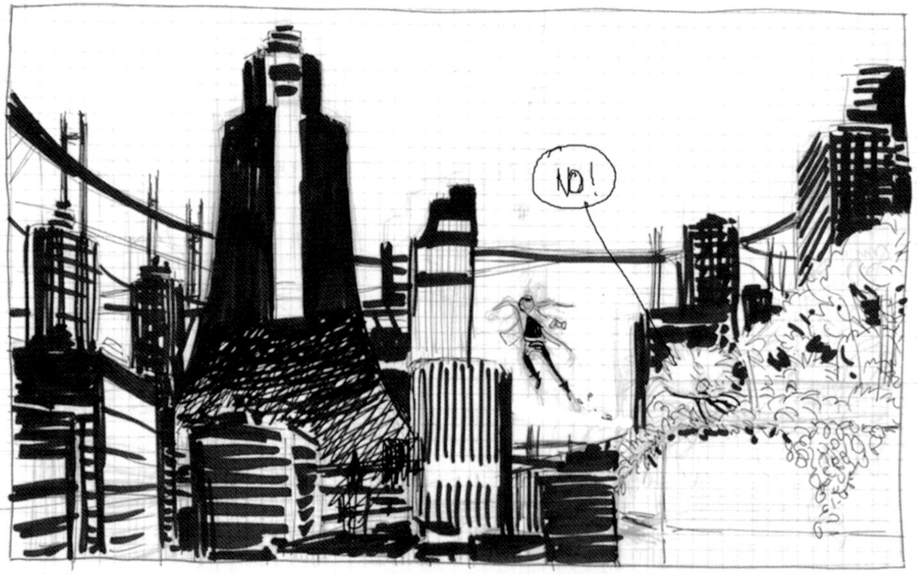
NO!

PAGE 5

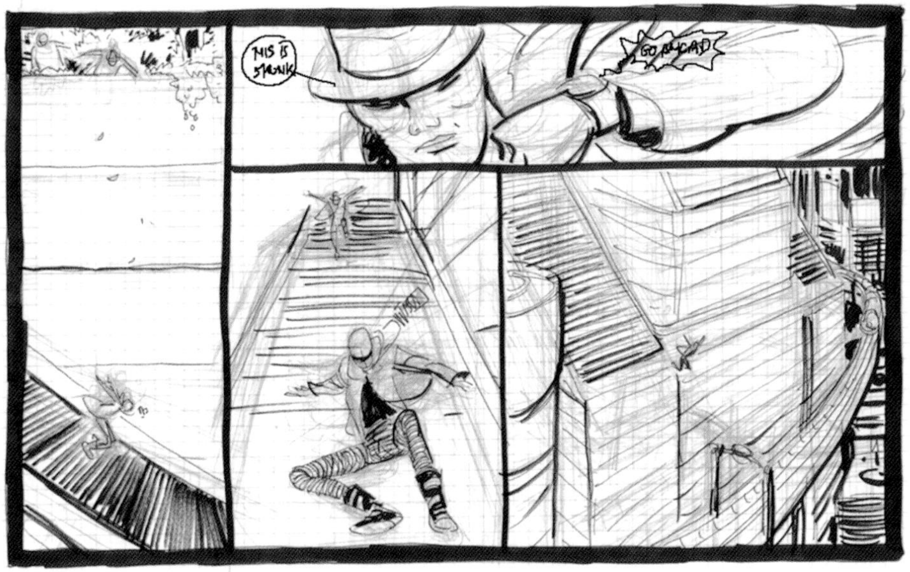
THIS IS STRUNK
GO AHEAD

PAGE 6

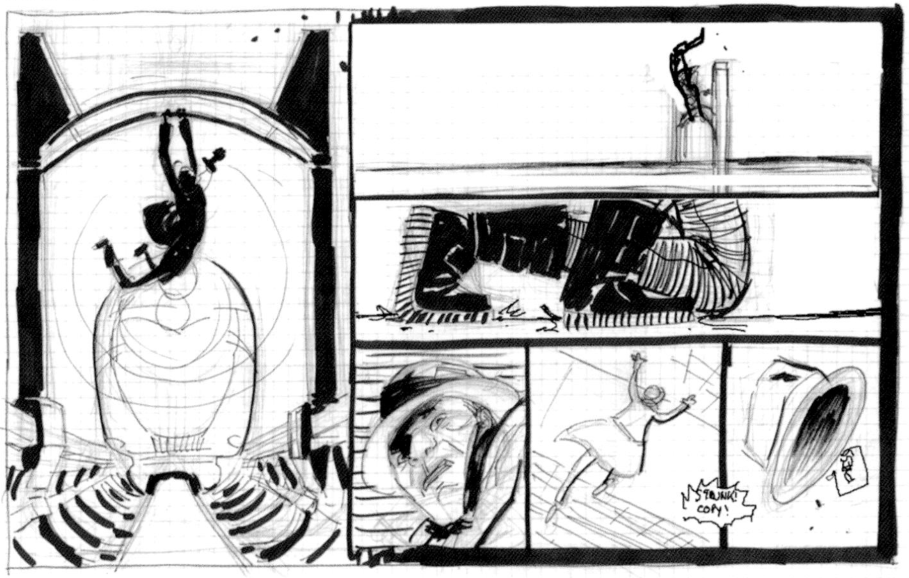
STRUNK! COPY!
PRESS

PAGE 7

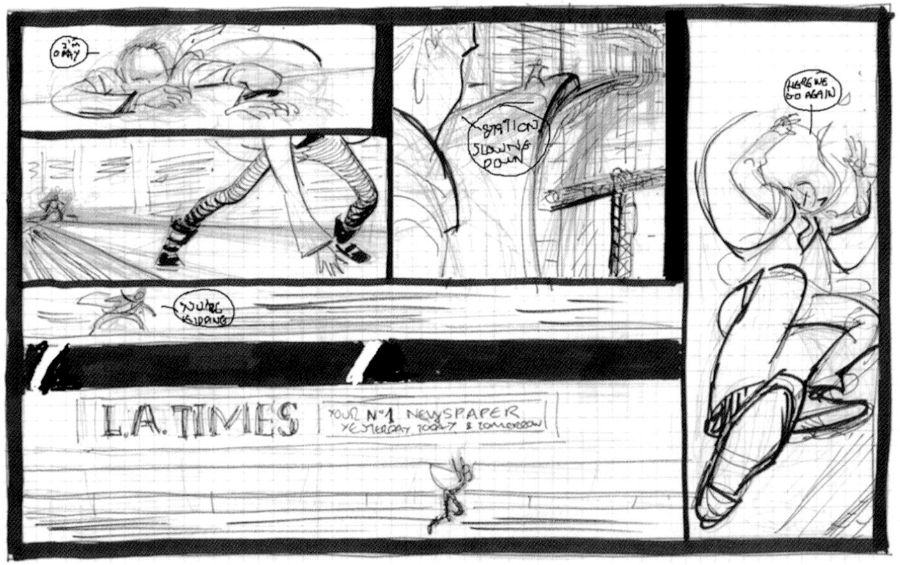
I'M OKAY
STATION SLOWING DOWN
HERE WE GO AGAIN
YOU'RE KIDDING
L.A. TIMES
YOUR Nº1 NEWSPAPER
YESTERDAY TODAY & TOMORROW

PAGE 8

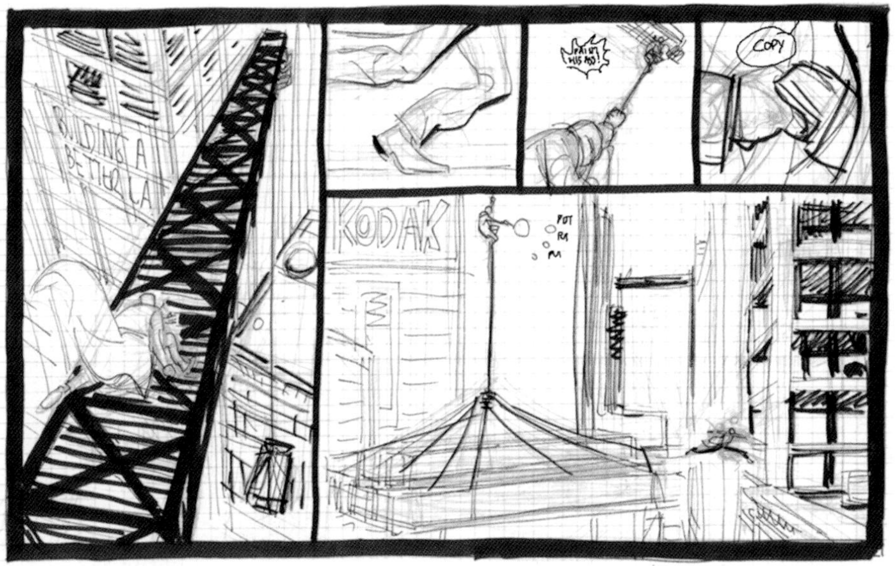
BUILDING A BETTER LA
PAINT HIS ASS!
COPY
KODAK
POT RA RA

PAGE 9

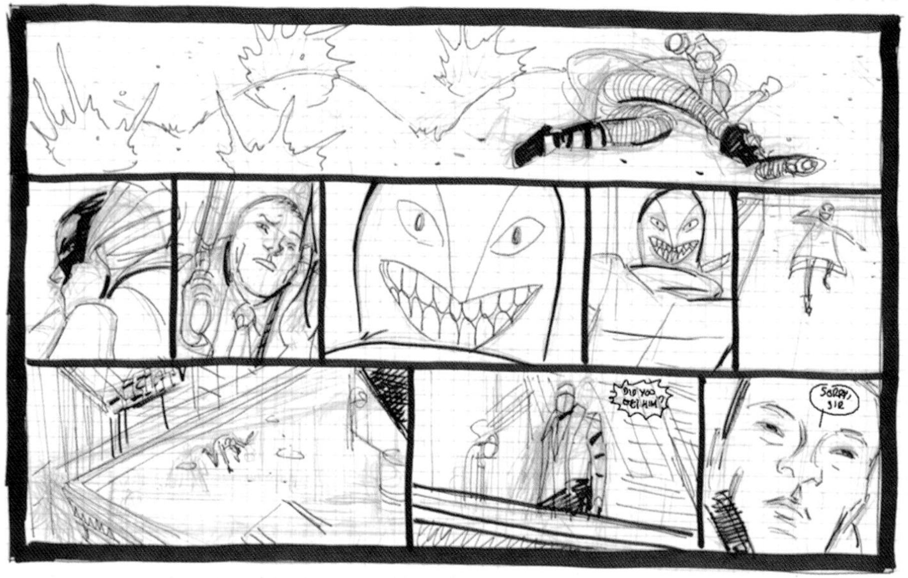
DID YOU GET HIM?
SORRY, SIR

PAGE 10

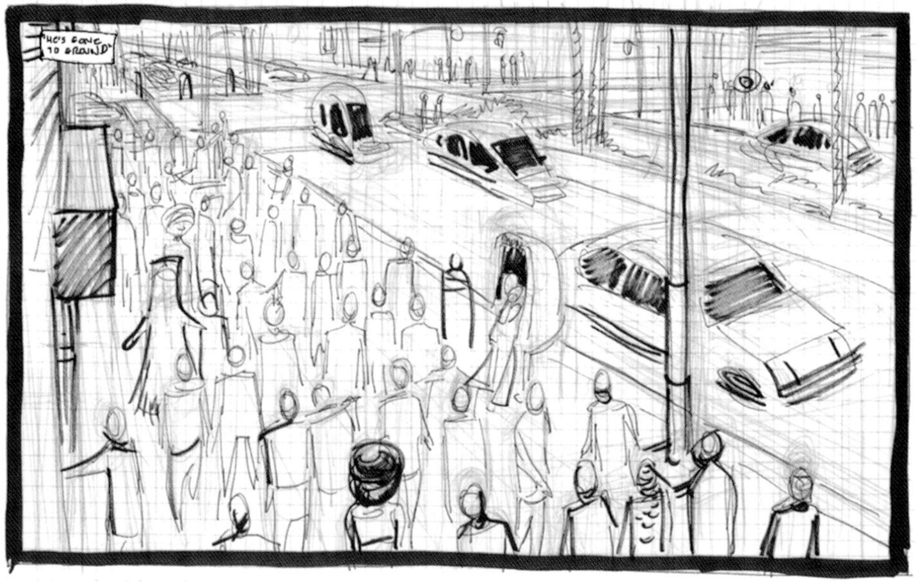
"HE'S GONE TO GROUND"

PAGE 11

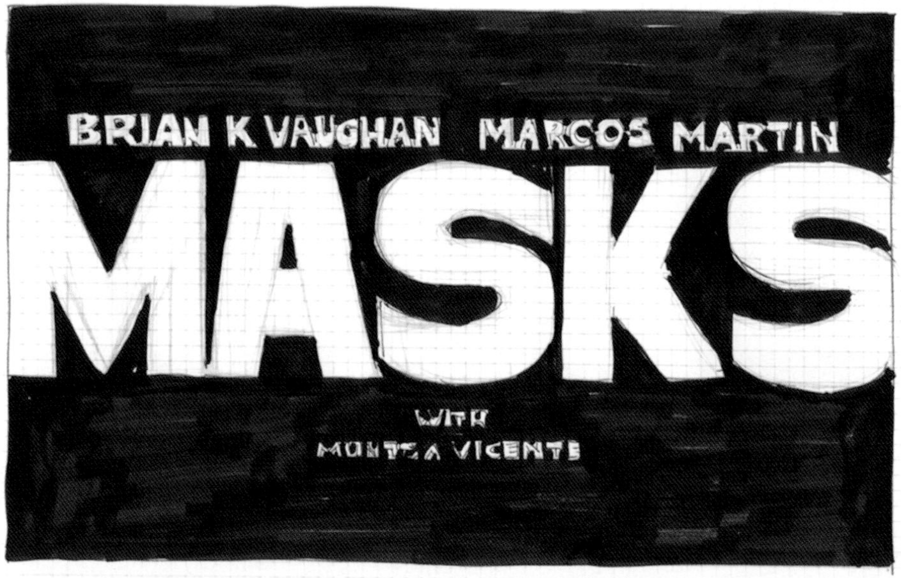
BRIAN K VAUGHAN MARCOS MARTIN
MASKS
WITH
MUNTSA VICENTE

From: Brian K. Vaughan
Re: Headline
Date: June 28th 2012 22:00:03 GMT+02:00

Hey, Marcos! I was just thinking about our story, and how these old-fashioned "automats" would be a perfect place for a private lunch in our future. No waiters, no receipts, etc. Might make for a cool location in an upcoming issue:
http://cityroom.blogs.nytimes.com/2012/06/17/revisiting-the-era-of-automatic-dining/

Anyway, your headline! If you have room for it, I was thinking something like "CRIME RATES NEAR HISTORIC LOWS" Something that suggests this masked future is actually safer than our present.

And for that album cover in P.I.'s office, maybe it's The Flaming Lips' fictional final album "Their It Was" (a play on their deliberately misspelled first album "Hear It Is")

And posters/paintings sound great, but I'd avoid too much existing imagery, since some companies/artists are litigious about existing images. I feel like P.I. would probably like old black and white detective or sci-fi movies. Maybe a few faded old movie posters in that style? I'm open to anything...

From: Marcos Martín
Re: Things
Date: July 12th 2012 01:53:17 GMT+02:00

Looks like we're going to have to start thinking of a new title... AGAIN.
http://www.comicbookresources.com/?page=article&id=39644

From: Brian K. Vaughan
Re: Things
Date: July 12th 2012 19:58:21 GMT+02:00

Shit. Sucks about our title, but the fact that they're using "Masks" for an Alex Ross project suggests that the title probably sounded a little too "superhero" anyway. Back to the drawing board...

From: Marcos Martín
Re: Pages
Date: August 14th 2012 14:09:23 GMT+02:00

Also, I've been giving some thought to our working title and I came up with a couple of possible options for your consideration: "(The) Private Eye" I think fulfills the same goal as "The Private Investigator" but it's open to different interpretations. And in the same vein, that could be further twisted into "The Private I". But that's perhaps going too far.

Anyway, I still like "The Private Investigator" but I thought it was worth exploring other possibilities. And again, I'm Spanish, so I'm not even sure how ridiculous these may sound.

Back to our private car elevator...

From: Brian K. Vaughan
Re: Pages
Date: August 15th 2012 01:32:55 GMT+02:00

OF COURSE! I actually had "The Private I" written down in my notes, but thought it was a little too cute. But I have no idea why I didn't just think of THE PRIVATE EYE, which is both as iconic as The private Investigator, but also, as you note, more poetic.

From: Marcos Martín
Re: Pages
Date: August 15th 2012 12:51:20 GMT+02:00

Great minds think alike! Let's settle for this then, at least, until someone takes it away from us again...

From: Marcos Martín
Subject: Domain name
Date: September 12th 2012 22:17:42 GMT+02:00

Brian!

So Jose (our web expert) tells me we need to come up with a domain name asap in order for him to go on with the programming. Unfortunately, I'm not sure I've been able to come up with anything usable. Here's a shortlist so far:

-Comicsauthors, Comixauthors or Comixcreators (if we want to keep it simple and yet, a bit obvious)
-Independentpanels, Panelsyndicate, Panelunion, Panelsunion, Syndicatedpanels (the comics element with our idea of some sort of guild or syndicate)
-Theguttersyndicate or Gutterguild (already dismissed, I think)
-Comicscomrade (if we want to go all communist)
-Foregroundcomics, Foregrounded, Offpanelcomics, (the)Offpanelists (using other typical comics elements)
-Bringtheflood (if we want to go all biblical. I wanted to use the idea of the cloud, but it seems all variations are taken)

I know. Shoot me now. But perhaps, there's something in these that might help you to come up with a better idea.

Right now, Badoonga, our working name for the mock-up page is starting to sound like a good option.

MM

From: Brian K. Vaughan
Re: Domain name
Date: September 13th 2012 19:11:15 GMT+02:00

Hm, I like something with OFFPANEL, but I see that's already the name of a popular comics podcast.

It needs to be something quick and memorable that isn't specific to this one project, but tells readers of any background that this is a site to get great, independently produced comic books for sophisticated adults. I like something simple like:

EverywhereComics.com

SplendidComics.com

FirstClassComics.com

Ugh, this is hard. I'll keep thinking. And sorry I haven't sent over that finalized dialogue for #1 yet! Hectic week...

From: Brian K. Vaughan
Re: P.I. #1 - Dialogue
Date: September 22nd 2012 02:18:33 GMT+02:00

Shit, I really liked PanelOne, too. That's just about perfect. Sucks that it's taken.

I love the idea behind Koomiks, I just think it sounds like a silly Muppet character.
The Esperanto word for comics is "Komikso," which sounds a little cooler to my ear... but of course, that's already taken.

Fuck, I just started typing random interesting words into GoDaddy and EVERYTHING is taken. Even SpaceDinosaur.com!

I agree that BrianAndMarcos sounds a little swishy, but what about combining our initials? MMBKV.com or BKVMM.com are each just five letters long, and they're both available.
I dunno, maybe we need some vowels.

Ugh!

From: Marcos Martín
Re: P.I. #1 - Dialogue
Date: September 22nd 2012 02:49:16 GMT+02:00

Panel one WAS perfect, so yes it was taken, of course. Everything's taken!

I also thought about the initials idea but they're too difficult to write and to remember. I don't know of any way to make that work. Also, we might end up sounding like an ad agency from the sixties.

We'll dig a bit more into the strange languages option. But right now, it looks like "PanelSyndicate" is in the lead.

From: Marcos Martín
Re: P.I. #1 - Dialogue
Date: September 24th 2012 21:01:49 GMT+02:00

Also, after much discussion and asking around we've finally decided on "PanelSyndicate.com" as the domain name since it seemed to gather the most consensus. I'm surprised to say most people really like it, actually. I hope you won't be too disappointed.
Anyway, it's already registered and ready for business! I'm actually excited!

From: Brian K. Vaughan
Re: P.I. #1 - Dialogue
Date: September 24th 2012 23:07:53 GMT+02:00

Awesome! Like all of your crazy ideas, PanelSyndicate has really grown on me. As always, I can't wait to take all of the credit when the site gets a million views.

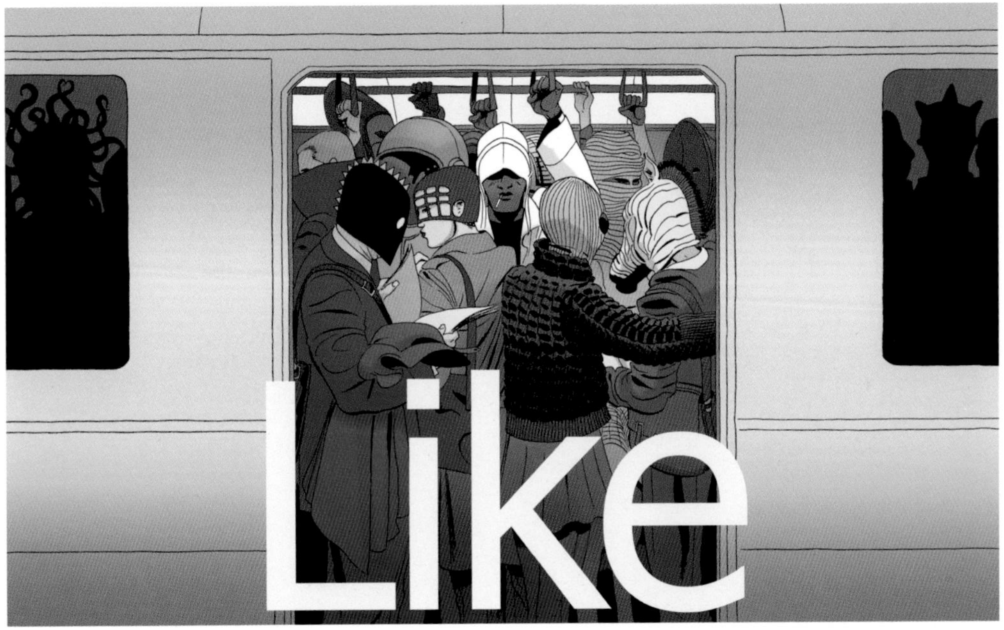
Like

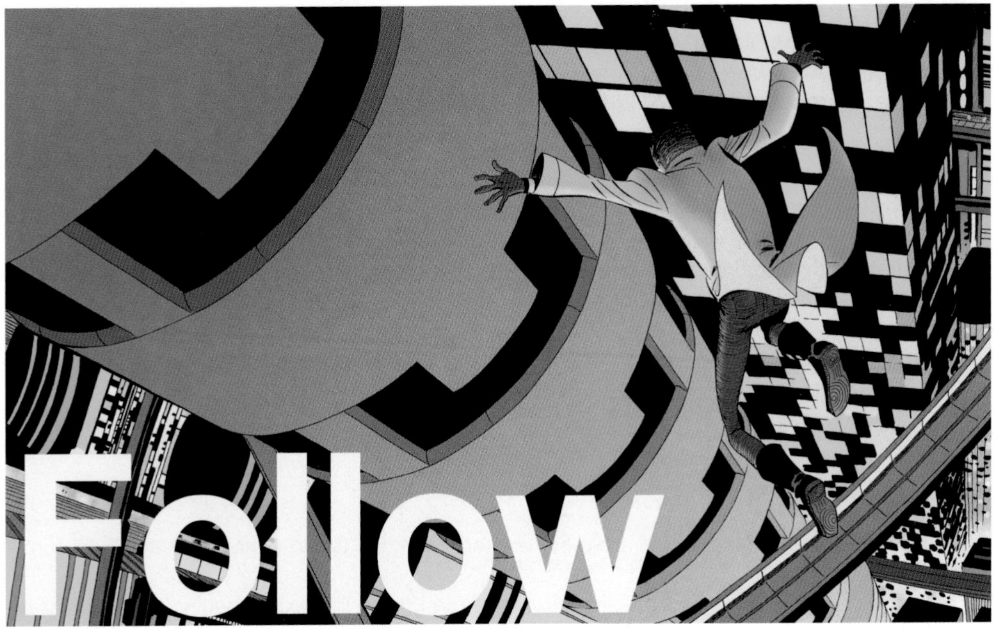
Follow

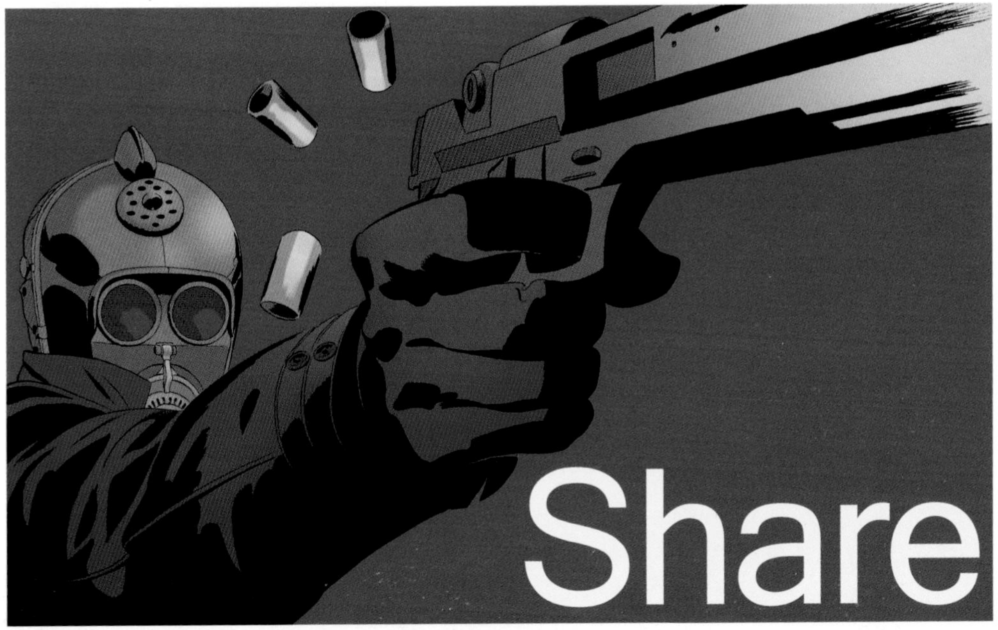
Share

From: Marcos Martín
Subject: Afterword
Date: March 18th 2013 20:25:00 GMT+01:00

Brian,

Well, it looks like people have at least noticed our teasers. Wonder what will happen tomorrow...

I'm attaching the final afterword after a couple of touch-ups on the fifth and seventh paragraphs (special thanks and contact info). Just want to run it through you first to make sure you're ok with it.

And I'll send you an email as soon as we've got the website up and running. Fingers crossed!

From: Brian K. Vaughan
Re: Afterword
Date: March 19th 2013 02:47:07 GMT+01:00

Looks perfect! Man, people are really excited, Marcos. Could tomorrow actually be fun???

Please let me know when the site is live and ready, and I'll start spreading the word far and wide late tonight!

From: Marcos Martín
Re: Afterword
Date: March 19th 2013 04:36:06 GMT+01:00

Site is now up and running and fully operational! Congratulations! We are now oficially crazy. :)
Do you know what time you will be sending our "Press Release"? I'd like to send the news to some Spanish sites, too, but I don't want to do it too early. Also, do you need me to send you the cover with the ad copy again?

Anyway, we did it man. For better or worse.